A CURABLE ROMANTIC

ALSO BY JOSEPH SKIBELL

A Blessing on the Moon

The English Disease

A CURABLE ROMANTIC

A NOVEL BY

Joseph Skibell

ALGONQUIN BOOKS OF CHAPEL HILL   2010

Published by
Algonquin Books of Chapel Hill
Post Office Box 2225
Chapel Hill, North Carolina 27515-2225

a division of
Workman Publishing
225 Varick Street
New York, New York 10014

This is a work of fiction. While, as in all fiction, the literary perceptions and insights are based on experience, all names, characters, places, and incidents either are products of the author's imagination or are used fictitiously.

A portion of this novel was published, in slightly different form, in *Maggid: A Journal of Jewish Literature.*

Library of Congress Cataloging-in-Publication Data
Skibell, Joseph.
A curable romantic : a novel / by Joseph Skibell. — 1st ed.
p. cm.
ISBN 978-1-56512-929-0
1. Jewish men — Fiction.   2. Vienna (Austria) — Fiction.
3. Freud, Sigmund, 1856 – 1939 — Fiction.   4. Esperanto — History — Fiction.
5. Zamenhof, L. L. (Ludwik Lazar), 1859 – 1917 — Fiction.
6. Warsaw (Poland) — Fiction.   I. Title.
PS3569.K44C87 2010
813'.54 — dc22   2010018605

10 9 8 7 6 5 4 3 2 1
First Edition

For my mother צילא רכל (ז״ל)
and for her mother אסטער רייזל (ז״ל)
for my daughter אריאל שירה
and for her mother באשע אהבה

קוק איך טרויעריק מיר אריין
אין דער מאַמעס אויגן:
ס׳האָט איר ליבשאַפט נישט געלאָזט
ווערן מיך אַ פויגל.

איציק מאַנגער
״אױפֿן װעג שטײט אַ בױם״

And in memory of my father
אייזיק אריעה בן יחזקאל הכהן (ז״ל)

מה עשה הקדוש ברוך הוא? נטל אמת והשליכו לארץ.
— בראשית רבה

And the Holy One, what did He do? He buried truth in the ground.
—Genesis Rabbah

A CURABLE ROMANTIC

BOOK ONE

A CURABLE ROMANTIC;

or, My Life in Dr. Freud's Vienna

I fell in love with Emma Eckstein the moment I saw her from the fourth gallery of the Carl Theater, and this was also the night I met Sigmund Freud. My seat had cost me nearly half a krone. For a full krone, I could have stood in the parterre, but that would have meant going hungry all the following day. I owned no evening clothes. Unbeknownst to my neighbor Otto Meissenblichler, a waiter at the Sacher, I regularly sneaked into his rooms when he wasn't working or on other occasions when he didn't need them and took from his wardrobe his black swallowtail coat, his black pants, his black tie, and his white shirt with the gold-and-onyx buttons, restoring the ensemble long before he returned from his own night out, which was usually early in the morning.

Otto possessed a dexterity with women that frankly eluded me, I who had so clumsily dropped and broken every heart so far entrusted to my care.

He was also taller than I, Otto was — perhaps his height accounted for his amorous successes — and his suit was at least two sizes too large. My neck swimming in his collars, his tie drooping to my sternum, his cuffs tucked inside my sleeves, his trouser crotch falling halfway to my knee — was there ever a more ridiculous figure than I?

What woman, other than his own mother, would find such a clown cause for sexual alarm?

None. I knew the answer was none, and so I kept my head down and my long nose in my program, hoping to command no more attention than a shadow if I failed to meet another's gaze. The men who glanced at me glanced away again quickly, wry grins concealed within their thick beards, and the women accompanying them looked straight through me.

I'd seated myself behind an enormously broad-shouldered man and his enormously broad-shouldered wife. The man's cape and the woman's fox stole, hanging like an arras from their shoulders, formed an impenetrable horizon beneath which I couldn't see the stage. I watched the audience, therefore, before the curtain, seated on the edge of my chair, peering through the aperture formed by the couple's shoulders, their heads, and their hat brims.

It was thus, my view framed by the little seahorses of their ears, that I caught my first glimpse of her, my Venus on the half shell, my ill-starred amorette: my Emma Eckstein.

WHAT DREW MY attention so irresistibly to her? Perhaps it was her broach that caught my eye. A silver angel pinned above her heart, the spangle glimmered and flashed, reflecting back light from the thousand and one gas lamps roaring in the hall. Beneath the pin, her bosom heaved in a pendulous panic as she stepped into the aisle. Verifying the seat number on her ticket stub, juggling her program against the reticule she kept in her other gloved hand, she searched the crowd in front of her (for her seat, I presumed) and behind her (for the companion from whom she'd become unintentionally parted), unable to find either, or both, or perhaps one without the other.

She was nearsighted — I could tell by the way she brought the stub to her face — but too vain to wear her glasses, allowing a squint to mar her forehead, puckering it with a scowl.

I couldn't help sighing. I've always responded, quite often foolishly, to beauty, but it's the eye, I believe, and not the heart or the groin, that is the organ of desire, the eye that in a convulsive ocular somersault literally turns the world upside down, defying the brain to make sense of it all.

But can the eye be trusted? That is the question. How clearly may it peer into the heart of our attractions, when it's the nature of beauty to beguile the eye and confound the mind?

And the Fräulein was indeed beautiful. Her nose was straight and fine, and her mouth almost too large for the trembling pedestal of her chin. Her hair, swept off her neck and pinned into place by an opal clasp, frizzled out in small exasperated tufts. She seemed older than I — she must have been nearing thirty — and yet she had about her a frazzled air belonging more properly to a maiden. And indeed, it was this sweet and mild confusion animating and irritating her every gesture that convinced me the alarums clanging in the belfry of my heart at the sight of her were genuine. I held my breath in anticipation of the arrival of her companion, hoping he would prove to be neither husband nor lover nor (in those strangely liberated times) both. However, the relief I felt upon seeing a mother and not a lover join my darling (already I was thinking of her in this way) disappeared as I watched the Fräulein, obviously chastened by her mother, attempting to decipher the elder woman's wishes, peering into her face as into a page of incomprehensible scribbling.

I followed their progress down the aisle through my opera glasses but lost sight of them when the head of the man in front of me threw itself up, a big fleshy mountain, between us. Rearing back, I jolted the glasses into the bridge of my nose and was blinded by a yellow flash of pain. Swerving my lorgnette in a panic to the right, lest I lose them, I found the Fräulein and her mother again on the far side of the woman's plumed hat.

They were speaking to a gentleman, a family friend by the looks of it, although upon closer examination — peering in, I refocused my lorgnette — I could see that the man's presence seemed to be rattling the younger woman. She seemed smitten by his person. Blushing compulsively, she dropped her head, unable to meet his gaze. Gripping her little purse by its chain, she let it dangle in front of her, as though to conceal the delta of her sex.

At that moment, I realized, with a riveting sense of shame, that I was staring at her lap!

My cheeks burned. I lifted my lorgnette and, in order to distract my gaze, took a better look at my rival. Bearded, well barbered, impeccably haberdashed, he was puffing on a slender green cigar. Steadying its nib with his thumb, he roared with laughter at some witticism or other of the mother's; tilting back his head, he exhaled, filling the air above them with a plumy smudge.

How I hated that man! I hated him the way one hates anyone who possesses what one lacks, whose sturdy happiness exposes how ludicrously constructed is one's own. I felt barred from the marvelous joke they were sharing, exiled from their witty conversation, not only by the distance that separated us—I was, after all, four tiers above them—but by my poverty, broadcast plainly to the world, if by nothing else, then by Otto's suit.

Lower your lorgnette, I counseled myself, look away, spare your heart! But instead I watched as the mother placed an ungloved hand upon the arm of the gentleman and caressed it. Meaningful looks were traded between these two. They'd agreed upon something—that much was clear—and as they turned towards the daughter to see if she concurred, and as she signaled her assent with an embarrassed charade of shrugs, I knew I possessed no hope of winning her.

My rival had bested me before I'd even announced my intentions!

THE HOUSE LIGHTS dimmed, the curtain went up, and I watched the play—half a crown is half a crown, after all—though I could barely concentrate on its plot. (Dr. Herzl's *The New Ghetto,* it had something to do with a count, a duel, a questionable marriage, and a coal mine.) When the gaslights came up, I stood in my box and peered over the heads of the couple in front of me to search the stalls for the girl in the lavender dress with all the extravagant flounces.

(Ah, that women no longer dress in this way, as though they were packages waiting to be unwrapped, is an understandable, if no less lamentable thing!)

I found her easily enough this time with my lorgnette. As soon as the curtain had fallen, she'd taken leave of her mother and was walking towards the lobbies. "Bitte!" I cried to my boxmates; standing, I bumped into their knees. My heart pounding, I charged out of the gallery through the corridor towards the staircases, where, hurrying, I leaned over its railing, searching the crowd below me for a glimpse of a lavender hem.

Pince-nez flashing, monocles glittering, well-dressed men stood in clusters, roaring their opinions about the play into one another's faces. Snaking through these dense knots of smokers and drinkers, I circumnavigated the ground-floor lobby, its red velvet wallpaper, its red velvet sofas, its red velvet chairs whirling about me in a hurricane of scarlet. However, the Fräulein was nowhere to be found.

Mildly out of breath, I could only chide myself: Did I really expect to find her in so large a crowd, a solitary queen inside such a busy swarm? And if I had, what did I next propose to do? Introduce myself? Declare my love for her perhaps? No, the quest had been a foolish one, impulsive and doomed. I was on the point of conceding as much when, as though alerted by a signal only they could hear, a rout of drunken loiterers moved off, scattering from the bar in several directions at once. Behind where they had only moments before stood, indeed stationed there as though by the Unseen Hand of Fate, was the well-barbered gentleman I'd seen speaking to the Fräulein before the curtain, his immaculately tailored person encircled by the whitish fumes of his cigar.

With no idea how much longer the interval might last, I seized my chance and placed myself beside him. As he was facing the bar, I leaned my back against it. As he was drinking a brandy, I ordered one as well, a fact he noted out of the corner of his eye, nodding almost imperceptibly in approval. With mirrors on all four of its walls, the little alcove seemed to repeat itself in an eternal stutter. Though a single chandelier dangled from the ceiling, a thousand appeared to have been strung, in long lines, back to a thousand distant vanishing points, and no matter which direction one faced, one could see the room from a dozen different angles. And so, although I was facing away from Dr. Freud, I was able to watch him while simultaneously watching myself. (Yes, the stranger was Dr. Freud. Why not reveal it now and get it over with? I'm not a novelist or a playwright, after all, that I must bait my reader's interest by withholding pertinent information.) Like everything else in the room, like the barman and the wall sconces and the chandeliers, Dr. Freud's figure receded into the mirrors' staggered horizons, replicated in ever smaller versions. I followed this unending trail of Freuds, moving my gaze from the back of one of his more distant heads to the front of a head less distant, jumping from mountain peak to mountain peak, as it were, moving nearer to the original, until I realized that he was doing the same with me and my many reflections, and although we were facing in opposite directions, we were very soon staring into each other's eyes. Dr. Freud seemed to note this queer fact at precisely the same moment as I, and a shockingly awkward intimacy ensued: one's habitual mask falls away and one feels naked, having presented his unguarded face to another man (better to rouge one's cheeks with the appurtenances then available to masculine physiognomy—beards, monocles, muttonchops, mustaches, dueling scars—so that if the mask slips, one mightn't lose face altogether).

Of course, it's easy enough to lionize Dr. Freud now, but even then, in the years before fame enveloped him in its luminous cloak, he possessed a brooding quality, a fierce, unblinking omniscience. His eyes were dark and lustrous, whereas mine were pale and myopically blue, and though I've no idea what Dr. Freud saw in them, as his glance swept over their surfaces, I've no doubt he saw everything there was in them to see. As his many reflections turned away from mine, I felt like a mouse that had been spared inexplicably by a cat and was alarmed, therefore, to find him now only a small distance from my shoulder, looking me straight in the eye. The looming geographies of his face, so near mine, were dizzying. Beneath the whiskery arms of his mustache, he drew on a yellow-green cigar, grinding its smoke between his teeth. Two fumes coiled out of his nostrils like a pair of charmed snakes.

"Dreary, wouldn't you say?"

I took a step away from him. "I . . . I beg your pardon?" I hoped to sound as though I'd only just noticed him, as though I hadn't been watching him the entire time, as though *I'd* been the one lost in thought and it were *he* who had pulled *me* out of the mists of my own foggy preoccupations.

"Why, the play and its themes," he said, tilting his brandy to his mouth.

I struggled in vain to recall the play. Though I'd been looking forward to it—it was the event of the season, as far as our little circle was concerned—I'd paid such scant attention to the opening act I could barely quilt together the fragmentary fabric of its themes. Dr. Freud had tossed me an opening, and I had dropped it, like a blind man juggling eggs.

His thumb against the nib of his cigar, he leaned in closer to me and murmured, "I'm speaking, of course, of the low social status of the race to which we both belong."

At these words, all thoughts of silly Fräuleins and lavender dresses vanished from my head. "Yes," I said, "and for my generation, it's even worse."

"Worse?" Dr. Freud said. "How so?"

"Our greater expectations, based upon your own generation's accomplishments, combine with our more limited economic possibilities, to make everything far worse."

I next expressed a regret that my generation was, in fact, doomed to atrophy.

"These are strong words," Dr. Freud said.

"Perhaps," I said, warming to my theme. "However, it's difficult to feel oneself destined for a higher purpose and still be uncertain of earning one's daily bride."

Dr. Freud's brow contracted. "Bride?"

"Bread." I corrected him as politely as I could.

"No, no, you said *bride:* 'And still be uncertain of earning one's daily bride.'"

"Surely you misheard me." Whatever I'd said, I'd meant *bread,* of course (*Brot* in German), and not *bride* (*Braut*). Dr. Freud grinned and bit into his cigar, rolling it in quick circles between his teeth. "And if I did, what of it? It's a simple and meaningless mistake," I said.

"Is it?"

"A mere triviality—yes!—an error in speech, and nothing more!"

With his elbow on the bar, Dr. Freud leaned his head against his fist. A thatch of his hair fell into his eyes. "I agree with you that these occasional lapses are quite trivial in nature, and yet I would suggest to you, on the evidence of my own medical researches, that there are no occurrences, however slight, that drop out of the universal concatenation of events or escape the tyrannical rule of cause and effect."

The universal concatenation of events? The tyrannical rule of cause and effect?

"You're claiming—what?—if I'm understanding you correctly that you can trace my silly verbal misstep back to the mental processes that caused it?"

"Certainly I can, and it shouldn't take long. However, to do so, I ask of you only one thing."

"And that is?"

"That you tell me, candidly and uncritically and without any aim whatsoever, whatever comes into your mind as you direct your attention to the misspoken word."

As Dr. Freud leaned in closer to me, I could smell the medicinal tang of brandy and tobacco on his breath, and I couldn't shake the suspicion that he was laughing at me, playing with me, as though it were all a merry game, or not a game, but a sport, since, like a fox beaten out of the hedges, I had no understanding of the rules that were to govern my painful exposure.

"Bit of a parlor game?" I said, attempting to make light of it all.

Dr. Freud tapped his cigar against the spittoon on the bar, letting a red plug of ash fall into it. "I've no idea what parlors you frequent, but I can assure you it's hardly a game." Once more, he confined me inside the prison house of his gaze. Indeed, I felt as though I'd been hauled by the imperial police into an interrogation chamber. However, what could I do? Refusing him was out of the question. Doing so would put an end to our conversation and irrevocably forfeit for me any chance of learning the Fräulein's name. (Though I knew not yet one syllable of it, I could practically feel my tongue and lips conspiring to pronounce it.) Slyly changing the subject would be impossible, I sensed, with a man like Dr. Freud. Ruled by his passions, he'd never permit himself to be distracted or put off. I had no idea how much longer the interval might last, and I made a quick calculus: though sounding my mental depths for the buried source of this verbal slip might take the entire intermission, thus depriving me of the moment in which I might steer the conversation towards my own uses (viz., the learning of Emma Eckstein's name), I was convinced the procedure would reveal nothing of consequence about me and that afterwards, having indulged my new friend in his harmless pursuit, I could more forcefully ask his patience in indulging mine.

"Good! Marvelous!" Dr. Freud said, clapping his hands. "Let us begin immediately!"

Exhibiting considerably less enthusiasm for the examination than he, I coughed into my fist and cleared my throat. "Well," I said, "if I recall correctly, I said something along the lines of 'It's difficult to feel born for higher things and still be uncertain of earning one's daily bread,' or rather 'bride,' as you maintain."

"And what springs to mind?" Dr. Freud said. "Quick! Quick! Don't give it too much thought."

I shrugged. "I don't know. The Lord's Prayer, I suppose."

"Ah, very good, the Lord's Prayer. 'Give us our bride, our daily bride,' eh?" Dr. Freud said this in English, and as he did, I began to feel the first stirrings of an inexplicable shame. "Yes, you see," he continued, "one might make a similar mistake in English, as well as in several other languages. In Hebrew, for instance, *kallah* is 'bride' and *challah* a sort of bread. Why, even an aristocratic Pole might confuse *pain*, 'bread' in French, with *panna*, the Polish word for 'miss.'"

I ducked my head. "Well, I suppose I'm not as cunning a linguist as you," I said, or rather tried to say. I'd attempted this riposte in English as well, but I'd tripped over the difficult locution and now blushed, hearing my own words.

Dr. Freud raised a well-barbered eyebrow. "A Latinist?" he chortled.

"Forgive me, Herr Doktor," I stammered, "if I've consulted you in any way!"

"Ah!" he crowed. "If only my patients were as honest as you!"

"*Insulted*, I meant!"

"There! You see? That's another aspect of these faulty speech acts. They're highly contagious, and quite so!"

"Yes, but what have you learned so far?" I said, hoping to master the situation. I could feel my cheeks burning.

"Not much." Catching the barman's eye, he waved two fingers over our empty glasses. I cringed: I could barely afford the first. "But let us continue. Now, if I asked you what thoughts the Lord's Prayer produces in your mind, you would say what?"

"Right off the top of my head?"

"Certainly right off the top of your head."

Feeling unfree to consider the matter for more than an instant, I answered him with the first thing that sprang to mind: "Why, Reni's *Gathering of the Manna*, I suppose."

"Ah."

"I saw it not too long ago in a cathedral in Ravenna." The painting still hung in my mental gallery, and I could see it clearly: Moses in his red cloak and sandals, two goat horns emerging from his head; winged babies tossing an invisible something from their nursery blanket of clouds; the crowds' arms raised to receive; a muscular man bending, lifting something from the ground, the thumb of his hand inside the handle of a clay jar, and not a crust of bread in sight.

"Why the Reni?" Dr. Freud asked.

"Bread from the sky, I suppose?"

"And of Moses, what thoughts?"

"The lawgiver?"

Dr. Freud stroked his beard. "Stern, harsh?"

"Implacable," I agreed.

"Ah . . . ah . . ." Dr. Freud raised a finger to his lips before pointing it at my face. His eyes narrowed. "And what crossed your mind just then?" He'd apparently seen me smiling at some private thought.

I touched my own finger to my lips and waved my hand before my face dismissively. I demurred. "It's hardly germane to our subject, I would think."

"However, you've agreed to tell me everything."

"Well, no." I sighed. "It's just . . . something just . . . crossed my mind . . ."

"Just now?"

"Yes . . . but it's really too intimate to pass on, and besides, I see no connection to our discussion and therefore no necessity in speaking the thought aloud."

"I'll be the judge of that."

"However . . ." I folded my arm.

"Of course," Dr. Freud snorted, "I can't force you to talk about something you find distasteful; but then you mustn't insist upon learning from me how you came to substitute the word *bride* for *bread*."

"Oh, very well." I capitulated before his greater will. "No, it's just" — I cast my eyes down at the carpet — "this idea of a daily bride, you see." I smiled at him imploringly. "The notion occurred to me that one might . . . possess, well, I suppose . . . six women then. One for each day of the week."

"Which would mean?"

I shot an embarrassed look at Dr. Freud. "A double portion on the Sabbath?"

He smirked and lowered his voice. "You've been married, I take it?"

"Indeed, I have."

"More than once?"

"Indeed."

"Twice, in fact."

"But how could you have guessed that?"

"Both marriages imposed upon you by your father?"

"That's correct."

"The first one a marriage of great love."

"Yes!"

"The second, less so."

I fell half a step back and took a hard look at the man standing before me. "Have we met before and I've forgotten it?"

"Your father forced you into these betrothals quite against your will."

"And now you're tweaking me for my absentmindedness, is that it?" I shook my finger at him, pretending to scold. "We've obviously discussed this matter previously."

"No, I assure you, we've never met; neither have I had the pleasure of making your father's acquaintance. Besides, he doesn't live in Vienna."

"He doesn't. That's correct."

"But in the East somewhere."

"Astounding!"

"In Galicia, I would imagine. In—?"

By reflex, I started to pronounce the name of my hometown.

"In Szibotya, yes." Dr. Freud finished the word for me. "I thought as much."

"But-but-but—how—?" I stammered.

"'But-but-but—how?' That is indeed the question!"

"Are you a mind reader or a conjurer that you've seen so deeply and so completely into the private recesses of my heart?"

"Not so deeply, neither so completely, and certainly not as private as you imagine." He downed his drink and pulled back the wings of his evening jacket, placing his fists in the small of his back. "A mind reader? A conjurer? No!" He laughed. "A humble man of science is all. In any case, you did most of the work yourself, preparing the way, as it were: a harsh father figure; give us our daily bride; 'a double portion on the Sabbath'; the invisible manna of the Reni symbolizing a kind of communal delusion. That you're from Galicia, anyone could discern from your accent. With Szibotya, granted, I cheated. You began to pronounce the name, and I'm familiar enough with the region, as many of my wife's cousins reside there, to have guessed the rest of the word."

Eying me pensively, he grew silent. Not a large man, he was nevertheless taller than I, and, for a moment, I had the impression that he was preparing to strike me. Instead, he reached out and lightly fingered the lapel of Otto Meissenblichler's jacket, a gesture against which, as I'd prepared myself for a blow, I couldn't help flinching. Noting this, he frowned.

"And now, despite the wretched history of your sentimental life and this absurd habiliment in which you comport yourself, you would have me introduce you to the young woman you saw me speaking to earlier in the evening." He released Otto's lapels and rubbed his thumb against his fingers, as though something disagreeable had adhered to them. "Unless I'm incorrect, and that is not the reason you have approached me after all." His glower proved to be beneficent. "No need to verify my surmisings, and, I assure you, denying them will do you no good. Her name is Emma Eckstein, and I would be delighted to facilitate your making her acquaintance."

"Emma Eckstein?" I repeated the words, frightened I might forget them if I didn't. "Forgive my amazement if I —"

"Oh God, no!" Dr. Freud roared. "There's nothing to forgive! Indeed, let the world gape in amazement. I'm prepared to accept its tribute!"

The bell for the second act rang out, summoning us to our seats. I reached into my breast pocket, but Dr. Freud touched my arm. "I'll see to this," said he. "You were gracious enough to indulge me in my little game."

We swallowed the last of our drinks, and he looked me up and down again, simultaneously appraising and dismissing me, I thought.

"Well then," he said, fussing with his matches, his coins, and his cigars.

"Thank you, sir."

"Enjoy the rest of your evening, young man."

"And you yours."

"I will, but not as much as I have this interval with you."

Feeling the moment called for some grand statement, and also fearing that he might too easily forget the promise he had made me, I cleared my throat and said, "My dear sir, I am a doctor as well."

"Yes, as the prescription pad in your left pocket testifies, although I suppose it might belong to the owner of the jacket."

"And so, let me assure you," I continued, blushing, "that despite the tenor of our conversation, my intentions towards the young lady in question are entirely dishonorable."

Dr. Freud smiled unhappily as I strove to correct myself. "Honorable, I meant."

"By the way," he said, escorting me to the staircases, "speaking of parlor games, you don't by any chance play Tarock, do you?"

"Tarock?"

"We're short a fourth for this Saturday's game."

"I never miss an opportunity," I said, although I had no idea what Tarock was nor how one played it.

Dr. Freud purred, "In any case, it's easy enough to learn."

"And Fräulein Eckstein?" I asked. "Will she be there?"

Dr. Freud stopped and placed both of his hands upon my shoulders. "The rules of the heart, as I think you'll discover, are somewhat more complex than those of Tarock." He handed me his card. "You do own your own clothing, don't you . . . Dr. Sammelsohn?" he said, reading mine.

"I have a suit, yes."

"Then I shall see you in it on Saturday night at eight o'clock sharp!"

He took his leave of me with a slight bow and descended the stairs, pushing through the turnstiles of men's canes and women's fans, while I climbed back to my place in the fourth gallery. When the final curtain rang down, I hurried out, thinking that if I could leave the theater before them and appear to have inadvertently crossed their paths, I might not have to wait until Saturday for—I glanced again at his card to remind myself of his odd-sounding name—Dr. Freud to introduce me to Frau Eckstein and her magnificent daughter. The crowds swarming through the theater doors were too dense, however, and I saw neither Dr. Freud nor the Ecksteins again that night. Still, I lingered beneath a streetlamp as couples and groups hailed cabs or drove off in private fiacres, in the hopes that I might.

Eventually, even the actors emerged in their ordinary clothing. Their faces still partially rouged, they bid each other good night in their large voices, their gestures not as bold as before, although still somewhat affected. Finally a workman in shirtsleeves fastened a velvet rope across each of the theater's doors, and I made my way home, my hands thrust into the pockets of Otto Meissenblichler's coat.

Though much about myself at that time embarrasses me still—the little mustache and goatee I wore in an effort to appear not more masculine, but less feminine; my unruly hair, worn in the Bohemian style; the little trinkets and fobs dangling from my vest, which, with the rest of Otto's ensemble, made up my apparel for the evening—there's but one thing I continue to scold my younger self for, and that is the alacrity with which he once again surrendered to his cravings for love.

Ah, just look at him! The poor fool! At last, he knows the beloved's name: "Fräulein Eckstein . . . Fräulein Eckstein!" It sweetens his tongue like a lemon drop when, in an ecstasy, he whispers it to himself: "Emma . . . Emma . . . Emma . . ." Why, he's practically dancing on the benches in the Stadtpark, swooning against the gas lamps, gibbering at the gibbous moon! No one is abroad at this late hour, and so he feels himself the only man awake in Vienna, the only man alive in the empire, or perhaps in the entire world, the lone vertical figure crossing the planet's horizons as it spins in its ethers, aroused by the perfumed caresses of Beauty herself.

(Oh, what an idiot I was!)

I knocked softly upon Otto Meissenblichler's door and, receiving no answer, let myself in. Crossing the rug in the half-light, I removed my suit and exchanged it for the one I'd left hanging there. Self-dramatically running my hand through my hair, I slipped back into the passageway and entered my own rooms. Tossing my hat onto the table, I flung myself, fully clothed, across the bed.

"O Noble Room!" I cried out softly. (How I cringe to report this!) "Witness for so long of my bitterest solitude! May you now serve as a sanctuary to my new and tender love for Fräulein Emma Eckstein!"

The evening restages itself, a delightful comedy this time, in the theater of my mind, and I watch it over again. With its sparkling lamps and its incandescent chandeliers, the Carl is an empire of light. The murals on the ceiling are neckbreakingly beautiful, adorned with harps and trumpets and a whirling zodiacal wheel. There are depictions of Nestroy in costume and of the Muses in none; and beneath it all, there he is, young Dr. Sammelsohn, his heart and eye aroused to a frenzied pitch, delighting in the brilliance of it all.

(Who could have known then that, only a few months later, the fool would learn to his peril that the heart, like the eye, is drawn not only to light but to the soothing ambiguities of darkness as well?)

❦ CHAPTER 2 ❧

I tended, in the meanwhile, to my chores at the Allgemeines Krankenhaus, fiddling, for instance, with the Helmholtz ophthalmoscope
and the Graefe knife, instruments whose uses I'd yet to perfect. Not
that I needed to. The majority of my patients were simple malingerers
feigning nearsightedness in the hopes of obtaining a government dispensation or a military deferment, and my most frequent prescription was
a sternly worded lecture: "Let me assure you, Herr Whomever," I might
say, "that I have no time for these sorts of duplicities and neither does the
emperor or his generals!"

However, nothing could have been further from the truth. I was an
unmarried man, living by himself in a city full of strangers: I had nothing but time. My hours were indeed so empty, I could hardly fill them.
As a consequence, I was incapable of arriving anywhere late, a source of
continual social embarrassment for me. Invited to dinner by my aunt
Fania and uncle Moritz, for example, I arrived never less than punctu-
ally, which was always too early. Caught out like actors behind a curtain
that has risen before its cue, Fania and Moritz made off-seeming conversation while seeing to the last of their preparations.

Naturally, I had no wish to repeat this error at the Freuds', certainly
not on the evening I was to meet the Fräulein, and so when the great
stone wheel of the week finally turned and Saturday finally dropped into
place, I sat at the window, self-imprisoned in my armchair, waiting for
the sky to fully darken. Then I dallied as I'd never dallied before. I dallied in choosing my clothing, in dressing, in bolting the door. I set the
hands of my watch back ten minutes and then, intentionally forgetting
I'd done so, I did so again. Descending the stairs to the street, I set out
as tentatively as a blind man without his switch and crossed the city,
stopping continually to ascertain whether I'd remembered my wallet.
Halfway there, I began to run, fearing I was late. Arriving at Dr. Freud's

landing, I stood frozen, listening to the sounds of my own breathing, until my self-consciousness grew too acute and I forced myself to ring the bell.

As I did, carillons bellowed eight chimes from a nearby church tower. In the half-light of the landing, I clicked open my watch. Factoring in the twenty minutes or so I'd set the timepiece back, I saw that it was precisely eight o'clock.

"Oh, but you're early," the maid said as she opened the door. She pointed to a bench stationed against the wall. "Sit in the foyer, and I'll interrupt Dr. Freud's meal with his family to inform him that you're here."

"I could come back later, if that would be more convenient," I said.

She pirouetted on the toe of her shoe. "Tell me, sir, what would be more convenient about receiving you twice."

I pointed to the wooden bench. "I'll just wait here then."

"As you wish." Curtsying, she abandoned me to the foyer.

My spectacles had fogged, and I'd taken them off to polish, and when Dr. Freud appeared before me, it was as a column of white-and-brown splotches. "Oh, no! She didn't leave you sitting out here by yourself, did she? You're not the bootblack, after all."

"There was a chair," I said.

"A bench," he said. "It's hardly a chair."

A large white napkin was pinned around his neck, and he seemed to be chewing the last of his meal. Turning from me, he gripped the knobs of the twin doors behind him and rolled them into their wings. He beckoned me into a sitting room and gestured me towards a red Turkish divan. "You'll be more comfortable in here, I should think." With a yank, he unpinned the napkin and spat something into it. Gristle, I thought. "And now, if you'll excuse me, I'm running late and must prepare for the others. I don't know what could be keeping them." Glancing at his watch, he bowed and retreated from the room.

I sighed and stood and looked out the window at the stand of snow-burdened trees that rose up behind the apartment's stables. What had I gotten myself into? I had no idea. Although it was nearly 1895 and although Sigmund Freud was, of course, Sigmund Freud, the truth was that no one yet knew it, perhaps least of all Sigmund Freud. Though he'd crafted a dozen or so monographs on various aspects of neurology, his foundational work on neurosis, on the dream, on the unconscious, lay very much ahead of him. Even *Studies on Hysteria,* the book he'd authored with Dr. Breuer and whose five case histories would soon become the creation myths of our new century, was months from publication.

As far as I knew, as far as anyone knew, Dr. S. Freud was a struggling neuropath, a nerve specialist, shocking his clientele — the hysterical daughters of Jewish Vienna — not with irrefutable evidence of their unconscious sexual crimes but with actual volts of electricity, electrotherapy being in those days very much in medical vogue. What no one knew, indeed what no one could possibly have known, was that having dispensed with galvanism and faradism in favor of hypnosis, free association, and a rudimentary form of the now-famous talking cure, Dr. Freud was preparing to shock an even more nervous clientele: the world at large!

(Or so the Freudians would have us believe.)

I HEARD VOICES from the foyer: the hearty, booming voices of men who share an affectionate regard for one another. Answering the door himself, Dr. Freud had taken their scarves and their winter cloaks and was carrying them bundled in his arms. With his cigar clenched between his teeth, he was urging the men into the sitting room.

"Ah, mais oui, notre docteur Königstein a disparu!" the first fellow said upon seeing me there. "Yes, he mentioned something about that, didn't he?" the second murmured before noticing me as well. I felt as though I were a riddle that suddenly needed solving. The two men stood frozen before me, one slightly ahead of the other, my unexpected presence forcing them to reconsider the informality of their poses. Though their backs stiffened, their faces retained their original gay expressions, and they resembled two schoolboys caught out in a prank.

"Oskar Rie," the first one finally said, his expression becoming more formal, his posture less so.

"Jakob Sammelsohn," I answered with a bow.

"And this, I'm afraid, is my brother-in-law."

"Rosenberg," Dr. Rosenberg said, reaching around Dr. Rie. Leaning his barreled chest forward, he awkwardly extended his hand.

"Dr. Sammelsohn and I met the other evening at the theater," Dr. Freud said, adjusting the green ceramic stove that stood in a corner of the room.

"Ah, the theater!" Dr. Rosenberg boomed.

"And he graciously allowed me to coerce him into sitting in for Königstein."

"Good man."

"A dreary play, wasn't it?" asked Dr. Rie.

Dr. Freud stood, wiping soot from his hands. "Did you think so?"

"I didn't see you there," Dr. Rosenberg said.

"Nor I you," Dr. Freud said.

"That's because I *wasn't*," Dr. Rosenberg barked.

(I shall let this remark stand as an example of Dr. Rosenberg's notorious wit.)

"Hennessy?" Dr. Freud said.

"Make it two."

"And little Königstein?"

"Ludwig, please!" Dr. Rie clucked his tongue.

"Whatever everyone else is drinking," I said.

"Good, very good," Dr. Freud said. "I'll bring the bottle down."

THEY WERE BROTHERS-IN-LAW, Rosenberg and Rie, although whose sister had married whom, I can no longer recall. Perhaps they'd married women who were themselves sisters. There was nothing remarkable in that. Dr. Freud's sister had married his wife's brother, which made Dr. Freud's wife his sister-in-law, and Dr. Freud his own brother-in-law, I suppose. As for Rosenberg and Rie, their close family ties and the fact that both men were pediatricians—Rie cared for Freud's own growing brood—had turned them into affectionate rivals whom Dr. Freud compared to Inspector Bräsig and his friend Karl, the one quick-witted, the other deliberate and thorough.

Dr. Freud's consulting rooms were in the downstairs apartment, and he led us there now, carrying the bottle of brandy on a silver tray. Inside, we lifted our glasses and drank, without irony, to the emperor, and then to Frau Freud and her children.

By the time we sank into the red velvet cushions of our chairs, I was pleasantly drunk.

Dr. Freud reached behind him for a letter box, which he placed in the center of the table. Wrapping his knuckles against its lid, he intoned the word *"Ispaklaria!"* When the box was opened, I half-expected to see a djinn rising from its velvety interior. Instead, Dr. Freud removed a well-creased deck of Tarot cards. "Don't worry, Dr. Sammelsohn," he murmured, shuffling, "I shan't be telling your fortune tonight." He plopped the deck down with a thump near Dr. Rosenberg's hand. Dr. Rosenberg lifted the top cards and tucked them beneath those on the deck's bottom. Dr. Rie removed a pen and an abacus from a side drawer and opened a scorebook. Without knowing precisely what I was doing, I raised my cards and hid my face behind their fan. Swords, wands, cups, pentacles swam before my eyes. I was uncertain whether I should admit outright that Tarock was a game I'd never played or whether the whole thing would prove simple enough for me to glean its rules from a round or two. Perhaps, I thought, the pleasure of trouncing me would distract my opponents from the fact that I had absolutely no idea what I was doing. Regrettably, however, the first thing I discovered about Tarock is that one plays it partnered, in my case, to Dr. Rosenberg, who, true to his name, sat across the table from me like a big red mountain. There would be no pleasure in my trouncing from his corner, only, I assumed, more abrasive comparisons to the absent Königstein.

I blushed. I was here under false pretenses and soon everyone would know it. In truth, I cared little for the hirsute pleasures of masculine society (whiskey, smoke, and cards) and was hoping merely to be delivered through it onto the receptive breast of its feminine counterpart. At every creak of the floor boards over our heads, I imagined Dr. Freud's wife, his daughters, his sister Rosa, and the Ecksteins, their guests, preparing to burst in upon us and insisting, as ladies will, that we surrender our cards and join them instead.

"Oskar," Dr. Rosenberg said gently.

Dr. Rie looked up from his hand. "Hm? Sorry. I suppose I'm a little—"

"You're sitting right of the dealer."

"—distracted." He nodded. "I know. However, I've just come from an unfortunate case."

"Oskar works with children," Dr. Freud explained to me quietly.

"Ah," I said.

"Heartbreaking . . ." Dr. Rie shook his head.

"Another dram of Hennessy?" offered Dr. Freud.

"Gratefully," Dr. Rosenberg answered for his brother-in-law, and Dr. Rie moved his glass an inch nearer to Dr. Freud. With a sigh, he opened the play.

"Anyone see the papers?" Dr. Rosenberg asked, as a way, I assumed, of changing the subject.

"Another article on Dreyfus, I take it."

"Poor devil."

"Still maintaining his innocence?"

"They've shipped him off, haven't they?"

"Why shouldn't he? He is."

"Innocent?"

"Of course he is! I was up all night, thinking about that poor wretch pacing that damned island." His face increasingly florid, Dr. Rosenberg downed another drink. Captain Alfred Dreyfus, a Jew in the French army, had been convicted of espionage against the state. The French had sent him to Devil's Island, and the newspapers were choking with the story.

"Perhaps we should immigrate to Palestine ourselves before they ship us all off to Devil's Island?" Dr. Rie suggested tartly.

Dr. Rosenberg made a sour face. "As long as Dr. Herzl makes me ambassador to Vienna, I'll consider it."

"To your cards, gentlemen, to your cards," Dr. Freud said. "We've centuries yet to speak of our redemption."

I coughed and brought my fist to my lips, clearing my throat.

"Ah, what's this? What's this?" said Dr. Rie.

"Königstein's replacement seems to be on the point of speaking," Dr. Rosenberg said.

"I'm afraid it's been a while since I last played," I said.

"Has it been?" Dr. Freud eyed me sharply.

"And I was wondering if someone might perhaps remind me of the rules."

"Ah, when exactly was the last time you played, little Königstein?"

"Never," I admitted.

"Ha! I'd thought not!" Dr. Freud roared.

"So I assumed."

"Yes, and I was wondering when you'd confess it."

NO WOMEN APPEARED that evening. In fact, we saw no one from the Freud family at all. As the hours grew smaller and the floorboards above our heads ceased their creaking, I could only assume the household had turned in for the night and that we were the only ones still awake in the building. Detachable cuffs and collars littered the tabletop. Cigars burned unattended at our wrists. I had no idea what time it was: the nicotine, the alcohol, the late hour had blunted my senses. Dr. Rosenberg drowsed between turns. The whole thing seemed like a dream and, indeed, at one point, Dr. Rie spoke so quietly to Dr. Freud, in intonations that were so intimate that although I was sitting no more than three feet from either man, I felt I was listening to a foreign language.

"You've seen . . . ?" Dr. Rie asked Dr. Freud gently, raising his eyebrows.

Dr. Freud lowered his cards and squinted at Dr. Rie.

". . . our friend?" Dr. Rie completed his thought.

"Oh, you mean . . . ?"

"The Fräulein," he confirmed.

"Oh, yes, that." Dr. Freud nodded. "Sad, a sad case."

"Pity."

"Indeed."

"And you saw her . . ."

Dr. Freud shook his head. "At the theater."

"When?"

"Oh."

"The other . . . ?"

"Evening, yes."

Dr. Rie emptied his chest of air. "All the Ninth District must have . . ."

"Must have been in attendance, quite so." Dr. Freud coughed. "And the mother as well."

The two shared a warm and liquid laugh. "Ho," said Dr. Rie, more softly still.

Dr. Freud drew upon his cigar. "Barely got away with my *life*!" Beneath its eagle's lid, his brown eye suddenly turned on me. Caught out eavesdropping, I pretended to arrange my cards, immersing myself in the fantastical images printed on each: the Fool, the Magus, the Lovers, the Wheel. Reassured that he was speaking privately, Dr. Freud continued, in a murmur, to Dr. Rie: "In any case, she's agreed to see me again, and I met with her for the week. The mother . . ."

"Coerced her?"

"Only in part, no, only in . . ."

"And can you . . ."

"Help her?"

Dr. Freud studied his cards.

"I remind you, Sigmund: 'Primum non nocere.' "

"Yes, and so I thought I'd have my . . ."

"Not Berlin!"

A low tone moved inside Dr. Freud's throat.

"Is that wise?" Dr. Rie said.

"We've discussed this before, Oskar."

"And I've expressed my concerns to you before."

"Your dislike of Wilhelm is . . ."

"Entirely personal? Admittedly. Nonetheless."

"Enough."

Dr. Rie sighed. "Well, at least I've said my piece."

(I'd understood not one word the two men spoke to each other. However, everything I needed to know about the Fräulein, I realized later, was hidden in their words, concealed as though in plain sight, though I was too foolish to know it at the time.)

Dr. Freud busied himself with the cards, the scorebook, the abacus. He looked at me again, but this time I was too hypnotized by fatigue to look away. "Oi-yoi-yoi," he said, stretching. He spat something into his kerchief. "It's early. It's late." He rubbed his face. He took his pulse and stood. "Well," he said.

"Am-um-uh-er-whaz?" Dr. Rosenberg muttered, flustered, waking.

"Time to go, Ludwig." Dr. Rie tapped him on the wrist. "Come on, old man. You've lost a fortune."

Dr. Rosenberg blinked into the room with a fearful uncertainty, squinting against the lamplight. "I . . . I was on Devil's Island," he said. "We all were!"

"No, no, you only dreamt it."

"Yes? And?" Dr. Freud said.

"Not good." Dr. Rosenberg gave him a frank look. "Not good at all."

Dr. Rosenberg pushed back his chair. Each man gathered his cuffs and his collar and stuffed them into the pockets of his coat. At the top of the stairs, the brothers-in-law exchanged fraternal kisses with their host. I stepped aside to wrap my scarf about my neck. It was then that Dr. Freud turned towards me and took my hand.

"Tonight was impossible, I'm afraid."

"The Fräulein?" I asked, peering into his face, hoping I'd understood him.

"But soon, soon, I promise," he said.

For the month that Dr. Königstein was away, tending to his mother's ill health, I lived on that promise, but like everything else Dr. Freud told me, it proved to be a lie. During this time, I never saw Dr. Freud during the week. On Friday afternoons, he either phoned me at the clinic or sent a telegram to my apartment, summoning me to the game. In truth, I dreaded these games of Tarock, mostly because the powers of observation that made Dr. Freud a master psychologist turned him into something of a cardsharp as well. He seemed able to anticipate my every move, and consequently, he and Dr. Rie took the lion's share of the winnings, a circumstance that allowed Dr. Rosenberg to blame his own lackluster playing, absent his traditional partner, on me.

To make matters worse, I now owed them a considerable amount of money!

Still, these men were cultivated fellows, accomplished in the medical arts. Their company was stimulating, their conversation invigorating and quick, and their acquaintanceship, I knew, could only help me, the youngest colleague at the table, in a professional way. Yet, even had I cared nothing for such things, I couldn't have refused Dr. Freud's summons, as doing so meant forfeiting all hope of gaining the Fräulein. My attempt to meet her on my own had utterly failed. Though I'd discovered the location of her parents' apartment and had traversed the length of the streets adjoining it to Dr. Freud's consultancy—the only destination of hers I knew for certain—hoping to meet her along the way, the time I could devote to such skulkings was limited, during the day, by my hours at the clinic, and during the night, by my fear that with the streets deserted and my person lurking too ardently in the shadows, I might be remarked upon and a policeman summoned.

Instead, I hoped she might contrive to make an appearance each week during the Tarock game on some sweetened pretext, such as bringing refreshments down from the kitchen in the company of Frau Freud or her sister, Minna, or her sister-in-law Rosa. However, as the women and children had been warned away from Dr. Freud's medical domain during the week—and rightly so: his patients relied upon his discretion—they continued to respect its territorial exclusion from their lives when, on Saturday night, he converted it into a private men's club. (Also, as I was later to learn, it was only in Dr. Königstein's absence that the games were even held at Dr. Freud's. The friends typically met at the Königsteins', and the family spent these evenings no differently than it did when its paterfamilias was out, all but unaware of his presence in the rooms beneath them.)

And so, I continued to slush my way through the snow or ride the trolley to Dr. Freud's home, no longer making the mistake of knocking on the first floor, but heading directly to the ground floor where I was heralded by a now-familiar chorus of masculine ribaldry and subjected to an endless iteration of Tarock hands that stretched to fill the hours until the very hours seemed to stretch.

I must admit, there were times when I doubted Dr. Freud's sincerity and was convinced he dangled Fräulein Eckstein over my head only because he saw in me a suitably incompetent replacement for Königstein, known to be the worst of the Four Cardsmen of the Apocalypse (as the quartet had fashioned itself).

"She's unwell," he told me on that second Saturday; and on the third, he said, "She's worse." On the fourth, he could only shake his head. "Of course, I'm not at liberty to discuss her case, but perhaps I can tell you this much as a colleague—although your interest in her isn't really collegial, is it? However, as her condition is highly unstable, an introduction to her at this time, I'm afraid, is absolutely out of the question."

"Gentlemen," he roared at the end of that final game. "A toast!" he said, pouring out four glasses and raising his own. "As we all know, Königstein will be returned to us next Saturday, Mother Königstein having made, I'm told, a remarkable recovery in the interim. Leopold will be back in his regular chair and our little malavah malkahs will convene, as is our custom, in his rooms henceforth. Your sitting in for him, Dr.

Sammelsohn—let me say it now, lest I forget to do so later—has been richly appreciated by all."

"Bah!" Dr. Rosenberg bleated with ill-natured good humor.

"We've warmed to your company. A real affection has grown up between us, and I daresay I speak not only for myself but for all of us when I say, Salut! We shall miss you."

Either Dr. Rie or Dr. Rosenberg began a round of applause before thinking better of it. I downed my drink in the silence that followed that aborted eruption. I understood I was being dismissed from their company and that it was unlikely I would ever see any of them again.

I BEGAN FOLLOWING him. Perhaps I should be ashamed to admit this, but sometime after that, I'd noticed him through the windows of the Guglhupf, the coffee house I preferred. In those days, I was quite regular in my habits, and so apparently was he, for exactly at the same hour each afternoon, he rounded the curve of the Schottenring out for a daily walk or, I presumed, visiting patients. Fearful he might recognize me, I turned from the window and watched him in the large mirror along the café's back wall; and only when he'd passed did I drop a florin on the table and take up my coat.

I'm not by nature a sneak, and trailing Dr. Freud was anything but easy. Despite his constant smoking and what I then considered his advanced age (he was thirty-nine; I, merely twenty-one), he was a vigorous walker. Small in stature, he nevertheless carried himself with a martial stride, his chest thrust out, his shoulders back, using his stick, as a punter might an oar, to thrash through the milling crowds—the women in their complicated hats, the men in their fur coats, the students walking five abreast. He reminded me of a locomotive engine, with great puffs of cigar smoke steaming out from beneath the brim of his felt hat, and my inclination to drop back to avoid being seen by him gave way to a very real need to keep up. I struggled to hold him in my sights, as the clusters of people that broke apart for him made no such scattering concessions for me.

There are no corners on the Ringstrasse, of course, and yet each day I managed somehow to lose him. What did I imagine anyway? That I could follow him to the Ecksteins and simply barge in behind him and force him to introduce me to their daughter? It was idiocy to think so, and at such moments I could only compare myself to him unfavorably. A man of impeccable habit, he arranged his daily labors with the precision of a military campaign: up at seven, with patients by eight, at table with his family at noon, followed by a walk and further patients and dinner at seven. Then cards with Minna and another walk (more locally, in the neighborhood, this time), and he was at his writing desk by ten, working into the small hours, whereas I was the sort of man who might leave his clinic for a coffee at noon and still be loose upon the streets two hours later, his patients wondering what has become of their doctor, the nurses uncertain where to look, and all because he's allowed himself to become fascinated to the point of lunacy by a woman to whom he has yet to address a solitary word and whose face, despite the magnification of his opera glasses, he has gazed upon from a distance of no fewer than one hundred meters.

Determined to return to my practice with as much dignity as I could, I strolled at a gentlemanly pace towards the cabstand until, after about five days of this nonsense, I caught sight of him entering Landtmann's Coffee House.

HE'D SEATED HIMSELF at a table away from the kitchens. I chose a seat in the adjoining room and ordered a Kaffee mit Schlag from an old waiter with a full mustache and the turned-out feet that mark a member of his trade. I pulled a newspaper from the rack and glanced up from it periodically, as a man will, without seeming to see anything, peering about the room and hoping in this way, were Dr. Freud to glance up at precisely the same instant, to meet his gaze. Dr. Freud, however, never lifted his eyes from his work, and so I said, "Ah-ha!" to no one in particular, as though delighted to have spotted a friend. I summoned a waiter and gave him my card and watched as he ferried it across the threshold into the adjoining room. Dr. Freud picked it up and read it and sighed exasperatedly through his nose. Peering around the waiter, he acknowledged me with a scowling nod.

"Ah, Dr. Freud," I said, approaching his table. "I trust I'm not disturbing your work."

"Dr. Sammelsohn."

I bowed timidly, the annoyed tones in his voice giving me pause.

"Imagine running into you here," he said.

"A pleasant coincidence."

"Is it?"

"Pleasant?"

"A coincidence."

"But of course it is!"

"Then why are you blushing?"

"No, I don't believe I am," I said, although pronouncing this inanity only made me blush harder.

Dr. Freud drew on his cigar. "Correct me if I'm wrong, Dr. Sammelsohn, but this isn't your regular coffee house."

"No, it isn't."

"Nor is it near your apartments."

"That is correct."

"In fact, before today you've never been here."

"In this coffee house, you mean?"

"And yet today of all days . . ."

"Voilà!"

"Suddenly you are here."

"Yes" — I made a great show of scrutinizing my watch — "and due back momentarily at the clinic. Seeing you from the other room, I merely wished to extend my hand to you in friendship and to wish you a pleasant afternoon. That's all. Good day."

Dr. Freud blew an orchid of cigar smoke into the air above his head, where it bloomed and withered.

"It's far from here, isn't it?"

"Far, Dr. Freud?"

"The Allgemeines Krankenhaus?"

"Yes, quite far." I had no choice but to confirm this fact: Dr. Freud knew the local geography better than I.

"And so your being here makes no sense."

I pretended not to understand him.

"As an alibi, an excuse, a story, a ruse!" he said.

"No, as matter of fact, it doesn't," I admitted.

Dr. Freud glanced about the room. He sighed. "Well, you might as well have a seat, then."

"No, no, I really must be getting back," I said.

Nevertheless, I pulled out a chair and joined him. Through the wide doorway, I could see the old waiter with the mustache and the turned-out feet arriving at my table and searching for the gentleman who, only a moment before, had ordered the Kaffee mit Schlag he was balancing on his tray. I attempted to draw his attention to me.

"Ah . . . ah . . . a-ha!" I said, half-rising.

"I shouldn't worry about it," Dr. Freud said as the fellow returned to the kitchen. "They've nothing but cups of coffee here."

As though proving his point, the old waiter was presently at our table, handing Dr. Freud his own cup and his mail, which, in those days, one could have delivered directly to one's table.

"Kaffee mit Schlag," I said, "bitte."

The waiter's eyes narrowed. He looked at me and then over his shoulder at my former table before snorting contemptuously and walking off.

"Ah! At last!" Dr. Freud said, kissing a blue envelope and—it was an odd gesture—placing it against his forehead. "A word from Berlin!" He tore the letter open. "Ah, it's better than I'd hoped," he said, still reading. "He's actually coming!"

"Who?" I said, but Dr. Freud, rereading the letter, apparently didn't hear me.

"Well," I said, "I have an appointment, and so I'm afraid . . ."

Dr. Freud glanced up from his mail. "You do have a curious relationship to the truth," he said.

"Do I? Well, nevertheless, I must go."

I rose from the table, but Dr. Freud gripped me by my arm. "Listen to me, Dr. Sammelsohn," he said. "Men of science, such as ourselves, cannot afford to lie. Even in our private lives, we must ally ourselves so completely with the truth that nothing will ever turn us from it. A man who fears what his neighbor thinks will achieve nothing in this life. Now promise me you'll discipline yourself in this way."

I nodded but said, "I just happened to be on this side of town, and so, of course, I thought I'd drop in for a coffee, as I'd never been here before, and when I saw you, naturally, I thought . . ."

Dr. Freud looked as though a consumptive had coughed in his face. "Very well then," he said.

I didn't know what to say. I stood before him, my hat covering my crotch, an Adam on the point of being expelled from Eden (and he, I suppose, the addlepated deity who had neglected to supply me with an Eve!).

"The truth?" I said, feeling suddenly invigorated by his admonition. "Very well then: here is the truth, Dr. Freud! Yes, I intentionally followed you here."

"Yes, I thought as much."

"I saw you on the street a few days ago, and I've been following you ever since. All week, in fact, if not longer."

"But why, Dr. Sammelsohn?"

"It's because of the Fräulein, naturally!"

"The Fräulein?" Dr. Freud shook his head.

"Fräulein Eckstein!" I reminded him.

He scowled. "Oh, but Dr. Sammelsohn, you know she isn't well. In fact, her behavior at the moment is highly unpredictable, erratic even. The excitement of a suitor, even one as ineffectual as a Sammelsohn, could prove the worst thing for her, although one never knows with hysterics." Hearing himself pronounce this diagnosis aloud, he said, "Although perhaps I've said too much."

"Nevertheless," I couldn't help pressing the matter, "I was hoping you would arrange a meeting with the young woman, as you promised me you would."

"What do you mean? I promised you no such thing."

"Well, then certainly you led me to believe that such a promise had been made."

"By whom?"

"By you, of course!"

"Then forgive me, Dr. Sammelsohn."

"I know, I know, you're busy, and the Fräulein isn't well."

"No, you needn't forgive me for delaying but for promising something I have no power to deliver and no intention of ever delivering, if indeed I did." Dr. Freud's upper lip curled in an expression of disgust. "A woman is not an object one simply hands over to another man, like a girl in a harem! Besides, on your salary, you'd be mad to think of marrying. Wait until you've established your own practice and even then, believe me, it'll be a stretch. I'm speaking from bitterest experience."

"But you mentioned to me that the Fräulein had expressed a desire to make my acquaintance as well."

"Did I?"

"Yes!"

"And did she?"

"Or so you told me. And on your word, I've been waiting all these weeks."

"But why didn't you say something to me about this earlier?"

"I was under the impression you were aware of the situation."

"I'm sure I have no idea what I might have said or done to have given you such an impression. Arranging these sorts of things is more in my wife's line of interest. You should have spoken not to me, but to Marty, although of course, I would have forbidden you from doing so. The girl is ill, Dr. Sammelsohn. I have no choice in the matter."

And with that, the subject was closed. It was as though he'd slashed the word *Finis!* across the bottom of one of his manuscript pages.

BUT THEN, OF course, he relented.

"Oh, what the deuce!" he cried. "Weren't we all young and in love once? Plus, and I tell you this in strictest confidence: the poor girl's developed too strong a dependence upon me. A suitor might be a healthy distraction, although one never knows with this sort of thing. Also, you'll get to meet Wilhelm, and that's the important thing, isn't it?"

"Wilhelm?"

"Wilhelm Fliess! He's coming in from Berlin especially for the Christmas party. Oh, he's an extraordinary fellow, Dr. Sammelsohn, a first-rate mind, and you really must meet him!"

Clipping the nib off a fresh Reina Cubanas, Dr. Freud added, "On Sunday evening, we're having a group of friends over, the Ecksteins among them. You'll come as well, and we'll put this whole messy business behind us once and for all, eh?"

That was Freud: quixotically blind to his own quixotic nature, just as I was blind to my own Sancho Panza–ish abilities to overlook his madness, explaining away his sudden surrender of professionalism and good sense until it resembled its very opposite, simply because I was getting what I wanted.

CHAPTER 4

I spent the week in a delirious cloud; and when Sunday morning arrived, pulling Sunday afternoon in its train, I was almost too nervous to alight from my chair. Only after the sky had blackened did I make my way beneath it to Berggasse 19. Crossing the threshold, I knocked upon the door of Dr. Freud's consultancy, and when no answer came, I knocked again. I checked my watch. Was it possible I'd gotten the date wrong? Or come too early? Could the party have been canceled? Knocking again, I succeeded in summoning no one to the door. I patted my gloves against the sides of my coat and considered leaving. Of the two prospects—never meeting Fräulein Eckstein and finally meeting her—I didn't know which was the more terrifying, and for a moment, I considered dashing out the door. Instead, I tramped up the yellow staircase to the Freuds' apartment, where, on the other side of the double doors, I could hear the sounds of festive company: blurred voices, spoons tinkling, decanters ringing against raised glasses, the periodic explosion of laughter.

Wiping my feet on the woven mat, I forced out a nervous breath. Either my life will change, I told myself, or it won't, although I very much hoped that it would.

Was it Dr. Freud or Frau Freud or the maid who answered the door? Memory has left no trace of the figure who met me there. I recall only the apartment light spilling across the threshold and jangling my already jangled nerves. Whoever it was took me by the arm and ushered me into the salon where two or three dozen people were already gathered around the Freuds' Christmas tree.

(Yes, the Freuds had a Christmas tree, the first I'd ever seen inside a Jewish home.)

The room glittered with the usual accoutrements of late-century masquerade: monocles, lorgnettes, pince-nez, stickpins, watch fobs gleamed

in the candle light. The women wore their usual assortment of impractical hats, the men beards of every chop and curl and color.

Sipping from the drink Frau Freud's sister Minna had given me, I
peered over its rim into the room, scanning the crowd like a scholar
skimming a text, searching for that rare word, waiting for its familiar
shape to leap out against the intentionally blurred page, when, quite
suddenly, she was there—Fräulein Eckstein!—standing between Drs.
Rosenberg and Rie.

"Ah, little Königstein!" Dr. Rosenberg called out, and the two men
gestured me towards their little trio. Before I could take a step in their
direction, however, Dr. Freud placed his hand upon my shoulder and
bellowed to the assembled crowd: "Mesdames et mesdemoiselles et messieurs, permettez-moi de présenter mon collègue—"

"And our indispensable fourth in Tarock," Dr. Rie piped in.

"Le jeune docteur Jacques Sammelsohn."

The introduction, barked out in this way, elicited a smattering of applause and not a little laughter. Caught out in the white-hot spotlight of
the room's attention, I performed my usual dance of nervous ticks: laughing through my nose, shrugging repeatedly, I coughed and dropped my
gaze, like a penitent's, to the floor, horrified by the sight of my antigrope-
los (which I'd neglected to remove upon entering the apartment). Thus
blinded to the room, I felt Dr. Freud push me into a cloud of extravagant
perfumes.

"Docteur Jacques," I heard him say, "Madame Amalia Eckstein et sa
fille, l'Emma incomparable!"

Now, as anyone with any experience of the world might have told
me, at the moment of capturing the long-sought object of my desire, I
felt nothing but a wounding sense of disappointment. The girl standing
before me was not the belle femme I remembered from the Carl. No, here
was a delicate child, an invalid, lovely perhaps, but obviously unwell.
She moved with a convalescent's gracelessness, her clothing seemingly
irritating her skin. The blush dappling her cheeks, I judged, was more a
consequence of fevers than of the womanly arts. She looked as though
she'd only just risen from her sickbed. Her hair, which I recalled as a
glorious crown, lay flat, and her bosom, which in memory had defied the

principles of Newtonian gravity, rested upon her chest like two apples fallen from a tree. Even worse: in her eyes, I saw no mirrored flash of recognition, no summoning flare of interest when she looked at me or heard my name. Although Dr. Freud claimed he'd mentioned me to her, and that she'd inquired after me, obviously she had not. Instead, she greeted me with a polite indifference, perhaps even a sense of irritation: she was here only to please Dr. Freud or her mother and had no interest in me.

"What a beautifully thick head of hair the young doctor possesses!" her mother cried.

"Maman!" The Fräulein dropped her gaze to the floor. "I'm certain Dr. Sonnenfeld has better things to do than listen to compliments about his hair."

Involuntarily I raised my hand and stroked my head as though calming an agitated cat. "Sammelsohn," I said, though no one seemed to be listening.

"Nonsense," Dr. Freud boomed. "Women are not the only vain sex, you know!"

He himself made a daily visit to his barber, keeping his appointment even on the morning of his father's funeral a few years hence. And in truth, I *was* vain about my hair and preferred to wear it, as I've said, in the unkempt Bohemian style that gave me, I imagined, the tousled, late-out-of-bed look of a man so preoccupied with his thoughts that pushing him back into bed and distracting him from those thoughts would be the only thing a woman might consider doing at the sight of him. I regret to say that the effect had so far worked upon no woman more brilliantly than it had upon Madame Eckstein.

(Perhaps because Dr. Freud had introduced us in French, I continued to think of her as *Madame* Eckstein. As with many of our Jewish women, there was nothing Germanic about her, not her face, which she rouged heavily, nor her shock of orange hair, nor her diamond-shaped eyes, nor her extravagant bosom from which emanated a soporific of lavender and organdie, the scent so pervasive it preceded her appearance into any room and remained long after her departure, serving as a kind of olfactory calling card.)

I blushed against her matronly advances, while Fräulein Eckstein, mortified by these same advances, blushed also.

"Stop it, Maman! You're embarrassing him!"

"But I'm not, ma fille. Use your eyes."

Fräulein Eckstein gave Dr. Freud a desperate look, which he ignored.

"He's so young to be a doctor!" Madame Eckstein whispered to him.

"Nearly thirty," Dr. Freud murmured in return.

"Doesn't look it."

"We'll talk, Amalia. We'll talk."

"Was I embarrassing you, young man?"

"Of course not, madame," I said. What else could I tell her?

"There, Emma, you see."

"Well, you're embarrassing *me*!" the Fräulein cried. "You all are!"

Madame Eckstein straightened her spine, and her bosom, that fragrant sultan's pillow, became a hard, imperial bust. "You shall not be rude to me, young lady!"

Bending at the waist, Fräulein Eckstein placed her hands upon her abdomen. "Oh! My stomach is in *knots*!"

"Are you all right, my darling?"

"No, Mother, I am *not* all right! It was madness to bring me here."

"I didn't insist, you know," Madame Eckstein told Dr. Freud.

"Didn't you?" the Fräulein cried.

"Emma, stop this wicked behavior!"

"Excuse me," said Fräulein Eckstein. "But I really must lie down."

"Dr. Freud, Dr. Sammelsohn," Madame Eckstein said, following her daughter from the room.

"*Sigmund!*" someone else cried.

Dr. Freud and I turned in the direction of this summons to see Frau Freud standing beside her sister Minna, both of the Bernays women with their black hair pulled back into a severe bun, each with her arms crossed, both tapping an irritated foot, both obviously annoyed about something.

E nter Wilhelm Fliess, the handsome ear, nose, and throat special-ist from cosmopolitan Berlin and the presumptive villain of our story. He was standing between the Freuds' green ceramic stove and their glittering Christmas tree, a yuletide drink in his hand. A gifted monologist, he had succeeded in luring the majority of Dr. Freud's guests to his corner.

He was a marvelously attractive fellow. Even I will admit that. His coal-black eyes and his jet-black beard glistened in the candlelight. Though his pate shone through his tonsure like a knee through a worn trouser leg, the receding hairline only made him appear more virile. I was especially struck by the audacity of his plum cravat. Here was a man, I told myself, who had fallen deeply, madly, and passionately in love with himself, and this was perhaps the only love he'd ever fully reciprocated.

Josef Breuer, Dr. Freud's mentor, had introduced the two men a few years earlier, and they had hit it off immediately. Roughly the same age, each newly married, both beginning their families and their careers, they even resembled each other: bearded Jews with penetrating eyes and straight, handsome noses. But there was another, even more striking congruity: in his theoretical work, each man was stepping outside the bounds of accepted medical practice, and to the late-nineteenth-century mind, Dr. Freud's mad-brained theories on dreams, on the unconscious, on sexuality, seemed no less far-fetched (if, indeed, far less fetching) than did Dr. Fliess's odd notions.

Scorned by a blinkered medical establishment, the two men sheltered inside each other's admiration, offering a sympathetic ear and an ap-proving bosom upon which to lay, figuratively at least, their heads. Meet-ing as frequently as their schedules permitted—in Germany, in Austria, in the little towns dotting the Italian border—for what Dr. Freud had christened their "private congresses," they shared their thoughts and gave each other counsel and encouragement.

And what were Dr. Fliess's radical new ideas? Well, principally, he had two. The first of these, the theory of periodicity, held that all life was determined by two powerful biorhythmic cycles. The more familiar of these, consisting of twenty-eight days, was feminine in nature, whereas the less familiar cycle of twenty-three days was masculine. By multiplying one of these integers against the other, or each by the difference between the two, and adding or subtracting the results, Dr. Fliess was able to find these numbers hidden, as a unifying pattern, in virtually all of creation.

Dr. Fliess's other theory, and the one that more concerns us here, pertained to that triangular mound of bifurcated flesh located in the center of the human face, by which I mean the nose. The nose for Wilhelm Fliess was what the psyche was for Sigmund Freud: the source of all human unhappiness as well as the locus of its cure. He'd discovered an ailment that he christened the nasal reflex neurosis, and in a seventy-nine-page booklet entitled *New Contributions to the Theory and Therapy of the Nasal Reflex Neurosis,* he'd reported on over 130 cases of it. Not content to have merely discovered the malady, he also devised its cure: heavy cocaine swathes, normal cauterizations, and if these failed, galvanic cauterizations.

"Now, when this treatment is followed," he told us that evening, sipping at his drink, "the nasal reflex neurosis will become the principal means of earning his daily bread for the general practitioner, and as a consequence, the immense multitude of neurasthenics will disappear. By that, I mean, of course, those unfortunates who, rushing from doctor to doctor and from spa to spa, make a *mockery* of our healing arts as they fall into the hands of all sorts of disreputable quacks!"

"But surely it's more complicated than you're making out," Dr. Rie suggested.

Dr. Fliess granted him a condescending smile. "We live in an age of miracles and wonders, Dr. Rie, miracles and wonders, as you well know, and as the frontiers of knowledge advance rapidly before us, we must hurry if we are to keep up. We must hurry. No, we mustn't blind our-selves to any new discoveries. Now, I'm well aware that the astonishing newness of my ideas too easily makes skeptics of otherwise fair and im-partial men, and accordingly, I've taken the precaution of documenting my researches with absolute meticulousness. With absolute meticulous-ness. For example, when the observation of blood in my infant son's urine led to my discovery of male menstruation—"

"Male menstruation?" Dr. Rosenberg nearly spat out his drink.

Dr. Fliess nodded. "—occurring every twenty-three days in both men *and* women, I took great pains to preserve the sheet and shirt with those precious traces of blood on them. Not merely as a means of silencing my detractors, mind you, but for the sake of posterity as well. For the sake of posterity as well. However, as a doctor committed to my patients, I'm willing to try anything if it means restoring an invalid to her health. Why, only recently, I cured a slight case of strabismus in a two-year-old by scraping his tonsil with my bare fingernail. How did I know the dis-eased tonsils were inhibiting the maturation of the child's eye muscles? Genius? Intuition? Call it what you will! It worked, ladies and gentlemen, it worked."

His ring twinkled against the lights of the Freuds' Christmas tree as he puffed on his cigar.

"Today, of course, everyone is crying 'Neurasthenia! Neurasthenia!'" Dr. Fliess cried, raising his hands and shaking them in the air, as though he were mimicking a man shrieking the word. "But I'll tell you this: most neurasthenics are simply poorly misdiagnosed wretches suffering not from neurasthenia"—again he raised his hands and shook them—"but from nasal reflex neurosis!"

"And the proof of this?" Dr. Rie countered.

Dr. Fliess smiled handsomely. "The proof of this is my testimony be-fore you tonight. Oh, I know, it's tedious to hear a man singing his own praises, but since you asked me and since I'm talking anyway, let me say only this. However, let me say it clearly: with my nasal therapies, I've suc-ceeded where master physicians have striven in vain to cure. Reviewing my cases at the end of a long week, I often astonish myself. No, I do."

He glanced over at Dr. Freud. The two seemed to be sharing some stimulating secret. It's well known now, of course, that in addition to aiding and abetting Dr. Fliess in his numerological preoccupations, supplying the data-hungry Berliner with all sorts of information — the birth dates and death dates of his family, the rhythm of Frau Freud's menses, the ebb and flow of their children's illnesses and of his own literary productivity — Dr. Freud twice allowed Dr. Fliess to operate upon his own nose as a cure for various cardiac complaints and that he recommended courses of nasal therapy to many of his own patients as well. Dr. Fliess typically swathed the postoperative nasal passages of these patients with lavish doses of cocaine, and this might go some distance in explaining the extraordinary benefit to mood perceived by all of them, including Dr. Freud, who, we now know, conducted an ill-considered love affair with the narcotic. Indeed, cocaine might go some distance in explaining Dr. Fliess's mesmerizing conversational style. His light-footed rhythms, his quicksilver connections, his inexhaustible fund of images all bear the cloven hoofprint of that old devil, although of course none of us realized this at the time.

"And let me tell you something even more marvelous and originally profound!" he cried out. "As our host has heroically shown — and cheers all around for Dr. Sigmund Freud!" — he raised his glass in Dr. Freud's direction — "neurasthenia in young people is caused by nothing less sinister than masturbation!"

Though he pronounced the word with a practiced frankness, several of the women in the room gasped, and suddenly I understood the Bernays sisters' consternated toe-tapping. Dr. Rie hemmed and hawed; Dr. Rosenberg threw his hands in the air; Dr. Breuer scowled behind his wispy beard; Dr. Rosanes laughed into his drink; but Dr. Fliess continued on as boldly as before.

"Naturally enough, bad sex behaviors in both genders affect more than just the nose. The nervous system is harmed as well, of course, but it's the nose that suffers most."

A woman moaned. "Good Lord, man!" Dr. Rie protested weakly.

Misunderstanding the nature of their distress, Dr. Fliess hurried to defend his thesis: "Let me assure you that I'm speaking here strictly from experience with my own practice in Berlin. Immediately after masturbation, one may observe a very characteristic swelling and a heightened sensitivity to what I call the nasal-genital spots." He tapped his nose twice with his forefinger.

"Sigmund, may I speak to you this very instant?" Tight-lipped and white-knuckled, Frau Freud gestured her husband from the room.

"That's the problem, you see," Dr. Fliess continued. "One may remove the painful spots — I've done it a million times: scrape, scrape, scrape!— but they simply return as long as abnormal sexual satisfaction is occurring. Now it's a well-known scientific fact that unmarried women who masturbate suffer from painful menstruation, along with neuralgic stomachache and excessive nosebleed. Who among us does not know this? And so you're correct, Dr. Rie: my nasal therapies are helpless, absolutely, in aiding these women *until* they surrender these vile practices."

He was losing his audience. This frank talk was costing him the attention of all but those of us in possession of a medical degree. Most of the women had already fled the room.

"Preposterous," Dr. Rie muttered.

"Preposterous?" Dr. Fliess glanced over our shoulders at the defectors. "No, but I shall tell you what *is* preposterous. What *is* preposterous is the fact that this condition, prevalent for so long in our society, has gone undetected, and that those daring enough to attempt its cure are laughed at and scorned and mocked and driven from our professional societies until we are nearly insane with bitterness and rage!" Dr. Fliess clapped the back of one hand against the palm of the other. "And yet, despite the opposition I have personally received on this score, I have persevered in devising a cure. A cure, yes! By altering the left middle turbinate bone in the nose's frontal third, precisely in 'the nasal stomachache spot,' as I have termed it, I have cured my patients not only of their abnormal sexual practices but of the neuroses these practices create as well."

"Nasal stomachache spot!" Dr. Rie harrumphed again.

Dr. Fliess was bristling now. "Yes. Unfortunately, however, as I've discovered, there is more profit in addressing oneself to laymen who are grateful for one's work than to professionals who, in their Latin-nomenclatured ignorance, betray that ignorance by scoffing!"

"Wilhelm, my dearest friend." Dr. Freud had at that moment reentered the room and was looking anxiously between the two men. "You've allowed us to detain you long enough. When you publish the rest of your beautiful novelties, as you must, you'll astonish more than a small group of sympathetic friends. You'll astonish the world. And although we can wait for that, our dinner, I'm afraid, cannot. May I invite everyone in to dine?"

(As for Dr. Fliess's presumptive villainy, I can say only this: In the coming months, a strange story was bruited about the cafés and whispered over in our little medical circles, to wit: that Dr. Freud, fearful that through his newly minted psychoanalytic bias, he may have overlooked a physical reason for Fräulein Eckstein's suffering, invited Dr. Fliess in to consult, and that Dr. Fliess had suggested to him that the Fräulein's hysteria was symptomatic of nasal reflex neurosis and had recommended, as a cure, the removal of the left middle turbinate bone of her nose. The story continues: having never performed this surgery, his own mad invention, before; indeed, having never performed major surgery at all; having previously confined his practice to simple cauterizations and cocainizations of the nose, Dr. Fliess botched the job and nearly killed the girl when he accidentally left a meter of surgical gauze inside her nasal cavity. This story, as my own narrative will demonstrate, is preposterous, of course, designed to blot out the true events, which I will now recount.)

Nothing was as I imagined it only an hour before. I could barely concentrate on my dinner. Frau Freud had placed me between Dr. Freud's sister Rosa and Heinrich Graf, her fiancé, and though they tried to include me in their conversation (something about the massacres at Aleppo), I could think of nothing but Dr. Fliess and his strange theories. Was it possible that masturbation actually disfigured the nose? And could the removal of the left middle turbinate bone truly relieve not only stomachache and uterine bleeding but also the psychic distress caused by masturbation? And *did* masturbation really cause psychic distress? (Or wasn't it the other way around? Speaking for myself, abstinence seemed to create as much psychic distress as did autoeroticism; and normal sexual satisfaction, as Dr. Fliess had so blithely termed it, would, I feared, create only more.)

Granted: there *were* similarities between the genitals and the nose. Both hung on the central column of the body without a complementing twin. In women, the nostrils resided above the mouth as did the oviducts above the nether labia; both were capable of bleeding. In men, the formal symmetry between the nostrils and the testicles, being external, was even more pronounced. I couldn't help glancing about the table at the twenty or so noses ringed about me. Sharp, flat, hooked, pug, aquiline, Greek, snub, hawk, celestial; this one wagging his, that one caressing hers; how shamelessly we displayed them in public; how baldly we allowed them to protrude into the open air—quivering, vulnerable, receptive! I blushed as the scrolled nostrils of the woman across from me seemed suddenly as enticing as might the dimples of her rump! How was it possible, I wondered, that neither law nor custom forbade the display of nose hair in public? The way it sprouted from some of the older gentlemen's nostrils in stiff tufts seemed almost lewd, as did the blue veins that stood out on the reddened skin of some of the coarser specimens on display. Beards, mustaches, side whiskers, even eyebrows now brought to mind only one thing: the littler beards we kept hidden beneath our trousers and our skirts. I dropped my gaze when this one chortled through hers or that one brought a handkerchief to his, pulling on it with sharp brisk tugs until he'd emptied it of its contents.

Frau Freud's cherried veal tasted like wood pulp in my mouth, and I'm afraid I availed myself too eagerly of the wine. It was bad enough that everyone appeared to be wearing a pornographic postcard glued to the middle of his forehead; worse was the disillusionment I felt upon finally meeting the great and brilliant Dr. Fliess. The dashing young genius from Berlin, about whom I'd heard so much, struck me as little better than a Bedlamite. I was aghast to watch him, seated at Dr. Freud's right, soliciting from those who'd been honored with chairs near his the dates of all the significant events of their lives, from which, like a fortune-teller, he was busy calculating the hour of their demise.

"Fifty-one months from your birthday," he said, adding up his figures, "fifty-one being twenty-three plus twenty-eight, minus the difference between them, which is five, multiplied by twenty-three squared, divided by the square root of twenty-eight . . . ah, yes, here it is. According to my calculations, you can expect to expire at precisely thirty-six minutes past two on the morning of March 14, 1938."

His dining companions appeared eager for this information and, once it had been revealed to them, delighted to possess it. Indeed, I watched with my mouth agape as Amalia Eckstein inscribed the date of her death into a booklet she withdrew from her purse, penciling it in as though it were a dental appointment!

(Proof of the prophet's worthlessness, I told myself, was the fact that according to his calculations, a majority of the people at the table were to perish in March of 1938.)

I could only shake my head. Dr. Freud had a weakness for gypsy-like parlor games, it's true; but Dr. Fliess had gone him one better. If, like an Hasidic rebbe, Dr. Freud could read a man's sins in the lines of his face, Dr. Fliess, like God Himself, knew the hour of his demise.

What did it say about Sigmund Freud, I wondered, that he revered a man of such low caliber?

STILL, ALL THIS was nothing compared to the heartbreak I had experienced upon seeing Fräulein Eckstein again. Never for a moment had I imagined that the woman whose picture I'd carried in my heart for over a month might feel only indifference towards me! It was madness to have come here, I told myself. I regretted pressuring Dr. Freud into inviting me to this odd Christmas soirée (in attendance at which there seemed to be only Jews; at a quick glance, I estimated that none of the guests had ever been within ten feet of a baptismal font!). Still, I couldn't help watching Fräulein Eckstein. The way she laughed at Dr. Fliess's calculations, hanging on to his every word, made me blind with rage. It pained me to see her eyes glistening with admiration for him while she sat with her fingers braided before her mouth and her nose laid out like a dainty for him upon the platter of her hands.

(Her interest in Dr. Fliess, it turned out, was completely counterfeit. As I would learn the next day, she was merely flattering him as a way of pleasing Dr. Freud.)

"Dr. Sammelsohn!" I heard my name called as though from a great distance. "Are you still with us, then?" I refocused my eyes, and the white and blue blotches before them unblurred into the person of Fräulein Rosa Freud, sitting beside me in a shimmering blue dress.

"Ah, Fräulein Freud," I said, "pardon me. I must have been daydreaming."

"I was only asking you whether you agreed that what Herr Graf just said was wickedly funny."

I looked at her fiancé, Graf. He smiled at me ludicrously, his watery eyes brimming behind his pince-nez. "Oh, well, no," he said with modest good humor, "it's nothing really." He smiled tenderly at Fräulein Rosa. "I was just saying that it's apparently not enough for Dr. Fliess to cure gynecological concerns, but he must stick his nose into Dr. Freud's neurosis as well."

Although this was the second time in as many minutes that she had heard the witticism, appreciative laughter fell from Fräulein Rosa's painted mouth. She reached across me to caress Herr Graf's hand, and the two retreated into the privacy of each other's gaze.

I'd never felt lonelier in my life.

What further disaster could befall me that evening?

"AH, DR. SAMMELSOHN, may I touch it?" Amalia Eckstein had sneaked up behind me when I'd stopped in the hallway to admire the Freuds' new telephone. A wooden box with a phallic-looking tube above two silver bells that resembled naked breasts—or so, in my current state of mind, the apparatus appeared to me—it was the first I'd seen in a private home.

"What in Heaven's name are you talking about?" I cried, turning in alarm. I had thought, of course, she had meant my nose.

"Why, your hair, you silly-billy," she said. "Because it's so extraordinarily thick and marvelous!" She lifted her hand and let it hover in the now-electric air between us. What could I say to her? That I'd prefer she didn't touch me? Of course, I did the only thing a gentleman could, which was to bow my head and offer it to her. "Oh! But oh—oh my! It's so much softer than it looks! So soft and so curly and so full! Oh—but it's an absolute delight!"

I felt as though I were being examined by a careless phrenologist. Her nails nicked the skin behind my ears. As strands of my hair became entangled in her rings, she simply plucked them out. Worse: she'd pushed the shelf of her bosom so near my face that my breath had steamed up my glasses, and when I heard Fräulein Eckstein's strangled cry—alas, the Fräulein had stumbled upon our unfortunate tableau—I had no choice but to read through the steamy lenses the horror etching itself upon her face.

"Mother!" she cried.

"Darling, you must come here and caress this young man's hair immediately! It's une expérience sensuelle."

"I will do no such thing! My God, Mother"—Fräulein Eckstein dropped her voice—"there are people in the other room!" Unable to force herself from the passageway, she covered her face with her hands, blocking out the image, and I feared she might at any moment faint.

"Madame, if you will excuse me," I said, stepping away from the mother. "Fräulein." I nodded to the daughter. As I approached her, however, she jumped away from me, as though I were a moral leper, and for the final time that evening, I gave up all hope of wooing her.

Dr. Freud beckoned me from the open doorway of his apartment. "Dr. Sammelsohn!" he cried, with Drs. Rie and Rosenberg standing on either side of him, like two thieves flanking the savior whose birthday they, in their strange way, had been honoring that night.

"I've invited the men and the women to separate," he explained to the Ecksteins and to me, "the women to remain above, nearer the Heavens, the men to descend into the nether regions, where each may partake of the activities biology has assigned them: the women to their chattering; the men to their brandy and cigars!"

Happy for an opportunity to escape, I offered Fräulein Eckstein an embarrassed bow and attempted to edge past her. However, she pulled me to her and held me so closely that when she spoke, I could feel her breath palpating my lips.

"Help me!" she whispered, as though it were a request I had too often refused her.

"Help you, Fräulein? Of course, I will, but how?"

"Lower you voice," she commanded me. "The others mustn't hear us."

I looked at her mother and at Dr. Freud.

"I've been trying to speak to you all evening."

I peered into her face. "Frankly I'm astonished to hear this, Fräulein."

"You're the only one who can help me."

I didn't know what to say to her.

"Will you?" she demanded.

"Of course, I will, Fräulein."

"Then why haven't you responded to me?"

I searched her face, understanding nothing of what she was saying to me. "Responded to you, Fräulein?"

"To my ads. In the newspaper," she explained. "In the personal advertisement section. I've been leaving you ads in the *Neue Freie Presse* for well over a month now!"

I continued to stare at her as though I were a village idiot who had never dreamt that men might communicate with each other by printing words in a newspaper.

"Of course," I said, shaking my head in an attempt to uncloud it. "I'll look for your notice there."

"The next one's scheduled for tomorrow morning."

"So soon, Fräulein?"

"And you'll read it?"

"Certainly."

"And if I've asked you to meet me somewhere, you'll meet me?"

I hesitated.

"I must speak with you," she insisted. "It's absolutely urgent. Not here." She glanced at her mother. "But in private."

Before I could respond, Dr. Freud called for me again. The Fräulein released my hand, and my fingers ached where she had gripped them. I saw that the other men had already left the apartment and were presumably descending the stairs to Dr. Freud's consulting rooms. I glanced again at Fräulein Eckstein. She seemed to have disappeared inside herself. It was as though the light of her face had darkened its flame. Dr. Freud and Madame Eckstein witnessed this strange phenomenon as well, and their eyes met in an unspoken moment of concern. A naïf, I imagined that they were congratulating themselves on the match they'd arranged between us. (With equal naïveté, I'd interpreted Madame Eckstein's flirtatiousness as nothing more sinister than motherly affection. Didn't all women fall in love with their daughter's suitors and, later on, with their husbands?) But I might as well have been blind. Indeed, of all that was occurring about me, I saw little; and of the little I saw, I understood even less.

With a bow to the women, I hurried down the yellow staircase after Dr. Freud.

"Come on, come on then!" he called up, seconds ahead of me but already at the bottom of the stairs. "The time until you meet again will pass slowly, so you might as well fill it with cigars and good company. Dr. Königstein has returned, as you know, and there's no telling when we'll next spend a sociable hour together. With your losses at cards tonight, you will handsomely repay me for whatever services I, in my capacity as Cupid, have rendered you. Although how could it be otherwise? Where there is Psyche, Eros must naturally appear!"

He addressed me from the doorway of his consulting rooms, a hard, mad glint in his eye. It was a look I recalled receiving before only from my father, a glance so lacerating I feared neither of us would avoid being cut to shreds by it.

That night, I couldn't sleep. I was too nervous about what I'd find in tomorrow's paper. Abandoning my bed, I fished the *Neue Freie Presse* from the trash bin, where it lay beneath a moist hash of coffee grounds and apple cores. I'd never concerned myself with these sorts of things, these personal advertisements, but I understood the city was mad for them, and now I saw why: who could resist the most private of correspondences carried out in this most public of places, clandestine meetings arranged before the entire world, the particulars of one's secret assignations announced via the public press?

> To the exquisite lady sipping coffee in the Café Griensteidl yesterday with a young child I took to be her niece; she so sympathetically shared her cream pitcher with a gentleman at the neighboring table and would do this gentleman an even greater kindness by indicating to Box 721, this newspaper, when and at what café he might return the favor.

Things were not yet as notorious in Vienna as they would later become, with everyone and his sister crawling into bed (sometimes with each other), but an air of promiscuity had already descended upon the city, sending its inhabitants scurrying for warmth; and where better to find that warmth than in the arms of a similarly invigorated other?

> The woman who, Wednesday last, during the Mozart at the Lichtentaler Pfarrkirche, caught the eye of the gentleman behind her, enraptured by the obbligati, is hereby begged for a longer interlude at a suitable hour to be agreed upon, he prays, through Box 456, this newspaper, at the convenience of her delight.

At the convenience of her delight? Is this what Fräulein Eckstein wanted? To declaim her love for me from behind a mask of serifed prose? If so, I suspected it had everything to do with her mother. Indeed, how intoxicating to conduct an illicit affair right beneath the nose of one's dueña. (Ah! the nose! the nose! I couldn't get Dr. Fliess's damned noses out of my brain!) I turned the pages of the paper and glanced through the ads once again. I was shocked to see that even the bite of an agonized conscience was inked in printer's black for all the world to see:

> My darling S., I live in terror over what my sister may or may not suspect. Leave no more letters at our home, nor will I meet you this afternoon in your laboratory. Communicate with me only through Box 621, this newspaper, and may God grant us the strength to stop, your loving M.

I cinched the belt of my robe tighter. How had I gotten myself into this mess? A day before, I might have been entranced by the naughtiness of it all. Now I only felt intimidated by the game. I was in over my head, and I knew it. True, I'd been ogling women for years, but nothing like this had ever happened to me as a consequence. And the truth of the matter is it had very little to do with me. Coincidence alone had placed Dr. Freud beside me at the Carl; happenstance had allowed him to read my mind—I didn't even possess courage enough to ask him for the Fräulein's name—and it was the Fräulein herself who had approached me at the Freuds' Christmas party. Left to my own devices, I'm certain I'd still be daydreaming about a nameless girl I would never see again. And wouldn't that be preferable? I had no head for this sort of thing! I could barely navigate the circles of the city. With a map Otto had given me when I'd first moved in, I'd plotted out my essential routes—from my apartment to the hospital, from the hospital to the opera, and lately from the hospital, my apartment, or the opera to Dr. Freud's. Despite my stalking of him, I had little idea where the rest of the city was kept, including, or rather especially, the offices of the *Neue Freie Presse*. Nor did I understand how one went about procuring for himself a "numbered box." Certainly the clerk who handled these transactions understood their licentious purposes. How brazen *was* the Fräulein, one had to wonder, that she could meet the wink of this fellow while filling out the requisite forms?

(Glancing through the advertisements, I soon discovered that there were many purposes, not all of them immoral, to which one might employ one's box: professors giving piano lessons advertised for students in this way, as did merchants searching for employees and tradesmen for customers. The libertines and demimondaines who flaunted their epistolary concupiscence in the broad daylight of newsprint did so under the protective banner of these more respectable burghers.)

It was nearly three in the morning when I threw the paper down. I lay on the sofa, and once again, I saw that hard, mad glint in Dr. Freud's eye. Looking deeper into it, I was repulsed by the homunculur portrait of myself reflected in its vacuum. Beneath his captious leer, I appeared not as I knew myself—a lovelorn chap searching myopically through the circular maze of Vienna for a woman who might love him with an ardor equaling his own—but as Dr. Freud saw me: a wild, slobbering satyr whose membrum virile, rising like a gnarled branch from the delta of his crotch, had become so inflamed, he'd stick it anywhere to extinguish its fire. My desire for love had somehow transformed me into a rascal who couldn't be trusted with the girls! Nor was this the first time I'd been exiled to rascaldom by the all-too-knowing gaze of another. My father's glance used to pierce my side in the same crucifying way. Hadn't I continually disgraced him, a boy with straw instead of thoughts inside his head, a balk of a son, compelled through life by no force greater than his own tomfoolery? As I crawled onto the sofa and stared at the ceiling, I knew a large part of the disgust I felt for myself belonged properly to my father.

He had failed to prepare me for life in every way.

ONLY TAKE, FOR example, the day he asked me into his study so that he might explain the mysteries of sexual union to me. This was a day I'd prefer to forget, though not one painful hour of it has escaped my memory. We sat opposite each other, my father and I, he behind a large desk piled high with bills and invoices, and I on a low, small chair before it. I was barely twelve.

"יעקב," he said, addressing me, as was his custom, in Hebrew: *Ya'akov* (Genesis 44:34). "ושמעת את כל הדברים האלה אשר אנכי מצוך למען ייטב לך" *Listen to everything I tell you, if you know what's good for you* (Deuteronomy 12:28).

His short beard had turned greyer and his face thinner since the discovery of my crime. Unable to eat or sleep, he'd become an emaciated version of himself. When he folded his thin arms against his chest, the sleeves of his kapote scissored against each other, producing sharp whistling noises. He opened his mouth to speak but could apparently find nothing to say. He walked to the window and peered through it. The wind nudged a few leaves an inch or two across the meadow outside. With his arms behind his back and his spine held straight and his blue-black shadow falling behind him, he resembled the gnomon of a sundial.

Neither of us had touched the tea my sister Reyzl had brought in to us. Our cups sat on their saucers, growing cold. When I lifted mine, my hand trembled so violently and the cup rattled so noisily, I had to put it down. Turning towards the sound, Father glowered, and my cheeks burned beneath his gaze. I knew what he was thinking: How is it possible that this creature, so alien to me in every way, this miscreant who's made a mockery of everything I know to be true, this reproduction that resembles the original not in the least, sprung from my inner being? And now to have to school this botch of a son in the lessons of manhood so that he might plant his own seeds and produce his own children who, God forbid, will resemble me even less!

The bitterness of my apostasy aside, it was a torment for my father to have to speak of these unseemly matters. And yet — he sighed — one is commanded to teach one's children; and no man is exempt from the directives of the Lord.

He picked up his tea and peered into the cup. His mouth an ugly gash, he sniffed at the drink, as though at the scent of curdling milk, before returning it to its place. He cleared his throat and rubbed his papery hands together, clapping once.

"אל־תיראי כי־לא תבושי," he said. *Don't worry, for I won't embarrass you* (Isaiah 54:4). "גשה נא" *Come closer* (Genesis 27:21). "ועתה בני שמע בקלי" *Now, my son, listen to me* (Genesis 27:8). "קראתיך בצדק ואחזק בידך" *I've called you for a righteous purpose and have taken hold of your hand* (Isaiah 42:6).

He seemed to be listening to his own words — they seemed to hover in the air between us — scrutinizing them as a jeweler might a string of diamonds, searching for a secret flaw. Finding none, he proceeded. "רק חזק ואמץ" *Only be strong and courageous* (Joshua 1:7) "החרישו אלי" *and listen to me without interruption* (Isaiah 41:1) "בן יכבד אב" *for a son will show honor to his father* (Malachi 1:6).

How may I explain these linguistic peculiarities of my father's?

By the time I was born, he refused to speak in any but the holy tongue. What were his choices? Yiddish was a mongrel pidgin, suitable only for women and illiterates. German—a barking, braggart's tongue—belonged to the children of Esau, and Father would have never dreamt of sullying the holy vessel of his mouth with its guttural frothings. As for Russian, it wasn't even a human language. Rather, it had been taught to the ancient Varangians by bears (hence the Russian proclivity for laziness and violence). French, something Father had picked up in his youth, my grandmother Sammelsohn having harbored unrealistic dreams of a diplomatic career for him, was, on the other hand, an all-too-human patois: curling the tongue, it trained it for duplicity. Why else did everything in it—taunts, curses, even the blackest of threats—sound like the sweetest of psalms?

For all his fanciful glossologies, Father might have languished in silence, had it not been for the holy tongue, although Hebrew presented its own problems: the language in which the angels beseech one another for permission to chant their unceasing praises, as well as the language in which these praises are unceasingly chanted, Hebrew was the language with which the Holy One had spoken the Heavens and the Earth into being. This troubled my father. How could he, mere ashes and dust (Job 42:6), speak the language of the Lord? Fearing the Holy One's sacred places (Exodus 19:30), he would have preferred the distant dove of silence (Psalm 56:1) to defiling the sacred tongue by straying from its words (Proverbs 4:5).

Fortunately, God Himself had commanded us to speak it, viz.: "ודברי אשר שמתי בפיך לא ימושו מפיך ומפי זרעך ומפי זרע זרעך אמר ד' מעתה ועד עולם" *My words, which I've placed in your mouth, shall not be removed from your mouth or from the mouth of your children or from the mouth of your children's children, thus saith the Lord, from now until forever* (Isaiah 59:21).

Still, painfully aware of his dismal humanity, Father leavened this celestial vocabulary with the earthier Aramaic of the Oral Law, hoping in this way to keep his feet rooted to the ground.

And did our Father find his powers of expression limited by this peculiar choice?

Not at all, not at all! On the contrary: "הפך בה והפך בה דכולה בה," he'd say: *Turn it and turn it for everything is in it* (Avos 5:26). Indeed, father's knowledge of the scriptures was so complete he was able to carry on lengthy conversations on a wide range of topics, once, for example, discussing his gastric pains with our family physician.

"וואָס איז דער מער?," Dr. Kirschbaum asked him, in Yiddish, of course.

"צר לי," Father said. *I'm in distress* (Lamentations 1:20). He pointed to his belly. "יש רעה חולה ראיתי תחת השמש" *There is an evil sickness I've seen under the sun* (Ecclesiastes 5:12).

"And your bowels?" the doctor asked, palpating him, "how are they?"

"נצמתו," my father said: *They've shriveled up* (Job 6:17).

"Any problems with flatulence?"

Father shrugged. "הקץ לדברי רוח" *Is there no end to these words of wind?* (ibid. 16:3).

Dr. Kirshbaum handed him a curative powder in a paper sleeve and played along. "רפאות תהי לשרך" *This will be a cure for your navel* (Proverbs 3:8).

Another time, when Father had ordered manure to be laid upon the orchards, he'd noticed the gardener boy idling about. "הנה זה עומד אחר כתלנו מציץ מן החרכים," he muttered. *There he stands behind our wall, peering through the lattice* (Song of Songs 2:9). He called to the lad. "הטה אלי אזנך והושיעני" *Incline your ear to me and help* (Psalm 71:2) "כי הנה הסתיו עבר הגשם חלף הלך לו" *for now the winter is past and the rains are gone* (Song of Songs 2:11) "הנצנים נראו בארץ עת הזמיר הגיע" *the flowers have appeared on the land and the time for pruning has come* (ibid. 2:12). Steering his charge towards the fertilizer, he commanded him: "ופרצת ימה וקדמה וצפנה ונגבה" *You shall spread it out powerfully westward, eastward, northward and southward* (Genesis 29:14) that it may "הפיחי גני יזלו בשמיו" *blow upon my garden and its perfume spread* (Song of Songs 4:16). But he cautioned him: "בני תורתי אל־תשכח ומצותי יצר לבך" *My boy, let your mind retain my orders*

(Proverbs 3:1), for "למה תשבת המלאכה כאשר ארפה" *why should the work be halted when I leave?* (Nehemiah 6:3).

As incredible as it may seem, those who knew my father as a young man claim that though he never uttered a word that couldn't be found in the Torah or the Talmud or the Commentaries or the Codes, he was a chatterbox who never ceased talking. However, as he grew older, the fear that he might tarnish the holy tongue through everyday use took hold of him, and by the time I was born, he'd ceased speaking in complete sentences and only whispered one or two phrases to make his will known. If our mother pleased him, for example, he might say, "מי ימצא" (*Who can find?*) or "מפנינים" (*greater than pearls*), and we understood that he was showering his abbreviated praises upon her. "אשת חיל מי ימצא ורחק מפנינים מכרה" *Who can find a noble wife? Her price is beyond pearls* (Proverbs 31:10). Or if, on a cold winter's day, I raced out to skylark with friends in the snow, he might block my path and hold out two woolen scarves to me and say, "קשרם," and I knew he meant *Bind them* as in "קשרם אל גרגרותיך" *Bind them about your throat* (Proverbs 3:3). On Sabbath evenings, after we children had been put to bed, we'd hear him, through the thin walls of our house, crooning *Song of Songs* to our Mother. Indeed, he did this so regularly that, after many years, if, in her hearing, speaking of agricultural concerns, he happened to mention "a flock of goats" (6:5) or, in looking at our ceilings, muttered something about "the beams of our house" (1:7), she was helpless to control her blushes.

My sisters—Gitl, Golde, Rukhl, Reyzl, Feyge, Khayke, and Sore Dvore—all older than I, understood him perfectly. Perhaps their education, occurring at home, had been more thorough than mine; perhaps, having known him when he'd spoken in complete sentences, they could decipher his shorthand more easily; perhaps they simply loved him better than I did and found it easier to indulge him. Whatever the reason, I couldn't understand a word he said. Taking pity on me, my sisters and sometimes even my mother translated his remarks into a warm and womanly Yiddish, and as a result, I seldom bothered listening to him at all, nor did I take seriously the obligation to learn the Torah backwards and forwards in order to understand what he was saying.

(A word of caution here: as my father's eccentricities were explained to me when I was a small child by my sisters, it's possible they thought to cast it all in a wondrous fairy-tale light, suspecting that I, a stubborn child, might be more amenable to the polylingual demands placed upon our family by our father if I could believe in their tales of talking bears and jabbering angels. It's also possible that I'm misremembering — *perhaps even intentionally!* — what was in fact no more than my father's not unusual penchant, given the time and place, for peppering his speech with scriptural quotations.

Be that as it may, when he towered over me that day in his office and said, "קדשים תהיו כי קדוש אני" *You shall be holy, as I, the Lord your God, am holy* (Leviticus 19:2), I understood from his tone that the preamble was over and the specifics were now to be addressed.

He sighed unhappily. "התיצב והכן לך," he said. *Stand erect and prepare yourself* (Jeremiah 46:14). "נערה בתולה שכבה בחיקך" *A virgin girl will lie in your bosom* (I Kings 1:2). "השמר והשקט אל־תירא ולבבך אל־ירך" *Be calm, fear not, let not your heart grow faint* (Isaiah 7:4). "ולזרק עליו דם" *Blood may be dashed* (Ezekiel 43:18) "וביום באו אל־החצר הפנימית" *on the day of a man's entry into the inner courtyard* (Ezekiel 44:27). "צר המקום" *The place is tight* (Isaiah 49:20). "הוא פלאי" *It is hidden* (Judges 13:18). "ככתוב" *For as it is written:* "בין רגליה כרע נפל שכב" *Between her legs, he knelt, toppled, lay* (Judges 5:27). "נפל איש אל־רעהו" *One fell against the other* (Jeremiah 46:16). "וישב על־ברכיה" *He sat on her lap* (II Kings 4:20). "ששון ושמחה ימצא בה" *Joy and gladness shall be found there* (Isaiah 51:3).

Something made him hesitate. "אהא הנה לו־ידעתי דבר," he said. *Alas, I know not how to speak* (Jeremiah 1:6). He scowled and wet his tongue nervously. "וידעת את אשר תעשה" *But you will know what to do* (I Kings. 2:9). He peered down at his hands, lying upon his desk. "יען אשר היה עם־לבבך" *Regarding your heart's desire* (I Kings 8:18) "כל אשר בלבבך לך עשה" *whatever is in your heart, go and do* (II Samuel 7:3). "הנה העלמה הרה" *The maiden shall conceive* (Isaiah 7:14). "זרעך יצא ממעיך" *Your offspring will issue from your loins* (II Samuel 7:12). "חבלי יולדה יבאו" *Labor pains shall come* (Hosea 13:13). "זעיר שם זעיר שם" *A bit here and a bit there* (Isaiah 28:10). "ונאמן ביתך עד־עולם יהיה" *Then your house will be established forever* (II Samuel 7:16). "אז תראי ונהרת ופחד ורחב לבבך" *Then you shall see and be radiant, eager and expansive shall be your heart* (Isaiah 60:5). "טוב," he said.

Good (Genesis 1:10). "לֹא־יִפָּלֵא מִמְּךָ כָּל־דָּבָר" *Now nothing will be hidden from you* (Jeremiah 32:17).

He had covered apparently everything and was at a loss now for anything further to say. He raised his eyebrows: two semaphores signaling *man overboard,* and mine, involuntarily, imitated his: I was lost at sea. We stared at each other in this way until he said, "עָשָׂה הָאֱלֹקִים אֶת־הָאָדָם יָשָׁר וְהֵמָּה בִקְשׁוּ חִשְּׁבֹנוֹת רַבִּים" *God made man upright, but he sought out other inventions* (Ecclesiastes 7:29). "שְׁאֵלָה" *Any questions?* (Judges 8:24).

I folded my hands and cleared my throat. Father's talk had included no pictures, no charts, no helpful graphs or diagrams of any kind—he hadn't so much as sketched anything in the air with his hands while he spoke—and I could imagine the sexual act only as well as I could, which is to say not at all, or rather בְּאַסְפַּקְלַרְיָא שֶׁאֵינָהּ מְאִירָה *as through a glass darkly* (BT Vevamos 49b).

"No, Father," I replied. "Thank God, everything has been sufficiently explained."

He sighed again, apparently in wild relief.

"וַיִּגְדַּל הַנַּעַר וַיְבָרְכֵהוּ ד'" *And the boy grew and the Lord blessed him* (Judges 13:24), he said, as a way of dismissing me.

For many years afterwards, this conversation comprised the entirety of my knowledge on the subject.

IT SAYS MORE about our town perhaps than about our father that he was not considered the least bit odd there. On the contrary, he was counted among Szibotya's principal citizens. O Szibotya, what a strange little town you were! Its streets were muddy whether it was raining or not, and the town square was rhomboidal. We faced east in our synagogues, as tradition demanded, aware that Mother Russia had imposed herself there between the Holy One and ourselves, like an imperial censor, and few of our petitions, we suspected, were being let through. Rumors of violence on the eastern horizon sent paroxysms of fear through our little town, and fire was a problem as well. Every few years, Szibotya burned to the ground, and every few years, for reasons that defied logic, we rebuilt it again.

The market was a shambles: moist barrels of glazed-eyed fish suffocating slowly; chickens, alive one moment, dead the next, their necks slashed, their feathers ripped out by gossiping matrons; legless men in wheelbarrows begging for crusts and, when crusts were scarce, for crumbs; porters sleeping on their boxes, shielding their eyes with their hats, their hands thrust into the mouths of their shoes, their most valued possession.

And there was nothing more terrifying than a visit to the tailor's shop. Zusha the Amalekite was the most frightening man I'd ever known. Because his big beard crept nearly to his eyes, I couldn't look him in the face. His hands were strong enough to break a boy in two, and his breath, which he expelled from his mouth in labored grunts, smelled as though field mice had been sucked into his lungs and died there. When, on his knees to measure an inseam, he placed his head next to mine, death seemed not only the inevitable but also the preferable consequence.

In Russia, it was said that Zusha had kidnapped boys from one town to serve in the army as the next town's quota, and when the first town paid him, he thanked them by stealing their children to serve as a third town's recruits. He'd made a small fortune in this way but he lost it all in bribes, fleeing from the tsarist police. Everyone knew the story: when his daughter, Frume-Liebe, slept with a Russian captain and had gotten herself pregnant, Zusha refused to let her see a doctor. Worse, when her time came, he tried to kill the baby, strangling it with a shoestring, and he would have succeeded, too, if his wife, Beyle, hadn't restrained him. Refusing to speak to her father ever again, Frume-Liebe denounced both of her parents to the authorities before running off with her lieutenant and abandoning her child. Stuck with the baby, a brain-damaged girl they called Ita, Zusha and Beyle raced across the border and returned to Szibotya, where Ita sat now each day in Zusha's shop on a high stool doing absolutely nothing. There was no point in sending her to school or in teaching her to cook, everyone agreed. She was an idiot first and last. Why, she could barely speak and only repeated whatever anyone said to her, but she had no idea what she was saying.

"שלום-עליכם, Ita," my mother greeted her, upon entering Zusha's shop. *Shalom aleykhem.* (It was my mother's task, of course, to take me to Zusha's for my wedding clothes.)

"Lech . . . umm . . . shlom," Ita repeated in her halting voice.

"You're looking well, Ita."

"Uhr . . . 'ooken . . . wuuh."

As Ita tried to repeat my mother's words, growing flushed at the prospect of a conversation, I hid behind her skirts, waiting for the terrible interview to end. Unlike with my father, conversation for my mother had nothing to do with the littleness of man in the face of God's terrible greatness. Talk was for her, instead, a way of bringing everyone closer to her. Large-boned and strong, she broadcast her affection everywhere she went, her words like love letters addressed to "Whomever It May Concern," and it was no different with Ita.

"Have a good Shabbos, Itale," she said, touching Ita's sticky hands.

"Gud . . . Szpass . . . 'uhn." Ita nodded and drooled, et cetera, et cetera. Her face was flatter than it should have been, and her eyes didn't focus, and when she breathed, a harp of snot vibrated inside her nasal passages. Because of Ita, I learned from an early age to keep immaculate care of my clothing. Adults commented upon it as though it were an oddity, but I would have done anything to avoid coming into Zusha's shop.

"Ah, so, this is the young man who's getting married then, eh?" Zusha barked out. Mother pretended not to hear him when he added, "Oh, yes, the whole town's buzzing with the news!"

I'D FALLEN INTO bad company, you see.

One afternoon, when I'd exhausted his stock without finding anything of interest, Avrum the Book Peddler asked me to stay behind. Perhaps he'd sensed my intellectual dissatisfaction — by age ten, the mandatory piety of my education had begun to bore me — or perhaps without my realizing it, when we were speaking, I'd pronounced some secret word that identified me to him as a fellow maskil. Whatever the reason, when his other customers wandered off to pray the afternoon prayers, Avrum made no attempt to hide his true feelings from me.

"Ah, just look at them, Yankl," he said, biting into his pipe stem, "running off to beg the Master of the Universe to do all the things He put them on this earth to do for one another." He shook his head, and I found myself shaking my own. Those little blackened figures scurrying across the town square appeared to me for the first time as benighted and pitiable creatures of limited intellect and daring, and I wondered how I'd never seen them before in this light.

"You like to read," Avrum said. Though it wasn't a question, his tone demanded some sort of confirmation, and I nodded in reply. "Good. I thought so. A smart boy like you. Well, for a smart boy like you, Avrum has a special trove of books. Or didn't you know about Avrum's special trove?"

He spoke in such a way that anyone passing by would neither hear what he was saying nor suspect it was of any special concern: just a boy and a peddler. Perhaps the child's mother had sent him to invite the man home for a meal or to pick up a special order. Avrum glanced over the swayback of his horse and combed the mare's mane until he was certain no one was watching us. Then raising the plank that served as a seat on his wagon, he brought out from beneath it a handsome traveling pouch.

"These might be of interest to you, who knows?" he said, handing me a couple of books and a number of pamphlets. For a boy like me, it was like finding a buried treasure. Still, I was unsure if I could accept them. "No, no need to pay for them," he said, "if that's what you're worrying about. If you enjoy them, good. If not, return them to me, no harm done. But there's only one thing." He attempted to make his face appear as benign as possible but succeeded only in making it seem sinister and cunning. "You might not want anyone to know what you have here. Your father, for example, or anyone with authority over you, your mother, for instance, or your teachers. We understand each other, yes? There's a new world coming, Yankl, but it isn't here quite yet."

A new world! I knew these words could mean only one thing: the coming of the Messiah, the return of Israel to its national borders, the restoration of our holy Temple.

"Pah—no!" Avrum frowned, coughing out a puff of smoke. "That's the *old* new world, Yankl! I'm speaking of the *new* new world."

He gazed over my shoulders at the horizon behind me where, I imagined, he could see the light of this new world dawning, although it was already almost dusk. Instead, he straightened up and said, "However, I see that your father has come to pray, and you'd better go join him."

"Oh, and Yankl!" he said, grabbing me a little too roughly by the collar. "This remains just between ourselves, correct? That's a good friend. Just between ourselves. That's right. Now go!"

I crossed the square, stopping to hide the books and the pamphlets in the coal bin on the far side of the old Beis Midrash. When I entered the synagogue flushed and out of breath, Father pierced me with his customary look. It was as though each time he saw me, he had to remind himself who I was; and when he remembered, his mood darkened considerably. I returned to the coal bin after dinner, and thus began my second education as over the next year or two Avrum supplied me with all sorts of books—Lilienblum's *The Sins of Youth*, Luzzatto's *Samson and Delilah*, Pseudonym's *History of a Family*. This last title was so inflammatory, Avrum told me, that its author couldn't even sign the novel with his true name and had to use the name of an ancient Greek philosopher who'd been executed by the government for his controversial views.

"Just like Jesus," Avrum said, spitting. "May his name be blotted out."

AS I SAY, this was my second education. The first began when I was only three.

When they told me I had to go to school, naturally I assumed they were joking, that it was some new game Mother had invented. My sisters will pretend to take me to this "school," to this cheder: a *room*—they couldn't even think up a proper name!—where they'll pretend to abandon me; I'll cry and they'll return; they'll dry my tears and, once again, when they're baking or sewing or cooking or cleaning, I'll be passed, like a newborn duckling, from one of their laps to the next. I was willing to play. But no, they assured me, it wasn't a game; every little boy had to go to school. "Then let me be a girl like the rest of you!" I cried, resisting so fiercely they had to pry my arms from Gitl's neck and carry me, kicking and screaming to this cheder. Clearly, I'd done something wrong. This *room*, as they called it, this school, was obviously a punishment of some kind. And I wasn't the only malefactor apprehended at whatever misdeed had sent me here. No, six or seven other boys, their dirty faces broadcasting blank stares, sat around a long wooden table, where we were all forced to read from books when anybody with any sense could have seen that none of us knew how!

I looked up at our keeper, Reb Sender. He had a thick black beard and bushy black eyebrows, but his crinkly face seemed kindly. If I behave myself, I remember thinking, Reb Sender will set me free, because unlike the other boys, who (it didn't take much imagination to see) really *were* savages, I didn't belong here. Surely Reb Sender will realize a mistake has been made in my case, surely he will send me home, if I show myself agreeable and compliant, and if I uncomplainingly learn to decipher those ugly black squiggles in the thumb-smudged books he kept thrusting beneath our noses even after we'd given up resisting and it was clear our spirits had been broken.

(The starchy smells of those books sent my head swimming, and most mornings I could barely keep down the breakfast of groats Reb Sender's wife made for us.)

Hoping for a commutation of my sentence, I finished the year's work in a matter of weeks, mastering both reading *and* writing, demonstrating in this way, I hoped, that I'd repented of whatever crimes had placed me in his care, that my character had been reformed, and that I could be safely returned to my former life.

This strategy backfired. Though I was the most docile of his students, as well as the most helpful *and* the most learned, I wasn't forgiven, but rather laden with extra responsibilities and doubly burdened with Reb Sender's loathsome praises. "Yankele, I don't know how I'd ever run things here without you," he told me repeatedly, his words throwing me into a panic. If I'm indispensable, I told myself, I might serve out my sentence and never be returned home!

I devised a new and desperate strategy: if I demonstrate to them that I am the worst lunkhead of all, disruptive and incapable of further learning, certainly they'll ask me to leave, as they did Ze'ev, a wild boy who peed into Reb Sender's hat, but my daydreaming and rude remarks only brought my teacher's attentions more virulently down upon my small person. There was no fooling Reb Sender. He was up to date on the most modern of pedagogical methods, and when he screamed at me or cuffed my ears, I learned my lessons fast.

Every day I tried a new scheme, and every day it failed; and in the end, I succeeded only in convincing everyone how appropriate school was for me, until finally there was nothing to do but fold my hands and sit at the table like the other boys and read aloud from the books when I was asked to. The dark swirls of the curly alef-bais were no longer the evocative Rorschachs they had once been. No, somehow, they'd become the very sounds they symbolized, and no matter how hard I concentrated, no matter how hard I tried, I couldn't unremember what they meant.

I'd been tricked, I realized. I'd been tricked and there was no way back to the happy, illiterate savagery I'd known before.

FORBIDDEN BOOKS WERE only the beginning. I began to smoke a pipe as well, and I knew no greater pleasure than hiding in my father's cherry orchards, lying on a bench in one of his gazebos, smoking bowl after bowl while reading the illicit books Avrum supplied me, versions of Tolstoy, Gorky, and Shakespeare, expanded and improved upon (פֿאַרגרעסערט און פֿאַרבעסערט, as their title pages attested) by our Yiddish writers, as well as several Hebrew novels written by these same wicked men. I took precautions, of course, hiding my contraband beneath a loose plank in the gazebo's flooring and concealing whatever book I was reading inside a folio of the Talmud, so if anybody chanced upon me, all he would see would be a young scholar absorbed in his learning, teasing out the arguments of Rava and Abaye over whose donkey should go first in a procession of scholars.

On the day Sore Dvore discovered me, I was reading a novel by Mapu. Even more entranced than usual, hidden inside a fine cloud of tobacco smoke, I didn't hear her calling me until she was only a foot or two away. Though I'd taken my usual precaution of concealing the forbidden novel inside a larger volume of Talmud, I'd lain on the bench with my head towards the house, so that all she to do was look over my shoulder for the charade to be exposed.

She had no choice but to report everything to our mother, of course, who had no choice but to report everything to my father, of course, who had no choice but to prepare for me whatever punishment I had forced him to conceive. After all, nothing less than my place in the World to Come was at stake!

Spewing forth a litany of curses (cf. Deuteronomy 28:15–68), Father dragged me to the rebbe, and I was made to sit between them as they hurled verse after verse of psalms over my head. (Though he'd married into an Hasidic family, Father was not himself a Hasid. He treated the rebbe of Szibotya with respect, but without reverence, and this was pleasing to the rebbe. The most learned men in our community, the two literally spoke each other's language and could converse in it for hours.)

"הושיעני מפי אריה" *Save me from this lion's mouth* (Psalms 22:22), my father pleaded. "יגון בלבבי" *My heart is melancholy* (13:3). "פסו אמונים מבני אדם" *Have truthful people vanished?* (12:2)

"ואהי תמים" *I'm perfectly innocent.* I quoted a verse (18:24), attempting to give testimony at my own trial.

"נתן בקולו" *He has raised his voice?* (46:7). The rebbe looked at me critically.

"הרף," my father whispered. *Desist!* (37:8).

It was decided the best thing Father could do was to marry me off—certainly at age twelve, I was old enough—and in this way saddle me, like a goring ox, with a wife and, may God smile upon us, with children, and quickly, too (my father emphasized), before I'd permanently deranged my mind with vile literature written by godless men who wanted only to destroy our people's name, and also (the rebbe emphasized) before rumors of my conduct circulated widely enough to destroy all chances of a suitable match with a good, pious girl, under the obligation to care for whom, he was certain, I would return to my former self.

Father shook his head. "חלה הוא" *The boy is sick* (1 Kings 14:5).

"שאי בנך," the rebbe counseled him. *Pick up your son* (2 Kings 4:36).

After burning the books and the pamphlets they'd found in my possession, the two negotiated my marriage contract with a family from a distant town.

. . .

IT PAINED ME that my marriage would be so different from my parents', whose courtship, by all accounts, had been a storybook affair.

Everyone knew that Father had been a sickly youth, so sickly, in fact, that no one had expected him to live. He was a sight to see: bruised patches colored the gaunt planes of his face; his chest sunk in so cadaverously his ribs could be counted with precision through his clothing, though he wore a jacket, a vest, a shirt, and a talis katan. When he coughed, spumes of bloody phlegm were torn from his lungs, which he spat into his handkerchief like dull red-green oysters. He carried a dozen fresh handkerchiefs with him each day, and each day these were ruined.

Forbidden by his doctors to attend school, he'd developed an invalid's propensity for study and dedicated the long hours in bed to the Talmud. Eventually his enormous learning entitled him, as was customary at that time and in that society, to the most covetable of rewards: a bride of his choice.

And by seventeen, despite his ill health, he'd conceived a burning desire to marry.

None of the local girls would have him, of course, and he was too aware of his deficiencies to force himself upon an unsuspecting girl through an arranged match. Partly to protect his pride and partly out of a fear of girls natural to an innocent young man, he was scrupulously forthright when it came to his courting, and naturally enough, the long line of maidens that paraded through my grandparents' parlor took one look at this scrofulous hairball of a boy, coughed up, it seemed, by an ailing cat, and remembered more pressing engagements elsewhere.

Many, I'm told, ran from the room without a word.

Father endeavored to remain philosophical—God must have His reasons for visiting this plague of horrified girls upon him—but the rejection took its toll, and his parents despaired. Grandmother Sammelsohn cried, wringing her hands and pulling at her marriage wig. This bride-hunting was too much for her baby's delicate constitution. The family physician and the family rabbi concurred. "The strain on his heart might prove mortal," Dr. Kirschbaum announced. "Though a man is commanded to marry," Rabbi Weissmann affirmed, "one may not sacrifice his life to carry out the commandments."

At one time adamant about his son's need to carry on the family name, eventually even Grandfather Sammelsohn agreed. The boy would never be healthy enough to find a wife, and no girl in her right mind would have him.

No one, however, bothered to ask Father his opinion, which he bothered to reveal to no one. Even then, he was an expert at effacing his true self. A lifelong invalid, he knew how to build a wall out of his symptoms and to hide himself behind it. Of course, he would never act against his parents' wishes, but the truth is, he never stopped praying for a bride.

IT HAD BEEN arranged for him to meet one last girl, and Grandfather Sammelsohn had been unable to send a letter in time to prevent her family from coming. They'd already begun the arduous trek from her town to his. (As Father was too ill to travel, the girls and their families came to him.) Grandmother Sammelsohn felt that canceling the tête-à-tête after the pains Mother's family had taken in getting there would be unseemly. "They'll come and go quickly enough," she said. "What difference does it make? One look at Nosn and they'll be out the door."

They waited one day, two days, three days for the girl to arrive, accompanied by her father and, no doubt, an uncle or two. They'd play out the charade one last time, their hearts no longer in it. Though they urged him to return to his bed, Father insisted upon waiting for their guests in his chair in the parlor, slouching with his legs pulled up high before him, his knees like doorknobs inside his best pants, a folio of the Talmud spread across his lap, his hair long and lanky, the odor of sickness hovering, like a rain cloud, almost visibly above his head.

The clock ticked loudly in the otherwise silent room. At last, they heard the rumbling of a coach approaching, then stopping at their door. Concentrating on his blatt of Gemara, Father listened to the clicking and clacking of passengers as they disembarked and the trill of his mother's voice as she welcomed their visitors into the hall. Father slouched farther into his black leather chair. One foot on its cushion, he crossed his legs, and his knobby knees were now higher than his head. (He was so thin his angular bones scraping against his clothing wore out the fabric in half the time it normally took.)

"Alter Nosn!" his mother calls in to him.

Pretending to be engrossed in his studies, Father pretends not to hear her. She enters the room with the small party of guests in her wake: my father's uncle, the girl's father, the girl's uncle, and the girl herself.

"Oh, look, he's studying," Grandmother Sammelsohn says, as though explaining a diorama in a museum. "Lost in thought. That's our Alter Nosn, I'm afraid."

Father stutters out a chain of syllables and looks up from his book, blinking at them, as though into new light. Unlocking his long body from the chair, he stands, waiting for what he knows is coming next: ill-concealed disgust, quickly minted excuses, a hasty retreat from the room. Everyone avoids looking at one another until the girl's father, seizing the moment and putting the best face on it, offers Alter Nosn his hand.

Careful not to smile, lest he reveal the rickety picket fences of his teeth, Father places his hand, a cold dead fish, into the older man's hand. (Years later, we would laugh at how Grandfather Horowitz reached into his pocket for a handkerchief and wiped his palm.) Everyone waits for the inevitable: the inevitable desperate looks between father and daughter, the inevitable noticing of the clock, the inevitable remarking on the lateness of the hour, the inevitable remembering of the pressing appointment, their inevitable and immediate departure.

Grandfather Sammelsohn clears his throat and is about to speak, when my mother says, "I fear it may seem rude" — occasioning knowing looks from every side — "but the long trip by coach has left us parched." They lean in: this is something they've never heard before. "And I do so worry over my father's health" — ah, here it comes, here it comes now, bring their coats, their hats — "and I'm wondering if we might trouble you for a place to sit and a glass of tea?"

That was my mother. She possessed a flair for the dramatic reversal. From the few photographs of her from that time, one can see that she keeps the great sweep of her caramel-colored hair in a high, muscular pompadour. Her cheeks radiate an ecstasy of blushing. Her white teeth flash each time she throws back her head to laugh. Her torso and rib cage are robustly articulated; her bosoms, straining against her bodice, are like two scoops of ice cream on a spoiled child's plate. Each of her arms is larger in diameter than my father's neck. Through the shimmer of her skirt, you can see the magnificent strength of her haunches, as strapping as a young colt's. And yet, at sixteen, despite her monstrously good health, there's nothing masculine about her at all. She's soft, spherical, thoroughly estrogenic, her hips muscularly wide as though engineered specifically for the vigorous work of childbearing.

And now it is my Grandmother Sammelsohn's turn to search for a polite excuse. With a mother's concern, she regards her future daughter-in-law, this Brünnhilde stepped off the stage of some Wagnerian nightmare, with unadulterated horror, certain that if her stick-figure son pursues a marriage to this Amazon, he will survive neither the rigors of his wedding night nor the travails of the marriage bed.

What to do?

Grandmother Sammelsohn coughs and fidgets. She fingers the watch she wears on a gold chain around her neck with her stubby fingers. She makes suggestive nods towards her brother, my great-uncle Chaim-Mottle, who, to her dismay, seems as enchanted as his nephew by this radiant, gracious horse of a girl, now serving tea and passing around the mandelbrot her mother baked for them.

Grandfather Horowitz, his plump hands on the head of his cane, his curly black beard bristling with pride, sits at my mother's side like a barker at a carnival showing off the strong man: Ladies and gentlemen, ladies and gentlemen! Behold this marvelous creation, this strapping lioness that I have produced . . . yes! . . . from my very own loins!

Had my father been a normal man and not a pious scholar, he would have been unable to take his eyes off my mother. As it was, she was so beautiful, he forbade himself to glance at her even once. Instead, crumpled up like a damp handkerchief in his chair, one long leg looped around the other, his chest sunken deeper than usual by his slouching posture, his pallor as moldy as cheese, he attempted, when the tubercular coughing to which he was subject permitted it, to make learned conversation with the men, quoting this or that Gemara, this or that Mishnah, this or that word of this or that sage, demonstrating his value as a potential husband to this vibrant girl, surprising himself, no less than the others, by the seductive brilliance of his remarks.

Indeed, Father was so smitten that at one point, when his and Mother's eyes accidentally met across the parlor table, he blushed so deeply his face took on the mottled color of a bruise. Embarrassed, he looked down at the crumbs in his lap and then raised his tearful, bloodshot eyes to take in the new family portrait before him.

Unable to suppress a grin, he revealed to the others all the grey luster of his translucent teeth.

IT WAS IMPOSSIBLE for Grandmother Sammelsohn to protest. How could she when her son had been refused by girls with squints and incipient mustaches and small disfiguring humps? As formal promises were exchanged over the dregs of Russian tea, she excused herself politely, went into her kitchen, and vomited. Her kerchief balled up in her fist, she beat her breast, wailing quietly enough that no one in the adjoining rooms might hear her.

She wasn't alone in her concerns. No one in the entire town expected Father to survive until the wedding. The strain on his heart would prove too great, they said. He was so skinny, you could almost see it (his heart, I mean) pounding like a fox against the bars of his rib cage whenever Mother walked into a room. The excitement was taking its toll. He could hardly sleep. He exhausted himself each night staring at the ceiling in anticipation of the dawn. In the morning, a day nearer to claiming his beloved, he was too excited to eat. He sat at the table and allowed Grandmother Sammelsohn to serve him, though he couldn't touch a bite.

How long could he burn like a Havdalah candle with all his wicks in flame?

"She'll be a widow longer than a bride," the townspeople whispered. "If she doesn't smother him with affection, she might just smother him," they didn't even bother to whisper. "Alter Nosn, eat, rest, consider your health!" my grandmother Sammelsohn pleaded with him, but all in vain.

Lovesick and simply sick, Father abandoned himself to the wedding preparations, studying through the long night, his body bent like a question mark over his Gemara, memorizing every word our Sages had uttered on the subject of spousal duty, so depleting himself in the process that eventually he could barely speak. His voice sounded like a piece of crumbled rice paper, all crackles and pops and sibilant hisses, and to everyone's surprise, when the morning of the wedding arrived, he was alive to see it, although how well was the question: his vision had begun to fail.

WHAT NO ONE understood, of course, was what my mother saw in him, and yet she seemed as smitten as he, and as eager to have the wedding contract signed. What no one knew, indeed what no one could have possibly known, is that for many weeks before they met, Father had appeared to Mother each night in a series of dreams. In one, he offered her an iridescent fish; in another, a basket of ripe fruit; in a third, a tin box filled with cookies shaped like the letters of the alef-bais. These, he hurled high into the air and, as they fell, they flashed out cryptic sentences in rapidly changing constellations. Upon awakening, Mother scribbled down what she could remember of them in a diary she kept near her bed. Realizing, too late, that in rushing to document this dream on a Saturday morning, she had unintentionally violated the Sabbath, she threw down the pen, and when she peered at the words again later, they made no sense to her at all: הײ, קיאָן ווי פֿאָראַס, דעטשיפֿראַנטע טשי טיאוין פראַזוין? רעבענו אַל לאַ ראַקאָנטאָ, אַל לאַ ליבראָ!

Using Almoli's famous dreambook, she took all sorts of arcane stabs at what this emaciated apparition might mean, never for a moment thinking his nightly appearances might contain the slightest bit of prophecy. Still, there is no dream without its interpretation, and in her prayers she begged her great-great-great-grandfather, the Seer of Lublin, to intervene on her behalf, to petition the archangel Gabriel to unlock the secret meaning of these visitations. The seer proved unable to move Heaven in this regard, however. Appearing to her one night in a luminous white robe, he counseled patience: "Wait, my daughter," he said. "The best is yet to be."

And so when she strode so purposefully into the Sammelsohn parlor, following her uncle and her father, and saw the wretched invalid sitting there like a waterlogged scarecrow, she couldn't help giving out a happy gasp of recognition. Here was the boy with the fish, the boy with the fruit, the boy with the cookies and the dozen and one other things he'd presented to her each night. The excitement she felt in having at last solved a puzzle and the dizzying sense of transformation it foretold stayed with her throughout their short engagement and did much to compensate her for the repulsion she felt at the sight of my father's physical person.

"Obviously God has intended me to marry him," she told her worried parents.

THE WEDDING DAY was sparkling, immaculate, the sunlight seeming to illuminate everything from within. The pink cherry blossoms trembled in the wind. The windows of the buildings along the main road, scrubbed clean for the occasion, dazzled the eyes of the only people up at sunrise to see them: the milkmen and the garbage collectors and my father who watched these men making their rounds from his room at a local inn.

Having slept not at all, he leaned against the window frame. He'd grown so thin that he no longer appeared to have one foot *in* the grave, but rather one foot *out* of it, as though, having died some months earlier, he'd remembered his wedding and had somehow managed to break free from his tomb. His arms and legs, thin to begin with, had grown thinner over the course of his engagement, and his brittle bones rattled and clicked as he dressed himself. He pulled up his breeches and belted his gartl and donned, for the first time, his stovepipe hat. Having made the necessary ablutions, having prayed the necessary prayers, he opened the door of his room and found, left there on a table by his mother, a breakfast of extraordinarily weak tea—a fleet trolling of the tea ball through the lukewarm water filled the cup with sufficient caffeine to remove from his truculent bowels the prune-sized turd that had been lodged in them since yesterday morning, causing him almost unendurable intestinal distress—and a bowl of unseasoned groats, softened by sheep's milk and flavored by three raisins.

(It's traditional, of course, to fast on one's wedding day and although Father would never, for a multitude of reasons, have eaten this meal,

Grandmother Sammelsohn had secured a rabbinic dispensation to feed him, to which, for her sake, he complied.)

Still, as he grasped the tray and teetered precariously over it, struggling to lift it, he couldn't help regarding it as though it were the last meal of a man condemned to death. He chewed his kasha as gingerly as he could (still his gums bled) and, after two bites, pushed the bowl away. He rose with difficulty and glanced one final time at the ghostly reflection of himself in the mirror, nodding towards it in parting, as though to an old friend he expected never to see again. He took up his hat and placed it on his head, attempting one last time to curl, with his fingers, the lifeless kite tails of his peyos. He gave the sleeves of his caftan a quick and inefficient brushing. Still the dandruff remained. Expelling a final preparatory breath, he opened the door and stepped out into the hallway.

AS FOR MY mother, she rose that morning from her own bed, all buxom and muscular, and stood with her bare feet planted squarely on the wooden floor. The sunlight streamed through the loose weave of her nightdress, silhouetting the curves of her powerful body. Her golden hair fell about her shoulders like a kilo of challah dough. She poured water from a vessel into a basin, left at sunrise by a servant at her door, and holding her hands before her, intoned the blessing in a voice as deep and as flowing as an ancient river. She splashed water onto her cheeks, already vibrant and red, and looked out the window, at her little town. "Today," she whispered to herself, "today today today," the word a tart mint on her tongue, sweet and biting.

Before she unties the crisscross of laces from her nightdress and opens its collar and pulls the shift over her head (at which point, out of filial restraint, I shall cease imagining her), she records the night's dream in her dreambook. She writes feverishly, attempting to crack the dream's bizarre code. She knows, from her beloved Almoli, that no dream is cast in stone (apparently not even a dream image may be graven) and yet the dream had terrified her. No matter how much she attempted to ring the image with an ameliorating hedge of interpretation, it remained as frightening as a snake in a rose garden; and she couldn't banish from her mind the image of my emaciated father in the costume of a circus strong man lifting her over his head, as though she were a set of barbells, while in a cage nearby, a panther devoured something struggling beneath a dirty bundle of rags.

FATHER DIDN'T DIE, of course.

According to my sisters, who loved these stories of our parents' courtship and who, I realize as I write them down for the first time, may have embellished them to suit the requirements of their girlish imaginations, Father didn't burn up like a stick of wood in the conflagration of our mother's nuptial passions. On the contrary, as Grandmother Sammelsohn was happy to remark at breakfast the following day, her son, though still decrepit, appeared unnaturally flesh-colored, heartier and haler than she'd ever seen him. He blushed, pleased. Turning even redder, he laughed off her suggestion. Glancing shyly at our mother, he remarked that he had merely finally gotten a decent night's sleep, and now it was our mother's turn to blush. Reaching for the groats, she overturned the pitcher of milk, and my father jumped up, with an unaccustomed alacrity, to call the maid in to tidy up the mess.

The next morning, he seemed even healthier, younger, less sallow, stronger. The change was obvious enough now that others, not only our grandmother, remarked upon it. Though my imagination stops firmly at the threshold of my parents' bedroom door, it seems that beneath my mother's muscular caresses, my father was kneaded, pounded, dandled, coddled, cuddled, cosseted, and suckled back to life. According to my sisters, this resuscitation continued over the seven nights of our parents' wedding banquet, until on the eighth night—and here I clearly detect the pastel mottling of my sisters' collective editorializing—it was as though our father had been reborn with a full head of black curly hair, twenty-eight milk-white teeth, virile lips of damask red, alabaster skin, and eyes as blue as an alchemical flame.

The truth? I can only assume that perhaps Father had had a touch of tuberculosis and that it had clouded his marriage prospects for a time. I suspect further that the picture we have of him as an obscenely wretched invalid has more to do with the exaggerated concerns of his mother—who first told these stories to my sisters—than with his true medical history. Certainly, the joyous life he shared with our mother, with whom no one could help falling in love, brought him a happiness and vitality unknown to him from his dry life as a scholar, bent over his books from morning till night, and I've no doubt that his work in the cherry orchards he purchased with her dowry was physically invigorating. Still, how different in every aspect is this love-intoxicated neurasthenic from the reprimanding scold I knew as a child! It's impossible for me to even reconcile the two. Could this man whom my sisters believed emerged, completely reupholstered, from our mother's embrace, be the same man I knew, twenty or so years later, as my father?

The two seemed nothing alike.

DESPITE HIS STORYBOOK romance, Father wasted no time in arranging mine as a punishment, and the day of my wedding quickly arrived. With a wife and soon, God willing, a family to care for, I would be forced to put aside my revolutionary ideas and return to the quiet ways of our people.

(In this, however, my father knew me not at all. I was less interested in the overblown political treatises buried in these novels than in the love stories their authors used as a palliative to entice their readers. I was like a child who pretends to be sick for the sugar water the doctor will serve his medicine in. If I could have had the story without the politics, the sugar without the medicine, the honey without the groats, I would have dispensed with them entirely. As far as I knew, however, it was only dashing young freethinkers that beautiful women fell in love with.)

Not wishing to seem completely old-fashioned, or perhaps even embarrassed by his own methods, Father insisted I meet the girl before the wedding. I was the first of his children to marry, after all, and though this wedding was being inflicted upon me — *not as a punishment, not as a punishment,* my mother kept reminding me, *but as a loving rebuke* — still, a wedding is a wedding, and everything must be conducted in an appropriate spirit of joy. One day, I would understand all Father had done on my behalf, and on that day I would thank him. Of this, my mother was certain.

I would have thanked him then and there, if it wouldn't have queered the deal. Fearful of that consequence, I kept my mouth shut, or if I opened it, I mentioned neither my gratitude to my father for having arranged this marriage nor for his having prepared me so thoroughly for the wedding night, but only the downtrodden masses, exploited by the landowning aristocracy and my admiration of the Russian narod. If all else failed, a word about Czech independence or the bloody mess in the Balkans, and Father would purse his mouth, his thin lips becoming a lily-white seam inside the opening of his beard—like many a saturnine fellow, his renunciative character concealed an emotional disposition—and return to his wedding plans with vindictive furor. Without another word, he canceled the meeting with my fiancée. She was no longer permitted to attend the gathering at our parlor. I alone would be exhibited to her family. They had a right to meet me, after all. In exchange for their generous dowry, they had more or less purchased me.

WE WAITED FOR the arrival of my future in-laws. Father had insisted I sit, as he had when meeting our mother, in a chair in the parlor with a folio of the Talmud spread across my lap. We heard the rumbling of a coach stopping outside our door. I pretended to concentrate on my Gemara, listening to the trill of my mother's voice as she welcomed in our guests. Father, pretending to hear nothing, busied himself with papers at his desk. Hands behind his back, he stared at a map of the empire framed upon the wall, and when Mother entered the room with the pantry of visitors behind her—my future father-in-law, my future uncle-in-law, my future brother-in-law—he waited before turning to greet them, pretending to be lost in thought over one of his many business deals, strategizing over his own empire, a miniature Franz Josef, with a look of pleasant surprise on his face.

"Ah!" he said at last. "I'd lost all track of the time."

I unfolded myself from my chair and stood, waiting for the introductions to be made.

"An industrious boy," my future father-in-law said, seeing me struggle to get out from under the folio of Talmud. He extended his hand and I offered him my own, a cold dead fish weighing approximately nothing, which is, of course, the appropriate warmth and weight of a scholar's hand. Then, et cetera, et cetera, the scene plays itself out exactly as you might imagine. While the fathers and uncles chat over cigars, the brother is dispatched to query me, as casually as possible and in such a way that I should be unaware of what he is doing, on the extent of my learning. They're marrying off their daughter to a budding scholar and want to make sure they've gotten their money's worth. Four years older than I, this brother is something of a dunce and knows a fraction of what I, even with all my heretical afternoons, know, and I make him pay for it, grilling him on this obscure point or that obscure point (many of which I make up out of whole cloth; and so patchy is his knowledge, he fails to detect the ruse), until, humiliated, he excuses himself from my company and, nodding to his father, gives me the familial stamp of approval.

"Very good, very good," my future father-in-law intones over elderberry wine. "Everything looks in order. On to the synagogue then, to check on the preparations there."

"Is everything satisfactory with your rooms at the inn?" my mother inquires.

I'll skip to the wedding itself, already the second in what I'm afraid will be a chronicle choked with weddings. It no doubt frustrated my father that the bride he'd chosen for me as a rebuke was acceptable to me in every way. Perhaps because my heresies had been conducted more or less in secret—I'd felt no need to broadcast my intellectual enlightenment to the world, nor even to our little Szibotya—my reputation was not yet in tatters, and I could attract a decent match, a bright, attractive girl, a healthy girl and one from a good family.

Hindele was all these things.

Not yet twelve when I saw her for the first time beneath the wedding canopy, her face behind a lace veil, she possessed, or rather was possessed by, the gawky beauty of a gamboling foal. Wide-shouldered, long of thigh, her head lowered demurely upon her slender neck, she had an awkward, charming grace, and though she only peeked at me, I couldn't take my eyes from her.

Her maple-colored hair, in a thick circuit of braids, formed a halo about her head. Her hands were whiter than the lilies she carried. Above a high collar, her chin trembled, and beneath the intricate lace of her shirtfront, her emergent bosom heaved with what I hoped was a nervous delight. What a sight we must have made, I not yet five feet tall, she a head taller, circling me the seven requisite times. In my Saturday best, a round fur hat upon my head, my peyos oiled and gleaming, I was intoxicated by her perfumes.

I looked at my father, watching the proceedings not a foot away, frowning so severely, the tip of his nose curved nearly to his chin. He looked at me with that same hard glint I would years later see flashing across Dr. Freud's handsome gaze: that maddening mixture of pride, envy, anguish, revulsion, and despair that marks a father's love for his son. I knew what he was thinking. He was afraid we were establishing a poor precedent. If a magnificent girl like this is the price one must pay for reading forbidden literature, what prevented the entire world from heading to our gazebo, prying loose its floorboards, unearthing my stash of heretical texts, my Mendelssohn, my Krochmal, and my Luzzato, rolling cigarettes and waiting for the inevitable discovery of their crimes with its swift, sweet punishment, for as my Hindele and I sipped from a single cup of wine, her face so close to mine we were almost kissing, I knew that even the most extraordinary piety would never have earned for me such an exquisite bride.

I awoke to the roiling of cathedral bells. I rose from the sofa, where I'd fallen asleep the night before, and pulled back the heavy curtains from the window. The light of a bone-grey sky pierced my eyes. The room was freezing. I wrapped myself in the afghan Aunt Fania had knitted me, and I found my spectacles and sat at my escritoire, with a piece of bread and a little pot of jam, to scribble down my dream.

I'd dreamt again of the yellow lion. She lay next to me in bed this time, nibbling at my throat; and I awoke, as I always did from these dreams, quaking in fear.

(I'd discussed the lioness with Dr. Freud. In his opinion, she represented nothing more than a wish to return to childhood. Somehow, he'd gotten it into his head that a porcelain lion had been a favorite toy of mine, although I couldn't recall ever having possessed such a thing, and nothing I said could dissuade him from his opinion.)

It was late, I knew. The morning's newspapers had long been printed and long ago delivered to the kiosks where they were now for sale. Fräulein Eckstein's advertisement had been waiting for me in one of them, I knew, since dawn. I had no idea how to proceed. I could have asked Otto Meissenblichler for advice, I supposed. As I've said, he seemed in possession of a never-emptying Wunderhorn of women. Literary houris, would-be actresses, bored schoolgirls, naughty Hausfraus, widows and virgins alike, seemed eager to immolate themselves upon the altar of his sexual genius. I ruled out knocking at his door, however. The last time I'd done so, I'd barely opened my mouth to call out his name when I'd heard it uttered by voices far sweeter and more plaintive than my own. The door of the bedroom flew open and, though I raised my arms against the sight and commanded myself not to look, no shield could prevent my beholding their four breasts and the two furry pelts that seemed to hang from their waists like scalps on a Red Indian's belt. The brazen skin of knee cap, hip bone, thigh, elbow, throat, belly, and buttock bruised my optic nerve until it failed and I went blind.

Besides, what help could Otto give me? We were too different, he and I. He was a voluptuary, a connoisseur of the actual, with no patience for the romantic chimeras that seemed to preoccupy me. While he was being caressed by two or perhaps even four arms, dandled by two or perhaps even four breasts, I was wooing two women, neither of whom was real: Fräulein Eckstein, about whom I knew nothing, and the fantasy of her I'd carried in my heart for the better part of a month.

Still, I dressed and made my way to the Stadtpark, passing newspaper kiosk after newspaper kiosk, until, finally, I plucked up the courage to buy a copy of the *Neue Freie Presse.* I sat on a park bench and opened its pages and found within it, exactly as I imagined I would, the advertisement Fräulein Eckstein had placed there for me, surrounded by a black border, a typographical enhancement for which, I assumed, she'd paid extra.

It read:

> To the kindly oculist who looked into a young girl's eyes last night —
> seeing what? I can only imagine: why do you ignore my messages? Meet
> me, I implore you, at least once, at the Café Pucher in the Kohlmarkt,
> noon, for Marillenknödel, today!

With jittering hands, I drew forth my watch from my vest and saw that it was already noon. I could have kicked myself. My first lover's assignation and I was already late! I stood and turned in all four directions at once. Dropping the newspaper onto the bench, I flagged down the nearest stroller, an elderly man in a black cloak with the white beard of a biblical prophet, and asked if he knew the shortest route to the Kohlmarkt.

"The Kohlmarkt?" he said to himself, squinting. "The Kohlmarkt?"

"Never mind, never mind!" I cried, dashing off. My heart was in my throat. If I were late, I feared the Fräulein might give up hope and leave before I arrived. I had no idea how many of her previous advertisements I'd left unanswered, but surely, after the first few dozen disappointments, one's expectations, as well as one's patience, diminish. However, even if I weren't late, I would have hurried. After all, how often does love summon you by name, or if not by name, by general description?

This thought produced a terrible fear in me. What if I'd read the wrong advertisement? What if the advertisement I'd read hadn't been intended for me, but for another one of Vienna's kindly oculists? After all, the Fräulein hadn't used my name. On what grounds did I presume I was the kindly oculist in question? Could I even be described as kindly? No, I couldn't be. When had I demonstrated even an ounce of kindliness towards Fräulein Eckstein (or towards anybody for that matter)? On the contrary, I'd been rude and sullen towards her at Dr. Freud's. What if I blundered into the Pucher only to discover one of my colleagues there dining on Marillenknödel with the lovely girl he'd met the previous evening, kindly Dr. Kessner, for instance, or kindly Dr. Loiberger, or any of the city's other oculists, many of whom, far kinder than I, might have made the acquaintance of a young woman who wished to communicate with him through an advertisement in the newspaper? And even if the advertisement had been written by Fräulein Eckstein for me—I was struck by an additional horror—what prevented one of my colleagues from imagining the note had been written for him? Or worse: what prevented *all* of them from arriving at the café precisely at noon under just such an impression?

By the time I reached the café's door, I was in a state of nervous collapse. I knew what I would find inside: kindly oculists, five to a table, each man looking at me in the same way I'd be looking at him, wondering, What the deuce is *he* doing here?

But of course, I found only Fräulein Eckstein, seated at a corner table, her elaborate hat peeking out from behind the front page of the *Neue Freie Presse*.

"Dr. Sammelsohn?" she called, lowering the paper and squinting at me. "Is that you?"

"Ah, Fräulein, good afternoon," I said, approaching her table, relieved to be the only oculist in sight. "May I join you?"

Oddly, this request seemed to have momentarily flustered her. "Oh!" she said, before saying, "No, of course. Certainly. Please, do. By all means."

"You're not waiting for someone, are you?"

"No, I don't think so," she said, smiling oddly.

I took the seat across from hers and thought to immediately make my amends. "You must forgive me, Fräulein. I've been irresponsible and I've come to apologize for my abstruseness and to make good any expense you've gone to on my account."

"Expense?" she said, tilting her head to the side.

"For the advertisements," I said.

"The advertisements?"

"In the newspaper."

The Fräulein laughed nervously. She shrugged, as though embarrassed, and smiled sweetly. "Forgive me, Dr. Sammelsohn, but I've no idea what you're talking about."

I leaned back and gave her a hard look. We seemed to have switched roles in the scene we'd played out the night before at the Freuds'. Perhaps this was all part of the velvety game of Viennese lovemaking, I told myself. Having arranged our assignation anonymously, we were required, I gathered, to continue the charade, pretending to have run into each other accidentally in order that it might appear so to the rest of the world.

"Ah. Never mind," I said, with a knowing air. "I'm obviously mistaken."

At this, the Fräulein seemed to relax. "In any case," she said, "it's nothing short of a miracle, running into you like this."

"A miracle, Fräulein?"

"Yes, as there's something I've very much wanted to ask you."

"A question, Fräulein?"

"No, a favor, really." She lowered her gaze. "Only I hope you won't think it too forward of me, if . . ."

"If what, Fräulein?"

"No, I can't," she said, blushing. "You'll think ill of me, I know."

"But I won't," I said. "I promise."

"You won't!" She playfully took my hands. "Do you really mean that, Dr. Sammelsohn?"

"I do, Fräulein." The touch of her fingers, even through the calfskin of her gloves, stirred me to my core.

She took a deep breath. Her chin trembled. "May I make a confession to you, Dr. Sammelsohn?"

I swallowed nervously. "A confession, Fräulein?" Things seem to be proceeding more quickly than I'd anticipated. "That's a bold word," I said.

"Yes, it is, isn't it? It *is* a bold word."

I was unnerved to find her staring so avidly into my eyes. May a woman stare so brazenly at a man and he not interpret it as a sexual provocation? However, drunk on her own liberated impulses, or mad with desire, or perhaps simply mad (what *had* Dr. Freud told me about her diagnosis? I struggled in vain to recall it), the Fräulein showed no sign of relenting, and it was I who finally looked away. Holding my hand and unwilling to surrender my attention, she lightly traced the lines of my palm with her finger.

"Emma," I whispered, although too quietly, I hoped, for her to have heard me.

"Dr. Sammelsohn," she said, "permit me to ask you a question?"

"A question, Fräulein?"

"A personal question."

"Well, all right."

She smiled shyly. "Do you love anyone?"

"I . . . I beg your pardon, Fräulein. Do I . . ."

"Love anyone?" she repeated.

I opened my mouth to answer her, but no words sprang forth.

"Ah, so you must!" She laughed, covering her mouth with her hands.

"Well," I murmured, "there *has* been someone of late, I suppose . . ."

"And who is she, if I may be so bold to inquire?"

"Oh, but I haven't the courage to tell you that, my dear Fräulein."

"No, now don't be shy," she said, leaning forward on her elbows. "We can share our secrets like girlfriends." Vexed, perhaps, at hearing herself describe me as a girlfriend, she corrected herself: "Or like a brother and sister. Oh, but you know what I mean. Sometimes a person loves another but doesn't feel free to declare that love. Isn't that so, Doktor?"

My stomach dropped, my vision narrowed. What had Dr. Freud told her? How much did she know about this last month, the month I'd spent pining for her?

"That's true," I said cautiously.

"Myself, for example."

"Yourself, Fräulein?"

She sighed and, crossing her arms, sat back in her chair. "There's no reason for you to know this"—her eyes followed someone walking across the room behind me and she lowered her voice—"but in the past . . ."

"Yes, Fräulein?"

". . . I've always been attracted to older men."

"To . . . to . . . to *older* men, Fräulein? But . . . but this was in the past, you say?"

"Oh," she said, "you know, with their dignified beards and their . . ." She brought her fingers softly to her lips. "How it must chafe to receive a kiss from a man with a beard . . ." She blushed again and giggled. "Although I must say . . . your little beard, Dr. Sammelsohn . . ."

"My little beard, Fräulein?"

". . . it seems so soft and silky, yes . . . Kissing you would be . . ."

"Yes, Fräulein?"

". . . a lovely experience, I imagine."

The conversation was getting away from us. An untamed horse whose reins we had dropped, it had broken free from the high road and was pulling us, exhilarated, into a forest of brackens and brambles. We must return to the high road immediately, I counseled myself, lest we be torn to shreds by this wild tangle of thorns! And yet, at the same time, no woman had ever spoken to me in so open a way, and the agony her voice occasioned in my person was not entirely unpleasant: an electrical storm sowed its turmoil in my breast, a siege of lightning lay claim to my undefended heart, a quiver of pangs shot, like flaming arrows, through my central nervous system, spiraling down to the core of my lowest self, where its havoc aroused my concupiscence from its long wintry slumbers.

"Fräulein Eckstein," I managed to say at last, "may I be frank with you?"

The time had come to bare my breast, to confess my feelings, to reveal the whole complicated mess I'd made of everything. Yes, it was time to throw myself upon her mercy, to declare my intentions, to risk all, like a gambler, on one fatal spin of the wheel—although how much of a gamble was it when she had all but declared her love for me—for me and my kissable little beard?

"I was hoping we might both be frank," she said, breathlessly, "and honest. Completely. Oh, how we allow our lives to become so *poisoned* with untruth! Dr. Sammelsohn, don't you find that's so?"

"I know. I know it," I said. "I lie. I do. All the time. Why, I lie to everyone. No, only the other day, I lied to the milkman. I did. 'Did you order butter?' he asked me, having failed to deliver it, and I said, 'No,' although, in fact, I had. I had ordered it."

"Then let us agree to speak only the truth to each other, Dr. Sammelsohn, shall we?"

"Fräulein, from now on, yes: the truth. Absolutely, agreed!"

"And let us bare our breasts together."

"Metaphorically speaking, you mean, of course."

"Shall I go first?"

"Or I. It doesn't matter."

"Let me then."

"As you wish."

"In that case"—she filled the bellows of her lungs with a fortifying breath, and her bosom lifted magnificently—"I must tell you, Dr. Sammelsohn, that I'm in love!"

"Ah! I knew it!" I couldn't help laughing.

"With . . ." As she said this, the color in her cheeks rose.

"With? Yes?" I said.

"Oh! But can't you guess it?"

"I can, but I must hear it from your own mouth."

"Very well then. Let me declare it openly and honestly. I'm in love, Dr. Sammelsohn—"

I clapped my hands. "Oh, Fräulein!"

"—with Sigmund Freud."

"With?"

"Sigmund Freud," she said. "As you, in your wisdom, have clearly intuited."

"You're . . . ?"

She nodded, her face bright with happiness. "I'm in love with Sigmund Freud." Leaning across the table, she took my hand again. She lowered her voice, scouring the room as though for eavesdroppers. "Oh my God, Dr. Sammelsohn! That man! But I don't have to tell you. He's just so handsome, and his theories are so brilliant and so bold!"

"You're in love with Dr. Freud?" I said.

She blushed now for a different reason. "But of course, you must really think me awful."

"Well, he *is* a married man, I suppose, and by all accounts quite happily."

"I know, I know!" She closed her eyes. "I'm just. . . it's just . . ."

I don't know why I was surprised. If one doesn't count Josef Breuer, Dr. Freud was the first psychoanalyst; and if one doesn't count Anna O., Dr. Breuer's patient, Fräulein Eckstein was the first psychoanalytic patient, and like so many who would follow her, she had fallen in love with her analyst. The blackness of her crime was far worse than if she'd simply placed herself between a wife and her lawful happiness, however: Martha Bernays Freud was a family friend; the Ecksteins and the Bernays were longtime members of the same circle. For all I knew, they might even have been cousins (as everyone else seemed to be).

"Well, one can't help one's passions, Fräulein," I told her as kindly as I could. "And certainly we don't choose with whom we fall in love."

Her face brightened at the prospect of this moral reprieve, and she wiped away a tear. "Do you really think that's true, Dr. Sammelsohn?"

"I do."

We were silent for a moment, and then she said, "And that's why I thought perhaps you could speak to him."

"Speak to whom?"

"To Dr. Freud?"

"Me, you mean?"

"Anything, yes, the slightest thing that you could say on my behalf, I'm sure, would be helpful. He's your friend, after all. Perhaps you could mention to him that you'd noticed my attraction, and then you'd be able to see in his eyes if there's any chance for me. And if there is . . ."

"Fräulein. . ." I said. Is this why she had invited me here? Is this what these weeks of newspaper ads had been about?

"No, of course, you're right. It was ridiculous for me to have asked you." She took a bite of her dumpling and chewed unhappily. Wiping a dab of jelly from the corner of her mouth, she smiled bravely and pushed her plate away. It was terrible to see the look of self-reproach pass over her. She glanced down at her watch and, biting back tears, said, "In any case, I've got two tickets for a quintet at the Urania this afternoon, and I'd very much like it, if you'd care to join me."

We met every day for over a month. Fräulein Eckstein seemed to have two tickets to everything and no one to go with. And it wasn't hard for her to entice me out of my apartment with the promise of a concert or a lecture or a play. Perhaps, I thought, this was what Dr. Freud had wanted all along: for me to distract the Fräulein, to get her out of his hair. Nevertheless, I found these enticements impossible to resist. Also, the Fräulein was so heartbroken and lonely, it seemed cruel to refuse her. We spent hours in each other's company, and during those hours though we conversed upon a broad array of topics, every word, I knew, anticipated only one thing: the moment when our conversation touched upon Sigmund Freud, as it invariably did, and we could begin discussing him in full.

I listened as attentively as I could, aware that my willingness to speak to the Fräulein about my rival was all that kept me at her side. In addition, my lack of censure won for me her complete confidence, and the intimacy of her company assuaged whatever conscience might have otherwise nagged at me as I indulged in the questionable pleasure of plotting to destroy Dr. Freud's marriage, even though doing so meant, in theory at least, surrendering to him the only thing I wanted, which was Fräulein Eckstein's love, her mineral, emotional, carnal, and spiritual love. Every evening and twice a day when there was a matinee, we'd scheme together, dreaming up remedies for her unhappiness, sometimes walking arm in arm, our heads pressed together in delicious conspiracy.

A typical conversation:

"Oh, Dr. Sammelsohn, if only Aunt Marty could feel my heart beating at the thought of him, she'd understand me, wouldn't she?"

"Certainly she would, Fräulein."

"And she wouldn't judge me too harshly, would she?"

"No! How could she?"

"She couldn't. No, you're right, because we're the same, aren't we?"

"Of course you are, Fräulein."

"We love the same man, don't we?"

"And that's what makes all this so damnably difficult: your kindness in not wanting to hurt her."

"Oh, I know! The thought of hurting her is just . . . so awful! I could never do it. And yet how could he not choose me over her, Dr. Sammelsohn?"

"He couldn't."

"Just thinking of it—oh, just feel what it's done to my heart!"

We were strolling in the ringing white sunlight on a bright winter's day when Fräulein Eckstein removed her hand from her muff and used it to place my hand over her heart. I tried to keep glued to my face the mask I wore with my patients, that of a concerned medical man, as we looked deeply into each other's eyes, our breaths steaming forth in clouds of condensation, my hand on the curve of her breast.

"Yes, Fräulein, it seems to be beating . . . quite beautifully."

It was all very confusing, I must say, and there were many times when I couldn't help feeling that the Fräulein was communicating to me a powerful desire to be kissed. I wasn't certain, however, as not two moments earlier, she'd been breathlessly describing her desire for a man who was clearly not myself. If I overcame my fear and kissed her and she didn't wish me to, I would lose her forever, I knew. On the other hand, nothing in the mores of the era would have allowed her, had she in fact wished to be kissed, to do anything other than what she was doing now, which was staring at me with a look of stupefied admiration, her eyelids lowered as though the sight of me had weakened her occipital muscles.

Invariably, of course, she'd turn away from me and say something along the lines of: "Oh, but he's just so very handsome, isn't he?"

"Dr. Freud, you mean?"

"With that beard and those eyes that pierce right through you!" She shook her head, as though she'd lost her train of thought. "Although you're rather good-looking yourself, Dr. Sammelsohn. Oh, not in a virile way, of course, like Dr. Freud, but still."

"Still." I offered her a weak smile. I could still feel the curve of her breast inside my palm, and these impoverishing compliments were, I knew, the price I paid for the hours I spent in her company.

"Oh, it's poor form, I know, to praise the looks of one man to another, and no woman ever would put up with such treatment! But you don't mind my speaking to you so forthrightly, do you?"

"Of course not, Fräulein. I find your candor refreshing."

"Because you're the only one I can talk to about any of this. You know that, don't you?" She placed her hand on her head, as though she had a headache. "It's odd, Dr. Sammelsohn, but sometimes I feel as though I've known you my entire life—do you feel that also?—as though we'd been children together."

IN THIS WAY, I learned the Fräulein's medical history. She'd been seeing Dr. Freud on and off for several years, she told me, though only at the insistence of her mother. In regard to what malady, she preferred not to say. "It's complicated." Dr. Freud was a family friend, and this inhibited her when he asked her, at the beginning of their daily hour, to tell him everything that passed through her mind. (Indeed, no psychologist today would treat a person from his own social set, but in the Vienna we shared with Dr. Freud, especially among its Jewish middle classes, finding a doctor one didn't know personally was a near impossibility.) At times, she suspected—correctly, I might add—that Dr. Freud's fledgling practice was struggling to take flight, and she worried that he'd taken her on only because he needed the money. "Not that Maman sent me to him as a charity case. God forbid!" It's just that sometimes—quite often—she felt that nothing was the matter with her. "Oh, I have my vacant moments, I suppose, when I lose track and I can't account for where I've been or what I've been thinking, but then aren't all women susceptible to daydreaming? It's all the needlework, Dr. Freud says, that makes us particularly vulnerable." Her mother, for example. "It's she who should be seeing a nerve specialist, and not I. But then you've met her yourself, haven't you?" No, it was her mother who had invented the canard of her ill health, "this so-called hysteria or dream psychosis or whatever it is," as a means of diverting attention away from her own psychopathologies. "Or whatever Dr. Freud calls them!" And the measure of her success had been that she was able to fool a man as formidable as Dr. Freud. "Although how formidable is he, really? Ask yourself: who published this account of Dr. Freud's brilliance, if not Dr. Freud himself? Have you ever heard another human being make a similar claim?"

Still, she couldn't help loving him. "He's a dear man, a true man, a beautiful man." Which didn't mean that she couldn't see through him. She could. "All those hours of psychoanalysis, Dr. Sammelsohn! You learn about a person — no, you do! — even if he *is* hiding behind a sofa." And in this respect, Dr. Freud was no different from any other man, "present company excluded": vain, posing, preening. "You could turn his head with a well-phrased compliment," something she'd done on numerous occasions, whenever she grew tired of his psychoanalytic probing. Oh, my, what a handsome tie, Dr. Freud, was all she had to say, and he was out from behind the analytic couch in a flash, sitting where she could see him, jabbering away about gabardines and silks, this weave versus that, and how normally expensive it all was but how he'd gotten it on the cheap thanks to the enormous esteem in which his tailor held him. "Only imagine!" At the end of such an hour, he'd gleam, *Why, Fräulein Emma, we've made wonderful progress today, haven't we?*

"His interest in my health is secondary to his interest in his theories (and everything comes third to his interest in clothes). If you appear better, he's glad, but only because it means he's been right. And if you dare to come to him cured of your symptoms by any other means — oh my, but he pouts for days! Every day — and he insists you see him on all five! — there he'd be, glum as a goose on Christmas Eve, in the vilest of moods! And everything's worse now, since he's given up tobacco. You can barely induce him to speak civilly! After a week of such treatment, whatever composure, whatever health, whatever happiness you've managed to win by this tonic or at the hands of that masseur is shredded and you're hysterical all over again! I don't know why I put up with it, but of course, I do. It's because I'm not well, you see?" She began to cry, and through tears, she told me that this was why she'd begun to put so much hope in Dr. Fliess's revolutionary new cures. "If my problems are nasal in origin, as he maintains, he'll be able to cure me with one quick surgery."

Still, she worried that by clinging to Dr. Fliess, she was betraying Dr. Freud and his superior, if at the moment less effective, methodologies. And yet it was Dr. Freud himself who was pushing her towards Dr. Fliess. "Am I such a hopeless case? Has he washed his hands of me?" Or was he beginning to chafe against her love for him, a love of which he couldn't be ignorant. "Perhaps Aunt Marty insisted he drop me! But that's impossible because he's promised to work with me even after Dr. Fliess removes the organic causes of my malady, although according to Dr. Fliess, such work would then be unnecessary." At times, she couldn't tell which would please Dr. Freud more: if she submitted to his friend or declared her allegiance to him, and all she really wanted was to be loved by him! "Is that so evil, Dr. Sammelsohn? I mean haven't I the same right to happiness as Martha Freud?"

CHAPTER 10

These conversations typically exhausted me, and I was happy to have finally reached our destination: the opera house. I surrendered our coats and scarves and the Fräulein's muff to the girl inside the cloakroom. A strong country type, she was an uncomplicated beauty, blonde and blue-eyed, with a peasant's firm bust. As she forced the wooden hangers into the shoulders of our coats, I couldn't help thinking that, were I Otto Meissenblichler, I might already have arranged a rendezvous with her for later in the week, perhaps for as early as the first intermission. Oh, how I longed to cast off this accursed virginity as though it were a pair of knickers I'd outgrown, but this was a feat, as far as I knew, impossible to accomplish on one's own, and I had little idea how one went about enlisting an accomplice in such a selfish pursuit.

When the cloakroom girl laid the chit for our possessions into my hand, her fingers grazed my upturned palm, and I ached against my shyness, against my inability to speak to her, indeed to say anything to her other than "Danke."

"Bitte," she said in return, laughing a little bit as though she knew what I was thinking.

"Ah, there you are." I found Fräulein Eckstein at the foot of the green-carpeted staircase, gloves in one hand, our tickets in the other. The last of the afternoon sun slanted through the transoms above the opera's many doors.

"Let's hurry," she said. "The curtain will be rising soon."

I offered her my arm, and we ascended the stairs, the good Viennese milling in groups or in pairs beneath every arch and in every arcade on the landings above us. I handed a white-gloved usher our tickets and followed him to a box on the first tier. The Fräulein sat in a red plush chair nearest the front. However, as though she were suddenly ill, she laid her head on the red velvet banister before her. Standing over her, I observed with concern the little beads of perspiration that had appeared along the piping of her neck.

"The Champagne you ordered, Fräulein," the usher said. A steward brought in a stand and a brass bucket, all frothy with ice. After proffering me its label, he plunged the bottle back into the bucket with an abrupt violence. I nodded, distractedly, in approval. Both men, impeccably trained, glanced not even once at Fräulein Eckstein, and the noise they made seeing to their work covered, perhaps intentionally, the moaning coming unmistakably from her throat.

"Fräulein, are you . . . is everything all right?" I asked when they had finally left us.

"Can it be locked?" she said, raising her head and nodding at the red plush door, closed now and so almost invisible inside the red plush wall.

"I think not," I said. "Are you well?"

"Of course, I'm well."

"In any case, there's no lock," I said, checking the door.

"It doesn't matter," she said. "I've reserved the box for us alone, and no one would dare enter without knocking."

Her face was ashen, her look oddly vacant. I had the eerie impression that she wasn't really seeing me but that something inside her was staring through her, using her eyes as though they were windows.

"You're certain you're up for an opera this afternoon?"

"Of course I am, silly," she said. "I'm fine."

She fluffed out her skirts and then, as though mesmerized by the rustling of her petticoats beneath them, continued to fluff them. "Oh, Yankl, have you ever seen such a marvelous dress as this!" I didn't know what to say. The overture had begun, and I sank into the cushions of my chair, easily the most comfortable I'd had for an opera. I wouldn't have minded sitting in the hardest seat in the back of the highest gallery, however, if it meant listening to the music in peace. In truth, the Fräulein's company was draining. Her emotional squalls exhausted me. Her needs were frustratingly impossible to satisfy, her problems evaded solution or were at least beyond my abilities to solve. All I wanted was to let the endless waves of Mozart's sublime genius wash over me and to forget about everything else.

However, the Fräulein would not stop talking.

"See to the curtains, won't you?" she said.

"The curtains?"

"Draw them."

"You'd prefer the curtains drawn, Fräulein?"

In those days, before Mahler took over as director and insisted otherwise, the house lights weren't dimmed during a performance; and those who didn't wish, for whatever reason, to be seen were invited to close off their boxes with a drape.

"Yes, pull the curtains," she said again.

"But what will people think?"

"It's better that no one see us together. What if Dr. Freud is here? Or, worse, my mother?"

Sighing, I did as she bid me and released the scarlet curtains from their braided ropes, plunging the box into an artificial red twilight.

"Good. Now pour out two drinks." She'd closed her eyes and had begun rubbing her temples with three fingers of each hand. I poured the Champagne and, holding both glasses, offered her one. She stood. Ignoring the drinks, she pressed both her hands against my chest before laying her head upon it as well, near my tie. I trembled against this unexpected gesture and dribbled a bit of the Champagne onto her dress.

"No, no, sha, sha, it's all right," she said, "it's all right, my darling." With her hand beneath my chin, she lifted my head, forcing my attention from the stains on her dress to her face. She brought her mouth to mine. "Oh, Yankl," she said, "you've no idea how long I've been missing you."

And then, of course, she kissed me.

It was a hard, frank, unpleasant kiss, nearly a bite really, her teeth rasping against mine. My upper lip, pinched between her teeth and my own, received a painful nip. The experience was disconcerting. (Quite literally: I forgot all about the overture.) Forbidding me to speak, she covered my mouth with her own.

"Kiss me, Yankl," she whispered. "Kiss me back." I'd stopped breathing and stepped back to look at her, hoping to regain my bearings. "Put the Champagne down," she ordered.

I was suddenly aware of the fluted glasses in my hands. "Of course," I said.

Woodenly, I turned towards the small stand, and thinking better of it, with the awkward air-bound grace of a marionette, I downed the first drink and then the second, before depositing the empty glasses there. My hands were trembling so, at least one of the glasses fell off the table and onto the carpet, which was, thankfully, too thick to break it. Like a schoolboy having performed a task for his master during the course of his being punished by him, I placed myself before Fräulein Eckstein again. She returned her hands to my chest, exactly as she had them before, as though she had memorized the proper attitude one must strike when receiving a kiss. I moved towards her, our heads tilting together first to the left, then, correcting, to the right, then to the left, et cetera, until they were properly angled. She laughed at me, and I could feel her breath in my mouth. My lips touched hers politely, inquisitively, deferentially, although obviously too tentatively for the Fräulein, who received them with the rapacity of a wolf, her mouth open and slavering. As though devouring it, she kept her mouth upon mine and pulled me in closer. I folded her into my arms, but soon she was sitting, pulling me on top of her, lifting her legs against my outer thigh, drawing me onto her skirt and her petticoats, so that I lay atop her frilly undershifts with my knees upon the floor.

"Here," she said, placing my hand beneath her bosom, and I could feel her heart heaving against the fabric of her garments. I lifted my neck and drew back to take a better look at her. Her eyes were closed, her nostrils flaring; a vein throbbed visibly in her throat. "Yankl, be my husband," she whispered. "Lie with me as your wife."

Conscious of applause sounding out on the other side of the curtain, I stood and moved far from her.

"Ha!" she laughed. "You haven't changed at all."

"I'm not certain what you mean by that, Fräulein?"

"Still with your head in the clouds."

"Fräulein, are you certain you're all right?"

"Pay attention, Yankl. Look at me." Staring me in the eye, she reached down with both hands and lifted up her skirts. It's difficult now, when in our modern era a woman wearing no more than a fig leaf is considered dressed, to remember how many undergarments a woman then wore, but I couldn't begin to number her silken petticoats, as she untied their colored ribbons and lay open their flounces. Lying back in the narrow chair, her skirts to her lap, she unclasped her blouse, exposing the ornate piping of her corset. With an agonizingly slow hand, she unbound the ribbons threaded through its seams and unfastened three enormous whalebone hooks. Gently, she picked up its now-freed halves, one in each hand, and parted it as though she were opening an oyster shell. The twin pearls of her bosom lay inside, exposed. "Husband," she said, a brazen look transforming her face, "do I please you now?"

"Fräulein," I said, knowing neither what to say nor where to look, unable to gaze upon her nakedness openly though less able to turn from it completely.

"Does this body please you better than the other?"

Mastering myself, I stared at my shoes. "Fräulein," I said, pleading with her, "dress yourself or I won't be held accountable for our actions."

"Tell me, Yankl," she asked, "how satisfied are you with your tailor?"

"With my tailor, Fräulein? Quite satisfied."

"I was thinking you should perhaps speak to him."

"Speak to him, Fräulein? But why?"

Her eyes dropped vulgarly and she laughed a small, pleased, whorish laugh. "Because there seems to be a slight distress in the fabric of your pants."

She was clearly in the grip of some severe form of hysteria. Indeed, there seemed to be two Emma Ecksteins—the one who had expounded at length upon her doomed infatuation with Sigmund Freud earlier in the afternoon, and this one, a second Emma, inside of which the first had all but disappeared, and who lay back in her opera chair now, her bodice unlaced and her bosom exposed. I knew of no way of calling the first Emma back. Her offer of herself had so rent the fabric of our normal conversation that I hardly knew what to say. She had also addressed me, as no one had in years, by my childhood name, and though I didn't realize it until later, we had slipped together into Yiddish. In fact, her German had become unspeakable, filled with all sorts of grammatical and syntactical errors.

"Fräulein Eckstein," I addressed her as tenderly as I could. "Emma," I said—for how could I speak to her formally when she sat before me three-quarters undressed?

"Don't I please you, Yankl?"

"Of course, you do. You're exceedingly pleasant, but the opera!" I said, clutching at straws. "We're missing the first act!"

"Be kind to me, Yankl. I've waited so very long for this moment."

"Fräulein Eckstein." I took a step towards her. Tentatively I lifted her hands from her open bodice and covered her bosom with her corset.

She pouted seductively. "No," she said.

"Sha, sha," I said, trying to button and lace up her clothing. Her ensemble was ridiculously complex.

"Yankl." She lowered her face and kissed my hands.

"But Fräulein," I said, "I thought you wanted to see the opera."

It's difficult to account for what happened next. I continued trying to dress her, my hand fumbling with the fabric. Her face, beset by a siege of neuralgic tics, became a fearful mask of incomprehension. With a too-real shriek, she looked me in the eye, as I was lacing up her blouse. "What in God's name do you think you're doing, Dr. Sammelsohn?" Her voice was entirely unlike the sultry sulk with which she'd moments before addressed me. "I beg your pardon! Unhand me this very instant, sir!"

Ah, here was the first Emma who had so inexplicably disappeared. And this was exactly what I'd feared, indeed what I've always feared with women. I had misunderstood her, I had misread her. Intoxicated by fantasies of sexual conquest—a conquest I wouldn't permit myself!—I'd placed myself in a position where I now seemed a fool. Or worse: a Bluebeard, a debaucher, a libertine. Though she had undressed herself, though she had plied me with Champagne, though she had ordered me to draw the curtains, clearly I had read vastly more into these things than she had meant. I shuddered to think what might have happened had I allowed my misperceptions free rein, giving into impulses from the darker hemisphere of my nature!

Without ceasing to scold me, Fräulein Eckstein turned away. Her chin tucked, her hands working between her bosom, she rebuttoned and relaced herself, relocking herself inside her garments. "Dr. Sammelsohn," she said, realigning her skirts, "you may fetch me a cab. You shall go out of this building, and you will summon it, and you will pay for it in advance. Here is the money that you will need." In her agitation, she riffled through her reticule, producing a small fistful of banknotes, which she dropped onto the floor between us. "You will return, without entering this box again, to inform me when my ride has arrived."

She spoke now in the clearest of German—what is more German than the imperative case?—and I turned sheepishly from her towards the curtains.

"Do *not* open the curtains!" she cried.

"As you wish, Fräulein."

"I only hope that no one of my acquaintance saw me enter this box with you, or my name—*and my family's name!*—will be ruined forever. Surely you understand that!"

"I'm certain no one saw us."

"How can you be so certain?"

"I can't be, Fräulein. No, you're correct there."

For the second time since the overture began, I became aware of the music outside our box. The singers had taken their places onstage. I'd read marvelous things about this production. I could never have afforded so splendid a ticket on my own. What a shame to let so magnificent a box go empty! But Fräulein Eckstein was right. Opening the curtains, broadcasting my face to the civilized world, the long-nosed leer of her seducer, was out of the question. Still, perhaps after bundling her into a cab, mightn't I return? What harm could come from my peeking through a breech in the curtain and listening to the rest of the opera?

Fräulein Eckstein finished dressing, and though I hesitated to interrupt her before she'd fully vented her spleen, neither did I wish to make her wait unnecessarily long for her cab. "Very well, Fräulein," I announced, "if you're through, I shall go in shame and disgrace and summon you your ride."

She turned quite suddenly. "No! Don't! Please don't leave me, Yankl, my husband, my lover! Don't leave me!" She crossed the few meters of red carpet that lay between us as though the earth had opened up behind her, and she threw herself against me, her mouth once more upon mine, ravenous for my kisses. Before I could kiss her or even refuse to, before I could utter a word of surprise, however, her nose started to bleed.

"Oh no!" she cried. Crooking her back like a hunchback, she tilted her head towards the ceiling to keep the blood from spoiling her dress. Her hands fluttered like hummingbirds on either side of her face before she thought to cup them beneath her chin. Holding one bloody palm above the other, her shoulders drawn in, she resembled a pitiable beggar. "Help me, Dr. Sammelsohn!" she shrieked in a whisper, not wishing, I presumed, to disrupt the performance or to draw attention to us here, illicitly hiding behind the velvet curtains.

I quickly pulled a handkerchief from my pocket. She seemed torn between accepting and rejecting it, apparently not wanting aid from the man who had nearly ruined her. With little choice, however, she took it and brought it to her nose. "Fräulein Eckstein," I commanded her. The situation was now a medical emergency, and I was obliged to take charge of it. "Sit down!"

Unwilling to sit in the chair where she had undressed herself, she moved to the one behind it. "This *keeps* happening and — oh! God! — it takes forever to stop!"

The amount of blood gushing from her nose *was* alarming. When she occluded the offending nostril, the blood simply ran out the other; if she pinched both at once, as I advised her to do, the blood pooled at the back of her throat, mixing with her saliva until she had to spit it out in bright livid plugs. My handkerchief, crumbled in her hands, soon resembled a butcher's rag, and her fingers, the front of her blouse and the knees of her skirt were stained with the wine-ish lacquer. I ran to summon help, and the house manager, appraising the situation, returned with towels from the tenor's dressing room. Holding the white cloths to her face, Fräulein Eckstein allowed this gentleman to escort her from the box and, presumably, down the stairs to the lobby. He rode with her, I later learned, in the opera's own fiacre to her family's residence.

I felt contemptible for failing to accompany her, but I knew my person was not desired. I attempted to concentrate on the performance, but I had no stomach for the contrivances of the plot and soon left.

CHAPTER 11

She spoke Yiddish to you?"

"Yes, and she called me Yankl."

"But perhaps you mentioned to her that you were called Yankl as a child, and she wished, for some reason, in addressing you to bring up memories of your childhood." Dr. Freud stopped to relight his cigar. He turned against the breeze, raising his shoulder as a windbreak. "It's not an uncommon diminutive in the mother tongue . . . and yet"—he shook out the match and threw it into the street—"it does strike the odd-sounding chord." He puffed on the cylinder with a smoker's relief, the nicotine visibly soothing his nerves. "Mention nothing of this to Fliess, should we encounter him on our walk today, an occurrence I think likely."

"Certainly I'll say nothing of Fräulein Eckstein."

"Not of the Fräulein, no, but of these," he said, raising the cigar. "The old charmer's back in town, you see, and at his command and for the benefit of my health, naturally, I've given up this filthy habit. I smoke the occasional one now and again simply to prove that I can stop whenever I wish."

We hesitated at the corner of Schwarzenbergstrasse to let a fiacre pass. The driver whipped his horses with a brutal fury, his passengers oblivious to his barbarisms, concealed, as they were, inside the carriage, wrapped comfortably beneath their heavy blankets. I could hear the high, fine tinkling sound of a woman's laughter coming from inside the coach as it sped past.

Dr. Freud scowled at the terrible sight. "You've put my work with Fräulein Eckstein back months now, or even years, I don't mind telling you. You realize this, don't you, Dr. Sammelsohn? Didn't I tell you she was too ill for a suitor? And yet you recklessly ignored my warnings.

And now just look at the mess you've made. Fräulein Eckstein's was to be the final history in our *Studies on Hysteria,* a case of my own to rival what Breuer has done with Pappenheim in 'The Case of Anna O.' I'll be months, mopping up the disaster you've created!"

Dr. Freud checked the pulse in his wrist, then in his neck, before spitting onto the curb. "I have such a headache," he said, closing his eyes and rubbing his temples. "And it's difficult to say if she's truly suffering from hysteria or if her troubles have a more physiological origin. Once again my lack of medical knowledge weighs heavily upon me. Perhaps I *should* have Fliess examine her after all."

"Is that wise?"

"Who else if not Wilhelm?"

"It's just that his theories seem so . . ."

But I had risked too much. Dr. Freud grew suddenly cold. Perhaps because it seemed so improbable to me, I continually underestimated his infatuation with this dubious friend.

"She acted as though she were possessed by a devil," I said, hoping to bring the conversation back to hysteria, knowing that Dr. Freud was obsessed with the subject.

He made a scoffing sound in his throat. "Oh, Dr. Sammelsohn." He shook his head. "If you only knew."

He explained to me that, in addition to hysteria's more dramatic and debilitating symptoms—all sorts of neuralgias, contractures, paralyses, hallucinations, et cetera—it was his and Dr. Breuer's great discovery that hysterics suffer principally from reminiscences.

"From reminiscences?" I said.

"Mm, yes, from memories," he said. "Specifically from repressed memories. Now these memories correspond to traumas the patient has allowed himself to experience only insufficiently. They are not, therefore, subject to the natural wearing-away process of normal memories. You see, Dr. Sammelsohn, the fading of a memory depends most importantly upon whether there has been an energetic reaction to the event in question, and by that I mean everything from acts of revenge to simple tears."

He drew on his cigar. "If the reaction is suppressed" — he shrugged — "the emotional charge attaches itself to the memory and manifests as hysteria."

In the great majority of cases, it was impossible to deduce the original trauma by interrogating the patient, however thoroughly one carried out these interrogations, partly because the experience in question is usually one the patient dislikes talking or even thinking about.

"In that case, one must hypnotize him and, under hypnosis, arouse his memories of the time at which his symptoms first appeared. When this is done, it's possible to demonstrate the connection between the hysterical symptom and its traumatic cause in the most convincing of fashions."

He had treated a clerk who'd become an hysteric as a result of having been beaten by his employer in public.

"The poor man suffered from attacks in which he collapsed into a frenzy of rage, without giving any sign that he was in the grips of an hallucination. Under hypnosis, I was able to provoke an attack in the patient who then revealed that he was living through the scene in which his employer had beaten him."

But it was not he, Dr. Freud was quick to inform me, but rather Dr. Breuer, who, in treating a spectacular case of hysteria in a local girl named Bertha Pappenheim, had stumbled upon a rudimentary version of the psychoanalytic technique as early as 1880.

"Now Breuer and I have found to our amazement that each symptom immediately and permanently disappears when the memory of the event that provoked it and its accompanying affects are brought into the light of analysis. This happens when the patient describes the event in the greatest possible detail, putting the affect into words. Hence: the talking cure. If a typical case of hysteria may be compared to a small shrine, Pappenheim's was the grand cathedral of Chartres!"

Highly intelligent, though intellectually understimulated, by her early twenties, Bertha Pappenheim had wrecked her health caring for her ailing father, and it was in the wake of his death that her symptoms first appeared: a squint, a nervous cough, violent mood swings, positive as well as negative hallucinations (she saw what wasn't there and didn't see what was). She suffered also from aural hallucinations and visual distortions.

At one point, she could perceive the world visually only in pieces, one narrow segment at a time. At another, she lost her native German and spoke only (and perfectly, I might add) in English. Indeed, when given a German text to read, she translated it instantaneously, without realizing she had done so. For a time, a part of her consciousness lived in the actual year 1882, while another lived in the year before. In fact, she reexperienced the events of 1881 each day with a perfect fidelity, as Dr. Breuer was able to verify by consulting the diary of her mother.

Only by having Fräulein Pappenheim recount the events of her trauma under hypnosis—one by one and in reverse chronological order—was Dr. Breuer able to relieve her of her symptoms. This was painstaking work, requiring infinite patience and infinite care; and the recounting succeeded only when Fräulein Pappenheim reexperienced these traumatic events with a full range of emotional responses. Fräulein Pappenheim herself coined the term *talking cure*—in English, of course—and in her lighter moments, she referred to the treatment, also in English, as *chimney-sweeping*.

"But I'll tell you a secret," Dr. Freud said, leaning against me, and suddenly the air was thick with a delicious conspiracy. "Though you must promise never to reveal what I'm about to tell you to a living soul, and I mean that, Dr. Sammelsohn. Not to a living soul!"

I promised him. I had no idea what he was going to say. I knew only that I must hear it.

"This is what really happened between Breuer and his patient." Dr. Freud raised his eyebrows. "On the evening of the day all of Fräulein Pappenheim's symptoms were brought under control, Dr. Breuer was called to her bedside one final time. The patient was confused and writhing with abdominal cramps. Asked what was the matter, she replied, 'Here comes Dr. B's baby! Here comes Dr. B's baby!' Breuer, of course, had no stomach for such things. He picked up his medical bag, returned his hat to his head, and fled. He held the key in his hand, Dr. Sammelsohn, he held the key in his hand, and he dropped it. He dropped it! Like a thief who runs at the first sign of trouble, he had the courage of the knife but not the courage of the blood."

It was clear from the vitriol in Dr. Freud's voice that his bitterness towards Dr. Breuer was far more complicated than he was letting on. He sounded like a suitor who'd been thrown over for a lover far less accomplished than himself. If this is how Dr. Freud treats his ex-friends, I thought, I'm glad to count myself among their opposites.

"Breuer aside, the Pappenheim case is foundational for our young science," Dr. Freud said. "The longer I've occupied myself with these phenomena, the more I've become convinced that there's a splitting of consciousness involved in every hysteria, a 'double self,' as it were. Ideas originating in this second self, which are available to both patient and doctor in a state of hypnosis, are otherwise cut off from the normal consciousness of the patient. In their secondary state, these notions seem to form a second consciousness, a more or less highly structured condition seconde, as I call it. During an attack, control of the body appears to pass over to the second self entirely, and normal consciousness is repressed. I'm afraid something like this has befallen our poor Eckstein. In any case, the report you've made is troubling, and I'll have to ask you to promise never to see the Fräulein again."

"Of course," I said quickly.

"I say this neither as her friend nor as yours but as a physician, *her* physician specifically."

"I will do whatever it is you advise."

Dr. Freud spat again into the curb. "God only knows what effects your afternoon tryst may have had upon her. You'll give me your word, then. You will neither see her nor write to her, nor will you respond to any correspondence from her, except with the most bland demurrals, as any gentleman would."

"After today, I'm not certain Fräulein Eckstein will ever wish to see me again under any circumstances."

"That's of course a woman's prerogative," Dr. Freud said, suddenly jovial and magnanimous again. "In which case . . ." He raised his eyebrows.

"Yes?"

". . . there's always the mother!"

He barked up an orotund laugh.

We were, by then, in the Prater, wandering along a rutted path before coming to a clearing near the Konstantinhugel where Dr. Fliess had asked Dr. Freud to meet him. He was waiting on one of the restaurant's verandas, dapper in a dark suit and a floppy bow tie. He finished the chocolate he was eating and, wiping his hands against each other, rose to greet us as we approached.

"Ah, Sigmund, good evening."

"Dearest Wilhelm, good evening, good year. You remember Dr. Sammelsohn, of course."

Dr. Fliess smiled at me with the icy grace of a reptile. "I'm quite sure we've never met. Or if we have, I don't recall it."

"The week before last Christmas?" Dr. Freud prompted him. "At the soirée?"

Dr. Fliess riffled his memory banks. Shaking his head, he made a clicking noise with his mouth. "Didn't leave an impression, I'm afraid." Nevertheless he took my hand. "There were so many fascinating people there."

At this, both men turned, as one, and looked at me. By their silent compact, I understood that they'd finished with my company and, too polite to dismiss me, were waiting for me to excuse myself.

"Well, I see you have matters to attend to," I said at last.

"Yes," Dr. Freud roared, "we're having our picture made." He smiled at Dr. Fliess. "A dual portrait. One that can be sent to all our mutual friends."

"What time is the appointment, anyway?" Dr. Fliess said.

"You'll receive a copy," Dr. Freud assured me.

"You'd better run," I said as Dr. Fliess drew forth his watch. "Good evening, gentlemen."

"Good evening, Dr. Sammelsohn."

"Good evening, Dr. . . ." Though Dr. Freud had just spoken it, Dr. Fliess had apparently forgotten my name already.

"Sammelsohn," Dr. Freud said sotto voce.

"Sammelsohn, yes, marvelous to meet you," Dr. Fliess said as I said, "Good to see you again."

The two men walked off, arm in arm, Dr. Freud nearly leaning his head against Dr. Fliess's shoulder. I waited a decent interval before following them the short distance to Brandstatter's Photographic Emporium. I watched through the large front windows as Herr Brandstatter greeted both men. A hunchback, he shook their hands while looking at his shoes. He posed them against a grey backdrop, Dr. Freud with his long white tie, Dr. Fliess in the rakish bow tie embossed with a field of golden keys. Warning them with a raised finger not to move a hair, Herr Brandstatter retreated behind his camera and hid himself beneath its hood.

He held up the pan, and the powder exploded with a flash.

THAT NIGHT, THINGS came to an awkward pass. In bed, I felt hands tickling me awake. I pulled the covers tighter about my shoulders. "Who's there?" I cried, squinting into the gloom, but I could see no one, even with my pince-nez on. As I was about to lay my head upon the pillow, however, a knocking sounded, and I got up, cinching the sash of my robe as I made my way to the door. A man is not made of stone, and though I'd pledged to do exactly as Dr. Freud had commanded, still, when I opened the door and found Fräulein Eckstein on the landing, dressed only in her nightgown and robe, her hair a mass of wet tangles, I had to let her in. What else was I to do? Send her away? Her clothes were damp from the night's mist, and her bare feet were scalded red from the burning ice of the sidewalks.

"Good Lord, Fräulein! Is that you?"

She said nothing. Her eyes were nearly closed, her jaw slack, and her mouth opened slightly. She reminded me of a blind man I'd seen as a child in a railway station. Abandoned by his companions, he moved tentatively, taking each step as though the floor beneath him might open up at any moment and the earth swallow him. As with the blind man, something prevented me from immediately offering Fräulein Eckstein my aid. She was sleepwalking. I hadn't realized this at first. Indeed, she was in as advanced a state of somnambulism as I had ever seen. Surely even Dr. Freud wouldn't insist I send her away in such a precarious state. On the contrary, my calling as a doctor demanded that I take the opposite tack. The little I knew of somnambulism suggested it was best neither to startle nor awaken the Fräulein. On the other hand, I couldn't very well leave a young woman, clad only in her nightclothes, standing at the door of my apartment and continue to live with my neighbors' approval.

"Come in, come in, you look frozen," I said as gently I could. To my relief, she took a small step forward. She hesitated as though puzzled at hearing my voice, but finally she crossed the threshold. I peered into the hallway before closing the door. No one was there. Fräulein Eckstein moved into the room, swaying slightly. Though her eyes were now completely closed, she managed somehow to avoid the furniture, a feat all the more remarkable as she'd never been inside my rooms before.

"Do you mind?" she said, sitting at the table beneath the lamp, where earlier in the evening I'd been reading Dr. Fliess's *On the Causal Connection between the Nose and the Sexual Organ*. Fräulein Eckstein picked up the book and tossed it aside. "Why do you read such rubbish?" she asked, still quite asleep.

I shrugged, wondering if the silent gesture would register with her in any way. However, there was nothing to say in the book's defense.

"Yankl," she said, sighing pleasurably.

"Yes, Fräulein?"

"Do you hear it?"

"Hear what, Fräulein?"

"The wedding music."

I shook my head.

"I'm listening to it now," she said. "Are you?"

"I'm not."

"And why not?"

"Because I can't hear it, I suppose."

Her brow puckered. "And why is that?"

"Well, I'm certain I don't know."

It's an unsettlingly intimate thing to sit with a person whose eyes are closed. Observing while unobserved, the eye takes in things it otherwise might never see. I leaned in closer to Fräulein Eckstein and looked at the little blue twigs of veins inside her lowered eyelids, the skin of which seemed more red and roughened than the rest of her face. Perhaps she's been crying, was my initial thought.

"Do you know how difficult it was to find you here, Yankl?"

"Here, in my rooms, Fräulein?"

"I've been walking and walking."

"I hope you haven't caught a cold."

"And no one saw me."

"No?"

"Because it's night."

"Ah, yes, that's very clever of you."

"I slept during the day."

"Did you?"

"Whenever I could."

"Although perhaps we shouldn't talk so much until you've properly awakened."

"In haystacks, in barns. I didn't know where I was going exactly or where I'd find you."

She sat with her back rigid and her hands on the table, one atop the other. So flat and lifeless, they almost resembled gloves. I played with my slipper, snapping my ankle, lifting my heel in and out of the shoe, a nervous habit. Neither of us spoke again for a minute, and I listened to the grandfather clock, ticking with its slight irregularity, in the corner of the room.

Finally she said, "Do you see them, Yankl?"

"See whom, Fräulein?"

"You don't then?"

"No."

"Do you see them now?"

"I see no one."

"Good."

"Is it?"

"Perhaps I've eluded them."

"I certainly hope so."

"Do you?"

"Very much so."

"Because I thought you might blame me."

"Blame you, Fräulein? But for what?"

"Oh God!" She startled.

"What is it?"

"They're here!" She trembled. "Are they here?" She turned her head, listening. "I think they're here!"

"No, no one is here, Fräulein," I said, but as I tried to reassure her, her breathing quickened and grew short. She lifted the backs of her hands to her face and held them there, as though shielding her eyes from an inordinately brilliant light. "I've harmed no one!" she called to whatever presence she imagined confronting her. "I've harmed no one but myself!" She stood. "It is owed me!" she cried. "Do you hear me? It is *owed* to me!" As though struck, she fell to the floor, cowering beneath her chair, sheltering there, or so it appeared to me, from a rain of invisible blows.

I stood and paced in frantic steps, first towards the door, then towards her recumbent figure, then towards the door again, undecided which was best—summoning help or seeing to her myself. Throwing medical caution to the wind, forgetting in my fear the old wives' tales (or was it hard, medical fact?) that forbade waking a sleepwalker, I grabbed her by her shoulders—her head was beneath the chair, her torso confined between two of its legs—and I shook her. "Fräulein! You must awaken!" I cried, but her convulsions worsened at my touch. As though beaten and kicked from every side, she screamed out, raging incomprehensibly, holding out her arm, reaching for my hand, as might a sailor being devoured by sharks before the eyes of his helpless crewmates. "Fräulein Eckstein," I cried again, and her trembling ceased immediately. Her arms, which had been protecting her head, fell away; the hinges of her elbows unlocked, her head dropped. I lifted the chair from over her and, kneeling again, supported her back, helping her to sit up. "Can you hear me?"

She opened her eyes. "Dr. Sammelsohn?" She expressed these two words as a question.

"Yes, Fräulein, it is I."

She looked searchingly into my face, as though trying to decipher a Chinese ideogram, then glanced about the room. "Oh, oh, but . . . how . . . ?" Sitting up, she gathered the collar of her gown. Looking at my nightclothes and at my robe, and then at her own nightclothes, she screamed—"God in Heaven, no!"—before fainting dead away. She couldn't have been more distressed had she regained consciousness in an opium den lying in the arms of a white slaver, it seemed. I picked her up, not an easy feat — she weighed nearly as much as I — and carried her into my bedroom, where I laid her down in my bed. I glanced out the window. It must have been nearly four in the morning. Though the sky was still dark, I knew there was only one thing to do: I must summon Sigmund Freud, her rightful physician, immediately. Making a quick calculus, however, I resolved to put off doing so for another few hours, until dawn, at least. The Fräulein could sleep in my bed. The poor girl had obviously exhausted herself. I would sleep on the sofa in the sitting room. As for Dr. Freud, whatever he could do for her at four in the morning, snatched out of his warm bed, groggy and ill tempered, he could do far better after a full night's sleep, or such was my reasoning.

Making certain Fräulein Eckstein was comfortable, I injected her with a hypodermic of a strong sleeping draught, which I kept in my medical bag. She relaxed, and her breathing lengthened. I covered her with blankets and made to leave the room. As I was about to close the door behind me, however, she startled me by addressing me in a voice that was alert and strong. "Yankl," she said.

"Yes, Fräulein?" I turned back, bending in through the doorway, staring at her form inside the darkened chamber of the room.

"There's no need to sleep so far away from me."

"Ah, yes, well, I think it's better that I do, Fräulein, and in the morning, I'll see to it that you arrive safely home."

(Perhaps the choral was old, I told myself, its potency expired.)

"Come lie with me, Yankl," she said.

"Fräulein."

"Please, because I'm so cold!"

I took my hand off the knob. "You're not cold," I told her. "It's the hypodermic I administered to you that's making you feel cold, that's all."

"But I *am* cold," she complained like a lost child. "I walked barefoot in the snow."

"Then I'll bring you an extra blanket."

"Open a light, if you don't believe me, and I'll show you the gooseflesh on my arms."

From this point on, my dear reader, I have nothing to say in my own defense and will make no attempt to justify anything I did that night. Telling myself I wished only to help her, as might any doctor in these circumstances, I lit a candle, believing its amber light would soothe her mind more calmingly than would the gas. The flame created an impenetrable shadow outside the oval of its light, and I could see Fräulein Eckstein inside the flickering penumbra, lying in the rumpled bedsheets. Her chemise was unlaced from its collar to its hem, and I couldn't help tracing with my eyes the lines of perspective that plunged across the rosy white expanse of her chest and her plump belly and the long stark avenues of her naked legs converging, as though in a single vanishing point, at the wild riot of curly black hair in her lap. She smiled almost imperceptibly, in triumph it seemed, one corner of her cheek and a single eyebrow rising. I couldn't help gasping at her beauty. She carefully opened the bodice of her chemise a bit farther, and her breasts commanded my attention as would two roses in a snowy field. A tingling needled my spine, more precisely than the needles of any Chinese doctor. I felt myself a character in a fairy tale, summoned to the bed of a wolf disguised as a sorceress. My hand trembled so, the flame guttered, extinguished in its own wax, and the vision of Fräulein Eckstein disappeared.

I struggled in the pitch to relight the taper.

"Yankl," she said, visible once again inside the flickering amber light.

I took a step towards the bed, convincing whatever part of me needed convincing that I was approaching her only for the purposes of carrying out a thorough medical examination.

"Fräulein Eckstein, you're sick," I told her, "you're ill."

She shook her head. "On the contrary, I've never felt better in my life."

"However, we mustn't do anything we might regret."

"No, I want to regret things, Yankl. Make me regret everything."

I swallowed nervously. "Very well then. Yes, I see. But you must understand that I promised Dr. Freud I wouldn't see you again."

"Dr. Freud!" she laughed out the name. "What a horse's ass!"

"He cares only for your well-being."

"He cares only for Dr. Fliess, and the worst part of it is he doesn't even know how lovesick he is — oh, the poor ridiculous puppy! 'Wilhelm this and Wilhelm that and, oh, my darling magician.'" She imitated Dr. Freud's voice to perfection. "It's really too disgusting!"

As tempting as it was to discuss Dr. Freud's incomprehensible admiration for the person of Wilhelm Fliess with another person as galled by it as I, I knew this was neither the appropriate time nor a suitable place.

"Perhaps Dr. Freud sees more deeply into Dr. Fleiss's character than you or I are able to," I said simply.

"Lie with me, Yankl," she said, quite suddenly.

"No, Fräulein," I demurred.

"Let me be a wife to you."

Not knowing how to respond, I chose my words carefully, speaking in my most medically avuncular manner: "I admit it's difficult in a situation such as ours, not to lose one's head . . ."

"No, lose it, Yankl," Fräulein Eckstein said, "and I'll lose mine as well."

My father had warned me against such women, and now his face appeared before me, its pinched, saturnine features, its thin mouth screwed down into a bilious frown, its nostrils curled as though against an odious stench. The face of a scold, colored in the dark hues of rebuke, it filled me with a half-forgotten bitterness for the way he'd insinuated himself between Hindele and me following our wedding. I'd resolved never to let him stand between me and a woman again. Before I could banish his caviling glare from my oculus mentis, Dr. Freud's face appeared there as well (as I'm certain it would in the coming century to anyone approaching Eros's sordid bed). Pert with derision, he leered at me like an anatomist peering into the eviscerated bowels of a cadaver, his face alert with disgust and fascination.

I reacted as negatively against Dr. Freud as I did against my own father: Who were these men to tell me who I could and could not consort with? True, I told myself, Fräulein Eckstein was in the thrall of a manic hysteria with elements of psychosis, but it's equally true that her madness only enhanced her beauty. She seemed a wild, ravishing thing, an animal, strong and omnivorous in her passions.

"What is it, Fräulein, you would have me do?" I asked, standing at her bedside. "Consider me your servant."

"Unsash your robe," she commanded me.

Betraying these betraying fathers, I obeyed her, my hands working as if on their own.

"Now shrug it off your shoulders and let it fall to the floor."

I did as she requested.

"Unbutton your nightshirt."

For that, I had to settle the candle on the table. Having done so, I complied, my hands, nervous and jittery, fumbling at their work.

"Now pull it off over your head."

Beneath my robe and nightshirt, I wore long lavender drawers, fashioned from lamb's wool. (These were extraordinarily warm in winter.) Fräulein Eckstein's eyes dropped vulgarly and once again she laughed that small, pleased, whorish laugh I'd heard that afternoon in the opera box. "Come here," she said.

My various garments about my feet, I hobbled towards her like a convict in leg irons. How may I put this without offending? Propped onto her elbow, she unbuttoned the lamb's wool and rummaged delicately through its central pouch, untangling the bobbin from the skein, as it were, firmly coercing what she found there to its full extension if not (such are the unfortunate effects of a lifelong abstinence) beyond. In truth, all this made me not a little uncomfortable. It wasn't so much the raw stark fact of my manhood negotiating the space between us — I'd never been held so matter-of-factly by a woman (or by anyone else for that matter) and though the attention my nether member received, at turns admiring and judicious, was not entirely unwelcome, nor were the many things its presence in the open air seemed to promise — still, this was an entirely different Emma Eckstein from the one I imagined I knew. I had previously thought her a typical höhere Tochter, a sweet woman-child, an innocent daughter, frazzled by her own femininity, an angel in the house, not the sort of wharf trull one encounters in the shadowy docks of Hamburg's rougher districts! Her vulgarity repulsed me and unstiffened my ardor. I swooned in confusion, not understanding how we'd gotten so quickly to this pass, and more than a part of me felt manipulated. My legs buckled, and I fell onto the edge of the bed. Keeping a small distance between us, I again stationed the candle in its holder on the table. For her part, lying next to me, she allowed her hand to fall against my thigh, its back nuzzling my crotch. Mesmerized against my will by her flesh, I reached out to her and, with a trembling hand, stroked her belly. She breathed in sharply, her gaze, beneath her slitted eyelids, never leaving mine. Her pelvis lifted involuntarily, as though an unseen hand had thrust her womanhood towards me. Daring to kiss her there, I again heard the same sharp intake of breath, like the sound of water hitting a hot griddle. With a startling quickness, she was on her knees and forearms, facing me, like a cat with its back caved in.

"Why did I run from you at the opera?" she asked playfully.

I rubbed the backs of my hands against her breasts which hung loose beneath her shift, two roses wrapped in silk. "Absolutely no idea," I said.

"Don't," she said. "That tickles."

I tried to kiss her, but she moved away. "Wait," she said, and she turned her back on me completely, lying on her belly, her arms beneath her chest. I leaned over her and kissed her neck, which seemed to elongate against the pressure of my kisses. Lying beneath me, Fräulein Eckstein turned her body around so that she faced me. I felt her arms, like snakes, coiling up my back, encircling my neck. She kissed me on the mouth and then, with an alarming strength, hugged me to her, her cheek hard against my cheek, burying my face in the pillow beneath her dampened hair. I was still sitting, and so my torso was pinned awkwardly against hers. I unfolded my body, bringing my legs onto the bed and pressing my body against hers fully. I could hear the brittle hair of her naked pubis crinkling against the crotch of my lamb's wool. We lay, kissing each other lightly.

"You have no idea," I said, "but I've been thinking of nothing but you since the moment I first saw you."

"You're such a charming liar," she said.

"No, Fräulein, it's true."

"How many woman have you lured into your bed with such charming lies?"

"Until now? None, quite honestly."

A proud gleam illumined her eyes, but immediately the look clouded over. "Never leave me," she said, tightening her arm around my neck.

"I won't."

"I mean it!"

"I promise."

"Swear to it!"

"I'd rather not swear, Fräulein," I said, and by then, we were both breathless with laughter.

"Love me then," she said, "finally and completely!"

Her tongue clanged inside my mouth like the clapper of a bell. Her elbows pummeled my soft belly as she unbuttoned my woolens. My spine rigid, my back raised, I pinioned myself inside the brace of her thighs, struggling to pull my long underwear off past my feet, and then, suitably unclothed, I once again pressed myself against her compliant body, kissing her wildly, with a lover's manic sorrow, my heart in anguish. I kissed her again and again until I felt something warm and liquid in my mouth.

"Fräulein Eckstein?" I said, removing my mouth from hers.

"No, it doesn't matter, it doesn't matter!" she said, holding me fast.

Her nose was bleeding again, so propulsively this time, in fact, that within moments, the blouse of her chemise, and her breasts beneath it, my chest and the bed sheets upon which we lay were soaked.

"It's nothing, my darling. No, it happens all the time these days and will soon stop. I promise you." She tried to kiss me again, but her mouth was so filled with blood that it dribbled down her chin until she appeared to be wearing a diabolical red goatee. I drew away in panic, but she held me tight, her hands on my arms, her legs encircling my waist.

"Let go of me," I cried, "and I'll summon help!"

"Always running, always running, little Yankele, you poor little thing. Well, run away then. Run away!" She pushed me off her, kicking me with one leg. As I tumbled out of the bed, she cried, "You disgust me!" I gathered my clothes from the floor: my long underwear, my robe, my slippers. But she held her arms out to me. "No, don't! I didn't mean it, Yankl. Hold me! Please: I'm cold!"

"I'll ring for help!" I said, departing the room.

"No, no, don't!" she shrieked so loudly I feared she'd rouse my neighbors from their moral slumbers, and they'd mass together, outraged, at my door.

I found my pince-nez and put them on. "Sssh! Fräulein Eckstein. Please! I'll stay in the room," I conceded, "if that's what you prefer. I'll do whatever you wish."

"This is *my* blood, Yankl!" she said. She stood on her knees in the rumpled bed sheets, her face smeared with it, her hands dripping, more blood cascading from her nose to her chest, her belly, her knees. Even her brow was smeared where she'd pushed her hair from her forehead.

"Of course, it is, Fräulein. It's your blood. Of course, it is." I tried to placate her. "Calm down, please. No one's suggesting that it isn't your blood."

"And who spilled it?"

This question confused me. "Who spilled it?" I said. "I'm sorry, Fräulein, but I don't follow your gist."

"Who spilled it, Yankl?" Her hands, curled into fists at her sides, opened and closed, as though in solidarity with the pumping of her heart. She looked like a ruffian spoiling for a fight, irritating her own anger as one might a maddened dog, waiting until it was frothing at the mouth and she had only to open a gate and release it for it to sink its teeth into the throat of her opponent: me.

"Well, I might have bumped into you too roughly," I admitted. "We'd both become a little extreme in our passion, I agree. But as you said, it's been happening a lot lately, all the time, as it did this very afternoon at the opera."

"You killed me, Yankl!"

"Oh, don't exaggerate, Fräulein Eckstein."

"You killed me!"

"And also please consider my neighbors, many of whom have to get up for work early in the morning."

With her bloody palms lifted to the ceiling, she stood on her knees. "How could you have killed me when I loved you so? I loved you so much, Yankl. My sweet Yankele."

I hardly knew the woman, and she knew me not at all. I'd been infatuated, it's true, off my head with dreams of her, but even as foolish a fellow as I would not confuse an attraction of that sort with the kind of love that kills.

"Fräulein," I said, "it's true I've allowed myself to become overly fond of you in recent days . . ."

She shrieked again. Still on her knees, she closed her eyes and dropped her head back. Her bared throat angled towards the ceiling, she cried out in extreme pain. She looked as though she were being whipped across her back, lashed with a strop wielded by the hand of an unseen tormentor. At intervals, she gasped, her chest buckling forward, her head thrown farther back, her face ecstatic with pain. Her hands were balled into fists. With each lunge forward, she dug her nails deeper into the meat of her palms, until they too were bleeding.

"Ah! . . . ah! . . . n'ah!" she cried. "God is merciful, Yankl! God is merciful, yes! Even when we spit in His face, even when He must rebuke us!"

She opened an eye and looked at me with a small sad smile: the very portrait of a loving penitent, though nude.

I stood at the door, my nightclothes in a bundle before my sex. I counted thirty-two invisible lashes until her rhythmic bucking came to an end.

"Oh, yes! yes!" she cried. "Oh, but do you see God's extraordinary mercy, my lover, my husband, my slayer?"

Finally she collapsed, falling sideways onto the bed.

(Today, of course, I would assume that in an hysterical frenzy of sexual excitation Fräulein Eckstein had brought herself to a climax, perversely enjoying my voyeuristic participation in her guilt-ridden self-degradation. Ignorant then of such things, I had no way of interpreting the gruesome masque she'd played out before me. All I knew, all I told myself, was that the hypodermic I'd given her seemed to have finally worked.)

I checked her pulse. It was dangerously faint. I covered her where she lay, not daring to move her, lest I awaken her again. I put on my clothes. Unable to find a fiacre at that hour, I ran all the way to Berggasse, bisecting the Ring, and by the time I got to number 19, dawn had announced its presence in the sky.

"Dr. Freud! Dr. Freud!" I shouted, following his sister-in-law in her nightclothes to their kitchen where I found Dr. Freud at his morning table. He looked up from his porridge and his Kaiser roll and took in what I'm certain was the ghastly sight of me, standing before him, unshaven, my hair wild and uncombed, my hands and face smeared with blood where, distracted in my haste, I'd neglected to wash them.

"It's Fräulein Eckstein," I cried.

"Emma?" he said, standing.

"You must come immediately!"

Along with throat catarrh and his heart troubles, Dr. Freud suffered from boils that made his every move a torment. Especially painful was a boil at the base of his scrotum, which, he told me, had lately grown as large as an apple. It was my misfortune to have bounded into his kitchen, my face and hands smeared with Fräulein Eckstein's blood, on the day he'd scheduled to have it lanced. Minna, serving him his breakfast, promised to ring the doctor and, if possible, to remake his appointment for later in the day.

"Thank you, my dearest," he said, rising from his place with a great show of pain. Wincing, he gathered up his things and, in a moment of pique, ground his cigar into his uneaten porridge.

"I'll hurry back and make sure she's still all right, then," I said.

"Still?" He glowered. "What makes you think she was all right to begin with?"

Moving gingerly, his legs slightly bowed, he grimaced again, and before I could answer him, he barked out, "Yes, yes, go on then, go!"

A half hour later, he was making his way painfully up the stairs of my apartment, a damp handkerchief pressed against his nose. "The suppuration is intolerable this morning," he explained.

I leaned over the railing and called down to him, "This way."

"I'm ascending as quickly as I can, Dr. Sammelsohn! Do not hector me!" He hesitated at each landing, puffing like a grampus. "Is there a spittoon anywhere on the premises?"

"None on the landing, I'm afraid."

He hawked up a viscid oyster of phlegm and spat it into an umbrella stand in the corner.

"Pity," he said.

A disgusted exhalation slipped through my lips before I could censor it. Dr. Freud eyed me coldly. "The body has its needs, Dr. Sammelsohn.

Now, show me to my patient, and while I see to her, perhaps you will be so good as to rinse her blood from your face and hands, so that you cease to resemble a Red Indian on the war path!"

He limped into my rooms. Taking a deep breath and surmounting his disgust, he entered my bed chamber. I called to him from the kitchen, where I stood at the sink, "I assure you, Dr. Freud, I had no intention of ever seeing the Fräulein again, exactly as I pledged to you."

I tamped my face with a towel. Through the bedroom door, I could see him examining Fräulein Eckstein, checking her pulse, her arm lifted awkwardly behind her back. She had fallen forward onto the bed, and I'd thought it best to leave her undisturbed when I'd fled the apartment in a panic. I explained as much to Dr. Freud.

"Dr. Sammelsohn, if you would, please help me turn her over." He was bitingly polite, and I felt appropriately bitten.

In concert, we each took one of her shoulders and lifted her up, placing her on her back. Her unbuttoned chemise exposed the length of her body: her breasts, her belly, her knee caps all lacquered and shiny with blood.

At that moment, Dr. Freud ceased being able to look at me. "Call an ambulance" was all he said, staring at his shoes.

"It looks terrible, I know," I said—and it did: the bed splashed with blood; the room, a shambles—"but she came here on her own. You have to believe that. She was sleepwalking, in fact."

"The ambulance, Dr. Sammelsohn. I'll take the particulars of the case from you later. At our leisure. Once the patient has been seen to."

"Of course."

Chastened, I went to find the porter. Before I left the apartment, I turned to watch as Dr. Freud buttoned Fräulein Eckstein's chemise with all the tenderness of a father. He'd neglected to remove his hat and was wearing it cocked onto the back of his head. "What has he done to you, my poor child?" he said, though she'd not yet awakened from the chloral I'd given her.

THE AMBULANCE ARRIVED, and the attendants bundled Fräulein Eckstein out, still unconscious, on a bier.

Dr. Freud turned on me quite suddenly. "You!" he said.

"Yes?" I asked meekly.

"Have you any coffee by any chance?"

"I'll set about brewing it at once."

Wincing, Dr. Freud sat down at my kitchen table.

"An unfortunate morning," he muttered, rubbing his face in his hands. He inspected the length of his beard, lifting it with one hand and letting it fall, his face a growl of self-disgust. In addition to the surgery for his boil, I'd kept him from his daily appointment with his barber. "Even my teeth feel gritty," he complained.

"Milk?" I asked, handing him a cup.

"Black."

"Black it is."

"Indeed."

Refusing to acknowledge the little laugh I'd presented to him in appreciation of his joke, he nailed me to the cross of my own guilty feelings with a dour stare. Sitting across from him, I turned my cup around and around on its saucer, waiting for him to speak.

"Can you please stop that incessant clattering!" He closed his eyes and brought his hand to the middle of his brow. "I have such a headache."

I released the cup.

He took his pulse. "I want a cigar. And I need more cocaine."

Dr. Freud treated the mild cardiac arrhythmia from which, during the time I knew him, he imagined he was dying, with unstinting, self-administered doses of cocaine. (If not the actual cause of his arrhythmia, the cocaine must surely have exacerbated it.) He painted his nostrils repeatedly until copious amounts of pus were discharged, after which he imagined he felt better. Now he blew his nose into his already saturated handkerchief. Attempting to wipe it clean, he daubed with the kerchief at the embouchure of his beard, spackling it further.

"Dr. Sammelsohn, if you would be so kind, rehearse for me the events leading to your appearance this morning at my breakfast table. And leave nothing out," he warned, "as it shall be I and not you who decides which details are of importance and which not."

He pierced me again with that terrible gaze of his. More than Fräulein

Eckstein's health, I realized, hung in the balance between us. Though I'd come to think of my longing for her as a month's folly, never to be reciprocated, the friendship with Dr. Freud that resulted from it was of great value to me. At the moment, however, that friendship seemed as precarious as Fräulein Eckstein's health. One ill-chosen word, I knew, and it would be lost forever and, through it, my citizenship in the brave new world I'd come to think of, prematurely, as my own. How much could I tell Dr. Freud without risking everything? In a moment of myopic, if not blind panic, I decided to leave out all the sexual details in order, I told myself, to spare Fräulein Eckstein and to guard her honor. Plus, what possible interest could Dr. Freud have in that aspect of things? (At that point, I knew nothing of his then-revolutionary interest in the psychodynamics of sexuality.) My hands fidgeted and ceased fidgeting with my coffee cup, and I poured forth the story as I thought he wanted to hear it, eliding over all self-incriminating details in the hopes of proving myself worthy of his continued esteem, meanwhile emphasizing my passivity in the whole bloody show: I'd been up late, reading Fliess, I emphasized for good measure, lost in my own thoughts, when Fräulein Eckstein knocked upon my door. Sleepwalking, she'd come to my apartment barefoot, without a wrap, in a state of dangerous psychosis. When she began screaming, I gave her a hypodermic of chloral to help her sleep the few hours until morning, placing her in my bed. All was well, until her nose began to bleed, and she began screaming, accusing me of having murdered her. Under the circumstances, had I really done anything he himself wouldn't have done, either as a doctor or a man?

With each and every word, however, I sensed I was only alienating Dr. Freud's affections further. Had I made an open and frank confession, revealing everything to him, including the small licentious particulars I'd edited out, the consequences couldn't have been worse nor the retribution harsher.

"You're lying!" he nearly shouted at me.

"Certainly not!"

"Then you're leaving something out."

"Of course, but nothing of consequence."

"What is it you're not telling me?"

"What do you imagine"—I coughed out a hollow laugh—"that I raped the poor girl in her sleep?"

"So that's it, then!"

"No!"

"Ach, this fucking boil!" he cried, adjusting his pants crotch and wincing again in pain. "Listen to me, Dr. Sammelsohn," he said, "I cautioned you, did I not, to stay well away from the Fräulein, and so you pledged to me that you would, but in your lust—and I do not use the term lightly—you failed to live up to that pledge, and now you have not only betrayed me, as a physician, as a colleague, as a friend, but you have perhaps done irrevocable harm to a young woman whose health is at this very moment dangerously compromised. Why, the Ecksteins are longtime family friends of ours! Did you think nothing of that? What am I to tell her mother?"

"I have no idea."

"You have no idea?"

I didn't know how seriously to take his question. He seemed to be simply throwing my words back at me, though I wasn't certain. Therefore, I shook my head and shrugged. "I really have no idea," I said again.

"Very well, then," he said, standing. "In that case, Dr. Sammelsohn, I regret to inform you that our acquaintanceship has reached its terminus. Make no effort to contact me either personally or professionally, as I assure you I will make no such effort, from my corner, to contact you. I expect you to have nothing further to do with the patient, even in the aftermath of her recovery, the prospects of which you have, I reiterate, severely compromised. Have I made myself clear?"

He didn't leave me a moment to reply.

"Then I shall take my leave of you."

"You're going?" I said, only now beginning to comprehend all that he had told me.

"I am, sir," he said. "Good morning and good-bye!"

MY DAYS AND nights were suddenly quite empty, emptier in fact than they'd seemed before I met Dr. Freud, when solitude was merely an unalterable condition of my life and not the result of my own wicked behavior. Before, I might have been content to eat a cold chicken wing at my desk while perusing a medical journal, followed by an early bed. Now, however, I couldn't tolerate being alone in my apartment. I made plans for every evening—concerts, lectures, operas, plays—though I could hardly afford to do so, and this met with disaster as well.

Let me explain: I was mad for the late quartets, that last flowering of Beethoven's difficult genius, and I had read in the papers that the Ehrstinsky Quartet were scheduled to perform the Grosse Fugue, op. 133. Rarely played, the piece is abstruse, perhaps even demented. I had read the score, but could make neither head nor tail of it, and was very much looking forward to the concert. I hesitated over purchasing my ticket out of fear of running into Drs. Rosenberg or Rie, certain each would have heard about my falling out with Dr. Freud or, if he hadn't, would embarrass me by asking friendly questions about this or that event to which I knew I would never be invited. I was concerned, also, that if by chance I encountered Fräulein Eckstein in the presence of these men, they might, with unintended or even purposeful malice, let Dr. Freud know that I had seen her. Though I told myself I had nothing to be ashamed about, I felt ashamed about everything. It was better to suffer in private, I knew; still, I couldn't abide the solitude of my apartments.

I arrived late to the Brahms-Saal of the Musikverein and surrendered my coat to the girl at the coat check. I stood in the back of the auditorium and calculated my odds: What were the chances, given her illness, that Fräulein Eckstein would even be here? And if she were, how likely was it that I might run into her? To further decrease the chances of our meeting, I forbade myself to look about the hall. I descended the aisle instead with my eyes cast down so that all I could see were the feet of the patrons seated on either side of the passage, having removed my eyeglasses as an additional precaution. Right or left? I asked myself, coming to a row that appeared in my blurred view to contain at least one vacant chair. My natural inclination was towards the left, and I disobeyed it, hoping, in breaking all habit, to further diminish the likelihood of encountering anyone I knew. I pushed my way to an empty chair and sat. I reached into my pocket for my pince-nez, which I fastened to the bridge of my nose, only to discover that I had placed myself directly behind Fräulein Eckstein. (Had this coincidence not happened personally to me, I would never have believed it possible!) My stomach sank. I inspected the room, but even with my pince-nez on, I could find no available seat nearby. I consoled myself with a single idea: Surely Fräulein Eckstein will not turn around? She was too well bred a girl for that.

She was wearing a dress similar to the one she had on that night at the Carl, and in what I considered too flirtatious a manner, bubbling over with whispers and giggles, she periodically leaned her shoulder into the shoulder of her companion, a gentleman whose most remarkable characteristic, from my vantage point at least, was his abnormally rigid spine. I sat up straighter, I couldn't help myself, and peered over their shoulders. They weren't holding hands; however, when making a point, Fräulein Eckstein not infrequently permitted herself to touch this fellow's hand, resting, as it was, on top of his knobby-headed cane.

"Stupid, stupid, stupid," I muttered to myself. Where is Dr. Freud, and why isn't he here to witness this? I wondered. What good does his forbidding me to see Fräulein Eckstein do if the taboo doesn't extend to all of masculine Vienna?

I was a man of science, trained to observe the most horrific of scenes while remaining inwardly calm. Compared to the gruesome demonstrations I'd been forced to watch in the course of my medical training—vivisections and such—how difficult would it be, I put the question to myself, to observe Fräulein Eckstein in the company of this other man? Perhaps the experience might even prove instructive. I might come to understand what my attraction to the Fräulein had been about. Almost immediately, however, the task proved beyond my meager strength. Though the last thing I wanted was to be glimpsed by Fräulein Eckstein or caught, having seemingly followed her to the concert, at the same time I couldn't abide being ignored by her!

The quartet mounted the stage, and the first violinist, his hair hanging down on either side of his forehead, began explaining the difficult piece, apologizing for it, really, while praising our willingness to hear all of the Master's work, no matter the costs to our senses. The comment elicited appreciative laughter. As it died away, I leaned forward and, hoping to invest the phrase with a credulous tone of surprise, muttered, "Oh—well—hello!" as casually as I could.

Neither Fräulein Eckstein nor her companion gave any indication that they had heard me. The people on either side of me took note, however, each presenting me with an arch glance before shifting away from me in their seats. Whether Fräulein Eckstein heard me or not wasn't simply an academic question. If she hadn't, I could repeat myself verbatim, with a little more volume this time; but if she had, no matter how genuinely I sounded my surprise, I would appear ridiculous. How many times may one be astonished by the same coincidence? (Not more than once, of course, is the answer.) Nevertheless, I decided to risk everything and repeated "Oh—well—hello!" at a louder pitch.

"Please!" the woman to my right exclaimed, and the fellow on my left shushed me as well. In reaction to the commotion brewing up behind him, Fräulein Eckstein's brother angled away from the noise. (Yes, this splendid fellow turned out to be not Fräulein Eckstein's lover, but her brother Friedrich, a noted Sanskritist and yogi: hence the impossibly rigid spine.) His movement left me an avenue, an opening, if I leaned forward enough, through which I could address Fräulein Eckstein privately, or at least away from the man and the woman on either side of me, which is what I did.

"Fräulein Eckstein!"

"Dr. Sammelsohn?" she said at last, turning towards me and peering behind her in the gloom.

"What a marvelous coincidence!" I boomed out in a whispered charade of confidence. "I sat here at random—completely at random!—with no forethought, with no design at all, absolutely randomly, and yet, well, here you are!"

"Yes, and it's good to see you." She smiled apologetically, a small, though not unkindly dismissal, before returning her attention to the stage.

"Yes," I said, attempting to prolong our conversation but without success.

Her brother lowered his head towards hers, and the two murmured conspiratorially. I couldn't make out what they were saying but assumed he was asking her to identify me. What could she tell him? Who was I to her? No one, really, just a man who seemed continually on the point of raping her, that's all. Friedrich Eckstein turned his head and, with one handsome eye, took me in. I nodded curtly, as though we'd been introduced as rivals.

Without answering my nod, he brought his attention back to the first violinist, who had taken his chair, garlanded by a wreath of applause. I could feel the man and the woman on either side of me regretting my presence between them. I crossed my arms and legs, hoping to disappear into myself. However, I could barely concentrate on the concert. The first violinist began with an aggressive attack, and the opening phrases, punctuated by silence, sliced the air like a series of sinister accusations. After an achingly beautiful motif, one hectoring note was shrilled out incessantly, until the piece sounded like a jig being danced by a man with a bullet in his brain. None of it made any sense to me.

"Bitte," I said, standing in a crouch.

"What *now*?" the woman on my right whispered explosively.

"Pardon me, excuse me, pardon," I said, moving down the row, knocking into knees at every chair, anger and pique washing over me from the four quarters of the concert hall. A scowl of annoyance burned into my back from the violist, peering over his music stand into the darkened hall, doing everything he could, short of leaving off from the music, to see what the commotion was.

I retrieved my coat and pushed through the front doorway and was once again on the street.

I WALKED UNTIL I reached the Prater. Its woods were dark. Women's voices called out to me from every direction beneath the trees. These were no sylvan nymphs, but prostitutes, and I wanted nothing to do with them. Or rather, wanting everything to do with them, I avoided them completely. Returning night after night to the grove where they lingered, lit by the garish lights of the amusement arcades, I could bring myself to approach not one of their number. And yet, for the better part of a fortnight, I ended my evenings here. Where else was I to go? Dr.

Freud had seen to it that I was accepted nowhere. When I dropped in on Dr. Rosenberg or on Dr. Rie or—why not mend fences?—on the Freuds themselves, the maid returned my card to me exactly as I'd placed it on the silver tray, as though it were too revolting to be touched.

I continued to see my patients during the day, but I no longer cared about catching them in their fakery. I prescribed government-issued spectacles for anyone with sufficient nerve to bluff through the exam. Let them have their imperial stipend! What did I care? After the night of the Grosse Fugue, as I came to think of it, I avoided all lectures, concerts, and plays. If, by chance, I had seated myself behind Fräulein Eckstein in a large concert hall, did I imagine I could drift through Vienna's other public venues without encountering at least one person who, poisoned by Dr. Freud, would cut me dead? I had neither the heart nor the head for such encounters, and instead I found myself in the late afternoons wandering through the Prater, waiting for the sun to set and for the fallen women to appear like overripened fruit beneath the trees, where the courage to purchase one reliably failed me.

I began attending a children's puppet theater in the park. Usually the only adult in attendance without a child in tow, I sat on the low bench, my hands laced around my knees, taking up as little space as I could. Without a child, I felt I had no right to more room. I felt like a clumsy giant sitting on the miniature bench, nodding and smiling with an exaggerated benevolence, in the hopes of reassuring the others—women, mostly: mothers and nannies—that I was as harmless as I seemed. (These many years later, I can only imagine that they saw me for what I was: a lonesome boy of a man lost in the capital city.)

Herr Franz's Marvelous & Astonishing Puppet Theater was no more than a wooden room, really. Its walls, once painted gaudily, were faded and stained. It was heated by a brazier of coals burning in the rear. Yellow tufts of winter grass not beaten down entirely by the feet of stamping children grew between the benches. The stage was a crude rectangle cut into the back wall. The curtains looked like old chintz drapes onto which were sewn moons and stars. A bracing wind might collapse the entire ramshackle structure in an instant, it seemed, and yet, when the barn door closed behind us and the stage lights ignited and the hurdy-gurdy began its warbling, I lost all sense of myself. Finally, in the darkened playhouse, I could breathe again. As the puppets strutted and fretted behind the proscenium, barking their dialogue out in comical dialects, I followed the story, whatever it was — tales from the Arabian Nights, from the Brothers Grimm, from the Ramayana — with incommensurable delight.

(Oh, the place was extraordinary. The puppet master Franz, a Jew from Galicia like myself, prided himself on a *Life and Death of Beethoven* performed each December in commemoration of the composer's birth, and it was here that I witnessed, over the course of a single night from dusk to dawn, Goethe's *Faust,* performed in its entirety.)

At times, I found myself envying the puppets, and not only for their lightness and agility. Though their limbs were wooden and their bodies fashioned from the flimsiest of fabrics, each was animated by a defining spirit, each exulted in his own character, reveling in it, as it were, no matter how many flaws it contained. It was exactly the opposite of real life: the sillier the puppet, the more trouble he brewed, the more joy he created, and the more beloved he became. No one asks a puppet to reform his character or to improve it through psychoanalysis, and though he may find himself a social outcast in the middle of the play, by its end, all will be right with him again, though he will have, in the meantime, learned nothing at all.

Sitting among the children, I reimagined my debacle with Dr. Freud as though it were being performed by marionettes. Half-daydreaming, I watched a marionette version of myself on the little stage falling in love with a marionette modeled on Fräulein Eckstein. From the breast pocket of Otto Meissenblichler's suit, too large for my wooden frame, occasionally bursts a velvet heart fastened to my chest by a spring. The stage is a reproduction of the Carl in precise trompe l'oeil. With a herky-jerky gait, tangling up in my strings, my enormous papier-mâché head filled with dreams, I rush down the stairs of the theater, searching for the beautiful marionette in her lavender dress, only to encounter a sinister Dr. Freud, smoking at the bar. O, what a villain is he! O, how easily one can recognize his villainy when he has been transformed into a puppet! Why, just look at that pointy beard and those glinting eyes and the

Mephistophelean cigar and the red devil's tail that continually escapes from a patch in the back of his pants with a loud *spronggg!* As a puppet, I'm as oblivious to his devilry as I was as a man in actual life. However, the delight my obliviousness creates in the audience of screaming children is a comfort to me.

"Would you like to come play cards at my house on Saturday night, eh?" Dr. Freud asks, and through a mechanism only Herr Franz understands, smoke actually comes out of his painted mouth.

"No! No! Don't do it!" the children scream from their benches, all mad limbs and terrified shrieks.

"Don't do it, children? Is that what you're saying?" I bounce lightly on my wooden knees, the string that lifts my hand lifts it to my head, and I scratch it in confusion.

"Yessss!" the children scream.

"Yes?" I feign bewilderment. "Yes or no? Which is it now?"

"Yes!"

"All right then, 'yes' it is." I turn back to Dr. Freud. "Why, I'd be delighted, simply honored, thoroughly and extraordinarily so, to come."

"Then I'll see you at eight. Sharp!" He leers, smoke steaming out his ears.

"At eight," I say, floating offstage. "At last my loneliness is over!"

The stage reddens with a hellish glow. Bobbing wickedly at the end of his web of strings, Dr. Freud confronts the audience of booing children. "You almost gave me away there, Kinderlach. But thankfully, Dr. Sammelsohn is as thick as the wood from which he's cut. Now, all I have to do is introduce him to Fräulein Eckstein, and his heart, that shabby pillow he keeps hidden behind his breast pocket, will be broken into a thousand pieces!" He laughs a devilish laugh: "Maw-haw-haw-haw-haw!" His strings slacken, and he bows evilly.

The children hiss and hoot.

(It's foolish, I know, to assume I'd be the central character in this comedy. Devil or saint, as far as history is concerned, Dr. Freud is always the star. And where do I imagine I'll end up, except as a tangled heap of string and fabric, moldering in the puppet trunk of history?)

D r. Freud had been emphatic that he never wished to see me again. He couldn't have made his desire less ambiguous had he nailed it, as a proclamation, onto the doors of St. Stephen's Cathedral, and so I was very much surprised, late one evening in March, as I was leaving the clinic, to receive a telephone call from him, requesting that I come immediately to his home.

"Or I can come round to get you, whichever is the quicker."

"No, I'll come to you," I said, still, after everything, deferential. However one might characterize the various stages of our acquaintance (surely not now as a friendship), he was always its senior partner.

"Take a fiacre, and I'll pay for it. And have the driver wait for us both outside."

I gathered up my medical bag and locked the examination room and bundled into my coat. I made my way to the street, where, after a short while, I was able to flag down a cab. Dr. Freud's home was near the clinic, and while I rode, I barely had time to think through this extraordinary development. Why, hardly a month ago, I'd been exiled by Dr. Freud, as though by the tsar, to the northernmost reaches of a social Siberia, and yet here I was, roused from the dead and summoned urgently back. Had my case been reviewed? Had I been found innocent of all charges? Or had Dr. Freud, digging through my file, merely discovered a new crime with which to charge me? I had little time to agonize over these concerns. I knew only that my throat was dry in anticipation. I asked the driver to wait at the curb, and I made my way into Berggasse 19. I had barely knocked at number 6, when Dr. Freud was at the door.

"Ah, Dr. Sammelsohn, you've arrived."

Forgive me, reader, if I belabor these five words: *Ah, Dr. Sammelsohn, you've arrived.* For the life of me, I couldn't mock out their deeper meaning. Was Dr. Freud glad to see me? Did he, in uttering them, mean to express, *Ah, Dr. Sammelsohn, thank goodness, you've arrived*? Or did something of his previous vexation darken their intent: *Ah, Dr. Sammelsohn, so here you are again, turned up like a bad penny*? His Tarock face gave nothing away, and I didn't know whether to throw myself upon his bosom, the prodigal son returned, or to remain distant, braced for further scolding. Also what matchingly bland phrase could I utter in return to cover the entire spectrum of his possible meanings?

"Yes, I've come," I said, keeping well away from him on the landing.

"There's so much you didn't tell me."

He turned to lock the door of his apartment. I stuck my hands into my coat pockets, where they might at least jangle my keys.

"I suppose I might have left out a bit of the sexual parts, it's true . . ."

"A bit?"

"Rather *all* of the sexual parts."

"I'd suspected as much," he said, dropping his keys into his own pocket. "And though you may feel the penitent's need to unburden his breast, I assure you I've no confessor's wish to hear the illicit details, and happily, except perhaps tangentially, your malfeasance in the case of Fräulein Eckstein is not at issue here."

He took my arm and escorted me down the staircase. Once again, I was hard-pressed to interpret the gesture: was he holding me, as one might a beloved friend, or as a jailor would a fugitive who could suddenly bolt? In either case, I felt constrained.

"On the contrary," Dr. Freud murmured, "I'm speaking of your wife."

"Of Hindele?"

"Rather of Ita." He purred the name into my ear, and my entire being went cold. In truth, I almost fainted. Indeed, had he not been holding my arm, I'm certain I would have tumbled onto the cobbles of the sidewalk. This was a name Dr. Freud and I had never spoken between us.

"Of Ita?" I repeated. I searched his face for clues.

"Let us get into the fiacre, Yankl, where we can talk more intimately."

How many thoughts can aggravate a man's brain at once? A hundred, two hundred, a thousand, more? At that moment, of those thousand buzzing, humming, blundering thoughts, I was aware of only one:

a desire to break from Dr. Freud and to run as far from him as I could. Unschooled in blatant arrogance, alas, I'd made a habit of ignoring my inner wishes or, more precisely, of concealing them inside a pantomime of decorum. I could no more act upon my desires with immediacy than I could break into a yodel in the middle of the Heldenplatz. Further: Dr. Freud's will was suppler than my own. Whereas another man might have bridled at his ambush with a stern counterattack—*As soon as you explain to me what this is all about, my dear fellow, then I'll happily accompany you*—or resisted him with more force and still been justified—*Kindly put it in a letter to my solicitor*—even had these replies occurred to me then, and not, as they did, long afterwards, I would have lacked the courage to utter them. *As you wish* is all it occurred to me to say.

"As you wish," I did in fact say, as Dr. Freud opened the door of the fiacre and, extending his arm, made certain I climbed in before him.

(It occurred to me to climb immediately out the other door and to sprint away, but to commit such an act, I'd have to have been a puppet in a commedia, and not a flesh and blood man in the farce he was making of his own life. And though I knew the chase would have delighted an audience of children, I also knew that the inexorable laws of drama would have demanded my capture, as apparently did the laws of God Himself.)

I leaned back against the seat and threw aside the woolen blanket, waiting for my nemesis to clamber in. Dr. Freud bellowed up an address to the driver and shut and locked the door. We sat side by side, he taking up more room than I, his elbow pinioning my arm against the seat. Perhaps the cocaine had anaesthetized his senses. In any case, he seemed unaware of the pressure he was exerting upon my arm.

The sun had set, and the lamplighters were about their sooty business. A freezing drizzle had crept in. The city was dismal and gloomy. There were few others on the streets, and the lonesome clip-clop of our horses' hooves resounding against the buildings chilled my bones.

Dr. Freud sighed and looked out the window on my side of the carriage. "You never told me about Ita," he said, glancing past me through the sleet-spotted glass.

"Has someone contacted you?"

I wouldn't have put it past her grandfather to have tracked me down in order to blackmail me by revealing everything to my new important friends. Of course, unless Zusha the Amalekite were a devotee of obscure neurological journals, he'd have never heard of Sigmund Freud. In any case, my fears were unfounded. Zusha, as I recall, was illiterate, in German as well as in the seventy other languages of the world.

"I'm not proud of what I've done," I told Dr. Freud.

"Nor have you reason to be."

"However, I was a child."

"As we all were once."

"Not yet thirteen."

"At sixteen, Alexander had conquered the world."

Gaslight from a streetlamp, as we passed it, fell across Dr. Freud's brow. He squinted, momentarily blinded, before returning his gaze to me. "I'm afraid I'll need to know everything. If you care at all for Fräulein Eckstein, Dr. Sammelsohn, your help will be essential because, frankly, I'm in over my head."

"But what has Ita got to do with all of this?"

"That will be made clear, my dear boy, but later, when we have the leisure to go into the thing in depth. First, I'll need to know from you, honestly and without expurgation, all that occurred between you and the girl."

"Between Fräulein Eckstein and myself?"

He shook his head. "Between you and this Ita."

"But Ita has nothing to do with Fräulein Eckstein or her hysteria, I assure you!"

Dr. Freud scowled from behind his whiskers.

"I promise you, Dr. Sammelsohn, all will be rendered clear. But a good deal of that clarity depends upon a frank and forthright confession from yourself."

"A confession?"

"That is perhaps an ill-chosen word."

"I've committed no crime."

"I didn't mean it in its juridical sense."

"I've done nothing with which to reproach myself. Neither with Fräulein Eckstein nor with Ita!"

"Ah." Dr. Freud dropped his head into his hands and rubbed his eyes with the meat of his palms until the gesture produced a small clicking sound. "The treacherous byways of the unseen world have perhaps put me into too ecclesiastical a mood. If so, forgive me." Lifting his head, he cast his now red-rimmed eyes over me. His voice creaked with emotion. "Dr. Sammelsohn, I don't by any means pretend to understand the entirety of human consciousness. In this regard, I'm very like one of those ancient cartographers who limned, with their gouaches and their oils, the boundaries of the then-known world. Though skilled sufficiently in their arts to encompass the globe, their work depended fundamentally upon the reports they received from men who set out to explore those regions, and whose work, in turn, depended upon the whim of this or that monarch or, later, upon the heads of some shipping or trading firm, who, in the first case, lusting for gold or spice, and in the second, for navigable trade routes, desired accurate maps to enable them to return to the new lands they'd conquered. In our young science, the cartography of the human psyche depends equally upon many such serendipities: the caprices of the maladies that afflict our patients; the caprices of the patients themselves, who may or may not seek treatment or who may or may not seek treatment from me; even then, what a patient chooses to reveal about herself in analysis depends upon a thousand and one incalculable factors, not excluding which tie or cologne I happen to be wearing that day and what memories these bring to mind. In this way, I'm not unlike Anaximander or Mercator or Americus Vesputius, those mapmakers who, for their work, relied upon the integrity and the veracity and the mathematical precision of their informants, most of which, one can only presume, were lacking. And just as these ancient cartographers might, at the limits of their knowledge, spell out the legend *Beware! Beyond this border: demons!*, so too the ancient psychologist, the priests and abbots of their day, faced with the vexing hysterias and neuroses of their parishioners, and the wild behaviors these diseases occasioned, imagined in them the thing they feared the most: demonical possession. Let me be blunt, Dr. Sammelsohn, there is no difference in outward appearance between a case of severe hysteria and one of demonical possession. But I confess to you, at the risk of sounding like a lunatic myself, that although

I know Fräulein Eckstein is suffering from the former, from all appearances, she seems to be in the grips of the latter."

"You're claiming—what?" I stammered. "That you believe—that is to say—that you imagine Fräulein Eckstein is possessed by a demon?"

"By a spirit of some kind; a dybbuk, let's call it; more specifically, by your wife. It's not my claim—I would never make such a preposterous claim—but hers. That is to say: your wife's."

"Ita's?"

"Ah, yes, that's right," Dr. Freud purred. "I keep forgetting. Concerning wives, you've had more than your fair share."

"There's no need to bait me," I said, bristling. "There's nothing one can do to change one's past."

"Perhaps you should tell that to your wife, Dr. Sammelsohn, as she seems to be laboring under an entirely different opinion regarding the matter."

"You speak of her as though you've recently seen her."

"In many ways, I feel as though I have."

Suddenly, Dr. Freud threw back his head.

"Ah! this damnable nose!" he cried.

Blindly unbuttoning his coat, he pulled aside its tails and searched in his trouser pocket for a handkerchief, which he brought to his dripping nostrils. "A moment and the suppuration will cease. You can use the time to tell me everything you need to. And leave nothing out! One never knows which detail might be the picklock to open any number of barred doors."

The fiacre rocked from side to side, the horses' hooves clopping out a snow-muffled tattoo. The sleet had stopped, but the night air was thick. I pulled the collars of my overcoat together with one hand. The mention of Ita's name had evoked in me a chilly fear. I leaned my head against the seat cushion and peered out the window at the sky. The moon was bleaching the clouds that covered it. There was nothing to do, I supposed, except to tell Dr. Freud everything, the truth, the same and simple truth I'd been avoiding mentioning to him or to anyone, for that matter, since I'd arrived in Vienna.

AS THE EMERGING moon cast everything in ivory tones, I painted for Dr. Freud a picture of myself as a child, a skinny youth with earlocks and a long caftan, a child so thin he barely fit into his clothes. My marriage to Hindele was proving a disaster. To begin with, at the age of thirteen, I had no idea what one did with a wife. As I've said, Father's instructions to me in this regard had been cryptic at best, and though, at night, in the tiny bedroom we shared, the sight of Hindele's maple-colored hair, unfettered from the prison of her marriage wig, was sufficient to arouse my manhood into a painful tumescence, as far as I knew there was no remedy for the distress her beauty provoked in me. Even the books my father had confiscated, though considered depraved, were of no help to me in this regard. Indeed, one could learn nothing from such books! Their authors, men of the world presumably addressing other men of the world, felt no need to follow their protagonists into the bedroom, or if into the bedroom, into their beds, or if into the barn, into the haystack. Though corrupters of youth and despoilers of our heritage, these authors preferred to drop a curtain between the reader and such goings-on, not only, I presumed, because such goings-on were known, at least in their general contours, to the reading public but also because publishing one's description of such goings-on was no doubt a chargeable offense.

Something happened to the lovers in these books, between the end of one chapter and the beginning of the next, but I had no idea what. All I knew was that a fervent discussion of politics and religion seemed to lead up to it. As a consequence, Hindele and I never touched. We lay in bed each night like two adolescent sisters, talking, as did the lovers in these books, about a better world and the mad revolution that would soon bring it into being. Along with the books, which Avrum continued in secret to supply me, I'd taught Hindele to smoke, and though we shared cigarette after clandestine cigarette (by the time we were divorced, she had developed quite a habit), and though she had a real head for philosophy and quickly fell under the sway of these very same books, the entire thing led to nothing more intimate between us than talk.

"Of course, we must free our own people from the tyranny of their superstitions!" she said one night as we lay chastely side by side. Propped up on one elbow, she allowed her hand to strum the covers. "The Czechs, the Magyars, everyone is ready to throw off the emperor's yoke, but even if we were free of imperial oppression, we'd still be slaves to an invisible God, which is far worse than a master of flesh and blood whom one can kill. Or don't you think so, Yankl?"

"Ssh," I cautioned her. "Or Father will hear you."

Though the house was large, its walls were thin, and especially if one wished to, one could easily hear everything that went on in the other rooms.

"Let him hear me, that pious old fraud"—after only half a dozen novels, Hindele had mastered the dialectic—"clinging to his antiquated ways, parroting the language of rabbinic oppression!"

I can't tell you how fetching she was in her transparent shift, pacing like a revolutionary in his garret, her cheeks in a high ruby blush.

"And not even real Hebrew, Yankl, but all those horrible quotations from the holy books."

I encouraged her, hoping to enrage her, to ignite her passions, as happened all the time with the cardboard characters in the novels we shared. What wouldn't I say to keep her fury aroused? It was like feeding logs into an already blazing oven, although to what purpose, I had no idea.

"Where and to whom shall he ever speak such a language?"

"Nowhere and to no one."

"In Palestine? Is that what he thinks?"

"Who goes there, anyway, but old people to die?"

"Our home is here, Yankl! Not in some imaginary dream world! Some land that even the Arabs don't want! Why, just look at my own father."

"Remind me again what it is you so despise about him, Hindele."

"I don't despise him. On the contrary, I love him, Yankl, and so I pity him. My pity for him—and, oh God, for my mother!—is the greatest proof of my love. Why, when I look at him, scurrying around, afraid of his own shadow, doing anything the rebbe tells him, I cry for our people, Yankl, I do!"

She'd become a wild river of a girl, and with snatches of the Song of Songs and the Mishnas and Gemaras Father had taught me concerning a husband's obligation to his wife roiling through my head, I had no idea how to stay afloat inside her passions. Younger than I, more fiery by nature, Hindele possessed the idealism of a twelve-year-old, which is precisely what she was. Her firebrand politics, her desire to ring down the hypocritical banners beneath which our families lived, were sincere, and they had transformed her. But with me, it was the opposite. I'd grown resigned, as Father predicted I would, to the life he'd set before me. I divided my days between learning the family business and learning the sacred law. I'd even advanced in my studies. My progress as a scholar increased in tandem with my growing unbelief. When I was a little boy, I believed everything I was told, that God Himself had authored the Torah, designing the letters down to the little crowns they wore upon their heads. It was enough for me to open a book and to gaze at the letters to feel the presence of the Holy One. What was there to understand? Now that I no longer believed that God had written the Torah, what it said had actually begun to interest me.

Still, Hindele would have none of it. She chafed under the rigorous strictures of our life. An eighth daughter to my mother, she was expected to cook and clean and was treated no differently from the rest. Secretly, she wanted to go to school, to study properly, to travel, to become a teacher or — God willing! — a revolutionary.

I can only wonder what life would be like for me now if we had remained married, if she hadn't objected to a meaningless remark Father made over the soup that terrible evening in coldest December. Both of our families were there. The Shabbos candles gleamed on the sideboard, bathing the room in a warm, tranquil light. Along one side of the table sat my sisters, all in a row, their hair freshly washed and plaited. My mother sat at the foot of the table, her blonde wig piled up muscularly upon her head. She was still a handsome woman. Near her was my mother-in-law, her many chins resting contentedly one on top of the other, and a string of pearls, lit by the candlelight, glimmered in the crevice of her bosom. Hindele's father, Reb Nuftile, sat near Father, the great mink wheel of his shtreimel resting on his head like the halo of a Christian saint. Next to me sat Hindele, of course, and on either side of us her siblings. Father conducted the business of the meal with a quiet dignity, unable to conceal his pride and his pleasure. Everything had turned out as he planned,

I recall thinking. My rebellion had been quelled. I had been repatriated to my native land, against which I had momentarily considered treason. All had been forgiven, and if now and then I indulged in the seditious literature that had marked my villainy, I did so only as a personal lark or a childish foible and not as a revolutionary act.

I breathed a quiet sigh of relief and even offered up a silent prayer of thanks. Indeed, I was so lost in these happy thoughts that I failed to notice the commotion that had stirred up at the table until it was more or less fully launched. Hindele and my father were speaking to each other in tones that, because each was trying to hold back his passion, sounded all the more passionate and severe.

Of course, Hindele respected the writings of the Sages, she announced, but as a source of interesting intellectual activity, pertinent perhaps in its own time, just as the thoughts of liberal rabbis and political reformers of our own age were pertinent to ours. "Consider the way we behave in our own houses of worship," she said. Loud, boisterous, incessantly shuffling. "Couldn't we take a page from our Christian neighbors who sit in their churches without saying a word, without moving a limb? And if you object" — as she knew my father would — "that we mustn't walk in the ways of the Gentiles" — he'd know the quotation: Leviticus 18:3 — "then why, when King Solomon enjoins us to learn from the ant" — Proverbs 6:6 — "and Job from the beasts of the fields" — Job 12:7–8 — "can we not learn from our neighbors who, unlike these lower forms of beings, are men of reason, like ourselves?"

Before either of our fathers could object, Hindele continued, her cheeks flashing an exalted crimson. "Why, if even Rabbenu Tam" — And what did she know of Rabbenu Tam? Nothing. She'd merely memorized Liebermann's famous essay — "says we should envy the nations of the world who serve God in awe and fear, then shouldn't we do everything we can to surpass their works many times over?"

Sitting at that table that night, wondering what in God's name had prompted my dear little wife to stand up to her father and father-in-law, I was of two minds. On the one hand, I was exhilarated to see someone, anyone, giving those two pious old maids a run for their money, and Hindele *was* magnificent, as only an idealistic twelve-year-old can be.

She stood with her fists clenched and her knuckles white with passion. (Girls were encouraged to read and learn in both our households; otherwise she would never have been able to find her voice, I'm certain.) On the other hand, these were our fathers, whose time, admittedly, was passing. They, and the men who thought as they did, were destined for the ash heap of history. To have a young girl urging them all the more quickly into that abyss couldn't have been a pleasant experience for either man. Nor for those of us who loved them and were forced to witness the spectacle. Even I recoiled from Hindele. I felt as repulsed as everyone else and wondered if I would ever be able to look upon her again with affection and desire, a moot point, as it turned out, as this was the last time I'd ever see her.

"Reb Alter Nosn!" Her father stood at the table. He jerked his napkin out of his collar and tossed it into his bowl of borscht. "How is it my daughter, whom I brought to you as pure as the whitened snows, has come to these heretical opinions while living in your home?"

Before Father could respond, Hindele supplied the unfortunate answer herself: "My husband and I read books together."

"Books!" Reb Nuftile exclaimed.

"Yankl!" Mother berated me.

"What sort of books?" Reb Nuftile demanded.

"Mama, it's not what you think," I said in my own defense.

Hindele gave me a burning look. What self-respecting maskil whines so miserably to his mother?

"No daughter of mine shall stay in such a house of apostasy!" her father roared.

"תהי-נא לך," my father shot back at him. *Take her then!* (Judges 15:2).

And so Reb Nuftile did. Forcing his wife, his daughters, and his sons up from the table, he escorted Hindele firmly from the room, from our house, and after the Sabbath from Szibotya and my life, from everything, in fact, except my memory.

"No need to show us out!" he stormed, standing at the dining room door. "And as for the blessings following the meal, that can be dispensed with at a table of idolaters. This food is hardly kosher. Ester!" he called to his wife.

AS I HAD been married against my will, so I was divorced against it. I'd never seen Father so piercingly splenetic. For six days, he said nothing, merely sat in his study staring out the window, his bilious mood infecting the entire house, radiating through it, poisoning its air like a sulfur, until the seventh day, when he stood up and, without a word, walked into town. Returning an hour before Shabbos, he announced that he had traded his son, as though I were damaged goods, to Zusha the Amalekite as a groom for his granddaughter, the idiot girl Ita.

"Father, no!" I pleaded with him, but he refused to hear me out. "I'm only a child," I protested. "I don't need to be married!"

"אל־תאמר נער אנכי כי על־כל־אשר אשלחך תלך," he said. *Don't tell me you're just a child, because wherever I'll send you, there you shall go!* (Jeremiah 1:7).

"No! I won't go through with it!" I shouted in his face.

My sisters restrained me as though I were a wild animal, while Father finished the verse: "ואת כל אשר אצוך הדבר" *And everything I order you to say, you'll say!*

Something broke inside me. Held down on all sides by my sisters' fourteen arms, I looked up into Father's face and saw nothing in it but unrelieved hatred. As the red-hot point of his anger scorched me, my world darkened. I couldn't believe he was willing to debase himself so thoroughly out of spite, but hatred for me had overwhelmed his sense of proportion.

All of Szibotya was invited to witness my humiliation. Every seat in our synagogue was full. Even in the women's section upstairs, amused faces glowered down at us, their eyes lit with the same glee they might contain at the prospect of a particularly naughty Purim spiel. Zealot enough to ruin his own reputation, to make a laughingstock of himself for the sake of his piety, Father was certain, I'm sure, that by conspiring in his own degradation for the sake of the holy Torah, his exaltation would manifest like a translucent halo above his head before the eyes of all the wedding guests.

Astonished to find myself once again beneath the wedding canopy, I felt like the Paschal Lamb: chosen, it's true, but as a sacrifice. Whose fault was it that I had strayed, that I had corrupted myself with forbidden books, if not Father's and the community he represented, all of whom had driven me to those books by the hollowness of their pietistic poses?

I looked at Ita, at her flat face and her little hump, at the strings of saliva that flew from her mouth whenever she became too excited. She'd already crushed and destroyed most of the lilies in the bouquet they'd given her, twisting their stems in her uncomprehending agitation. Though any romantic hopes for herself were futile, what right had they to make a mockery of them? How could they so willfully blind themselves to the fact that beneath her concave, narrow chest, unconnected to her malfunctioning brain, beat the still quite feminine heart of a young girl, who, despite everything (this much was clear to see), wanted only to be loved?

I could barely look her in the eye, neither in the good one, nor in the one with the drooping lid. I endured the ceremony, in order not to embarrass her, but I'd hatched a plan.

"Ita, my dear," I spoke as gently as I could when, after the ceremony, we were left alone in a private room, as is our religious custom.

"Muh dee-uhr," she repeated numbly. As you will recall, such repetitions formed the whole of her vocabulary.

She in her virginal white, I in my Hasidic wedding garb, we sat on either side of an elegant table set intimately for two and piled high — the vindictive irony of my father knew no bounds! — with the finest of foods: whole broiled chickens sprinkled with rosemary, roasted potatoes, savory onions, spicy kasha, exotic grapes, prunes, raisins, nuts. I stuffed everything I could into the small bag I had concealed beneath my talis katan.

"Ita must listen now," I instructed her.

"Eee-taw mush l-l-l-lee-sun," she said, nodding, her eye with the drooping lid glazed and unfocused, the other one sharp and clear. With an upward motion, she rubbed her wrist against the bottom of her nose and smeared away the snot.

"Yankl must go."

"Unkull gaw?" she said, picking at a scab on her dirty knee.

"Yes. Far, far away. To Vienna."

"Unkull gaw fuh wai?"

I had my doubts about how much the poor girl understood. Surely she possessed no accurate sense of time or distance, nor enough mind to imagine that a life with me was what this wedding was supposed to mean. Surely an hour after I climbed out the window (for such was my plan), she would forget about the events of this late afternoon, this odd wedding, no different, really, from the thousand and one cruelties to which she'd been subjected during her short life. Marrying Ita in a mock ceremony and having to kiss the bride was a game that not only the cruelest children but all of us had played. Still I was struck by the tears that appeared in her downturned eyes.

"Ita, listen," I whispered.

She nodded, and her mouth was open. She breathed through it, and I could see her tongue twitching like a restless sleeper in its bed.

"They will ask Ita where Yankl go."

"Wuh Unkull gaw?" She seemed in all sincerity to have asked this question, although I knew that was impossible. Agitated, she further twisted the lilies she was still holding in her small, stubby hands.

"Ita must tell them . . ."

"Eee-taw taw-al," she confirmed in her plodding, monstrous voice.

"Say to them: Yankl goes to liberate the masses from religious and political oppression."

She repeated the sentence in her sluggish, slurred way, faltering over the final difficult word.

"Oppression," I repeated.

"Uh-preh-shzun!"

"Again!"

"Ug-gun."

"No, Ita. Say 'oppression' again."

She tried the sentence again.

"Good, Ita!"

"Goo Eee-taw!" She pointed to the cleft of her chest.

"Tell them: Shame on you, you pious frauds."

She gargled the phrases fiercely.

"Tell them that Ita looks forward to the day when you bourgeois parasites will be lined up against the wall and shot."

She repeated my words as well as she could, and she surprised me by spitting on the ground.

"Good enough," I said.

"Nah, naht eee-nuf," she said.

"No, it is, it is, it's good enough, Ita."

"Eee-nuf," she seemed to plead suddenly, reaching out to me, but of course she had no idea what she was saying. "Yunkull!" she shrieked.

I had by this time pulled back the heavy drapery and had opened the window and was already halfway out of it, sitting with one leg dangling over the outer wall and one leg on the sill.

"Ita, what is it?"

She spoke with more difficulty than usual. "Eee-taw . . . iz . . . bride tew you."

"No."

"Iz bri-i-id!" she insisted.

"It was a joke, Ita, a silly joke. A trick, that's all."

"D'rik?"

"A play. Like a Purim play."

"Boo-reem?"

"And now that play is over, you see, or almost. One scene more to go. Where has Yankl gone? . . . Ita?"

"Unkull gaw li-ber-ate maz-sez frahm ree-lee-jee-uss a-an-duh pol-eee-tee-kul . . ." she faltered.

"Oppression."

"Upp . . ."

"It's not important. They won't listen to you anyway."

"Up-reh-shzun!" she said.

"Good. And who's to blame?"

"Sh-sh-shay-mmm awn ye-e-u pi-jus . . . frowds!" she cried with a sense of conviction that was truly alarming.

"Good for you, Ita," I said. "Excellent, excellent. That's fine. But now I've got to go."

"Taw lee-ber-ate maz-ses, Yunkull?"

"Yes, to liberate the Jewish masses, Ita. One poor Jew at a time. Starting with myself."

"Guh-buh, ma-iiii huh-huhzs-bund," she said softly.

"No, Ita, not husband, not really. It was only a play."

"Bor-eem p'lai."

"Yes, that's right, a Purim play."

She cut a forlorn figure, with her hump and her paralyzed arm and her drooping eyelid and the shapeless white dress they had made for her out of God knows what cheap muslin.

"Good-bye, my love," I whispered to her as sweetly as I could.

"Guh-buh, mufh luh-fff?"

I was about to drop from the window to the ground when she called my name, her face straining, as if she were actually thinking and the effort were costing her.

"Ita?"

"Huhzs-bund?"

"No."

"Huhzs-bund!" she insisted.

"No, no husband, Ita. A play."

"Yunkull *eez* huhzs-bund!"

"No, Ita not wife. Yankl not husband."

"Raabai sez!"

"It was only a play."

"AND?" DR. FREUD said.

I looked through the window of the fiacre. We were far beyond the Ring now, in a district I didn't know. "I jumped from the window," I told him. "I couldn't even see where I landed; my eyes were filled with tears. An hour before, I'd hidden a tailor's shears in the bushes behind the synagogue, along with a darning needle and a thread, and a mirror. I ran until dark, and I kept running, following the roads, navigating by moonlight and starlight until sleep overtook me. I awoke at dawn the next morning and ate an entire chicken. My wedding feast! Then I set about my work. Two snips and my earlocks were gone. A little tailoring, a little darning, a little thread, and my telltale caftan was an inconspicuous short coat. I regarded myself in the mirror. I was, I thought, utterly transformed. I was picked up later in the day by a merchant on whose spice cart I rode all the way into Vienna. I looked up my uncle Moritz, the family heretic and Father's bête noire, against whom I'd been warned my entire life, and of course, he took me in and treated me quite warmly, even seeing to my education. Though he begged me to do so, I never bothered divorcing Ita, knowing that it played no practical purpose. They were never going to marry her again. Even those cruel people couldn't have been *that* cruel."

Dr. Freud was quiet, and I was quiet as well.

"Dr. Sammelsohn — may I ask?" he said, licking the inside of his lips. "Did you ever speak to Fräulein Eckstein about any of this?"

"Most assuredly not."

"Nor about Hindele, your previous wife?"

"Nothing at all."

"Nothing about life in Szibotya?"

"I assure you, Dr. Freud, on the occasions Fräulein Eckstein and I met, I could barely get an edge in wordwise."

"Troubling," Dr. Freud said. "Troubling, indeed. And yet, as scientists, there is naught for us to do but analyze each datum as it presents itself. Let me apprise you on how things currently stand."

ACCORDING TO DR. Freud, after the episode in my apartment, he'd renewed his efforts with Fräulein Eckstein and all seemed well for a time, until inexplicably the patient began hemorrhaging again from her nose. Her nasal passages swelled, and a fetid odor set in.

"I tried irrigating her," he said, "but there seemed to be an obstacle inside. I called in Dr. Gersuny, who inserted a drainage tube into her nose, hoping things would work themselves out once a discharge was reestablished." Dr. Freud shook his head. "Two days later, she was bleeding again, profusely this time. As Gersuny wasn't available till evening, I called in Dr. Rosanes, who started cleaning the area, removing blood clots, and the next moment, for no discernible reason, out shot a flood of blood."

"Oh my!" I said.

"Yes," Dr. Freud said. "The Fräulein turned white, her eyes bulged, she lost her pulse. Rosanes quickly packed her to stop the hemorrhaging, but the poor creature was quite unrecognizable, lying flat on her back. That's when something quite strange happened."

"And what was that?"

"A foreign body came out."

"A foreign body?"

"Ita," he confirmed, looking at me with a seemingly infinite need for compassion. He raised his chest and sighed. "I felt sick," he confessed. "After the Fräulein had been packed, I fled to the next room and drank a bottle of water. The brave Frau Doktor, Fräulein Eckstein's sister-in-law, was kind enough to bring me a small glass of Cognac, and I became myself again. What could I do? Nothing. And so I arranged for the poor unfortunate to be brought to the Sanatorium Loew, where we are going now, and when I returned to the room, shaken, she greeted me with the condescending remark, 'So *this* is the strong sex!' Only . . ." He hesitated.

"Yes?" I encouraged him.

"It wasn't Fräulein Eckstein speaking."

"No?"

"But Frau Sammelsohn."

"Ita, you're saying?"

"Oh, yes," Dr. Freud said warily.

"And," I stammered, "what exactly made you think it was Ita who was addressing you?"

The tone of my voice had sharpened to a lethal point, and Dr. Freud was forced to reconsider his approach.

"Dr. Sammelsohn, I apologize for throwing all this at you as though it were a bucket of water and you had caught on fire. How did I know it was Ita? An excellent question. Well, the voice was different, for one thing, and she introduced herself to me as such."

It was hard to know how to reply. The urbane, skeptical man of science had simply disappeared. Before my very eyes, Dr. Freud had transformed himself into just another credulous Jew. I looked down at my hands and brought my fingers together.

"Forgive me, Dr. Freud, for my"—I struggled to find the appropriate word—"blockheadedness, I suppose you'd call it, but are you suggesting to me that Ita has died, an occurrence of which, until this very moment, I've learned nothing, neither from my sisters nor from my mother, whose correspondence I receive periodically, and that she has returned to haunt me, through Fräulein Eckstein, as a dybbuk?"

"No, of course not!" Dr. Freud cried. Relaxing a bit, he even laughed. "To believe such a thing in this age of electrical lights and gramophones . . ." He ruffled his hair with his hand, knocking his hat askew. "No, as I've said, it's clear that yesteryear's demonical possession corresponds entirely to the hysteria of our time. However"—and here he grew rigid and troubled again—"one cannot dismiss out of hand one's patients' delusions without threatening the therapeutic bond, you see. And so I'm afraid we've no choice but to accept—provisionally, provisionally, of course—whatever the patient brings to us until we can demonstrate to her the falseness of her own claims."

Dr. Freud reminded me of a story he'd told me once before: encountering Bertha Pappenheim (the not-yet-famous Anna O.) in the throes of an hysterical pregnancy, calling out 'Here comes Dr. B's baby, here comes Dr. B's baby,' Dr. Breuer had run from her bedside all the way to Italy, fleeing the scene and, in his bourgeois cowardice, leaving his patient in less competent hands.

"The instant Breuer told me this story," Dr. Freud said, gritting his teeth, "I resolved never to allow myself to be similarly unmanned by a lack of analytic nerve."

WE RODE FOR a moment in silence, the tattoo of the horses' hooves muffled by the snow.

"It's odd," I said.

"Yes?"

"But as a child, I was present at a dybbuk possession."

With his handkerchief pressed against his nostril, Dr. Freud eyed me with a somewhat astonished, somewhat indulgent look of irritation. "My God, Sammelsohn, you're like Burton returned from Medina with a thousand and one tales of the mysterious East!"

"Well, it's not the sort of thing one talks about freely," I confessed.

In fact, these were tales I'd never told anyone, but especially not Dr. Freud, who, regarding them with his jaundiced medical eye, I feared would see in them evidence for all sorts of psychopathologies on my part. Also, although I knew them to be true, somehow in the bright splendor of Vienna, they seemed, though exotic or odd or piquant, utterly and ultimately false. And yet my friend Shaya and I *had* hidden beneath Khave Kaznelson's bed the day Vladek the Wagon Driver entered her as a dybbuk.

He was a terrible man, this Vladek, a drunkard who, it was said, murdered his customers if he suspected they were carrying diamonds or gold. Leaving the bodies by the roadside, he'd claimed that bandits had done the killings and sometimes wounded himself in the foot or the arm in order to make his story appear more convincing to the police.

Of course, at first no one knew that it was Vladek who had entered Khave's body. Summoned to her bedside by her frantic husband, the rebbe asked the spirit to identify itself.

"Who are you, spirit?" he demanded, speaking as forcefully as I'd ever heard him, and he was one of those screamers whose shrill exhortations could make the wood mites fall out of the ceiling beams of the shul.

"Why should I talk to you, you filthy Jew?" the voice roared back in a coarse, masculine way. "Send for a priest! I'm a good Christian and demand a proper exorcism!"

The rebbe would hear none of it. "Since, wicked creature, you have taken it into your head to inhabit a goodwife of Israel, a lamb for whom I am the shepherd, you shall deal with me instead."

"A goodwife?" the voice scoffed. "Now there's a laugh!"

"Silence!" the rebbe demanded.

"Why, when I could tell you a story or two?"

As though with one breath, a gasp erupted from the crowd ringing Khave Kaznelson's bed.

"I want the children out of here! out!" the rebbe screamed.

We thought we were safe enough, Shaya and I, unseen beneath the bed, huddled on our stomachs, our fists balled against our ribs, but over Shaya's shoulders, I saw two large hands appear, then the tip of a beard, then an angry eye. As the hands manacled themselves around

Shaya's ankles, I felt the same thing happening to mine. The next thing I knew, we were sliding away from each other. "Yankl!" he cried, throwing out his hands like rescue ropes before him. I did the same, our fingers locking, but we were dragged apart, lifted out on either side of Khave Kaznelson's bed, and held there, each of us in the arms of a strong man, like Torah scrolls on either side of the bimah during the blessings for the month of Teves. Of course, we struggled to break free, but we were helpless to do so.

However, when Vladek spoke next — "Why bother me? What trouble am I causing you?" — everyone seemed to forget about us. Held above her bed, I saw with my own eyes that Vladek's voice emanated not from Khave Kaznelson's mouth, but from her throat, where there was an unnaturally large bulge.

"The children," the rebbe commanded, "remove them, I say!"

We were trundled out, passed from hand to hand, like buckets in a fire brigade.

"I, Vladek the Wagon Driver, am a murderer! Cursed be the law of God which seeks my destruction!" was the last thing I heard before the bedroom door was slammed. We raced outside the house, but the children watching through the windows were already four lines deep, though the curtains had been drawn, and no one could see anything at all.

AS I FEARED, Shaya and I were summoned to the rebbe's study that evening. Naturally enough, we believed we were in trouble, and naturally enough, we'd each constructed an alibi that exonerated himself while incriminating his friend. Sitting outside the rebbe's door on a cold, hard bench, I'd noticed that the nails of my hands were black beneath their tips. I scraped the dirt out with the corner of a tooth and had my hand in my mouth when Reb Yudel opened the study door. "Have you no shmatte?" he asked with a scowl. "Well then, wipe the spittle on your pants." I rubbed my hand against my knee, while Reb Yudel muttered, "Stupid boy."

It seemed to take years to cross the room with Reb Yudel pinching at our necks. Our legs moved numbly; we didn't seem to be advancing at all. The rebbe sat in the corner of the room behind his desk, reading by candlelight, half his face illuminated by the flame, the other half in shadow. He seemed not to be getting any larger as we approached him, until suddenly, there he was, an enormous figure looming above us.

"Sit," Reb Yudel commanded us, and we sat. Or more precisely: he dropped us into our chairs. After what seemed like a thousand years, the rebbe looked up from his book, the one eye lit by the candlelight peering at Shaya and me, before gravitating slowly upwards towards Reb Yudel. "Thank you, Yudel," the rebbe said. "You may leave us now."

I could hear Reb Yudel's footsteps receding behind me, though I dared not look. His departure seemed to take forever, during which time the rebbe kept his gaze in alignment (or so I calculated) with Reb Yudel's back. His soft, papery hands, though one clutched the other, hardly seemed to be touching. Finally, the click-clacking of the door's opening and shutting sounded and after an eternity of silence, the rebbe lowered his gaze and took us in.

"Quite a show this afternoon, gentlemen, quite a show," he said. "Now, I'm certain neither of you have ever seen such a strange thing in the whole of your lives. Am I correct? However, rest assured, the poor miscreant has confessed his crimes to me, and I have sent a quorum of honest men out to put markers at the graves of his victims and to unbury the loot he has hidden in the woods. And yet"—the rebbe sighed—"that's the least of my concerns tonight."

The rising moon filled the little window in the wall behind him, its light illuminating his shoulders with a glowing mantle. His eyebrows, thick and wiry, were as tangled as two blackberry bushes. As I studied his face, they looked suddenly out of place, as though a prankster had cut off someone's mustache and glued it, in two pieces, over the rebbe's eyes.

"Are you familiar with the term *dybbuk*?" he said, clasping his hands together and learning forward on his elbows. "I thought not. However, I'm certain you know that the human soul is a spark of the Holy One's light. Of course, you know this—you're children and still see things clearly—and so you also know that just as one flame can be made from another flame without diminishing the first, the soul of man, like a wick properly trimmed, may burn with the radiance of divine light. Now, our sacred Torah tells us that God is an all-consuming fire, and yet it also tells us that those who cling to God are alive today—not consumed by the fire! How can that be?" he demanded. "Which is it? Which is the truth?" he shouted, slamming his hand against the desk. "Is the Lord an all-consuming fire or a being to whom we may cling and not burn up?"

I was afraid he expected one of us to answer the question, but before we could speak he continued on in a calmer voice. "Now, the teachings of the Eternal are perfect. You know this. God isn't a man that He writes and blots out. God forbid! There are no contradictions in His holy teachings. And so which is it then? Is the Lord an all-consuming fire or may we cling to him and not perish in the flames? Ah, but I see that you're ahead of me here, my dears. Yes, you are, you're quick, and that is correct: fire is not consumed by fire. The fiery soul of man cannot be extinguished in the burning embrace of Heaven. And yet, and yet, my good boys, there are souls, souls of the dead, who naturally fear this divine conflagration. We see this in life all the time, do we not? How a man runs and returns, runs and returns . . ."

He sat for a moment with his arms crossed, looking from one corner of the room to the other, as though at a man running and returning, and finally, he spoke again. "The Judge of the Universe is, thank Heaven, a fair judge. He cannot be bribed. Indeed not. The Heavenly Court runs according to the same strict system of justice as, l'havdil, our Emperor's Court. How could it be otherwise? There is an Eye that sees, and an Ear that hears, and each of us must give an accounting of his own life. Each of us—why, both of you, for that matter—will stand trial in the Heavenly Court. Yes, that's true. One day, you will be required to defend every one of your deeds, may they all be for good, my darlings, may they all be for the good!"

He sighed, and his face grew sad.

"However, just as there are men in this world who owe and do not hurry to repay or who, having committed crimes, connive to put off their punishment, so there are souls—the souls of the blackest of sinners—who prefer to put off such a reckoning in the next world for as long as they're able. Refusing to submit to divine justice, these souls wander the great broadways and desolate plains of the other world, a world that touches our own—can you feel it, children? can you? I know you can—at various points and most rapturously, I'm told, though I've never experienced it myself, in our holy city of Jerusalem, may we live to see the day of its redemption, when the Holy Messiah will make known His holy name, may it be soon in our times, amen!"

His face grew tender. "There are doorways, my dears, doorways to the next world and doorways back, and there is no doorway more open than the human heart. Only with his heart may a Jew serve the Holy One. But out of fear, the eye of the heart darkens, and we mistake the blessings the Holy One renders us for punishments. There is no punishment, my dears, but sometimes the Holy One blesses us with a very harsh Hand. And so it is with these errant souls, upon whom the Holy One causes to descend a horde of unruly angels. But is there no place where a soul like this may shelter from the pangs of her tormentors? I can see the question in your eyes. You're sweet children, you're dear, sweet children, and you're wondering: How could God allow these demons to torment a poor and naked soul, tearing into it, as though into its flesh, with their whips and their cudgels and their chains? And also what kind of repentance may a soul sincerely make under such extremities? And you're right. No, of course, you're right, it isn't just!" He shook his head. "It isn't just. And so, in His mercy, which is infinite, the Holy One extends shelter even to those souls who refuse to submit to His judgment, permitting her to hide in a rock or an animal or, may God protect us from such plagues, in the body of a human being. Is the Merciful One not merciful? He provides shelter even for the soul who flaunts His justice, spitting into His face, as it were, God forbid. However, just as, at dawn, all eyes turn to the east, so all souls, no matter how degraded they've become, seek a reunion with the Beloved of all Beloveds, perhaps without even knowing it, for by hiding in a human being, the dybbuk gives herself away, doesn't she, and why would she want to do that?"

The rebbe stared over our little trembling shoulders, as though, without making a sound, someone had entered the room. He smiled gently, as one might at a friend one hasn't seen in years. "You know," he whispered over his interlaced fingers, raising his woolly eyebrows, "this is not the first dybbuk to whose aid I have been called." He leaned in closer to us.

"Perhaps I shouldn't be telling you this." He glanced about the room like a sneakthief. "But will you promise never to reveal a word I say to you to another living being? Not even to your own mothers or fathers?"

Shaya and I nodded mutely.

"And not even to talk of it among yourselves after you leave this room?"

We silently agreed.

He snarled. "You know what happens to little boys who break their promises, don't you?"

We shook our heads.

"No, and you don't want to know either!" Finally, he sat back in his chair. "So it's agreed, then? The following will remain strictly between the three of us here tonight? Good. Now as I was saying: Khave Kaznelson's was not the first dybbuk to whose aid I had been summoned. Nothing remarkable about that. But would it shock you, my dears, if I told you that the last time had been more than three hundred years ago?" He raised his furry eyebrows. "And what if I added that it was neither as myself as you see me now, nor in this town, nor in this life that I performed this good deed?" He crossed his arms. "And yet it was so."

A strange smile illumined his face, and soon his entire countenance was glowing. He sipped his tea, seeming to delight in the simple drink. "The year was 5336, the month Adar, and I, a young rabbi in Genoa, was summoned to the bedside of a maiden by the name of Bianca. Oh, children, you have never seen a maiden as beautiful as this Bianca. She lay perfectly still in her bed, as though in a trance, her eyes shut, her mouth slightly parted, not moving, barely breathing. And yet, as soon as I entered her room, she turned her face from me.

"'Who are you?' I commanded instantly.

"'No, I shall not speak to you,' she cried.

"As with Vladek the Wagon Driver today, she addressed me in a voice not belonging to herself. A low-pitched growl, it was deeper in timbre than a woman can properly make. She spoke to me in Italian, of course, my language at the time. Ah, children!" the rebbe said, interrupting himself. "How I loved those Petrarchan sonnets! I composed literally thousands of them. Ah," he sighed, "life to life, so much is lost. In any case, I was not to be put off.

"'Look at me!' I insisted.

"'I cannot,' she demurred. 'I cannot gaze upon the holy light shining from your face.'

"Ah, a flatterer, I thought.

"'Spirit, do not flatter me,' I said.

"'But I don't,' said she or he or whoever it was inside of her. 'Everyone knows of Rabbi Leonardo Emanuel. Beyond the Heavenly Curtain your name is whispered with reverence and trembling.'

"'Look at me,' I commanded again, 'and tell me your name.' But he did not. 'I order you to obey me,' I said, and not then and not later, but eventually the dybbuk obeyed. His name was Bernardo Messina. I had known him in my youth, and I knew him for what he was: an apostate who'd been hanged as a horse thief.

"'Also,' he confessed, 'I sired many bastard children, their mother the wife of my tutor. I've lain as well with my stepmother's daughter and with my stepbrother as well.' Brazenly, he added: 'Or even better.'

"'Vile creature!'

"'Oh, Leonardo, if you only knew the half of it!'

"'Still, death has undone you,' I reminded him.

"'As it will us all,' said he.

"Now, children, listen to me, this Messina had repudiated the One True God and His Holy Torah, and had embraced the Trinity as part of a scheme to defraud a brotherhood of monks who'd hoped to redeem him from his evil ways, but who, under his influence, had succumbed, instead, like him, to pederasty and to other such abominations. How he met his death is too gruesome a story to recount. Embittered over his fate, he made it his business to mock both of the faiths he had traduced. Accordingly, every morning and every evening, when the church bells rang, Messina forced Bianca to recite the customary Christian prayers, which she did with alarming fluency. When her parents witnessed this for the first time, they were aghast, and they sent for me. Though time was of the essence—I knew not how long the maiden could endure alive with Messina inside of her—I realized that there was much to learn from him, from studying him, before releasing him from her mortal coil.

"To begin with," the rebbe said, "his voice. I'd noted that it seemed to emanate from the young girl's neck. Now, this was a curiosity to me and, to resolve the puzzle, I asked him many questions concerning the nature of his form.

"'I know not,' he replied.

"I asked about its volume: 'Is it like a goose egg, or the egg of a hen or maybe a dove?'

"'More like a dove, I think.'

"'Where are you inside the young woman's body?'

"'Between the rib cage and her waist on the left side.'

"Her lips never moved during the course of this interview, and when I'd exhausted my line of questioning, I pleaded with Messina to let the young woman speak on her own behalf, so that I might interview her as well. Naturally, he was reluctant to do so, hungry for attention, as all such sinners are, but I appeased him. How, you wonder? An excellent question! I flattered him, my dear children! Yes, I flattered his bravery, his intelligence, his cunning. I laughed with him over the fools he'd made of those dunderpated monks. Eventually believing I was his friend, he complied, and agreed to release the poor girl from his power.

"Along with my students (whom I'd summoned to me), I watched in alarm as the egg-sized protuberance that had been visible near the girl's throat began to move from where it had stationed itself in order to speak out more clearly. It moved first across her chest, then down to her side and finally to the place beneath her rib cage where it normally lodged. It resembled nothing so much as a small mouse moving beneath the blanket of her skin. The young woman appeared in extreme pain during this procedure. She writhed, dampening her sheets with bucketsful of perspiration, and when finally she opened her eyes, she stared at us in wonder

"'Can you see me, child?'

"'I can.'

"'And you can hear me?' I asked.

"'Yes, although you are speaking as though from a great distance away.'

"'I will come closer now, my dear,' said I, moving nearer to her bedside.

"Someone, a relative, her mother perhaps (I no longer recall who) brought me a chair, and I sat in it, pondering what to do next. After a fervent, though necessarily brief prayer, I decided on a course of action. I ordered the room emptied, except for my most trusted pupil, Benyamin Navarro, whom I stationed by the door. Knowing that from there, he would not be able to hear us, I returned to the maiden.

"'Daughter,' I said softly.

"'You speak so calmingly, Rabbi.'

"'I'm here to aid you, my dear child.'

"'How could you minister kindness to a girl as wicked as I?' she said. The strain of the ordeal overwhelmed her, I'm afraid, and she began to cry. I handed her my kerchief, and she wiped away her tears. She brought the kerchief to her mouth, bunched up, like a rag, you see? But beneath it, unbeknownst to me, she was drawing the waters of her saliva together in her mouth. 'Rabbi Leonardo,' she said tenderly.

"'Yes, my daughter?'

"'May I tell you what I think of your kindness?'

"'Certainly, my child.'

"With a great hawking sound, she coughed up the phlegm and, using her mouth and tongue as mortar and pestle, mixed it into a gelatinous mass, which she unceremoniously spat into my face!

"'Messina!' I roared.

"'Look, Leonardo,' Messina spoke again, but this time using the face and mouth of the young girl, his deeper voice issuing, as naturally as it could, from her lips. 'Do you think she's as innocent as she pretends? Do you think she's so meek and mild, this daughter of Israel?' Using her own hands against her, he began to rub her private places, grinding her hips in an unbecoming manner. 'Take me, Rabbi Leonardo!' he howled. 'Come to me like a lover!'

"Now, this perfidy wasn't enough, but he ripped at her bodice and, exposing her young breasts, picked one up in each hand and pressed them together like two pumice stones, whispering lasciviously: 'Spill your seed across my chest so I'll remain a virgin.'

"'Dastardly creature!' I screamed at him. 'Desist immediately! Or I'll—'

"'Or you'll what?' He flung the question back at me as though it were a slur. And when I stammered mutely, wiping his spittle from my beard, he let out another long and maddening laugh. 'This is what she dreams of every night, Leonardo, I promise you,' he said. 'And not only that but this.'

"And here, he turned her over, exposing her bare rump to the cold air of the room. 'Enter her from behind, like a dog. Or a monk,' he laughed. 'That's what she wants.' Forcing her head down onto her pillows, he lifted her backside and, with his hands grasping each cheek, spread them far apart."

At that moment, the rebbe looked at Shaya and me quizzically, as though, until then, he had forgotten to whom he was speaking.

"Yes. Well"—he coughed—"perhaps these are not the sorts of details I should be sharing with small boys, but I want you to understand the gravity of the situation."

"But Rebbe," I asked him, "what did you do?"

"What did I do?"

"How did you help Bianca?"

"And Bernardo," he said.

"And Bernardo?" Shaya asked.

"Why, of course."

"But why would you ever help Bernardo?" I said.

"Now, don't forget, my dear children, I'd been summoned to Bianca's bedside to aid and assist not one lost soul, but two, his as well as hers. No matter how much he had blackened the shroud of holiness that was his birthright, no matter how many blasphemies he'd recited, no matter how many sins he'd committed, his was still a soul in dire straits, and I had commended myself, years before, to its aid."

"So what did you do?"

"Exactly! What did I do? What could I do?" he said. "'Be still, Messina!' I shouted. 'Dress the maiden and desist from your vile rogueries.' Of course, he didn't listen to me, and so I had no other choice. I stared into the young girl's eyes and recited a verse from the Psalms of King David: 'הפקד עליו רשע ושטן יעמד על ימינו' *Set a wicked one over him and stand the Satan at his right!* I recited it three times. Then three times backwards: 'ימינו על יעמד ושטן רשע עליו הפקד.' Then three times reversing all the letters: 'ונימי לע דמעי נטשו עשו וילע דקפה.' Until the poor devil could withstand no more.

"'Enough!' Messina yowled, quickly buttoning up the girl's blouse and covering her knees. I took the opportunity to intone the kavones proscribed by the most secret of our holy books and called upon the aid of certain angelic forces.

"'Leave her,' I commanded again, and again the young girl began to writhe in pain, her hands clutching at her sheets, her head jerking backwards and forwards. Vomit frothed from her mouth, and I was alarmed to see that her throat had swollen dangerously.

"'She seems to be choking!' I called to my student, and again I recited the formula.

"'Leave, I order you, without harming her in any way!'

"Quickly I called in the rest of my students and set them to reciting all the Psalms from their beginning. That did the trick—aha!—and I had him on the run!

"'Promise me . . .' Messina choked out, but the girl's thrashings were so terrible, he could barely get a word out.

"'Promise you what?' I roared over the din.

"'I will not harm her if . . .'

"'Yes? If? If what?'

"Every word was a torment for him: 'If you . . . will promise . . . to . . . recite . . .'

"'Recite? Recite what, Messina?'

"'. . . Kaddish . . .'

"'Aha! The Kaddish prayer?'

"'. . . on my behalf!'"

The rebbe folded his arms. "Though they desire nothing but the good, still their ways are crooked from long habit, and one must negotiate with these wretched souls as one would with a shtreimel-maker in midwinter.

You must be precise about all foreseeable conditions and occurrences. I reiterated the bargain he proposed to strike: 'You promise to leave this poor girl without harming her in any way, neither physically or spiritually, and you will cease your wanderings and submit to the righteous judgments of the Heavenly Court, if I promise to recite the prayer for the dead on your behalf?'

"'For the full eleven months!' he cried. He, too, was being careful, indeed exquisitely so, with the terms of our agreement, as much hung in the balance.

"'For the full eleven months!' I agreed.

"'So you've promised.'

"'And so it shall be done, Messina!'

"'Swear it!'

"'No, Messina, you swear!'

"'I swear!' said he.

"'On what?'

"'On the One True and Holy God and upon His Sacred Torah!'

"'Then it is promised,' said I.

"'And I am released,' said he.

"At that moment, a bitter wind from the sea blew open the windows of the girl's room. I could hear the sound of wild horses neighing somewhere nearby in terrible distress.

"'Rabbi, help me!' the maiden cried out, but in two voices at once, her own and Messina's. Her body pitched and jerked so fiercely, it seemed at times to be suspended above her bed, the sheets billowing in a furious bedlam. At odd moments, I could, when the covers lifted from her thrashings, see the mass, the lump, beneath her skin, moving from her chest to her waist and down her legs and finally to her foot. She shrieked in pain. The sound was like a bow being raked across the bridge of a violin. Her foot, pushing out from beneath the covers, swelled to twice its size, and then, with a spurting starburst of blood, the nail of her little toe popped off. And it was by this egress that the spirit of Bernardo Messina ultimately left her body.

"'Call a physician!' I roared at my student Benyamin Navarro. 'A doctor!' Navarro shouted out the door. A rank miasma filled the air above our heads. 'Blessed is the name of the Lord,' I could hear Messina's voice crying out. 'And blessed is his servant, Rabbi Leonardo Emanuel!'

"The miasma was sucked out the window by the vacuum of a windstorm, a minor hurricane, and everything returned to normal order. I waited until the doctor came. He bandaged the girl's toe and gave her a sleeping draught. Resisting sleep at first, however, she called me to her side. 'Rabbi Leonardo,' she said.

" 'Yes, my child?'

" 'I have a confession to make. I've recently succumbed to the beliefs of the so-called enlightened ones, and though I outwardly maintained a pious face, inwardly I'd begun to doubt and mock the existence of God and the authority of his holy Torah. I know now that by opening myself to these doubts, I made a space for the evil dybbuk who violated me. Know now and hear me clearly that I repent and again believe and affirm my belief in the oneness of the holy name, blessed be He.'

"Children, never has a face appeared so radiant to me as did hers in that moment. 'Sleep, daughter,' I counseled her. 'Sleep, my child, for you will not be troubled by unpleasant dreams tonight. This much I assure you.'

" 'Our work here is done,' I said, taking leave of the grateful household. To the girl's father, I said, 'My young pupil will remain in the hall to recite psalms throughout the night. Make certain he has enough to eat and to drink.'

"I returned to the synagogue, and in the morning, during my devotions, I recited the prayer for the dead on behalf of the penitent Bernardo Messina, as I continued to do faithfully and consistently for the mandatory eleven months, after which the old rascal appeared to me in a dream, bearing with him, as a gift — would you believe it? — a magnificent and handsome stallion!"

B y the time I'd finished telling my tale, the evening had grown quite late. The streets were drowsing under their snowy garments. In the glow of the gas lamps as we drove past them, I could see the gleam of a rueful squint in Dr. Freud's eye. Condescending, benevolent, it was the indulgent look with which an adult meets the story of a child's love affair. *Now, now,* it seemed to suggest, *you may feel such things are real, but because I am older and wiser, I know better; and when you are older and wiser, you shall know better, too.*

With the tip of his cane, Dr. Freud worked some detritus off the bottom of his shoe.

"A boy is taken to the circus," he said with a sigh, "and there, because he witnesses acrobats whirling in the Heavens, he believes not only that people can fly but that there is something wrong with him for not being able to." He shook his head. "Ah, how we prefer our illusions! Why, even the simple workmen you tend to as a doctor prefer to be thought of as blind."

"Yes, because the government insurance compensates them and they're let off from work."

"A man is always well compensated for his blindness," Dr. Freud told me.

He trimmed another proscribed cigar, making a great show of lighting it, the sulfurous match illuminating his face in reds and yellows. He drew the flame through the rolled cylinder. With his hands on the top of his stick and the cigar cradled between his fingers, he gazed out the window into the inky shadows blotting the facades of the buildings we passed. This was the Freud he would soon bequeath to history: the skeptical unriddler of Sphinxy riddles.

His neck swathed in woolen scarves, he blew out a frank-smelling puff of smoke. "Two dybbuks for one village rabbi. That's statistically excessive, don't you think? Even if the two episodes occurred hundreds of years apart!"

"I assure you I wouldn't know." I was miserable at having given him a stick with which to beat me in the ribs.

"Still one might have a sense of what is statistically normal, even in the realm of the paranormal."

"I'm not a statistician."

"I never implied that you were."

"Nor a historian."

"Granted."

"I only told you what I saw with my own eyes or heard with my own ears."

"Saw with your own eyes, yes, but admittedly only for the briefest of moments and in an emotionally roiled state, which is to say, while being jostled by a stranger who held you captive." Dr. Freud sat facing me, his shoulder pressed against the seat. "Now, isn't it more likely, Dr. Sammelsohn, that what you mistook for an unnatural bulge in that sick woman's throat was a tumor or a goiter which, under normal circumstances, she kept hidden under a high collar or beneath a shawl, women being in reality the vain creatures we have long imagined them to be; or more likely than a tumor, her breast, unintentionally revealed in her delirium, and occasioning in you, in conjunction with the swaddling sensation of being held so tightly, an almost unbearable sense of returning to the helplessness of infancy? Instead of a breast, you willed yourself to see a lump, and imagined, for cultural reasons, that this lump was a dybbuk. In this way, you avoided confronting your amorous feelings towards your own mother, while remaining within the charmed circle of the pious whose members would otherwise have condemned you for the only-too-normal, in a boy of that age, ogling of a woman's undressed bosom."

"And the rebbe and his story? How do you explain that?"

Dr. Freud looked at me as though he were a con man sizing up an easy mark. "I cannot, of course, say what that gang of men was doing in that poor woman's bedroom, an activity whose discovery was so dangerous to them that they felt the need to post guards at the door, but I've no doubt from my own experiences with such charlatans, that your rebbe would have exploited any occasion to promote the notion that a not small portion of the fealty one must swear to the Creator of the Universe may be justly allotted to him as the Lord's emissary. In this way is propped up the rigid scaffolding of a strict social and legal hierarchy that not coincidentally enshrines him at its summit."

Dr. Freud drew his watch from his vest pocket and tilted its face towards the candle burning in the cab's lamp. "In any wise," he said, winding it and holding it to his ear, "one shouldn't underestimate mankind's capacity to delight in all sorts of sheer nonsense."

THE FIACRE DREW up to a building I didn't recognize. Dr. Freud paid the fare. "Come along, Dr. Sammelsohn." He'd leapt from the cab and was stamping his walking stick upon the ground in a pantomime of impatience. "The hour is later than I'd anticipated."

I climbed out and followed him to the gate. I'd never been to the Sanatorium Loew before. The building was part of a large estate once belonging to a Count von Esterhazy who, as I dimly recalled, had gone mad after donating it to the city as a clinic, becoming, in effect, the first recipient of his own charity. We crossed the clinic's gardens, and Dr. Freud let himself in with a key. "Physician's privileges," he murmured. "And there's no need to disturb the staff." He guided me into the foyer. "This way," he said.

A nurse in a starched white bonnet sat behind a reception desk. Dr. Freud nodded to her, and she nodded in return. "Dr. Freud," they said to each other simultaneously, he identifying himself, she confirming that she knew him.

Taking my arm like a chatelaine, he led me down a long passageway. "Fräulein?" Dr. Freud opened the door to Fräulein Eckstein's room, and though he called in, he elicited no response.

I held back in the hallway. "Come in, Dr. Sammelsohn," he whispered.

Walking through the darkened room, Dr. Freud reached for the gas lamp and adjusted its flame. Nothing he had told me on the drive over had prepared me for the sight that greeted me now: Fräulein Eckstein lying in her bed, her face a ghastly white; her eyes wide open; her mouth a gash; her tongue sticking out at the ceiling; her legs stiff; her arms rigid at her sides, their fingers splayed; with barely a twinge of life in her.

We stood on either side of the bed. Holding a small candle, I examined her. I had the impression of a prisoner gagged and bound. The eyes especially—I cannot describe them as *hers*—were haunting: empty, ringed in black; and though she stared up at the ceiling, it was as though her eyes saw nothing themselves, but were being used, as windows, by a being inside her. As with Khave Kaznelson, she possessed a lump, an unnatural bulge, beneath the skin of her throat.

Dr. Freud placed his palm on her forehead, and Fräulein Eckstein's body seemed to relax.

"She's had a bran bath," he told me quietly, "and I earlier gave her a massage. Now I have only to hypnotize her, and we can begin tonight's session."

Dr. Freud spoke to her in a voice too low for me to hear, while lightly pressing her body in various places. Slowly, Fräulein Eckstein's mouth opened, and to my surprise, words were pushed through it like letters being pushed through a mail slot.

"Yankl . . ." she said in a voice unrecognizable as her own.

Dr. Freud gave me a significant look, as he reached down to take Fräulein Eckstein's pulse. "You see, madam. I've kept my promise," he said.

Madam, not *miss*: I assumed this choice of words was all part of Dr. Freud's therapeutic acceptance of Fräulein Eckstein's delusion, but it chilled me to hear the word spoken. In reply, Fräulein Eckstein's head was turned—I can only speak of her in the passive case; she seemed a puppet in the hands of a will greater than her own—and made to look at Dr. Freud. There was no mistaking the expression affixing itself to her face. I'd never seen a man appraised so dismissively, as though he were no more than an errand boy. (How different this face was from the adoring face Fräulein Eckstein normally presented to him.) For his part, Dr. Freud took the slight in stride and set about checking other of the patient's vital signs.

"Unhand her!" something or someone seemed to shriek from inside

Fräulein Eckstein's body. "There'll be time enough for these procedures! You can draw up her death certificate if you must keep yourself busy."

Dr. Freud relented and backed away. From the shadows, he prompted me silently. I cleared my throat. "Ita?" I said, addressing the voice.

Color flushed beneath the skin of Fräulein Eckstein's face. Though its features remained as rigid as before, the skin radiated a girlish blush. "You know me then?"

"Why wouldn't I?" I said.

"How have you been keeping, my darling husband?"

How to describe this odd phenomenon? The rigid features had disappeared and Fräulein Eckstein's face resembled a translucent mask through which another's features were discernible. The impression was similar to seeing a real face beneath the reflection of one's own on the surface of a lake.

I asked her the first thing that came into my head. "How is it that you can speak now?"

"Oh, Yankl—or Kobi—or whatever it is they call you now—are you still such a stupid boy?"

Uncertain how to proceed, I glanced at Dr. Freud. He signaled with a slight upward movement of his chin that I should answer her honestly. And so, crossing my arms, I said, "Well, that's a difficult thing to evaluate subjectively, I suppose."

"No, no, you're right," she said. "You're quite right." And she laughed grimly. "Better to allow others to decide who's clever and who's dull."

"MAY I SIT here?" I gestured towards a chair.

Fräulein Eckstein nodded, which is to say her head shook as though it had been had grabbed by its hair. I turned to Dr. Freud. He was standing in the shadows thrown off by the gas lamps. He nodded as well, and I drew the chair closer to Fräulein Eckstein's bedside.

Fräulein Eckstein's head swiveled on its neck so that it now faced me. I looked into her eyes. Beyond the two little images of myself I saw trapped in their glassy surfaces, I saw nothing of Ita. "Perhaps I can relax and inhabit her fully?" the voice inside the Fräulein suggested.

Again, I looked at Dr. Freud, a little grace note of a glance; he nodded back with an equal quickness.

"I think that would be all right," I said, sitting up straight and preparing for the interview.

"Only don't hurt her," Dr. Freud commanded.

"Of course not," the Fräulein said.

Dr. Freud and I watched as Fräulein Eckstein writhed in her bed. The little bulge I'd noticed protruding from her neck was hidden from my view beneath the bedsheets. If it moved beneath her gown like a mouse beneath a tablecloth, I didn't see it. In the next moment, Fräulein Eckstein's arms and legs came to life, and she stretched. Her face lost its pallor, and when she spoke, the words were no longer shouted through the aperture of her open mouth, but were clearly shaped and articulated by it.

"Oh, oh my, but that's so much better, really," she said, sitting up in her bed and pulling her legs beneath her in a girlish way. She let her hands fall into the circle of her lap. "May I take your hand, Yankl?"

"Best not," Dr. Freud cautioned.

Fräulein Eckstein turned to him, as though surprised to find him still in the room. Hadn't she dismissed him? For a moment, it seemed as though she were considering screaming at him but had decided, in my presence at least, to forego all unseemly behavior.

"As you wish," she said sweetly, so sweetly, in fact, I could think of nothing but the poisoned sugar people leave out for rats. I folded my arms and sat back in the chair with my ankles crossed, letting a forelock of my hair fall charmingly across my brow. I hoped to look as sympathetic and bemused as I could, as though I were a bachelor uncle whose precocious niece had run away to join him in the city. There was no question but that such an uncle would send the girl back home, but he would do so without reprimands or censure, so as not to impair the child's affection for him.

"Ita, Ita, Ita," I sighed, attempting to credit Fräulein Eckstein's delusions as much as possible, as Dr. Freud had instructed me to do. "I'm afraid my relations with my family have been . . . well, shall we say, *strained* since the night of our . . . can we really call it a wedding? I think not. Communication hasn't been as constant as familial affection might otherwise allow, and I'm afraid I hadn't, until now, been apprised of your death."

It felt an odd thing to say to a person.

"So no one told you about it then?" she asked.

I raised my palms in a gesture of helpless sorrow. "No, but permit me to extend my condolences now."

Her features contracted behind the mask of Fräulein Eckstein's face until she resembled a badgered dog.

"Oh, Yankl, Yankl!" she cried, sobbing into Fräulein Eckstein's hands. "I know you didn't love me. I may have been an idiot, but I wasn't a fool!"

I handed her my handkerchief.

"Thank you," she said.

"No, no, please," I said.

She daubed at her tears.

"You're very kind."

"It's nothing."

She drew a shawl about her shoulders and attempted to gain control of her weeping. I looked at Dr. Freud. I have to say: the mise-en-scène was disconcerting. Though the body belonged to Fräulein Eckstein, the voice wasn't hers at all; and this confusion of identities was maddening. To whom was I speaking? To Fräulein Eckstein or—but no, it wasn't possible!—to Ita Sammelsohn? A poisoned headache stirred up behind my eyes, and I understood no man at that moment better than I did Josef Breuer. Like Dr. Breuer, all I wanted was to flee. Who wouldn't prefer a trip to Italy to this stuffy bedchamber and these difficult psycho-pathologies? However, as I'd been deputized by Dr. Freud, I felt duty-bound to carry on as competently as I could. It was my job to test the weave of Fräulein Eckstein's impersonation and reveal whatever holes I could find in the fabric.

"When you say you knew I didn't love you, Ita, what exactly do you mean?"

She laughed. "Oh, you'd be surprised at the things I understood, Yankl."

"For instance?" I probed as delicately as I could.

"Of course, no one imagined I understood anything at all."

"That was Szibotya," I said, as though this explained everything. "They treated me the same way."

"And so no one feared speaking in front of me."

"Ah, yes, I remember. That's true." I said this as much to Dr. Freud as to Fräulein Eckstein.

"Or even committing the most horrible sins in my presence."

"Really?"

She shrugged a single shoulder. "Even if I knew what I was seeing, what did it matter? Who could I tell? God in His Infinite Wisdom had denied me the power of speech, and I was little more than a parrot. But then you know all this."

I listened grimly, aware that Dr. Freud had seated himself behind her bed with a sheaf of paper on his knee and a pen in his hand. I didn't understand by what psychic mechanism Fräulein Eckstein could appear to know so much about Ita's childhood, and I suddenly found myself worrying lest some youthful indiscretion of my own might next be laid upon the table for inspection. As though reading my thoughts, Fräulein Eckstein shook her head and said, "No, you were kind to me, Yankl. You didn't make fun of me. Not like the other boys, who were so cruel! And your mother was always very sweet."

"You remember my mother?"

Fräulein Eckstein nodded. "Your sisters treated me with compassion as well, as did your father, whenever he noticed me, which wasn't often."

"My father," I said softly, shaking my head.

"Now there was a man consumed with his own affairs!"

"Oh, yes." I nodded.

"Chief among them"—and here, Fräulein Eckstein cut me a sly, sideways glance.

"Chief among them, Ita?"

"Chief among them"—she paused again, it seemed, for dramatic effect—"an unrequited passion for Blume Levanthal."

Dr. Freud, who had hitherto written nothing, began scribbling madly.

"Blume Levanthal?" I laughed hollowly, the way a man in a duel laughs, thinking the bullet has missed him before realizing it has pierced his heart.

"Or didn't you know this?"

"No, Ita. I didn't."

"Oh, yes." She eyed me sharply. "How your father used to pine for that woman! A woman forbidden to him in every way: by law, by custom, by his own sense of decency; and yet he couldn't banish her from his heart. How do I know this, you're wondering? I can read the question in your face, and it's a good question, Yankl. The answer is: I used to see him in the forests."

"You used to see my father in the forests?"

"My grandfather, may his name be blotted out, used to leave me there, in the hopes that a wild animal would devour me, or a Russian use me and slit my throat. I was a stain on the family honor, after all. Ha! The family honor! Can you imagine a greater absurdity! But God creates the cure before the disease. Weren't we taught that, Yankl? And invariably, in the woods, there would be Reb Alter Nosn, reciting his reams of poetry, all dedicated to an appreciation of the breasts and the hair and the neck and the ankles and the matronhood of Blume Levanthal, Motkhe the Shochet's wife."

This was a picture of my father I had never seen, a page in the family album no one had ever shown me, and to my relief, I found the depiction hard to credit. And yet, as Fräulein Eckstein prattled on, she somehow caught my father's likeness perfectly. The narrow chest, the little pouch of his stomach sutured up inside his vest, the scholar's stooped shoulders, the rabbit's foot of white in the middle of his otherwise sable beard, the glittering pince-nez, his habit of wetting his lips with his tongue before speaking, signaling to all that he was on the verge of some important pronouncement. I could see him as though he were standing before me, but never never *never!* had I imagined him, secreted in the woods, declaiming songs like a Persian poet drunk on the corporeal splendors of an unremarkable little woman called Blume Levanthal.

"Oh, yes" — Fräulein Eckstein must have noticed the twin veils of disbelief and confusion dropping across my face — "he could get quite rapturous at times, waving his arms about, fashioning a laurel of fallen leaves and wearing it as a crown. 'Ah, Ita,' he once told me, 'I'm an autumnal poet, don't you know—not yet dead, but old enough to know better, and still a fool.'

"'Steeh uh foo?' I repeated in my idiotic way."

A line of cold electricity shot down my spine as she spoke in the dirgelike singsong so familiar to me from my childhood.

"'But what are you doing out here in the woods alone, child?' he'd say. 'It isn't safe.' 'Nin't sa-af!' I'd say. 'Oh, no, it's not, Ita,' he'd reprimand me as though I'd not repeated, but had actually contradicted, what he'd said. 'Sit here'—he'd place me on a log—'and I'll take you back into town with me when I return. Your grandfather must be worried sick. There's no minding a child like you, is there? First, however, you'll make a splendid audience for my verses.'

"Who else could he recite them to? And so I sat on my log, and I watched him rummage through his pockets for the little scraps of paper on which he'd composed those secret odes.

"'Ah, yes, here's one. Now tell me what you think?' 'Wah *e-i-oo* t'enk?' I'd struggled to ask. 'What *I* think, Ita? Why, you're such a delightful child. *I* think it's a masterpiece.' 'Eee-tah dee-liii-t-fuh?' 'Yes, but don't let that go to your head, like with that rascally son of mine, mollycoddled by his seven sisters and his mother. I do what I can to toughen him up, don't you know, but they're spoiling him.'

"And afterward, Yankl, he'd escort me back into town. My grandfather always pretended to be surprised—in the bustle of the business day, he failed to notice my absence—and grateful for my safe return. It was all a sham, of course, acted out for the benefit of Reb Alter Nosn, the town's wealthiest and, outside of the rebbe, most knowledgeable man."

"Concerning my father?" I couldn't help asking.

"Yes, my darling?"

"Did he ever act upon these . . . ?"

"Passions of his?"

I shrugged as casually as I could. "I'm only wondering, is all."

"Not that I'm aware of, except, of course, in the writing of his verses."

"Which he never showed to Blume?"

Fräulein Eckstein's face took on a sweetness that had lately become foreign to it. "I have no firsthand knowledge of this, but I think it unlikely," she said. "He was as powerless to act upon his feelings as he was to not feel them. In any case, I found him a kind man."

"Did you?"

"Yes, and that's why on the day he came to ask for my hand, I felt I could trust him." She looked at me coyly. "Because the thing is," she hesitated, all blushes and palpitations, "or perhaps you didn't know this, Yankl, but . . . I always loved you." She lowered her eyes. "But you knew that, didn't you?"

I was silent for a moment. "No, Ita. I didn't."

"Right," she said, tart and business-like again. "How could you? There was only one way I could ever make my love known to you and that was if you'd said you loved me first. Then I could repeat the words to you."

She threw herself back onto her pillows.

"Oh! I don't really want to tell you how many hours I spent dreaming of just such a thing. I was a foolish girl, really, but a girl nonetheless, though one with a face as flat as a skillet and a glazed eye and a nose that never ceased running. Who could ever love such a creature? Certainly not the great Ya'akov Yosef, the rich and spoiled son of Reb Alter Nosn, pampered by one sister after the next, each more beautiful than the last!"

"Well," I said, "I suppose you have every right to be bitter."

"Oh, you have no idea!"

"Still, I think this has gone on far enough —"

"Let me finish, Yankl!"

Dr. Freud stood abruptly. "Dr. Sammelsohn, is there any reason we should hear nothing more of this?" he said.

"None," I admitted, looking down at my hands. "None, but my own sense of personal embarrassment."

"The truth is the truth whether it's spoken aloud or not," he lectured me.

"Well said," Fräulein Eckstein concurred.

Dr. Freud cut her a dismissive look. "Frau Sammelsohn, I think you'll find that your flatteries benefit either of us but little."

"Ha!" she sneered "The beard speaks! Remind me again, Yankl: who is this hatless rabbi?"

"He isn't a rabbi, Ita."

"No?" She laughed. "How can he not be? Why, just look at him: he's got fanatical piety written all over his ugly face!"

"He's a doctor, Ita, and a very good one, and one whom I think can cure you."

Dr. Freud cleared his throat. "A moment with you, Dr. Sammelsohn."

"Forgive us, Ita," I said, backing away from her bed.

"We'll return shortly," Dr. Freud said. "Is there anything we can bring you? Tea perhaps? Or a toddy?"

Fräulein Eckstein looked at him as though he had gone mad. "And what would a disembodied soul need with such refreshments?" she exclaimed.

"An excellent point, madam." Dr. Freud bowed. "In that case: excuse us. We'll see ourselves out."

WE STOOD OUTSIDE her door and, for the first time, the thought struck me like a thunderbolt: Ita is dead. The shock of learning of her demise had been lessened, I suppose, by her presence in the room. By the end of our interview, I'd banished the hope that Fräulein Eckstein's condition represented some sort of psychic splitting into two distinct persons, à la Bertha Pappenheim, a phenomenon that, as Dr. Freud kept insisting, was absolutely common in cases of hysteria. Indeed, in years to come, this would be the strategy apologists, citing Dr. Freud himself, would employ to make sense of all dybbuk possessions, blurring the distinctions between the hundred or so documented cases, until each one fit a nice, tidy pattern: weren't they all women, silenced by a masculine cabal, who in sickness had found the voice they could never claim in health—a hectoring, sneering, scorning, accusing, threatening, ridiculing, blaming voice? Was it any different from hysteria, which also allowed its victims to leave off caring for their fathers in their sickbeds, or for their husbands in their marriage beds, or for their children in their cribs, to cease their running and fetching and consoling and feeding and comforting and suckling and coddling and copulating with, on, and for the men who denied them free use of their wills, harnessing their bodies, as though they were mules, to their own vile needs instead?

One thing baffled me only, and it was this: although this last description might be applied in some degree to Fräulein Eckstein, who bowed to her mother's will and lived in the shadow of her brilliant brother, and who additionally allowed herself to be passed between Dr. Freud and Dr. Fliess as though she were the key to an apartment the two men shared, it applied even more to Ita, bartered away by her hateful grandfather to my unloving father as a convenient albatross to hang about my penitent's neck. If the Ita in Fräulein Eckstein's bed—sharp-tongued, well spoken, no longer docile—represented a Fury released from the dark wells of repression, why would Fräulein Eckstein's hysteria choose Ita as its unrepressed agent when, in life, Ita was far more oppressed than Fräulein Eckstein had ever been?

I'm certain this is what also baffled Dr. Freud and forced him to reconsider the social banishment to which he had consigned me. He'd called me in as a consultant, much in the way that he had, days before, made use of Dr. Rosanes and Dr. Gersuny. If I could determine that the personality presenting itself to him as "Ita," claiming to be my spurned second wife, was no such being, but was instead a fabrication of Fräulein Eckstein's mind, constructed out of odd remarks about my former life she'd chanced to overhear, he could rule out the far-fetched but seemingly inescapable diagnosis of demonical possession and treat her for the hysteria with which he was medically as well as philosophically more at home.

Unfortunately, I had no doubt that the figure I'd been addressing, the figure hiding inside Fräulein Eckstein like a fox inside a rotting log, was Ita, an Ita, it was true, in all outward manifestations different from the one I'd known—this Ita could speak; she could reason; she could add and subtract, I wagered, if I had need to put her to the test—and yet it was clearly the same girl.

However, Dr. Freud would hear none of it. "I think you'll find that Fräulein Eckstein's symptoms, *including* her secondary personality, will immediately and permanently disappear as soon as we succeed in bringing to light the memories of the events by which these symptoms have been provoked."

"And to do that?" I asked.

Exhausted, I pushed my hair back with both hands.

"We must simply allow the patient to describe whatever she wishes in the greatest detail possible, letting her put all her affect into words."

"But it's *not* Fräulein Eckstein we're speaking to."

Dr. Freud pinned me with a look of indulgent condescension. "Dear boy, my dearest boy, do you really expect me to believe that we're dealing with a dybbuk? You might as well suggest that Moses parted the Red Sea!"

"Do you really believe Fräulein Eckstein capable of concocting such atrocious verse and in Yiddish besides? But that's the very least of it. Why, everything she says—"

"Dr. Sammelsohn, Dr. Sammelsohn, let's be honest. Is that really a portrait of the father you knew? Think, man!"

He let a moment pass.

"No," I conceded.

"Well?"

"But I can't claim to have known the man completely."

"You're unaccustomed to the ingenuity of this disease. Don't lose your scientific objectivity! No matter what this Ita tells you, no matter how realistic or truthful she seems, no matter how much Fräulein Eckstein's knowledge defies logical explanation, no matter how close to the raw bone her sharp points might probe, I'm counting on you to keep a part of yourself in reserve, by which I mean the finest part: the physician. Whatever Fräulein Eckstein is feeling towards you is simply a manifestation of a symptom lying deep in her unconscious mind. One must remain intellectually aloof in order to provide relief for this poor suffering woman. I brought you in only because Fräulein Eckstein, or Ita as she fashions herself in her condition seconde, was demanding your presence here. I understand you're not trained in the art of our young science. Perhaps it's foolish of me to trust this part of her analysis to a novice, and yet, under the circumstances, what else could I do?"

Dr. Freud searched my face to see if I understood all he had told me.

"And this portrait she painted of my father?" I'd already willed myself to believe in its authenticity. It was pleasing to me to imagine my father as a lovestruck poet reciting verse in praise of Blume, the wife of Motkhe the Shochet, while wandering in the deep forests of Szibotya.

"A complete fantasy," Dr. Freud said, "and I'll prove it to you. May I ask you — who among the circle of your acquaintances does this image of your father most resemble?"

I thought for a moment. "Why, myself, of course."

I felt myself scowling at the obvious truth of what Dr. Freud was telling me.

"Precisely," he said. "Hysterics and neurotics are extremely sensitive people, Dr. Sammelsohn, not the dégénérés and the déséquilibrés Professor Charcot would have us believe. Why, you'd be surprised how much they can divine about the person to whom they are speaking. And don't forget, Fräulein Eckstein has spent more than an hour or two in your company, sometimes intimately."

Blushing, I recognized that what Dr. Freud was saying was in all probability true. The hated image of my saturnine father, graven for so long upon my heart, once more bled through, like a graffito on a whitewashed wall.

"Why, as a student in Paris, at the Moulin Rouge, I upon several occasions witnessed so-called mind readers performing these very same sorts of tricks. We're always giving away clues to ourselves, Dr. Sammelsohn. We have only to open our eyes to read them in others."

"I suppose you're right," I agreed.

"Come along now," he said, and together, we reentered Fräulein Eckstein's room.

We found her on her back in the same horrifying posture as before: her eyes opened wide; her mouth a horrible gash; her tongue extended towards the ceiling; her arms and legs stiff; her toes and fingers splayed.

Dr. Freud went to her side and, as I had seen him do before, he gently laid his hand upon her brow. "Under the pressure of my hand," he commanded, "you shall come back to yourself, my child."

At this, Fräulein Eckstein's posture relaxed and the patient turned onto her side. Bringing her knees to her chest, she hugged her pillow against herself. "I don't feel well," she murmured, gazing at Dr. Freud through a squint.

"No," he said simply. "I wouldn't think so."

"But it's so sweet that you're here with me, Dr. Freud. Are you finding my case very interesting?"

"Can you see and hear me, Fräulein Eckstein?"

"Silly . . . man . . ." She spoke with the weariness of someone who, having been awake for ages, might drop into a dream at any moment. "Silly, beautiful man. Of course, I can see and hear you . . . only, why are you standing so very . . . very far from me?"

"How far do I seem?"

"It's a long . . . long tunnel. You're so distant . . . but your voice is so sweet and so manly . . . I'd recognize it anywhere."

"Fräulein Eckstein!" Dr. Freud raised his voice, but the patient had already drifted back into her trance. "Fräulein Eckstein!" he called again.

"Fräulein Eckstein, Fräulein Eckstein!" the Fräulein's other voice cried out, seeming to emanate once again from inside her throat. The creature before us opened a single truculent eye. Dr. Freud's back stiffened.

"There's little you'll be able to do for her as long as I'm here," Ita said. "You know that, don't you?"

Dr. Freud exhaled heavily. "Yes, madam, I know that. And how long do you imagine that will be, if I may inquire?" He sounded as though he were almost speaking to a taxing house guest.

"How long?" Ita laughed.

"Yes, madam?"

"Why, forever, I suppose."

"Oh, I'm afraid I cannot permit that."

"But I have no intention of leaving."

"None whatsoever?"

Ita shook Fräulein Eckstein's head, rising upon one elbow in her bed. "Why, just look at these tiny ankles and this graceful neck! She's not the most refined of beauties, admittedly, but compared to the stubby, flat-chested drab in which I was formerly imprisoned, Eckstein is a playground of wonders. Oh God, I feel so . . . womanly!"

Dr. Freud raised a well-barbered eyebrow and sighed.

Ignoring him, Ita turned her attention to me. "Yankl," she said, "why don't you kiss me?"

Until that moment, I'd been happily overlooked, like an actor who, having played his scene, now watches the drama from the wings, in costume still, it's true, but no longer in character. Indeed, I was shocked to hear myself addressed and, like an actor, by a name no one in my daily life ever called me. "Kiss you?" I said, all out of breath, as though I'd been forced to rush back onstage to deliver my lines.

Ita pouted fetchingly. "You know you've been wanting to ever since you saw me at the Carl."

"That was *you,* Ita?"

"Why, of course it was me, silly boy. Now come over here and kiss me, my darling."

This feminine command produced in me something of a dither; and the truth is: had Dr. Freud not been present, I might have succumbed. Fräulein Eckstein's dulcet body, combined with Ita's vulgar sensuality, stirred me to the core. My practice confined me, most days, to my clinic, and I had rare occasion, either professionally or otherwise, to visit women in their nightclothes. Ita had saucily untied the laces of Fräulein Eckstein's gown, and inside her blouse front, the gentle chiaroscuro of her emancipated bust nearly robbed me of coherent speech. Also, the sweetness of being addressed by my childhood name in my native tongue by someone who knew me, indeed, who *loved* me, as a child was more than I could bear. Had the Sirens sung not a high wild sexual keening to the sailor Ulysses, but a lullaby in his native Greek, I'm certain no deckhands with their ears stuffed with swab could have prevented him from tearing loose the ropes that bound him to the mast and plunging into the perishing oblivion of his own orgiastic desires. Though my childhood had ended bitterly, Ita's purling Yankls and her Galician vowels returned it to me as though it were a cherished parcel I'd dropped in my haste to flee from home. Now I wanted nothing more than to erase the distance I'd placed between me and my former self, to collapse the intervening years, to enfold myself inside Ita's arms, finding in her bosom the lost caresses of my mother and my sisters and my wives. I flashed an angry look at Dr. Freud; the thought pounded in my brain: Why shouldn't I kiss her? By the laws of God and man, she's my wife, after all!

"No! Don't!" Dr. Freud said, grabbing me by my arm.

Had I actually taken a step towards her? Or had he read my mind?

"She's not your wife," he insisted. "In addition to everything we've discussed, and even if all the impossible things you believe to be true *were* true, still, the dead have no such claims upon the living."

"Let him go!" Ita shrieked, turning Fräulein Eckstein's hands into dainty fists, which she shook angrily in the air.

"Madam, I won't!"

"But he wants me!"

"No, madam, he does not want *you*, but the whole lost world of his youth!"

Naturally, in the cold light of day, everything seemed different. Though at first I could barely drag myself out of bed and had to force myself into the clinic, as the hours wore on, I realized that Dr. Freud was almost certainly correct. Clearly I couldn't trust my own impressions. Guilt had kept Ita's memory alive for too long in my conscience. Lying like a poisonous snake in the deepest coils of my mind was the guilty expectation that one day I would have to face her again, that one day I would have to stand trial before her for the harm that I, in my role as my father's victim, had caused her. Certainly, my aggrieved conscience made me a less than objective witness in evaluating Fräulein Eckstein's medical situation. Equally deluding was the unresolved business with my father. With the extraordinarily refined sensitivities granted to her by her disease, Fräulein Eckstein had divined my most vulnerable secrets and had told me everything she imagined I wanted to hear. Had she been a con artist or a spiritualist, and not an invalid, she no doubt would have already emptied my bank account.

No one, I had to remind myself, was denying the reality of the demonical possessions of yesteryear. Those poor sufferers *had* ranted and raved, they *had* taken on different identities, they *had* spoken in foreign languages and in different voices, exactly as the testimonies we have of them describe. Drs. Freud and Breuer's great contribution to the enlightenment of the human race was not to deny these sufferers their symptoms, but to see more deeply, and less naïvely, into their medical causes.

Dr. Freud insisted I join him the next evening at Fräulein Eckstein's bedside, and having persuaded myself that we were dealing with nothing more extraordinary than a complex symptom of an acute hysteria, I entered the sanatorium, my heart lighter than it had been when I'd left it the evening before. If these symptoms occasioned guilt and embarrassment in me, I told myself, it was not because I was facing the wife I'd abandoned, but because I was working without the rigorous psychological training Dr. Freud had imposed upon himself. I marveled at his ability to keep his head in the choppy waters of Fräulein Eckstein's delusions.

When I arrived, he was carefully massaging the patient's body, and so I entered her room and took a seat as far from her bed as I could, watching as Dr. Freud placed a faradic brush on Fräulein Eckstein's constricted arm.

"That hurts a little bit," she told him.

"I can stop it, if you wish."

"The massage is better, I think."

"Whichever you prefer."

"The massage," she said, and he began to softly stroke her epigastrium. "Ah, ah, yes, that's . . . that's so very nice."

"Here?" Dr. Freud murmured.

"A little lower."

"Now?"

"Lower still, I think."

"Good?"

"Ah, quite good, yes." She gave out a luxurious sigh and gently stroked Dr. Freud's hand as it caressed her. "May I ask you a question, Herr Doktor?"

"Of course, my Fräulein."

"Is my case enlightening to you?"

"Enlightening?"

"Psychoanalytically speaking, I mean."

"Quite."

"More enlightening than Dr. Breuer's famous case?"

"Oh, considerably so."

"And you'll publish it?"

"I hope to, yes."

"And it will make your name?"

"Who can say, Fräulein?"

"No, I'm sure that it will."

Dr. Freud drew in a deep breath. "But perhaps, in order for that to happen, you will tell me a bit more about the wedding."

"Ita's wedding?" Fräulein Eckstein asked.

"Who else's?"

It was only then that I realized Dr. Freud had been hypnotizing Fräulein Eckstein. As he continued to stroke her lower abdomen, she looked dreamily at me. She was in a partial trance, it seemed, and finally she pointed towards me with her chin. "Do you know how much I've suffered for that one?" Squinting, she looked me in the eye.

"Perhaps you'd like to tell me," Dr. Freud said.

The Fräulein was silent for a long moment.

"Of course, I knew the wedding was all wrong," she said at last. "I bleated my refusals after Reb Alter Nosn had left our house, until Grandfather finally had to beat me."

Fräulein Eckstein's eyes were fully closed, and Dr. Freud gave me a significant look: the patient had succumbed again to her condition seconde.

"But I thought you loved our Yankl," he whispered.

Fräulein Eckstein opened her eyes, and both she and Dr. Freud looked at me as they spoke to each other. Ita had fully emerged.

"I did, but I knew they were forcing him, you see."

"Ah," Dr. Freud said.

"Still . . ."

"Yes, madam?"

"I hoped I could make him a good wife."

"Of course," he said.

"That somehow he might come to love me, if he could see me as you see me now. Because you love me, don't you, Dr. Freud?"

With both hands, Dr. Freud grasped her hand. "Yes, madam. Very much so. I do."

She pressed his hand against her cheek and, quite suddenly, grew bitter. "But thanks to the hideous body in which God had confined me, I knew he would hate me, that he would blame me, when all I wanted was for him to love me." She dropped Dr. Freud's hand and turned on her side in the bed in order to address me directly. "I wanted you to love me, Yankl!"

"Must I really be involved in this, Dr. Freud?" I said from my distant perch.

"Patience, Dr. Sammelsohn," he cautioned me.

Fräulein Eckstein again took Dr. Freud's hand and held it to her breast. "I prayed for it all night and all day in my bleating sheep's tongue. I stood among the women in the synagogue, so that when they called out 'Amen,' I could repeat the word and have the merit of their prayers. Oh God, what a joke we were, Dr. Freud!"

"A joke, madam?"

"What a poisonous little tale Mendele could have made of us!"

"Ah, excellent." Dr. Freud nodded.

"An intelligent boy caught reading worldly books is punished by a forced marriage to the village idiot! Oh, but then even the great Mendele Moykher-Sforim wouldn't have seen what an idiot that idiot truly was. He would have painted me in tragic tones, Dr. Freud, but . . ."

"Yes, madam?"

"You have to understand: I wasn't a victim."

"No?"

"Because I conspired in my own humiliation, you see? Oh, I schemed along with the rest of them, placing myself in the center of their storm, fussing like a bride over every detail of her wedding, of her dress, of her bouquet. Do you remember the lilies, Yankl?"

Fräulein Eckstein turned to me. I nodded my head.

"His father spared no expense, Dr. Freud. My God, it was the most beautiful wedding Szibotya had ever seen! The synagogue lit by a thousand candles, the chupah made of Chinese silk."

"The chupah was *not* made of Chinese silk," I told Dr. Freud.

"The mayor, members of the Jewish council, the richest women and their husbands watched from the upper-story windows of their houses as our wedding procession marched down Szibotya's muddy little streets. Yankl's sisters, no doubt forced into it by their father, carried my train!"

"That much, I admit, is true."

"The evening before, Dr. Freud, my grandmother even took me to the mikve. Oh my God, I almost died! My soul nearly left my body! I never *dreamt* I'd come as a bride to the mikve, never dreamt a man would take me as his lover. What am I saying? It's all I dreamt about! But then"—her shoulders fell and she addressed me with an ugly sneer—"then I saw you beneath the chupah, Yankl, and I knew what a charade it all had been."

"A charade, madam?"

She lay again on her back, and gripping Dr. Freud's hand again, she placed it on her heart.

"I died in that moment, Dr. Freud."

With his other hand, he stroked her forehead.

"Died, madam?"

"I knew I was being murdered. And who was murdering me? You, Yankl? Or your father? Or perhaps my grandfather? Was he finally succeeding, twelve years after tying the shoestring around my neck? Or were my murderers the townspeople, the mayor, the men of the Jewish council and their obscene wives, or the rebbe, for that matter, none of whom dared to confront your father!"

Crossing her arms, she eyed me critically. Dr. Freud had retreated behind the head of her bed and, in the silence that followed, all I could hear was his pen scratching across the pages of his notebook.

"Are you listening to this, Dr. Freud?" Ita called over Fräulein Eckstein's shoulder, although she kept her eyes fixed on me.

"I'm listening, madam."

"Because there he was, biting his lip beneath the chupah. He could barely look at me, and when he did, Dr. Freud, all I saw was that same scheming I'd seen on his father's face the day he entered Grandfather's shop to negotiate with him for the bride. I tried to smile at him, but of course, what did I know from smiling? I must have looked like a gargoyle, my mouth pulled into a horrible grin. Jewish weddings are short, thank God, and it was over before I knew it, and we were being escorted by the assembly into a private room for our moment of seclusion. The table was set with the finest meats and wines, fruits all the way from Africa! I told myself: Though I'm repulsive, though I've nothing to compare with his beautiful Hindele, still, a boy is a boy, isn't that right? He'll consummate the marriage, I thought, if only out of spite: ruin the bride and throw her back into their faces—eh, Dr. Freud? And so I leaned against the sofa, with my rump raised towards him, the way I'd seen dogs do in the street. But of course, it was all horribly wrong."

"Ita," I said quietly, "I was thirteen. I knew nothing of such things. My marriage to Hindele had been completely chaste."

She wiped a tear from her eye. "Oh, this Eckstein!" She regarded her damp hand with an air of irritation. "She's so *sentimental*! She's been crying over me ever since I entered her." She dried her hands on the bed quilt. "Is this what a woman's heart is like? Or is it just the Viennese?"

A MOMENT PASSED, and a sly look crept across Fräulein Eckstein's face. "Do you know how I managed it, Yankl?"

"Managed what?" I asked with no small amount of exasperation.

"Getting inside of her. Do you have any idea?"

"Of course not."

"Shall I tell you then?"

I sighed. "If you wish."

"Unfortunately, as you'll one day discover, everything they told us is true."

"What do you mean, Ita? Everything they told us?"

"Oh, all those horrible old tales. You thought they just meant to scare us, but that's because you're clever. Just like your precious friend here, Dr. Freud, you know nothing except how clever you are! But in the true world, Yankl, in the world of truth, it's well known that a sinner like me can only enter a vessel that's already been cracked. Eckstein's vessel was cracked." She smirked. "And do you want to know why?"

"I think that's quite enough!" Dr. Freud roared. He stood and threw down his papers. "This is nothing but gossip and petty slander, madam, and I beg you to desist from saying anything further!"

"But it's all part of my case history, isn't it, Herr Doktor?"

"You and I know what you're referring to. That is sufficient."

"Yankl," Ita whispered to me, "Eckstein abuses herself."

"Oh, cruelest of harpies!" Dr. Freud nearly screamed.

"Ah," Ita laughed, "he speaks to me as though I existed! I'm flattered!"

"You're nothing but a wretched incubus! You know that, don't you?"

Without going into vulgar detail, I will only report that Ita was not shy in using Fräulein Eckstein, along with a pillow, a hand mirror, a hairbrush, and a candle, in a graphic demonstration of her claims.

"Help me get her back into bed, Dr. Sammelsohn!" Dr. Freud exclaimed when Ita, having made her point, left the Fräulein in an exhausted, exhilarated heap upon the floor.

"It's nothing that she and I haven't gone over a thousand and one times during her analytic hours," Dr. Freud confessed to me as he took her under the arms and I lifted her legs, and together we carried her back into bed. "Though I'm sorry you had to witness it. I think our work is over for the night."

"No!" Ita shouted. "*I* will decide when our session is over!" She kicked off the covers we had so carefully tucked in for her and stood on her knees on the bed, clearly not the same woman who had just spent her vital energies so frivolously.

"Fine, madam," Dr. Freud said, hectored, exasperated. "Continue. As you wish. Certainly. Please."

"However, Ita." I could hold my tongue no longer, and I stood at the foot of her bed in order to challenge her. "You said Fräulein Eckstein's deviance was a sufficient opening to allow a wretched sinner in. But how is it that you're a sinner at all? What sins can a village idiot perform?"

"Not many, it's true," she said, as though charmed by this challenge. "Sinning takes imagination and concentration, two traits the faulty machinery of my brain couldn't quite manufacture, isn't that right? And yet, somehow, I managed to perform the blackest sin of all."

"No, Ita, you didn't!"

"I couldn't have done it without your help, Yankele—thank you very much—or without the help of the entire town, for that matter. But surely one of your sisters wrote to you about it?"

"My father forbade all such communication."

"Then you truly didn't know?"

"There were things I felt it best to leave in the past."

"Things, Yankl?"

"Forgive my rudeness, Ita. Not things, but people, events."

She gave out a small, harsh laugh. Leaning forward on her knees, she placed her hands on her thighs and gave me a bitter look. "Then let me fill you in, my darling husband. Let me fill you in."

• • •

ALERT TO THIS summons, Dr. Freud returned to his paper and his pen
behind the bed; I returned to my chair.

"You remember the wedding feast they laid out to mock you?"

I started to answer her, but found that my voice had fled.

"Oh, I'd never seen such food in all my life, Dr. Freud! I didn't understand the insult Reb Alter Nosn had intended with it, you see. The
wheels and cogs of my brain couldn't decipher irony. I saw only a delightful wedding feast, paid for by the man whose secret companion I'd
been on his lonely sojourns in the forests. This is how he repays me for
my faithfulness, I thought. But then you didn't know that man, did you,
Yankl?"

"I knew only the abrasive pietist, concerned lest one yod or tittle of
the law should pass away."

"Mm." She nodded. "I watched in amazement as you stuffed as much
food as you could into that little sack of yours. And when you taught me
those awful slogans, you were no better, really, than your father. I was a
stick you two used to pummel each other. If there's anything I've learned
in these dark realms, Dr. Freud, meeting other souls who lived in opposition to the will of Heaven and who, in death, oppose it still, it's this: evil
is committed by people who, having been harmed themselves, feel justified in harming others. On our wedding night—ha! despite everything, I
still think of it as that! So let me be more accurate: on the day your father
rubbed your nose in your sins, using me as a piece of filth, you saw me
as no better, and why should you have? Oh, if only you could have seen
me playing my part, Yankl! Sitting alone, nibbling the few figs you'd
seen fit to leave me. Didn't they fit into your sack or did you actually for
a moment consider my hunger? I'd been fasting all day, in the manner
of a good, pious bride, fasting to atone for my sins and for those of my
husband, so that I could come to you with all the innocence of a baby,
enter the marriage newly born like a baby entering the world. On the
other side of the door, I could hear the klezmorim playing one tuneless
tune after another. How many guests remained in the great hall, waiting
to see the joke through to its end? Did anyone suspect the denouement
you'd contrived? I'd exhausted myself in tears long before I heard a commotion stirring up on the other side of the door. I could hear question

marks gathering there, as though in a printer's bin. Preparing to meet the wedding horde, I dried my eyes on the hem of my gown and finally, after much knocking and pounding, the door flew open.

"With your father and my grandfather at its head, a quorum of men entered the room. Perhaps they'd expected to find me with my throat slashed or the two of us self-poisoned, although I doubt it: we were Jews, and though a legalistic cruelty isn't beyond us, murder and suicide are quite beyond our Pale. No doubt such were their pious fantasies that they expected to find us reconciled to our new state, you happily chastened and no longer playing the rebellious son.

"'Where's Ya'akov?' your father demanded, and it was with all the concentration and intention I could muster that I didn't repeat what he had just said, but instead, I squinted my eyes and summoned forth to my lips what you had told me to say: 'Unkull guh lee-ber-ate de mah-sez, et cetera, et cetera. Sh-sh-shay-mmm uhn ye-e-u pi-yus . . . frowds!' For some reason, this phrase was quite easy on the tongue, and I couldn't stop repeating it. I must have been shrieking it still when Grandfather stepped forward and slapped me in the face. Your father rebuked him, then left me in his care. 'But I don't want her!' he shouted at your father's back. 'She's your daughter-in-law now! You take care of her!' Your father was already at the window like a police inspector surveying the scene of the crime.

"'Where is Yankl?' your mother said, entering the room. 'Gone,' one of your sisters said. 'He's gone?' 'The boy's gone,' your father told her.

"It was as though you had done something completely outside the realm of the possible, as though you'd become a Moor or turned yourself into a bird. After all, Jewish sons do not run away, just as Jewish fathers do not force their children to do anything that is not ultimately for their own good.

"'אוי לי,' your father cried, 'שהחרבי את ביתי והגליתי את בני' *Woe is me that I have destroyed my house and exiled my children* (BT Berachos 3a).

"The look on his face was unbearable to see: it was the face of a man who'd gone too far and who now understood that his actions were irrevocable. Far worse was the look on your mother's face: bitter, accusing, naked, perhaps for the first time, of all illusion. She saw her husband as she'd never seen him before: as the man who had now irreversibly embittered her life. If, in this instance, I, a mere village idiot, could see their entire life passing between them, as though in a moment of divine judgment, what did the others in our little mob of outraged citizens see with their fuller powers of comprehension? The exasperation knitted into your mother's brow seemed to say: *It's bad enough, oh, it's bad enough, all these years, you've gone out into the forest like a madman with your poems, and we humored you; you've hungered after that repulsive little troll Blume Levanthal and I ignored it; but now you've driven my only son from our house, and I can no longer bear you!*

"You could almost hear the one small chamber of her heart still open with affection towards him buckling. He seemed crushed. His beard seemed to whiten before our eyes. The hook of his scholar's stoop, always rounded like a question mark, ceased signifying intellectual inquiry and now broadcast dumbfounded incomprehension. As for myself, I became aware of the fact that everyone in the room was looking at me. I understood I was a problem without a solution, a bloody mark upon their lintel signifying to the Angel of Life that he may as well pass over their houses and withhold his blessings. To your father, I was proof of what an ornery fool he was. To your mother, I was a hostage who would never be redeemed, held in captivity forever against the return of her son. I seemed to have exchanged a family who wished me dead for a family who wished I'd never been born. I was moving up in the world, but at that moment that thought was of little comfort to me. All I could think of was you, Yankl. Yes, you! Oh, how I loved you! How I wanted you! Oh, and the children I wanted to give you! As tempers reached their boiling point, as accusations and recriminations, long simmering, bubbled over, while no one was looking, indeed while your father and mother were arguing over what was to be done with me, I slipped out. Nobody saw me, or if they did, no one alerted anyone else, and I made my way to the river. For where else do heartbroken girls go?"

"Ita," I said softly, "tell me you didn't."

"Drowning myself was easy, Yankele. No one had ever taught me how to swim, and I'd heard enough love stories to know that at the moment

I jumped into the waters from a rocky ledge, you would appear on the horizon to save me."

"You *drowned* yourself? Ita!"

Fräulein Eckstein's face reddened with the memory. "The water was cold, and I was crying, of course. I was a foolish girl. Crying as the water covered me like a goose-down quilt on a cold winter's night. 'This will be my wedding bed,' I told myself dramatically. 'These hard river rocks will be my pillows.' I grew drowsy and, for a moment, I slept."

Dr. Freud lifted his eyes from his notes. His pen stopped scratching. We both waited for her to continue.

"But only for a moment." She smiled, in triumph, like Scheherazade, content to hold her listeners in a chasm of silence between one part of her story and the next.

"And after that?" I finally said.

"Well, after that," she said, "I was no longer cold, nor wet, nor even in the river. I sat upon its banks, watching the poor, wretched girl below me. She looked like a rag doll that had been tossed into a puddle by a careless child. 'Who is that unfortunate girl?' I asked, not expecting a reply, and so I was stunned to hear a voice very near my ear whispering, 'She doesn't concern you anymore.'"

CHAPTER 16

And who was it who spoke these words to you?"

"Oh, Yankl, I'd never seen anyone so beautiful!"

"Yes, but who was it?" I insisted.

"Impossible to say!" Once again, she was on her knees on the bed, her arms spread wide apart, describing the scene. "Because the being had four faces."

"Four faces? Ita!"

"A man's, a woman's, a lion's, and a child's — oh, and magnificent fiery wings!"

I glanced across Fräulein Eckstein's sickbed and met Dr. Freud's skeptical expression. With his eyebrows raised, he seemed to be stroking the inside of his cheek with his tongue. Ita didn't notice, however, and continued with her story.

"It dropped its cloak about my shoulders and pulled me away from the water.

"'There's no time to mourn now,' the woman said.

"When I refused to budge, the lion produced a mirror from inside the cloak, and the child held it to my face.

"'Look,' the bearded man commanded me. And, oh, Yankl!" Ita raised her hands to her cheeks. "The face in the mirror had no features. It was a radiant, honeyed flame.

"'Leave this,' the lion said, puffing out its chest and pointing with its chin towards the rag doll in the river. Her wedding dress had grown brown in the water. It looked as though it'd been steeped in tea.

"'She's no longer your concern, nor mine, nor ours,' they said all at once, their wings rustling with fire.

"'This is who you are,' the man said, tapping his finger on the mirror.

"I looked again at the rag doll and then at the mirror. 'Oh, if Yankl could only see me like this,' I thought. In response, the woman pronounced a word that sounded as though it were formed completely of vowels, a word I recalled never having heard before, but which I nevertheless recognized as my own name."

"Can you transcribe it for us?" Dr. Freud asked.

"I'll try."

Taking a piece of paper and his pen from him, Ita curled her tongue against her upper lip—she had never been taught to write—and scratched out in a very childish hand the name by which she'd been addressed: אַאְעְאֵאָאֶעֶעֶווֹיא.

"Something like that, I think."

"Hm," Dr. Freud said.

"The man stroked his beard, the woman crossed her arms, the lion shook his head. 'Child,' he roared, 'come along with us. You mustn't resist.'

"'Yankl is gone,' the man said, and the child piped in, 'Come on, אַאְעְאֵאָאֶעֶעֶווֹיא, you're in enough trouble as it is.' But still I refused."

"You refused, Ita? But why?"

"I may have spat in God's face, Yankl, I may have thrown away the life our Father in Heaven had given me, but I was a bride, and a bride who was still a virgin. I *too* had my claims, and I wasn't going to be denied!

"'Oh dear, oh dear, here we go again,' the lion roared unhappily.

"'If you persist in this, אַאְעְאֵאָאֶעֶעֶווֹיא,' the woman warned, 'the horde will soon descend.'

"'The horde?' I said.

"'In the morning,' the child told me, 'you'll hunger for evening. In the evening, you'll pray for dawn.'

"This was disagreeable news indeed, but still, I kept my resolve. 'Is there no place then,' I asked, 'where I may shelter in the meantime while waiting for Yankl to join me?'

"'Each time we meet'—the bearded man sighed—'you ask the right wrong questions.'

"'We've met before?'

"'Oh, many, many times.'

"'Short lives and violent deaths seem to be your métier,' the lion roared.

"'We meet as though between the acts of a very long play,' the bearded man said, and the woman added: 'Although not so long usually in your case.'

"'About this sheltering,' I said.

"'Oh, אַאְעְעָאָ אָעְ עְעוּוִיא, don't be foolish now.'

"'Tell me!' I insisted.

"'As we are bound to the truth, we shall tell you.' The man instructed me: 'You may shelter in a stone, in an animal, or in another human being, though I promise you you'll find no peace there. You laugh?' he said to me. 'You think this is amusing?'

"I looked again, knowing it was for the last time, at the body of that poor drowned girl, lying among the river rocks. 'Poor Ita,' I thought. 'Well, this ended badly,' I said.

"'It *will* end badly,' the bearded man corrected me. 'While you continue to resist, things are far from over.'

"'Bless me then, angel?' I asked them shyly.

"'Alas, poor אַאְעְעָאָ אָעְ עְעוּוִיא,' the woman said, 'there isn't time.'

"It chilled me to the bone to see the angelic being raise all eight of its eyes and gaze past my shoulder. I turned to look at what they were seeing."

"And what were they seeing, Ita?" I said.

"Oh, Yankl, on the horizon, under a purple sky, moving as though in a dirty rain cloud towards the promontory upon which we all stood, was the horde."

She stared into the space before her, as though witnessing it all again. "I'd never seen such a rude and murderous crew, certainly not in the previous world, with their dirty black wings and their sharp claws and the hideous insignias inked all over their reptilian skins.

"'Are these angels as well?' I asked.

"'Of a sort,' the man said.

"'Demons,' the woman elaborated.

"'A subcategory,' the child explained.

"'Good-bye for now, darling אַאְעְעָאָ אָעְ עְעוּוִיא,' the lion roared. 'If I were you and if you sincerely mean to resist . . .'

"'Yes, angel? Counsel me, please!'

"'. . . I'd run!' said he.

"In a twinkling, he or she or they or it were gone, and I was left to face the advancing horde alone."

Ita swallowed and wet her lips. "Oh, what a sight these dark angels were, Yankl! Their noses were so long, they drooped to the middle of their chests. Flames shot out of their nostrils. Their burning cudgels had charred their skins. Their sooty wings beat at their dirty backs. The black leather harness each wore was studded with spikes and gleaming metal bits. Among them were men and women, brothers and sisters it seemed from the similarity of their features, and only because the laws of forbidden intercourse do not apply to angels was I able to get away from them. For just as they'd spotted me, just as the chase was about to begin, each of these dogmen, their uncircumcised members grown as long as curved scimitars at the smell of their frightened prey, grabbed a sister by the hair and threw her to the ground where, growling and biting, they mounted her for their pleasure, three or four brothers to a sister, as the women were in the minority. The other males stopped to watch, laughing their cruel laughter, pulling their brothers off and replacing them when their patience wore thin. Immortal, they seemed to delight in thrashing one another to within an inch of their eternal lives, slitting open one another's bellies, for example, and yanking out one another's intestines, bashing one another's heads in, the recipient of the blows more aroused, it seemed, than his tormentor.

"How much of this horror can I relate to you? Only one more thing: as I stood watching this terrible sight, these dark angels kept their eyes, seven to a skull, fastened upon me, man and woman alike, as if to tell me that it didn't matter, that they had all the time in the world, that I was going nowhere and could never run far or fast enough to elude them. And yet they were clearly urging me on, if only for the sport of it, I thought. What pleasure would there be in it for them if I submitted? I understood as much and, when they contrived to look away, their attention drawn to the yelping of one of their sisters as she climaxed, flailing beneath the weight of her brothers—two of whom sat with their knees upon her outstretched arms and two upon her outstretched legs—I fled. I fled, knowing that my capture was inevitable, knowing that if they caught me, they would abuse me horribly, hurling me from one end of the universe to the other, like a ball in a game of toss. My escape was from any reasonable point of view futile. Is there any place where God's will may be overturned? But the dead are only human, and are therefore subject to self-deception, isn't that correct, Dr. Freud? And so I ran. Or rather, they let me run. The pleasure for the pursuer is not in the capture, but in the heart-thumping terror of the chase, fear making sweeter the lashings and the beatings. I ran, the horde on my heels, my back lashed by the teeth of their whips, their garlicky breath in my ears, until suddenly in my terror I recalled the words of my guardian—'In a stone, in an animal, in another human being'—and I jumped inside a granite crucifix stationed over a grave. At least here, they were powerless to touch me. Unfortunately, though, I couldn't bear the idolatrous spirits inhabiting the stone, and I leapt into a rock. Lifetimes later, it seemed, this rock was thrown by a small boy into a stable. My presence there drove the horses mad. One beast, in its fright, beat against the rock with its hooves until I was driven out. The punishing horde was waiting for me still, I knew, but somehow I was able to dive headfirst into the entrails of a cow. I hoped that its slaughter by a kosher butcher would at last atone for my sins and end this long, mad dash, the ultimate point of which I was beginning to forget. The stench of the beast was intolerable, however, and I jumped into a horse, and when I overheard the coachman saying he was traveling to Vienna the next day, I couldn't believe my good fortune. All of a sudden, I remembered the object of my desire."

"Which was?"

"Why, you, of course, Yankl! You! I was nearer to you than I had ever been."

I blushed at these words. "*I* was your goal?" I said.

According to Ita, it was not out of spite or rebellion that she'd refused to submit to the Heavenly Tribunal. Neither was she afraid of the punishments waiting for her there. She knew what she had done: she was a suicide, a sinner as black as any, blacker than most, in fact, and although she might believe she was driven to it by other hands, she was realistic enough to know that, as a defense, this tack would be laughed out of the Heavenly Court by the Heavenly Judges, who, unlike their human counterparts, could not be moved to pity. Submit, she knew, endure the shaming fires of Gehenna, and be cleansed, made new and as white as a freshly laundered shirt. (The more time she spent in the corridor between lives, the clearer her memories of her previous visits became. How clearly she now recalled the steam-cleaning each soul receives at the end of its sentence, the great, steaming machinery through which each is pressed, before being hung to dry, wrinkleless and crisp, and placed into a zygote by the same angelic hands that secrete the scent inside each rose.) It would have been easy to turn herself in, to surrender, if it weren't for the thinnest hopes she still had of attaining her goal, which was (I blush to transcribe this): me. When at last the coachman arrived in Vienna, she knew her wanderings were nearing their end.

Leaning forward in bed, she exclaimed: "Don't ask me how I found your Fräulein Eckstein, Yankl. Accept that the Hand of God aids saints and sinners alike. What in a novel might be called coincidence is merely the invisible machinery of Heaven awkwardly revealing itself, and there I was. How glorious is our Lord, Yankl; though I spit in His face, He opens His hand to satisfy the desire of every living thing. Fräulein Eckstein's hand opened to her desire as well, as I explained earlier, indeed as I demonstrated, and I slipped in thereby, lodging between the blooming rose of her old maidenhood and the storehouse of mulch and dreck. In life, I'd learned to expect little, and so I was happy there, until one evening — oh, one glorious evening! — she accompanied her mother to the Carl. And that's where I saw you. Yes, my love! Way, way, way up in the fourth or fifth gallery. And I knew it was only a matter of time before I would draw you to me, using Fräulein Eckstein as an old paillard might a young boy to sexually ensnare the child's mother."

Ita looked out brazenly from inside Fräulein Eckstein's face. "And the rest you more or less know," she said with a little shrug.

I looked at Dr. Freud, seated behind the head of her bed. He wore his Tarock face, letting nothing show. How absurd we seemed, he and I, how ill prepared for such a cosmic turn of events, with our late-empire beards, and comical pince-nez and other turn-of-the-century sartorial fripperies. Ita, on the other hand, seemed as happy as a hypochondriac to have two such attentive suitors at her bedside.

"And so there we are," she said, leaning back comfortably into her pillows.

THERE WE WERE indeed.

"Do you mind if . . . if I take a sip of your water?" I said to Fräulein Eckstein, or to Ita, or to whomever. What did it matter? I'd asked only out of politeness, and neither of them responded. My hands trembled as I poured a glass from their bedside pitcher. (Yes, *their*. It was impossible for me to think of them now as other than two souls residing in a single body. They were like flatmates who'd outgrown the small apartment they nevertheless continued to share.) "Sorry," I said, bending down with one of Dr. Freud's massage towels to mop up the water I'd spilled.

"Dr. Sammelsohn, why don't you sit down!" Dr. Freud said sharply. "Either the water will dry of itself or we'll send for a nurse to sop it up."

"Yes . . . thank you," I said. "I think I will." I sat and brought the glass to my mouth, sipping inexpertly and choking as a result.

My life felt like an ill-fitting suit someone else had picked out for me; I barely recognized myself in it: Was I truly the sort of man who could drive his wife to murder herself?

"Stop luxuriating in your guilt," Dr. Freud said to me.

I raised my eyes to find him and Ita (or was it Fräulein Eckstein?) staring at me, Dr. Freud with his invasive gaze: the seer, the knower of open secrets, the diviner of poorly hidden things. It was alarming to find myself the object of their attentions. Of all the characters in this strange drama, I imagined myself far from being its protagonist. Wasn't I the most minor of players here: an insignificant consultant called in by the great doctor; a forgettable suitor to the mysterious patient; a husband for no more than a few hours to the avenging Fury; the wayward, problematical son to the extraordinarily successful businessman and scholar? Who was I to find myself the author of everyone's sorrows? The answer resounded simply and clearly: You are Ya'akov Yosef Sammelsohn, murderer of your wife.

"May I see you in the passageway outside?" Dr. Freud said, gesturing with his head. I rose from my chair, knocking into the table as I did and tipping over the glass I'd left there. The rest of the water ran off the table onto the chair and dribbled onto the floor. Torn between honoring Dr. Freud's wishes and mopping up the spill, I hesitated so that Dr. Freud had no choice but to bark: "Leave it, Dr. Sammelsohn, leave it! I need to speak with you this instant!"

In the passageway, he lit a cigar.

"Ah," he sighed extravagantly. "Nicotine is a slow poison, and yet, in moments of extreme agitation, a poison can also be a balm. Would you care for one?"

"No, thank you," I said. I couldn't imagine anything less agreeable.

Dr. Freud blew a poisoned fume into my face. "Well, I'm done with them now, you know" — he patted his breast pocket — "and carry them only for emergencies."

I didn't know what to say. Was he deluded? joking? mad? The man smoked incessantly! He smoked like a badly ventilated stove! His clothes reeked of tobacco and sulfur, his teeth were a sooty grey, the pores of his face were coated with a translucent lather of nicotine. Identical to the writer's callus on the middle finger of his right hand was a smoker's callus on the middle finger of the left. A close inspection of his coattails and his pant legs revealed a thousand tiny burns. I'd never in the course of our acquaintance seen him without a cigar, and yet he held rigidly to the fiction of his abstinence, and until that very moment — I was shocked to realize — I'd never thought to question this fiction myself. Why, if you had asked me, I would have told you that, yes, except on the rare festive occasion or under duress to calm his jangled nerves, Dr. Freud is no longer a smoker. And so, when he told me, "Dr. Sammelsohn, there *is* no Ita. The woman you imagine in your fervid guilt-filled fantasies having killed is naught but a complex symptom of hysteria," I was, for the first time in our association, inclined to disbelieve him.

"You can't tell me I wasn't speaking to my wife."

"To your former wife, if indeed she is dead, and dead by her own hand, which I very much doubt."

"But you heard her yourself!"

He clicked his tongue with a condescending clack. "You have no idea how real these delusions may seem. The appearance of a second personality is often, if not always, presented in a deceptive manner, its pathogenic material belonging to an intelligence not inferior to the patient's normal ego, but I assure you, Dr. Sammelsohn, even were I inclined to accept as real the possibility of a dybbuk possession, I'm experienced enough in these matters to distinguish between an actual person, be she alive or dead, and an hysterically induced condition seconde. When I say that the pathogenic material behaves like a foreign body, and that its treatment proceeds, too, like the removal of a foreign body from living tissue, I assure you, Herr Doktor, the foreign body I have in mind is a tumor, and not a dybbuk!"

"But—"

"No, no, you see, you must learn to listen to the discourse *within* the discourse. When Fräulein Eckstein, speaking in the voice of Ita, confesses that she conspired in her own humiliations, she has told us everything."

"How so?"

"Well, what was Ita after?"

"Love," I said.

"And whom does Fräulein Eckstein love?"

"Why, you, of course."

"And what could be more humiliating than these hysterical antics she's putting herself through. You see? Only ask yourself: can you imagine a more efficient means for keeping me at her bedside?"

"But—but—but," I stammered, gesturing towards the wall behind which Fräulein Eckstein lay, "the things she knew . . . Fräulein Eckstein couldn't have known them!"

"Oh, well, there are more things in Heaven and Earth, Horatio, et cetera, et cetera, and the geographies of the mind, believe me, Dr. Sammelsohn, are stranger than any Baedeker might reveal."

"So I didn't kill her?" I asked meekly.

"Send a telegram home to your sisters, if you doubt me, inquiring after the health of your wife, Ita."

"I've resolved to do as much already."

"Although, I assure you, there's no need."

"Still."

"And if you're intent on this foolish gesture, may I dare to counsel you, as an older friend?"

"Yes. Please. Certainly."

"Along with the telegram, send a get." Here, Dr. Freud meant a rabbinic decree of divorce. "Divorce yourself from this poor girl. Remove the twin albatrosses of responsibility and guilt that hang around your neck. Stop paying interest on your father's debt. He's the moral bankrupt, not you. Do yourself, as well as the girl, this service, and I promise you, you shan't regret it."

"But of course you're right."

"What stuff and nonsense they've filled your head with." He touched my hair affectionately. "Mine, too, of course. Oh, yes, I had a religious upbringing—strict, too—a Hebrew teacher, Hammerschlag by name, the whole bolt of cloth. But with the tools of scientific objectivity, you understand, I've been able to put it all behind me. And when you witness my curing of Fräulein Eckstein with the young science of psychoanalysis, you, too, will know beyond a shadow of a doubt that dybbuks, demons, ibburs, and such like, are nothing more than the fairy tales we use to enslave ourselves to our own fears. Why, religion is nothing but a prison house constructed by the inmates themselves; the clerics, the guards we appoint above ourselves. Man will do anything not to confront the empty, howling wilderness that is the universe God abandoned long ago, this terrifying no-man's land filled with chaos and desolation."

Dr. Freud blew another choking plume of smoke into my face.

"I'll send the telegram first thing," I said, coughing.

He didn't quite laugh at me, but a subtle smirk destroyed the handsome symmetry of his face. "Do," he said, amused.

Quietly, he opened Fräulein Eckstein's door and peered in. Standing on tiptoe, I looked over his shoulder and saw that Fräulein Eckstein had returned to her previous stuporose state: limbs rigid, mouth opened, tongue protruding.

"We've done enough for one evening, I think," Dr. Freud said. "I'll only just slip in and give her a posthypnotic suggestion that upon awakening tomorrow, she will remember nothing of what she has told us. You should get some sleep, Doktor. You look done in. And besides, it's nearly day."

He was correct. The once darkened windows of the hallway were beginning to glimmer with light.

CHAPTER 17

I was as good as my word. After a few hours' sleep, I ventured out, freshly shaven, to the telegraph office, and by late morning, I'd received a reply from my sisters, confirming everything Ita had told us the night before:

SZIBOTYA, 5 MARCH 1895

DARLING BROTHER, IT IS WITH GREAT SORROW THAT WE INFORM YOU BELATEDLY OF THE DEATH OF YOUR GOOD WIFE ITA MAY GOD FORGIVE HER BY HER OWN HAND FOLLOWING YOUR WEDDING. BLESSED BE EVEN NOW THE TRUE JUDGE. FATHER HAS FORGIVEN NO ONE IN THE MATTER INCLUDING HIMSELF. WITH LOVING REGARD, YOUR SISTERS, GITL, GOLDE, RUKHL, REYZL, FEYGE, KHAYKE, & SORE DVORE

I presented the telegram to Dr. Freud at Landtmann's that evening, where he'd invited me to dine. "I was prepared to follow your advice," I said, "but as it turns out, a get will not be necessary."

"No? And why is that?" he said, digging with his fork into his Spätzle.

I could almost not pronounce the words. "Because Ita is dead, I'm afraid, and by her own hand—just as Fräulein Eckstein's dybbuk claimed—hours after our wedding. As you can see, this telegram"—I nearly waved the thing in his face—"which I received not more than a few hours ago, confirms her story in its every detail."

Dr. Freud took the telegram and said nothing. Having read through it, he seemed to forget that it was in his hands, until, finding it there, he read it again. Finally he spoke. "Dr. Sammelsohn," he said, a shrewd look bruising his face, "I feel confident in ruling out a practical joke on your part, but can I be as confident in doing so on the part of your sisters?"

I was appalled. "I assure you they are not people inclined towards such cruel humor."

He was pensive. "One cannot, I suppose, in good conscience suspect the telegraph operators of such an elaborate ruse."

"No," I said, reaching out to retrieve the telegram—the document, one of the rare communiqués I'd received from my family in the years since I'd left Szibotya, was precious to me—but Dr. Freud ignored my hand.

"How much pleasure the retreat from reason gives us," he said, shaking his head. "How happily we surrender to the allurements of sheer nonsense." He gazed into the middle distance before focusing his eyes on me. "Do you realize how long this occultish business has been going on? Why, since the days of the Bible! No, only listen to this!" He shifted through the pages of his little notebook. "Both Kings Saul and Ahab were said to be possessed by evil spirits, and the Gospels several times refer to the casting out of the same. First-century Galilee seemed to have witnessed a pandemic of demonical possession. Even Josephus describes an account of a Rabbi Eleazar withdrawing the spirit of a dead sinner through the unfortunate victim's nostrils by applying a ring that contained a magical herb to his nose."

"He took the dybbuk out through the victim's nostrils?"

"Yes, I wrote to Wilhelm immediately, of course." Dr. Freud breathed on the lenses of his glasses, befogging them and wiping them clean. "Don't be taken in, Dr. Sammelsohn. Everywhere, these stories are the same, the symptoms exactly as we find them in hysteria: frenzy, contortions, trembling; the revelations of dark crimes and scandalous tales; the exposure of local secrets. A rabbi or a healer is called in, and finally the spirit, supposedly homesick for the divine realms, agrees to depart and undergo her rightful punishments, and when she does—ah, and here is the essential thing, Dr. Sammelsohn, the essential thing that gives away the entire game—when she does, the route of her departure must be strictly negotiated, lest it wreak havoc upon the body of its captive."

"I don't understand," I said. "How does that give the game away?"

Dr. Freud lowered his voice and made certain no one was listening to our conversation. "Well," he said quietly, "according to all this nonsense, a spirit will often insist upon leaving via the route that causes the greatest damage to the organs: through the eye, resulting in blindness; through the mouth, with a great shattering of teeth; through the ear, deafness; or even through the throat. Often, a plate or a window will break, as proof that the spirit is departing."

"Yes? And? So?"

"But surely you're not so naïve! How can one read a fairy tale of this sort as anything other than a transparent attempt on the part of the pious to cover up the violence wreaked upon the poor hysteric by her so-called healers? My impression is that they raised the stakes against her, taking sexual advantage or otherwise physically harming her, until she was forced to feign a cure simply to save her own skin."

"And the proof of that is?"

"Why, the clues are everywhere."

"For example?"

"For example: while it's apparently demeaning for the soul to leave through the anus—and you're perfectly aware of the biblical prohibitions regarding anal intercourse, which would perhaps have given even our abusers pause—it's said to be unclear whether the genitals are suitable for that purpose. In one purported case, a spirit exiting in this regard created a monstrous hemorrhage. Here, clearly, the patient was violently raped. There's no other explanation for it. Another declared its intention of leaving the body of its captive only on the wedding night during the nuptial cohabitation. Here, the patient was obviously coerced into a marriage she herself did not want or seek. And often enough, though the cure is reported to be successful, the patient fails to survive it."

"And so you're suggesting?"

"I'm suggesting nothing, Dr. Sammelsohn. As a scientist, I'm stating unequivocally that these so-called dybbuk possessions were nothing but the last cry of outrage on the part of the victim against her abusers after a long history of misuse, and it's now well known that such treatment is often the *cause* of psychopathology."

"And has Fräulein Eckstein been subjected to such misuse?"

"Of that, I cannot speak to you."

"No, of course not," I said.

I was silent for a moment. Dr. Freud gave me a severe look. "May I be blunt with you, Dr. Sammelsohn?"

"Go on," I said.

He leaned in towards me. "No, it's only that I'm wondering if there isn't some reason that you might prefer it if Fräulein Eckstein's case were not one of hysteria, but indeed rather one of demonical possession."

"On the contrary!" I sputtered. "I have every reason to hope otherwise!"

"Yes, I understand that, and yet you appear constantly to be advocating against that very hope."

"Well . . ." I said to no purpose.

"When one would imagine, given the circumstances, that you'd be clutching at any of the many scientific straws I'm constantly providing you."

"Yes," I admitted, "it's . . . mysterious . . . quite, even to myself."

"I can only speculate, of course," Dr. Freud said, "but I imagine, if we probed deeply, we'd find buried beneath this refusal of yours to submit to reason a long-cherished childhood wish. When reason becomes an impediment to pleasure, I think you'll find that it's the first thing a man throws overboard."

He paid the check and began gathering up his notes.

"In any case," he said, "I hope to make an end of this wretched case tonight."

AT THE SANATORIUM, following her bran bath, Dr. Freud pressed his hand against Fräulein Eckstein's forehead and, hypnotizing her, commanded Ita to speak. "Frau Sammelsohn," he summoned her. Though I'd resolved, out of scientific scruple, to banish my belief in the authenticity of Fräulein Eckstein's condition seconde, Dr. Freud's addressing her by this name continued to embarrass me, reminding me, as it did, of the many ways in which I'd harmed Ita while she was yet alive. Amid a rippling of neuralgic facial tics, Ita swam to the surface of the pond, so to speak, animating Fräulein Eckstein's face. She looked like a sleeper waking, uncertain where she was. Seeing Dr. Freud, she scowled however, and things took an ugly turn.

"Oh, Yankl," she cried, "what does this horrid man want from me now?"

"Good evening, madam," Dr. Freud said.

She placed a hand distractedly upon her forehead. "I can barely re-member half of what we talked about last night! He's making me forget things! He's forcing me to forget you, Yankl!"

"He only wishes to aid you, Ita. His motives are charitable, I assure you."

"But he's an unbeliever!"

"Rather a freethinker, madam," Dr. Freud corrected her, "my thoughts free to go either way."

"Isn't my presence here proof enough of the unseen world?"

"I admit you're highly convincing," Dr. Freud said. He was a well-oiled flatterer when he wanted to be. Clasping his hands together, eager to be done with her, he next said, "However, the hour grows late, and if we're of like minds, perhaps you'll permit me to proceed with the cure."

"The cure! Your precious cure! That's all you care about, isn't it?"

"But surely you have no wish to remain in your current state?"

"How many times do I have to tell you, Doktor? *I am not ill!*"

"Not ill, madam, no, but it's abnormal for you to remain here, not only for Fräulein Eckstein, about whose welfare I'm certain you're concerned, but for yourself as well."

"I'm happy where I am, thank you very much."

"And these paralyzing attacks from these so-called angels of destruc-tion—they don't concern you?"

"There's nothing you can do to alleviate them."

"Are you so certain?"

"Is the doctor Moses that he speaks directly to God?"

"Not Moses, no, but a humble neuropath, and yet I know a thing or two."

"Oh God, Yankl! Get rid of this horse's ass! There are things I need to discuss with you in privacy."

I felt compelled to rise from my chair each time Ita addressed me, like a prisoner in the docks, a murderer finally caught and captured and tried. "There's nothing you can't tell me in the presence of Dr. Freud, Ita," I said. "He's here with no design other than the restoration of pro-portional health to everyone involved in the affair."

I sat.

"What are you paying him?" she asked.

I rose again. "The Ecksteins are seeing to his fees."

"Oh God, why do they waste their money! Can't you see he's a complete quack!"

"Don't insult him, Ita."

She pointed with both hands to her chest. "*She* may be ill, but there's nothing wrong with me."

Dr. Freud seemed to laugh and sigh at the same time. He looked at me wryly as though to say, *Why on earth did you marry such a shrew?* But then, of course, he remembered why, and nothing less than complete sympathy showed upon his face. And then, of course, he remembered that the patient lying in bed before us was not, in fact, the shrew I had married, that I had, in fact, never married a shrew. I had been married to the village idiot, a docile, inarticulate unfortunate who had nothing in common with the impersonation of her Fräulein Eckstein had thought, in her illness, to contrive.

"Madam," Dr. Freud said, "though I am, as I say, a freethinker, I am not without an appreciation for the exigencies of the soul. It can't be easy for you to resist the gravitational pull of Heaven."

"What do you even know about it?" Ita said glumly.

"These myriads of destructive angels, though terrifying and grave, are nothing, I'd wager, compared to your own inner wish to relent, to surrender to divine justice, and to finally do what's right according to divine will."

Ita laughed. She crossed her arms. "Never!" she said.

"And why not?"

"Let's just say I want what's owed me."

"And what is that, madam, exactly?"

"And what *is* that, madam, exactly?" she sneered.

I didn't know how Dr. Freud withstood the hatred directed towards his person, projected, as it were, upon the screen of Fräulein Eckstein's lovely face. Many times during these sessions, I was reminded of the high esteem, indeed the admiration and the amorous affection, Dr. Freud was accustomed to meeting in Fräulein Eckstein's glance. How hard it must have been for him to see this same face pressed into the service of such hateful sneers.

("As you know only too well, Dr. Sammelsohn," Dr. Freud explained to me when I mentioned these concerns to him later, "no Jew manages to reach the age of maturity without having hardened himself to the derision he meets with from all sides in this world. Such is my lowly state that I expect no better from the Jewish dead in the next.")

"And what exactly is owed you?" Dr. Freud reiterated, pressing forward. "You yourself have implied that the universe adheres to a strict form of justice, stricter than any that can be petitioned for on this side of the veil. Make plain your demands and if indeed something is owed you, I will not cease from my advocacy on your part until these just demands are met."

Ita raised an eyebrow and pinned Dr. Freud with a tart and saucy look. "You have a daughter, I believe," she said.

"Three," Dr. Freud said, the proud paterfamilias, "the youngest not yet a year."

"And I'm certain you harbor, Dr. Freud, as any father would, great hopes for their futures."

"Great hopes, madam, indeed."

"Should one of them die young—and I regret to inform you that I have heard it whispered from behind the divine curtain that such is the fate of your . . . Sophie—"

Dr. Freud's face lost all color.

"—wouldn't you feel recompensed if, as I assure you will be the case, as an adult, your Sophele finds love and a husband, and through her husband, children, and through her children, a sort of immortality?"

"Sophie?" Dr. Freud whispered, stricken. "But when?"

I stood. "Dr. Freud, perhaps we should leave off pursuing this line of inquiry!"

"Quiet, Dr. Sammelsohn!" he roared. "I will decide what it is I wish to know and what not!"

"But I implore you!"

"Nineteen hundred and twenty," Ita stated flatly. "Influenza. Her death will be painless, or nearly so, at least for her, if not for you, and quick."

THIS WAS A side of Ita I'd never known.

"How ugly you've become in your beautiful new body," I whispered to her, appalled.

"Excuse me for a moment, if you will." Dr. Freud stood and bowed. He staggered from the room with all the grace of a broken toy.

"Such cruelty, Ita! Such wanton cruelty!"

"You've fallen in with bad company, Yankl."

"Who I choose to spend my time with is of no concern of yours," I said, pacing the floor before her bed.

"But I'm your wife."

"Were. You were my wife!"

"Ha!"

"You know as well as I you have no legal claims."

An ill-concealed smirk distorted Fräulein Eckstein's face.

"Don't laugh," I said. "It's not amusing."

"A legal claim!" she trumpeted. "Why don't you call a policeman if I'm bothering you."

"Perhaps I shall."

"Go ahead, Yankl. Have me arrested."

"Oh!" I turned away from her in disgust.

I looked through the window. The sanatorium grounds were dark. The trees pressed against the black sky like shadows falling across a darkened body of water.

"I'm not the only one here who has caused another unhappiness, you know."

"I know, I know, Yankl!" she said, leaning forward in her bed and speaking in an excited tone. "But that's only because of the body in which I was imprisoned."

"Surely you don't really believe that, Ita."

I turned to face her, and our eyes met, too intimately, I'm afraid.

"I do," she said deeply.

"I was happily married," I said to her as matter-of-factly as I could.

"Yes, to that little—"

"Stop it!" I raised my hand. "I won't have Hindele's name besmirched! Not by you. Of all of us, she's innocent of having ever caused you harm."

"Since when can't a wife be jealous of her husband's previous wife?" she said with a trill of girlish laughter.

I sat in the chair by her bed and looked at my shirt cuffs poking out from beneath my coat sleeves. Any other man, I was certain, upon learning that his hated wife had years before killed herself, might pause a moment in the course of his day and allow himself to feel a small self-inflicted stab of remorse. He might reflect upon the death that one day awaits us all, feeling, if only for a small moment, a mixture of pity and regret, before sighing with relief, *Ah, at last, at last, that's over and done with!* Never for a moment would such a man imagine being called away from the busy happiness of his life, from the productive routines of his work, to converse and bargain with this dead wife, debating the merits of her claims against him and the others who had driven her, according to her word, to her unhappy death. Never in all my time in Vienna had I heard of anyone being hounded by a dead wife, called away from his cards or his dinner to answer a comparable summons from the spirit world. Why should I, who am remarkable in no other way, be thus honored? Certainly my crime is no blacker than many a rake's. Surely Ita's heart was not more broken than many a young maiden's. Of all the spurned girls in Europe—left at the altar, impregnated, abandoned, trifled with, deflowered, lied to, seduced, defiled by an employer and dismissed from service by his wife—why was Ita the only one who, having destroyed herself, managed to return from the silent world of the dead to complain about the whole sad affair?

It's a peculiarity of us Jews that we tend to drag our history along behind us, clattering and clanking like tin cans tied to the tail of a frightened dog, and the more we attempt to outrun it, the louder and more frightening it becomes. Still, it's nearly impossible for me to describe the shame of being haunted by a dybbuk at the dawn of the twentieth century, as though I were nothing but a benighted Ostjude!

I looked about the sumptuous hospital room with its fine rugs and its warm, roaring fire. What was I doing here? It was madness to have accompanied Dr. Freud to Fräulein Eckstein's bedside, madness to have remained here, and as soon as he returned, I intended to quit the case, leaving it entirely in his hands. My oath as a doctor, in fact, compelled me to excuse myself and hand Fräulein Eckstein's treatment over to a physician with no personal stake in the matter.

I glanced coldly at Ita. As though reading my thoughts, she glared back at me. We were for the first time behaving like a husband and wife! Having pummeled each other verbally, we next subjected each other to an icy, biting silence, at the frozen arctic of which, the knob of the door finally turned, and Dr. Freud reentered the room. Ita ignored him, preferring to glower at me, her arms crossed beneath Fräulein Eckstein's bosom. I was troubled to see that Dr. Freud's eyes were gleaming with an odd and incandescent light. His gestures were overenunciated, as though he were an orator addressing an audience seated in the high rows of an amphitheater. *Cocaine:* the word shot like a whining arrow through the din of my otherwise noisy brain. Stung to the quick by Ita's prophecy, he'd no doubt availed himself of his favorite alkaloid balm.

"Ah! Ah! Ah!" he called to us from the doorway, sniffing like a Frenchman in a cheese shop. "And how is our young couple getting along then?"

The malicious tone in his voice unnerved me.

"Oh, this is intolerable!" Ita shrieked. "This is who you bring to help me? This hophead in love with a charlatan!"

"Wilhelm's no charlatan," Dr. Freud said, understanding Ita, I thought, a little too quickly.

"How can you prefer that idiot to Breuer?"

Dr. Freud shrugged loosely. "He's a little unorthodox, perhaps."

"A little unorthodox!"

"But everyone loves and respects him."

"Idiot!"

"Dr. Freud, it's late," I said, appealing to his better self.

"Right, right," he said, sniffing as casually as he could. "I'm not completely ignorant of our traditions, you know. Unbeliever!" he muttered to himself. "I've read deeply into many of its more esoteric concerns, but you didn't know that, did you? Yes, enough to know that a soul cleaving to another being—you see, I'm even conversant with the appropriate terminology—that such a soul, in a state of metempsychosis, often feels she's left something undone on this side of the veil. Or isn't that correct, madam?"

For all their antagonism, Ita and Dr. Freud shared an odd, teasing rapport; and I remembered that, without Dr. Freud's knowing it, it was Ita who had sat through those many long hours of psychoanalytic therapy with him, concealed, as she was, inside Fräulein Eckstein, his patient.

"Shall I tell you what I want then?" she nearly spat at him.

"Yes, madam, please do." Dr. Freud nodded.

"Just say it out plainly?"

"Without censoring yourself. Absolutely."

Ita swallowed and moistened Fräulein Eckstein's lips.

"Come on, come on!"

"You're right, of course. It would be easier and more beautiful to accept the ways of our Lord, whose teachings are without flaw. Even now I can hear the angelic hosts singing His praises in their celestial choirs. Can you hear it, either of you? Yankl, Dr. Freud?"

Dr. Freud and I listened, but I could hear nothing outside of the rapid fluttering of Fräulein Eckstein's breathing and Dr. Freud's dripping sinuses.

"But you're forgetting one thing."

"And what is that, madam?"

"I am or at least I *was* a woman, and the heart I possessed and still possess is a woman's heart."

"And a woman's heart must know love," Dr. Freud said, anticipating her meaning.

"Surely, even an apostate like you cannot deny that God has decreed it thus."

The words, spoken so simply and with such honesty, pierced my heart. I couldn't look Ita or Fräulein Eckstein in the face and instead turned my gaze towards my shoes, hiding like whipped dogs beneath the curtains of my trouser legs.

"Madam," Dr. Freud said softly, "may I take your hand?"

No longer a wild mare spooked by every noise, Ita breathed deeply— Fräulein Eckstein's chest bellowed out with air—and gently lay one of Fräulein Eckstein's hands, palm upward, on the blanket. Dr. Freud took it and held it between both of his.

"Put yourself in my place, Dr. Freud. My soul, like all souls, was perfect, but through no fault of my own, it was confined in a narrow, mangled body. You've heard the tale of my grandfather and the shoelace, thanks to which I was like a princess in a decrepit prison tower. Anyone who wanted to hurl insults at me could degrade me in any way they chose. I couldn't answer them back. I had no protector. Then by chance, against all odds—only consider!—this horrid creature found herself married one day to the very boy she'd loved her entire life."

"Yes, madam, go on."

"However, when our wedding was at last performed, as I'd always hoped it would be, the groom chose not to consummate the union, but to flee. And who can blame him? Still, the heart is an obdurate little muscle, and it wants what it has been led to believe rightfully belongs to it."

"And what is that, madam? Let us be specific."

"If I tell you, will you aid me in securing it for myself?"

Like a too-smug smuggler approaching his final border, Dr. Freud turned and gave me a triumphant look. "Frau Sammelsohn," he said, "I will do so, if in turn you will promise me that upon receiving whatever you desire, you will peacefully depart from Fräulein Eckstein's body without harming her in any wise, neither physically, mentally, psychologically, nor spiritually. You will further promise to forgo your life as a fugitive, sheltering no more in bodies that are foreign to you, but will remand yourself immediately to the Heavenly Courts, where you shall be tried and judged and sentenced in accordance with divine law."

I was struck dumb. Had Dr. Freud never bothered to read mythology? Did he have no idea what happened to people who make pledges and promises before understanding their implications?

"And you will say Kaddish on my behalf?" Ita negotiated her counter-terms.

"I'm no shul-goer, madam," Dr. Freud demurred. "In all honesty, my attendance at such a task, as honorable and noble as it might seem, would be spotty at best, but I will see to it that a mature boy of impeccable character, a scholar and a Hasid, is hired for the requisite period of eleven months to perform that which you ask."

"I do have a husband to mourn for me, you know."

Both Dr. Freud and Fräulein Eckstein looked at me, their gazes boring into my hands and feet, crucifying me to the cross of their examination.

"I assure you he cannot be relied upon in this regard either," Dr. Freud said simply.

"That's only too true, I suppose." Ita sighed, rubbing her arms unhappily.

"Madam, I will be frank with you. Under other circumstances, I would recommend a complete psychoanalysis. Only in this wise might we get to the bottom of your long unhappiness. However, the procedure is not only lengthy but expensive. You have no funds, and no way of procuring funds, and I'm afraid Fräulein Eckstein is equally poor in time. She cannot afford to linger in the twilight in which you've placed her for the duration a proper analysis requires. So in lieu of offering you my healing arts, make known to me your request and, if, as I say, it is within my power to obtain it for you, under the agreement we have set out, obtain it for you I shall."

"I have but one request."

Dr. Freud clapped his hands. "Then make it known and consider it yours!"

"You're a gracious man after all," Ita said, unmanning us both with her charm.

Dr. Freud bowed. "I thank you sincerely for the compliment."

"I underestimated the caliber of your character when I previously maligned you."

Ita seemed to be putting off making her request known. Was she fearful of the destructive angels waiting for her just outside the limits of our perceptions? Or was she too thoroughly enjoying our bedside attention to move on? Or did she, like all of us, have no wish to secure what she wanted if it meant ending her life?

"Come, come, let us cease this endless handln, my dear Frau."

"A bride dreams only of one thing, of course." Ita grew girlish beneath the mask of Fräulein Eckstein's face. "The only thing I desire with all my heart is, of course, to lie with my husband as his wife."

Though I'd anticipated as much, I sputtered wordlessly in protest. Ita reached out to me from her bed. "Yankl, I don't blame you, I don't blame you, my darling, for turning away from me before! But look now! Look at the lovely body I've brought you!" She tossed aside the bedsheets. "You yourself were attracted to her at the Carl!"

"Ita! Ita, it's impossible," I stammered. "Why, it . . . it would be . . . *rape!*"

"Rape, between a man and his wife?"

"Dr. Freud, for Heaven's sake! Help me!" I pleaded, but Dr. Freud was strangely absent, staring at the nails of his hands.

"I want you!" Ita cried. "Let me die happily and fulfilled! Yankl, look at what I'm offering you!" With nimble fingers, she began untying the laces of Fräulein Eckstein's gown.

"Stop!" I exclaimed, and in frustration, Ita dropped onto her stomach and pounded her fists against the mattress.

"Why won't you love me? Why won't you love me?" she wailed into her pillows.

I yanked Dr. Freud up from his chair where he'd been sitting glassy-eyed like a Chinaman in an opium den and pulled him into the hallway outside.

re you mad?" I nearly shouted.

Dr. Freud grimaced. "What would you have me do?" he said. "Flee like Breuer at the first mention of gynecological matters? He held the key in his hand, Dr. Sammelsohn, he held the key in his hand! But unwilling, or perhaps constitutionally unable to use it, he dropped it!" Dr. Freud rubbed the underbridge of his nose. "For all his mental acuity, there's nothing Faustian about poor Josef, I'm afraid."

I confess this reference to Dr. Faust unnerved me. In retrospect, one must really question the all-too-German enthusiasm for this work: an aging scholar trades his soul to the devil for vast knowledge and a wealth of depraved experiences, only to repent in the end and, through a loophole of Christian piety, be exonerated and forgiven. I'd only recently seen the play, Parts I and II, performed at Herr Franz's Marvelous & Astonishing Puppet Theater, with puppets, as Goethe had first envisioned it. With this experience fresh in mind, Dr. Freud's condemnation of Dr. Breuer rang differently in my ears than it did in his own, I'm certain. In his love of the play, seeing its protagonist as a paragon of Promethean daring, stealing fire by hook or crook from the Heavenly realms, Dr. Freud was typically German; I, on the other hand, preferred Dr. Breuer's cooler head and calmer passions.

"In these sorts of situations," Dr. Freud said, "as indeed in all areas of my life, I have been no more courageous than most men; indeed, quite often less so. If I have tended to overcompensate for feelings of inferiority and cowardice, I've done it while quaking in my boots, so to speak. Until I met Wilhelm, that is."

"Until you met Dr. Fliess, you mean?" I begged for clarification.

"Wilhelm cares nothing for the wisdom of pedants or the small, passionless victories of sober men working in somber laboratories, each afraid of his own shadow. For Wilhelm, it's the grand gesture or nothing, the electric leap, riding along the clouds in no sturdier chariot than his own brilliance. Who else would have dared to place the nose so centrally in the sexual life of man? Not I, I can tell you that, nor you, Dr. Sammelsohn, nor Dr. Breuer, who is for me all I fear becoming. Why, he stood at the very gates of Hell and could not bring himself to enter its sacred precincts. And I believe we are now at a similar pass."

We? I thought. *We?* It was simple enough for Dr. Freud to say *we*. No one was asking him, for the sake of scientific inquiry, to drop his drawers and climb into bed with the soul of his dead wife and the body of a more or less perfect stranger. Granted, the more or less perfect body of a stranger, and one I had admired to the point of wishing for nothing more than this very invitation; and yet, though I might have wished to possess Fräulein Eckstein body and soul, it was not without the consent of their rightful owner.

"I know what you're thinking, Kobi." *Kobi?* Dr. Freud never called me by this name, and I felt odd hearing it from his lips. "Your thoughts nearly float across your face. If I were being called upon to leap this moral barricade, I too would hesitate, and that is why I must tell you this: in similar situations—"

"Similar situations?" I barked incredulously.

"I said *similar,* not *identical,*" he scolded me. "We were all young and virginal once. Even I, Kobi, though you might find that hard to believe. Of course, it's true, my earliest sexual experiences were at the hands of a Christian nurse my parents employed, who used to take me with her to Mass when I was no more than eight. But no! When I say 'in a situation like this,' I mean one that gives a person pause and calls out of him all his reserves of courage to perform. In finding myself in such a situation, I now recite a simple formula: I ask myself a simple question."

"And that question is?"

"What would Wilhelm do?"

"'What would Wilhelm do?'"

"If ever I find myself hesitating before the herd mentality of our so-called peers or betters, that is the question I put to myself, 'What would Wilhelm do?' and arriving at an honest answer, I follow its exact course."

I was appalled to see him blushing like a schoolgirl.

"Sigmund," I said, assuming at first that in fair play I could call him by his first name as well, but feeling woefully uncomfortable doing so, I quickly corrected myself, "Dr. Freud."

"Perhaps I've given too much of myself away, and you will no longer credit me with authority. But certainly you're no stranger to him. Though you're not as intimate with him as I, you've seen his bold ways, his intellectual decisiveness. You've seen him raise the banner of his own brilliance atop intellectual and scientific peaks no one else has the courage to ascend. How many centuries have men stared at the nose of his neighbor before seeing it for the erogenous organ it truly is?"

I collapsed into a chair. My head swimming, but barely, in confusion, I watched as my thoughts drowned one by one. If Dr. Freud could mistake that crazy-eight-ball Fliess for a paragon of intellectual attainment, what else was he mistaken about? Perhaps I'd grown too used to thinking of Dr. Freud as wise and all-knowing. The habit was so engrained in me, I wrote off his odd love of Dr. Fliess as a quirk having nothing at all to do with the rest of his character, rather than seeing it for what it perhaps was: the ill-placed foundation stone thanks to which the entire structure of his personal integrity might eventually collapse.

"What in God's name would you have me do, then?" I whispered hoarsely, scarcely able to speak.

"Not run away, as Breuer did to Venice, forgetting everything he'd seen, letting his bourgeois concerns for his petty name cripple him at the threshold of a major discovery, like the little old lady that he is! No, Kobi, let neither of us turn away from this new continent, simply because it is as-yet unmapped; who knows what treasures, what spices, what new species of herbs and medicinals we might find inside its unwalked geographies! 'What would Wilhelm do?' That's what you should be asking yourself!"

I nodded unhappily, though in truth, this was hardly the question ringing in my ear, its tail raised in the interrogative, like a snake preparing to strike. The actual question piercing my flesh, like so many arrows into St. Sebastian's, concerned only one thing: ESCAPE: avenues of; possibility vs.

impossibility of; saving face while in the act of; near; narrow; rescue in the absence of; daring last-minute; see: DEUS EX MACHINA!

"I'll tell you what I imagine Dr. Fliess would do." Dr. Freud drew my attention back to himself, though there was no need for him to say anything. I knew only too well what that unthinking psychopathic narcissist would be up to at this moment. As soon as it had entered my mind, I tried to banish the picture of him, with his jacket off and his braces undone, his trousers in a puddle at his feet, his manhood protruding from beneath the tails of his shirtfront as though it were Pinocchio's nose!

"What you're asking of me is impossible," I said. "To begin with, it's immoral."

"How is it immoral?"

"It's rape."

"But it's not rape at all!"

"Perhaps not in the name of some greedy pleasure, but still it's rape."

"I'm surprised at you, Dr. Sammelsohn. You're certainly not thinking very clearly."

"I'm not thinking clearly?"

"No, not at all."

"Very well then. Won't you enlighten me, please?"

Dr. Freud sat in the armchair opposite mine and looked at me with a weary condescension that belied the watery gleam in his eyes. "You are convinced, as I am not yet convinced, that the soul of your dead wife is inhabiting the body of this other. To believe this, you must a priori believe that souls are constant in ways that bodies are not. The body is no more than a garment the soul puts on and takes off. That is to say, if you can claim to recognize Ita without her body, then her body is in some essential way not *her*. Agreed? Neither then is Fräulein Eckstein's body *Fräulein Eckstein*. Wherever Fräulein Eckstein is at the moment, she is not in her body, and if we can speak of her thus, then we can say that she is *not* her body, and therefore one cannot violate her by conjoining with a body that is not *her*, at least not at the moment, but is, rather, in some more essential sense, Ita. Why, you could no more kill me by stabbing a knife into my suit as it hangs in my wardrobe than you can violate Fräulein Eckstein by lying with Ita at this very moment."

"And yet," I protested helplessly, "despite the confirmation from my sisters via their telegram, you yourself remain unconvinced that Ita is anything more than a symptom, a condition seconde, brought upon Fräulein Eckstein as a result of her hysteria."

"My mind is as yet unresolved on the matter, it's true," Dr. Freud grumbled.

"And if your diagnostic suspicions prove correct, then you will have urged me onto a woman—"

"—who in her condition seconde has herself requested that you make love to her."

"Which she does only because she's ill, deluded, and not thinking as herself."

"I never claimed the matter was morally simple."

"But just look at me!" I cried.

"I am," he said. "Now tell me what it is you imagine I see."

"To begin with: I'm no Casanova."

"No, that's plain and clear."

"And my experiences in these matters have been quite circumscribed."

"You've been married twice as well as divorced and widowed one time each."

"While remaining as virginal as a young maiden!"

"You're more naïve about the young maidens in Vienna than perhaps you ought to be."

"Nevertheless: I stand before you thus."

"Oh, Sammelsohn, Sammelsohn." Dr. Freud shook his head. "How often does love call us by our proper names and summon us to its altar?"

What was there to say in response to such a question? Nothing; and so I merely hung my thumbs in my vest pockets, curling my lower lip over the fringe of my mustache. Dr. Freud made everything sound so simple: "Give Ita what she wants, free Fräulein Eckstein from her possession, enjoy yourself with a clear conscience, and walk away free of guilt, not only from this encounter but from the wreckage of your second marriage as well."

"And if the being who addresses us is not in fact Ita, but some aspect of Fräulein Eckstein, what then?"

"Listen, Chrobak once sent me a patient to whom he couldn't give sufficient time. After eighteen years of marriage, the woman was still a virgin, her husband being impotent. Taking the man aside, Chrobak told him plainly: 'The sole prescription for such a malady is familiar enough to us, but we cannot order it. It runs as follows: Rx Penis normalis; dosim repetatur.' The entire thing, I wager, would be, in one way or the other, curative for her."

A squalling storm had broken out, its heavy drifts turning the black night outside the sanatorium windows a chilling bone white. I shivered. It was already quite late. Dr. Freud had secured permission to attend Fräulein Eckstein around the clock. Aside from a night nurse stationed at the front desk, the only staff abroad at this hour were one or two cleaning ladies, old drabs in babushkas, mopping the floors and gossiping to each other in their low country dialect.

"A STOUT DRINK should do you good."

I didn't see where Dr. Freud had suddenly produced a bottle of his favorite Hennessey from, but he seemed so certain of himself and I so filled with doubts, I greedily accepted the drink and threw down nearly a fourth of the bottle. "Take some in to Ita," he advised, steering me towards Fräulein Eckstein's door. His keen interest in the proceedings displeased me greatly. Certainly Fräulein Eckstein, and Ita by extension, remained Dr. Freud's patient and not mine; but this encounter — so long dreamed of, so often deferred — belonged not to Dr. Freud, but to me, and though he'd facilitated it, I couldn't help resenting his proprietary interest in its outcome.

Nevertheless, I entered the room. Emma, Ita, whoever it was, lay in bed with no light on. Receiving no response from the sleeper, I went to the window and stood watching the snow fall in silent drifts. I could feel a chill on my cheeks through the thin window pane. Was Dr. Freud correct? Could I free Ita from her unnatural sorrow simply by offering myself to her as a husband? Could such lechery ever truly appear heroic? What would my father say? (Of course, wasn't this, in some way, exactly what he'd wanted?) But how would Fräulein Eckstein, returned to herself as a consequence, view the act? What would her mother think? Or her father, for that matter? Or her brother, the famous Sanskritist? Perhaps he'd challenge me to a duel! Say what you will about Dr. Breuer, it was unlikely he would perish at dawn in a field facing down a bullet fired at his all-too-timid heart by a male member of the Pappenheim clan, while his seconds looked on helplessly. However, as I stood over Fräulein Eckstein's body and gazed upon its perplexing convexities—she lay in her rumpled sheets with one arm flung over her head and the other across her belly, her hands grasping at nothing, her tousled hair freed from its public poses, her mouth open as though in a sigh—I admit that all thoughts of right and wrong left my head. Only a fool inquires into the morality of a rose, I told myself; a sensible man simply surrenders to its fragrance and its beauty.

"Ita?" I called softly, shaking her gently. "Ita, my darling?" She stirred, but did not awaken. She moved her head, squinted her already closed eyes. Rubbing the back of her hand violently across her nose, she clacked her tongue twice against the roof of her mouth and uttered the words: "Soup, now, I suppose." She exhaled and grew still. There was room on the bed next to her, and so I placed first one knee and then the next upon the mattress. I knelt beside her, trying to disturb her as little as possible. I leaned in to kiss her, balancing on one hand, my knuckles pressing against the bed. My jacket had a too-constricting effect on me and so, standing, I removed it as quietly as I could and hung it on a peg on the back of the door. As long as I was at it, I uncuffed and rolled up my shirtsleeves, tucking my cuff links into my breast pocket.

"Ita?" I said again, and again I received no response.

A decision had at this point been made, I suppose. Unlike Dr. Breuer, I had committed myself to receiving the full force of love the patient held for me. At the time, however, I was thinking not of decisions and principles, but only of roses and perfumes. I convinced myself that I would kiss her only, cuddle her as a father or a brother might, profess my affection for her, and let her decide what our sexual destiny would be. I wanted merely to demonstrate to her my carnal availability should she truly, as she claimed, wish to avail herself of it. The door was locked. I'd checked it more than once. Dr. Freud, in any case, was on the other side, serving as a sentinel with his Hennessey. I climbed again upon her bed, balancing on my knees as precariously as before. Again, with one hand on the mattress, I leaned in towards her, my lips on the delicate hinge joining her neck and her shoulder. I kissed her, inhaling all the scents of her soaps, her bran baths, her shampoos, her laundered clothes, the lingering musk of her anger. She breathed out hummingly and giggled. Emboldened, I kissed her cheek. With her eyes closed, she laughed against the pressure of my mouth upon her face. When I kissed her lips, they did not pucker against mine, but lay unpursed. The sensation was coldly unpleasant, not unlike, I imagined, kissing a corpse. She turned from me—I must have been disturbing her slumber—her shoulder angled against my check, her breast falling innocently into my open palm. Beneath the thin flannel of her night blouse, her nipple seemed to have shaken off its own slumbers, lifting its little head from the pillow of her flesh.

"Ita?" I said, kissing her now behind her ear, untying her collar, cupping my hand around her warm breast. "I'm here—just as you've asked me to be."

Reader, how happy I would be to skip over this next part, but as I have committed myself to the whole bolt of truth, no inferior remnant will do. Still, it's impossible to convey the horror of what next occurred. As I cupped my hand around Fräulein Eckstein's breast, a masculine voice rang out, filling the room, like a sonorous gong, with its castigations: "Dr. Sammelsohn," it cried, "what on earth are you doing? Are you out of your mind!"

I removed my hand from the patient's chest and peered over my shoulder towards the door where I imagined I might face my accuser. No one, however, was there. Assuming the voice belonged merely to my conscience, I sighed with relief until it addressed me a second time: "We're not behind you."

"No?" I said into thin air.

"Rather you hold us in your arms."

I looked at Fräulein Eckstein. She stared at me with an unnerving intensity. Her mouth was agape and the deep ringing voice emanated—I was horrified to realize this—from somewhere within her! I dropped her instantly—"I'm terribly sorry, my good sir!"—and jumped away from the bed, unrolling my cuffs and wrapping myself in my jacket. "Of course, I didn't realize . . ." I began, but I could think of nothing further to say.

"He's stunned! Ha! Yes, stunned into silence! We tend to have that effect on people."

It was true: I was stunned into silence, and I was speechless to deny it. I was as mute as a man who has bitten off his own tongue and, gasping in alarm, accidentally swallows it.

"May I ask the name of the one who is addressing me?" I finally managed to say.

With an athletic grace I'd never seen in her before, Fräulein Eckstein stretched out on the bed and kicked off its covers. She lay on her side, propped up by her elbows, and cocked her head against her fist. An ironic look played across her face.

"It never changes, does it? 'Tell me your name.' That's always the first thing they ask."

The rude shocks kept coming! Before I could respond to this odd statement, a second voice, also from inside Fräulein Eckstein, responded to the first: "Only too true, too true," it said.

This voice was masculine as well, with a lilt similar to the first's. My ear couldn't quite place the accent. Its geographies were unknown to me. What distinguished it from the other voice was a certain raspiness; and each time it sounded, the Fräulein's physique took on a more hulking aspect. "That's *him*?" the raspy voice cried. Making use of the Fräulein's body, its possessor seemed to glare out of it at me suspiciously.

"Ya'akov Yosef ben Alter Nosn?" the other inquired politely, inclining Fräulein Eckstein's chin in my direction. "That *is* you, isn't it?"

The two seemed to be sharing Fräulein Eckstein's body, taking turns with it, as it were, like two men peering through a tiny window, each stepping back to let the other have a look before stepping up again.

"We've heard so much about you," the gentler voice said, before whispering to his friend, "Not as prepossessing as she made out."

"She's in love," the huskier fellow replied, also in a whisper. "You know how she tends to exaggerate things."

Fräulein Eckstein sat upon her mattress in an attitude that was shockingly gruff, one foot flat upon the floor, the other tucked beneath her thigh, her legs uncrossed and parted. Periodically, she scratched herself—under her arm, along the inseam of her crotch, at her throat as though whiskers were irritating her skin. When the two beings inside her conversed, not with me, but with each other, her head moved first to the right, then to the left. The effect was not unlike watching a madman having a conversation with himself. The two, it seemed, were brothers, for despite the well-known folkloric prohibition against an immortal surrendering his name, they were only too happy to introduce themselves to me.

"What are you going to do with it, anyway?" the gentler one asked. "Besides, who can pronounce it correctly?"

He identified himself as אשריל.

(This, in any case, is my rough typographical approximation of the word he spoke. In truth, when I asked for the spelling, he grew uncharacteristically truculent and employed all manner of diversion to dissuade any further inquiry along these lines. "What are you planning to do? Put it in a book?" he snarled. In pronunciation, the name sounded something like a blowing wind, and I soon realized it belonged to the angelic being who had met Ita after she'd parted so violently from her life.)

"As we always do," he said, sighing. "The poor thing is as addicted to unhappy lives as an addict to his morphine."

"And your brother?" I asked him. "What role does he play?"

Before the brother could answer, אשריל brought Fräulein Eckstein's hands together, in a gesture of supplication. "Dr. Sammelsohn? Pardon us, but the space here is hardly sufficient for one of us, never mind two."

"Would it terrify you horribly if we left this sausage casement and revealed ourselves to you in a less narrow guise?"

"It's difficult to judge such things in advance," I said.

"A sensible man." אשריל nodded.

"Just how terrifying are you?" I asked.

"Oh, horribly," the brother said with a laugh. "Not at all," אשריל promised in the same breath. "Don't listen to him. Stop it now, שמנגלפ! He's only joking."

(It was then that I caught the brother's name. It sounded like water draining from a tub.) What could I do? I'd witnessed so many frightening things in the last few days. I couldn't imagine surrendering to my terror now. Instead I said, "Certainly. Do as you wish. Whatever makes you comfortable."

"Then on that wire that stretches from wall to wall, and upon which nurses hang a curtain to allow their patients to dress and undress in modesty, hang a curtain yourself, a sheer bedsheet, and we will appear behind it in order to address you."

I did as they asked, finding exactly what they'd requested in a trunk at the foot of Fräulein Eckstein's bed. How much time passed in this way, I cannot say. Time seemed of no importance here, until I thought of poor Dr. Freud, waiting outside the door, imagining God only knows what perverse raptures Fräulein Eckstein and Ita and I were committing in our odd ménage a trois.

"You might as well invite him in, your friend," אשריל said.

"Ah, yes, that's right," שמנגלפ added. "He's sleeping outside the door, isn't he?"

"You'll do well to have someone with whom to share the experience."

"Creatures such as yourself—"

"By which he means human beings."

"—tend to forget."

"They forget what they've forgotten."

"And then that is forgotten as well."

WERE I FLUENT in all the tongues of mankind, still I doubt I could accurately describe what happened next. Two pops sounded, each with an electric flash. Fräulein Eckstein twice jerked up and then lay still, stiller than I'd seen her since I'd entered the room. A great wind whooshed by me; the gaslights flickered before failing. The bedsheet I'd hung across the wire billowed out with a boisterous flapping before falling perfectly silent and still. Behind it, as though projected upon it from the rear, was a small, round point of light that grew steadily in size and brightness—I was reminded of the headlamp of an approaching locomotive—until it illuminated the entire sheet. Outlined in an even brighter light were the figures of two broad-shouldered men, one lithe and graceful, the other hulking with a dog-like snout.

The hair on the back of my hands, on my scalp, on my neck, tingled.

"You called me?" Dr. Freud said, entering the room, although of course I hadn't. Or had I? Perhaps I'd shouted out his name in alarm, though I wasn't aware of having done so. "What's this?" he said, closing the door behind him and taking in the curious scrim.

"Shlomo ben Ya'akov, welcome." Together, the spirits addressed Dr. Freud formally by what I assumed was his Hebrew name.

"I've never seen this before in a case of hysteria," he whispered to me. "You must admit: the disease has a stupefying sense of imagination."

שמנגלפ snickered and scratched his crotch.

"Who are you, if I may be so bold?" Dr. Freud stuck out his chest, assuming his most martial stance. "Before you answer, I ask only one thing: that you not terrify us, so that we may keep our wits and not act out of fear."

"Who are we?" אשריל thundered. "Who are we?"

Dr. Freud nodded. I swallowed nervously.

"We are we: אשריל!" he shouted.

"And שמנגלפ! Who did you imagine we were?"

I could feel my knees shaking; Dr. Freud swayed a bit.

"Oh, let's stop this nonsense," אשריל suddenly said to his brother. To us, he said, "Gentlemen, forgive the theatricals. Such an easy joke is difficult to resist. However, allow us to come directly to the point. Why, in fact, are we here? We're here because we're in need of your assistance."

Dr. Freud and I turned towards each other: neither of us knew what to say.

"How can you help us, you're wondering?" אשריל said. "As you may have assumed, we are from the angelic orders."

"It's my job," שמנגלפ explained, "to pursue and torment the accused, along with my pack of thugs, for as long as she insists on running from us. אשריל, on the other hand, meets with her between each life to offer counsel, assistance, and guidance, as it were."

"Which she has rarely, if ever, taken."

"Never, as a matter of public record."

I once again saw the afterworld as Ita had described it: a desolate place of howling winds and raw elements, but connected to our world somehow, so that an errant soul might slip through.

"You are correct, Dr. Sammelsohn," אשריל said. "There are points of connection where Heaven and Earth meet."

Dr. Freud narrowed his eyes. "And you claim that Ita eluded you through one of these . . . cracks?"

אשריל sighed miserably. "Let us simply say: We see אַאְעְאָאָאְעְ עֶעוּוִיא more often than we wish. Every few years, as a matter of fact, each life darker than the one preceding it."

"Time before this time," שמנגלפ confided to us, "she murdered two babies."

"Before that, she poisoned her husband *and* his business partner."

"With whom she was maintaining amorous relations."

"Then there were the epidemics."

"The choleras."

"The plagues."

"When she worked in that kitchen that time, you remember," שמנגלפ reminded his brother.

"Her lives, as a rule, tend towards the unhappy and the brief."

"And the painful."

"Oh, yes, the painful. For all concerned."

"Ourselves not in the least."

At this, Dr. Freud uttered a guttural sound, though so quietly I imagined I was the only one who'd heard him. Having rejected fantasies of divine justice and retribution as nothing more than a system through which a priestly elite might control and exploit the credulous masses, he was having none of it now.

"And what exactly is it that you want from us?" he demanded.

Behind the bedsheet, the two figures, outlined in white light, looked at each other. If I had to translate that look—the hunch of their powerful shoulders, the swivel of their muscular necks—I would say that something in Dr. Freud's truculence displeased them.

"Well, to be blunt," אשריל said formally, "the first thing you must do is call a rabbi."

"Someone," שמנגלפ said, "who understands and reveres the power of Heaven."

"No, I forbid it," Dr. Freud said.

"Oh?"

"I won't have a religious functionary, some pious clerk, interfering with my case."

"*Your* case?" שמנגלף said. "What a queer phraseology!"

"Though you and your brother may claim to be here on behalf of Frau Ita Sammelsohn, late of this world, I, Dr. Sigmund Freud, have been called in to assist Fräulein Emma Eckstein and am employed by her family to do so."

"Shlomo ben Ya'akov!" אשריל cried.

"You may address me as Herr Doktor, my good sir!"

"Very well then, Herr Doktor, if you insist on remaining in charge of this 'case,' as you call it, you shall need candles."

"Black tapers," שמנגלף supplied the commentary.

"A ram's horn."

"Make it two. They break easily. Oh, and white robes for the quorum."

"And what exactly are you proposing?" I asked.

שמנגלף turned to אשריל. "It seems you'll have to explain it to them from the beginning."

"אַאְַעְֶאָאַַעֶעוּוִיא must be persuaded to leave," אשריל said. "That is what is being proposed. Now, very generally, this is an impossible task with a dybbuk. And knowing אַאְַעְֶאָאַַעֶעוּוִיא, I can assure you it's unlikely she will choose to depart on her own."

"And if she leaves?" I said.

"Upon her bodily eviction, she will be taken into the sling and tossed from one corner of the universe to the other until she comes to understand something of the unmarrable perfection of Heaven. In its mercy, Heaven cast her into a body in which it was assumed she could do no further harm. But mischief and quarrelsomeness are the lot of women, I'm afraid."

"She only wanted to be loved," I said in her defense.

"Loved?"

"Justifications! Excuses!"

"Those who blacken the name of Heaven always have a perfectly good reason for doing so."

"Make no mistake," שמנגלף told us. "She'll be driven out by the usual means: incense, prayer, psalms, supplications, and the recitation of the holy names. The holy light is ultimately impossible to resist."

"Alas, we cannot undertake this exorcism ourselves," אשריל explained, "and in an age of true piety, we would never have appeared to the likes of you, but what can we do? If you can't perform this ritual, I implore you: Call for Rabbi Chajes!"

"I think not," Dr. Freud barked.

"Then go to the Ger Rebbe. I believe he isn't far from here."

"That charlatan?" Dr. Freud said with real disgust.

"Patience," אשריל counseled שמנגלפ, who had begun growling like a wild dog. "Control your wrath, my brother."

"Listen to me, you two," Dr. Freud said, a little too brusquely, I thought. "I have already negotiated the terms of her surrender with the patient."

"By raping her?" אשריל cried.

"How, sir, can you pretend this disgusting sexual obsession of yours is a medical therapy is what I'd like to know!"

"Otherwise," Dr. Freud said, keeping hold of his temper, "all I can propose is a long course of psychoanalysis. That is your only hope of a permanent cure. But I warn you, the therapeutic procedure moves by slow advances, by means of many false starts, and by as many retreats. If you're going to hang in there for the entirety, you're going to need the patience of Job, and it's expensive besides."

"Is there no way . . ." I started to say.

"Proceed, Dr. Sammelsohn," אשריל encouraged me.

"Well, I was just wondering, if there is no way to simply talk her into surrendering to your authority. Perhaps you'll let me try. If I can do that, will you promise me she'll go straight to the highest Heaven, to the very Garden of Eden, suffering no further torment at the hands of your brother and his band of thugs?"

The angels laughed and, almost against our will, Dr. Freud and I laughed with them. The sound of their laughter was so glorious, so marvelous and appealing, that my shoulders relaxed completely. I stopped glowering and squinting into the too-bright sunburst beamed at us through their curtain. Dr. Freud actually leaned his shoulder against mine, having lost his footing, and the sensation of his arm touching mine was so pleasant, I made no attempt to move out from beneath his weight, and he no move to correct his stance.

"Ah, a noble heart," said אשריל.

"If completely misguided," שמנגלפ said.

"I'm afraid what you propose is impossible. Though you married her, believe me, you do not know this girl."

"But if I'm able to convince her?" I said.

"Ah," שמנגלפ sighed.

"If you can induce her to leave on her own volition, then, yes, I will personally see to it that she is returned to the highest spheres without physical suffering. However, she must leave on her own volition. Which is to say: without any sexual coercion from you."

"I understand," I said.

"And as for you, Herr Doktor," שמנגלפ said.

"Yes? As for me?" Dr. Freud said.

"May a worm grow in your jaw, you godless Jew!"

"I wanted only to help," he said cravenly.

"Our time here is short," אשריל said. "We shall be waiting." He clapped his hands. "If psychotherapy is your approach, do with it what you can."

"No, wait!" Dr. Freud cried, appearing to suffer a terrible moment of regret. "I'll summon the Ger Rebbe! I'll produce the white robes and the black tapers!"

"Too late, too late," שמנגלפ and אשריל both cried out together, as the light behind the scrim began to fade. As it disappeared, I realized it was morning. Dr. Freud and I stared at each other in the rough, raw light of dawn, our eyes red, our faces creased like clothes that have lain too long in their traveling cases.

Before we could say a word to each other, Fräulein Eckstein sat up in her bed and screamed: "Help me! For God's sake, somebody please!" For the first time in my dealings with her, I couldn't tell who was pleading for my aid. Was it Fräulein Eckstein or Ita?

And for the first time, it no longer seemed to matter.

CHAPTER 19

D
r. Freud's initial attempts to perform psychoanalysis upon Ita failed utterly. The cards were stacked against him. She had disliked him from the first, seeing in his desire to banish her (as any doctor would a painful symptom) a shadow of her grandfather's aggression towards her. Dr. Freud's need to prove to her that she was nothing but a figment of Fräulein Eckstein's diseased imagination— combined with his eagerness to rid the world of the pious fairy tales we'd all had stuffed down our throats—bought him little of her sympathy and nothing of her trust. Also, she considered psychoanalysis a pale substitute for the cure he had originally promised her: that I would lie with her as my wife. On most days, she wouldn't speak to him at all, and she refused to permit Fräulein Eckstein to emerge in his presence. Dr. Freud sat behind her bed where Ita couldn't see him, hoping she might forget exactly who was there with her. When she did speak, she cursed at him, flying into rages, sometimes even spitting at him or slapping at his face. She threw Fräulein Eckstein's hairbrush and mirror at him, and accused him of a litany of crimes, secret sins he had perhaps actually committed, choosing to do so, after hours and hours of silence, when her nurses were in the room.

The consultants Dr. Freud called in—Drs. Breuer, Gersuny, Rosanes— were helpless to assist him. In their presence, Ita was a model patient. Unfamiliar with her voice, these physicians couldn't tell it apart from Fräulein Eckstein's. In response to their medical inquiries, the patient complained of nothing except that her doctor seemed to rely too excessively upon physical examinations, rectal and vaginal, which he performed, absent the proper equipment, with his tongue.

When even Dr. Fliess began doubting his reports, Dr. Freud almost washed his hands of the case.

At the same time, although the sanatorium was quite a distance away for me, I made it my custom to visit Ita for a half hour every evening after work. I was motivated in part by a professional solidarity with Dr. Freud. We disagreed over one thing only: whether the two angels we'd encountered in Fräulein Eckstein's room were symptomatical or cosmological in nature. I insisted upon the latter, Dr. Freud upon the former.

"Those so-called visitors from the spirit world," he constantly tried to assure me, "are nothing but the old symptom reappearing elsewhere, under another guise and with a greater intensity." He'd draw upon his cigar and blow out a noxious puff of smoke. "Breuer and I call this phenomenon 'joining in the conversation,' and it typically represents the illness's last stand."

"How do you mean?"

"Well, you see, the symptom increases in intensity the deeper we penetrate into the relevant pathogenic memory until suddenly it manifests elsewhere — as though *another* symptom has joined in the conversation! This signals the end, and the symptom soon diminishes or vanishes completely. Also" — here, he lowered his voice — "much of what you and I imagine we experienced together was due not only to our extreme exhaustion and the stressfulness of the scenario in which we found ourselves, as well as the inordinately late hour, but also — I'm convinced of this — to our ill-advised use of cocaine."

"But I partook of no cocaine!"

"Then to our exhaustion, to the stress of the scenario, to the latish hour, and in your case, Dr. Sammelsohn, to Hennessey and the effects of coital frustration."

I could only demur. There seemed to be no talking him out of this position, and though disagreements of lesser import would in later years drive the likes of Adler, Jung, and Ferenczi from the embrace of his affection, my sympathy for Dr. Freud, as well as his for me, remained (at this point) unimpaired, perhaps because, no matter how much we disagreed over the phenomenon of the angels, we had experienced it together.

My concern for Fräulein Eckstein was, by now, more than professional. Seeing her in the moments before Ita, sensing my presence in the room, animated the Fräulein's face with her own, I could only shudder at the ravaged woman lying before me. Despite Ita's girlish attempts to resuscitate her figure with grace and charm, Fräulein Eckstein was wasting away; and as I observed her physical dwindling, I couldn't hide from myself the knowledge that I was at least partly responsible for it.

You must understand: as my infatuation with Fräulein Eckstein diminished, my affection for Ita had grown. I'd discovered that we shared a world: a time and a place, and a complete cast of characters from the long-lost Szibotya of our childhood. I'd never before stopped to consider that our wedding had been forced upon her as well, and with as little sympathy shown to her as had been shown to me. Though in wildly differing ways, we'd been hurt by the same people at the same moment. With my vision corrected, I no longer saw Ita as a tool used against me, but as a fellow victim done a similar act of unkindness. Truth be told, though we had not married out of love, and though death had ended our nuptial agreements, we remained married nonetheless by the cruel experience of our wedding, and so I indulged myself (though, as I say, for no more than half an hour a day) in the pleasure of her company. As my affection for her grew, however, so did my concern for her ultimate fate: what was to become of her? In truth, she was everything the angels insisted: cruel, vindictive, haughty, caustic, dismissive, even murderous. (If, in Fräulein Eckstein's wasting body, she could have overpowered Dr. Freud, I've no doubt she would have strangled him to death and left the Fräulein to pay for her crimes.) And yet, because she reserved her bitterness for others, principally for those who had harmed us in our youths, I delighted in her gossipy excoriations and her dead-on impersonations of them. These held a very real pleasure for me; and over the course of these few weeks, we started to resemble newlyweds not a little. Entering her room, my heart would lift, and I'd call to her pleasantly. She'd respond, delighted to see me. I'd sit upon her bed and reach for her hand. She'd sit up, as an invalid might, and in a voice at times faint, at times strong, tell me of her day, of her therapeutic encounters with Dr. Freud, of the strategies she'd employed in outmaneuvering him. I laughed with her against him. We ridiculed his vanity, his overweening pomposity, his outrageous infatuation with the donkey-headed Fliess. She commiserated over the social tumult he'd put me through, pleading with me to drop him as a friend. Despite her disastrous suicide, or rather because of it, she'd become something of an actual wife to me and, if only for twenty or thirty minutes each evening, I finally experienced what my father in his rage would have denied his only son: the loving ministrations of a devoted wife.

"Are you getting enough to eat, Yankele?" she'd typically say to me. "Because you look so thin and peaked. Are you sleeping enough? You can sleep with me here if you wish," she'd say, making this offer in a low voice, all innocence and voluptuous generosity.

On other nights, she'd confessed her most intimate fears: "Oh, sometimes, Yankele, when I huddle against this Eckstein, I can't tell who is clinging to whom, and we wail over our fates like two lonely spinsters! All she wanted was to give Dr. Freud a case that would make his name! They'd tour the continent together, staging demonstrations in the capitals of the world. He'd come to love her, to prefer her, not only to his wife but to that sister-in-law of his (with whom she's convinced he's having an affair, though perhaps it's just her jealousy that tells her so). What will become of us, Yankl? Eckstein's dying, I'm dead, and both our loves are thwarted!"

Each night, as I bid her good evening, placing a firm and brotherly kiss upon her brow, she'd pull me to her, holding my hands against her breasts, imploring me, so that Dr. Freud, settling now into his chair at the foot of her bed, couldn't hear: "Lie with me, Yankl! Make me your wife — ravish me, claim the tokens of my maidenhood — they belong to you! — and I'll release all my captives. I swear it. You, Dr. Freud, Eckstein. I'll gladly burn in Gehenna if I can burn in the fire of your embrace first!"

I admit: these pleas became increasingly difficult to resist. I was a bachelor, after all, and a sexual maladroit, a man without a mistress in a world where unmarried women did not lie with men except if they were hired to do so. (Married women, then as now, slept with whomever they wished.) Only one thing kept my resolve in check: I didn't trust Ita. I trusted her neither to do what she promised nor to refrain from committing worse crimes once her demands were met. As every schoolboy knew, a dybbuk may use any opening to enter the body of a sinner. If I

kissed her lips or plunged into her body via its even more enticing ori-
fices, I feared she'd abandon Fräulein Eckstein and take up permanent
residence inside me, thus effectively fulfilling the commandment for a
man and wife to become one flesh.

(A curious note: Though Dr. Freud admitted to believing in none of
this, the day after our encounter with אשריל and שממגלפ, he paid a young
scholar, one of Rabbi Chajes's boys, to hang a mezuzah on the doorpost
of Fräulein Eckstein's room. "Why not?" He shrugged casually. "The
sickrooms of Christians all have crucifixes on their walls.")

CHAPTER 20

Certainly the tools of psychoanalysis were as precise as any surgeon's scalpel, but a doctor's instruments are only as profound as the doctor himself. This much was clear to Dr. Freud. Though he continued to work with Ita nightly, and though she began to submit grudgingly to his psychoanalytic probing, hers was proving to be an even more demanding case than he'd originally thought. Unlike with his normal run of neurotics and hysterics, it was no longer a question of uncovering a single childhood trauma buried beneath the rubble of a disintegrating personality. With Ita, there was no primal scene, no early experience of seduction, nor even a small chain of events that, once interpreted, would magically relieve all of her symptoms. Instead, she presented Dr. Freud with a series of lives. Her psychoanalytic history chronicled well over five thousand years, with one life ending (usually in disaster) and another beginning (always bright with hope and a breathtaking sense of innocence), each life ignited, like a chain smoker's cigarette, by the fiery destruction of the one preceding it.

Dr. Freud began to worry that in rejecting notions he'd previously considered superstitious trifles — reincarnation, divine justice, the constant identity of the soul — he had unnecessarily limited psychoanalysis's scope. True, not every patient would be able to recall all of her past lives; not everyone would be fortunate enough to attend her analytic hour in the guise of a dybbuk — certainly the constellation of events allowing Ita to do so would be difficult to replicate in the laboratory of clinical practice — still Dr. Freud was at times hopeful, at times despairing, that he'd soon discover a way to reach all his patients and not merely the dead ones, until each could make a full accounting of his soul's entire history.

"And yet, at other times, and more generally," he confessed to me, one freezing April evening at the Guglhupf, where he'd asked me to join him,

"I feel like the Sorcerer's Apprentice. As soon as I've solved the issues of one of Ita's lives, another five appear!"

"Ita's lives?" I said, and he nodded. "If I'm understanding you correctly then, you now believe you're speaking with Ita?"

"Believe? Disbelieve?" Dr. Freud puffed on his cigar. "Science is not a church, Dr. Sammelsohn, that I must formally declare my vows before entering its precincts. Do I believe I'm speaking to your former wife? Not at all! I've merely silenced my critical apparatus long enough to listen to the wishes of Fräulein Eckstein's other voice, a voice that has gone to great trouble to make itself known to us, and to address it in the language of its choosing. From Dr. Breuer's poor example, you see, I've learned the importance of acknowledging the dignity of *all* hysterical symptoms. And yet . . ." I waited for him to continue. "We must be strict with ourselves." He sighed and looked at his hands. "If we admit that these miraculous stories from the ancient past are beyond our testing; if, in our opinion, they cannot be substantiated; mustn't we concede that they cannot, strictly speaking, be disproved either? In the absence of hard, scientific evidence that dybbuks *don't* exist, isn't it more scientific to hold out the possibility that they might?"

"I'm astonished to hear you say such a thing," I told him.

"Our science is young, Dr. Sammelsohn, and we've no idea where these procedures will lead us. Perhaps only when we're done with the voyage will we know for certain where we have been. In any case, thank you for meeting me here tonight."

Dr. Freud called for the waiter and instructed him to push two tables together. He next unrolled an enormous chart across the two tabletops. From his medical bag, he took out pens and bottles of ink, the sort medical illustrators use, and, from the inside pocket of his vest, a small quantity of scraps.

As he unfolded these, I saw that his handwriting covered both sides in chaotic fashion.

"Notes from another mad session," he explained. "Tonight's, in fact. Many of them concerning you." He removed his coat and hung it on the back of his chair. "Let me just ink these in and I'll explain everything to you at once."

He bent over the chart and, consulting his notes, began filling in the data. I'd never seen him quite so excited. Pacing round the tables, the way an artist might a half-finished canvas, he slurped at his coffee without looking at the cup. His hair hung down in loose strands before his eyes. His tie was unknotted, his vest unbuttoned. Ink colored his fingers; and his cuffs, despite the precaution he took, were soon busy with stains.

"Waiter!" he cried again after a moment, standing back to judge his work. "Two more coffees, and make them strong—oh, and two snifters of brandy as well!"

Returning to the chart, he corrected some small slips of his pen with a chamois. The waiter brought our drinks, placing everything on a table nearby, his calm manner in direct contradiction to Dr. Freud's agitation, an agitation that was proving contagious. I was trembling with nervousness myself.

"Given the depth of the psyche," I said to Dr. Freud, "mightn't it be preferable to remain blind to one's former lives? Perhaps man is not meant to know himself quite so completely."

Dr. Freud held his notes before his face and squinted to read them. "This isn't the best place for this work, I'm afraid," he said, moving closer to the lamp.

I continued, "If Heaven or happenstance or even human incuriosity sees fit to erect a curtain between who a man thinks he is and his deeper self, should a man really take advantage of a rip in the fabric to peek through that curtain?"

Dr. Freud grunted noncommittally.

"Mightn't one be opening a Pandora's box that could affect the course of one's entire life?"

Dr. Freud glanced up, frowning like a man who'd bitten into an unripe lime. "Don't be absurd, Dr. Sammelsohn," he said, cleaning his pen with his tongue and drying it on his chamois, and instantly I felt that he was right. Only a man content with his own smallness would walk away from the Faustian bargain: isn't knowledge of one's true self worth losing everything, including one's soul? and didn't Dr. Faust beat the Devil in the end, simply by proclaiming his belief in God? or was it his belief in Christ?

If the former, I felt emboldened; if the latter, not as much.

Dr. Freud rolled down his sleeves and clipped his cuff links through his cuffs. He buttoned his vest and laced the golden chain of his watch through the slits in its fabric. With a lighted cigar in his hand, he brushed back his hair. Raising two fingers to his lips as though he were about to whistle, he instead fixed the part in his mustache.

"Come. Let us have a look," he said. "It's a trifle inelegant perhaps, but it was the only way I could keep track of all the information Ita was spewing forth."

He and I bent over the chart spread out across the two tabletops. In scarlet ink, Dr. Freud had sketched in all the incarnations Ita had recalled, as though each were an entry in a genealogical record of a large family, with lines branching off from each persona to its relevant events and relationships.

For example:

HERMAN WEISENTHAL, merchant ———— marries SOPHIE neé GOLD
(b: Berlin 1776; d: Philadephia 1801;   (b. Freiberg 1774; d: ? 1843)
in the Americas from 1790 on)

Suicide; suspected arson   children: Jean-Paul (b. Phila. 1795)
                                                                   Dora (b: Phila. 1796)
Seduced by father LEOPOLD
(who, between lives, Ita realizes
is "BASHAN")

(see: AVIDAL)

In blue, he'd charted the incarnations of Zusha, Ita's grandfather, who appeared now as her husband, now as her wife, now as her master, now as her lover, her owner, or her slave. Across the long plain of Jewish history, these two had shared a combustible relationship, taking turns murdering or being murdered by each other. Discovering each other in every life, one always taking the other by surprise, one always gaining the upper hand, neither seemed to realize that a person pays in the next life with his own for the lives he takes in this one.

Charted in green ink, my father (or his various incarnations) appeared periodically as well, always at a polite distance, always facilitating, through his ignorance, the meeting of these two incompatibles.

"Of course, the whole thing is necessarily simplified in this graphic form," Dr. Freud told me. "Every detail is highly overdetermined."

In gold, he'd documented the appearance and disappearance of a fortune Ita had spent all her lives chasing. Having earned it in one life, she'd lose it in the next, only to inherit it in another after Zusha had stolen it during a life in between. In a similar vein, in pink, Dr. Freud had traced a strain of syphilis Ita first contracted in the eleventh century from a parish priest. Dr. Freud cracked his knuckles and pointed at the chart. "Follow the chain of syphilis, Dr. Sammelsohn, and you'll see that time and again, every few lives, Ita reinfects herself. It goes round and round in a configuration I can only describe, on this chart anyway, as a double helix."

(Once again, as with the cocaine—but more on this below—a blind Freud had found his way to a treasure that, for whatever reason, he couldn't see.)

Pointing with his pen, he brought my attention to other entries marked in red. "Look closely here, Dr. Sammelsohn, and you can see the amazing role fire seems to play in so many of אַאָעָאַאַעָעָעָעוויריא's lives." He tapped his chart with an unlit cigar. "Here, as you can see, she destroys a country church, burning its congregants and its vicar to cinders, only to suffer the same cruel fate three-quarters of a century later as a burgher in the Alps. Here, she drowns her own children; there, a thousand years later, she is drowned. Here, she swindles; there, she is murdered by swindlers."

"And what's all this?" I said, pointing to various mathematical calculations littering the margins of the chart.

"Nothing, just nonsense," Dr. Freud said, "just some details of each person's nose and various notations concerning cycles of twenty-three and twenty-eight, information I'd gathered in the hopes of enticing Wilhelm's interest in the project, but I'm sorry to say he considers the work beneath his scientific dignity, and I've come to doubt the data is of more than dubious value."

I could feel Dr. Freud watching me.

"You're looking for yourself, of course," he said.

"Of course," I admitted.

"Yes, but, you see, I've intentionally left *you,* as an item, off."

"And why is that?"

"So that, having arranged to meet you here tonight, I might show you the chart and consult with you upon its meaning without compromising your medical objectivity. Your collaboration is proving far too precious for me to render its potency null by implicating you into the equation. Tonight, after you've taken a look, I'll go home and fill in the rest. I have only to ink in the matters pertaining to you. I possess a certain amount of information about where you, or more precisely your soul, has been for the last few thousand years."

"But . . ." I could only protest.

"Also," Dr. Freud said, stopping me, "I'm not certain at this point how much of this information I can share with you without violating Ita's confidentiality, to say nothing of Fräulein Eckstein's."

"Of course," I said. Once again, I'd underestimated Dr. Freud's integrity, and once again, he'd proven me deficient in my esteem for him. Here was a man of unbending medical scruple, of unfailing principle, or so I thought until, unable to constrain himself, he said, "Oh, what the deuce! It's really too exciting to keep to oneself—and who else, other than Minna, can I discuss it with?" He spoke in a rush, hurriedly inking in all the data that pertained to me. "Marty takes no interest in these things. The sexual component of my work disgusts her. She's a lovely woman, and a man couldn't ask for a better mate, although that's the problem with a perfect wife, isn't it? It's impossible to divorce her! Ha! Upon what grounds? You see? There are none!"

Wiping the nib of his pen, he pinned me with his gaze. "Now we must clear our heads for the great work that lies before us. Mankind, I'm certain, is not yet prepared to accept the gift I'm on the point of bestowing upon it: the truth about our many lives and the effects each has upon those that follow. You shall be my test case, my first audience, Dr. Sammelsohn. Come," he said, leaning in. "The chart is complete and, for the moment, up to date. Now tell me what you think."

He pointed with the two fingers that held his burning cigar.

"Here," he said. "Look here. This is a most important thing. You see this cinnamon-colored line I've only just inked in?" He directed my attention to a long golden-brown ribbon of ink that, as a dotted line, spiraled though the various stages of Ita's long trek.

"I see it," I said, bending nearer, "though the light is rather poor. However, what does it represent?"

"Love." Dr. Freud grinned mischievously. "Real, actual, consummated, mutual, fructifying, and revivifying love. But as you can see, my dear young man, the line is segmented and broken. Nowhere on the chart is it complete. Follow its path and you'll come to realize what I have realized these last few weeks working with our friend. Though in each of her many lives, Ita experienced a profound longing for another—that person appearing on my chart in amethyst—the timing of these encounters has never been right, was, in fact, almost always horribly wrong, and decisively so—off sometimes by a few days, sometimes by hours, sometimes by entire centuries. Here, for example, as a fuller's apprentice in Babylon, she's conceived a passion for her master's wife that is never consummated. Seven hundred years later"—he pointed to the bottom of the chart—"we find that same soul, as a young page, pining for a knight who has no interest in him, except as a convenient source for an occasional moment of sexual gratification."

"I'm the fuller's wife?"

"And the page. Again and again, through the millennia, the theme plays itself out in a thousand different variations. In each life, circumstances throw you together, and, in each life, fate keeps you from merging."

"And Ita knows all this?"

"In part, but only in part. And that's why she has been so insistent upon consummating your marriage. No longer can we imagine her the disappointed bride of a single night. Alas, she has been hungering for you over the course of many thousands of years." Dr. Freud pointed to the top of the first page. "Almost as far back as it goes, days before the giving of the Torah at Mt. Sinai, actually, when Moses separated the men from the women, you and she, newly liberated from your slavery in Egypt, made plans for a clandestine rendezvous. You were to meet her in her tent. Although I should say 'meet him in *his* tent,' for as you can see, in this encounter, she was the male"—he pointed to an ancient-sounding name inscribed upon the chart in scarlet—"yourself the female." Another name in purple. "Fearful of breaking the prophetic law, you avoided her that night and for many nights thereafter. Alas, she seems to have been among the scoundrels committing sexual revelry at the base of the Golden Calf, all of whom, as you know, were subsequently slaughtered by the Leviim, along with Moses."

"Along with Moses?" I said.

"Hm, they slaughtered him as well." Dr. Freud looked through the scraps of his notes. "Or I believe that's what Ita told me. She was an eyewitness, after all. However, since then, it's been the same thing over and over again. Perhaps even as paramecia, you two couldn't quite come together."

"And if I choose to consummate my marriage with her now?"

"To liberate Fräulein Eckstein or something like that?"

"And Ita and myself."

"Break the long chain of karma, to quote Fräulein Eckstein's brother?"

"Yes, certainly."

"Well." Dr. Freud swallowed the last of his brandy. "You would be doing several things at once: primarily, you would be stealing from me the most important patient and the most essential case I've yet to encounter in all my researches; and for that reason alone, I cannot permit it. Secondly, can we really trust Ita to make good her promises? I think not. Further, who knows what might happen if, after thousands of years, you two consummate your love? The entire city might burn up in the conflagration! And lastly, there's a concern about what the sexual act with Ita, perpetrated through the vile use of Fräulein Eckstein, might do to Fräulein Eckstein, for whose care, as I've never ceased to remind you, I remain responsible."

"But you yourself tried to convince me doing so was morally reasonable."

"See: reason one."

"Surely you're jesting!"

"No, Dr. Sammelsohn, I assure you I am not. I can't lie to you: this case could make my name, and I'm not going to rush through it as I did, damn it, with that damned cocaine!"

(As a young medical man, having pioneered the research into cocaine as an ophthalmological anesthetic, Dr. Freud left off from his work in order to visit his then fiancée, Martha Bernays. While he was gone, his friend Carl Koller perfected the practical application, work for which he was subsequently nominated for a Nobel Prize.)

I didn't know what to say. With both hands, I pulled back my hair. My limbs felt light, my head woozy. I looked at Dr. Freud's chart, spread out across the two tabletops, the new additions glinting under the gaslights as the fresh ink dried. I peered out the café window. It was past midnight. We'd been talking for hours. A fierce snowstorm had blown in.

"But this is preposterous!" I said.

"What exactly is preposterous?" Dr. Freud returned.

"That you should put establishing your name before the well-being of either of your patients! I don't know what to say, but . . . I won't stand for it. Good night, sir!" I tramped out of the café, a dramatic exit whose drama was spoiled by the fact that, dizzy with the new information I'd been absorbing, I'd left my coat behind. Rolling up his chart, binding it with a pale blue ribbon, Dr. Freud looked up from this task when I reentered the café. "I've forgotten my coat," I explained. He squinted in incomprehension, apparently not having heard me. "I've forgotten my coat," I said, a bit more forcefully this time.

"Oh, oh, yes," he said. "Well, mustn't go out without that. Not in this weather."

"Good night, then," I said, grabbing the garment.

"Good night, Doktor."

"We'll speak," I said, attempting a note of reconciliation.

I walked out into the night. My head was on fire. Had I really been chasing Ita through the world for thousands of years? And if I had, what did I intend to do about it now? My first impulse was to flee the city. Perhaps Dr. Freud was right. If a simple love on a small scale can scald a person beyond recognition, what of a love that stretches through millennia, binding the living and the dead, a love so ruthless it cares neither how many hostages it takes nor how many corpses lie in its wake? I certainly wasn't prepared for such a love; and besides, as I kept reminding myself, Ita was dead. What kind of lover would a dead woman make, to say nothing of a wife? What sort of home might we build together? What sort of children did I imagine she would give me? No, a future with Ita was nothing but a silly daydream. The most I could hope for was a night or two of passion. Although what was wrong with that? With the door of Fräulein Eckstein's hospital room secured and locked, the three of us might come to an understanding and finally know the vivifying pleasure of physical love. Indeed, as Dr. Freud himself had pointed out—before he countered his own reasoning—the body in question was and was not Fräulein Eckstein's. And though I'd come to realize that it wasn't Fräulein Eckstein I'd fallen in love with, but rather Ita, sheltering inside her, I wasn't, in all honesty, indifferent to the beauty of Fräulein Eckstein's body, even in its present state. And mightn't the experience be beneficial for her, or even especially for her, if, as a result, Ita released her from her grasp? Still, I wasn't convinced, even in our enlightened age, that an encounter of this sort wouldn't adversely affect her chances for a decent marriage. Still, what was the alternative—contacting Rabbi Chajes at the Seitenstettengasse Shul and asking him to round up eight Jews besides ourselves (seven if Dr. Freud consented to join us) to serve as participants in an exorcism? Hadn't I left all that behind? The superstition, the guileless piety, the seeing of the Divine Hand beneath every crack in the sidewalk! It was 1895, after all, the modern age! If, as a child, I'd known enough to reject my parents' beliefs as foolish, was I really to adopt them now as a grown man? And even if I ran to Rabbi Chajes's and asked for his help, I knew he'd laugh me out of his office. Here, in the West, even the religious scoff at the wonders we, in the East, take for granted!

And yet I'd never felt like this before. The experience was absolutely new to me, and it filled me with an enormous sense of contentment and glee: I was loved. *I was loved!* I, Ya'akov Yosef Sammelsohn, was loved with a love spanning aeons and generations! And thanks to the young science of psychoanalysis, for the first time in all my various lives, I understood something about the long history Ita and I shared and could now make an informed decision regarding it. How, under such circumstances, could I let such a love slip through my fingers?

I'd intended to return home, to sleep perhaps for an hour before trudging into the clinic, but instead I found myself walking all night, sipping from the bottle of brandy I'd taken, without Dr. Freud's noticing, from the Guglhupf. It was nearly dawn, however, and I was lost. None of the streets were familiar to me, the district completely unknown. And yet, when I raised my head—mirabile visu!—I saw that I'd somehow arrived at the Sanatorium Loew, its long marble edifice glinting in the new morning light. It looked different from the way I remembered it. I'd seen it only in the dead of night, when the gas lamps made everything dilapidated and sad. In the freshly minted light of a sparkling winter day, the building seemed bright, even iridescent.

Go home, run home, go! No good will come of this! I cautioned myself as I opened the gate. Go home! I admonished myself, and I ignored these admonitions as I made my way through the foyer into the mezzanine and down the hallway to Fräulein Eckstein's door, knocking upon it as softly as I could.

"Ita?" I stuck my head into her room provisionally. "Darling, are you here? Are you awake? Can you rouse yourself, my dear?"

The body in the bed began to stir. Lifting her head from the pillows, she sat up and looked at me. However, it was not Ita, but Fräulein Eckstein who greeted me.

"Oh, Dr. Sammelsohn?" she said. "Is that you? Why, you look a mess!"

(My clothes were damp and my hair wet from my long night's walk. Also, thanks to the brandy, I'm certain I had the disreputable look of a man who'd been drinking all night. Which is exactly what I was.)

"Have you come to rescue me?" She laughed gaily. "Or abscond with me? I hope so. Because I must tell you, Dr. Sammelsohn, I'm feeling ever so much better."

"Would you like that, Fräulein? If we ran away together?"

"Why is it, Dr. Sammelsohn," she said to me, "that you and I have not fallen in love with each other?"

"Why not indeed, Fräulein?"

She took my hand. "Wouldn't we have made a suitable pair?"

Although her tone was flirtatious, she seemed to have meant her question earnestly. Arrested by her flirtatiousness, I looked into her lovely face. Before I could answer her, however, before I could say anything at all, in fact, the expression of hopeful curiosity vanished from it. It was as though someone had pulled her away from a window, a window at which, in the next moment, the face of her captor appeared.

"Yankl?" Ita said, equally pleased and surprised to see me. "What are you doing here?" She closed the neck of her gown demurely. "And so early?"

"Do you mind if I sit down, Ita?"

"Oh, my hair must be a fright." With both hands, she touched her hair, but made no effort to comb or untangle it. I drew my chair near to her bedside.

"No, you look lovely."

"Flatterer!"

"But you *do*."

She gave me a frank look. "You've been speaking with Dr. Freud, haven't you?"

"I have indeed."

"And how much has he told you?"

"Everything."

"Everything?"

"Enough."

"And now? What do you intend?"

At that moment, a white-hatted nurse stuck her head into the room. "Ah, I see you're awake," the nurse said.

"I am," Ita answered, as sweetly as Fräulein Eckstein might.

"Are you hungry?"

"Oh, simply ravenous!"

She carried in the tray. "Good morning, Doctor," she said to me, eying my wet hair and my miserable-looking clothes. "Is everything all right with you, sir?"

"Nurse." I nodded in greeting. "Thank you. Yes, I'm fine."

She placed the tray near Fräulein Eckstein's bed. Laid out upon it were a soft-boiled egg in an alabaster cup, pats of butter, a hard roll, jam, coffee, and a small glass of prune juice.

"We have to keep up our strength," she cautioned.

"We certainly do," Ita sang out.

She tucked in the corners of Fräulein Eckstein's bed before leaving us to ourselves again.

"You know, she's right," Ita said to me when she'd gone. "If I don't feed and care for this old body, giving it the proper nourishment, doing my twenty minutes of calisthenics and walking every day, poor Eckstein might waste away, and then where would I be?"

"You've thought of everything, haven't you?"

Ita's face hardened; she stopped chewing her egg; she held up the little spoon, making her point. "Let me tell you something, Yankl," she said. "I'm not going back. I'm never going back, not into a disgusting animal nor into a stone! You've never experienced coldness until you've lived as a stone, to say nothing of *slowness*! Oh, the tedium!"

I couldn't help laughing. "You're quite a charming woman."

"Stop it!"

"But you know that, don't you?"

"Well, if I didn't, you've been telling me it for thousands of years."

"Have I?"

"According to Dr. Freud."

"Well, I mean it this time."

"As you have all the other times," she said.

"And yet?"

"You've never acted upon those feelings."

She was right. She was right. Stung, I stood and paced the room. I turned my back upon her and stared out the window, though I could still feel her eyes upon me, watching my every move. "Ita," I said, "you know as well as I the dead have no claims upon the living."

Though I couldn't see it, I sensed her gesture: a small victorious shrug. "I'm not interested in laws," she said, "neither God's nor man's."

I watched through the window as sheaths of ice dropped from the branches of a tree and fell silently into the snow.

"Don't you imagine you'll be punished severely?"

"I'll deal with that when I have to."

I turned and, without success, tried to read her face. "You have no intention of keeping your bargain, do you?"

"My bargain?"

"Of surrendering Fräulein Eckstein if your demands are met."

"No." She laughed. "Why should I?"

"You really are wicked, aren't you?"

"Oh, you have no idea, Yankl. You should see the despair that greets me every time I die. Poor אשריאל. How he shakes his head over me, always hoping for even the slightest bit of moral improvement, but I always disappoint him. He has the patience of a saint, though I suppose an angel would."

I couldn't help smiling.

"I'm glad I amuse you," she said.

I had to admit it: she looked stunning in her bed, radiant, as only an invalid can, with fevers, her hair a wild mess about her shoulders.

"Why do I run from you?" I said. "Tell me that, Ita. Why have I run from you through all these many lives?"

Though the entire room separated us, we were now looking directly into each other's eyes. I could feel the winter's chill through the window panes on my back.

"Yankl," she said, naughtily. "Come here, my darling, and I'll show you why."

"No, Ita," I said, dropping my gaze and losing my nerve.

I looked out the window again, and when next I turned to her, I was alarmed to see that she had unbuttoned Fräulein Eckstein's gown and unlaced her chemise and pulled both garments from her shoulders. With both hands, she lifted the Fräulein's small breasts and held them up to me. At the sight of her flesh, mine began to yearn for hers, tingling, as though under the electric pulse of a faradic brush. She smiled a small smile of barely concealed triumph.

"Let me lock the door," I heard myself saying, and soon, my hands were fumbling with the key. I crossed the room and sat next to her. The bed was high, and I am short, and so I sat on the edge like a child, my feet not quite reaching the floor. I kissed her, my chest constricting in a wild spasm. Indeed, I could barely breathe. Below my cravat and through the fabric of my shirt, beneath the wings of my vest and under the lapels of my suit, I could feel Fräulein Eckstein's soft breasts hardening, as my lips grazed hers.

"You don't know how long you've been waiting for this, Yankl, but I do."

"Ita." I gulped for breath.

She placed a hand tenderly on my cheek. "Darling, let's not speak."

"But I love you," I said. "That's all I wanted to say."

She leaned back and looked at me as though I'd suddenly gone mad.

"I mean it," I told her. "I love you. Is that so very strange?" I moved in to kiss her again, but she pushed me away, both of her hands flat against my chest.

"And you expect me to believe that?"

Her question caught me off-guard. "Why wouldn't you believe it?"

"I wasn't born yesterday, you know."

"To say the very least."

"No, and neither were you!" She crossed her arms angrily. Looking away from me, she recrossed her arms and sneered, as though she sensed she were being made the butt of some unfortunate joke.

"Ita, surely you must know by now that I'm sincere in my affections."

"Right, right, right." She laughed an ugly little laugh. "If it weren't for Eckstein, do you really think you'd even be here?"

"If it weren't for Eckstein?"

"'If it weren't for Eckstein?'" she mimicked me, lowering her voice and parodying mine.

"What does Fräulein Eckstein have to do with any of this?"

"You know you only want to save her!"

"But I don't!" I cried. "I mean, certainly, I did. At first. No, you're right. At first, it was true. I was appalled at her situation. But now . . ."

"But now?" Ita hugged her knees to her chest and planted her chin on top of them.

"But now — oh, it's so difficult to say this, really. But now I don't care a *fig* about Emma Eckstein!" The truth of this sentiment was terrifying to speak aloud, and I retreated from it immediately. "No, of course, I do. I do *care* about her. Of course, I care. Who wouldn't? Don't misunderstand me. I think it's terrible what's happened to her, unfortunate in the extreme—"

"Yes, it's unfortunate." Ita sneered again. "It's unfortunate that I'm so very evil!"

"But even under these circumstances, Ita"—I sighed—"I don't want to lose you."

She closed her eyes and cocked her ear towards me. "You don't?" she said in the voice of a little girl. "Really?"

I grasped her hand and kissed it. "Ita, listen to me. I've hungered for you—if Dr. Freud's psychoanalytic techniques have any scientific validity, and I believe they do—for well over three thousand years! And now I'm simply fed up with waiting."

"You are?"

"Yes! That's what I've been trying to tell you."

"And you love me?"

"I do."

She leaned back against the pillows of her bed. She laughed, showing all of Fräulein Eckstein's pretty white teeth. "You love me?"

"I do, Ita. Really."

"Really?"

"Yes!"

She kissed me. But then her face darkened, and her hands began to tremble. I doubted at first what I was seeing, but it appeared that tears had moistened her eyes. She bowed her head and brought her two hands, flat against each other, to her face, pursing her lips against her two index fingers. She took a deep breath and closed her eyes. When she opened them again, she looked at me before her expression crumbled into a ruin of despair.

"Yankl," she whispered, shaking her head. "I want to be worthy of your love."

"Worthy?"

"No, I want to be worthy of you."

"But you are worthy, Ita!"

"No, I'm not. Just look at me! Look at me, Yankl," she said with real disgust. "I can't stay here."

I attempted to kiss her again. "But of course you can," I said, cupping her breast in my hand.

"No, don't. Don't!" She pushed me away. "It's too . . . vulgar!" She frowned.

"Vulgar?"

"Our meeting like this! Oh, Yankl." She stroked my face, drawing me near. She kissed me again, her tears spilling onto my cheeks. "But you're so sweet. No, you're so good, my darling, you're so very good and so very sweet."

"But I'm not, Ita. I'm not good, nor am I sweet, but I love you, and I want to make love to you right now." I could think of no other words with which to press my case.

"Hold me, Yankl. Hold me in your arms."

I embraced her more completely.

"Yankl?"

"Yes, my darling?"

She took a moment and exhaled a deep breath. "I have to leave you now."

"No. Certainly not."

"No, I think I have to leave you."

"Ita! Please!"

She brought her fingers to my lips, as though to silence me, and I kissed them, and she kissed my lips through them.

"I'll be so lonely without you," I said.

"Then promise me you'll wait for me," she said.

"But you're not going anywhere."

"Promise me, Yankl!"

"Of course I promise," I said.

"Swear to it!"

"Very well. I swear."

"Swear on all that is holy that you'll wait for me to be reborn; swear, Yankl."

"Of course, I swear that I'll wait for you to be reborn, my darling."

"On God's holy name and on His holy Torah."

"I swear!"

"Good," she said. "Now I can go. But how?"

"Go? Ita, no. You mustn't! You can't! Not yet."

"Through her ear?"

"Through her ear? No, we'll discuss all this later, darling, after we've made love."

"Through her skin, Yankl, bursting through? No, that's no good. Through one of her toes?"

"Let's just put this off for an hour, shall we?"

"I can't, Yankl. You have to understand. It's not honorable. It wouldn't be honorable or fair to the Fräulein. It's not right, and it's certainly not worthy of your love. Of *our* love! Now that we've found each other again! Please, Yankl. Help me return to God."

There seemed to be no dissuading her. Any idiot could see that, and as I sheltered her in my arms, I could feel her hold over Fräulein Eckstein weakening, her grip on the Fräulein giving way, surrendering, the way an orange peel, sliced into, begins to release the meat of its fruit.

"But how shall I do it, husband?"

"Let me think," I said, and I thought back to that odd night all those many years ago when the rebbe had called me into his chambers with my friend Shaya and told us of the exorcism he'd performed hundreds of years before as an Italian rabbi in Padua. Through what avenue had he commanded the darkened spirit of Bernardo Messina to depart from that poor Jewish maid? Was it the ear? Or did that result in hearing problems for the girl? Was it through the skin? Certainly not. The wound would have been too great, too punitive, too dangerous. I remembered something Dr. Freud had said about Josephus, a Rabbi Eleazar, and a magical ring. Was it through the nose? Did he pull the spirit out through the nose? Something about the nose seemed to ring a bell.

"You're certain?" Ita said, looking nervously into my eyes.

I shrugged. "That's what I seem to recall."

Her trembling had grown unusually fierce and the entire bed— indeed, the entire room—seemed to be shaking.

"Yankl, my husband," she said.

I held her as tightly as I could. "My darling?"

"Kiss me one last time in this world, but do so quickly." Mustering all her strength, she attempted with only limited success to quiet her tremors, and I kissed her as passionately as her trembling permitted me to do. "Darling, don't leave me until I'm completely gone."

"I shan't," I promised.

"Although you'd better stand away."

Reluctant to abandon her, I nevertheless placed myself against the nearest wall. She lay back in the bed, rigidly at first, but relaxing by degrees. Fräulein Eckstein's body began convulsing, opening and closing like a pocketknife. These muscular contractions were so fierce that at times she appeared to be hovering in the air, twisting this way and that, shaking and shouting like an epileptic during a seizure, calling out so frightfully, it's a wonder she didn't succeed in summoning the entire nursing staff to her room. I recoiled to see her hammering her head against the pillows, beating with her fists against her thighs, screeching horrible garbled sounds, screaming like someone whose tongue had been anaesthetized. Now she seemed to be choking, strangling, her eyes wide in horror; now laughing, as though tickled to the point of nausea. She tried to sit up, a rasping noise coming from deep within her throat. Her arms flailing, she fell back into the sweat-stained sheets. She jerked her lower body up and down. At this point, my vision darkened, I must have been losing consciousness, and I saw, or imagined I saw, a cloud or a gaseous fume forming above her bed. Ring-shaped, the color of a bloody sunset, it seemed to be swirling around her bed, and for a moment I imagined I saw אשריל and שמנגלפ's faces inside it. Fräulein Eckstein struggled in an agony beneath it, until with a propulsive burst, something unseeable exploded through her left nostril with a small starburst of blood.

"Yankl, my husband, my lover!" Ita called to me, though no longer from inside Fräulein Eckstein's body. I looked about me and saw nothing other than the Fräulein lying lifeless and bloody atop her blankets and her sheets. Ita's voice came from inside the rose-colored fumes. "Farewell for now, my darling!" she cried, her voice ringing with a tone of happiness. I was chilled to hear the sharp sound of glass breaking, and a tiny, round opening appeared in the hospital window as though someone had shot a bullet through its pane. The bloody plume was sucked, as though by a vacuum, from the space above me through this hole, and I nearly fainted to hear אשריל and שמנגלפ's voices calling out.

"A noble heart," אשריל said.

"Yes," שמנגלפ said, "and he has already received his reward."

CHAPTER 21

I woke up, days later, in Dr. Freud's consultancy. I looked at the ceiling. A thin veil of cobwebs hung from a beam. Dr. Freud's hand pressed against my forehead, knocking clumsily into my nose. "Sorry," he said, readjusting his position. His hand was dry and scratchy. His face was near mine—he sat in a chair next to the sofa—and his breath was a mixture of tobacco, peppermint, and inadequate dental care. I closed my eyes and was instantly asleep.

When I awoke next, I was in my own bed. I had no idea how much time had passed, nor how I'd gotten there, but I opened my eyes to find Dr. Freud's bearded face looming over me again. I felt my head; it was bandaged. Weighed down by the covers, I struggled to sit up.

"Ah, thank Heavens, you're awake," he called. "Although I wouldn't move too fast, if I were you."

"But what has happened?"

"It's unclear. The police say they found you, drunken and bareheaded in the snow."

"And Fräulein Eckstein? How is she?" I said, but before he could answer, I was again fast asleep.

I was able eventually to awaken and to stay awake, and, when I did, I found Dr. Freud sitting in a rocking chair near my bed, sipping at a cup of tea. My landlady brought in soup for me, and when I'd sufficiently regained my strength, Dr. Freud and I had a frank talk. He'd been none too pleased, he told me, stopping by Fräulein Eckstein's room the day after I'd last seen him, to discover that Ita was gone. "You really gave no thought at all to my scientific researches, did you, Dr. Sammelsohn?"

"It's hardly my fault," I said. "All I did was to declare my love for Ita and suggest that she depart Fräulein Eckstein through the nose. Everything that came in between those two events transpired without me."

"The cause denying responsibility for the effects!" Dr. Freud said sharply. "Well, no matter." He put down his tea. "Fortunately I've managed to gather enough data to rock the very foundations of the scientific world!"

Before he could do that, however, he'd seen to Fräulein Eckstein's nose. "It was in a state of ruin," he whispered. This was partially my fault and partially Ita's. Mine, because my instructions to her had been imprecise — I should have commanded her to leave, not *through the nose,* but *through the right or left nostril* — and Ita's, because in her recklessness to scale the barricades of Heaven, she'd taken less care than she might have otherwise done.

As a consequence, the Fräulein's nose had caved in. Tapping his own nose, Dr. Freud said, "The left middle turbinate bone seemed to have shattered completely."

He'd called in Dr. Fliess from Berlin, of course — whether because he thought Dr. Fliess the most competent man available or because working with a doctor from out of town might safeguard his own reputation, I cannot say. Neither can I say whether it was earlier or during these procedures that Dr. Fliess left the meter of surgical gauze inside Fräulein Eckstein's nasal cavity. My sense of time is woozy, and though I retain no high opinion of Dr. Fliess's medical finesse, I wouldn't put it past Dr. Freud to have made up the entire tale, just as many now suspect he made up the story of Bertha Pappenheim's hysterical pregnancy, just as there are those who believe that Dr. Jung made up the story of Dr. Freud's love affair with his own sister-in-law. These giants of scientific integrity apparently feel no comparable scruple regarding the truth when it comes to the character of their enemies and former friends.

Still, true to his word, Dr. Freud wrote up his notes and presented the case as a paper, on April 21, 1896, before the Society for Psychiatry and Neurology in Vienna. He knew the lecture, entitled "The Aetiology of Hysteria," would be revolutionary, presenting, as it did, not only Ita's case history but Dr. Freud's radical new theory that the origins of hysteria lay not in early sexual traumas, as he'd until then maintained, but in "dybbuk seductions," as he termed them, and other forms of spirit possession. As a therapy, Dr. Freud recommended extensive past-life regression by means of a psychoanalysis and, if need be, hypnosis.

Needless to say, the lecture met with an icy reception, eliciting from Dr. Richard von Krafft-Ebing the now-famous retort: "It sounds like a scientific fairy tale!" Dr. Freud's colleagues rose up as a group, not to denounce him, as one might expect, but to protect him from himself, and the talk was universally suppressed.

Eventually, under pressure from the group, Dr. Freud recanted everything.

Now, according to Dr. Freud, God was nothing more than a symptom of our child-like longing for a father who might exorcise the terrors of nature, reconcile us to our deaths, and compensate us for our suffering and privation.

When we spoke of the matter later, he went so far as to claim that I'd hallucinated the entire affair, including our conversations in my bedroom, while I lay, drunken and bareheaded, in the snow—a claim impossible for me to refute. In his memoirs, he distanced himself even further from Fräulein Eckstein's case: "If the reader feels inclined to shake his head at my credulity, I cannot altogether blame him," he wrote, "though I may plead that this was at the time when I was intentionally keeping my critical faculty in abeyance in order to preserve an unprejudiced and receptive attitude towards the many novelties coming to my notice every day. However, I was at last obliged to recognize that these scenes of seduction had never taken place and were only phantasies which my patient had made up or which I myself had perhaps forced upon her."

As fairy tales go, Dr. Freud's was neither the sweetest nor the most imaginative, but it served the traditional purpose of fairy tales: lulling its listener into an uncritical sleep.

I saw little of him after that. Our paths never seemed to cross. I can only assume that the sight of me, loveless and forlorn, waiting for my soulmate to be reborn, reminded him too much of his own intellectual duplicities, or perhaps he merely thought me the most gullible of fools. Whatever the reason, my invitations to him were politely, if firmly declined; his and Marty's ceased coming to me altogether. Thus began the systematic suppression of everything that occurred between Dr. Freud and myself. (Even in Dr. Freud's famous "Irma" dream, the dream that unlocked the secrets of dream interpretation for him, I appear, concealed, though in plain sight, as a *Sammelperson,* a composite.)

BOOK TWO

MILOJN DA JESOJ;

or, My New Life in the Esperanto Movement

CHAPTER 1

I tried to get on with my life. What else was there for me to do? I threw myself into my work; and when I wasn't working, I read voluminously; and when I wasn't reading, I dragged my body out on long walks, dressed head to toe in widower's black. I wound up most evenings at the Prater, and though I continued to patronize Herr Franz's Marvelous & Astonishing Puppet Theater, I avoided the prostitutes who hung their wares in the park nearby, fearing that in my misery I lacked the fortitude to resist their squalid charms.

Inside Herr Franz's, I found myself ogling every newborn daughter in her pram, hoping to catch in her unfocused eye a glint that might say to me: *Yes, Yankl, it is I, your beloved Ita, newly reborn! We've only to wait another eighteen years, and we can be married again!*

(The only thing I understood with certainty during this difficult time was that no mother enjoys having her infant daughter stared at in this too-inquisitive way by a stranger in a puppet theater with no children of his own to justify his presence there, and who, really, can blame her?)

O, IF ONLY I could have ended this book with the scene of Ita dashing headlong onto the ramparts of Heaven from the rumpled sheets of Fräulein Eckstein's hospital bed! What a glorious drama that would have made! Life, however, does not end where our storybooks do. Or at least mine didn't. No, the obdurate and all-too-actual world with its crush of petty demands and its dulling routines soon swept me off the high cliffs of my romantic folly, and I was drowned in the wild, raging river of ordinary, everyday life. Though I'd renounced all women in the wake of Ita's miraculous ascension, and though I intended to keep the pledge I'd made to her — that I would wait for her — the heart is crooked (ah, but who doesn't know this?) and it wasn't long before I met another woman.

Just as Dr. Freud played the cicerone in my love affair with Fräulein Eckstein, so Dr. L. L. Zamenhof, in Vienna at the time for an ocular refresher course, played it here. I had no idea who he was, nor any reason to have known him. The era of his greatest fame still lay far in the future. And although he was the second great man I had the privilege of knowing, he couldn't have been less like Sigmund Freud had he resolved to be unlike him in every way. They had but one characteristic in common: the utter havoc each man brought to my life, and though I imagined my friendship with each would lead me out of the labyrinth of Ita's attraction for me, both men only dropped me, panting and breathless, at her gate.

WITH LITTLE TO do in the aftermath of my second expulsion from Dr. Freud's life, I rededicated myself, as I've said, to my work, and as a consequence of the advances I made at the Allgemeines Krankenhaus, I'd been asked by my superior, Dr. Koller, to present an ocular refresher course at the university on his behalf. The seminar had been an ordeal from top to bottom. I'd never stood at the head of a class before, and certainly not one filled with doctors, and my nervousness conspired with my sense of inadequacy to such a degree that I had to force myself each day into the lecture hall, where I hacked my way through the curriculum, my wits as dull as a rusted machete, and by the end of the week, I wanted nothing more than to sit in my darkened rooms and breathe in the musty vapors of my more private unhappinesses.

Must I rehearse the litany of my woes? Ita was gone; Dr. Freud had rebanished me to a social Siberia; I was living without apparent remedy for the unnatural widowerhood I'd acquired through the most unworldly of means; and though I'd been married twice, I'd yet to taste the nectar of carnal love. Worse: I'd been driven, by my father, from our family, and though my uncle Moritz had sponsored my medical studies in Vienna, I seemed to have remembered nothing at all and felt a complete fraud standing before this colloquium of esteemed colleagues, most of whom, at week's end, were exiting the surgical theater.

As I waited for the elderly woman upon whom I'd performed the day's final demonstration (a double iridectomy) to awaken from the chloral I'd

administered—I'd begun to fear I'd murdered the poor unfortunate—
Dr. Zamenhof descended the aisle and approached my lectern in order
to thank me for what he said had been an enlightening week. "I had absolutely no idea, no idea of the advances Major Smith had made in the
Punjab treating pterygium!" he told me. "Absolutely none at all!"

As he offered me his hand, it was all I could do not to giggle. It's difficult to credit my reaction, but there was something silly about the man.
His pale eyes glittered merrily behind his tiny spectacles, and his beard,
an elegant square, was parted fussily down the middle. (Once a fiery red,
it seemed to have burnt down to a crisp grey ash along its edges.) Scrolled
towards their ends, his mustaches lent him a hint of flamboyance without turning him into a dandy, and his eyebrows, flown perpetually at
high mast, inflected his face with a perpetual air of wonderment. Were
it not for the great hairless dome of his cranium, I might have thought
he was a child masquerading as an adult, sent in to the surgical theater
as practical joke, although, of course, I knew of no one who might play
such a joke on me.

His voice was high and quavering; his manners, fusty; his clothing,
old-fashioned though meticulously cared for (a sure sign of poverty, I told
myself). Nevertheless, something about him reached me in the depths of
my Arctic loneliness. I found my mood lightening in his presence, and
when he asked for directions to Papagenogasse, I surprised myself by
offering to accompany him there.

"Splendid! Excellent!" he cried. "I don't wish to rush you. Your patient
has not yet recovered from the chloral. However, I'm afraid I'm late as it
is for a meeting."

"A meeting?"

"Hm," he said. "With a group of language enthusiasts." And for some
reason, he blushed.

STROLLING ALONGSIDE DR. Ludovik Leyzer Zamenhof was a bit like
walking beside a potbellied stove: there was something warming about
his company. My ear had not yet dulled to the comical element in his
voice, and each time he spoke, I found myself giggling. As he scurried
through the maze of our city in his black bowler hat and his black frock

coat, he reminded me of a character from a fairy tale, a mouse, perhaps, that had been transformed into a man, and no one seemed more delighted by this transformation than the little mouse himself. He seemed to be what Frederick Eckstein, in a lecture I'd recently attended on the *Kama Sutra* (hoping in my loneliness to reacquaint myself with his sister), had called a vidushaka, that rare fellow the mere sight of whom makes one want to laugh.

These were difficult times for him, he said, and although he was recounting to me the story of his failures, he did so with such good humor that neither of us could help laughing. His original practice, somewhere out on the frozen Russian steppes, had failed. He was ashamed to admit it, but he'd been consistently outearned by a local faith healer called Kukliński. The few patients who did seek him out were often too poor to pay him, and it was he who, upon leaving their hovels, would press a ruble or two into their hands. And when a patient died, he renounced his fees completely. "How could I accept their ruble without a cause?" Eventually, he abandoned generalized medicine for ophthalmology, "a branch of our medical arts in which even the sickest of patients reliably fails to die," but his new practice in Grodna collapsed when a second oculist moved into town. Now, at the urging of his father-in-law, he had returned to Warsaw. Worn out by competitors, he'd opened his shop in the poorest of neighborhoods, tending to the poorest of Warsaw's Jews, half-blind vitamin-starved wretches with recourse to no other physician. As a consequence, his practice was booming, although few of his patients could pay him in cash. Instead, in exchange for his services, he accepted milk and butter and eggs and cheese.

"And once even a live chicken. A rooster," he told me glumly.

I shot him a questioning look.

"No eggs there, I'm afraid."

"And this language of which you're an enthusiast?" I said, hoping to brighten the conversation.

"Oh. Esperanto, you mean?"

"I've never heard of it."

"Well, it's not a native language, but rather a human invention, intended to be an international language. Its creator is speaking at the meeting tonight."

"Its creator?"

He shrugged, as though the subject were of little importance to him. "No one knows much about him. A modest man who wishes only to give the world what he is able, he signed his original work with a pseudonym: Dr. Esperanto. In la lingvo internacia, you see, the word means 'one who hopes,' and though he never intended to call the language anything at all, the name stuck and appropriately so, in my opinion."

At that moment, a pall fell over the conversation. At least it did for me. I could think of no one but my father. A polyglot by political happenstance (as I believe I've described him), he looked upon the several languages available to him with horror. They were like whores in a brothel to him: there were too many to choose from, and though one differed from the others in the ingenuity of her form, they were, in fundamental use, the same: vessels of sin, corruption and waste. The labia of speech were no less a snare than the labia of sex for him, and wanting no stranger's tongue in his mouth, he avoided all languages but those of our holy books.

Though Dr. Esperanto's aim—to join all humanity and not to separate from it—was diametrically opposed to my father's desire, his methods appeared the same: to eschew all but two of the languages available to him.

(Once again, I cannot keep a secret: this mysterious Dr. Esperanto, although I would not know it for another half hour, was none other than my companion for the evening, too modest to have boasted of his accomplishments to a new friend.)

However, it didn't matter whether Dr. Zamenhof was Dr. Esperanto or his least devoted acolyte: his similarity to my father proved too potent a brew, and I wanted nothing but to depart from his company immediately.

"Well, here we are then, I believe," Dr. Zamenhof said, stopping before a large apartment house and rapping upon its door with the knobby end of his umbrella. "Perhaps you'll join us for the evening?"

"Ah, I think not," I said, inventing the first excuse that came to mind. "I'm late as it is, I'm afraid, for a dinner appointment with a dear friend who's recently been unwell."

"A young woman?" Dr. Zamenhof asked, his eyebrows rising an inch higher than their usual high station upon his forehead.

"A young woman?" I said, abashed. I dropped my gaze and stared at my shoes. "No, I'm afraid not. A few years ago, you see, I had a rather harrowing experience, and not with one woman, mind you, but with—"

However, at that moment, the door opened, and Dr. Zamenhof, who'd only been half-listening to me out of politeness anyway, turned from me completely. "Ho, Fraŭlino Bernfeld!" he cried, and with the woman who appeared at the door, he began rattling off sentences whose meanings I couldn't for the life of me decipher—although we were all Jews, I felt myself the Jew among them, excluded, by language and education, from their society—until at last Dr. Zamenhof spoke the only words I might at that moment have understood, my own name: "Doktoro Sammelsohn!"

For my sake, he added in German, "May I present to you Fräulein Loë Bernfeld."

I NODDED IN greeting, willing my face to work, to move, to mechanically reproduce a smile, stunned, as it was, into paralysis by Fräulein Bernfeld's beauty. I'd never seen a handsomer woman. Her eyes were as dark and as rich as two chocolate drops, and her hair, a magnificent blonde conch, was shot through with caramel highlights. Her mouth seemed to express half a dozen emotions at once: she bit her bottom lip insecurely; pursed her lips impatiently as I detained her guest at her door; sent a dimpled pout of reassurance towards him, growing cold upon her stoop.

"Unfortunately," I was suddenly aware of Dr. Zamenhof saying, "Dr. Sammelsohn has a prior engagement and won't be able to join us this evening."

Loë Bernfeld gave me an uninterested look. "A pity," she said, although she didn't seem to mean it, or rather she meant it only in the most impersonal of ways: my absence from their meeting, though a pity for me—who in his right mind would give up a rare chance to hear Dr. Esperanto?—as well as for the cause—which could always use an additional friend—would not be a pity for her. On the contrary, she seemed content to continue living, as she had her entire life, without me.

The same, in regards to her, I'm afraid, could no longer be said of me. Before I could announce a revision of my plans, before I was able to utter even one syllable of protest, Dr. Zamenhof was once again thanking me for an invaluable week. His patients, he said, if not his practice, would profit greatly from all I'd taught him. Our good-byes thus exchanged, he offered Fräulein Bernfeld his arm, and the two entered the building, chatting away fluently and with great affection in a language I couldn't understand at all, until finally the door was shut between us.

I STOOD UPON the Fräulein's stoop, the cold night air cutting like a razor into the skin of my cheeks. I looked down Papagenogasse in both directions. Gas lamps flickered on all of its corners.

"Fool!" I cursed myself, striking one hand against the other.

All my life I've struggled at playing this role of myself, this absurd part Heaven has assigned me, never quite rising to its improvisatory demands, never responding with sufficient promptness to this or that cue, never quite certain whether the scene called for a hero or a clown, and it was no different that evening. Not knowing what else to do, I knocked upon Fräulein Bernfeld's door, and in an instant, Dr. Zamenhof was once again before me.

"Perhaps I will join you after all," I said.

His face transformed into a hieroglyph of wonder. "But your friend?"

"There is no friend."

"No friend?"

"I only said there was."

"But why on earth would you contrive such an excuse?"

I exhaled and inhaled. What could I say to him? Could I really tell him all about my father and his odd linguistical notions and my consequential marriages to Hindele and Ita, and the effect it had all had on me when he'd mentioned Esperanto? Why not throw in the whole messy business about Dr. Freud and Fräulein Eckstein while I was at it? Instead, I opened and shut my mouth; I shook my head and raised my shoulders in a pathetic little shrug, a miscellany of gestures Dr. Freud would have deciphered quickly enough ("Ah, the father again?") whereas all Dr. Zamenhof said was, "Oh, well. Come in, come in then, do." He giggled. "You must be freezing out there!"

And so saying, he offered me his hand.

• • •

NO SOONER HAD I entered Fräulein Bernfeld's apartments than I regretted the bold impulse that bid me rap upon her door. Granted, she *was* an attractive woman, and I'm certain I've all but exhausted the subject of my weakness in this regard. Still, hadn't I learned enough from my recent drubbing at the hands of Cupid's thugs to know that what I was experiencing was nothing more than a fine aesthetic appreciation for the excellent way Fräulein Bernfeld's skin draped itself so cunningly over her well-knit bones? Smitten, as I too habitually was, by the beauty of a woman's face, I had allowed myself to forget the havoc such behaviors had previously caused me.

More important, I reminded myself, I'd pledged myself to Ita. I'd bound myself to her by an oath. And besides—I couldn't help noting with a certain peevishness—Fräulein Bernfeld was paying no attention to me at all.

Indeed, no one was. As soon as we'd crossed the threshold of her rooms, the dozen or so men and women gathered there rose to greet Dr. Zamenhof. Offering him their hands, presenting their cheeks to his for kisses, they ignored me completely. Still ignorant of the fact that he was the (at least in this room) quite famous Dr. Esperanto, I was confounded by the reverence shown him, a man who, as far as I knew, was nothing but a struggling oculist. Though I'd accompanied him into the apartment and was introduced by him to all, none of the warmth with which he was greeted spilled over to me. Indeed, those who didn't glance at me with hostility, as though my friendship with him somehow threatened theirs, greeted me indifferently before turning their love-struck gazes back to the little man who, no matter where he stood, seemed to be standing in the center of the room, his every need, despite his protestations, a matter of great urgency, this one taking his hat, that one dusting snow from his lapels, this one bringing him a chair, and all of them jabbering away, some fluently, others less so, in the euphonious gibberish he'd been conversing with Fräulein Bernfeld in at her door.

Summoned by the whistle of a teakettle, Fräulein Bernfeld dashed into the kitchen, leaving the lamp on inside her bedroom, where she'd taken Dr. Zamenhof's things. Two curtained doors separated it from the sitting room, and though she shut them, they'd neglected to catch, and I blushed to see the rough peasant's afghan thrown across the bottom of her bed.

"Dr. Sammelsohn," Dr. Zamenhof said, watching me too closely, I feared, "sit anywhere."

"Yes, please do, everyone," Fräulein Bernfeld called out, returning. "Make yourselves comfortable, do."

I took a chair nearest the back wall. In the excitement of Dr. Zamenhof's arrival, no one had taken my coat, and I let it hang, cape-like, from my shoulders. Miffed at having been overlooked, I cocked my hat onto the back of my head but was unable to bear keeping it on indoors and instead placed it on my knee, my hand upon its crown. With my other hand, I fiddled with my umbrella, which I also retained. I was on the point of leaving—in fact, I'd already stood and was edging towards the door—when Fräulein Bernfeld approached me with her teapot and a platter of mandelbrot.

It was an awkward moment. Gripping her tray with both hands, horrified to see that no one had taken my things, she was nevertheless incapable of doing so, while I, holding on to them and seeing her distress, could do nothing to relieve her of her tray. We were clearly at a social impasse, and the evening, which obviously meant so much to her, had come to a grinding halt. She gave me an imploring look, and as though I were rescuing a damsel from some dire mishap, I tossed my hat onto my head, draped my coat over one arm, hooked my umbrella over the other, and gallantly grabbed hold of her tray.

"May I, Fräulein?"

Relieved of her burdens, she quickly relieved me of mine before bundling them from the room. When she returned, I was able to give her back her tray, and she apologized, in a whisper, for having neglected me, while I, whispering as well, apologized for having allowed myself to have been neglected. The looks we traded, I was astonished to note this, were humming with the kind of mutual curiosity that charges the air between a man and a woman. The Fräulein seemed to be studying me as though seeing me for the first time, not as a blurry figure in the background of Dr. Zamenhof's magnificent portrait (which is how I appear in all other chronicles of Esperanto, I'm afraid), but as a subject in a portrait of my own.

When at last I reclaimed my chair and she filled my teacup, she steadied my hand, which I'd lifted towards her to make lighter her work, by placing her fingertips gently upon the top of it. The year was 1899, and one would have been hard-pressed to find a more erotically charged gesture in polite company. How long had it been since a woman had touched me? If one didn't count my frustrated encounters with Fräulein Eckstein or, more precisely, with Fräulein Eckstein's body, nor my clumsy attempts at lovemaking, as a boyish groom, with Hindele, my first wife, the answer was: forever. It'd been forever, which is to say: I'd *never* been touched by a woman, excluding my mother and sisters whose touch, it goes without saying, had none of the effect Fräulein Bernfeld's was having upon me.

"Good?" she whispered hopefully, as I sampled my tea.

"Very good, Fräulein." I pursed my lips in a gentle, affirming moue, and as I watched her wending her way to her chair through the knees and feet of her other guests, the axis of my little world began to shift; as the ruby blush that dappled her throat deepened as she stood more formally before the little crowd, I knew I'd lost my heart to her.

I BEGAN RETHINKING my priorities. It was absurd to hold back from life on Ita's account. In truth, she was as good as dead to me. (What am I saying? She *was* dead to me! And to everyone else, for that matter!) And wasn't it high time I put the unfortunate chapter behind me? One need only consider the practical implications of the pledge I'd made to realize how impossible it was to keep. After all, I had no guarantees Ita would even be reborn during my lifetime. Perhaps we'd had our one and only encounter for this go-round. Must I spend the rest of my life alone, not knowing whether she would reappear before my own demise? And if she did, how was I even to recognize her or she me? Though according to the paranormalists who credit such beliefs (the transmigration of souls, et cetera), we've all been reborn countless times, who among us has the least memory of his former lives or of the people he knew in them? No, the prospects seemed doubtful at best.

Also, if I was scrupulous with myself, I had to admit that, although at times I was bereft without her (indeed, many were the nights I lay in bed, restaging our tender farewell in the theater of my mind), at other times, I could only feel I'd survived a narrow scrape. Ita had been a dybbuk, after all, the blackest of sinners in direct rebellion against the Heavenly Court, and a suicide to boot! It was with only a little distance between us that I was able to see her for what she was: a wicked demon who in no wise would make a suitable wife.

If Dr. Freud's original speculations were correct—and though he'd burned his chart, its inky lines remained vibrant in my memory—Ita and I had been chasing each other, with little to show for it, for millennia. What was one tender hour compared to a history of five thousand bitter years? No, I told myself, in all likelihood, it was Dr. Freud's final view that was correct: a belief in reincarnation belonged not only to the childhood of mankind but to my own childhood, and as a consequence, I was particularly susceptible to it. And at times, it's true, the fantastical story of my love affair with Ita seemed just that: a fantastical story. As the weeks and the months and even the years had passed, she seemed less and less real to me each time I thought of her, until I hardly thought of her at all; and though I'd pledged never to forget her, I did often forget her for long stretches of time.

I crossed my arms and shifted in my seat.

There was still the issue of the vow. I'd sworn an oath to Ita, and there was no denying that. The matter, however, wasn't as simple as it might, at first blush, seem. Even if Dr. Freud *weren't* correct, even if I *hadn't* hallucinated Ita's ascension (as he maintained) while lying drunk and bareheaded in the snow, even if I *had* sworn an oath, pledging (as I recalled) my eternal fidelity to her, one needn't be a Talmudist to ask if such an oath, made outside the presence of two proper witnesses, is binding under Jewish law? The answer: it is not. Though, as we've seen, the dead may break the holy Law, like the living, they're helpless to revise it; and though a promise is a promise, and an oath an oath, without two Sabbath-observant witnesses, neither constitutes a binding contract. In fine: even if I hadn't hallucinated Ita, I owed her nothing; and if I had (I suppose this goes without saying) the same conclusion obtained.

Viewed in this light, the affair seemed, at best, a regrettable error of youth; at worst, some terrible form of psychosis on my part. But either way, for the first time since that morning of April 1896, the astonishing events of which may or may not have occurred in the Sanatorium Loew, I felt free to move on with my life.

AND NOT A moment too soon.

Fräulein Bernfeld held the fingers of one hand locked, scroll-like, inside the fingers of the other beneath her handsome bosom, and had begun addressing her guests. "La nuna tasko donas al mi grandan plezuron," she said.

I'm reconstructing this dialogue, of course, after having learned Esperanto myself. At the time, I had no idea what she was saying, a circumstance she herself must have remarked upon, because having made her small speech welcoming her guests and introducing "nian Majstron, kiu bezonas neniun prezentaĵon," she returned to her former chair, before thinking better of it and placing herself next to me. No words needed exchanging. Her look of compassion told me everything: she was here to translate Dr. Zamenhof's speech so that the evening might not be a complete loss for me, the lone anaglot (Esperantically speaking) in the room.

In order to do so as quietly as possible, she sat nearer to me than she might ordinarily have. Her throat was so near my face I had to continually suppress an impulse to kiss it. Again and again, I reminded myself—and in the strongest of terms—that Fräulein Bernfeld was a stranger to me, and one who had given me no indication that she felt a complementary attraction towards my person. Perhaps she felt nothing for me beyond a hostess's pity.

Dr. Zamenhof stood before the room now, nervous and ill at ease, looking exactly like what I knew him to be: a failed oculist.

"Karaj samideanoj," he said.

"Dear comrades," Fräulein Bernfeld breathed into my ear, and though she was translating a highly technical talk that was public and open to all, whispered, the words issuing from her mouth, coupled with the heat of her breath on my face, thrilled me like the most collusive of secrets.

"Ĉiuj ideoj, kiuj estas ludontaj gravan rolon en la historio de la homaro havas ĉiam tiun saman egalan sorton kiam ili ekaperas . . ." Dr. Zamenhof said.

"Every idea that plays a grave . . . no, rather," the Fräulein corrected herself, emphasizing the revision by gently tapping my hand, "an important role in the history of mankind has in every era the same fate when they first appear."

"Ah," I said, looking deeply into her eyes.

"Clear?" she said.

". . . la samtempuloj renkontas ilin kun rimarkinde ostina malkonfido . . ."

". . . the people living at the same time — samtempuloj: literally same-time-people: contemporaries — encounter them with a remarkably obstinate . . ." She thought for a moment. "Hm . . . malkonfido?"

The word struck me as odd. "Faithlessness?" I suggested.

"No. Literally un-confidence, *mal-* meaning 'the opposite.' The prefix cuts the necessary vocabulary in two, you see? It's really quite clever." No longer translating, Fräulein Bernfeld lowered her voice even further and told me that "Tolstoy himself learned the grammar in only two hours."

"Tolstoy?" I said.

"Hm," she said. "Well enough to read it" — she shrugged a delightful little shrug — "if not to speak it."

"Did he really?"

"Yes, really," she said.

A s the evening drew on, I came to realize that Dr. Zamenhof was not, as I'd presumed, merely one of the evening's enthusiasts. He was the honored guest, placed at the very heart of this devoted circle, its members sitting almost literally at his feet. Nor was he merely first among equals here. On the contrary, he had *invented* Esperanto, created it on his own as a usable international language, so that men ("And women," Fräulein Bernfeld reminded him sternly) might communicate across national borders, and even, in the same city or town, across cultural and ethnic divisions as well.

"Let me understand this," I said, as we took our seats in Fräulein Bernfeld's parlor after the other guests had departed. "This isn't just some interesting . . . intellectual game or rarefied philosophical quest?"

"On the contrary," Dr. Zamenhof exclaimed.

I knew, as every schoolboy did, that philosophers like Leibniz and Descartes had attempted a universal language and had failed utterly. As with alchemy or the search for Ali Babi's cave, I'd assumed the search for a universal language was merely one of the chimeras that had bedazzled our benighted race during the quainter centuries.

"Certainly," Dr. Zamenhof said, "these men were more illustrious than I, but I would suggest to you they were after something altogether different."

"And what was that?"

He exhaled a line of cigarette smoke. "They were seeking a langua philosophica, the lost language of Eden, a language so pure there would be no difference between a word and the thing it described, whereas my ambitions" — he ducked his head — "are not as grand as that."

"No?"

"No, I merely wish to end the enmity and hatred that divide the peoples of the world."

He gave out a comical little shrug and, once again, I found myself nearly laughing in his face. Surely this was all an elaborate joke. The man couldn't be serious! Inventing a language seemed impossible enough; promoting its uses to the four corners of the globe more impossible still; that it might affect some essential transformation in the hearts of mankind seemed a hope so far beyond the concept of possibility as to be inconceivable.

However, one look at Dr. Zamenhof's face told me he wasn't joking. "Even as a small boy," he said, "I knew this hatred wasn't right."

He'd grown up in polyglottal Białystok where, he told us, the Russians, the Byelorussians, the Germans, the Poles, and the Jews misunderstood one another in a scramble of languages, often with fatal consequences, especially for the Jews.

"Perhaps it was childish hubris to think so . . ."

"No, no." Fräulein Bernfeld shook her head quietly: she knew better than that.

". . . but by the age of fifteen, I'd formed a plan, you see." He leaned in and tapped me on the knee, rearresting my attention. "I promised myself that when I was older—old enough for people to take me seriously—I would abolish this hatred."

I leaned back, smiling politely. Had I wandered into a tale from the *Arabian Nights*? Were these people mad? I wondered. For an instant, I felt supremely uncomfortable in their presence. Not knowing where to place my eyes, as one does in the presence of the mad, I looked at the silver coffeepot stationed on the table between us. In the convex mirror of its belly, our little party was replicated in miniature: our heads large bells at the top of skinny elongated necks. For all its distortion, the picture seemed accurate enough: surely I'd stumbled, Alice-like, into a Mad Hatter's tea party.

Once again, I eyed the door, thinking that now was the time to take my leave. Before I could prepare my excuses, however, the burning touch of Fräulein Bernfeld's cool fingertips was once again upon my hand. "Coffee?" she said, pouring a cup for me and for Dr. Zamenhof and then for herself.

"Ah, yes, very good. Thank you, Fräulein," I said, arrested in my place.

"IN THE BEGINNING," Dr. Zamenhof continued with his story; he'd considered reviving one of the classical languages—Latin, Hebrew, or Greek—but these, he knew, would be too difficult for the poor. "Besides"— he sipped his coffee—"there were so many new things in the world, for which I'd have to invent new words anyway, that I told myself, why not go ahead and invent an entirely new language?" Also, it'd become clear to him that the only language suitable for these purposes had to be a neutral language.

"A neutral language?" I said.

"Belonging to no one and to everyone equally." Initially he believed that the shortest words would be the easiest to memorize, and he contrived a series of arbitrary monosyllables: ab, ac, ad, ba, ca, da, e, eb, ec, be, ce, et cetera. "But even I, their own inventor, found their meanings impossible to learn." In his next attempt, he selected roots from Latin, German, and Russian, and standardized them with simple regular endings. Thanks to the English he was then learning in gymnasium, he felt free to abandon the difficult declensions and conjugations that mar the faces of so many native tongues. "And then," he exclaimed, "I had a completely unexpected breakthrough! Oh, it must have been 1878 or 1877. I was walking down the street, just a schoolboy in his uniform, when I chanced upon an ordinary signboard, hanging in front of an ordinary shop, something I'd passed a thousand times before, I'm certain. However, this time, immersed in my linguistic preoccupations, my mind perceived it as though it were lit by a great and shimmering light."

"And what did it say?" Fräulein Bernfeld asked, breathlessly.

"Shveytsarskaya," Dr. Zamenhof said.

Fräulein Bernfeld and I traded blank faces.

"A porter's lodge." Dr. Zamenhof shrugged. "Nothing remarkable in that," he agreed. "However, farther down the lane, there was another sign above another shop, this one reading Konditorskaya: a confectionery. Now, you see, the skaya in both, signifying place, was the same, and at that moment, I was like Saul on the road to Damascus. I realized that if I built my language upon a foundation of affixes and suffixes, why, I'd be able to bend a finite number of roots into the service of an infinite vocabulary. Now, the idea took hold of me, and I was on fire! My hands, my feet were trembling, and all those intimidating grammars and dictionaries I'd been pouring over, night after night, in my little room suddenly fell away."

Though full of faults and nothing like the Esperanto he'd spoken that evening in Fräulein Bernfeld's parlor, the language was tried and tested and officially consecrated on December 5, 1878 ("although this was according to the old Russian calendar"), when, with a few friends and his brother Felix, young Ludovik made speeches and sang songs in it around a birthday cake his mother had prepared especially for the occasion.

"That's the Russian Empire for you," Dr. Zamenhof said. "Meetings were forbidden, and a birthday party was the only subterfuge my dear mother could think of to conceal what we were about."

Remembering one of the songs he'd written for the day, at Fräulein Bernfeld's insistence, Dr. Zamenhof threw back his head and sang a verse of it in his high, quavering voice, his cigarette burning down between his fingers:

> Malamikete de las nacjes,
> Kadó, kadó, jam temp' está.
> La tot' homoze en familje
> Konunigare so debá.

"Hatred of the nations," he translated for us. "Fall, fall, it's long past time! United as one family will be all mankind!"

AS ONE MIGHT imagine, the child met with nothing but scorn. A family friend even convinced his father that the boy's single-minded dedication to this utopian folderol was a dangerous idée fixe which, if left fixe, would lead ultimately to madness.

"And so Father locked everything away in a cupboard," Dr. Zamenhof said, hazing his lungs with a deep draft of smoke. "All my dictionaries, my grammars, my translations, the verses I'd composed, promising me that if, when I'd finished my medical studies in Moscow, I were still interested in all this . . . rubbish . . . he would make it available to me again. Naturally, I obeyed him. After all, what son could go against his father's wishes?"

He looked at me, expecting some sort of masculine sympathy, I supposed, but of course, I could show him none.

"Two years later, when I came home for the winter holiday, however, I announced to my father that although I would continue with my medical studies, as he wished, the aim of my life had not changed. I asked to be released from my promise and to have my papers returned."

His eyes sparkling, his lips smirking inside his bristling beard, Dr. Zamenhof paused at this chasm in his story and waited for us to prompt him to jump across it.

"And what happened?" Fräulein Bernfeld finally said.

"Well, my mother broke instantly into tears."

"Oh, no!" Fräulein Bernfeld cried, practically in tears herself.

"My father had burned it all, you see."

"No!"

"No, it didn't matter, fraŭlino. No," he comforted her, "silly girl, don't be so silly. I was like Moses, trudging up the mountain for a second pair of tablets. I'd forgotten nothing. How could I? I knew my language as well as I knew my Russian. Remorseful, Father released me from my promise, and I continued on exactly as before."

"Oh, Majstro," Fraŭlino Loë murmured, her cheeks reddening.

"Tush—no!—silly girl! Doing everything a second time merely helped me improve the language, and the only thing that stopped me after that, of course, was the appearance of Volapük."

"Volapük?" I said.

"Hm," Dr. Zamenhof nodded, squinting through a cloud of cigarette smoke.

"It was all the rage for a time," Fräulein Bernfeld informed me.

"Perhaps you've heard of Johann Martin Schleyer," Dr. Zamenhof said, "a Catholic priest living in Baden? No? Well, they call him the living Tower of Babel. Knows seventy languages, reportedly."

I shook my head. None of this was familiar to me.

"According to the legend," Dr. Zamenhof said smirkingly, "this Herr Schleyer had been turning the idea of an international language over and over in his head—one of his parishioners had been unable to write a letter to his son in some faraway country, I believe—until finally, growing tired of his procrastinations, who should appear to Herr Schleyer in the middle of the night, but God Himself, suggesting that it was high time the good Father got started on the work. Now, it's not every day that God appears to you, even in a dream, and so Herr Schleyer began his work immediately."

"And this was Volapük?"

Dr. Zamenhof nodded, taking another sip of his coffee. He wiped his lips on his napkin. "Herr Schleyer published his project in 1880, and in quick order, Volapük societies popped up across the globe. There were over a hundred thousand adherents in the beginning. Now, I'm not certain how many of these actually spoke Volapük, mind you, but obviously the time was ripe for an international language."

"And in 1884—" Fräulein Bernfeld began to say.

"Yes, in 1884 . . ." Dr. Zamenhof nodded. "Go on, tell him."

Fräulein Bernfeld, slightly annoyed at being even so gently ordered about, fixed me with a doleful look. "No, I was only going to say that in 1884, the first Volapük World Congress was held in Germany, wasn't it?"

"Yes." Dr. Zamenhof nodded. "And the second in 1887 and a third in 1889."

"At the first two, all business was conducted in German."

"But by the third, Volapük was the language of the day."

"Policemen, concierges, even waiters in the coffee houses, addressed the congress attendees in Volapük."

"I considered renouncing my own project and working in support of Herr Schleyer's, but after reviewing his work, I saw that as a language, it was much too odd and baroque."

"And in another few years—"

"Ah, yes." Dr. Zamenhof nodded sadly.

"—it was dead."

"The whole thing came crashing down—infighting between the president of the Volapük Academy, who advocated reforms, and Herr Schleyer, who, as God's emissary, was disinclined to heed the concerns of mere mortals. Its failure brought terrible harm to our cause, I must say. Now, Herr Schleyer can't be blamed for the fact that his work proved impractical, and yet it's thanks to his failure that the world cooled towards every other artificial language, and we're paying a steep price for it now."

Fräulein Bernfeld seemed pleased that I was taking such an interest in her Majstro. As she later told me, she was often saddened by the way so many samideanoj ("comrades," or "people of the same ideas") grew tongue-tied around him. A terrible irony, this: the acolytes of his international language found themselves often too nervous in the Majstro's presence to say anything of value to him in it. Also, Dr. Zamenhof quite clearly had no talent for managing their adulation. His conspicuous humility, a strategy for subverting their adoration, I suppose—he hated the sobriquet Majstro, for instance, but could never bring himself to correct the people who used it—only increased the ardor of his disciples.

"Anyway, in 1887," he told us, "I was ready to publish a pamphlet of my own. On that day, I stood before my own Rubicon. Once my brochure appeared, I knew I would never be able to return to the life I'd previously known. I knew what fate awaits a doctor who, relying upon the public for his livelihood, occupies himself with fantastical schemes. I was risking my future happiness and that of my family, and yet what else could I do?" He gave out a little shrug. "I crossed my Rubicon."

He pulled on his cigarette and sighed, exhaling a melancholic cloud of smoke.

"As for Esperanto, I make no grand claims for it, except that it's easy to learn, and my hope is that it will ease the way for mankind to reunite into a single family." His voice broke, and tears moistened his eyes. "Until then . . ." he said, shaking his head. "Oh, the things men do to one another . . ."

"Oh, Ludovik." Fräulein Bernfeld reached across the arms of their chairs and took his hand. As she held it to her cheek, I feared that I'd misread the nature of their friendship. Perhaps, in my attraction to Fräulein Bernfeld, I'd too naïvely assumed that she and the good doctor were no more than passionate friends committed to the same cause. At this tender moment—gone were the polite Fraŭlino Loës, the formal mia Majstros—they were suddenly Ludovik and Loë, and I wondered: was she, and not poverty, the reason Dr. Zamenhof had traveled to Vienna sans famille?

"AĤ, MIAJ KARULOJ," Dr. Zamenhof said, "it's late."

With a raised knuckle, he dabbed the tears that had fallen from Fraŭlino Bernfeld's eyes.

"I'll walk you to your hotel," I announced, a bit too brusquely, I'm afraid. Neither Dr. Zamenhof nor Fräulein Bernfeld had recovered from their weeping, and I must have sounded like a policeman ordering the survivors of some tragedy home before they'd come to grips with whatever terrible thing had befallen them. Dr. Zamenhof folded Fräulein Bernfeld's hands together and kissed them gently. With an equal tenderness, he kissed her forehead. "Baldaŭ, baldaŭ," he said, comforting her, and I had to wonder: Did he mean "soon" (*bald* in German) as in *Soon, soon, we shall be alone, without this prying lummox Sammelsohn to indulge our carnal passion for each other*? Or did he rather mean: *Soon, soon men will be able to speak to one another across cultures, and no one will savagely beat his brother to a pulp*?

I felt like a cuckold, the sharpened points of my jealousy sprouting like horns from the corners of my skull, and I hoped that, if Dr. Zamenhof and Fräulein Bernfeld weren't indeed lovers, they might misinterpret my hectoring not as jealous raillery, but as a new convert's enthusiastic desire to spend more time alone with his Majstro.

Keeping hold of Fräulein Bernfeld's hand, Dr. Zamenhof turned to me. Here was the same penetrating gaze I'd seen glancing off Sigmund Freud's brow, a gaze that bore in, seeing everything. Dr. Zamenhof's look was leavened with a sweetness missing from Dr. Freud's. Whereas Dr. Freud seemed to see a wild beast, trussed up in a suit and masquerading as a man, Dr. Zamenhof saw its opposite: an angel who, convinced he was a man, had forgotten the most essential thing about himself.

With Fräulein Bernfeld's hand in his, he reached for mine. "Isn't it only right that two such good friends of mine should become friends to each other?"

Fräulein Bernfeld, looking annoyed, dropped her head and lowered her eyes.

"Do we have a little something for Dr. Sammelsohn?" Dr. Zamenhof inquired of her meekly.

Nodding, she broke away from our trio, taking a half step towards her bedroom, before thinking better of it. "Oh!" she exclaimed, tapping her forehead. "I've left it in the kitchen."

Dr. Zamenhof smiled beneath the scrolls of his mustache, as though to sweeten any disagreeable reaction I might have towards Fraŭlino Bernfeld's ditheriness, but of course I had none. The woman couldn't have been more charming. Her confusion had caused a blush to once again dapple her throat, and it stained her skin from her high collar to her scalp.

"Forgive my detaining you, Dr. Sammelsohn," she said, emerging from the kitchen, all business again, a slender green pamphlet in her hand.

I read the cover, printed in a motley of typefaces:

Dr. ESPERANTO'S
INTERNATIONAL
LANGUAGE
Introduction
AND
COMPLETE GRAMMAR
For Germans
Price 40 Pf.
WARSAW
1889

"Thank you, Fräulein," I started to say or perhaps did say, before correcting myself and addressing her in Esperanto: "Dankon, fraŭlino?" I turned to Dr. Zamenhof for confirmation that I'd pronounced these words correctly.

"Jes, jes, 'Dankon, fraŭlino,' certe," he said encouragingly.

"Dankon, fraŭlino," I addressed Fräulein Bernfeld directly with a bow.

"Ho!" she cried.

"Ho, ve!" Dr. Zamenhof reiterated.

"Tre bone, Doktoro Jakovo!"

"It rolls off the tongue quite musically," I said, and the two friends exchanged knowing looks.

Dr. Zamenhof raised his eyebrows. "And to think you almost didn't come with me tonight."

"Yes, and to think!" I said.

I WALKED HIM to the Hotel Hammerand, our hands thrust deep into the pockets of our coats. The bitterness of the night made conversation difficult, and neither of us seemed inclined to talk in any case. I was thinking of the Fräulein, daydreaming of her (though it'd been hours since the sun had set). I have no idea what Dr. Zamenhof was thinking; however, at one point, he sighed so deeply, I peered into his face and gave him a concerned look. Suddenly aware of himself, he presented a mandarin's smile to me and shook his head.

"There's one thing that's still troubling me," I said.

"Only one?" he said, placing his arms behind his back.

"It's the question of the Tower of Babel."

"Ah, yes, I hear that all the time."

"Does the good doctor really intend to reverse a Heavenly decree?"

Dr. Zamenhof fell silent for a moment. "I believe you've forgotten your Bible, Dr. Sammelsohn."

"How so?"

"Oh, it's the same with everyone, I suppose. Everyone remembers chapter eleven of the book of Genesis, in which God punishes the builders of the Tower by confusing their language and scattering them across the face of the earth, correct?"

"Correct."

"But who remembers chapter ten?"

I looked at him blankly. "Chapter ten?"

He nodded. "Yes, chapter ten, in which the sons of Noah divide into seventy nations, each dispersing to its own land with its own language, all described by the Torah in the most naturalistic of ways. The towermen's sin was not in the speaking of a common language—oh, no, Dr. Sammelsohn!—but in their rebellion against Heaven. With the memory of the flood still fresh in their minds, they built their tower as a means of escaping the next deluge, without having to examine their deeds or repent of their evil ways. Now, we Esperantists are not in rebellion against Heaven — Heaven forbid! — rather, we're engaged in the very work of Heaven itself."

"Which is?"

"Which is to bring Heaven to Earth and not the other way around. It's precisely because I am, like you, a Jew from the ghetto that the idea of uniting mankind came into my head in the first place."

I nodded, understanding him at once.

"No one can feel this unhappy separation as strongly as a Jew. And one day, when our people will have reacquired our ancient homeland, we will succeed in our historic mission, of which Moses and Jesus and Mohammed all dreamt."

"And that is?"

"That is, uniting mankind in a Jerusalem that will once again be the center of universal brotherhood and love."

"And for that we need a neutral language?"

"Or do you suppose we can achieve all that with Yiddish," he barked out, laughing, "a jargon that doesn't even possess a proper grammar?"

We'd arrived at number 8. The lights inside the Hammerand had long been doused. Through the front window, we could see the deskman dozing at his station. A single red-and-black tassel attached to a key dangled from its slot in a warren of pigeonholes behind him. This was, I presumed, Dr. Zamenhof's key.

"Well," he said, peering through the darkened glass.

"It's been a pleasure, Doctor."

"No, no, the pleasure has been all mine."

I held up his little green book. "I shall look forward to reading your pamphlet."

"It's freezing, and as much as I would enjoy continuing our conversation inside by a warm fire, I have much correspondence yet to attend to tonight."

"For the movement?"

"Precisely so."

"Then I shan't keep you, Doctor. Adiaŭ."

"Ne, ĝis la revido, mia bona doktoro," he said. "I feel certain that we shall meet again."

"Then I shall look forward to that splendid hour."

We each removed our right glove to shake hands and, in a spontaneous surge of affection, gave each other kisses, first on the right cheek, then on the left.

"Ĝis la revido, mia nova amiko."

"Ĝis la, Majstro."

"Adiaŭ."

"Ĝis," I repeated, before stammering "Auf Wiedersehen," and then "אַדיע און אַ גוט יאָר!"

(Though we'd said good-bye a dozen times in three different languages, it was only when I'd said it in Yiddish that I felt I'd bid him a proper farewell.)

CHAPTER 3

That night, I couldn't sleep. I tossed and turned in my bed. How blind could I have been? Here, at last, was the great and noble cause for which I'd been longing ever since אשריל and שמנגלפ had appeared to Dr. Freud and me in Fräulein Eckstein's hospital room! Harmony among nations, peace throughout the world, a universal brotherhood obtained through the promotion of an international auxiliary language—what could be more high-minded or more noble than that?

Unlike Dr. Freud, I had felt unfree to deny the experiences we'd shared in the company of the Angelicals. On the contrary, Ita's plight had convinced me that there *was* another world, higher and truer than our own; and although I couldn't return to the ways of my father, redonning the black garments of piety and reburdening my neck with the yoke of the Torah—I was a modern man, after all, and had no wish to reembrace the superstitious folk customs of previous generations—still, I was too much of a Jew not to hear the voice of Heaven hectoring me.

(If, beneath its constant assault, my hearing sometimes dulled to its summons—well, that was to be expected: I was only human, after all.)

The more I thought about it, the less absurd Dr. Zamenhof's dream began to seem. Musical notation, weights and measurements, railroad gauges, the Braille alphabet had all been internationalized recently. Why not a universal language?

I kicked off my bedclothes. My apartment was freezing, and I draped Aunt Fania's afghan about my shoulders. With chattering teeth, I dashed barefoot to the kitchen and brewed myself a cup of coffee. It was nearly four in the morning, but what did I care? I was too excited to sleep.

I retrieved Dr. Zamenhof's booklet from the inner pocket of my overcoat and carried it to my desk. I cracked it open and read it through. Its introduction contained much of what he'd told me the evening before. He began charmingly enough: "The reader will no doubt take up this little work with an incredulous smile, supposing he is about to peruse the impractical schemes of some burgher of Utopia." Still, it was clear, Dr. Esperanto claimed, that if the Great Wall of China separating national literatures were to fall, and people the world over could read the same books, their ideals, their convictions, their desires, and their goals would become aligned, and men would unite in a common brotherhood. Even without this utopian folderol, the immense importance of an international language to science and trade had to be admitted. Previous attempts had failed only because they were either too simple or too complex or too arbitrary. In short, there were three difficulties to overcome: the language must be child's play to learn, its learners must be able to communicate with people of other nationalities whether the language is accepted universally or not, and some means must be found to overcome the natural indifference of mankind to the entire question. Dr. Esperanto had solved the first problem—"My entire grammar can be learned in one hour"—as well as the second—"With the complete vocabulary required for everyday use printed on a single page and available in any language for a few pennies, one may enter into an intelligible correspondence with a person of a different nationality." As for the third and most intractable problem—convincing humanity to overcome its stupidity (these are my words, of course, and not his)—Dr. Esperanto had included in his booklet eight mail-in promissory notes, each stating that "the undersigned promises to learn Dr. Esperanto's language, if ten million people publicly give the same promise."

These notes, easily detachable from the back of the book, were to be mailed in to Dr. Esperanto, c/o Dr. L. Zamenhof of Warsaw.

Additionally, the booklet contained six literary specimens, including the Lord's Prayer ("Patro nia, kiu estas en la ĉielo, sankta estu Via nomo"), and the first verses of the book of Genesis ("Je la komenco, Dio kreis la teron kaj la ĉielon"), as well as the Sixteen Rules of Grammar and a pocket-sized crib with a bilingual vocabulary list comprising the then-extant nine hundred root words.

As I read over these, my eyes began to glaze, and I saw in the book's pages not Dr. Zamenhof's words, all pressed in their starched serifs, but the face of Loë Bernfeld, superimposed, like a rotogravure, upon them.

"Oh, Fräulein Bernfeld," I murmured, "speak to me of genders, of numbers, and of cases!" Instead she spoke of a new world, a happier world, her dark blonde hair undone, the collar of her blouse unbuttoned so that if I tilted the book at an angle—oh, thrilling prospect!—I could peer down her collar and see the indentations of her bare throat.

A door in the hallway creaked, and I was suddenly awake. The cold, hard pages of Dr. Esperanto's booklet stared back at me. Fräulein Bernfeld was gone. The sun rose late at this time of year, and it was still dark outside. Amazingly, I discovered that I'd committed most of Dr. Esperanto's grammar, through this odd somnambuliterary process, to memory. *Faster than Tolstoy! Ha!* I flattered myself, dressing for the day. Also I was not, as I expected to be, the least bit tired. On the contrary, I felt as though I'd slept in the softest of beds for a solid week!

Bound for the clinic, I knocked into Otto Meissenblichler's latest süss Geliebte as she slipped out his apartment door. We greeted each other through a squall of guilty blushes and embarrassed guten Morgens. She had the blurry look of someone who'd put on her clothes after having taken them off without sleeping in between. Well, I told myself, Herr Meissenblichler is not the only one with a new love this morning! This thought of Fräulein Bernfeld reminded me of Dr. Esperanto's pamphlet, and I returned to my apartments to retrieve it, so that I might take it with me. Nine hundred root words were no small matter, and I wanted to begin on them immediately. As I dropped the booklet into my coat pocket, one of its promissory notes fell out: "I, the undersigned, promise to learn the international language, if ten million people publicly give the same promise."

Ten million people! I had to laugh. It seemed an enormous amount. After all, how many copies of his little booklet had Dr. Zamenhof printed, anyway? Nevertheless I signed the note and deposited it in a mailbox, thinking more of Fraŭlino Bernfeld, I have to admit, than of the other nine million nine hundred and ninety-nine thousand nine hundred and ninety-nine samideanoj, of whose number, that morning, I was proud, thrilled, in fact, to count myself.

• • •

I WROTE TO the Fräulein immediately upon arriving at the clinic and received her answer by return post. I tore open the envelope, lavender in both color and scent. Though I'd addressed her in German, she'd written to me in the international language, and it took me the better part of an hour, locked inside my examination room (with my patients amassing outside) to decipher her short message, working between her note and Dr. Zamenhof's list of root words. As her office was not far from my clinic—she aided her father, Hans Bernfeld, in his trade—she suggested we take our lunch at the same hour. She would walk towards the hospital, I towards her father's office, and arriving in the middle, we could share our lunch in a coffee house while studying la internacian lingvon, or chatting in it when my skills became proficient to do so. Unfortunately, today she'd already scheduled the hour and the next day's as well, but the day after, she was free, and she would keep the time open every day henceforth, if I found myself in agreement with her plan.

I wrote back to her immediately, struggling with the brave, new words, even when it came to signing my own name: "Doktoro Jakovo Jozefo Sammelsohn." Samelson? Samelsono? Zamelzono? I was uncertain if Esperantistoj Esperanticized siajn nomojn, but I proceeded to do so with my own name, further announcing my allegiance to a cause that, I knew, was as near to Fraŭlino Bernfeld's heart as the breath inside her lungs.

EACH DAY, FOLLOWING our lunch, Fraŭlino Bernfeld and I walked the Ring, arm in arm, in a comradely fashion. I must say: it was a delightful experience, speaking this silly, made-up language with a woman as beautiful as she. And indeed, I cherished it as a delicious irony that on the Ringstrasse, that grand Deutschophonic wreath of a boulevard, the international language should prove, for the time being at least, the most private of idiolects. We could confer in our natural voices at their normal volumes with no one understanding us, and except for the very real fear that we might be arrested as foreign spies, we could speak our minds openly. The intimacy was exhilarating. I felt as though I'd inhaled a draft of Ramsay's newly discovered helium gas: my voice sounded funny to me, and I felt as though I were floating above the clouds. As far as I was concerned, I'd found my happiness in the fraŭlino's person. When I was away from her, I could think of nothing but being with her again; and when I was with her, I could think of nothing at all; and it was difficult for me to believe that I could feel this way if she in fact felt differently towards me.

However, since our first meeting in her apartment, when those looks of erotic curiosity had passed between us, she seemed to have reconsidered her attraction to me. Or perhaps I'd misinterpreted those looks in the first place. Naturally, I longed to clarify our standing, and yet I knew enough about myself to know that the anxiety attendant upon such an ambition would spoil my attempts to achieve it—indeed, each time I took a step closer to the subject, I could feel the fraŭlino gliding away—and so I pushed for nothing.

We were in her mind, it seemed, merely *geamikoj,* "friends" in Esperanto, *ge-* being, as she informed me, one of Dr. Zamenhof's most forward-thinking inventions, a prefix indicating that the word following it refers to members of both genders. "You see, Dr. Sammelsohn, hidden in the international language are all sorts of—oh, let's call them linguistic promissory notes for the future." Pro la venonto, she said: literally, "for that which will be coming." "But then I see you're laughing at me."

I looked into her lovely face. Snowflakes glimmered in her hair and on her eyelashes and were melting on her cheeks.

"I'm laughing, fraŭlino, yes, but not at you nor at what you're saying. I'm merely happy to be in the company of someone who cares so much about something besides herself."

She laced her arm again through mine, and we took a step forward. "These are, of course, just thoughts of my own. I haven't spoken to the Majstro concerning any of this, you understand." However, along the same lines, she'd noted other treasures hidden inside Dr. Zamenhof's work: whenever possible, for example, thanks to the prefix *mal-,* words for negative things appeared to have no linguistic substances in themselves, but were merely the shadowy negation of their solar opposites.

"For example?"

"Oh, I don't know . . ." she said. A pensive look dimpled her brow. "There's no word in Esperanto for 'old,' for example. 'Old' is simply *malnova,* 'not new'; or *maljuna,* 'not young.'"

"Yes, I see, and what else?"

She squinted at the horizon of rooftops. "Well, theologically speaking, we say that evil has no substance in itself, that it's only the absence of good, and interestingly enough, the Esperantan word for 'evil' also has no linguistic substance either. It's simply *malbono*, the 'un-good.' 'Darkness' is the absence of light: *mallumo*. 'Sadness' is *malgajeco* or *malĝojeco*: 'joylessness.' The Majstro has never spoken or written about this openly. But in this way, I believe, the structure of the language harmonizes with its greater agenda."

"Which is?"

She looked at me, as a schoolteacher might a student who'd mastered the entire curriculum, but still had no idea what the purpose of his lessons were. "Why, to produce goodness, of course!"

"Of course," I said. "And I'm certain you're right, fraŭlino, although," I couldn't help teasing her, "in my own review of Dr. Zamenhof's root words, I've noticed one or two exceptions to your rule."

"Such as?"

"Well, the word *war*, for example," which I uttered, by necessity, in German, "is *milito*, not merely *malpaco*, the 'un-peace.'" I felt cruel for having brought this vexing example to her attention, but charmed by the utter seriousness with which she approached it as a conundrum. Only because she took Dr. Zamenhof's creation so seriously did a contradiction in its formation trouble her so deeply, whereas you or I might have simply shrugged off the entire thing. The day Dr. Zamenhof coined the word *milito*, we'd tell ourselves, was a day on which he was simply inattentive. Perhaps an abnormally heavy lunch had made his mind sluggish, and he'd forgotten his own secret principles.

"Yes, I'd noticed the same thing, and I've been meaning to write to the Majstro about it."

"Or perhaps war isn't always a bad thing, fraŭlino."

"Now you're just being stupid, Dr. Sammelsohn!"

"Just as love isn't always a good thing."

"Isn't it?" she said, brushing my comment aside as lightly as she could. The truth is: I'd been waiting for the moment in which to bring the subject up. I could barely choke out the word *love*, it made me quite nervous to do so. And no sooner had I pronounced it than I felt a chill move in between us. The fraŭlino stepped away from me and pretended to stare at a part of the street where nothing exceptional was occurring.

"Or have you never loved unwisely, fraŭlino?" I asked her as innocently as I could.

"That's not really an issue here, Dr. Sammelsohn." She brushed my question aside. "Although I applaud you for bringing up the word *malsaĝe* as an example of what I earlier meant. Proving your point, Esperanto also graces us with the word *stulte,* from which we may derive the noun *stultulo,* which is a double for the word *idioto,* fools being apparently so abundant Dr. Zamenhof felt the need for more than one word to encompass them all."

"So the answer to the question is 'no' then, I take it?"

"The answer to which question? I believe we were discussing war."

"The question of whether you've never loved unwisely." I trailed along behind her. "Or been loved in a way that was not pleasing — malplezura — to you?"

"Malplezuriga," she corrected me. "However, I think we've exhausted the usefulness of this particular topic." She turned on me fiercely, her expression a warning not to proceed with my reckless flirtations, and suddenly, the day was no longer as pleasing (malplezura? malplezuriga? malplezuriĝa?) as it had been. I peered into Fraŭlino Bernfeld's face. She seemed to be biting back tears. Obviously I'd touched something in her to a degree I hadn't intended.

"I have to go now," she said.

"I apologize, fraŭlino, if I've —"

"No, I'm sorry. I'm so sorry. There's another appointment I've just remembered."

Without another word, she dashed into the street.

"Wait, fraŭlino!" I cried.

"What? What is it?" She hopped back onto the curb to confront me. "What is it that you want from me, Dr. Sammelsohn?"

I didn't quite know what to tell her.

"We'll still be skating on Saturday, won't we? That's all."

She huffed out a breath, sighing so deeply, her rib cage seemed to collapse in upon itself. A vaporous cloud of condensation formed outside her mouth. The wind whipped her hair into her mouth, and she pulled it out with a mittened finger. Finally, she laughed and said, "I suppose we have to. Because you're hopeless. No, you are! You can hardly conjugate your participles."

MY FEAR WAS that someone in our circle had told her of my past. Dr. Freud perhaps. I knew he couldn't be relied upon for his discretion, and the history of my sentimental education *was* appalling: twice married, once divorced, once widowed, I remained a stranger to the ways of carnal love (despite the fact that my second wife, as a vengeful dybbuk, had kidnapped the body of the woman I was then courting and held it for ransom, demanding that I make love to her in exchange for the woman's freedom). Naturally, I attempted to conceal this history from Fraŭlino Bernfeld, and had I been her only source of information, doing so would have been an easy task, since everything she knew about me I had told her in a language in which I could barely express myself with subtlety.

Dibuko? Transmigrado? Metempsikozo?

There were concepts to which, I felt certain, Esperanto never had to bend itself.

(Leafing through *La Plena Vortaro de Esperanto kun Suplemento* and *Le grand dictionnaire espéranto-français* many years later, however, I was surprised to find the second and third words, if not the first, listed in the very forms I'd imagined for them.)

Despite my fears, Fraŭlino Bernfeld continued to see me, and I was overjoyed to find her on Saturday, already laced up and on the ice at the Heumarkt Rink. I sat down near a brazier and pulled on my own skates. The day was cold, and my muscles were stiff, and I had to dig into the ice to keep up with her. I had promised myself, come what may, that today I would declare my love for her. I would take my chances, and there would be no turning back. However, though we skated side by side, chatting amiably, she dashed away consistently at the first sign of a romantic declaration on my part. "Fraŭlino Bernfeld! Wait! There's something I've been meaning to say to you," I cried after her. But she pretended not to hear me over the glistening whiz of the ice, hurrying off, as an undulating

line of skaters whistled past me. My balance was thrown, and my legs
went out from under me, and I dropped into the path of what looked, as
he bore down upon me, like the national champion, moving with all the
weight and speed of a locomotive engine. Unable to stop himself, he leapt
over me instead—I was helpless to suppress a shriek—and skidded to
an abrupt halt. I raised my arm, shielding my eyes against the prismatic
sheen of icy sparks that fell across me, and struggled to sit up.

"Are you all right, sir?" he called out, resting his hands on his enormous thighs, his cheeks a cherry pink, steam issuing from his mouth.

"Fine, I'm fine," I nodded irritably, muttering an unprintable epithet beneath my breath, unable to rise before Fraŭlino Bernfeld, having
turned in time to witness my humiliation, skated to my aid.

"Mia doktoro! Kion vi faras?"

Seeing me stand and reassured of my well-being, the brawny skater flew
off, but not before giving Fraŭlino Bernfeld a brisk masculine appraisal,
ogling her person from the top of her hat to the point of her blade.

"Let's get a warm drink, shall we? Some hot chocolate?" she said.
Holding me by the arm, she led me through the kaleidoscopic shiftings
of the skaters to the other side of the rink. We hobbled into the shelter.
"Sidu ĉe la tablo, Doktoro, kaj me alportas du varmajn ĉokoladojn."

"Jes, jes." I obeyed her, seating myself at one of the shelter's tables
while she went off to get two hot chocolates. Feeling miserable, I watched
the skaters whistling through the grey shafts of winter sunlight outside.
The hut was heated by a number of braziers, and I was soon uncomfortably hot and had to unbutton my coat and unwrap my scarf. Waiting
for the cocoa, Fraŭlino Bernfeld had begun a spirited conversation with
the older man behind the counter, the owner of the concessionary by
the looks of it. He had sucked in his belly and was standing straighter
than he was clearly accustomed to. Fraŭlino Bernfeld rarely seemed to
observe the transformation her presence occasioned in the men she encountered. For all she knew, the world was universally populated by a
race of straight-spined, courteous gentlemen with little to do but pay
exquisite attention to the woman standing before them. I couldn't help
but sigh. If this is the effect Fraŭlino Bernfeld has on all men everywhere,

what chance do I have of successfully suing for her affections? Indeed, what was I, really, but one more flirtatious concessionaire?

She picked up the steaming cups and made her way back to our table. "There now," she said, setting down the drinks. "What a pleasant fellow." With her chin, she gestured over her shoulder towards the man.

"Was he?" I said, unable to muffle the petulance that crept into my voice, although I knew it did nothing but make my company a burden to her, more especially in comparison with the other men who so agreeably surrounded her.

"I must remind myself to carry a stack of promissory cards. You don't have one on you, by any chance?"

"I haven't, no."

"Pity," she said. "He seemed interested. I think he'd make the pledge."

She wore a large hat with a wide brim and a woolen scarf with tassels. With the soft points of her elbows on the table in a rustic manner, she held the mug of steaming cocoa in both hands and raised it to her lips. She kept it elevated before her face, looking over its rim at me, her head to the side in an expression of curiosity, as though she'd just noticed something about me that she'd never seen before.

"Are you all right, Dr. Sammelsohn?"

I gave her a chagrined look. "Am I all right, fraŭlino?"

"That is to say: you're not unwell?"

"Unwell?"

"Are you feeling well?" she added helpfully.

"As a matter of fact, no, I'm not."

"Oh dear." She returned her mug to the tabletop and assumed a serious manner, putting aside, as a concerned friend must on behalf of a friend, the frivolities of chocolate. "You're sick then, I take it?"

"In a manner of speaking, I suppose I am."

She edged back in her chair. "It's a private matter?"

"Until now, it has been, yes."

"Then perhaps it should remain so." She made a small gesture with both hands as though she were drawing a border between ourselves and the subject. "I apologize," she said. "I didn't mean to intrude."

"But you're not, fraŭlino, and perhaps it's time the malady were made known."

"You *are* sick?"

"I am, yes."

"Oh!"

"Lovesick."

Amo-malsana, I said, an awkward construction, I'm afraid, Esperanto having no real word for "sick," sickness being merely the absence of health. I preferred it, however, to amo-naŭzita — nauseated by love — although at the moment, I was so nervous this second construction did, perhaps, more accurately describe my feelings. It troubled me, if only distantly, that the international language lacked the subtlety that enabled one to express a pleasant misfortune in it. One fell in love, linguistically at least, in much the same way one fell down a staircase: the chaos of tumbling, of leaping, of trilling uncertainty, of not knowing what the next step might bring were similar, I thought. The neologism must have taken Fraŭlino Bernfeld a moment to decipher, for her expression of perplexed concern did not, for that moment, change. Then, all at once, she glowered at me with an almost too beautiful mask of irritation, exhaling briskly through her nose.

"You're *in love*?" she said. She sounded annoyed.

"I am. Indeed."

"With a *woman*?"

"Of course, with a woman! What do you take me for?"

"No, I meant: do I know her?"

"Ho, Fraŭlino Bernfeld!"

"Who is she?" she demanded. "Someone I know?"

"Yes, she's someone you know." I could take no more of this wretched playacting. "You know the woman quite well, in fact, fraŭlino, as she is no one but yourself!"

"Oh . . ." she said, and then: "Oh."

It's difficult to describe the shifting expressions with which Fraŭlino Bernfeld met my declaration. Her face brightened and darkened. She smiled and unsmiled. She looked like a person approached on the street by a beggar who makes a number of pleasant inquiries, drawing his interlocutor into a warm conversation, doing everything he can to make it seem as though he is not a beggar, before finally asking for five kronen. Indeed, Fraŭlino Bernfeld couldn't have appeared more appalled if I had, in fact, asked her for five kronen.

"Mi povas nenion fari," I said meekly. *I can't help it.* I took a sip of my cocoa and fiddled with my scarf.

"Of course, you can't." She placed her hands around her mug of cocoa and stared unhappily into it. "However, I must tell you that I'm not . . ." She hesitated, and I waited in an agony of impatience for her to finish the sentence. "Not free," she finally said, and the sad, consoling smile she offered me disappeared as quickly as it was offered. "I'm not free."

"Of course not. How could you be?" I said. "A woman as beautiful as yourself."

"No," she said, and she brought her fingers to my lips, where she left them. "Don't misunderstand me. I haven't pledged my heart. It's my father who has arranged everything."

Ah, of course! The mighty Hans Bernfeld would never leave his only daughter's marriage to chance.

"I liked you from the moment we met, Dr. Sammelsohn, I really did. You were so charming and so sweet and so silly, but . . . I wasn't free. Despite my attraction to you, which," she lowered her voice, "was intense, I knew I couldn't get to know you in that way. I never imagined you'd really become interested in Esperanto, but I was hoping you might, so that we could continue seeing each other. Indeed, it was all I wanted, and when I received your note, I was so happy. I was so happy, Dr. Sammelsohn. You were interested in Esperanto, after all! Although what I really wanted you to be interested in was me. Although then I couldn't have permitted myself to see you. You understand. I enjoyed our afternoons so much, but each time I thought you were on the point of declaring yourself, I tried to distract you, to change the subject, anything, because once you had declared yourself, it would be impossible for us to continue meeting under the pretext of language lessons, and then I knew we couldn't meet at all!"

"Ho, fraŭlino. I've been so thoughtless!"

"No, no, it's all my fault," she said. "I've been so stupid! I only see what's in front of me! And I had no right to lead you on!" She couldn't have studied my face more intently were she preparing to reproduce its features for an art examination. "Ho, Doktoro Sammelsohn," she murmured, "mia dolĉa Doktoro. Now that we've been honest with each other, and now that we know that we both feel the same way, what I've feared would happen has happened, and we must stop seeing each other."

I moved my chair closer to hers and held her hands beneath mine. She was right, of course, and there was no use in fooling ourselves. "I'll miss our daily hour together," I said, as nobly as I could.

"And I as well." A tear fell down her cheek.

I swallowed with difficulty. "Well, farewell then, fraŭlino."

"Farewell then."

She nodded. Still, neither of us moved. She continued to study my face, and I hers. Gently, she uncurled her hands from inside mine and placed them upon the table. I acknowledged the finality of the gesture and began to stand, but before I could, she was pressing my hands again, keeping them locked tightly inside hers.

"Must we really stop?"

"Of course, we must."

"Must we?"

What could I say? At a moment like this, a man of integrity, his declarations of love having been firmly, if regrettably declined, would protest that he could do nothing more than remove himself altogether from the young woman's life. A man of substance would never permit himself to be demoted from a potent rival to an unthreatening friend, a sexless eunuch, invited into the most private chamber of the young woman's heart, but barred forever from crossing the threshold of her more sublime affections. Happily for us both, I was not a man of integrity, but rather (as I'd been told my entire life) one of little substance.

And so, I heard myself saying: "Mia kara fraŭlino, if we promise never to act upon these feelings, and to never mention them again, not even to each other, to deny their existence as much as possible, even to ourselves, to root them out of our hearts as though they were emotional weeds, appearing to the world to remain exactly as we have for these last several months, as friends devoted passionately not to each other, but to a common cause, then I see no reason why we cannot continue on as before."

"Oh, Kaĉjo? Do you really think so?"

"If it would make you happy, fraŭlino, I would do anything, yes."

Another tear rolled down her cheek, falling slowly inside the track left by its predecessor. She pressed the back of her hand against my cheek. "It would make me so very happy," she said.

"Then," I said with as much emotional detachment as I could feign, "I will see you home today, and I will very much look forward to our hour of language instruction on Monday."

WE WERE PLAYING with fire, and we both knew it, though of the two of us, I had the less to fear.

As the winter worsened, we abandoned the Ring and took refuge in various coffee houses, principally my own, the Guglhupf, where, sitting by a roaring hearth, we chatted through the darkening afternoons, sharing questions about participle formations and adjectival agreement, or quizzing each other, with homemade memory cards, on the latest words coming out of Warsaw. I had no idea who my rival was. Fraŭlino Bernfeld discouraged all questions concerning him. Though she didn't love him, and though he cared little for the cause, still, he was a good man. At times, she even felt sorry for him, blundering so optimistically into what promised to be a loveless marriage. I sensed this pity for him as a danger to myself. It could so easily uncurdle into actual love, and so my strategy was simple: I made no emotional demands upon Fraŭlino Bernfeld. Rather, I contrived to appear for our daily hour in the guise of my finest self, masquerading, in this way, as a utopianist, a dreamer, and a sexual renunciate, knowing that, in doing so, I would best this Herr Whomever, whom I felt certain was taking no similar precautions against me while in the company of his fiancée. And why should he? Knowing nothing of our rivalry, fearing it not in the least, he wished to be loved not for his best self, but, in the way of all men, for his true self. And this, I knew, would be his undoing.

We both looked forward to our hour together as the sweetest part of our day. The fraŭlino enjoyed my company clearly—I won't say she *preferred* it, having no idea how much she enjoyed *his*—and she made a virtue of our self-willed naïveté: as long as we remained convinced that our love was as hopeless as we claimed, she could continue my lessons with an easy conscience. She was like a missionary's daughter tutoring a lovesick cannibal, never imagining that her own heart might be at risk. She enjoyed flirting, moth-like, with the immolating fires of our mutual attraction, bathing in the heat of my yearning admiration. Our conversations were filled with utterances we stopped ourselves from making, with sighs that revealed as much as they concealed, with soul-stirring glances that, while breaking no code of decorum, were, at the same time, too intimate, too frank.

Each afternoon, at our farewell, we indulged ourselves in an exquisite drama of passionate renunciation.

"Adiaŭ, mia fraŭlino."

"Adiaŭ, mia doktoro."

"Ĝis."

"Ĝis la."

A look darkens her eye.

"What is it, my dear friend?"

"Nothing."

"I know."

"If only—"

"Yes, but we must not speak of it."

"No, of course, you're right, and so . . ."

"Good-bye."

Still, neither of us moves.

"Is it hard on you, Doktoro?"

"Terribly hard, fraŭlino."

"And yet you bear it?"

"Gladly."

"I feel so cruel."

"Don't. Never. Not for a moment. No."

"Oh," she sighs.

And I sigh as well.

And of course, it didn't last, nor could it. As high-minded as Fraŭlino

Bernfeld may have been, and as dutiful a daughter, no one, and certainly no woman, is without her vanity. Though we'd agreed upon remaining friends, and though (in her thinking) I'd forfeited all hope of her love, the truth was she had yet to surrender possession of mine for her; rather, she kept it, like a secret cache of chocolate from which she occasionally nibbled. How pleasant to flatter oneself with the hopeless love of another, how pleasing to imagine oneself so beautiful a woman, so rare and exquisite a specimen, that a man might choose a life of celibacy rather than coronate another woman upon the throne of his heart, a woman inferior, perhaps, to the original in all qualities but one: her actualness. And isn't it among the heart's greatest sorrows to realize that a person we've rejected, though once hopelessly enamored of us, has found a new object for his love?

At our bimonthly Esperanto meetings, which I attended regularly, I bestowed my attentions a little more ardently upon a young lingvistino named Suzanne Kiniower. She was sweet enough, if a little sad and too insecure to suspect that my attentions towards her were anything but real, and too used to romantic disappointment to depend upon them continuing.

"We merely shared a dinner," I informed Fraŭlino Bernfeld the following afternoon at the Gulphupf, when she'd all but forgotten herself and accused me of emotional treachery, "as du samideanoj might. Fraŭlino Suzanno merely wished to go over the differences between active and passive participles" (one of the most difficult features of Esperanto, I'd found).

"As though you're an expert!"

"Of course, I'm not an expert, but I feel more secure in the topic than she. And in any case, what am I supposed to do with my evenings? Sit at home like an old maid?"

"Do you find her attractive?"

"Ho, fraŭlino! What a question!"

"Do you?"

"Of course not!"

"More attractive than me?"

"We've been over this a thousand times. What does it matter who I find more attractive? You're affianced."

"Please stop reminding me of that!"

I feign an exasperated indulgence, crossing my arms and fiddling with my cuff links. "Do I complain when you go out with *your* fiancé?"

"It's hardly the same thing."

"No? And how is it different?"

"We're engaged! We *have* to spend time with each other."

"Now you're not making any sense."

"I can't believe you could be so hateful!"

And on and on, until at last she is apologizing, in tears, kissing my hands and begging me for my forgiveness: "Oh God, I've put you through such hardship! And it's my own fault. No, it is. I'm so selfish and so cruel!"

The other advantage I held over my rival was the fact that, with my increasing fluency, I'd become even more convinced that Esperanto's goal of universal understanding *was* a cause worth fighting for (or rather worth *not* fighting for). For most of the world, certainly, the enterprise seemed quaintly absurd, I supposed, a subject for the opéra bouffe: world peace and universal brotherhood obtained through the use of an artificial auxiliary language. But was there ever a more excellent goal? And did it matter that, in order to reach this summit of human excellence, one had to babble like a baby in an imaginary tongue? I was ashamed of myself for ever thinking of Dr. Zamenhof as a crank and of his followers as utopian lunatics. Had my heart so hardened that it couldn't be moved by a Zamenhofic belief in the ultimate goodness of man? What of value was ever obtained by cynics and realists anyway? Indeed, what sane-seeming man ever achieved anything of value? What modest clerk, hoarding his meager wages, ever advanced the cause of humankind one jot? With a renewed sense of high-mindedness, I plighted my troth to our movement, not caring whether doing so made me more attractive to Fraŭlino Bernfeld or less, though I knew it made me more attractive.

And this is what finally doomed her engagement: the fact that she could admire me without reserve. Like her father, her fiancé, I gleaned, merely indulged her passion for Esperanto. (It was more than a passion; for a time, along with W. H. Trompeter, the German surveyor, Fräulein Loë Bernfeld was one of Dr. Zamenhof's most generous benefactors.

Indeed, there were times when she kept the entire movement financially afloat.) While conceding that an international language might be a boon to trade, neither Hans Bernfeld nor his future son-in-law found himself attracted to its utopian underpinnings, and both, I'm told, considered it a frivolous and womanly affair.

The more indifferent I seemed as a lover to Fraŭlino Bernfeld and the more dedicated as an adherent I became to our cause, the more profoundly did she endure the weight of her unhappy betrothal, and the more inflamed became her jealousy when I dallied with other women, until, one black and wintry afternoon, when I'd seen her home, entering with her into the foyer of her apartment building in order to escape, even for a brief moment, the miserable cold, I bid her quickly adiaŭ and tipped my hat.

However, as I turned to leave and as she turned from me to ascend the stairs, our wrists lightly touched. The spark of skin against skin was like an electric convulsion that bound us in its current. Like the heads of two electric eels, our hands slithered around each other's arms until they found one another. Our fingers intertwined. Something sharp on her ring nicked my skin. We were facing now, moving towards each other in the moist chill of the unheated foyer, her arms bracing my neck, my arms her waist. She lifted her mouth to mine, her lips parted, and I kissed her, my pince-nez steaming up and blinding me until, jostled by her hungry mouth, the lenses, perched until then crookedly upon my nose, fell from it altogether. (The fear that they might be damaged, pressed between her body and mine, was undermined as I reassured myself: You're an oculist, idiot, and can replace them at cost!) Breathing in the rainy scents of her skin, biting into her pillowy lips, her head falling back as I kissed her plump throat, which trembled beneath my mouth like a small, captured rabbit, I listened to her murmur quietly and achingly, her breath a wet rasp in my ear, her open mouth tracing a moist line across my cheek until it again found my mouth.

Then suddenly her mouth abandoned mine. Her head dropped against my breastbone. She hid her face between the lapels of my coat. With her hands grasping onto my suit jacket, she pressed her elbows into my abdomen, bracing herself against me. Was she trembling or laughing or weeping? I had no idea. I kissed the top of her head and tried to kiss the tops of her hands, but she lowered them away.

"Ne, ne, ne," she cried, her forehead still pressing against my chest.

"Fraŭlino," I whispered.

"I've got to go," she said, without looking up at me. "Mention this to no one."

But instead, some force propelled her, and she was instantly kissing me again, her mouth expressing beyond its physical powers all the yearning we'd renounced for each other for so long. Unable to face me, she gathered up her sopping hat, which had fallen to the ground and, modestly raising her skirts, ran for the staircase, tripping on a loose cobble before falling to her knee.

"Fraŭlino!" I cried, reaching out to her.

"Ne, ne!" She blindly gestured me away. "Estas nenio. Bonan vesperon, Doktoro Sammelsohn, bonan vesperon."

Righting herself, she ascended the stairs and, without a glance backwards, disappeared onto the landing above.

On Monday, as I knew it must, a note from Papagenogasse arrived for me at the clinic. I put off opening it for as long as I could, stashing the envelope in my pocket but immediately taking it out again. I hid it beneath a pile of patients' charts and managed to forget about it for all of ten minutes. I was on the point of placing it in my medical bag when my hands, acting on their own, picked up a letter opener and tore the envelope to shreds.

With the deepest of apologies, Fraŭlino Bernfeld begged to be forgiven for the forfeiture of our lesson for the day. On Tuesday, it was the same: "Morgaŭ, morgaŭ, mi promesas!" However, the morrow brought only another lavender note, and this one, instead of begging off for the day and promising me the morrow, canceled our lessons until I should hear from her otherwise.

I wasn't surprised. When had my love life ever run smoothly?

Having failed to thwart the will of my own father, a petty tyrant with no real power, what hope did I have, standing against Herr Bernfeld, a man of actual substance and means? Still, I kept up my daily Esperanto studies, telling myself that there was no point in falling behind from despair, although who was I deceiving? I had no one to speak the language with, and in any case, I could barely concentrate on my studies. I began a translation into Esperanto of Dr. Freud's new book, *The Psychopathology of Everyday Life,* but lost heart early on when I came across the aliquis dialogue, a barely fictionalized account of my first conversation with him, designed obviously to eradicate all further traces of me from his life. I lived through my days like a sleeper who forces himself to remain in bed, hoping to begin redreaming a beautiful lost dream. Every hour, I checked the post, and when finally I received a letter from the Bernfeld residence on Papagenogasse, it was not in its customary envelope nor, as I saw when I'd opened it, was it in Fraŭlino Bernfeld's pretty hand.

Instead it was a note from Herr Bernfeld himself, summoning me to his club:

18 March 1902
Dr. Sammelsohn,
    I would be grateful to you for the favor of a face-to-face encounter.
            Sincerely,
            Hans Bernfeld

A face-to-face encounter? As I scanned the page, the disagreeable thought struck me that I'd been summoned to a duel! Such things were not uncommon in Vienna, even among its Jews. Indeed, the young members of these new Jewish fencing clubs proudly displayed, to the left of their mustaches, the cicatrices that now destroyed the symmetry of their faces as for centuries they had those of their Catholic brethren. In a panic, I read the note again. Although there was nothing friendly about Herr Bernfeld's missive, on closer inspection, neither did its intent appear lethal. Granted, the word *favor* seemed tipped with poisonous sarcasm, and the term *face-to-face* brought to mind an image of fisticuffs and bloodied noses; but otherwise the note was emotionless, brief and to the point. More important, I knew the meeting it proposed was my only chance of ever winning Fräulein Bernfeld's hand. Our broken appointments spoke eloquently of a good daughter obeying even the harshest decrees of her stern but loving father. She had obviously gone to him immediately and told him everything; and as immediately, he had forbidden her to see me. The swiftness of her petition followed by his prohibitory decree were testaments to her feelings for me and to the threat my person posed to her father's plans. Indeed, were I nothing more than a harmless language enthusiast, one more of the utopian cranks she welcomed into her apartments, our daily meetings would have been allowed to continue, as a fatherly indulgence to a daughter's tenderhearted folly. If nothing else, for the first time, my feelings for a woman were being taken seriously, though this was hardly encouraging: when it came to fathers and weddings, my history was dismal.

I wrote back my willingness to meet Herr Bernfeld and received a time for our appointment from his secretary, an Herr Emmanuel Gold-berg, by return post.

THE DAY OF my summons was one of those dark, cruel days too often imposed upon the Viennese during the winter. The sun never breached the woolen skies. I trudged through the snow, its flakes stinging my face, as though I were facing down an army of Chinese physicians. Taking every precaution, I'd bundled up in a cocoon of heavy winter clothing: a shapeless coat, thick gloves, a hood worn beneath my hat. Through an oval in its front, my face was exposed as little as possible to the elements. Around my neck, encircling it three times, so that it covered my chin, my ears, and even the tip of my nose, I'd wrapped a long scarf, and yet I trembled as I crossed the threshold into the Arcadia Club, and surren-dered my things to the steward who greeted me at the cloakroom—if *greeted* is the word for such a sneering reception—impatiently holding out his hand for each item as I hurried to unbutton, unlace, unlatch, un-loosen, and unravel the various garments I'd worn, until finally, I stood before him naked of my winterwear, weighed down only by an anxiety that rose in my solar plexus at the thought of my next task: winning from Herr Bernfeld the right to court his only child and heir.

A servant of the club addressed me: "This way, sir." Like the cloak steward, he too wore a splashy uniform—a taupe jacket with large brass buttons, militaristic epaulets, and a diagonal sash of deepest purple. On each pant leg was a raised satin band. This is the costume of servitude, I told myself, and yet I couldn't help feeling that my worsted suit suffered in comparison. I tried in vain not to gawk at the high ceilings and the murals and the domed skylights above me as the steward, inured to such splendor, led me into one well-lit sitting room after the next. Equally in vain were my attempts not to nod at the gentlemen who sat in their over-stuffed chairs, breaking off from their cigars and their newspapers and their business deals to watch, in silence, as I was escorted past them. The steward slowed his pace before two large oaken doors and leaned his ear against the wood, rapping lightly. I heard no reply, but the boy nodded, as though confirming for himself the sound of an answering command. He opened the door and, standing beside it, ushered me through.

The first thing I noticed was the large fireplace recessed into the room's high wall. It was nearly six feet tall and eight feet long, and the roaring flames were so loud I was uncertain I'd actually heard Herr Bernfeld's voice rising above them in greeting. He was seated at his desk in a sumptuous robe of blue brocade and matching velvet slippers. Outside the tall windows, the whitened city looked like a dreamscape dreamt by this regal man, this sultan sitting in the Saharan warmth of his own private chambers. Without acknowledging me, he continued signing checks inside the pages of a thick leather exchequer.

"Sit down, I said. Please."

So, he had addressed me after all.

"There." He nodded towards a well-polished table in another part of the room. I did as I was commanded, thinking first to sit with my back to him, then taking the chair opposite, so that I might watch him at his work, regretting, of course, the little hop-hop movement I'd made switching from chair to chair. Though Herr Bernfeld never raised an eye from his exchequer, I was certain he had nevertheless seen my embarrassing indecisiveness.

He was a tall man with a full head of black hair and a high, wide forehead. His rectangular beard fell nearly a foot and a half beneath his chin. His nose, straight as a letter opener, was perfectly equidistant between the southern tip of his beard and the northern pole of his widow's peak. The tight curls of his hair were so dark and lustrous, they nearly gleamed beneath the nimbus of the electric lamps. I'd never seen a man as virile nor as handsome among our people. He raised himself from his desk, and although his chest was narrow—he seemed constructed entirely out of rectangles—his waist was narrower still. Squinting myopically, he nodded in my direction and, though I nodded in return, a moment after doing so, I realized my mistake. He hadn't nodded at me, but past me, at the steward who was placing a silver coffeepot upon the table.

"Danke, Werner." Herr Bernfeld remained standing as the young man set the table. As though propelled by a will greater than my own, I rose from the chair and stood as well. Only when Werner had finished did Herr Bernfeld condescend to sit, looking up at me quizzically, as though my inexplicable standing were a puzzle.

Not a single word passed between us as I skulked, like a disobedient dog, back into my chair, slouching, then thinking not to slouch, then slouching out of nervous fatigue. Herr Bernfeld squinted at me, as though not quite certain he was seeing some amusing detail. He reached into the breast pocket of his gown and, with two long fingers, drew out a monocle at the end of a glittering chain. Placing it like a communion wafer inside his mouth, he sighed and befogged the glass on either side. Removing a silk monogrammed kerchief from his sleeve, he rubbed the lens between its folds before dexterously screwing the monocle into place. Half his vision thus improved, he looked at me again, having apparently confirmed with his half-naked eyes the presence of whatever amusing thing he'd previously seen.

"Allow me to pour," he said, reaching for the coffeepot and quickly filling our cups. "I won't waste any more of your time, Dr. Sammelsohn. It has been made known to me that you and my daughter have conceived a sentimental regard for each other, a circumstance that you are no doubt astute enough to know greatly displeases me. My daughter is my only child and the child of my late wife, whom I loved deeply. I had already, I thought with my daughter's consent, arranged a suitable match for her with a man her social equal, a match that, until you arrived upon the scene, she showed no signs of rejecting. And yet, now, here you are, the rude fact of you, sitting across from me, listening to me insult you, too convinced of the rightness of what I'm saying to even contradict me."

I tried to drink my coffee, but my hand was quaking too violently, and I returned the cup to its coffee-splattered saucer.

"Whether I am unworthy of your daughter's love, my good Herr Bernfeld, I cannot say. All I know is that I love your daughter very much, and against all odds, she seems to love me as well."

"If you truly loved her, Dr. Sammelsohn, as you claim, and if, additionally, you were a man of substance, you would, for her sake, renounce that love."

"If I were I a man of substance?" I returned. "How am I not a man of substance?"

Herr Bernfeld smiled at the simplicity of my question and answered me as one might a simpleton: "Why, just look at yourself!"

Indeed, so imperious was his command that I did exactly as he bid me. I lowered my chin and took a long look at myself or as much of myself as I could see from this vantage: my chest down to my feet, roughly the whole of myself minus my head and neck. From this view, it wasn't clear how I differed so radically from the statistical norm. I raised my eye and met Herr Bernfeld's monocled gaze. Though neither of us spoke it aloud, the word *idiot* seemed to hover in the atmosphere between us.

"Your daughter, Herr Bernfeld, if I may say so, is the most idealistic person I've ever known. Her belief in the goodness of mankind has completely transformed me."

"Every person is idealistic in his youth, Dr. Sammelsohn, just as everyone in his infancy cannot control his bowels. My apologies. I see by the look on your face that my analogy disgusts you."

I shrugged, not knowing where to look.

"Listen to me, Dr. Sammelsohn. The world is not intended to be a paradise, and all of us must eventually be expelled from whatever Edens we might cling to. When you have lived as long as I, you'll find that innocence has a way of calling forth its own traducing."

"Were you never an idealist yourself, sir?"

"I was. Indeed, I was quite the romantic. A man would have to be heartless not to be, and a fool not to outgrow it. Of course, every Jew wishes to summon the Messiah, to draw him down, through the force of his own goodness, from the throne upon which he sits chained in the Heavens. But one might profitably ask: Who has chained him there, if not the Lord Himself, the devil being a theological convenience we Jews, in our purest theologies, though not in the way you yourself were raised, forbid ourselves? And who has ever gone against God and won? Only ask yourself that. In the meantime, there's actual work to be done. As Ben Zakkai teaches us in our holy books: 'If you're planting a tree and the Messiah arrives, finish planting the tree, then go and greet the Messiah.' "

"But, my good sir, isn't that exactly what Dr. Zamenhof is doing, with the help of your daughter? Planting trees for our future?"

"Yes, I know of your Dr. Zamenhof. Much of my money has gone into sustaining his utopian schemes. He'd like to turn the entire world into Jews."

"Into Jews?"

"Certainly! Just as we possess a despised and ridiculed jargon that allows us to communicate with ourselves, as one family, across national borders, so, if Dr. Zamenhof has his way, will the entire world soon possess such a jargon. In this way, he believes he can smuggle our people into the great family of man while no one is paying attention. But, you see, there's one problem."

"And what is that?"

"They don't want us in their family."

They don't want us in their family. These words resounded for me in a thousand different ways. Herr Bernfeld didn't want me in his family, neither apparently did my own father, just as the world wanted nothing to do with any of us.

"With all due respect," I said as politely as I could, "it is to be hoped that through the work of people like Dr. Zamenhof and, to a significant degree, your daughter, this deplorable state will be revised."

"And then all men will be brothers, or something like that?"

"Exactly."

"You're familiar with the Bible, I presume, a man like yourself."

"Of course."

"You've read deeply into the genesis of mankind."

"Naturally."

"You've been immersed by your teachers in all the commentaries; you've turned the text inside and out and have examined it from a thousand different angles."

"It was the way I was raised, yes, of course."

"Then tell me, my dear young fellow, how many brothers did the earth require before one murdered the other?"

I could say nothing.

"Precisely," he said, having won the point.

"But certainly . . ." I deferentially gestured for permission to rebut him.

He nodded. "By all means, please go ahead; speak."

"Certainly in the five thousand years separating the murder of Abel from our own present moment, mankind has progressed, if not a little.

Besides, with Esperanto, we're not talking about some great altruistic sacrifice, but about a thing that is universally good for everyone. As Dr. Zamenhof clearly points out: since it's universally recognized that an international language is not only possible but that it would bring only good to mankind, if we didn't rise to the occasion, why then, as a race, we'd have to deny to ourselves even the smallest bit of elementary intelligence."

"Which I'm fully prepared to do."

"Surely you don't mean that, sir."

"You can't change the nature of man, Dr. Sammelsohn. The wicked will always destroy the naïve and the meek. Why? I don't know why. Perhaps it gives them pleasure. The Tower of Babel will always crumble beneath the weight of its many builders. But those of us who, like myself, accept the world as it is, who accept people as they are, who don't wish to reform anyone from his warring ways, can make a handsome profit from this eternal warring and, with that profit, build schools, fund hospitals, endow laboratories, plant a few trees, as you say, while fools like you go rushing off to greet the Messiah."

"Surely, you don't include your daughter among that list of fools?"

Herr Bernfeld leaned in towards me. "Let me tell you something about my daughter, Dr. Sammelsohn, shall I? Every day for eight months when she was nine years old, she begged me for a certain locket. We used to see it in the front window of a jewelry shop we passed on the Prinsengracht each morning as I walked her to school. It wasn't very expensive, but it was too expensive for a nine-year-old child. However, after eight months of her haranguing me, against the advice of my wife, I relented and bought Loë this necklace. She wore it straight through for three weeks, and after that, we never saw it again. 'And where's your pretty golden locket?' I said to her one day. 'Oh, Papa, I tired of it,' she told me. 'So I threw it in the canal, and now I want a horse.'"

He tossed his head back and roared with laughter, his mouth opened so wide, I could see all his bright and sparkling teeth. He caught his breath and unscrewed his monocle and wiped away the tear that had formed in his eye.

"'Oh, Papa, I tired of it, and so I threw it in the canal, and now I want a horse!'"

He laughed again, patting me sympathetically on the arm. "Would you care for a bite of breakfast with your coffee?"

"Thank you, no." I shook my head.

"Bread and jam?"

"No."

"An omelet? The chef here is excellent."

"No, thank you."

"A bowl of groats?"

I shook my head again.

"Well," he sipped his coffee, "and now I suppose you're wondering what I plan to do about this regrettable state of affairs, and the answer to that question may surprise you."

I raised an eyebrow.

"Nothing," Herr Bernfeld said, as though he were a chess champion explaining an unbeatable move to his opponent.

"Nothing?"

"Nothing at all." Though his beard was as thick as a mink's carcass, I had the impression he was grinning behind it from ear to ear. "I can't afford to estrange myself from the affections of my only child. She's too precious to me for that. I am, however, though I have loved but one woman in my life, no stranger to the ways of women. This"—he raised his nose, as though the word were repugnant to him—"romance of yours is entirely mismatched, it suits neither of you, it will not last, nor will it culminate in a marriage. Rather, it will crumble under its own weight. Exactly like that nonsensical language you promote. Of that I have no doubt, nor does a specialist I've consulted in the matter."

"A specialist?"

"A neurologist I see from time to time," he lightly brushed off the issue.

"May I inquire into his name?"

"Of course, although it's of no moment in our discussion: his name is Sigmund Freud."

"Ah."

"You know him, I believe."

"Yes, too well, I sometimes think."

"Yes. He said as much."

"Or perhaps not well enough."

"However, his professional opinion is in complete agreement with mine. Sooner, it is to be hoped, rather than later, but ineluctably, your friendship with my daughter, built upon so faulty a foundation, will crumble. And I ask myself, if this is so, as I and Dr. Freud believe, why, Dr. Sammelsohn, should I take a stand against you, intervening in a domineering and unattractive way, and thus jeopardizing the only thing that matters to me — the love of my daughter — when personal history, character, her character specifically, but yours also, will eventually do the work of a thousand chaperones?"

"And if it doesn't turn out the way you imagined?"

He smiled icily. "Well, it's not for nothing that our enemies accuse us of poisoning their wells." He clapped his hands lightly against his thighs. "Good! Well then," he said, "I've enjoyed our chat. Thank you, Dr. Sammelsohn, for accommodating me into your busy schedule. Under other circumstances, I daresay I might have treasured your acquaintance. As it is, I shall bid you good day."

Though I saw Herr Bernfeld make no move to summon him, instantly Herr Goldberg was at my side, escorting me from the room. Before I knew it, I was back in the bitter cold, the severity of which mattered little to me now. I took a step towards the clinic. I couldn't believe it! The old man had all but bowed to the ineluctability of Fraŭlino Bernfeld's and my love! Despite his stern posturings, what was he but an old toothless tiger, growling for the sake of pride and fooling no one with his bite? Besides, I was certain in time I could make him like me. Upon what I based this certainty, I have no idea. (Unable to charm my own father, what hope did I have of charming Fraŭlino Bernfeld's?) Still, I'd enjoyed his company, as he claimed to have enjoyed mine. Indeed, I felt sorry to leave him when our interview was finished. He was an undeniably attractive fellow, powerful, purposeful, and I could have listened to him for hours. His magnificent daughter, it turned out, was only the tail of an even more magnificent kite! In the face of all this, what did Dr. Freud's treachery matter? Love had triumphed! Or if not triumphed, it had certainly prevailed. At least it hadn't been entirely defeated. I loved Fraŭlino

Bernfeld; she apparently loved me, and as long as this held true, what force of nature, what human being, could come between us?

It was all I could do to deliver myself to the clinic. Every fiber of my person ached to bisect the Ring and detour by Fraŭlino Bernfeld's apartments. Despite everything, I was no Casanova. Duty called, and I obeyed its summons and was rewarded for my diligence by the midmorning delivery of mail. Among the white envelopes, like a lilac blooming on a snow-covered hilltop, was a note from Fraŭlino Bernfeld, the first I'd received in weeks. I tore it open.

"Oh, what a wise and noble father Heaven has provided me!" she wrote.

Ah, just as the old devil had predicted, his acquiescence to our love had elevated him even higher in his daughter's esteem while leaving my status more or less the same. I impatiently skimmed through these paternal encomia for something more immediately concerning my own person: Fraŭlino Bernfeld's proposal that we meet again daily for our hour of language lessons beginning that very afternoon over lunch in her apartments.

The favor of a reply was requested.

"Jes, jes, milojn da jesoj!" I responded rapidly.

"Very well, but I'm not sure you can actually say that in Esperanto," she lectured me, meeting me at her door and holding up my note, having underlined my awkward, homemade idiom—milojn da jesoj: a thousand yesses—in red.

"I don't care," I said, taking the note from her hand and ripping it in two.

"Oh my!" she cried. "But we're in high spirits today!"

Her maid Käthe helped me off with my heavy cloak.

"Hang them over the tub, Käthe," Fraŭlino Bernfeld commanded, and when the girl had left the room, I took Fraŭlino Bernfeld's hand and kissed its furrowed knuckles before pressing my lips against the softer skin of her inner wrist. She closed her eyes and inhaled sharply through her fluted lips. The little sizzling sound of her breath cut electrically through me.

"Mi estas tiel feliĉa," she said, looking quite handsome in the grey light of the foyer, her hair an extravagant mane, her chocolate-drop eyes peering into mine.

"Sed ne tiel feliĉa kiel mi."

"We must go and tell our good friend."

"Dr. Zamenhof, you mean?"

"The poor man." Fraŭlino Bernfeld shook her head. "From his last letters, it seems he's practically near despair. To know that his work has brought together two such happy lovers would cheer him, I think. It's not right, Kaĉjo, that we should be the only happy ones, is it?"

I followed her to the table and to the meal Käthe had prepared. "I suppose I can cancel Monday's patients and Friday afternoon's, and we can go for a few days."

"Marvelous!"

I took a sip of the wine. "But shouldn't we write him first?"

"No," she said, stirring her soup, "let's let it be a surprise."

The idea struck me as a poor one, but who could refuse Fraŭlino Bernfeld anything? Certainly not I, and so we made our plans: we would take the train to Warsaw to surprise Dr. Zamenhof with a visit, during which time we would announce to him our new love and (according to my own private scheming) our engagement. I wasn't clear exactly how I planned to propose to Fraŭlino Bernfeld; I only knew that I would not return to Vienna without having done so.

CHAPTER 5

The sky was a milky grey, and the afternoon couldn't have been duller. At three o'clock, I sent the last of my patients home and locked the clinic doors. Fraŭlino Bernfeld and I were to meet at the Südbahnhof. Arriving late, I caught sight of her, arriving later still. Our trip would consist of no more than two days of travel with two days in Warsaw, and I was perplexed to see her strolling down the platform followed by a porter toting a small caravan of boxes and bags. I'd packed only one small suitcase for myself, and her mountain of luggage made me nervous. As far as I was concerned, the Russian Empire was a wild and lawless place. One never knew when a maniac with a revolver or an agent of the secret police might step out from behind a baluster. Fraŭlino Bernfeld's bags would not only draw attention to us, but they'd make a dash to freedom all but impossible.

"I don't understand. Why would anyone want to assassinate you from behind a baluster?" she asked, when I'd confessed these fears to her.

"My dear fraŭlino, I can't pretend to understand the reasonings of a madman."

"And what information could you possibly give to the tsarist police?"

"None, and as a consequence, they'd never stop torturing me."

"Tip the porter, Kaĉjo, and stop worrying. These bags are going only one way."

I did as she bid me.

The train ride was uneventful, and we arrived in Warsaw early the following day. Fraŭlino Bernfeld wrote out the Zamenhofs' address, 9 Dzika Street, for the coachman on a white card with a small mechanical pencil she kept pinned to the lapel of her frock. The man grimaced, eying our luggage. With so many colorful bags and gifts piled onto his groaning droshky—I could only imagine him thinking—he'd be a horse-drawn advertisement for marauders! He rubbed his hand across his whiskery jowls, and when he removed it, in place of his frown was the grin of a plucky hero, minus a few teeth. Dangerous though it was, *he* would ferry the Fräulein to her destination, with me along for the ride. He gave me a hard and penetrating look. Who was I, anyway—her brother? her accountant? an annoying pest she wished to be rid of immediately? He would get her there, even if it meant leaving me in a roadside ditch.

We climbed into his cab. Warsaw seemed lost in a kind of grimy melancholia. Even the late morning fog felt dirty on my skin. The seats in the droshky were stained, and our horse limped along, farting, indifferent to the oaty detritus soiling its hindquarters. As we journeyed on, the streets became narrower and even more crooked, and we were almost face-to-face with some of the taller people walking along beside us. I reached for the latch on the droshky's door and secured it. Fraŭlino Bernfeld's face tightened into a look of uncomprehending concern.

"How nervous are you really?" she asked.

"A little less now," I assured her.

She brought the droshky's blanket to her chin and sighed.

As the alphabets on the shop signs began changing—from Russian and Polish, to Polish, to Polish and Yiddish—I gathered that we had entered the Jewish Quarter. A raw-boned woman with an expressionless face stood in one doorway, watching us pass. Another sold herbs and tea from inside a coal bin's delivery door. A white-haired man sat on a stone curb. Another in a worker's cap tugged on a cigarette. Porters dozed on their boxes, as they did in Szibotya, their hands inside the mouths of their shoes. Wafting in and out on the wind was the sound of an ill-played hurdy-gurdy.

Finally, our coachman stopped before a large four-story building. "Dzika," he cried, before whistling for a porter. Together, the two unloaded Fraŭlino Bernfeld's things. I kept an eye on both men as they worked, certain neither could be trusted. The odors rising from the street—horse piss, manure, rotting fruit—added to my unease. I paid the cabman, tipping him excessively, as Fraŭlino Bernfeld had instructed me, although I suspected he was already taking advantage of our unfamiliarity with the currency. At the urging of the porter, we walked ahead of his wobbly cart, though I kept turning around to affirm that he was still here, fearful the moment I ceased doing so, he would sprint off and disappear with our things through some crack in a wall where we'd be helpless to follow him.

"Ah, yes, here it is." Fraŭlino Bernfeld pointed with her umbrella to a sign that hung beneath a pair of outsized spectacles. A dozen or so dirty faces crowded the consultancy window to get a look at the princess in her elegant blue cloak, standing beside her mountain of luggage. Drawn by the commotion, Dr. Zamenhof soon appeared at the door, dressed in his white medical smock. I saluted him with a little wave of recognition, which he didn't seem to see. Irritation pinched his features as though he were considering an annoying puzzle that required an immediate solution: *What is everyone gawking at?* His eyebrows ascended, like hastily raised flags, as the pieces came together. Panic contorted his face. At last, he'd been caught out, his secret life exposed! (Again I told myself we'd done wrong by not notifying him of our plans.) His look of bafflement was followed by a grimace of resignation. There was nothing to do but present the most pleasant of faces to the world, and to the lovely people who had so kindly thought to surprise him. Still in his smock, he ran into the street, as though his only desire were to offer these two lost grandees directions for safe passage out of the neighborhood again.

"Majstro!" Fraŭlino Bernfeld called, oblivious to Dr. Zamenhof's embarrassment. He smiled tightly, his cheeks as red as polished apples, giving no indication to anyone who might be looking on that this gloriously eccentric title belonged to him.

"טראָג די וואַליזעס אַרײַן איו שטיב!" He directed the porter through the courtyard to the apartment upstairs.

"זיכער, מײַן הער!" the porter said.

"לאָמיך אים העלפֿן," I offered.

"גיך!" Dr. Zamenhof cried.

He didn't greet us. Instead, casting a fearful look over his shoulder, he corralled us into the whirlwind of his activity, imploring us to גייט! גייט! גייט! off the street and through the squalid courtyard, into the precincts of his slightly less squalid home.

"No one here knows of my work in the greater world," he explained to us, his voice tight, as though there might be spies hidden in the barrels inside the courtyard, "and it's just as well. No one wants a utopian crank as a doctor." He muttered this last in Esperanto, leaving the porter, who'd been following our conversation in Yiddish, gawking.

"Klara!" he called to this wife. "Say hello to our guests! They're special people. Introduce yourselves, everybody. Oh, and kisses all around!" He backed through the door, his arms raised, his hands opened, his fingers flicking, as though the kisses he metaphorically tossed out were hard candies. His figure darkened the doorway for an instant, and he was gone. I watched him through the window, a moment later, dashing across the courtyard below, avoiding the barrels and the goat, and disappearing at last through the inner door of his clinic.

Flummoxed into speechlessness, Fraŭlino Bernfeld and I turned to greet Dr. Zamenhof's wife. As small and as child-like as her husband, Klara Zamenhof stood in the kitchen wringing her hands. "I- I- I . . ." she stammered, her unhandsome face convulsing into the most womanly of tears. "I don't know what to say. Dr. Zamenhof is . . . my husband has been . . . well, he's simply not . . ." She collapsed into a chair at the kitchen table, and Fraŭlino Bernfeld was immediately at her side. She nodded to me, indicating that I should see to the porter, who needn't witness such an intimate scene.

"פֿאַר דיר," I said, slipping the man a ruble or two. "And no need to mention any of this to anyone . . ."

"זיכער, מייַן הער! זיכער!" he said.

"I'm LOË BERNFELD," Fraŭlino Bernfeld said, "a friend and an admirer of your husband; and this is Dr. Jakob Sammelsohn, a friend and admirer of . . . well, I suppose of mine." She said this last playfully. Avoiding my eye, Sinjorino Zamenhof nodded towards me in welcome.

"Is there sugar?" Fraŭlino Bernfeld asked her gently.

Sinjorino Zamenhof again nodded her head.

"And cream?"

Wordlessly, she pointed towards various of her cupboards.

"Dr. Sammelsohn, please sit with us!" Fraŭlino Bernfeld said.

"Jes, mia fraŭlino," I said, and I sat, fearful that my least movement or my most casual word might send the sinjorino into another paroxysm of tears. Clutching the sugar, the milk, the cups, and the saucers all against her chest, Fraŭlino Bernfeld brought everything to the table and dispensed three cups of spicy Russian chai from the samovar.

"Dr. Zamenhof isn't well, you say?"

"Oh, Fraŭlino Bernfeld!" Sinjorino Zamenhof said. "I can't tell you, I simply can't . . ." With that, her shrieking began anew, each hand worrying the other, as though trying to tear its twin to bits. As her wailing once again subsided, the realization seemed to descend upon each of us that we were, in fact, strangers to one another. An embarrassed silence overtook us, a silence filled only with the scrapes of cups on saucers and the sounds of needlessly cleared throats. I busied myself with my tea, hoping, in the meantime, that someone other than me might find something pertinent to say.

"Oh God!" Sinjorino Zamenhof moaned, once again tearing at her hair. With a gentle authority, Fraŭlino Bernfeld took hold of her hands. As though speaking to a serious-minded child whose day had been ruined by the pranks of a naughty sibling, she urged Sinjorino Zamenhof to unburden herself and to tell her everything. Though considerably younger, Fraŭlino Bernfeld was the taller of the two, and as Sinjorino Zamenhof began to unleash her lamentation, she so resembled a child, I half-expected her to climb into Fraŭlino Bernfeld's lap.

"Oh, they've been bad enough," she said, "these years in Warsaw, an absolute horror, you've no idea! No specialist ever practiced in this neighborhood before, and my husband treats factorymen, seamstresses, laborers for forty kopecks a visit! Forty kopecks a visit, seeing thirty or forty patients a day!"

"That's fairly excessive," I told Fraŭlino Bernfeld.

I myself saw no more than twelve.

"And from those who can't give forty, he takes twenty; and when twenty is impossible, why, he gives the medicine away! What else is he to do? Turn people away?" Her father, who had always supported Lutek's work, she told us, was now giving them a monthly stipend. "A terrible humiliation!" And yet what were they to do? They couldn't refuse it. "My husband's nerves are wrecked, and his body won't long endure the strain. He's on his feet all day and up all night at his typewriter! Why, he's even hallucinating," she whispered, "and that's not to mention the worry over his own father." It seemed that Dr. Zamenhof's father had lost a coveted position as a government censor, having been accused of letting a passage injurious to the tsar slip through in some publication or other. "But this is ridiculous!" Sinjorino Zamenhof wailed. "The article was nothing but a warning against intemperance!" Still, the old man had an enemy, a certain Zusmen, a drunkard himself and a baptized Jew. Zusmen had hated Markus Zamenhof forever without end, amen, and it was he who plotted the affair, and now it was all they could do to salvage the old man's teaching post. "That alone cost us five thousand rubles in bribes," the second half of her dowry, the first having long ago disappeared in printers' costs. "No one wants a doctor who devotes his every spare moment to humanity! If my husband drank like Zusmen, may his name be blotted out, or played cards like the other specialists, why, he'd be booked with patients, and patients who can pay! But no, instead, every night—oh, every night!—he's up till all hours, rattling away on his typewriter, corresponding with colleagues and collaborators over this or that linguistic question. It's all maddening! And now there's all this trouble because of Count Tolstoy!"

"Count Leo Tolstoy?" I said.

"Mm." Sinjorino Zamenhof nodded.

She considered her tea before pushing it away.

ASKED BY THE journal *Posrednik* to give his opinion on Esperanto, Count Tolstoy had responded that learning Esperanto was an appropriately Christian activity, as it promoted understanding between peoples. Dr. Zamenhof quoted Tolstoy's remarks in his own journal *La Esperantisto,* and the two men began a correspondence that led to the publication in Esperanto of Tolstoy's famous letter, "On Reason and Belief," a work considered subversive by the tsar. As a consequence, *La Esperantisto* was suppressed, and Dr. Zamenhof's attempts to continue sending the gazette to subscribers in plain, brown envelopes brought the authorities down even more furiously upon his head. The magazine was banned, and Dr. Zamenhof lost all contact with the Russian Esperantistoj, nearly sixty percent of his following.

"And so we're doomed!" Sinjorino Zamenhof cried. "Doomed!"

To keep her husband's spirits up, she'd made him a little sign, which she'd posted on his typewriter, an ugly old black Blikensdorfer, that read NI LABORU KAJ ESPERU! (*Let us work and hope!*), but both of these were becoming harder every day.

"Oh, how difficult, how truly difficult," Fraŭlino Bernfeld said, "to do the good and to be so good." She cradled Sinjorino Zamenhof's head against the soft pillows of her bosom and kissed her forehead as tenderly as a mother might a child's.

"Ne, ne." Sinjorino Zamenhof resisted the praise, it seemed, by habit. She began to pull away but was clearly exhausted, and Fraŭlino Bernfeld's greater strength prevailed.

"שאַ, שאַ, שלאָפֿט זשע אַ ביסל מיט מיר," Fraŭlino Bernfeld said. *Ssh, ssh, sleep a little here with me.*

In response to this gentle command, spoken not in the language of a new and braver world, but in the old and fearful one of our childhoods, Klara Zamenhof did exactly that: she slept. Looking over Sinjorino Zamenhof's shoulder at me, Fraŭlino Bernfeld pulled the corners of her mouth down in a comical expression of happy disbelief, as though we were the parents of a rambunctious child we thought we'd never get to sleep.

As Sinjorino Zamenhof snored, her nose cushioned against Fraŭlino Bernfeld's breast, I took a moment to study her face. Unlike her husband's, all ovals and rings, hers was composed principally of vertical lines. The nose was long and sloped, and the chin so pointed, in profile it resembled the tip of a slender moon.

"Ho, Klara dormas, ĉu ne? Bone, bonege," Dr. Zamenhof said, having climbed up from his clinic via an interior staircase. He seated himself at the table, surveying the odd scene—the unexplained presence of Fraŭlino Bernfeld and me, his wife slumbering on a strange woman's breast. He picked up Klara's teacup and, tilting it towards himself, swirled it, as though trying to reanimate its contents. Bringing it to his lips, he sniffed it before deciding against taking a sip. Beneath the weight of Dr. Zamenhof's slumbering wife, Fraŭlino Bernfeld pointed with her chin towards the samovar.

"Tason da teo, Majstro?"

"Ne, ne," he said, refusing her offer of tea.

He lifted his hands vertically, palms faceward, and rubbed his eyes, forcing his glasses onto the dome of his head where they remained even after he'd lowered his hands. "I was sleeping as well. Astonishing!" he said. "No, I fell asleep right on my feet, standing in my consultation room. I started to dream. I was in Veisiejai again, still so hopeful and . . ." He scowled at something neither Fraŭlino Bernfeld nor I could see.

"Majstro?" she said sweetly, and I heard the note of concern ringing in her voice.

"Estas nenio, ne," he assured us. *It's nothing.* "It's only sometimes I'm not certain who is here, you see, and who isn't. Still, nothing to be concerned about."

"If you would prefer to lie down, Majstro . . ."

"I sent them home, my patients. No, I did. 'The shop is closed,' I told them, 'in honor of the princess who has traveled from so very far away . . .'" Bothered again, he scowled at something visible only to himself. "Stop it!" he cried, and quite suddenly he was shouting: "I'm not! I'm not, and no, I won't!" To us, he calmly said, "There. You see: I'm not." Enraged again, he cried, "How could you just burn everything, as though it were all—"

"Lutek?" Now he had woken his wife. "Please, just stop, stop it, please, Lutek!" she pleaded and, once again, she succumbed to tears.

"I'm hungry," he told her simply, and from his intonation, I couldn't make out whether this was an explanation, a request, or a complaint. "But I'm also tired." He looked at me and said, "The little creatures go right through the walls, don't they?"

"The little creatures?"

"Psft!" He made a noise similar to air coming out of a bicycle tire, his hand trembling in a motion representing quickness. "Or am I only imagining it?"

He stood, then seeming to forget the purpose of his standing, said, "What was I after?"

"Dr. Sammelsohn, go with him," Fraŭlino Bernfeld said quietly.

"Yes, yes," Dr. Zamenhof said, scowling again at the oppressive presence in the room. He confided to me: "Klara would rather I didn't see them, don't you know?"

"Didn't see them?" I said.

He leaned in and whispered to me: "But I can tell you've been swimming in the ethers, haven't you?"

I didn't know what to say.

"No need to confirm or deny it. I know." Then: "Come and I'll show you my consulting chambers. Was your trip to Grodna pleasant?"

"To Warsaw, Majstro."

"To Warsaw, of course." He smiled painfully.

Before departing down the stairs, I turned back for a reassuring glance from Fraŭlino Bernfeld, sitting so vibrant in blue, next to Sinjorino Zamenhof in her matronly grey.

"Let's open these packages Dr. Sammelsohn and I have brought you, shall we? I think we'll find something we can use to make ourselves a fine dinner. And—look!" She opened the first of her many boxes. "Ludilojn por la infanoj!"

There was a tin train, a teddy bear, and a little wind-up frog sitting on a big bass drum.

DR. ZAMENHOF'S CONSULTANCY was on the ground floor. The room contained two overstuffed armchairs and a sofa. He threw himself onto the latter, though not without effusive apologies. Four outdated eye charts lined the walls; a stained basin stood near the window. Framed portraits of his parents glowered down at us from above his writing desk, next to a drawing of Oedipus embracing Antigone much in the same way Fraŭlino Bernfeld had been holding Sinjorino Zamenhof in the kitchen. When I turned from the drawing to remark on this similarity, I discovered that Dr. Zamenhof, like his wife, had fallen fast asleep. How odd! I thought. No one seemed capable of staying awake in this house—though I admit the poor man was clearly exhausted. So tiny, he fit, head to toe, on the sofa, he slept on his back with his mouth open, his hands forming a bridge across his belly. His snoring was considerably less masculine than his wife's. As always, he reminded me of a child, now playing at some game in his father's clothes with a Purim spieler's beard glued to his face.

I made a note to myself to forward a few eye charts on to him — these yellowing ones were a disgrace — as well as some medicines our clinic kept but no longer used, though I doubted much of it would find its way across the Russian border.

The late winter sun had almost disappeared, and outside, the snow was savaging the dirty court. The goat shivered, tied to her stake. I crept into an armchair as quietly as I could, fearful of waking Dr. Zamenhof. Suppressing a cough, I crossed my legs, uncrossed, and then recrossed them. Unidentifiable sounds came from various parts of the house. Water dripped from the water tank into the basin. For a moment, I could barely recall who I was or what I was doing in this strange room in this strange house in a foreign city in a distant land ruled not by our well-meaning emperor, but by a twisted Jew-haunted tsar. The world and everything in it seemed so tiny and fragile. Was it really impossible to escape the past? to refashion the world? Everyone seemed so filled with hatred. Zusmen hated Dr. Zamenhof's father; Tolstoy loved Christ, but hated the tsar; the tsar hated Tolstoy because he loved Christ. The Russians hated the Germans, the Germans hated the French, the French hated Dreyfus, and everyone hated the Jews. My own father had driven me from my home. I imagined people the world over, sitting in their parlors, hating one another, while Dr. Zamenhof, exhausted from his efforts to deliver them from their self-destructive passions, slept. How many dictionaries, how many grammars, how many vocabulary lists would it take before the world was reconsecrated in all its pristine glory? Or, I shuddered to think, was my father right to turn his back on the world, seeing it for what it was: irredeemably violent, venal, base?

Someone peeked into the room, but by the time I raised my eyes to glance at the door, whoever it was had gone.

"Write it down!" Dr. Zamenhof suddenly cried, sitting up. He looked at me oddly, as though he couldn't quite remember who I was.

"Certainly. I shall," I assured him.

"Ah, thank you," he said, stretching out again and falling instantly asleep.

I don't know how many more hours passed before Dr. Zamenhof next awoke, shouting "Ho ve!" but by then, the sky had darkened completely. He righted himself on the sofa. I lit the lamp, and he squinted against the light.

"Feeling better?" I asked, returning to my chair.

He sighed and lit a cigarette and shook out the match. He shrugged. "America is lost," he said. "Ten years ago, the American Philosophical Society rejected Volapük and took up its cudgels on behalf of Esperanto, but nothing has come of it, and no other endorsements have followed. Everything has stalled. There's no money to publish anything new. Everything will have to wait. Ah, Dr. Sammelsohn, we were so very close . . . One leap, one great leap forward. I imagined that was all that was necessary and yet . . ." He exhaled a melancholic cloud of cigarette smoke. "I've gone nearly mad with despair . . . Money, people, work. I've dragged my wife and my children — oh God!" His voice broke. "Look at Schleyer and Volapük. A million adherents and it all fell to pieces!"

"Volapük is not Esperanto, Majstro."

"Still, still." He shook his head. "Ten million promissory notes! What was I thinking?"

"Yes," I admitted, "I'd wondered about the mathematics."

"People share books, don't they?" He looked at me helplessly. "They'd study the language in small groups, I thought, wouldn't they?"

"Surely they do," I said.

He grew glum and small again. "Russia, the empire, America: gone. I don't understand. Why was I allowed to come this far, but no further? And who can say that it all won't simply disappear?"

"It won't."

"But surely that's what they told Herr Schleyer."

"Herr Schleyer didn't have a Loë Bernfeld backing him, for one thing."

Dr. Zamenhof smiled at the mention of Fraŭlino Bernfeld's name. "She loves you, you know," he said, tamping out his cigarette. "No, I saw it that first night. In Vienna. I did. And her love, Dr. Sammelsohn, is a rare gift from Heaven."

"Is it?" I said, remembering only too well the last time Heaven thought to send me a woman. "Well, whether Heaven concurs in my choice or not, I seem to have purchased a ring." I retrieved the jeweler's box from the pocket of my jacket, where its presence had been irritating me all day. Dr. Zamenhof clicked open the box and admired the small diamond inside. "I've committed myself to proposing marriage to her before the two of us return to Vienna."

"Ho! Klara will be so pleased. No, it will vastly lift her spirits."

Dr. Zamenhof closed the box and handed it back to me. Our conversation stalled, and in the lull, he seemed to recall his problems all over again.

"You've done so much," I reassured him.

"I've done nothing but dream."

He sighed again.

"Trompeter lost interest," he said.

"The land surveyor?"

"But the rich are like that, aren't they? Still, he gave generously to the cause. But he insisted on reforms, you see. And I told him it's not yet time. When we're stronger, then we can reform and improve the language. However, not until then. Reforms would only signal to the world that the time to commit to an international language has not yet arrived, that a new and better language is just over the next rise, you see?"

"Is there no hope then?"

He shrugged. "Lately, I've been receiving letters from a Frenchman. A marquis."

"A nobleman?"

"Yes, and from the sound of it, quite wealthy. Well connected. Seems to know everyone."

"A beacon of light."

"From Paris, no less!"

"The capital of the world!"

"Precisely!"

"And his name?"

"De Beaufront."

"A marquis, you say?"

"Yes, a marquis."

We heard someone descending the stairs. Dr. Zamenhof and I both assumed expectant looks and turned, receptively, towards the door. Fraŭlino Bernfeld stopped at the threshold and braced her arms on either side of the doorframe. "Dinner, darlings!" she called out.

"Oh? Yes?" Dr. Zamenhof's eyebrows lifted, and his eyes sparkled like a baby's beneath the glittering circles of his glasses.

"Yes, Sinjorino Klara and I have managed to cook up quite a banquet between us!"

DINNER WAS A feast of Roman proportions, the courses spread out on top of the Zamenhofs' sideboard: sparkling pear wine, crescent kipferl with a cherry marmalade, wild garlic soup, roasted buckwheat salad, sweet wine from the Neusiedlersee, spicy goulash, chopped Kaiseshmarrn, Baltic Sea bass with sweet peppers, cabbage noodles, marinated kippers, and for dessert, a plum Knödel. In their finest clothes, the Zamenhof children, Adamo kaj Zofia, sat as quietly as mimes auditioning for a circus. Eleven and ten, they too were fluent in Esperanto and followed our conversation easily. Their father, that mad, shy, wonderful genius, stood at the head of the table, pouring goblets of pear wine for the adults and tart raspberry juice for his children, his good spirits returned to him by the company, the sleep, and the food. He toasted our love, Fraŭlino Bernfeld's and mine, comparing it—rather too extravagantly, I thought—to the great romances of literary history, to Tristan and Isolde's, to King Solomon and the queen of Sheba's, to Rabbi Akiba and the daughter of Ben Kalba Savuah's, and finally to Klara's and his own.

Fraŭlino Bernfeld blushed. Sinjorino Zamenhof clapped her hands in delight. As Dr. Zamenhof carved the roasted goose, and young Adamo and little Zofia ferried slices around the table for everyone on the family's finest china, we all chattered away in that strange language our host, as a remarkable boy, had invented. There was so much goodwill in the room, I felt as though my life were only now beginning, or else beginning anew. Everything seemed possible! Sitting at the Zamenhofs' table, laughing, drinking, eating, chatting, I felt as I once did, long ago, before my father sent me to school, when I'd spend each day being handed from one sister's lap to the next to my mother's, the entire world, as far as I knew its boundaries, made up of womanly flesh.

Before I knew exactly what I was doing, I had cleared my throat and tapped my water glass with my spoon. Standing, I nervously fingered the jeweler's box in my coat pocket. "Estimataj sinjorinoj kaj sinjoroj!" I announced. *Esteemed ladies and gentlemen.*

"Hear, hear!" Dr. Zamenhof happily threw his arm across the back of his chair. He grinned mischievously at his wife, who scowled playfully back. Somehow, I saw, he had found time to inform her of my intentions! Fraŭlino Bernfeld folded her small hands together and, with her elbows on the table, leaned her chin against her knotted fists. I looked at the children. Did they know as well? Young Adamo paid me no mind, but Zofia seemed on the point of swooning. Even a neighbor, Seidman, and his wife had crept into the apartment and were standing outside the dining room door, quite obviously waiting for my proposal.

I began, stumbling over my words: "First, allow me — rather permit me — or rather allow me to permit — I mean to *thank* all the womenfolk of the household, including the neighbor, Frau Seidman — "

"You're welcome, Dr. Sammelsohn!" Frau Seidman called in from the adjoining room, occasioning much laughter.

" — for preparing such a fine and elaborate feast. Kudos to Loë Bernfeld and to her maid Käthe, without whom et cetera, et cetera, ad infinitum, and so on."

From around the table: laughter, raised glasses, gentle applause. Dr. Zamenhof pounded his tiny fist against the table top, and the crystal shook.

I coughed into my hand. "I've never been to Warsaw, as you know, and I simply wished to say . . ." Naturally, I hesitated for, at that very moment, it occurred to me that although I'd been wedded twice, I'd never personally asked for a woman's hand. In the past, my father had simply found the girl and insisted I marry her. This brave new world of proposals and rings and public speeches was an unknown continent to me, and it was only after I'd stepped foot upon its shore that I realized how lost I was inside it. Proposing marriage to a woman in front of seven strangers, it very quickly occurred to me, was a mad undertaking. Should Fraŭlino

Bernfeld refuse me, the evening would be spoiled for everyone, myself not in the least.

Nevertheless, I steeled myself to carry on, if only because it meant standing up to my father. How better to repudiate him and all he'd done to me than by marrying a woman as magnificent as Fraŭlino Bernfeld and on my own authority to boot? Of course, doing so meant betraying all hope of a future rendezvous with Ita. In this lifetime, at least. Not that I hoped for such a thing. I didn't. In fact, I dreaded it. Indeed, the prospect filled me with terror. Ita had a temper and a vindictive streak, and I trembled at the thought of one day having to explain to her that somehow, between her death and her rebirth, I'd — promises and pledges aside — married someone else.

The happy, drunken, sated faces around the table all looked up at me expectantly, except for Fraŭlino Bernfeld's. She kept her eyes on the tablecloth, lightly fingering its pattern.

I cleared my throat again. "It's been quite cold since we arrived," I said. "Yes, and . . . but . . . the welcome couldn't have been warmer."

An impatient murmur substituted for the applause I'd anticipated.

"And so" — I raised my glass and took a deep breath, my voice trembling — "I'd just like to say to Fraŭlino Bernfeld . . ."

The Zamenhofs and their neighbors quieted down. You could practically hear the snow falling outside. Everyone stole a look at Fraŭlino Bernfeld before attending to me again.

"Fraylin Bernfeld. Rather Fraylin Loë," I said. "My darling . . ."

Fraŭlino Bernfeld raised her eyes and met my gaze. Two crimson smudges reddened her cheeks. Her lips parted, the adhesive membrane of each separating from the other slowly; the tip of her tongue probed the opening, breeching the white border of her teeth, wetting her lips, as she prepared, it was clear, to answer a question about which, given the conspiratorial nature of the household, she must surely have been forewarned. I'd switched to Yiddish for the benefit of the Seidmans, and I stared as intently at Fraylin Bernfeld's mouth as might a dentist, trying to discern if the tip of her tongue was poised to rise against her palette in order to pronounce the word *ja* or lowered against her bottom teeth for *neyn.*

"Darling," I heard myself saying, "thank you so very much for proposing this wonderful adventure and . . . and also for buying the train tickets."

I sat, and as I did, I hit the table with my knee, causing my water glass to tumble. I caught it before it fell, but a measure of the liquid flew out. From all sides, napkins were thrown towards me to stanch the spill. After a dulling moment, Sinjorino Zamenhof said, "Zofia," and the little girl got up to help her mother bring in the Knödel.

"I don't think I could ingest another mouthful," I said unhappily to no one in particular.

FRAŬLINO BERNFELD CONTINUED doing her best to cheer up the household, hiring a seamstress to mend the children's clothes and a cleaning woman to straighten up the rooms. I was ordered to stand in for Dr. Zamenhof in his consultancy, so that he and the fraŭlino might spend our two days in Warsaw with their heads pressed together, poring over the proofs of her Dutch-Esperanto dictionary and her translation of *La Dua Libro.*

(Her clothes so reeked of Dr. Zamenhof's constant cigarette smoke that, back home in Vienna, she simply threw them out. "I'll never get the smell out of my hair," she said, "but it was worth it.")

Between the two of us, we contrived never to be alone during the remainder of our stay, and the opportunity to propose marriage continually failed to present itself. It was just as well, I supposed: just as a refusal at the dinner table would have ruined the rest of the evening, so a refusal at any time would have ruined the rest of our trip. Better to propose after we'd left, I told myself; and mindful of my promise not to return to Vienna without having done so, I decided to offer myself to Fraŭlino Bernfeld in marriage at some point during the train ride home.

We took leave of the Zamenhofs at dawn and traced our way in a hired droshky back to the station, where in the café, we breakfasted on strong coffee, brown bread, and pungent cheese. We ate quietly, I nervously leafing through the morning papers. Soon the sun penetrated the black drapery of sky, lighting all of Warsaw with its filmy light. When the train to Vienna juddered to life, we paid our bill and strolled across the platform to the track, no longer burdened with Fraŭlino Bernfeld's many packages. We sat in a compartment across from each other, our knees bumping. Fraŭlino Bernfeld opened the window, and the air, though soot-stained, seemed fresher than the stale air of the compartment. Though I held the newspaper before my eyes, I read nothing in it, too busy rehearsing my opening gambit, too conscious of the little jeweler's box in my pocket, cutting into my ribs. When we finally pulled out of the station, I folded my newspaper and glanced at Fraŭlino Bernfeld, swaying softly to the rhythm of the train.

"Anything interesting?" She nodded towards the newspaper. I shook my head. "Lutek needed a little bolstering, don't you think?" she said a moment later.

"Lutek?" I said.

"He asked me to call him that. *Majstro* apparently embarrasses him."

"Yes, so I understand."

Fraŭlino Bernfeld gazed out the window and said, "Klara's fortunate to love such a worthy man, to sacrifice so much for everything he believes in."

"Although could you really be happy living as they do?"

"What woman wouldn't be?" she said simply.

I nodded, although this was a vexing turn. I couldn't tell by her tone whether, in her estimation, I belonged to this pantheon of worthy men for which one might sacrifice everything or whether I was barred from it completely. I glanced out the window, lost in thought. Was I the sort of man who believed in the exalted things a woman could happily sacrifice herself for? It was hard to say. What *did* I believe in? I'm certain, from any objective point of view, I appeared committed to no cause greater than my own happiness; and even there, I worked at it fitfully enough. Less a cause, it was more of a hobby, something to do with myself when I was bored. I couldn't hide from myself the fact that in all likelihood I was exactly the sort of man who served as a deriding counterexample to Dr. Zamenhof: a proper medical man committed in his spare time to nothing more exalted than the playing of cards and the drinking of whiskey. (Although, in fact, neither of these pastimes appealed to me. I much preferred dropping in on Herr Franz's puppet theater for the late matinee.)

"I'm sorry you never met my mother," Fraŭlino Bernfeld said.

I turned from the window, grateful for this change of subject. "As am I," I said.

"She was quite beautiful."

"I could only imagine." I was too nervous to add *like her daughter.*

Fraŭlino Bernfeld told me how fortunate her father had been to marry a woman whose every waking moment was committed to the welfare of her husband. According to his daughter, the illustrious Herr Bernfeld could never have achieved all he had without his wife's support. Why, with it, he was able to stride the globe as a colossus, her love giving purpose and meaning to his extraordinary business skill. Without a family to cherish and raise, Herr Bernfeld's wheelings and dealings would have had no more significance than a long and lucky day at the roulette table.

I could only scowl. This last confused me greatly. Was Fraŭlino Bernfeld offering herself to me, advertising the advantages of married life, or was she rather letting me know that such a marriage was beyond my means? Certainly I could never compete with these great striders of the globe, Dr. Zamenhof and Herr Bernfeld, the one linking all of humanity with the invisible telegraphic system of a universal language, the other overseeing an invisible empire that stretched from São Paulo to Johannesburg to Constantinople to Rome.

"Ah, look! The Vienna Woods!" she said, pointing out the window. "We're home at last!"

I fingered the little box inside my pocket but seemed incapable of withdrawing it. Concealed from the world, we huddled as closely as was publicly decent in the fiacre on the ride to her apartment, the blankets pulled to our chin. Still, I was helpless to broach the subject. When I saw her to the door, she laid the palm of her gloved hand against my cheek in what I interpreted as a gesture of regretful farewell.

I rode home, the interior of the cab redolent with her perfumes. I climbed the front steps of my building and limped down its familiar passageway. I'd been gone only a few days, but everything seemed smaller, stuffier, greyer. Inside, I dropped my bags to the floor and threw off my heavy coat. I set the coffee to boil. What else was I to do? Redon my coat, dash out into the freezing maw of winter, return to her apartments, and pound upon her door?

"Yes! Yes! Yes!" I answered myself, but still I did nothing; and it was precisely at that moment that a banging sounded at my own door. Perhaps because I was expecting no other face or form than Fraŭlino Bernfeld's to greet me there, the identity of the stranger who crossed the threshold and threw herself upon my neck was an even greater puzzle to solve than it might have otherwise been.

CHAPTER 6

Uncle Moritz and Aunt Fania weren't certain you were home. Were you away?"

"Was I away?" I answered numbly.

"In any case, I thought I'd wait in the coffee house across the road and see if you came back. I wasn't sure I'd recognize you." She picked up her bag again and faced me. "Are you going to stand there all day? Or are you going to step aside and let your sister in?"

A grown woman now, Sore Dvore gripped the handle of her bag with both hands, shrugging against its weight. I stood on the other side of the door, my hand on the knob. She had, from any objective point of view, explained everything: she was in the city; our aunt and uncle had suggested she contact me, though they weren't certain I was in town; she'd come anyway and waited; when I arrived, she'd crossed the street; and now we were standing across from each other at my door.

However, though I could understand every word she said, I couldn't make sense out of any of it.

"Yankl?" she said. "Is there a reason you're not letting me in?" Like everything else my sister said, this question baffled me completely.

"A reason?" I said, unable to think of one. "I don't think so."

"Then may I come in?" She laughed, and I stepped aside. "You act as though you've seen a ghost." Sweeping by me, she lugged in her bag.

"A ghost?" I said, shutting the door and following her into the parlor. "Why on earth would you say such a thing?"

"Are we all so very ethereal to you?"

She removed her hat and unbuttoned her winter coat. I took a step towards her.

"Sore Dvore," I said.

"Sarah is sufficient." Tying up her hair, with her hat pins in her mouth, she said, "I've dropped the Dvore completely."

"I never expected to see you again."

She held her things out to me, but my mind was too cloudy, and I couldn't think to take them. Finally she laid them across the arm of the divan. "May I sit?"

I motioned her to a chair. "Please."

For some reason, I neglected to sit myself.

"Why don't you sit as well, Yankl?"

"Of course," I said, doing so.

We looked into each other's faces. The youngest of my sisters, she'd been the closest to me in age, and I hadn't seen her since she was fourteen. Now she was grown. Though her thick hair was, like our mother's, the color of golden raisins, she and I resembled each other not a little.

She crossed her arms. "That little beard of yours is charming."

I shrugged, embarrassed. "I'm a bit vain about it, I suppose."

"Oh!" She clapped her hands, remembering something. "Mama sent along some things."

"Ah! Very good!"

She reached into her bag, but then thought better of it. "I'll unpack it all later."

"How is she, anyway?"

Sore Dvore looked at the twin knobs of her enskirted knees and placed her hands in the vale between them. "Not good, I'm afraid."

"I'm sorry to hear that."

"Things have been hard since you left."

"Well, you can tell her when you return that I'm well, that you saw me, and . . . and that I'm well."

"That's just it," she said, raising her voice as I left the room to bring in our coffees. "I'm not going back."

"Father drove you out as well?" I said lightheartedly, sticking my head out of the kitchen, as though my expulsion from our family had been a merry joke and not the defining catastrophe of my life.

"Not at all. Oh, not at all," she said. "On the contrary, I'm on my way to Palestine."

"Ah, to Palestine?"

"With Father's blessings, yes. Thank you," she said, reaching for the coffee. She took a provisional sip. "Oh, but that's strong!"

"He gives out blessings now as well as curses?" I asked. "Sugar?" I handed her the bowl. "Perhaps it will sweeten the bitterness."

I had intended not to mention our father, and I cursed myself for bringing him up. This silent curse penetrated the air between us, and I found it difficult to say anything afterwards. Ignoring my diffidence, Sore Dvore unpacked the bread and the cheeses and the briny olives and the salty fish Mother had sent, either as a gift for me or as traveling food for her, it was never made clear, and as she did, she told me all about her life: she'd had become an ardent Zionist. She had, in fact, attended the first Zionist conference in Basel.

"Oh, Dr. Herzl's speech was simply electrifying, Yankl! Do you know him, Dr. Herzl? Because he lives in Vienna, doesn't he?"

I spun my coffee cup on its saucer like a top, admitting that although I did not know the great Dr. Herzl, I had called upon him once, inquiring for him at the offices of the *Neue Freie Presse,* where he worked.

"Yes? And? So?" Sore Dvore leaned forward excitedly.

"Well." I shrugged, embarrassed. "Perhaps I didn't enunciate his name clearly," I said, explaining that I had been taken to meet not Dr. Theodor Herzl, but Dr. Theodor Hertzka, also a writer at the paper, also the author of a utopian novel, although his, *Freiland,* unlike Dr. Herzl's *Altneuland,* had nothing to do with Palestine or a Jewish state. As my interview with Dr. Hertzka wore on, I became confused: why on earth would the great Zionist leader go on and on about public land reforms and urge me to emigrate, not to Palestine, but to British East Africa, where advocates of his ideas had recently founded a model community?

"But for that," I told my sister sheepishly, "I might be a Zionist as well."

(These sorts of confusions continued to dog my life. For example: arriving in the Promised Land myself, years later, a Zionist in fact, if not in theory, I made a fool of myself by purchasing a large bouquet of roses and hiring a taxi to Bethlehem one bright and ringing morning so that I might lay them as a tribute to the Yiddish poet Itzik Manger beneath what I'd anticipated would be a plaque erected for him in Manger

Square. How fortunate, I told myself on that bright day, how fortunate it is to live in one's own country where one's own squares may be named in honor of one's own poets!)

Sore Dvore brushed bread crumbs from her hands and laughed politely before going on to paint for me a picture of her last few years. She had read Dr. Herzl's pamphlet in the very gazebo where I had done my reading and had become enflamed with the idea of immigrating to the Holy Land. She'd joined Szibotya's Zionist group, Khibat Zion, and with its three other members began raising funds to send a pioneer to the altneu homeland. When the first congress was announced, however, the group elected to apply its funds to sending a delegate to Basel instead, with Sore Dvore the unanimous choice.

"Oh, Father must have had a fit!" I said.

"On the contrary," she told me, "he approved wholeheartedly."

"Approved?"

"What sort of life was there for me in Szibotya, Yankl? Backwards old Szibotya! Father not only made the first but, as it turned out, the largest contribution to our cause."

She leaned in, and her face grew serious. "Also," she confessed, "I have a lover."

"A lover? Really?"

"Are you shocked?"

"Would you prefer me to be?"

"Of course!"

"Then I am."

"Sincerely?"

"If that's what you wish."

"No."

"Then no."

"Good."

"And the name of this mysterious suitor?"

"Zelig Mintz." They had met, she told me, at the Congress, and this Zelig Mintz had already settled in Rosh Pina. They were to meet up there, God willing, and be married shortly after her arrival.

I smiled as though at an astonishing turn of events, although in truth, my heart was breaking. How dare that old tyrant dismiss on her part the very crimes for which he'd prosecuted me so severely! Had I been caught reading Dr. Herzl's pamphlet (or even the newspaper for which he wrote!) there wouldn't have been wives enough in Galicia with which to punish me! Now this same despot who had driven me from his garden was financing my sister's move — in the company of unbelievers! free-thinkers! Zionists! — to Palestine? It made no sense. It was one thing for me to have changed. After all, I'd been caught and captured, tried and convicted, punished and exiled, sent out of the Pale on my own, and at so very young an age, but what, I wondered, had happened to my father? With a sudden rush of memory, I recalled that it had been Sore Dvore who had found me that morning, happily smoking and reading in our Father's gazebo, Sore Dvore who had reported my black crimes to our Mother.

"So there I was, Yankl," she was saying, "a girl alone in Basel."

"Yankl," I said with a sneer. I discovered I couldn't help regarding her now with a certain bitterness.

"But why are you laughing?"

"Oh, it's just no one here calls me that."

"No? And what *do* they call you?"

"Kobi."

Sore Dvore folded her arms and tilted her head to one side. She squinted at me and pursed her lips. Her gaze seemed to weigh a thousand kilos and, beneath its derision, all my careful sartorial choices — my unkempt Bohemian hair, my dainty little goatee, my haute optique pince-nez — seemed like the crudest of masquerades.

"Kobi?"

I raised my eyebrows and nodded.

"Oh, but that just isn't *you*!" she cried.

Of course it wasn't me. Or at least not to Sore Dvore. Naturally, to Sore Dvore, I would only be what I had always been: a wretched little malcontented Yankl, reading his forbidden books, and smoking his forbidden tobacco out among the cherry trees.

"Fitting or not, it's what I'm called."

"Kobi, then, it is," she said, sounding slightly rebuked.

"Although my fiancée occasionally calls me Kaĉjo."

"Oh, so you have a fiancée again?"

I couldn't help noting that a poisonous tone had crept into her voice as well. I stood and walked to the window, parted its curtains with two fingers, and looked out into the night, trying to regain my composure. Taking a breath, I turned to face her again, hoping to bestow upon her the full force of my charm.

"Zionism, eh? Palestine! Marvelous! Simply marvelous. It's only there that a Jew can live as a man. However, did you know I'm somewhat involved in a great social movement myself?" Leaning against the wall, I crossed one ankle over the other and laced my arms across my chest. Perhaps it was only my imagination, but Sore Dvore once again seemed to be suppressing her laughter, biting into a slice of bread with a thick piece of cheese and olives on top of it, in order to conceal her grin.

"Oh?" she asked, chewing. "And what is that?"

"Esperanto."

She shook her head.

"It's a universal language movement."

She brought her napkin, in an emergency, to her open mouth, and I saw that I had imagined nothing. Unable to suppress anything now, she struggled between swallowing her food and spitting it out in order not to choke, her shoulders shaking in helpless convulsions.

"Oh, Yankl!"

"*Kobi!*" I corrected her, although I wished I hadn't. Whining, I never felt more like a Yankl in my life.

"What's the idea there? That everyone will speak—" She laughed so hard, she nearly choked. "That everyone will speak the same language and then . . . ?"

"Yes, and then, slowly, over time, of course, not all at once, mankind will be reunited into one family."

To calm herself, she'd taken a sip of coffee, but in reaction to this last, she spit the mouthful back into her cup. Particles of masticated cheese, olives, and bread floated in it like bits of fish food in an aquarium.

"Oh God, Yankl—I mean *Kobi*!" she corrected herself quickly. "I'm sorry, I'm sorry, I'm just so sorry!" She shook her hands out in front of her, as though they were wet and she were trying to dry them. "I don't mean to laugh." But then something made her laugh even more furiously.

Finally I could take no more of it. "And now, *Sarah*," I pronounced the name as snidely as I could, "let me ask you a question. Just what language does Dr. Herzl imagine we Jews will be speaking with one another when we all return to our newly regained homeland?"

"What language?" She laughed once more, wiping a tear away with the heel of her hand. "Why, German, of course."

I scoffed. "Proof of the prophet's excellence!"

"Well, certainly not Hebrew! As Dr. Herzl says in *The Jewish State:* 'Who among us can even ask for a train ticket in that strange tongue?'"

(Unuvojan bileton al Jafo, mi petas, I thought to myself unhappily.)

"Sore Dvore, let's be honest now," I said. "As noble as your Drs. Herzl and Nordau might be, as splendid as is their goal, do you really imagine that the attainment of universal peace and brotherhood through an international auxiliary language is any less realistic than the restoration of the Jewish homeland in ancient Palestine? I don't mean to be cruel, but do you really suppose that a precious Viennese feuilletonist, a failed playwright, whose plays are completely tedious, by the way, your noble Dr. Herzl, for all his impressive demeanor, might in any way perform as an effective figure on the stage of world history? Only look at the facts: the Ottoman Empire would have to collapse. Our empire, God forbid, would have to collapse. The Kaiser of Germany would have to have a complete change of heart. Europe would be plunged into war. And yet somehow you think these kings and sultans will simply fall at the feet of a little Jewish journalist who spent two weeks holed up in a Paris hotel scribbling his now-famous pamphlet? No, even if you will it, it's still a dream. And even *were* it to happen, the land isn't *arable*! No one wants it! No one even lives on it now! Who's going to till the soil? A bunch of soft-palmed yeshiva bukhers or neurotic salon Jews who don't know that potatoes grow in the ground and not on vines?"

She was nearly red-faced with anger herself. "And I suppose, *Kobi*, it's more realistic to assume that millions of people, in learning a new language, will suddenly become the best of friends?"

"Through free and open communication, yes, as Dr. Zamenhof imagines it, men of goodwill will come to see that there's much more binding them than dividing them, and quite so."

"Well, and the only argument against that is—"

"Yes, Sarah, what *is* the only argument against that?" I nearly shouted at her.

"All of world history!"

Alas, for that well-phrased triumph, I lacked a retort.

"As though people who speak the same language have never for a day oppressed one another!" Though I'm sure she meant it not at all in this way, the cataclysm that was my truncated childhood suddenly entered the room. Not that Father spoke the same language as the rest of us, but very nearly, and hadn't he oppressed us all?

(Or was it only me?)

"You're talking about Father now, aren't you?"

"No, I'm not talking about Father, Kobi. I'm talking about you!"

"Me?"

"How could you just abandon that poor girl to her fate?"

"Ita, you mean?"

"She threw herself into the river! Must I remind you of that, Yankl? She threw herself into the river!"

"Yes? And? So?"

"Because *you* left her, Yankl! You abandoned her! On her wedding night!"

"It wasn't because *I* left her, Sore Dvore! It was because Father forced me to marry her!"

"But she *loved* you! Anyone could see it in the way she looked at you. Even I could see it."

"And did I love *her*, Sore Dvore? Could anyone see *that* in my face? Did anyone even bother to look into *my* face? And what about Hindele? Does it matter whom she loved?"

"You destroyed everything when you left!"

"You say that, Sore Dvore, as though it were my fault."

"Father was never the same again!"

"Good!"

"And neither was Mama."

"Well, for that I'm sorry. I truly am. But what was I supposed to do? Remain married to the village idiot for the rest of my life!"

"Don't call her that!"

"It's not my fault Mama married a madman!"

"Yankl, you made us all so very unhappy!"

"Yes, and I suppose when everyone was happy except me, unhappiness didn't matter."

"You should never have read those books."

"And you should never have told them I was reading those books! Why couldn't you just have kept your damnable mouth shut!"

"Don't be cruel!"

"But no! You had to run through the orchards, shouting your discovery to the entire world—'Yankl is reading forbidden books! Yankl is smoking forbidden cigarettes and reading forbidden books!'—so that Father had no choice but to—"

"Yankl, I was a child!"

"Sore Dvore, *I* was a child!"

"We were children."

"Yes, and so it made us easy prey."

She made a small tsk-ing sound with her mouth. "You poor boy!" she said, raising her arms and offering to embrace me.

"No! Get away from me!" I heard myself shouting. "Get out! Now! Please! Leave me!"

After a moment of silence, she began bundling her things.

"Well," she sighed, standing with her suitcase at the door. "I'll leave you then."

"Good!"

"Please, Yankl."

I said nothing.

"I'll give your love to Uncle Moritz and Aunt Fania then," she said.

"I'll see to it myself."

"Yankl . . ."

God damn you! God damn you! God damn you! I wanted to cry, but instead I said, "Ah, forgive me, dear Sarah. I'm so very sorry I shouted at you. I'm afraid it's been a rather trying day." Apologizing again, I picked up her suitcase and offered to accompany her to the station, which I did. I even waited until her train left, waving as it pulled out.

And we never saw each other again.

It wasn't only Szibotya, of course. The entire world was changing and at a dizzying rate. The quarter century preceding my birth had witnessed a bumper crop of innovations: the sewing machine, the gyroscope, the glider. Trains suddenly had sleeping cars. Your neighbor suddenly owned a washing machine, a bicycle, and perhaps even a typewriter. Thanks to the internal combustion engine, automobiles now ruled the road. Strange lights controlled the flow of traffic. Elevators took you to the tops of impossibly high buildings made of steel, and an arsenal of new weaponry—the machine gun, the torpedo, dynamite, barbed wire—made the too-terrifying art of war obsolete.

However, all this was nothing in comparison to what followed: the phonograph, the lightbulb, the player piano, the dishwasher, the gramophone, the motor-driven vacuum cleaner. Cinemas, motorcycles, cash registers, fountain pens, seismographs, metal detectors, steam turbines, radar, toilet paper, rolled photographic film, pneumatic tires, Cordite matchbooks, escalators, diesel engines, a veritable tower of innovation and ingenuity at the summit of which stood the triumphal figure of man. When the World's Fair opened in Paris in 1900, its grand boulevards and its broad pavilions, its elevated trains and its moving sidewalks, its Ferris wheel and its Eiffel Tower (lit to heaven with garish electrical lights) announced to the world one thing: the future was no longer a thing of the past! It had arrived, it was here! And we were living in it!

Everything that could be dreamt could be built—and what couldn't be dreamt?—including an international auxiliary language!

It was thanks, principally, to the Marquis de Beaufront, the French aristocrat Dr. Zamenhof had mentioned to me, that Esperanto had not sputtered out in Russia. No, having carried the dying torch to Paris, the marquis illuminated the entire world from there. Esperanto societies now spanned the globe. Hundreds of Esperanto magazines had sprouted up, and somehow Dr. Zamenhof had even found the funds to publish the *Universala Vortaro,* a universal dictionary, with three thousand root words translated into French, English, German, Polish, and Russian.

(Fraŭlino Bernfeld undertook the Herculean task of compiling the Dutch-Esperanto entries, and we spent many long nights working head to head on an enormous card catalog of her own devising.)

All across Europe, high-minded people had begun gathering for congresses, and Esperanto was no exception. In 1904, 180 Esperantists had met in Calais, and the event had proven such a success that la Société pour la propagation de l'espéranto proposed a larger congress in France for the following year.

Fraŭlino Bernfeld and I were of course excited by the news, although we'd heard via post that Dr. Zamenhof would be unable to attend. Money was a problem, as well as his increasingly frail health. But these were the least of it. As unfathomable as it might seem, at age forty-five, Dr. Zamenhof had been drafted into the Russian army to serve as an oculist in Manchuria! Worse—as Klara wrote us, clearly in distress—he was insisting upon going! At the urging of his friends however, he was made to see the light. His heart, never strong, could never have sustained the rigors of army life. And indeed, not only was he granted a medical exemption, but his doctor ordered him into the hospital for an immediate week of rest.

When the news went forth that the Majstro would be attending la Unua Universala Kongreso, Fraŭlino Bernfeld arranged for us to meet up with the Zamenhofs and their new baby in Berlin so that we might travel the rest of the way with them to Paris.

DR. ZAMENHOF KISSED my cheeks in the Zoologischer Garten station. "I'm only doing this," he confided to me, "because it's become more and more clear to me each day that my face and name somehow make Esperanto palatable to the common man. Ideas and principles stir only the cold hearts of the intelligentsia, I'm afraid."

Fraŭlino Bernfeld embraced her Majstro warmly.

"Ah, when will you two finally set the date?" he asked, his beard bristling with goodwill at the sight of the two of us together.

Fraŭlino Bernfeld's face reddened and not because she was blushing. "Here's Klara!" she said, waving to Dr. Zamenhof's dour little edzino, trundling off the train with the toddler Lidja in her arms. They ran to greet one another, and Dr. Zamenhof cast me a puzzled look.

"I'll explain later."

"Certe, certe."

"And in private."

"I hope I haven't misspoken."

"No, no."

"But how many years *has* it been now?"

"Well, that's a bit of a sore subject, I'm afraid."

Though Fraŭlino Bernfeld and I spent nearly every day together, growing closer and dearer to each other, in the few years since we'd returned from Warsaw, I'd been unable to bring myself to propose. The words *Fraŭlino Bernfeld, will you marry me?* were often upon my lips, and yet I seemed incapable of summoning breath to utter them. The question lingered, unasked, in all our conversations, and though Fraŭlino Bernfeld tried to remain at all times pleasing and lovable (for what man proposes marriage to a vexed harridan?), almost anything could set her off. A wedding dress in a shop window, a baby pram in a park, an old wife buttering a roll in a café for her elderly husband, and she became instantly petulant, sulky, punitive, and severe. Even the sight of the Christ child and the Virgin Mother embittered her, and replicas of these were displayed, of course, all over Vienna. Also, it was impossible to jolly her out of these moods once one had captured her. Speaking sweetly to her was unfeeling condescension; returning her coldness only drove her further away. It was like trying to talk two cats out of a tree at once: every attempt to bring down one merely let the other climb higher and farther. If I bought a new suit, she criticized my taste: "Still a Galitsyaner, I see!" If I dropped my keys, she laughed: "Well done!" If I ordered for her in a restaurant, she felt demeaned; if I didn't, ignored. If I called her on the telephone, the sound of my voice seemed to multiply her burdens; if I refrained from calling her, her voice, the next time, dripped with recrimination. (Her father, I imagined, was watching it all from the side, pleased to have his expectations realized.) Naturally, I became confused! When Fraŭlino

Bernfeld was away from me, I hungered for her, but as soon as we were together, I longed to be rid of her again. At times, I could barely stand the sight of her, though this was only because the sight of me seemed to repulse her so. And yet there were days on which marriage, weddings, children, and babies didn't seem to matter to either of us, and on those days, everything between us was again as sweet as it had always been.

The train blew its whistle; the engine juddered to life. Though we'd ridden to Berlin in first class, continuing on in that manner was too much of an extravagance for the Zamenhofs, and rather than embarrass them, Fraŭlino Bernfeld had booked the rest of our trip alongside them in third. We squeezed into our new seats, bumping the knees of our fellow passengers, none of whom I suspected knew they were traveling with a visionary whose name they would, in the next few years, know as well as they now knew Galileo, Darwin, and Copernicus.

Dr. Zamenhof took the baby from his wife while she settled in. As the train lurched forward, Klara asked for the child to be returned. "Oh, give her back to me, Lutek." She was an older mother, and the unexpected joy of having a small child to care for at her age was clearly something she cherished. Things had been so desperate for them for so long, and yet now here she was on her way to Paris, a new mother traveling with her husband whose great work was at last being feted. The little family seemed to radiate a kind of joy, palpable, I thought, to everyone in the car. When I turned to Fraŭlino Bernfeld to confirm this impression, however, she gave me a look that was so black, it was nearly blinding.

Dr. Zamenhof opened his briefcase and placed it upon his lap as a makeshift desk and immediately set to work.

"Paĉjo has so many letters to write, Lidja," Sinjorino Zamenhof said to their daughter, her lips pressed against the crown of her head. "Ah, look, Lilke, cows!" She pointed out the window as the German countryside rolled by with its chocolate-colored cows and its green farmland and its distant church spires.

"Forgive my rudeness," Dr. Zamenhof apologized, "but I must attend to my speech."

"Ah! You're giving a speech?" I said.

"Of course, he's giving a speech," Fraŭlino Bernfeld said.

Sinjorino Zamenhof smiled to herself.

Dr. Zamenhof sighed. "If I had my way, I'd be a simple Esperantist, like everyone else, merely one of the people."

"But you're not one of the people," Fraŭlino Bernfeld said, as cordial to him as she had been uncordial to me.

"A congress speech!" I said, ignoring Fraŭlino Bernfeld's coldness. "What a marvelous idea! I wasn't thinking! But of course, we must make an occasion of it. Hundreds of years from now, when the extraordinary work you've done" — I looked at our small group — "that we've all done has so transformed the world that its inhabitants will look back, shuddering at our times as though at a savage, barbaric epoch, the day the creator of the universal language addressed the first of his followers will stand out, like the Buddha's Sermon of the Flower, as the inaugural act of a new and transcendent age!"

Dr. Zamenhof started to blush, but somehow forced himself not to, as though he feared blushing would signify not modesty but rather a false modesty overlaid upon a base of secret pride.

Fraŭlino Bernfeld pulled in her cheeks as though she were sucking on a sour candy. "Oh, do shut up!" she said.

Everyone pretended not to hear her.

"פֿון דײַן מויל אין גאָטס אוירען אַרײַן," Dr. Zamenhof whispered. *From your mouth into God's ears.* Then, like a cabaret emcee moving out of the white hot spotlight, he stepped back, as it were, and let his speech take center stage. "I'm planning, as is only appropriate, to end my little speech with a prayer."

"Are you now?" I said.

"That's lovely, Lutek," Fraŭlino Bernfeld said. "No, it really is. Just lovely."

Sinjorino Zamenhof distracted herself by primping the baby's blanket, as though she understood that her pride in her husband might irritate his lack of vanity.

"And have you finished it?" I said.

"Stop pestering him!" Fraŭlino Bernfeld said.

"Am I pestering you, Dr. Zamenhof?"

"In draft only," Dr. Zamenhof answered me carefully, unwilling to step into the middle of our quarrel. "Some of the rhymes are proving difficult."

"And may we hear it?"

"If he doesn't wish to read it, Dr. Sammelsohn, you mustn't force him!"

"As a matter of fact," Dr. Zamenhof said, "I *would* like to try it out before presenting it to the entire congress."

"Then by all means," Fraŭlino Bernfeld said. "By all means. Of course."

No one knew how many attendees to expect. For all we knew, there might be more listeners in our little third-class rail car than at the congress and so we settled back into our seats, while Dr. Zamenhof, a cigarette dangling between his fingers, riffled through the papers stacked atop his briefcase. With the cigarette between his lips, he squinted through its smoke. "Ah, yes, here it is," he said. He removed the cigarette from his mouth and looked shyly about him. Certain no other passengers were listening, he began: "Al Vi, ho potenca senkorpa mistero . . ."

Directly addressing the mysterious *Vi* of the Universe, the You who without form flows like a fountain of love and truth and life into the heart of every living being, the You who created and rules over a perfect world that we have bloodied with our wars, the prayer promised that we will strive beneath the green banner of Esperanto until all mankind is united in complete harmony and that, at the end of our struggles, despite the hindrances, the walls that divide us will crack and tumble with a mighty roar, so that truth and love might at last come into their own.

The last stanza, exhorting brothers to come together and join hands, concluded with a remarkable line:

> *Kristanoj, hebreoj aŭ mahometanoj*
> *Ni ĉiuj de Di' estas filoj.*

Yes, yes, yes! I thought. All men, Christians, Jews, and Muslims, *are* brothers. They *are* children of one God. Isn't that exactly what my old father couldn't see? Of course, he had sufficient reason not to see it. Even as we hurtled along towards our congress of utopiaj samideanoj, the tsar's army was firing on unarmed workers, nationalist strikes were whipping

up across the Russian Empire, and as always, the easily distractible ku-
laks were being easily distracted from their own misery and encouraged
to inflict it upon Russia's poor Jews instead, in the face of which Dr.
Zamenhof's all-too-Jewish utopianism might seem laughable, and yet
the sponsors of our congress—I reminded myself—were not unworldly
Jews, like Dr. Zamenhof and me, but worldly, realistic Frenchmen—
Europeans, vraiment!—as devoted as was our Majstro to the cause of a
universal language.

"It's a fine piece of work," I said, genuinely stirred.

Dr. Zamenhof handed the pages to Fraŭlino Bernfeld who had asked
for them. She dampened them with her tears. He rummaged through
his briefcase again, once again letting his cigarette dangle between his
lips, squinting through the smoke, unable to find whatever it was he was
searching for.

Finally, he gave up the search.

"My mother was a believer," he said, crossing his legs and letting his
briefcase drop. "My father an atheist." He looked out at the landscape,
his eyes misting over. "As a child, I too believed in God and in the immortality of the soul, exactly as our rabbis taught us. I don't remember
precisely when I lost my faith, but I do recall that I reached the highest
peak of my unbelief at the age of fourteen or fifteen, and that this was the
most tormented period of my life."

"But why, Majstro?"

He gave Fraŭlino Bernfeld a sad smile, his mustaches crinkling. "Life
lost all sense and value." He shook his head. "I couldn't help but regard
myself and other human beings with contempt. What was man then, but
a piece of meat, created without reason or purpose to live for an instant
before two eternities of darkness? What was I living for? What was the
point of all my learning? It all seemed so senseless and absurd . . ."

He stared out the window again. Fraŭlino Bernfeld looked at her
gloves, folded in her hand; Sinjorino Zamenhof at the top of little Lidja's
head; Lidja looked at me. Dr. Zamenhof clucked his tongue against the
back of his teeth. He lit another cigarette and drew its smoke deep into
his lungs. "But then," he said, "I don't know why, but I came to feel that
this was impossible, that death couldn't be disappearance, that some law

of nature existed beyond the limited sight of our eyes, and that there was something reserving me for a higher purpose, although at the time I had no idea what it was, of course."

"Of course," Fraŭlino Bernfeld whispered serenely.

I leaned forward, wanting to tell them all about Fräulein Eckstein and Ita and about how Ita and the two angels had appeared to Dr. Freud and me, and how Dr. Freud had denied everything; I wanted to tell them that the experience had made me want to dedicate myself to some higher calling, so that when I encountered Dr. Zamenhof and Esperanto, I had seen the hand of God in it. But before I could clear my throat, Dr. Zamenhof had laughed a bitter little laugh of self-mockery.

"Of course, I can prove nothing," he said. "And in matters of faith, what is proof, but the poorest of excuses to believe? In Białystok, where I was a boy—can you believe it?—even in this modern age, we were still bedeviled by our so-called saints who advanced all sorts of mad schemes to keep their minions in line."

"What sort of schemes?" I wondered aloud.

"Oh, the usual bag of tricks. Dybbuks, demons, wicked children in the service of the devil, that sort of thing: the closed fist of a punitive God."

Fraŭlino Bernfeld laughed scornfully, as did Dr. and Sinjorino Zamenhof. It was a dry, sophisticated laughter, the knowing laughter of those who had freed themselves from a jail that the other inmates believe is locked, but that, in fact, isn't.

"Thank God, that world is gone for good," Dr. Zamenhof said, exhaling a gust of smoke.

OUR TRAIN ROARED into Paris on the morning of July 28. It was barely ten o'clock and already the sun had turned the city into a brick oven. Furnace blasts of heat reached us as soon as we exited our car and descended the platform. We were all perspiring instantly, squinting against the glare piercing the glass ceilings. Dr. Zamenhof threw his hat onto the back of his head and daubed at the dome of his skull with a green handkerchief. Pigeons and sparrows swooped into the open building, creating a ruckus. Fraŭlino Bernfeld, irritated, it seemed, beyond redemption, grew more irritated still. As I watched the muscles of her face tighten, I counseled myself to stay out of her way. In this intense light, I wanted to avoid everything that might worsen the headache I was already feeling coiling up behind my eyes.

The Parisian Esperantists were feuding, and so no one had come to meet our train: the prize of greeting Dr. Zamenhof was apparently too precious to be either lost or shared, and it was thought best that no one should win it at all. At one point, their jockeying over who should host Dr. Zamenhof in Paris had grown so divisive that various camps begged him not to come at all. As a consequence, Dr. Zamenhof had insisted upon arriving as a private man. Still, none of us had imagined the Parisians would take him at his word. Lidja began to wail, unhappy in the heat, and we couldn't decide whether it would be more expedient to phone someone and wait or to simply hail a taxi for ourselves. My hands in my pockets, I paced up and down the platform among the milling crowds, as far from the others as I could get without seeming to have abandoned them, each biting hiss of steam from the stationary trains cutting through my head.

"Ah, here they are, here they are!" we finally heard, as an ebullient convocation of men, dashing down a brass staircase, approached us, easily recognizable as Esperantists by the queer language issuing from their mouths. None of us, of course, had ever heard la lingvon internacian spoken with a French accent. Enunciated thusly, it seems a far lighter, airier, and more complex act of parolation than it did coming from our own throats.

"We were looking for you in the first-class compartments," one of these gentlemen said, roaring with laughter.

They surrounded Dr. Zamenhof, each jabbering away with greater or lesser fluency, each introducing himself, each extending his hand, each offering to carry this or that bag, and all so cheerfully and musically, it was impossible for me, probably even more so for poor Dr. Zamenhof, to distinguish one distinguished gentleman from the next. It was only after I got to know each personally that I was able, in retrospect, to reconstruct the scene: here was General Hippolyte Sébert, fit in his midsixties, taking command of the platform as though it were the sight of a great battle, barking out orders, and sending for a porter after personally welcoming each member of our party to Paris. Next to him, offering his long-nailed hand to Dr. Zamenhof, as though it were a rare object d'art, was Professor Théophile Cart. Nearly sixty himself, he wore an inverted pyramid of a beard and a dashing white mustache. His broad-brimmed hat was cocked at a rakish angle, and condescension dripped from him like water from a rain barrel during a monsoon. He had hailed a porter of his own, a rival, and apparently a bitter one, of the porter General Sébert had summoned, and as we all tried to make pleasant conversation, the porters scuffling and arguing behind us created much distress.

There was Alfred Michaux, pushing an exasperated sigh through his long, battered nose. The organizer of the congress, he wore a white straw Panama, and I couldn't help noticing that his ears stuck out at a fifty-degree angle from his head beneath its brim. Well over six feet tall, with a beard as luxuriant as a mink's tail, he towered over the Zamenhofs. It was perhaps to distract them from the embarrassment of the battling porters that he asked Madame Zamenhof if he could hold the baby. When she nervously surrendered Lidja to him, Michaux lifted the child high above his head, giving out a whooping cry. To the delight of everyone and to my surprise, Lidja laughed happily, though Michaux had thrown her, with her eyes unshaded, through a penetrating beam of austere sunlight. Charles Lemaire was there as well. A handsome blond businessman with a florid mustache, he held the distinction of being the second French Esperantist, the first man recruited by the first French Esperantist, the Marquis de Beaufront, who (as Monsieur Lemaire was now explaining to Dr. Zamenhof) sent his profuse apologies. Alas, the marquis was ill and recuperating at his country estate in Rouen. Gaston Moch, arriving on his bicycle later than the others, greeted our party before strutting purposefully ahead of it to whistle down a squadron of taxis, into which we all piled. Michaux, who'd made certain he'd gotten into Dr. Zamenhof's taxicab, gave orders to the driver in French to carry Mademoiselle Bernfeld and me to the Hôtel le Pangloss, after which he would accompany the Zamenhofs to Dr. Javal's home, where it had been decided they would stay.

"Mia kara amiko," Dr. Zamenhof whispered, clutching my arm as I made my way out of the cab, "would you mind terribly coming along with me to meet Dr. and Madame Javal?"

"Not at all," I said, "not at all," although I felt torn in two. Here he was, holding on to my wrist, pleading with me to see to his needs, while Fraŭlino Bernfeld, in a seemingly eternal sulk, tapped her foot impatiently on the curb. Holding a parasol to block the sun, she gave up on me and moved, with a breathy rasp of exasperation, into the hotel foyer.

"Only let me arrange for our rooms and see to Fraŭlino Bernfeld and I'll be right out."

"Bone, bonege, dankon."

Framed by the window of the cab, Dr. Zamenhof resembled an orphaned child, captured and taken far from his home. He was overwhelmed, intimidated even, I sensed, by this festive delegation of Frenchmen and by the irresistible beauty of Paris, and he needed a friend at his side, someone who had known him a bit longer than the others had.

"YOU ONLY?" FRAŬLINO Bernfeld said, standing at the front desk with a bellcap, her bags stacked upon his trolley.

"I thought you'd want to rest," I said as tenderly as I could.

"Rest?"

"Hasn't it been a long journey?"

"Years!"

"Darling, please . . ."

"Fine! I won't go with you then!"

"Come, if you wish. You know the Majstro finds your company stimulating."

"The Majstro?"

"Yes."

"But not you?"

There was clearly no way to win this. "And I as well," I said as patiently as I could. "I merely thought you'd prefer to freshen up after the tiring journey."

"How very thoughtful of you."

"Is that not the case?"

"That is indeed the case."

"Then why don't you go to your room and rest?"

"Because I was hoping to spend the afternoon walking in the city with you."

"Something which you failed to mention to me, of course!"

"Must I explicitly mention everything that a more ardent man might simply take for granted?"

Although he was pretending not to, I could tell that the bellcap was listening to our every word.

"What am I to do with Dr. Zamenhof then? Refuse him in his hour of need? He's in over his head, fraŭlino. He's drowning with these people."

"Oh and you're not, because you're so very worldly!"

"I'm not worldly, no. Of course not. That is correct. But they have no interest in me and I therefore cannot disappoint them."

"Right, right, why should they take an interest in you?"

She crossed her arms and expelled a breath harshly through her nose.

"Fine!" I said. "I'll tell the Majstro I shan't be going with him then."

"And turn me into the villain?"

"Fraŭlino Bernfeld!"

"Dr. Sammelsohn!"

I couldn't help gritting my teeth. "Go up to your room and I'll be right back. I'll ring for you after you've bathed and napped."

"No. Just go! Go! Go with him! He needs you."

"And you're certain you don't?"

"I've never been more certain of anything in my life!"

"Very well then!" My head was pounding. "Good-bye," I said, hurry-ing away, lest she once more change her mind. I crossed the foyer and went back out into the dreadful summer sun, preferring its heat to the hell Fraŭlino Bernfeld was making of my life. I climbed into the cab and settled in across from Dr. Zamenhof and Monsieur Michaux.

"Ĉu ĉio estas en ordo?" Dr. Zamenhof inquired, somewhat nervously. *Is everything in order?*

"Jes, jes, certe," I nodded, attempting to smile as simply as I could.

"Avant!" Michaux called up to the driver.

"Does anyone mind if I pull down the shade?" I said, hoping to block out the sunlight and coddle my aching head. However, doing so only made the car hotter, stuffier, and dark.

OUR TAXI CROSSED le pont Alexandre III, with its golden statuary, and turned onto le boulevard de la Tour Maubourg, stopping, not far from the Seine, at number 5. We all climbed out. Madame Javal saw to Madame Zamenhof and the baby first, wisely guiding the travel-worn mother and her fussing child up the staircase to rooms that had been set aside for them. A retinue of servants in livery darted in and out of the house, pulling bags off the car and carrying them in through secret passageways.

"Monsieur le Docteur, my husband, is waiting for you in his library," Madame Javal told us.

"I'll show them in," the gracious Michaux offered. He wasn't intimidated, as Dr. Zamenhof and I clearly were, by the opulence of the Javal home. He led us briskly up the stairs to the house's topmost floor. I hadn't seen anything as opulent since Fraŭlino Bernfeld's father had me tossed out of the Arkady Club. Dr. Émile Javal, as Dr. Zamenhof and I knew from our medical work, was eminent. With one of his students, he'd radically improved the ophthalmometer (a device I used daily in my practice), and with another, he'd advanced the world's knowledge of optics and astigmatisms. He'd invented the stereoscope and the tachistoscope and a dozen other such scopes, and had been, from all appearances, rewarded handsomely for his labors. On every landing, alternating with antiques, were prototypes of Dr. Javal's inventions, exhibited in glass cases.

We found our host sitting in his library in a chair near an oval window, overlooking the river, a writing plank laid out across his knee. There was something wrong-seeming about the impression he made, and it was only moments after we'd entered the room that I realized he wasn't looking at his work nor out the window, but *towards* it, wearing the sort of smoke-tinted eyeglasses Chinese judges wore in the fourteenth century to conceal their expressions in court.

"Javal," Michaux called to him softly, and only when he raised his head, looking not at us, but merely in our direction, did I realize, with a clanging sense of alarm, that the poor fellow was blind.

"Jes, jes, bonvenon, bonvenon," he said, sure-footedly navigating the space between us, searching the air for our hands. Out of compassion, one couldn't help correcting as he corrected, thus inadvertently moving one's hand away from his in trying to move towards it. Nevertheless, he greeted us warmly, in the French manner, with kisses on both cheeks. A blackthorn switch was fastened by a cord to the buttonhole of his lapel.

"The variety of handclasps is infinite," he announced in a resonant voice. "I've learned with some surprise that a person who is both blind and deaf and who consequently comes into relation with another only by hand, sometimes recognizes a handshake after an interval of several years."

"Is that right?" Michaux asked.

Dr. Javal nodded. "In Japan, I'm told, the blind have the monopoly on massage. Had my loss of sight been accompanied by a falling into poverty, I should not have hesitated to make myself skilled in that art."

He gave us a clear and concise explanation of his malady: "Glaucoma. First the right eye. Sclerotomy. Iridectomy. Complete vision loss. Then the left, which we treated with pilocarpine."

"Ah," Dr. Zamenhof said professionally.

"However, it did no good. I asked Priestly Smith—you know of him?"

"I've heard of him, of course."

" — to perform an iridectomy."

"And?"

"Too late."

"A pity."

"Still, a man doesn't need his eyes to think, nor to dictate, nor even to write, for that matter." Dr. Javal gestured to the writing plank, and I saw that it was no ordinary escritoire, but another of his marvelous inventions: a scotographic tablet, the apparatus had a stationary rim at its base in which the writer placed his elbow and a ratchet that moved the paper up a centimeter each time the writer passed from one line to the next. With this and an American fountain pen, Dr. Javal was able to create a page as impeccable as any example in a Spencerian handwriting manual.

(Dr. Javal, I soon discovered, let his blindness interfere but little with his life. One had only to witness him bicycling around Paris on the back of his two-seated tricycle to take the full measure of the man.)

"I've had to give up research and consultation, of course, although this isn't an absolute," he said.

"No?" Dr. Zamenhof asked politely.

"My successor at the Sorbonne does me the great kindness of coming and telling me from time to time what is being done at our laboratory, and if some former patient of mine insists upon consulting me, well, I call in my old assistant who details the invalid's condition for me. It gives me the illusion of being useful as a physician. Mostly, however, I've dedicated myself to writing and to other intellectual endeavors these last few years. To your Esperanto, for instance, Dr. Zamenhof."

"To *our* Esperanto," Dr. Zamenhof corrected him.

"To which," Michaux boomed, "Dr. Javal has generously dedicated his funds and his own vital energies."

"And for which we are profoundly grateful," Dr. Zamenhof said.

A servant brought in coffee and pastries, and we were invited to sit. A bullet-headed man, Dr. Javal kept a wonderfully serene expression on his face, though I admit the tinted glasses were unnerving. His beard was a tangle of blackish wires, shot through with grey, and his hands were as thick as a butcher's. Yet one had only to watch him preparing the pousse-café to see the great skill his surgeon's hands retained. Ascertaining the precise location of the cups, the sugar cone, and the sugar nips, he unerringly ferried three perfectly nipped pieces of sugar into each cup before pouring a perfectly measured dollop of cream into each as well—he must have been counting silently—a dollop that raised the level of each beverage a perfect two centimeters beneath the lip of each cup. His own cup he then brought, lacking indecision, to his mouth.

"Ah!" He swallowed this first sip with a great show of gustatory delight. "Eating and drinking is for the blind the greatest of pleasures. Especially, may I say, in excellent company." Crossing his legs, he leaned back in his chair and clapped his hands together. "Now, Dr. Sammelsohn . . ." he said.

"Yes?" I said, leaning forward.

"Tell us . . ."

"Yes?"

"You're a friend of Dr. Zamenhof's?"

"I am."

"And an oculist as well?"

"That is correct."

"In Vienna?"

"Yes."

"And an acquaintance of Sigmund Freud, I believe."

"Correct."

"And so you know Dr. Breuer, I presume?"

"Slightly."

"An excellent man."

"So I understand."

"Related to me through marriage."

"That I didn't know."

"Next time you see him, ferry to him, if you will, my kindest regards."

"I will."

"And welcome to Paris."

"Thank you."

"And to our home."

"Thank you again."

"It's good to make your acquaintance."

"And yours."

Done with me, Dr. Javal turned to Dr. Zamenhof. "And now, Dr. Zamenhof, let us hear, let us hear: How did the three Zamenhofs and their friends enjoy their journey? Was your arrival in our magnificent city satisfactory?"

Faultlessly polite, Dr. Javal allowed Dr. Zamenhof to warm to his company by relating nothing of importance. In this way, the two men, who knew each other only through a correspondence conducted in neither man's native tongue and dominated by Esperantic concerns, might relax together, if only for a moment, before rolling up their sleeves and digging into the work that obsessed them both. Dr. Zamenhof chatted amiably, enwombed in a shroud of cigarette smoke, while Michaux listened avidly.

The light pleasantries exhausted, the subject moved on to the congress, and the three men discussed Dr. Zamenhof's Parisian itinerary for the next few days. This included a trip with Dr. Javal to visit the minister of education, and another with Professor Cart to tour the offices of the new Esperanto Printing Society. A formal banquet at the Hôtel de Ville and a party at the top of the Eiffel Tower were part of the festivities as well. Interviews with journalists couldn't be avoided, Dr. Javal warned Dr. Zamenhof, despite his well-known reserve.

Sitting a little to the side and trying not to think of the tongue lashing I would receive from Fraŭlino Bernfeld when I returned to our hotel, I reflected upon how gratifying it must be for Dr. Zamenhof to have such high-minded and accomplished men rallying to his cause. If only his father could see him! Or more to the point: his father's notorious friend, the one who'd warned Markus Zamenhof that the boy's invention was nothing but a sign of incipient madness! And what of my own father? How astonished would he be to see me sitting here, invited as a guest to this magnificent home on le boulevard de la Tour Maubourg, sipping pousse-café with intellectuals and aristocrats? (Oh, how I would have loved to have blackened his eyes with the sight of me here!) But fathers, I mused, in relation to their sons at least, were as blind as Dr. Javal.

After a bit, Michaux rose and apologized. He was late for a dinner appointment and must excuse himself. "Please don't get up," he said to Drs. Javal and Zamenhof. "And don't let me further interrupt your conversation. Carry on, do. Although, Dr. Sammelsohn, if would you be good enough to walk me out, there's something I'd like to discuss."

"You might not want to leave those two alone together for the nonce," he told me at the front door, towering over me by at least a foot and a half.

"And why is that, sir?" I said, looking up into his face. Dr. Javal seemed nothing if not absolutely dedicated to the Majstro.

"I'll say nothing more," he continued, sotto voce, "in the hopes that it will come to naught."

"Very well then," I said, inspired by his sense of gentlemanly decorum. We shook hands, my head barely reaching the tip of his beard. When

I returned to the library, Dr. Zamenhof and Dr. Javal instantly ceased their talking.

"Dr. Sammelsohn is one of my dearest friends and a confidant," Dr. Zamenhof said, breaking the awkward silence. "I assure you there's nothing you can say to me that can't be said, in confidence, before him as well." Dr. Zamenhof's gentle eyes crinkled in an almost Oriental expression of glee. I nodded back, grateful for the compliment.

"Very well then." Dr. Javal sat a little higher in his chair. He cleared his throat unsuccessfully and was forced to take a sip of coffee. He smoothed down his beard with three brisk strokes, achieving nothing: the tangled wires remained every bit as tangled as before. "This is difficult for me to say. And I know that you have worked for a long number of years perfecting la internacian lingvon, Doktoro Ludoviko, and that during that time, you've been fair and open-minded about considering various reforms. Some would say too fair, too open-minded."

This was true. It was well known that in 1893, having founded the League of Esperantist, an organization comprising any and all subscribers to *La Esperantisto,* Dr. Zamenhof (under pressure from Trompeter, then his main backer) called upon its members to propose any changes each thought necessary, after which all suggestions would be submitted, as referenda, to a democratic voting procedure, an approach that meant that anyone with forty kopecks for a subscription to the gazette had as much say in the shaping of the language as its most subtle and sophisticated speakers, including its creator. Dr. Zamenhof not only excluded himself from the voting but adamantly refused the many blank ballots sent to him by subscribers who urged him, the only man qualified to make such decisions, to use their votes in whatever manner he saw fit. Even with the vote thus potentially weighted against him, a clear majority was obtained in favor of keeping the language as it stood.

(What is less well known—and what certainly was not known to Dr. Javal—was that before the vote Dr. Zamenhof secretly urged members of the St. Petersburg Esperanto Society, whom he knew to be conservative in all matters of reform, to purchase multiple subscriptions to *La Esperantisto* so that their agenda might carry the day. Dr. Zamenhof felt an artist's love for the details of his creation, I think. After all, he'd spent eighteen years, lavishing upon it all the love and attention one might upon a beloved child.)

"But none of that was in the least scientific," Dr. Javal complained, and not without cause. "Science is not a democratic affair, and very little of value has ever been created by committee, if anything at all."

Dr. Zamenhof nodded silently, apparently forgetting for a moment that Dr. Javal was blind. "Jes, estas la vero," he finally thought to say. "Daŭrigu." *Yes, it's the truth. Proceed.*

"If nothing else, our congress next month will demonstrate the ease with which Esperanto can be used in conversation, in presentations, in literature, and in drama, but it may also reveal certain flaws and failings, and many reforms will then suggest themselves to us from practical use."

Dr. Zamenhof began to say something, but Dr. Javal, seemingly unaccustomed to being interrupted, raised one of his thick butcher's hands—"Let me finish!"—and Dr. Zamenhof of course relented.

"You merely wish to demonstrate, I know, a liberal openness to new ideas, as well as an antipathy towards appearing—forgive the unfortunate religious analogy—as some sort of language pope, unlike Herr Schleyer, demonstrating, in the meantime, your benevolent regard towards humanity as a whole. I know you offered the language gratis to the American Philosophical Society and have made no financial profit from it aside from what an author of books in any language is entitled to expect. Your integrity—let us be frank, your *saintliness*—is not in question here."

Time was getting away from us. The late summer sun shone through the oval windows of Dr. Javal's library so fiercely, I had to cup my hand to my forehead to shield my eyes. I knew, with a queasy sense of certainty, that the longer I remained, the more irate Fraŭlino Bernfeld would become. I pulled my watch from my vest pocket, wondering if the slinking sound of the chain sliding against itself might signal a sense of boredom to the alert ears of the blind Javal. He turned his head slightly, so that his cochlea was facing me. I coughed and crossed my legs, hoping the sound of my pants scissoring against themselves might hide the fact that I had opened my watch.

Dr. Javal opened his own watch—the face had no glass—and gently probed it with his thumb. "Seven o'clock, Dr. Sammelsohn. Is there somewhere you need to be?"

"He's left his fiancée at the hotel, I'm afraid," Dr. Zamenhof said.

"Ah!" Dr. Javal chuckled merrily.

"Fraŭlino Bernfeld is not actually my fiancée," I corrected Dr. Zamenhof.

"Hence, the lower boiling point for her womanly irritations."

I was flummoxed. Why was it that everyone seemed to know so much more about women, as a general subject, than I?

"We'll have you back to her by the next hour," Dr. Javal promised.

"I assure you there's no hurry."

Though Dr. Javal was blind, I could swear at that moment that in response to my patent naïveté his eyes met Dr. Zamenhof's in a conspiracy of gentle mockery. With his big, blocky hands, he poured us each another splash of coffee, spilling not a drop. "Where was I?" he said.

"Reforms," Dr. Zamenhof said unhappily, two lines of smoke streaming from his nostrils.

"I'll be blunt in the interest of love." Here, Dr. Javal smiled in my approximate direction. "Though I can find little fault with your beautiful creation, Doktoro Ludoviko, there is but one thing, one small but not insignificant thing that I must, as a man of science, as a physician, and most important, as an ophthalmologist, protest."

"And that is?"

"Its use of accents."

I leaned forward, interested again.

For the sake of clarity and simplicity ("one symbol, one sound"), Dr. Zamenhof had freed Esperanto of the clutter of blended consonants. To this end, its orthography employed six accented letters, five with a circumflex accent (ĉ, ĝ, ĥ, ĵ, ŝ) and one with a breve (ŭ). Though the accented letters serve as a flag—the informed reader knows immediately that he is reading Esperanto and no other of the hundreds or thousands of languages beside which it will live worldwide—they present a certain difficulty when it comes to most, if not all, typewriters and printing presses.

These practical concerns were not, however, at the heart of Dr. Javal's reservations. Leaning forward in his chair, he allowed his voice to drop. He sounded as though he were sharing with us an as-yet undisclosed scientific discovery. "I've become convinced through my researches and also through my work with patients for over forty years that, along with yellow paper, seemingly innocuous graphological accents create a dangerous level of eye strain, needlessly subjecting the precious organs to threat, and often resulting in damage that can lead to blindness."

Now it was Dr. Zamenhof and I, as though we were one man staring at himself in a mirror, who offered each other identical looks of astonishment. The presumption seemed absurd. But how could we say as much? We were both lowly oculists, Dr. Émile Javal a world-famous ophthalmological authority. His inventions, which we used every day in our dusty, shabby consultancies, stared down at us from their immaculate exhibition cases, accusing us, as it were, of reckless behavior, of inventing, in Dr. Zamenhof's case, and of promulgating, in both of our cases, a language with a typography so dangerous, reading it might — what? — scratch the cornea? How sharp did Dr. Javal imagine those circumflex accents to be? (As sharp as Louis Braille's awl?) And yet how could we argue the point with a man who was, in fact, blind? (I made a rough calculation: from things that had been said during our conversation, I'd gathered that Dr. Javal starting losing his sight as early as 1884 and was completely blind by 1900. He'd become an ardent Esperantist only in 1903, so at least his Cassandra-like warnings were made without personal grudge.)

"You're considering the argument's merits," he said into the silence, although clearly Dr. Zamenhof was considering nothing of the sort. The argument had no merits. Why not imagine *t* as a dangerous dagger or *y* as a low-hanging branch? How could a circumflex accent be any more straining to the eye than, say, an ampersand, that convoluted piece of plumber's piping?

"Your remarks are quite just," Dr. Zamenhof said, as politic as ever. "The accented letters are an inconvenience, and truly, I would be happy if they'd never existed. However, now is not the time to speak of reforms . . ."

"Ah, Captain Lemaire," Dr. Javal said, before Lemaire had entered the room. "How good of you to join us."

The dashing young businessman, pushing his hair into place, found us in the library. He had, by his own report, driven to the Javals' on his motorcycle.

"We were just discussing the supersigns."

"Ah, yes, the accents, Dr. Javal," Captain Lemaire said, taking a seat. "A very dangerous affair, that."

"As I was saying," Dr. Javal confirmed.

"And who should know better?" Captain Lemaire said.

Dr. Javal pursed his lips and honked out a little one-note laugh, as though wildly flattered by Captain Lemaire's tribute.

Reaching into the inner pocket of his jacket, Captain Lemaire said, "And because we both feel so strongly about the issue" — he removed a portable exchequer and a pen — "and because we understand how much time and effort go into a question of this magnitude, we're prepared to finance your work on the necessary reforms with a check, from the two of us, worth two hundred fifty thousand francs. That should cover all your expenses, Dr. Zamenhof, don't you think?"

A quarter of a million francs! Having recently converted my money for the trip, I knew this was no small fortune. In those days, a newspaper cost half a franc, a glass of beer ten centimes. A Parisian laborer made between four and ten francs a day; a professor between thirty-two hundred and eighty-five hundred francs a year. A quarter of a million francs was unheard of. Dr. Zamenhof and, if the money were well managed, conceivably all of his descendants unto eternity, would never have to work again.

"Why, you could move here to do the work," Dr. Javal said, gesturing towards the oval window of his library and, through it, to the Seine and to the exquisite city spread out below it. "Quit Warsaw and live among us in Paris where you properly belong."

Not content to dangle the offer before Dr. Zamenhof in a theoretical or abstract way, Captain Lemaire filled out the check, endorsed it with his signature, removed it from his exchequer, and placed it delicately upon the coffee table so that Dr. Zamenhof could clearly read what was written there. No one seemed to know what to say. In a silence full of barbs, I felt a stab of sympathy for Dr. Javal. Silent, we were as good as invisible to him. Or perhaps not. He cocked his ear and shrewdly said, "Think on it, that's all we ask. Sleep on it, and we'll speak of all this later."

CHAPTER 8

I returned to the hotel, registered for my room, and was stepping away from the front desk when the concierge, a small man with a waxed mustache in the shape of an archer's bow, called out to me. "Monsieur le Docteur?" he said.

"Oui?" I said.

"La mademoiselle has left this for you."

"Ah, merci."

Inside the metal cage of the elevator, I tore open the envelope and read Fraŭlino Bernfeld's note:

Kapdoloron, mia karulino.
Vidos din morgaŭ
L.

I sighed with relief. Fraŭlino Bernfeld had suffered a headache and would see me, her darling, in the morning. If unwell, she'd probably have gone early to bed and would consequently have no idea at what hour I'd returned nor how long I'd been away and therefore wouldn't be especially angry with me. Nevertheless, after unpacking my own bags, I descended again in the lift and found her suite.

"Fraŭlino Bernfeld, mia kara," I knocked softly upon her door. "Estas mi." I leaned an ear against the door and heard a flurry of rustling: bed-clothes, skirts, God knew what else. "Fraŭlino?" I knocked again. "How is your head, mia karulino?"

"Foriru!" she cried. "Go away! I don't ever want to speak to you again!"

"Dr. Javal was quite long-winded," I told her. "Open the door and I'll tell you all about it."

A surprisingly crude epithet followed, attaching itself to Dr. Javal's good name.

"Would you like to get dinner?"

"Leave me alone, I said!"

A rather dour-looking couple made their way down the hall past me, the woman in furs, the man in a black homburg. Feeling as though I'd been caught out in the commission of a crime, I greeted them as graciously as I could, raising my eyebrows towards the gentleman, as if to signal to him, by semaphores, the message *Women!* He scowled at me in return, his chin dimpling.

"Fraŭlino Bernfeld!" I whispered when the couple had finally passed. "Let me in and we'll discuss this. Please?"

Her voice rose in volume and pitch with each word—"If you don't leave now, I! WILL! SCREAM!"—until she was, in fact, screaming.

"Everything in order here?" The man in the black homburg turned back, as did the woman on his arm. She stared down at me furiously from behind her nez retroussé.

I had no choice but to depart the hallway immediately.

In the morning, Fraŭlino Bernfeld did not join me for breakfast in the hotel café. Rather, pretending she hadn't seen me at my table, she let herself be called over by a small crowd of samideanoj and persuaded to eat with them instead. Though I eyed her continually between paragraphs from behind the duck blind of my *Le Figaro,* she disappeared without a good-bye, timing her departure so perfectly I missed it. Since Dr. Zamenhof was being taken by Dr. Javal to visit the minster of education that day, I was left on my own.

I saw nothing of Fraŭlino Bernfeld the following day. She refused to accept or return the messages I sent hourly to her room. She begged off from the tour of the Esperanto Printing Society, led by Professor Cart; and when, afterwards, I arrived at the elaborate banquet hall of the Hôtel de Ville, I discovered her place card had been separated from mine. My seat, a place of honor, I had been originally told, was now farthest from the podium and nearest the kitchens. And although she *did* attend the party at the Eiffel Tower, somehow among the crowd and the buzzing journalists peppering Dr. Zamenhof with silly questions in le restaurant russe, she managed never to find herself next to me, though, nauseated with vertigo, I spent the evening pinging and ponging from the tower's north side to its west side to its south side to its east side in search of her. Days passed without a word, and when Dr. Zamenhof asked me to travel with him to Rouen to visit le Marquis de Beaufront, I was happy to have a reason to quit Paris.

LE MARQUIS PIERRE Josselin Gerard Eugène Albert Louis de Beaufront was France's preeminent Esperantist. In 1888, while on vacation in Antibes, he had encountered a review of Dr. Zamenhof's *Dua Libro* in an illustrated gazette, and from that moment on, he had devoted himself to the movement. Indeed, it was through his efforts alone, as I've said, that Esperanto had even survived. As Dr. Zamenhof's sole Western adherent, it was the marquis who had smuggled la sanktan lingvon out of tsarist Russia, as it were, to Paris, whence its light soon spread to the rest of the world.

The marquis was truly indefatigable. Not only had he founded la Société pour la propagation de l'espéranto and established the journal *L'Espérantiste,* he'd set up classes in Paris with a tiered series of competency exams. Further, he seemed to know everyone. His address book bulged with eminent names, and he'd blazed through it, winning an ever-growing number of France's intellectual and scientific luminaries to the cause. Indeed, it was thanks to the marquis that men such as Lemaire, Javal, Cart, and Sébert were counted among Esperanto's most devoted friends.

"We owe him much," Dr. Zamenhof said to me, riding in the car we'd hired to ferry us to Rouen. He picked a twig of tobacco off his tongue and dropped it onto the car floor with a fluttering of his fingers. "He really *is* Esperanto's Second Father, as he's called. And unlike Dr. Javal, who is a thousand times his moral superior, the marquis insists with real passion—certainly with more than I could ever muster—that the language must never be reformed or changed." Dr. Zamenhof looked moodily out the window. "How can one not love a man like that, foolish though he may at some times be?"

The villa where the marquis lived was perhaps the most beautiful I'd ever seen. A palace at the end of a long winding drive, it sat atop a tall green hill. It took our taxi nearly twenty minutes to carry us from the front gates to the house itself, where the butler seemed perturbed that we had rung at the front door. It was only after we'd been redirected to a small cottage in a nearby grove that the truth began to dawn on us: the marquis was not the master of the house, nor even a guest here; he was, rather, an employee, a tutor hired by the estate's owner, the Graf de Maigret, for his children.

As Captain Lemaire had explained, the marquis had not come to Paris to greet the Majstro owing to ill health. By all reports, ill health plagued the poor fellow, and upon entering his cottage, we found an invalid lying in his bed, his long, thin body hidden beneath half a dozen quilts. The marquis seemed to be drowsing, and Dr. Zamenhof was forced to clear his throat in order to announce us.

"Dr. Zamenhof?" the Marquis de Beaufront said weakly. "Is that really you?"

"Along with a friend, yes," Dr. Zamenhof said. We took a step nearer the marquis' bed. "May I present to you Dr. Sammelsohn?"

"Ah," the marquis said, raising himself on an elbow and squinting at us, an unalloyed look of disappointment transfiguring his face.

"If the marquis is too ill to receive us," Dr. Zamenhof suggested, taking the poor man's pulse, "we'd be only too happy to return at a more convenient time."

Of course, he was only being polite. There *was* no other time. It'd been difficult enough to fit this trip into his busy schedule.

"Such small men," the marquis said, taking a better look at us through the pince-nez he'd fished out from the blouse of his nightshirt. Frowning critically, he laughed at himself. "I had expected — I don't know what — a colossus, I suppose!" The marquis fiddled with his hair, which he wore in a long hank on one side of his head in order, I assumed, to cover his baldness. "In any case, I apologize for meeting you in this state of dishabille."

"And what exactly ails the marquis?' I asked as politely as I could. I had the uncharitable impression that all those blankets were piled on top of him not so that he might sweat out his fevers, but rather that he might simply sweat and appear, therefore, feverish.

"Non, non, non," he said, "let us say *tu* with one another, shall we?"

He graced me with a benevolent smile. "Let us be duzenbrüder, as the Germans so aptly phase it."

"Good. Thank you." Dr. Zamenhof meekly bowed his head, as though the marquis had bestowed upon him a significant favor.

"Now, do, come, sit near me, here by my bed," the marquis ordered us gently, "so that we might talk."

Dr. Zamenhof and I found rustic chairs in the kitchen and brought them to the marquis' bedside.

"Very well then," the marquis said. "Shall I relate to you how I came to be ill?" Before speaking further, however, he leaned over his bedside table and retrieved a wet towel from inside a pewter bowl. "One moment," he said, dampening his face; when he removed the cloth, the twirled ends of his mustache, which had previously pointed towards the ceiling, pointed towards the floor, and his short beard glistened with the droplets of water. "Ah, that's so much better. The visions are starting to recede now."

"Visions?" Dr. Zamenhof said.

With one trembling hand, the marquis waved aside the question. "It's my own fault, really. Though who wasn't young and foolish once?" He searched our faces for looks of sympathetic approbation. "It all began when I was a fellow at Christ Church, Oxford, I suppose. By the way, that's the only diploma of mine Father ever kept. He had no interest in anything else, really. Indeed, everything else"—he gestured with an extravagant flick of his wrist—"he threw out. But Oxford—oh, my, how that impressed him! But Papa was like that, I'm afraid. My dissertation in theology he lost on a hunting expedition, before he'd a chance to read it. Or so I assumed. He never told me what he thought of it, in any case. I rarely saw him. I was raised by the servants, I suppose one could say."

The marquis poured a small amount of medicinal powder into a glass of water, stirred the mixture, and drank it down.

"I'd been handpicked by Max Müller to work as his assistant. I was so naïve at the time I had no idea who Max Müller was nor that he was world-famous. Nevertheless, it was my job to assist the great man in his translation of the Rig-Veda and the Upanishads. English, I knew, of course, from my granmamá, who looked after me in the summers, but at the time, of my twelve languages, Sanskrit was the shakiest. And so I did what any young man would have done, what you yourselves would have done in my place, I suppose. Over Christmas, I traveled to India to improve my grasp of it; and there, to my enduring shame, I left, though only for a short time, the straight and true path of our church. I apprenticed myself to a yogic master called Swami Sri Giri. Now Swami taught me, imperfectly as it turned out, the Vedic art of slowing down, if not stopping altogether, the beating of one's heart. Despite the dangers to myself and despite repeated vows on my part not to undertake these rigorous devotions alone, I couldn't help myself—I was *that* hungry for spiritual enlightenment—with disastrous results, naturally." He gestured ruefully to his diminished body. "My health was wrecked. I came down with a terrible case of typhus in a filthy hotel room in Lhasa, waiting to be summoned for an audience before the Dalai Lama. The day was rainy, torrential, as I recall, but I went to him, sick though I was, and I'll never forget what his Holiness told me. 'Monsieur le Marquis,' he said, taking my hands in his, 'a dark time is coming. If we do not protect ourselves from deceptive acts, everything we hold dear may be exterminated.'

"Now, he thought he was speaking of Tibet, of course, but I knew better. He was speaking of Dreyfus. What else could it be? And why else would he have confided this warning to a Frenchman?" The marquis lay back in his sickbed. "In any case, my health was gone, and when I returned home, I discovered that the family fortune had been lost as well. I was only twenty-two at the time."

He cleared his throat and hid his hands inside the sleeves of his worn gown. "One does go on, doesn't one?" He wagged his finger at us. "But then you've drawn it out of me. How did we even get on to this subject in the first place?"

Before either Dr. Zamenhof or I could speak, the marquis had sent his charge, one of the Graf's littler sons, into the kitchen for a coffeepot and pastries, and the child was now struggling underneath the enormous weight of the tray.

"Another napoleon?" he inquired. "They're quite good."

"Quite good," Dr. Zamenhof agreed.

"From the finest patisserie in all of Rouen!"

"Thank you," I said, taking another one, although I'd had quite enough of the hard dry things.

The marquis watched the boy leaving the room with the heavy tray. Crumpling up a half-finished letter that lay on his bedside table, he said, "Pay no attention to this. I place intentional spelling errors in all my correspondence in order to test the children."

With two twisting moves of his hands, he resharpened the points of his mustache. He glanced out the window, and the lenses of his pince-nez filled with a white light.

"Now," the marquis suddenly said, "you must hear me out on this." He clutched Dr. Zamenhof's hand. "Now you must promise me that Esperanto shall never be reformed. You remember how you erred in '94, offering the language up to the reformists! Why, if it were left to you, you would have torn your work to bits long ago! But in the meantime, either Esperanto has become stronger or you have become weaker. You know with what constancy I've always supported you, and I'll continue to act in this way. Still, I must tell you the truth: your genius is so great that it seems to actually rob you of your ability to perform in the role of master over the rest of us. Now, we must swear to each other, as duzenbrüder, as samideanoj—which is a term, did you know, Dr. Sammelsohn, that I myself coined—but more important, as men who have given the best of their lives to our cause, that we will stand firm against these disastrous calls for plibonigoj, for so-called improvements and reforms. As you know, as everyone knows, as I myself have written to you countless times, bowing to the perfection of Esperanto, which I recognized immediately, I abandoned my own Adjuvanto."

He pronounced the word as though it were the name of a long-dead mistress.

"Adjuvanto, Dr. Sammelsohn," he said to me, "was my own universal language scheme and the work of a considerable number of years. Indeed, I was quite far along with it, but it was nothing compared to Esperanto." The marquis shook a scolding finger at Dr. Zamenhof, who, by habit, had begun to demur. "You see, that's his problem. He's too modest. No, he is! And where will they stop, these reforms? Today it's the accented letters; tomorrow the accusative -*n*; on Wednesday, this one can't bear the Slavonic roots; on Thursday, another thinks the vocabulary must be more French. Who knows what Friday and Saturday will bring? The only thing I can assure you is that there'll be no resting on the Sabbath. And in the meantime, what will happen to my grammar and my textbook?" His voice sharpened to a querulous point. "These are real books, Majstro, and not the little pamphlets you yourself have distributed. Our adepts cannot be expected to replace their entire libraries! And furthermore," the marquis said with a sudden ferocity, "it works! Esperanto *works*! Why, the language is perfection itself!"

"On that score, Marquis," I said, in the hopes of hurrying the conversation along, "you and I are in complete agreement."

The marquis sipped his coffee in a distracted manner and stared out the window. He sighed, as though he'd been charged with a necessary task he found distasteful.

"And yet," he said, "the thing we all must remember is this: France is not Russia. And though you Russians might model yourself upon our superior culture, the exchange is like a river: it does not flow backwards. Here in France, we are coldly intellectual. We are rationalists—we pride ourselves on this—with no warmth in our hearts left over for any sort of mysticism, whether Russian or Jewish or"—here, he curled up his nose—"Jewish, especially in light of ex–Captain Dreyfus whose shame continues to taint our nation. Now don't misunderstand me: I cannot blame the Jews, like Javal, who blind themselves to Dreyfus's perfidy. How could they not side with the traitor as one of their own? However, the Frenchmen who do so disgust me."

Dr. Zamenhof shifted in his hard wooden chair. Our time was growing short, and the marquis' falling out with Dr. Bourlet had yet to be resolved. Now was perhaps the only time before the congress a rapprochement might be essayed between these two former friends. Since arriving in Paris, Dr. Zamenhof had been beaten and battered with the news of their squabble. Before our cab had even pulled away from the train station, Carlo Bourlet had stuck his bearded face in through the window and said, "Before the day is through, Majstro, a word, please, about these publishing contracts!"

There'd been no time to speak of it then, but the following day, Dr. Bourlet pulled Dr. Zamenhof aside. "Though I'm loathe to bring up a delicate matter, Majstro, I must, concerning Monsieur de Beaufront."

Dr. Bourlet had gone to great lengths to secure a publishing contract for Esperantan books with Hatchette & Co., a leading Parisian firm. When the director of that firm insisted that everything be overseen by a French agent fluent in the international language, Dr. Bourlet had recommended not himself, but the marquis. Upon careful examination, Dr. Bourlet was consternated to see that the contracts the marquis arranged ceded to himself the lion's share of the profits, while binding Dr. Zamenhof to the firm more or less as a slave for the rest of his life. The contracts furthermore gave the marquis the right to approve or disapprove all such books published by Hatchette, while restricting the rights of Esperantists to publish with other firms, thus conferring upon his person all the powers of the Christian savior on Judgment Day: he alone would choose between the saved and the damned.

"No one is suggesting that the marquis will misuse these privileges," Dr. Bourlet told Dr. Zamenhof with an unhappy smile, "but it certainly gives him an enormous amount of clout over his friends as well as his enemies in the movement."

"I'm not a legal man," the Marquis de Beaufront said with a sigh, when Dr. Zamenhof at last broached the subject, "and I can assure you I take no delight in having exposed myself to the animus of so many of our friends. Surely you believe that, don't you?"

"Of course," Dr. Zamenhof said.

"The discussions were well beyond my competence. Indeed, it was criminal of Dr. Bourlet to place me in this situation! I had absolutely no idea what that Hatchette fellow was proposing. He spoke in circles, he flattered me. 'Sign this, sign that,' he said, shoving the papers in my face. Now I don't wish to speak ill of anyone, but Bourlet certainly seems to have used me as his straw man."

"The contracts will have to be redrawn," Dr. Zamenhof said.

"That goes without saying," the Marquis de Beaufront agreed. He hugged his thin arms and looked out the window again. "I'm a victim of a terrible misunderstanding."

"Ah, yes," Dr. Zamenhof said.

"It was all an honest mistake."

"Of course it was," Dr. Zamenhof said, "and I'll try to make Dr. Bourlet see it as such."

I could only sigh. Esperantists battling each other and refusing to
speak? It's not exactly what Dr. Zamenhof had in mind back in 1878,
singing songs around a birthday cake. Do human beings really require
a universal language in order to misunderstand each other? or to refuse
to speak to one another? If samideanoj couldn't attain a common understanding, what hope was there for the rest of the world? Not much,
it seemed.

On the drive back to Paris from Rouen, Dr. Zamenhof and I rode
in silence, he no doubt reviewing his conversation with the marquis or
perhaps thinking about the world and all its troubles or else making
plans for the congress in the days ahead; and though I was happy to have
accompanied him on this difficult excursion, I had only one thought in
my head and that thought, of course, was: Loë, Loë, Loë.

Finally, on the day we were to depart for Boulogne, Fraŭlino Bernfeld and I found ourselves standing near each other on the platform of the train station. With a distracted air, as though she were trying to recall who I was, she explained to me that she'd decided not to ride in third class with the Zamenhofs, but to continue on in first class, blaming a headache.

"Besides they don't need me looking out after them anymore. They've quite arrived, haven't they? After a week in Paris, they're as famous as Ali Baba and his Forty Thieves!"

"Fraŭlino Bernfeld," I began to plead with her.

"Dr. Sammelsohn?" she addressed me in a formal tone, as though we had not spent years courting, but had only recently met. The look of remoteness was so innocently and yet so furiously displayed upon her face that for a moment I found myself believing it as well, or if not believing it then at least behaving as though we were strangers. So although I wanted to say, Fraŭlino Bernfeld, my darling, let us tear up our tickets and find a rabbi and persuade him to marry us immediately, all I in fact said was: "Can I help you with your bags or at least summon a porter for you?"

"I can manage quite well on my own, Dr. Sammelsohn, thank you very much," she said, turning on her heels. "Ĝis la revido!"

ĜIS LA REVIDO?

Were these to be the final words Fraŭlino Bernfeld addressed to me, a jocund-sounding lie uttered in the language of universal truth? Ĝis la revido. She had no intention of ever seeing me again. If our paths crossed at the congress, as they were certain to — these were not yet as well attended as they would become in later years — she would no doubt confront me from behind a similarly unbreachable fortress of elegant manners and amiable words. As I took my small, uncomfortable seat in third class, I did so unresigned to my fate: Fraŭlino Bernfeld was no longer, if she had ever been, mine. Everything had come about exactly as her father had predicted. (Or perhaps even mandated.) But it was true: for all my fopperies, I remained a backwards Galitsyaner, unschooled in the gay sciences, a novice in the matters of the heart. Had I learned nothing of women since my father revealed the mysteries of sex to me, without the aid of helpful diagrams, by quoting the Hebrew scriptures? I slumped in my seat, or as much as the cramped space permitted me to, and sighed. No one took notice. Sinjorino Zamenhof was busily teasing a cooing Lidja. Dr. Zamenhof was working away, his briefcase serving again as a makeshift desk. I had to wonder: Was Fraŭlino Bernfeld merely elongating the emotional distance between us so that I would be forced to cross it, striding resolutely towards her in order to unelongate it, or did she truly wish never to see me again? I sighed a second time, so lost in my own thoughts that I must have been staring at Dr. Zamenhof for a long minute or two before realizing he was looking back at me.

"Daydreaming," I explained. "I'm sorry. I didn't realize."

"Ne, ne, ne," he said, chuckling. "I was staring into space as well."

The train shook us from side to side and for a moment we said nothing further. Though I couldn't bear to bring it up myself, I wanted nothing more than for Dr. Zamenhof to inquire after the state of Fraŭlino Bernfeld and my romance. On the one hand, I'd had enough of older men — my father, Fraŭlino Bernfeld's father, Drs. Freud and Fliess — meddling into my affairs; on the other, I felt so terribly hungry for even a morsel of paternal advice.

Sinjorino Zamenhof took from her large handbag three ham sandwiches wrapped in butcher paper and offered one to her husband and one to me. I shook my head. Though years out of Galicia, I still couldn't bring myself to eat pig of any kind. (Ita's fate had convinced me that there was indeed a God in Heaven and that despite Heine's famous assertion, forgiveness might not be His métier. It was one thing to shake off the yoke of the Commandments, quite another to appear before the Heavenly Courts with spicy kielbasa on your breath.) Dr. Zamenhof, however, accepted the sandwich absentmindedly, chewed a few bites before wrapping it up carefully and returning it to his wife. She rewrapped it even more carefully before tucking it inside her purse.

I watched Dr. Zamenhof working. He seemed oddly calm for a man who stood on the razor's edge between success and failure: here, in Boulogne, his life's work would be validated or found wanting. Or perhaps he merely appeared calm in comparison to me. As our train finally pulled into the little station, my heart began to race. I pressed my head against the window, planning my dash out of the train, so that I did not miss Fraŭlino Bernfeld.

Somehow, however, she managed to leave the train, hire a coach, check into her hotel room, and disappear among the townspeople without letting me spy her even once. The deskman had been given strict orders not to reveal the number of her room to anyone who might inquire after it. "Especially," he added, referring to a note Fraŭlino Bernfeld had obviously given him, "'a man of medium build, pince-nez, and a messily out-of-date bouffant,' a description that, I'm afraid, Monsieur, fits you perfectly," after saying which, he had the nerve to unfold his palm in search of a gratuity!

WITH LITTLE ELSE to occupy me, I changed into the white linen suit and the white straw boater Fraŭlino Loë had purchased for me, and walked the tiered streets of Boulogne down to the beach. My pant cuffs rolled up, my socks in my pocket, I strolled along the sea, carrying my shoes in my hand.

The sky was a summer blue with a pyramid of clouds stacked far out beyond the seawall.

There was only one thing to do, really, or so I told myself. I must break with Fraŭlino Bernfeld immediately and free her of the emotional entanglements remaining between us. As the sea licked my feet, I knew with absolute clarity that this was the manly course to take. I'd wasted too much of her time, drawn too heavily against her emotional reserves with no hope now of ever repaying her. There were two problems, rising like mountains between me and this goal, however. First: in order to carry out my plan, I'd have to communicate it to Fraŭlino Bernfeld, an occurrence she seemed too skilled at preventing. Not including our encounter in the train station, I hadn't seen her from a distance of under ten meters for the better part of the week! How could I break off relations with her if she refused to acknowledge my person? (By note, I supposed: handwritten, sealed, entrusted to the concierge who would ferry it to her rooms or hold it for her at his station.) Against the horizon of this plan rose the second mountain: the simple fact that breaking off with the fraŭlino was the last thing I wished to achieve by declaring myself in support of such a resolution. Indeed, I only wanted to suggest a parting of the ways in order to have her talk me out of it. Which is why a letter wouldn't do. In epistolary form, I could be crumpled up, torn to pieces, shredded to bits, passed from hand to hand between scornful girlfriends, or worse, discarded unread. No, my only hope was to stand before her in person and to appeal to as many of her senses as possible, trusting not alone in sight, but also in smell, taste, hearing, and (I trembled to consider it) touch. Then when I offered, like a man, to release her from our unofficial bonds, the intimacy of the moment would call to mind other such moments, and she, in tears, could make a great show of appealing to my sentiments. Once she had fallen to her knees and wetted the hem of my trousers with her tears, I could descend (as would any man not fashioned of stone) from the high rock of my noble intentions, in order to reconsider my resolve and reconcile with the poor creature.

But first, of course, she'd have to relent and agree to meet me!

I looked ahead at the shoreline curving off into the distance. All about me, French families were frolicking with their children. What my father had maintained appeared to be true: even when they were scolding them, the French sounded as though they were instructing their children in the most sublime of philosophies. I couldn't help thinking how different my life might have been had I been raised in this milieu! Stumbling late into work, tumbling out of the bed of my lust-crazed wife, downing the darkest of coffees with good pals at the local café, putting in a few carefree hours attending to my patients (most of whom, blinded by syphilis, accepted their fates, ne regretting pas), I'd lunch on red wines and creamy cheeses and spirally mollusks before engaging in a session of dizzying lovemaking with my underaged mistress, never for a moment feeling the slightest pang of guilt, never anxious that my sybaritic ways might be a hollow, shallow waste of life. And why should I, when the long history of rebukes received from my parents, from my teachers, from my headmasters, from my employers, from my lovers, from my spouses sounded as sweet as an air by Couperin? Addressed in this way from childhood on, who wouldn't become a lovable scoundrel, an endearing rogue helpless against his own endearing rogueries?

But instead, I was a God-bedeviled Jew, burdened with so many commandments, it didn't matter whether I kept them or not, I was always falling behind in my accounts.

I'D STAYED LONGER on the beach than I'd intended, and by the time I thought to return, the sky was already darkening. My hotel was a tiny building, indiscernible in the distant landscape above me. The air was chilling gradually, and I shivered a little inside my sea-bespattered clothes. My muscles ached, my stomach groused, and I had no choice but to tramp back to my hotel, wending through the tiered streets of the little city. My mood was lightened somewhat when, nearing the hotel, I crossed a town square and saw an unworldly sight. Flying, it seemed, from every flagpole and hanging from the balconies of every building, was the Esperanto flag with its green star of hope. Though the opening ceremonies were hours away, outside the City Theater where we would be meeting later in the evening, crowds had already begun to gather, forming themselves into smaller groups, little knots of new and instantly intimate friends, all (as I could hear more clearly with each step I took) speaking Esperanto! I stopped beneath an electric lamp and took in the amazing sight: here were Englishmen, Frenchmen, Germans, Poles, Russians, Danes, Dutchmen, Turks, Latvians, and Letts chatting away. Three fellows with a guitar, a fiddle, and a bass were even singing songs in Esperanto! Surely, this isn't France, I told myself, but the very Gates of Heaven!

My joy in the moment could only have been greater if, according to the cliché belonging to every solitary person, I'd had someone to share it with. Knowing there was no chance of locating either Fraŭlino Bernfeld or her room, or of persuading the one, if I happened to find both, to let me into the other so that we might step out onto its balcony and take in the gratifying scene, I decided upon alerting the only other person I knew who might enjoy the spectacle as much as I, if not more so. I slapped my forehead. But of course! Dr. Zamenhof must experience this!

I wasted so little time throwing on my shoes that I neglected to roll down my pant cuffs. What a sight I must have made, rushing through the austere lobbies of the Hotel Boulogne with my boater on the back of my head and my pants nearly as high as a boy's knickers. I didn't care, however. I felt as larky as a schoolboy on his birthday, bounding up the stairs.

The door to Dr. Zamenhof's suite was open, and as a colloquium of voices issued from it, my knocking apparently went unheard. Torn between twin rudenesses—the rudeness of barging in or of knocking again, loudly enough this time to be heard—I chose the middle ground: to walk away and to return later, when the heat of the conversation had died down. I hesitated long enough to permit myself to overhear some of the conversation. I was only human, after all. Indeed, holding my breath, I even pushed the door in a bit, or enough at least to get a view of the room's inhabitants: these were Dr. Zamenhof and six or seven of the French Esperantists.

His tie hanging loosely around his unsprung collar, Dr. Zamenhof looked small and tired, defending his position against the blows of this illustrious armada of French intellectuals.

"Please please please!" one of them was saying. "No one is telling you what you can and cannot do, nor what you can and cannot say."

"You are the Majstro!"

"Certainement!"

"But, however . . ."

"I would hate to think I left Russia and came to France only to be censored by enlightened Frenchmen." (Though I strained at first to identify the other speakers, I could easily discern Dr. Zamenhof's voice, not only because it was familiar to me but also because of its sad tones and its soft lisp.)

"Heaven forbid!" someone said.

"It's just that when, last week, we discussed the matter, before your arrival, all of us at Professor Cart's apartments—"

"You've already discussed this?"

"In good faith."

"You sent us a copy of your speech, and naturally we read it, and naturally having read it, we met to discuss it. There is nothing devious in that." This was Michaux, I believe. "And on the assumption, I might add, that that's exactly what you had meant for us to do with it all along."

"If you didn't wish for our advice, why consult us beforehand?"

"You've no idea how the Dreyfus case continues to divide all of France." I recognized the voice of Dr. Javal.

"Émile, no one has said anything against you Jews," Professor Cart said, meaning both Dr. Javal and Dr. Zamenhof, I supposed. "Dreyfus is an individual, we understand that, and not a representative of his . . ." Professor Cart searched for the appropriate word, with how much repugnance, I couldn't tell, before offering "race."

"Guilty or innocent as he may be," someone else cut in.

"Guilty or innocent? Of course, he's guilty!"

"Oh, and where's the evidence of that?"

"A man needn't be pardoned for crimes he didn't commit!"

"He's petitioned for a retrial. Does that sound like a guilty man to you?"

"No, only a foolish one. Captain Dreyfus is a fool."

"At last, we agree on something!"

"Having been twice traduced by so-called French justice —"

"How dare you speak in this way!"

"— he puts his hopes in it for a third try? For what reason? To wind up again on Devil's Island!"

"Where, I should say, he belongs!"

"Gentlemen! Gentlemen!"

"You can see, Dr. Zamenhof, that even among ourselves the matter is highly combustive."

Standing in the hallway, I remembered my first Tarock game with Dr. Freud and how obsessed the pediatrician Rosenberg was by the fate of poor Alfred Dreyfus, at that time still pacing the rocks of Devil's Island. By 1905, Captain Dreyfus had been court-martialed, publicly degraded, deported, imprisoned, conspired against, defended (most audibly and to his eternal credit by the novelist Émile Zola), rioted over, retried, reconvicted, and pardoned (as were all those who had conspired against him). Did he have any idea how his figure still haunted our continent?

"Javal, speak up! Tell him. You're a Jew as well and know the dangers," General Sébert prompted his friend. "Public opinion—against you, against the movement—will be stirred up in a moment if the general population realizes who you actually are, Dr. Zamenhof."

"All we're asking is that you drop the final stanza of the prayer."

"I think the entire prayer is a poor idea."

I heard an exasperated sigh, followed by a buzzing conspiracy, murmured on the side en français.

"Now you're being extreme," someone said.

"Extreme? We are men of science. Esperanto is a scientific endeavor! Let us leave the God of Israel out of it entirely!"

"If I may. Please," Dr. Zamenhof said in his small, piping voice.

"Let him do as he wishes."

"We've spoken and I hope not out of turn," one of the men said to Dr. Zamenhof.

"'Do as he wishes?' We know what he wishes, which is precisely what we're here to prevent him from doing!"

I'd heard enough and slipped down the passageway and up the stairs to my own room. Dr. Zamenhof had read us a draft of his speech on the train, and we had found nothing offensive about the speech or the prayer. It wasn't even a prayer, really, but a poem, addressed to "Vi," the powerful and incorporeal You of the Universe, ending with what I thought was a final, stirring sentiment: "Kristanoj, hebreoj aŭ mahometanoj / Ni ĉiuj de Di' estas filoj."

But apparently the Kristanoj wanted little to do, publicly at least, with la hebreoj.

NEEDLESS TO SAY, the joy I'd felt in the town square ebbed away. I stood before the full-length mirror, drawing on my formal clothes, newly purchased. Gazing at my reflection, I began to wonder if I were being too naïve. Did I imagine everything Dr. Zamenhof hoped to achieve could be won without a fight? (Of course, had I imagined a war around Esperanto,

I would never have imagined a civil war fought between brothers on the same side.) Perhaps this wasn't a war at all, I told myself, but simply a case of the French, natives here, offering sound advice to a conquering foreigner. Perhaps an invocation of universal brotherhood among Jews, Christians, and Muslims *would* rankle to the point of offense. Still, hadn't Dr. Zamenhof been clear from the start that Esperanto was not and could never be simply a useful tool for international scientific and cultural and mercantile exchanges?

No, without the "inner idea," it was nothing at all.

The time was late, and I'd had nothing to eat. A woven basket in the shape of a wunderhorn had been delivered to my room with chocolates, pears, and a small bottle of brandy inside. I wolfed down a pear, eating over my cupped hand, my back hunched over like a question mark, in order not to spill its juices onto the satiny fabric of my suit. I should have eaten the pear first and dressed afterwards, but I didn't think of this in time. It seemed ridiculous to dress, undress, eat, and dress again. I hid the chocolates inside a kerchief, which I stuffed into my jacket pocket, hoping they wouldn't melt. Realizing that they would, I unwrapped them and popped them—one! two! three!—into my mouth. "Pah!" I said, licking my lips. I daubed at my mustache with a hand towel, took up my top hat, and departed the room. The brandy could wait until I returned.

ALL FOUR GALLERIES were full, and I was among the last to squeeze into a seat near the back of the auditorium on the ground floor. I was hoping, vis-à-vis Fraŭlino Bernfeld, to repeat the incredible good fortune I'd had with Fräulein Eckstein when I found myself in the Brahms-Saal of the Musikverein sitting directly behind her. However, I put no stock in this hope. I had no idea if Fraŭlino Bernfeld had even remained in France for the congress. I felt I hardly knew her anymore and could no longer anticipate any of her decisions. And certainly, if an Esperantist as essential as the Marquis de Beaufront could stay away, Fraŭlino Bernfeld's premature departure needn't signal to anyone a lessening in her ardor for the cause.

Everyone was in evening dress, including some red-fezed Turks. The crowd was growing not restless, but restive, from a giddy sense of anticipation. I found myself sitting on the edge of my seat, peering over the shoulders of the people in front of me, trying to get a look at the dais, although nothing upon it had changed since I'd entered the hall. Though I couldn't see him, I assumed the orchestra leader must have entered the pit, because the first few rows broke into an applause that undulated over the auditorium until even the back rows, myself included, were applauding—not so much in response to the conductor, I think, but as a form of insistence that the proceedings begin. Finally, the notes of the "Marseillaise" were enunciated by a solo bassoon, accompanied, after a measure, by a cello, before the sound of everyone rising drowned out this odd arrangement. By the time we were all on our feet and could hear again, the anthem was all brassy and polished, as one usually hears it. We remained standing, at its conclusion, as the luminaries ascended the stage, led by the quite tall Michaux. He was followed by Dr. Zamenhof, who, naturally, looked even more like a child next to him; then Professor Cart, Dr. Bourlet, and Rector Boirac in full academic regalia; General Sébert with a chestful of war medals; Dr. Javal with his blindman's switch; and three or four local dignitaries: the mayor, a town councilor, the president of the chamber of commerce.

The mayor, a tall man with a shock of white hair, was the first to address the crowd—disappointingly in French, with Dr. Bourlet translating. Tears welled up in my eyes: I felt as though I were witnessing a piece of metal rusting at the beginning of the Bronze Age. Never again will one man need to translate for another before a third! The world in which such things happen is as doomed as the Mayan Empire!

The president of the chamber of commerce stood next, a portly man with a black beard and the closely cropped hair of a recently freed convict. Unlike the mayor, he welcomed the crowd in Esperanto, and the crowd roared back its approval.

When he was done, all heads turned toward Dr. Zamenhof.

Six hundred and eighty-eight pairs of eyes, half as many pairs of glasses, pince-nez, and lorgnettes, half again as many monocles were raised to get a better look at this little elfin man whose odd preoccupation with boundless love had somehow radiated out of the dingy court on Dzika Street to all points of the globe, and in response to which we were all here now, laughing good-naturedly, as the giant Michaux placed a wooden crate behind the flag-draped lectern and returned again from his seat to drastically lower the height of the carbon microphone.

Despite the grey in his beard, Dr. Zamenhof looked like a studious eight-year-old as he peered into the assembly. Even with the aid of the crate, he seemed to struggle to look over the lectern, the lights glittering off his spectacles. This was the first time many in the audience would hear la lingvon internacian spoken in an accent other than their own. It's one thing to converse with your neighbor in an international auxiliary language, quite another to speak to a man not from half a block, but half the world away.

Dr. Zamenhof cleared his throat. He seemed on the point of speaking, when he twisted his body away from the lectern to pick up a glass of water someone had left for him inside the hollow of the stand. Sipping, he spilled a line of water into his beard and had to pat it dry with a kerchief he pulled from the breast pocket of his evening suit. Evidently, the top of the lectern was raked, and having attempted to balance the water there, Dr. Zamenhof thought better of it and, corkscrewing his body again, returned it to its place inside the lectern.

He looked into the audience, his eyebrows rising even higher than usual.

"Estimataj sinjorinoj kaj sinjoroj," he said and, at the sound of his high, slightly shrill voice, a thrilled cry of greeting rose to meet him. Dr. Zamenhof smiled. The ferocity of the crowd's affection had evidently taken him by surprise. "I greet you, dear colleagues," he said slowly, enunciating clearly, seemingly looking into everyone's face, "brothers and sisters from the great worldwide human family, who have come together from near and far, from the most diverse nations on earth, to clasp hands in the name of the one great idea, which unites us all."

Clearly calming his own nerves, Dr. Zamenhof let the next roar of applause crest and die away. He took another sip of water, his hand trembling, then raised his head and peered over the tops of his glasses at the people seated above him in the galleries.

"I greet you also, glorious land of France"—here, a chauvinistic whoop was raised—"and the beautiful town of Boulogne-sur-Mer"—the same, if not quite as forceful—"both of which have graciously offered to host our congress."

Dr. Zamenhof bowed towards the row of officials seated behind him—as though caught in a white-hot spotlight, these men straightened up in their chairs and, with nods, acknowledged the audience—and the applause revved up again.

"I express also my heartfelt thanks to those persons and institutions in Paris who, during my journey through that glorious city, expressed to me personally their sympathy for our cause, namely the minister of public education"—boisterous applause—"the City Council of Paris"—louder—"the League of Language Instruction"—wildly—"and many eminent men of science."

The man in front of me, nodding his head and clapping enthusiastically, leaned over to explain something to the woman seated next to him, and that was, of course, when I saw her. Seemingly as thrilled as I by the moment, Fraŭlino Bernfeld had turned back in her seat. I saw her caramel-colored hair first and her gracious slender neck. She was scanning the crowd, searching for someone. Certainly not me, I thought, until her gaze fell on mine, and she nodded a hello that seemed as sweet as those I'd received from her when we were at our happiest. She scowled slightly in a question, as though asking me, *Why are you sitting so far in the back?* to which I shrugged and pointed at my new Parisian wristwatch and shrugged again, indicating that I'd come too late. The man in front of me leaned back and directed his attention again towards the stage, blocking the fraŭlino from my view. But at least I knew she was here, still in France, still in Boulogne, here in this auditorium now, not more than ten rows in front of me.

"This present day is holy," Dr. Zamenhof was saying, and I noticed the French Esperantists on the dais shift unhappily at the mention of this word. "Our congress is modest," he admitted. "The outside world knows little about us, and the words we speak here tonight and in the coming days will not fly via telegraph to every city and town in the world." He shook his head, smiling benevolently, as though congratulating us for the courage and the prescience that had brought us here, long before the rest of the world had even heard of Esperanto. "No crowned heads or prime ministers have come here to change the political map of the world, no luxurious clothes or impressive decorations shine in this room, no gun salutes resound around the modest building in which we find our- selves; and yet"—he let a caesura dangle tantalizingly—"through the air of this auditorium fly mysterious sounds, quiet sounds, inaudible to the ear, but sensible to every sensitive soul." The chamber grew hushed, as though each of us were listening for these quiet noises. "It is the sound of something grand that is now being born," Dr. Zamenhof assured us. "Through the air fly mysterious phantoms!"

He made a fluttering motion with his hands, and I thought I saw Dr. Javal sigh. Rector Boirac and General Sébert's eyes met discreetly: the cause has been lost, surrendered to mysticism.

"The eye does not see them," Dr. Zamenhof said, "but the soul senses them. They are images of a time yet to be. These phantoms fly through the world, taking on form and strength, and our children and grand- children will see them, will sense them, and rejoice."

I peered, as discreetly as I could, at the people sitting near me. No one seemed offended. On the contrary, a kind of light seemed to be beaming from everyone's face.

Dr. Zamenhof brought his fist to his lips and cleared his throat. "In the ancient past," he continued, one hand caressing the other, "which has long disappeared from the memory of humankind and about which history has preserved nothing, not even the smallest document, the hu- man family separated, and its members ceased understanding one an- other. Brothers created in one image, brothers possessing the same ideas, brothers carrying the same God in their hearts, brothers who should have helped each other and worked together for the happiness and the glory of their family became foreign to each other. Separated seemingly for all time into enemy camps, they began waging an eternal war."

(Here, I stopped listening for a moment. Dr. Zamenhof's description of the ancient family had made me think too much, and too uncomfort- ably, of my own. Hadn't we separated and ceased understanding one another, exactly as had the family of man? In our case, however, there seemed little hope of reconciliation.)

"Prophets and poets dreamt about that nebulous time in which we would again understand each other, again join together in one family; but this was only a dream. One spoke about it as though about some sweet fantasy, but no one took it seriously, no one believed in it. And yet, now, for the first time, the dream of a million years begins to become real. In a small city on the French seashore, people from diverse nations have come together and are encountering one another on an equal footing, not mute and deaf, but truly understanding one another, speaking like brothers, like members of one nation. Yes"—he stamped his foot—"often people from different countries meet and understand one another; but what a great difference between that understanding and ours. In our coming together, there exists neither strong nor weak nations, nor privileged and unprivileged, no one is humiliated, and no one embarrasses himself. For the first time in human history, we, members of very different peoples, meet, not like strangers, nor like rivals, but like brothers who understand each other mutually, man to man. Today inside the welcoming walls of Boulogne-sur-Mer, we meet not as Frenchmen and Englishmen, not as Russians and Poles, but as human beings. Blessed be this day, and great and glorious its consequences!"

Not another blessing, I could almost see Professor Cart thinking, as he rolled his eyes, dropped his patrician nose into his hand, and stared at the floor. And yet, of all those in the auditorium, the Frenchmen on the dais seemed to be the only people fidgeting. Despite his high, thin voice, Dr. Zamenhof had mesmerized the entire room.

"We met today," he said, bearing down on his theme, "to show the world, through irrefutable fact, that which until now it has refused to believe." Behind his shining spectacles, his eyes were enflamed with what I can only describe as a sort of divine madness. I felt I was listening to the words of an ancient prophet or seer. "We will show the world that mutual conversation between people of different nations is not some fantastic dream, but a beautiful reality!" he nearly shouted. "Our grandchildren will not believe that it was once otherwise."

As he picked up his pace, his cadences grew more rhythmic. "Whoever says that a neutral artificial language is not possible, let him come to us, let him walk the streets of Boulogne-sur-Mer in the coming days, and if he is an honest man, he will go out into the world and he will loudly repeat that Yes! A universal language is possible. Not only possible but easy, very easy, to learn!"

A knowing laughter, from several corners of the auditorium, reached Dr. Zamenhof, and its gentle sound seemed to calm him. "It's true," he admitted, "that many of us still possess our language imperfectly. But compare a novice's stammering with the perfectly fluent speech of a more experienced person, and an honest observer will see that the cause of this stammering lies not in the language itself, but only in the insufficient practice of the speakers."

His demeanor grew solemn, and the audience, attuned to his every mood, seemed to grow somber as well.

"Eighteen years have passed since the day Esperanto appeared in the world. Eighteen years is a long time — oy vey! — a very long time." At the sound of these words — ho ve! in Esperanto — I watched a collective chill run through the men on the dais. "In this great space of time, death has stolen a great many of our most fervent campaigners. Since citing each name would be an impossible task, I will list only a few." Dr. Zamenhof mentioned specifically Leopoldo Einstein, Josefo Wasniewski, and "the unforgettable" W. H. Trompeter. "Beside these three, there is also a great — oy vey! — a very great number of people" — again, the Frenchmen trembled — "who are not able to see the fruits of their labors." (What was Dr. Zamenhof doing, I wondered? Deliberately rubbing his Jewishness in their noses? Did it matter that he had pronounced the phrase in an Esperanticized fashion as ho ve?) "They have physically died," he said, "but they have not died in our memory. I propose, esteemed ladies and gentlemen, that we honor their memory by rising from our seats." Dr. Zamenhof raised his voice, as though offering a toast. "To the shades of each fallen Esperantan warrior, the First Esperanto Congress expresses its respect and a pious salute!"

We all stood and took in the moment in silence. At a nod of his head, Dr. Zamenhof indicated that we had stood enough, and we sat. Nervously, he seemed to turn completely away from the luminaries on the dais, easing them out of his purview, positioning himself fully towards his audience, his voice once again trembling.

"Soon the labors of our congress, dedicated to the brotherhood of mankind, will commence, but in this solemn moment, I feel the desire to make my heart light through a prayer, to turn to a certain very high force, invoking its help and its blessing. At this moment, I'm not from a specific nation, but am simply a human being; in this moment, I'm not a member of one particular religion, but am only a man. And in the present moment before my soul's eyes stands only this very high moral Force, which each human being senses in his heart, and to this unknowable Power I now turn with my prayer."

Dr. Zamenhof gazed towards the ceiling. The men on the dais crossed their legs and shifted unhappily in their seats. With his eyes closed, Dr. Zamenhof recited his poem from memory: "To You, oh powerful and bodiless mystery, most powerful ruler of the world, great fountain of love and truth and of ever-lasting life . . ."

To the Vi of the Universe, to the Cosmic You, Dr. Zamenhof pledged to work for the reunification of mankind, beseeching this Mysterious Power for His blessing and promising that, under the green flag of Esperanto, we will tear at the walls separating people until they crack and fall, and love and truth rule the world.

For a moment, I wasn't certain if Dr. Zamenhof had finished. He stood perfectly still, not looking at his text. He seemed to be reconsidering ending his prayer where he had and moving onto the final stanza. After all the ho ves and the blessed be this days and the invocation of mysterious invisible phantoms, would a call to unity among monotheists really have exposed him as a Jew? He gazed at the audience in a sort of sorrowful way, as though certain he had transgressed against their affection for him. But no, he had only to move an inch away from the lectern to signal that he was done, and the applause was a wild and inspiring roar of love and approval. Cheers rang out, shouts of "Vivu Zamenhof!" and "Vivu Esperanto!" People were weeping openly and yet the ferocity of the response didn't undo the holy-seeming atmosphere in the hall.

The French Esperantists stood and congratulated one another, their postures and physical attitudes broadcasting broad relief, as though we'd all dodged a bullet. After acknowledging the crowd's response, Dr. Zamenhof turned to the Frenchmen. I saw him nod subtly to the auditorium, shrugging, his eyes twinkling in triumph, as though to say, *These people seem to have no problem whatsoever with my prayer.*

"KAĈJO! KAĈJO!" FRAŬLINO Bernfeld called to me through the ecstatic, departing crowd.

"Fraŭlino! Here I am!" I cried.

She ran up the aisles, oblivious to the angry looks she was receiving from people as eager to depart the hall as she, oblivious as well to the indulgent nods surrounding her: here was clearly a woman in love. Even I could see that (though I admit, at one point, turning to look behind myself, imagining, if only for a moment, that she might be calling to a person, improbably also nicknamed Kaĉjo, who was, by some extraordinary coincidence, standing behind me).

"Wasn't he marvelous!" she said breathlessly. Without hesitation, she laced her fingers through mine.

"Absolutely!" I said. "Absolutely marvelous!"

"And to think, we were here. We were *here*, Kaĉjo, alive today, to see it!"

"Alive to see it, yes," I repeated, as though *I* were the village idiot, unable to speak my own thoughts but only repeat the words she had addressed to me. We were in the lobby now, no longer surrounded so tightly by others, and soon we were outside in the square among the jubilant throngs.

"I've been a fool," she said.

"No, it's I who have been foolish, fraŭlino."

"I was so sad, Kaĉjo, so sad, but now I'm so happy. I'm so happy, I could . . . I don't know . . ."

"What, fraŭlino?"

"Kiss someone! I don't know . . ." She blushed.

Though I realized she was all but inviting me to kiss her, I wasn't entirely sure. Perhaps she was merely reporting a fact concerning the quality of her happiness, describing it in a piquant way, never imagining that the metaphorical kiss she claimed to want should come from me, but rather, less improbably — for sake of example — from her mother and, if so, placed not upon her mouth, but upon her forehead; or upon her cheek, if from a father or an uncle; and in an extreme case, upon her hand, if by a rogue like me who really wanted nothing more than to devour her whole, beginning with her mouth. Out of fear or perhaps to mask my own lustful affections, I looked at her idiotically, as though I were not her lover, but her best girlfriend, sympathizing with this desire of hers without understanding how she expected me to fulfill it.

She took hold of my hands and said, "Let's take a walk," and so we did, wandering away from the theater and through the tiered streets of Boulogne, leaning into each other, recounting the highlights of Dr. Zamenhof's triumph. ("Lutek should never have compromised his visionary idea for their practical concerns," she said. "The French understand nothing about what the world thinks of them.") The pressure of her arm against mine was such an agreeable sensation that I resolved to volunteer myself immediately should Fraŭlino Bernfeld again mention a desire to kiss someone. Unfortunately, the question never came up, and eventually we found ourselves in the sand, along the shoreline, the surge of the ocean more virile than I recalled it being during the afternoon. The rising moon bisected the sea with a shimmering band of phosphorescence, the moving crest of each wave sparkling with reflected starlight.

We strolled past the statue of Victory straining to offer a laurel wreath to San Martín enthroned upon his horse.

Fraŭlino Bernfeld was shivering, and I offered her my jacket. "Cold?" I asked.

"No, no, I'm fine," she said. However, I insisted, and she allowed me to drape my coat about her shoulders. "That's better, yes, thank you very much."

She turned up the collar, and her white hands held the jacket front together from inside, the tips of two fingers crooking out.

"Fraŭlino Bernfeld." I cleared my throat.

"Hmn?" she murmured questioningly, looking at the sea.

"I was wondering," I said, "earlier when . . . you mentioned being sufficiently happy to . . . to . . ."

"Kiss someone?"

"I was wondering, yes: did you have anyone specifically in —"

Before I could finish my sentence, her arms had snaked out from beneath my jacket and her hands were grasping the back of my neck. With a gentle tugging, she brought my head down to hers. My coat slid off her shoulders and fell into the sand. I had opened my mouth and was on the point of protesting in order to rescue the jacket—it was brand new, after all—when Fraŭlino Bernfeld's upper lip filled it. (My mouth, I mean.) Her bottom lip slid wetly across my chin, and as it did, I thought it best to ignore the jacket, for the time being at least, lest I miss what, in my state of idiocy, I imagined would be a celebratory and thus solitary kiss, and not the first in an endless banquet of kisses. Fraŭlino Bernfeld's lips were soft and pillowy, and my lips seemed to sink into hers with the slow dulcet movement of a cherry blossom falling into a pot of honey. Because I didn't wish her to think I possessed any notions of taking advantage of her—though in a public place, we were, as far as I could tell, completely alone and blocked from view by the colorful fence surrounding the children's playground we were sheltering in—I began to pull away. Fraŭlino Bernfeld's hands tightened about the back of my neck, and she brought me to her again. Her mouth widened, gnawing at my own. A soft, purring murmur juddered inside her throat, and in truth, I nearly swooned at the sound of it. Though we were hardly moving, our two heads seemed to be lunging at one another rhythmically, until my hat fell off. I don't know where my hands were before this, but Fraŭlino Bernfeld's hands somehow found them and placed them upon her lower back. She pulled me towards her, until my chest was pressed into the soft upholstery of her upper torso. Still devouring my mouth, she dropped her chin, so that my chin was now nearly grazing the upward-thrust pillows of her bosom. Her head dropped back and some sort of instinctual knowledge took over in me. Without hesitation, I kissed her along the inside of her neck. Her hands, rising across my back, found my hair. Her fingers entangled themselves in my locks and, yanking on my hair, she forced my head down until the buttons of her blouse raked against my cheeks. My pincenez, for a while sitting askew, fell off the bridge of my nose and dangled between the columns of our bodies. With my mouth pressed against the fabric concealing her breasts, I allowed my hand to spider its way up her midsection, thinking she might at any moment, in a fit of modesty, brush it aside, as, of course, it was her absolute right to do. A gentleman, I felt it only correct to give her fair and ample warning of my intentions. Counter to my growing disbelief, my hand however was allowed to proceed unimpeded, until at last it attained the desired summit.

Fraŭlino Bernfeld shuddered.

Her mouth again found mine, her tongue licentiously searching mine out. Our knees gave way, and we were standing upon them. I could feel her hands working frantically, and when she once again forced my head onto her breast, I was surprised to find her bodice unbuttoned. As I (quite presumptuously, I felt) licked along the line where her bare chest met the cups of her brassiere, her hands, knotted into jittery fists, pummeled my sternum as she worked to unbutton the rest of her dress's front. Unable to wait, she yanked the two halves apart. Three buttons flew off with little percussive sounds and were lost in the sand. Kissing me still, she reached blindly across the sand for my jacket, and when she had it in her hands, she broke off from me. I looked into her eyes, questioningly. Keeping my gaze, she stood and retreated a step or two. She looked back towards the high cliffs and the little town. No one could be seen. Except for ourselves, the beach was uninhabited. While I remained on my knees, Fraŭlino Bernfeld pulled her dress off her shoulders. She let the top of her corset fall and climbed into my jacket, sliding her arms into its arms. In the moonlight, I could see a brace of sand falling from its shiny black satin. Covered now with the jacket, Fraŭlino Bernfeld let the top of her dress fall to her waist. She returned to me with a sultry air that was, quite frankly, alarming. Kneeling beside me, she locked her mouth onto mine and pressed her weight against me until I had no choice but to fall backwards onto the sand, moving my legs, with difficulty, from beneath me. She laughed with her lips still hard on mine, and I could feel her teeth. When I laughed in response, our teeth ground together. Her nipples emerged from beneath the lapels of my evening coat, and the black satin sliding against their extended flesh was nearly more than I could withstand. She removed whatever it was that was fastening her hair and threw it—a metallic glint in the moonlight—into the mouth of her shoe.

She shook out her hair, the milk chocolaty tresses falling onto the shoulders of my evening coat. "Now where were we?" she said.

"I believe I was offering to kiss you," I said, "if, in your happiness, you still feel the need."

Again she knelt beside me, her skirt and long underskirt a bell of fabric surrounding her legs. With her arm on my shoulder, she distracted me with a kiss, while with her other hand she fiddled with the buttons of my braces and with those of my trousers. Stupid! I thought. You should have unbuttoned them yourself while she had moved away to retrieve your jacket! But I'd been afraid of seeming too forward, of appearing to push myself upon her. What if I were misreading her signals? She dug, like a child digging in sand, through the various fabrics of my crotch, until she found at last what had been long buried there. Almost painfully, my manhood stood, uncustomarily erect. I couldn't help gasping out a high, helpless breathy gasp, and Fraŭlino Bernfeld smiled shyly. Schooled at her father's expense from an early age in the equestrian arts, she dispatched one leg across my supine body and straddled me before I'd completely anticipated her intentions. She settled herself upon me as though she were settling into a hot bath — slowly, degree by exquisite degree, her face contorting in a momentary grimace, until she sighed and seemed, at least provisionally, to relax. Lying on the sand, I held myself upright using my elbows as supports. Bending low, Fraŭlino Bernfeld pressed her breasts against my chest, kissing me in the crook of my neck, her breath blossoming against my skin, concealing us, as it were, behind the curtain of my jacket above and of her skirts below. If we were, Heaven forbid it, espied from a distance, I've no doubt we would have resembled either a man in a formal jacket raping a young maiden or a sartorial hermaphrodite falling to its knees on the beach, sobbing at some unimaginable tragedy.

Now I understood the presence of the book I'd seen her stashing so furtively inside her traveling case, Dr. Albrecht's notorious *Mysteries of Females or, The Secrets of Nature*. She had wisely prepared for the moment, researching it, while I, as ignorant as I had been after my father's frank talk, found myself still in the dark. I couldn't even say for certain what exactly I was feeling underneath her skirts. Cobbling a mosaic out of various sculptures and monuments I'd seen in museums, stops on a recent sightseeing tour, and the collection of pornographic postcards Otto once left inside his evening coat, I tried to conjure a picture of what might be going on between the straining obelisk of my lap and the Arc du Triomphe of Fraŭlino Bernfeld's, but of the images of the female nude I kept inside my head, none were specific enough to satisfy my current needs. Everything seemed soft, wet, and enfolding, but was that simply her sweat-bedewed thigh or actually, in fact, the soft and encompassing caresses of her vulva, the thought of penetrating which was enough to prematurely release the wellsprings of my masculinity.

I was alarmed to hear a garbled, strangled growl flying from my throat. My feet and head seemed to be pulling apart, trying to dash down the beach simultaneously in opposite directions. I may even have fainted before instantaneously coming to.

"Oh?" Fraŭlino Bernfeld said, raising herself up and looking perplexed as though, having come for the first time to the end of this sticky business, she couldn't quite understand what had earned the enterprise its exalted reputation. Her look of confusion was immediately covered by one of benediction as she came near me and kissed my eyelids, my forehead, my nose, and finally my mouth. Groggily, I accepted and returned these kisses, feeling somewhat humiliated. One of her breasts grazed my mouth, and I tried to suckle at it sleepily, but it moved past too quickly as she stood. She turned her back and dressed. I lay in the sand and let my head fall into it. I gazed up at the stars, a galaxy of brilliant points in a black shroud. I staggered up, intuiting that it was not gentlemanly to exult in my own deliquescence while Fraŭlino Bernfeld apparently could not in hers. (I'd learned enough from reading Freud to know this little.) I buttoned my pants and my braces. Fraŭlino Bernfeld was once again fully clothed with my jacket over her shoulders. I walked the beach the few paces towards her and stood behind her, kissing her neck and cupping her breast in my hands. She closed her eyes and leaned against me, before removing my hands, firmly and decisively.

Lowering her head, she covered her eyes and began to weep.

"Ne, ne, mia karulino, ne, ne," I said soothingly.

I turned her around, so that she was facing me, and she collapsed against my chest. I enfolded her into my arms. I felt horrible. She had given me her maidenhood, but clearly I was the only one who had profited from the exchange, and now she was ruined. Had I forced her into this? Perhaps by withholding a marriage proposal for so long, I had driven her into degrading herself, simply to secure my attention. I never felt lower or meaner in all my days, and I recoiled against the heartless cad I'd become. A creation of my own era—who isn't?—there was but one thing I could do.

"Fraŭlino Bernfeld," I said. "Loë. Ŝa, ŝa, ŝa, mia kara, mia dolĉa knabino . . ."

My words, however, only seemed to make her cry harder.

I held her by her shoulders, so that she faced me squarely. I took a breath, and at last I said the words I'd been meaning to say for so very long: "Karulino, edziniĝu al mi."

"Kio?"

"Estu mia edzino. Mi petas!"

"Ho, Kaĉjo!" She lifted both hands to my face and covered me with her soft, sweet kisses. "Jes," she said.

"Vere?"

"Jes, mi diris, jes, mi volas, jes!"

CHAPTER 10

The rest of the congress passed in a blur. There were concerts, speeches, balls, banquets, day-trips, and performances of various plays. Dr. Zamenhof's own translation of Molière's *Le Mariage Forcé* seemed to particularly delight Fraŭlino Bernfeld, although I found the depiction of Sganarelle, the reluctant bridegroom, a bit mean-spirited.

Early on the Sunday immediately following Dr. Zamenhof's speech, the Majstro roused me from my bed and asked me to go with him to the local church. He wished to attend a mass there. "In a spirit of openness and brotherhood," he told me. I had little enthusiasm for the gesture, noble though it seemed. Sore and chafed from my deflowering of Fraŭlino Bernfeld, I worried that something about me, forever and irrevocably changed, would publish to the onlooking world that I was now a mad sex fiend. Staying in bed, lolling lazily in the sheets, my reserves spent and renewing, I had only to close my eyes, and I could see her again in my jacket, bearing down on me, her breasts like the mountains of a long-sought homeland coming nearer and nearer as the pilgrim returns.

But who could refuse Dr. Zamenhof anything?

"I didn't bring a talis," he fretted, as I found my clothes in the morning's near darkness, my legs, my arms, my hips aching sumptuously. "It's been years since I've had the need to don one."

"They'll have them there, I suppose."

Apparently, however, Christians pray without the need of special garments. This was our first surprise upon entering the cathedral in the fortified old city. The second came when a man, the priest, ran up to us as we entered the narthex, his mouth bent down so violently at the corners, it resembled one of the circumflex accents Dr. Javal so worried about.

"Your hats, gentlemen, your hats! Show some respect, please! You're in the house of the Lord."

"But . . . but we have no other head covering," Dr. Zamenhof explained, whispering with an air of profound embarrassment.

"Off! Off!" the priest said, snapping his fingers. Meekly, we removed our hats. I'd never been in a church before and, of course, neither had Dr. Zamenhof. As we walked in and looked for seats, I tried to take in the sights without appearing like a novice. There were icons, paintings, figurines, statuary tacked up in every niche and on every spare inch of every wall. There were half a dozen confessionals—these reminded me of changing rooms on a beach, though built more solidly—and an odd statue of the Virgin Mother and her infant son inside a boat. The place looked like a cluttered secondhand shop, visually noisy, if not cacophonous. A small girl in a blue dress approached Dr. Zamenhof as we settled into our pew. Go away! Go away! I thought, wanting to fade anonymously into the crowd. I could sense the eyes of the entire congregation upon us, watching with interest our little dumb show. My thoughts, however, and the pleading scowl they no doubt produced on my face, had no effect upon the child as she thrust a small book at the good and now-famous Dr. Esperanto.

"Sir, may I have your autograph, please?" she inquired sweetly.

"Not here," Dr. Zamenhof whispered kindly in her ear. "This place is a sacred place."

He arranged to meet with her outside after the service.

"But they write on their Sabbaths," I whispered, leaning in to him.

His features became fixed in a look of momentary perplexity.

"What?" he whispered back, eying me above the rims of his spectacles.

"I said that, unlike us—although not unlike you and me—they write during their Sabbaths."

"Ah, yes, so they do, so they do. Of course," he said, clucking his tongue. He twisted his neck, looking into the church behind us. "I suppose it's too late to call her back."

"Yes!" I said quietly, as the priest was walking towards us again. What have we done now? What have we done now? I thought, but thankfully, he moved past us and ascended the apse.

ON MONDAY AT 10 a.m. sharp, the first of the general meetings commenced, and the hard work of organizing an international movement began. Citing fatigue, Dr. Zamenhof turned the proceedings over to Rector Boirac as the de facto president of the congress. Firmly, but with his usual tact, Rector Boirac opened the first meeting with a discussion of Dr. Zamenhof's *Declaration of the Essentials of Esperantism*, in which our Majstro laid out, in his usual clear and concise fashion, the tenets of our movement. A fundamento was established—though a liberal one, consisting of nothing more than Dr. Zamenhof's Sixteen Rules of Grammar, the eighteen-hundred-word *Universala Vortaro*, and the practical *Ekzecaro*, or exercise book—and from this, it was declared, no one could deviate while still calling himself an Esperantist. (These texts, down to their typos, so the joke went, were to be sacrosanct.) Any other ideas or hopes linked to Esperanto by its proponents were each man's private affair, for which Esperanto could not be held responsible.

This became known as the Boulogne Declaration.

Later in the week, an official language committee was proposed and voted in. There was a great deal of resistance to an international organization, however, and Dr. Zamenhof's long-cherished hope of founding a league of Esperantists was roundly defeated.

"It's impossible, I suppose, to rule a group of individualists and eccentrics," Fraŭlino Bernfeld whispered to me, as we sat in on the proceedings. As always, she was correct: how *does* one organize a bevy of mavericks, visionaries, oddballs, loners, and utopianists? The question was even more thorny since the French had joined the fray: children of the 1870s, they'd all been schooled in the rampant individualism characteristic of their age. Still, I confess, the issues under discussion impressed me less than did the fragrance of Fraŭlino Bernfeld's perfume and the slightly wet feeling of her skin. (Though by the sea, the days at Boulogne, by noon, grew quite hot.) The two of us found every opportunity, every opening in the official schedule, to casually wander away from each other, strolling with apparent aimlessness, often in opposite directions, so that as we arrived at her suite or at my room no one might come to know of the hours we spent together in bed, refining and perfecting the activities we'd discovered a mutual interest in that night upon the beach.

Fraŭlino Bernfeld's bed became a garden of delights, a haven of long, languid afternoons with the cool sea light frizzling in through the gauze of her drawn curtains. Focusing our attentions exclusively upon each other, we were only dimly aware of the shadows that fell across us, crossing the bed and the floor, climbing the wall, circumnavigating the room like the gnomon of a sundial, as days passed in this fashion. While others' often booming voices filtered through the open window from the square below, we spoke only in whispers and half phrases. Everything was succulent and wet. Beads of perspiration fell from my nose onto Fraŭlino Bernfeld's breast beneath me. The valley of her neck, where I planted my kisses, was slick. Our arms were slathered, our hair moist and dripping. As the hours ran down and the time for emerging again into the congress drew near, we finished our slow, bleary, convulsive lovemaking with climaxes that were but anticlimaxes, so rich and deliriant had been everything preceding them. Indeed, there was something disappointing about finally uncoiling the tensed spirals of the kundalinic snakes curling deep inside our groins, as doing so meant a cessation of the forever forward motion of uncon-cluded desire. Afterwards, we bathed, like children, in the tub, Fraŭlino Bernfeld sitting and I lying with my legs around her hips, or I sitting and she holding me in the brace of her long, smooth legs.

Much, of course, had been said throughout the congress on the now-proven utility of Esperanto. The language was flexible, pliant enough for every use from casual conversation to the ordering of a drink in a bar; one could give a speech in it or run a meeting with it or employ it in the highest of literary endeavors. I can attest, however, as could Fraŭlino Bernfeld, that the international language is suited, as well, for the mani-fold uses of love. As we had, in Berlin before boarding the train to Paris, agreed henceforth to speak only in the international tongue with each other, we made no exceptions, whispering words of passion, in the ex-quisite privacy of our bedchambers:

"Via buŝo je la ektuŝo donacas tute jam sian molecon de veluro!"

"Ho! Mia amanto, mi ludos viran rolon kun plezuro, rajdonte vin kun arta kokso-lulo!"

"Dum inter viajn du fermurojn, mia kara, premiĝos mia kapo kaj mia lango vibros kun fervoro!"

Sed, sufiĉe, leganto, mi estas maldiskreta kaj ĉi tiuj aĵoj estas neniom da via afero, vere!

Exhausted and enthralled, by the last hours of the congress, I felt drained, emptied, tapped, but deliriously happy. My lower limbs were as rubbery as a trio of garden hoses, and it was soon sufficient to merely see Fraŭlino Loë or to fall asleep near her in the afternoon or to catch sight of her talking, across the room, in a passionate debate. I had, I thought, no further need to touch her or to kiss her or to stroke her so that the sweet waters of her desire welled up for me, until in fact, I did touch her or kiss her or stroke her, and then I was on fire for her again. In public, we made our plans and parted as abruptly, as coolly as possible, meeting at her door or at mine or, as our desire grew too insistent, in the servants' stairwell or in the laundry room, bribing this laundry maid or that steward to lock the door and look the other way, so that, at the last moment of the congress, after the group of delegates had been photographed in impressive rows upon the hotel lawn, when every man threw his hat into the air and, with a crying hullabaloo, shouted out, Vivu Esperanto! Vivu Zamenhof! Vivu Michaux! I, standing among them, added my own vivuojn—Vivu Fraŭlino Loë! Vivu Amo! Vivu Sekso!—before searching with the other men among the earth-downed hats for my cherished square-crowned derby.

THINGS COULD NOT have been more different than they had been the last time the five of us stood together in Berlin's Zoologischer Garten station. As Fraŭlino Loë and I took leave of the Zamenhofs, seeing them to their rightful train, I took a moment to reflect. Though only one month had passed, our lives had all changed radically. Fraŭlino Bernfeld and I were no longer bitter opponents, as we had been when we were last here. Esperanto, once the strange hobby of an odd fifteen-year-old boy, was, if not completely established, known beyond the circle of its adherents and well on its way to transforming the world. Dr. Zamenhof was world-famous. He should have been pleased, but no, he was restless instead.

He'd realized, he told me as I escorted him between trains, that although a universal auxiliary language might ameliorate differences in speech and nationality, differences in creed remained a sticking point. "Hasn't this been made abundantly clear by the French Esperantists' refusal to allow me to recite the final stanza of my prayer?"

He was right, I supposed. If most of humanity, worshipping the same God, felt free to oppress and even kill those who offered their praises to that God in an insignificantly different manner, would a common language really pour a cooling water over their raging tempers? Would it do anything other than allow one man's murderer to explain to him, clearly and fluently, the precise theological reasons for which he was being murdered?

"No, clearly something more is needed," Dr. Zamenhof said, and with a certain modest pride, he revealed to me that, one night at the congress, unable to sleep, he had locked himself inside the sitting room of his suite. Dressed in his pajamas and night robe, pounding away at the typewriter he'd borrowed from the concierge, he'd composed a new pamphlet. Buoyed, no doubt, by the sheer giddy, ridiculous successes of the First Universal Congress occurring all around him, he'd invented a new scheme to further redeem humanity from the dark night of its eternal slumbers. People would scoff, he knew; they'd throw that old quotation of Kant's at him — that nothing straight was ever built from the crooked timber of humanity — but what did he care? "If eighteen years ago, I'd listened to these scoffers, why, I'd've never published my grammar, and eighteen years later, I wouldn't have been standing in front of nearly a thousand Esperantists!"

Indeed, the language he'd authored as a "mad" boy in Białystok was now being considered for inclusion in the curricula of all French schools by the French ministers of justice and education!

And so that night, in a burst of electric white heat, he had created Hillelism, or — more properly, in Esperanto — Hilelismo, named after Hillel, the first-century Galilian rabbi who'd been Jesus's teacher, one of whose guiding principles was "Do not do unto others that which is hateful unto you."

"Just as Esperanto is a neutral universal auxiliary language," Dr. Zamenhof explained to me, "so Hilelismo will be a neutral universal auxiliary religion!" He ducked his head. "Say what you will, call me a naïve dreamer, but that morning, as I lay my head upon my arms at the desk in my hotel suite and fell asleep, I dreamt of Hillelist temples, exalted palaces of music and light, erected in every city in the world — cities renamed according to Hillelist-Esperantan principle: Berlino, Nov-Jorko, Jerusalemo—where Hileluloj from different lands were gathering to practice a general religion for all of mankind, one that was emptied of superstition, meaningless ritual, and hate-filled dogma. Oh, Dr. Sammel-sohn, in my dream, I stood in one of those green-domed temples—yes, I did!—and I listened to a mighty orator intoning (in Esperanto, of course, so that everyone might understand) the words of all the holy teachers of mankind—Moseo, Jesuo, Mohamedo kaj Budho. And there were angelic choirs singing hymns based upon the psalms, but with all the violent and ethnocentric parts excised. Impossible?"

"Who can say?" I said, laughing.

"Why, five years ago," Dr. Zamenhof went on, "Boulogne would have seemed equally impossible, a mad dream, and yet we dreamt it, and—now, look!—it's real."

He kissed me and Fraŭlino Bernfeld good-bye, and he boarded the train, helping Klara and Lidja inside. When he turned back to us, he said, "I feel so restless." He rubbed his hands together excitedly. "There's just so much to do!"

FRAŬLINO LOË PROVED equally restless.

Foolishly I'd imagined our engagement would distract her from her desire to be married, that an engagement, like a new toy for a child, would be sufficiently interesting in itself. This wasn't the case. On the contrary, the engagement proved a thing of no value. It was like a pair of trousers delivered by the tailor before the rest of the ensemble: there's nothing one can do with it but lay it aside and wait for the jacket and vest to arrive. I couldn't even distract Fraŭlino Loë's attention with the purchasing of rings, as her father, following Dr. Freud's instruction not to stand in our way, had given her her mother's band to use. A furious impatience seemed to propel Fraŭlino Loë. If I had a heller for every time she said, "Darling, please, don't you agree it's time we set a date," I'd have had no need of a dowry.

As for me, it's no exaggeration to suggest that the prospect of a wedding filled me with terror. I tried to explain this reaction to myself by using Dr. Freud's new methods of self-inquiry. Given my history, it was clear that a wedding, specifically my own, should be a source of anxiety. After all, when had I not been emotionally brutalized at a wedding?

But these were only the lies I used to justify my reluctance. Had I revealed them to Dr. Freud or to any one of his acolytes, a growing number of whom were now working as psychoanalysts in Vienna, I've no doubt that he (or they) would have believed them. At times, I actually believed them myself. But at other times, I couldn't conceal the truth from myself. As much as I loved Fraŭlino Bernfeld, I could never flee the hectoring voice that hounded me, crying, Wait, Yankl! Don't do anything rash. You pledged yourself to me and it's only a matter of years before I am reborn!

That voice belonged to Ita, of course, though I'd last heard it issuing from the throat of Émile Boirac, Dr. Zamenhof's great friend and the newly appointed president of the Esperanto Language Committee.

RECTOR OF THE Universities of Grenoble and Dijon, and a philosopher of no small renown, Émile Boirac was an ardent, if amateur paranormalist. In addition to his work on behalf of Esperanto, Rector Boirac's contributions to world culture include coining the term *déjà vu*. He was also the first man to define *metagnomy,* knowledge acquired through cryptesthesia, later known as ESP.

Late one evening at the congress, Fraŭlino Loë and I stumbled across his demonstration of psychic conductibility by accident. Having spent the greater part of the night ravishing each other, we thought to slink down to the hotel kitchens to beg (if the staff were on duty) or to steal (if they were not) a plate of food. In a parlor off the main lobby, we noticed a rather large crowd of samideanoj seated across from a long table and, intrigued, we slipped in among them, unnoticed.

Rector Boirac stood at one end of the table, his great shock of electric white hair looking at once distinguished and mad. He wore a sturdy brown suit, a brown bow tie, and a brown vest. Near him was an empty kitchen glass stationed upon a saucer and a pitcher filled with what looked to be ordinary water.

On the other end of the long table sat a woman, the upper part of her face concealed by a black handkerchief knotted at the back of her head.

One could make out the small triangular tip of her nose and the dimpled point of her chin, but little else. Her hands rested, palms downward, on her knees.

The crowd breathed in an air of silent expectation.

Having concluded his preparations, Rector Boirac addressed us now, clapping his hands together. "Estimataj gesinjoroj," he said. "Will a volunteer kindly determine that Fraŭlino Zinger cannot see through the cloth I have draped about her eyes?"

A young man, standing up, gave an abashed nod of greeting to the audience from which he'd only just separated himself. Obeying Rector Boirac's instructions, he waved his hand before the blindfolded face of Fraŭlino Zinger, an attractive Polish Esperantist whom I'd noticed, glancingly, before Fraŭlino Loë and I had reconciled.

"That's hardly sufficient, Sinjoro Diderot."

Sinjoro Diderot nodded unhappily.

"Of course, do not harm her," Rector Boirac said, whereupon Sinjoro Diderot swung his arm across his own chest, as though it were a tennis racquet, and volleyed the back of his open hand towards Fraŭlino Zinger's face, stopping an inch away from it, in reaction to which Fraŭlino Zinger flinched not at all. "Any doubts?" Rector Boirac asked his audience, leaning on the table with both arms. "No then?" Not a word from any one of us. "Multajn dankojn, Sinjoro Diderot. You may return to your seat."

Sinjoro Diderot bowed towards the rector and towards Fraŭlino Zinger (though she of course couldn't see him) before melting back into the crowd.

The rector turned to the masked woman. "All is well, fraŭlino?"

"All is well, Sinjoro Rektoro."

It was nearly three in the morning, but Fraŭlino Loë and I exchanged glances, eager to see what might happen next. Rector Boirac cleared his throat. "May I trouble one of you to send to the front, wrapped in a kerchief as an added precaution, a smallish object of negligible value?"

The crowd drew its attention in towards itself murmuringly, various ones half-standing and peering over various other one's shoulders, until a man in the center elected himself our volunteer. Concealing something in a silk kerchief, which he'd knotted into a small bag, he passed the item to a woman in front of him who did the same to a woman in front of her, et cetera, et cetera, until a diminutive man in the front row delivered the little wandering rucksack into Rector Boirac's hands.

"Now!" Rector Boirac ran his fingers through his white hair, ruffling it further. "I shall, as a further precaution, stand well behind Fraŭlino Zinger, far from her on this side of the table. I shall turn my back to the room and untie the kerchief, and then I shall place the item, which is inside it, into my mouth, at which point, Fraŭlino Zinger, as I am now asking her to do, will identify it and, if she can, describe its particulars to us in detail."

As promised, Rector Boirac turned his back on us. His shoulders juddered as he untied the cloth. He flung the handkerchief across his shoulder for safekeeping. His hands moved to his mouth, and when he turned to us again, it was filled, it seemed uncomfortably so, with the object in question. His snowy eyebrows raised as high as imperial flags, he rolled the object across his tongue as though he were sampling a new wine.

Fraŭlino Zinger hesitated. "Is it . . . ?" she said.

"Mmjes?" Rector Boirac answered, keeping his mouth tightly closed.

". . . a ruby-encrusted tie clasp?"

Rector Boirac's face brightened with a look of triumph.

"With . . ." the Fraŭlino stuttered, her brow knotted beneath the black kerchief, "I don't know why I want to say this, but . . ."

"Mm? Mm-hm?" Rector Boirac nodded.

". . . an inscription on the back that reads . . . oh my, but that's very strange." Fraŭlino Zinger seemed to strain behind the black blindfold, leaning forward as though peering into a difficult text. "'Festina lente'?" she said slowly.

Rector Boirac spat the object from his mouth like a man spitting out an ill-fitting set of dentures and held it up for all to see. It was indeed a tie clasp with a red line of stones set into it. "Sinjorino, mi petas," he said, holding the little stick before the eyes of a woman seated in the first row, "would you kindly read to the assembly the inscription on the back of this tie clasp?"

The woman made a great show of finding her glasses inside her reticule before settling them onto the bridge of her nose. Growing impatient, Rector Boirac smiled over her head towards the rest of us. Finally, the woman read the words in a plumy English accent: "Festina lente," she confirmed. She translated: "Hurry slowly. Or in Esperanto: Rapidu malrapide."

Rector Boirac quickly removed the object from before her eyes. "Sinjorinoj kaj sinjoroj!" he said, holding the tie clasp up to the sound of applause. He returned to the table, doused the tie clasp into the water glass, in order, I assumed, to rinse it of his saliva, and placed it on the kerchief in which it had been wrapped. He stood with his arms behind his back, his broad belly pushing forward, rocking on his heels. He reminded me of a happy schoolboy, having successfully concluded a science report. "I will now demonstrate the conductibility of psychic force," he said. "May I trouble one of the ladies for an ordinary hat pin?"

His request was immediately fulfilled, the pin passed from hand to hand until it reached the rector's own. "Please note," he said, silencing us by pointing a finger towards the ceiling. "Fraŭlino Zinger, have we discussed what I am about to do?"

"No, Sinjoro Rektoro."

"You have no idea what I am about to do?"

"None whatsoever."

She spoke with a calm I found unnerving. She swallowed, and I watched her throat move. It felt odd watching someone who couldn't watch you back; and apropos of nothing, I have to say, she possessed a not unattractive bosom.

"Good, good," Rector Boirac said. "Now Fraŭlino Zinger, you can hear by the sound of my voice that I am standing far away from you, yes?"

"Yes, Sinjoro Rektoro."

"You can feel that there is no one else near you?"

"Correct."

"Your hands are placed palms downward on your lap?"

"They are."

"Very good. Excellent." Rector Boirac then pricked his hand with the hat pin.

"Ho!" Fraŭlino Zinger cried out, clutching at her own hand.

"Please show your hand to the audience, my dear."

Fraŭlino Zinger obeyed, and the audience gasped: her hand was bleeding from a small puncture wound. With exquisite care, Rector Boirac approached her and settled a clean handkerchief into her hand.

"You're bleeding, my dear," he said to her quietly. "It will soon stop, and there is no need to worry."

"Impossible," Fraŭlino Loë murmured, leaning into me. Her fingers laced inside mine, she pressed her shoulder against my shoulder.

"Now ladies and gentlemen," Rector Boirac roared, "watch closely." He filled the glass on the table with water from his pitcher. "As you can probably hear, Fraŭlino Zinger, I have filled a glass with ordinary water from the kitchen." She nodded. "I ask you to concentrate as fiercely as you're able and to project your sensibility, your mental or psychic sensibility — if you're understanding me — into this glass of water."

"My mental or psychic sensibility? Into the glass of water?"

"That is precisely what I'm asking you to do, my dear."

"I hope I'm doing what you ask correctly."

"Well, we shall soon find out, won't we?"

Like a skilled magician, Rector Boirac silently drew our attention, with one hand, to the hat pin, which he held high in the air with the other. Transferring it to the other hand, he used it to prick the surface of the water in the glass, and each time he did so, Fraŭlino Zinger gave out a little jump. "Oh! — Oh! — Oh!"

Rector Boirac filled a second glass with water and placed it on the side of the table nearer Fraŭlino Zinger. He inserted the ends of a single copper wire into each glass. "Behold!" he finally said. Each time he plunged his finger into the glass nearer him, Fraŭlino Zinger shrieked, as though he had poked her in the ribs. When he swished a pencil in the air above the glass, she ducked her head, covering it with her hands, as though to avoid a blow. After Professor Boirac silently removed the wire from his glass, these same movements had no effect upon the woman at all.

"Hah?" Fraŭlino Loë cried, grasping my hand.

"And now," Professor Boirac began another demonstration, but Fraŭlino Zinger interrupted him.

"Why is she saying those things, Sinjoro Rektoro?"

"I'm sorry, mademoiselle," he said. "But why is who saying what?"

By the look transfiguring his face and also by his dropping into French, Rector Boirac made it seem as though this was not part of his scheduled routine.

"Do you not hear it?"

"No, mademoiselle," Rector Boirac said, turning towards the crowd, "we hear nothing."

Fraŭlino Zinger nodded patiently as though listening to an invisible someone whispering into her ear. "I'll ask him, but I've no idea if he'll agree."

Leaning both hands against the table, Rector Boirac looked into the eyes of the crowd with as much astonishment as we were projecting towards him, I'm sure.

"Professor Boirac, forgive the intrusion," Fraŭlino Zinger said, "but a poor soul asks permission of the great philosopher and scientist to speak."

"Ho, he's gotten more than he's bargained for tonight, old Boirac," Fraŭlino Loë murmured, squirming happily at my side.

"It's all part of the charade," I told her. "These two are clearly in cahoots."

"You think so?" Fraŭlino Loë said.

"There's no other explanation for it, is there?"

Someone nearby shushed us.

"The spirit knows of me?" the rector was saying.

Fraŭlino Zinger seemed to listen to the invisible presence as though she were taking dictation. "Here," she finally said, "where time does not bind us, and there is no future and no past, the good professor's book *L'avenir des sciences psychiques* is widely admired and even more widely discussed."

Rector Boirac seemed openly pleased with this late-breaking news from the other world. "Remarkable!" he exclaimed. "The book is only half-begun and sitting, still in drafts, in the top drawer of my desk back home!"

(He wouldn't, in fact, publish it for another twelve years.)

"Well, here, it's all the rage," Fraŭlino Zinger told him.

"Oh, this is nonsense! These two have clearly rehearsed all this!" I said.

"Ŝa, Kaĉjo!" Fraŭlino Loë whispered, tapping me on the knees.

Though seemingly wildly flattered, Rector Boirac was ever the cautious technician. "And how does the spirit propose to make itself known to us?"

Fraŭlino Zinger held another silent conference with her invisible correspondent. Finally she said, "The spirit asks that I make my body available to her."

Rector Boirac grunted. "It would be better if I availed my own body for that purpose"—he fretted over the issue—"though I'm reluctant to surrender the high tower of scientific objectivity. Will the spirit assure us no harm will come to the fraŭlino through this agreement?"

"The spirit promises," Fraŭlino Zinger said, "although she says it will exhaust me."

"And Fraŭlino Zinger, are you willing?"

"I am, sir."

"Well then," Rector Boirac said, "I suppose I agree as well."

With that, Fraŭlino Zinger stood and laced her hands in front of her diaphragm. "The spirit will inhabit my body as a hand inhabits a glove, using my throat and my voice but for her own purposes." She stood firmly on the balls of her feet; and though she was blindfolded, her face, still behind the black cloth, seemed to transform.

"There is someone here in the room with us tonight," the fraŭlino said, in a voice not quite her own.

"Someone?" Rector Boirac inquired.

"A man who has forgotten a promise he once made."

"To you, Spirit?"

"Indeed, to me."

A queer feeling passed through me; I won't deny that. Fraŭlino Loë's brow beetled, and I could feel her peering into my face, delighted by the show. Without returning her look, I manufactured a small frown meant to convey my complete and utter incomprehension at the turn the proceedings had taken.

"And will you identify this man, Spirit?"

"Oh, there's no need of that. He knows who he is."

"Ah," Rector Boirac said. "Naturally, naturally."

Blinded by the black kerchief, Fraŭlino Zinger nevertheless seemed to peer into the crowd. "He's here. There." She pointed with her chin. "Sitting with his whore."

The audience, gasping collectively at this pronouncement, began to search within itself for the guilty party.

"Don't pretend to her that you don't know what I'm talking about," the spirit cried.

Oh dear, I thought.

Fraŭlino Zinger's movements seemed delayed, slightly staggered, as though the impulse behind each was being mediated through the brain of a second being. "I only want what was promised me. He told me he loved me. And he promised he'd wait for me, and now I'm alive again!"

"Alive again?" Rector Boirac asked, maniacally scribbling notes.

"Oh, the poor thing!" Fraŭlino Loë whispered to me.

"Is this making sense to anyone?" Rector Boirac asked.

No one answered him, naturally, and before I quite realized what I was doing, I had stood.

"Rector Boirac," I announced to the room in general, trying to seem as patently unmanned as I could, "I have no idea what any of this means, nor who this spirit, if spirit she is, might be. But as a medical man, I must tell you that the fraŭlino appears to be in the grip of some terrible hysteria, and I must advise putting an end to this demonstration before she is harmed. I fear that the strain might prove injurious to her health."

I hated to sabotage the explorations of an honest researcher, and I presumed I could explain everything to him later on in private, but at the time, I was a wreck, fearing what might next be said in Fraŭlino Loë's presence.

"Don't you dare touch me!" Fraŭlino Zinger screamed the moment Rector Boirac took a step towards her. "Dr. Sammelsohn!" she sneered. "You don't think I know what happened on the beach the other night, but I do! And I'll be happy to gossip about it all night long!"

"Kaĉjo!" Fraŭlino Loë whispered, clutching my hand.

"Spirit!" I said fiercely. "Do not add slander to the list of your sins while you're yet burning in Gehenna!"

"But I'm *not* in Gehenna!" she wailed. "Thanks to my husband's goodness, as I'm trying to explain to you, I was spared the fires of Gehenna, and now I've been reborn!" Seeming to peer over her shoulder, Fraŭlino Zinger suddenly exclaimed, "Oh, no! They're coming! I have to get off the line."

"Line?" Rector Boirac squinted.

"None of this is allowed," she told him. "Listen to me, husband," she called generally to the room. "Meet me tomorrow night at midnight in the ballroom on the mezzanine and I'll explain everything to you there! The fraŭlino's getting too weak! I can't hold on to her."

"Ita, wait!" I cried, and for a moment, everything was quiet, and in that silence, I heard only one sound: Fraŭlino Loë saying, "Ita?"

As Fraŭlino Zinger crumbled into a heap upon the floor, half the room ran to her, while the other half, in search of a credible explanation, turned to me.

"Husband!" Rector Boirac suddenly exclaimed, as though Ita were now using his throat as a megaphone. "Don't forget—you pledged yourself to me!"

IT WASN'T EASY, but no matter how much Fraŭlino Loë needled me about *Who is this Ita?* or *How did Fraŭlino Zinger know those things about you? about us?*, I feigned absolute and total incomprehension. I imagined myself a soldier captured by a cruel enemy, who would stop at nothing to break the truth out of him.

"No, I have to say I'm as confounded by it as you are, my darling. Flummoxed, really. In the cold rational light of day, none of it seems real."

"And did you ever know someone called Ita?"

"No. Well, yes, I suppose, I did. Once."

"Oh, Kaĉjo!" She surrendered to tears.

"But no, it was nothing like that! No, no! She was only a poor idiot girl in our town—"

"A poor idiot girl?"

"Yes, who could barely speak."

Having cracked under Fraŭlino Loë's line of questioning, my new strategy was to tell her as much of the truth as I needed to in order to keep her away from the rest of it.

"She simply repeated the last words anyone said to her."

"Oh, how awful!" Fraŭlino Loë stirred her coffee.

"Yes, her grandfather had tried to strangle her with a shoestring after she was born, or so the story goes, and this resulted in some sort of permanent damage to her brain. Both my parents were very kind to her, as was my entire family, actually. My father even tried to find a husband for her, but of course, that proved a total disaster."

"Of course."

"Precisely."

Taking a sip of her café au lait, Fraŭlino Loë stared out the café window towards the beach. As she swallowed, I watched the muscles of her throat working. She really was an extraordinarily good-looking woman. Her brow creased, and she pierced me with a hard look. "But how is it then that you thought you recognized her voice?" she said.

"Sorry?" I said, pretending not to hear her over the din of the espresso machines.

"If," she reiterated, "when you knew her, she could only repeat what other people said to her, how is it you thought you recognized her voice, during Rector Boirac's presentation, when she was speaking in full sentences? You called her by name, I thought."

"Yes, that's exactly what makes it impossible upon further reflection. It couldn't have been the Ita I knew at all. Which makes me shudder to imagine that someone was watching us on the beach the other night."

"Oh God! But who? Fraŭlino Zinger, do you think?"

"Or Boirac, more likely."

"It's too horrible to contemplate!"

"I know, my darling, I know."

I'd gotten myself into a terrible quandary. Fraŭlino Loë sensed—correctly, I might add—that I was concealing something from her, most likely an affair with the not unattractive Fraŭlino Zinger, conducted in the early days of the congress before she and I had reconciled. (Certainly, as an explanation, an affair with a beautiful Esperantistino made more sense than did the transmigration of my long-dead wife inside her handsome body. It wasn't inconceivable that a jealous Fraŭlino Zinger might have followed us to the beach, observed our lovemaking, and in a fit of spleen announced our affair to the world.) Regrettably, however, although Fraŭlino Loë's suspicion about Fraŭlino Zinger kept her well away from the truth, it opened an emotional chasm between us. Having created this chasm, all I wanted to do now was leap across it and confess everything to her, the story of my marriage to Ita, her suicide, her reappearance in Dr. Freud's consulting rooms, et cetera, et cetera, but the thought of Fraŭlino Loë's father prevented me from doing so. His face seemed to hover in the air between us, and I could only see myself as I appeared to him, a credulous Galitsyaner, an Ostjude, a demon-riddled Jew from the Near Orient. If Fraŭlino Bernfeld came to see me in this way as well, the wedding, I knew, would be off; and while all I wanted was to prevent that from happening, I also wondered if I weren't making a terrible mistake. Ita obviously possessed a devastating and primitive attraction for me, as I apparently did for her; and if Dr. Freud were correct (before he'd suppressed his original theories) we'd been chasing each other for millennia; and unless I imagined it all (as he now maintained), I *had* pledged myself to her, although (as I continued to insist with pharisaical obstinacy) not before two kosher witnesses.

Still, who, given the choice between a beautiful, penetratingly intelligent, and idealistic woman of astounding physical passion and a vindictive murderous shrew, hesitates even for a moment—especially when the former is alive and the latter less so—except a credulous Galitsyaner?

The way forward seemed clear, and yet that clarity didn't prevent me from leaving the warmth of Fraŭlino Loë's bed the following night on the pretext of sneaking back into my own rooms as I always (although usually much later) did, so that I might awaken in my own bed and appear to all the world as though I'd slept there.

Instead, I made a quick and carpet-quieted dash down the hallway to the stairs and into the lobby, where I innocently slowed my pace before dashing up the opposite staircase to the mezzanine. While in the lobby,

I nodded, with a counterfeit nonchalance, to the deskman who, with one cheek pressed against his fist, was sleepily reading through Dr. Zamenhof's *Dua Libro.*

Only one of the ballroom's many doors, the last one I tried in fact, was unlocked and, as I slipped through it and it closed behind me, the light from the lamps in the hallways was eclipsed.

"Hello?" I called out quietly into the darkness, as a clock in the corner of the room struck twelve. "Anybody here?"

The night sky, through the tall windows, offered the barest of light, and I was on the point of searching through my pockets for a match when I felt a presence behind me. An instant later, a pool of candlelight made a puddle at my feet. Before I could turn around to face whoever was behind me, a hand was laid upon my shoulder and, though I might have anticipated it, I nearly jumped out of my clothes with fright.

"Ho, Dr. Sammelsohn," Fraŭlino Zinger said, for it was she, as I saw when I turned at last to face my interlocutor. "I didn't mean to frighten you."

With one hand, she held a candlestick before her breast — the flame illuminated her face from below in a striking chiaroscuro — and with her other hand, she reached out to calm me. I must confess: the intimacy of the moment, the sensation of her flesh against mine, the way the light exaggerated the curve of her bosom, our whispered conversation, her eyes searching mine over the flame of her candle, made me nearly forget my purpose in coming here, or rather nearly made me substitute a second purpose for the first. Also, her face, no longer blindfolded, was lovelier than I recalled.

"I wasn't certain anyone would be here," she whispered. "I almost didn't come myself. It all feels a bit strange and otherworldly, doesn't it?"

"Indeed, it does, fraŭlino," I said with a gentle laugh.

"And the other night exhausted me. I slept through an entire day of the congress today, but I was willing to do it all again."

"And why is that, fraŭlino?"

She shrugged her pretty shoulder. "For the sake of love, I suppose. Shall we sit here?"

She took me by the hand to one of the tables along the dance floor, and we sat with our chairs nearer to each other's than propriety allowed. The fraŭlino's candle was the only true light in the room, and we were forced to huddle near it. I peered nervously into the blinding darkness surrounding us, wondering if anyone were hiding in the gloom. However, I seemed to be the only man fool enough, the only fool man enough, to have answered the spirit's call. As I glanced past the candlelight at the fraŭlino's delicate face—on the point of speaking, she had lowered her head modestly and wet her lips—I wondered if the story I'd invented weren't true. Perhaps a jealous Fraŭlino Zinger had contrived last night's performance and to-night's séance (for that is what I felt certain we were doing here) as a way of stealing me from her rival. Upon more sober reflection, a caper like this seemed as impossible to have planned as to pull off.

"I must say, Dr. Sammelsohn, all this is very strange to me, and I don't know if it will make any sense to you, either. However, the spirit who used my body last night—if that is indeed what happened—asked me to assist her in delivering a message to whoever arrived here this evening."

I nodded and swallowed nervously.

"She said that this man would understand everything."

"I can't say that I will, fraŭlino, but I will try."

"She's near," the fraŭlino said, "but too weak to speak. Last night al-most did her in, she says."

"Ah," I said. I didn't know what else to say.

"But she asks if I might touch you?"

"I suppose that will be all right," I said, "if it will help bring this epi-sode to a definitive conclusion."

Fraŭlino Zinger shyly raised her hand. She hesitated before placing it on my cheek, which she lightly stroked. I looked into her face and was moved by the expression of tenderness I found there. She sighed and seemed to relax a bit. She drew her attention inward. Once again, as on the evening before, she seemed to be listening to a voice I couldn't hear, aware of a presence I couldn't see. Finally, she said, "The spirit is speak-ing to me now, and she asks me to tell you that you're looking quite well and also very handsome." Fraŭlino Zinger nodded. "Tak tak," she said in Polish, though clearly not to me. "I will. Yes, I will." To me, she said, "The spirit apologizes for her rudeness yesterday. Your friend seems to be taking good care of you, and she's happy for that, she says, though of course, she couldn't help her jealous feelings. She says you'll understand that."

"Of course," I said.

"And she regrets her unseemly behavior."

"I assure her there's no need to apologize."

"May I hold your hand, Dr. Sammelsohn."

"Fraŭlino," I demurred, "I'm not certain that would be—"

"It will aid in the connection."

"Well, certainly then."

The fraŭlino took my hand in both of hers. She caressed my palm with her fingers, before bringing it to her lips.

"Fraŭlino," I remonstrated with her.

She nodded, seeming to concede the appropriateness of the rebuke, and she closed her eyes. Oddly, I could feel her hand growing first cold, then warm.

"Are you all right, fraŭlino?"

"The spirit wants you to know that she has been reborn."

"Yes, she has already mentioned that."

"And that she will see you in Paris."

I almost laughed. "But I have no plans to return to Paris, fraŭlino."

"It will be difficult, she says, but she will make herself known to you there."

I shrugged. I could see there was no use in arguing the point.

"In Paris, she will return to you, her dear husband, the love that you gave her in Vienna and that has so transformed her."

"But how will I know her, fraŭlino? Ask her that."

"Only . . ."

"Yes?"

Fraŭlino Zinger's voice darkened, and its tone became aggressive with threats. In fact, she glared at me, her face a sneer.

"Only do not marry that whore, Yankl! I forbid it!"

"Ita?" I said, looking into the fraŭlino's fiery gaze. "Is . . . is that you?"

"I'm warning you!" she said, pointing at me with her finger. "You know I have a temper, Yankl. Don't provoke me! Or I won't be held accountable for my actions!"

"Ita, that's sufficient," I said.

We sat for a moment in silence. Someone outside in the passageway coughed.

"Fraŭlino?" I said softly. "Are . . . are you all right?"

She cried out, "Kiss me, Yankl! I haven't much time here."

The fraŭlino threw herself upon me, though that justifies my behavior not at all, and I'm afraid the kiss we shared grew more passionate than either of us intended. I was kissing her neck when, with a sudden in-breath of air, she bolted upright, her spine rigidly straight, and collapsed into my arms, unconscious.

"Ita?" I cried, holding on to her lifeless body. "Fraŭlino?"

I had no idea what to do. I couldn't leave her here, nor could I, even at this late hour, carry her through the hotel to her room, the number of which I didn't even know. I gathered her in my arms and, holding the candle away from her, stumbled across the dance floor to the ballroom's door. Peering out, I saw that the passageway was empty. I dashed across it and barged into the woman's powder room, where I left the fraŭlino lying on one of its fainting couches.

Despite everything, Fraŭlino Loë and I were married in Geneva on the second day of la Dua Universala Kongreso. Dr. Zamenhof's opening address once again inspired me to throw caution to the wind and to marry on Switzerland's neutral soil. Somehow the sight of this tiny, myopic Jew, thundering out his polemic with all the fire of an ancient prophet, stirred in me a corresponding fire. Dr. Zamenhof was no longer the meek little fellow he'd been a year before, capitulating to an army of French intellectuals. He'd endured a year of calumny from the critics of Hilelismo, and it had toughened him up. (Perhaps because he'd signed the work pseudonymously, as "Homo Sum," his critics felt free to fall upon him like a pack of hungry dogs.) Catholic priests from eastern Europe ridiculed Homo Sum for his theological naïveté, meanwhile accusing him of betraying Christ their Lord. The response from the godless West was no better, and perhaps no critic was as vile as the Marquis de Beaufront. Dr. Javal had warned Dr. Zamenhof that France would never be receptive to these sorts of ideas, and the marquis picked up the flag of mockery and marshaled himself beneath its garish colors.

Dr. Zamenhof had hoped to introduce Hilelismo or Homaranismo, as he now called it (dejudaicizing its name, I suspect, in an attempt to conceal its origins), to a broader audience in Geneva, but the polemic against it had grown so bitter that Dr. Javal advised him against coming to the congress altogether, where a showdown with the marquis couldn't be avoided. That old military strategist General Sébert insisted, on the other hand, that Dr. Zamenhof had to be there, lest his absence deal a devastating blow to all that we'd managed to achieve so far.

Sick over the fracas and simply sick, Dr. Zamenhof retreated to the spa at Bad Reinerz to take the cure, and it was there that General Sébert surprised him with a visit and convinced him to attend the congress, though both men agreed, over sulfurous glasses of Mineralwasser, that the time for Hillelism or Homaranismo (Sébert: "Or whatever name you wish to call what is in fact Heaven on Earth") had not yet arrived.

"Kara Generalo," Dr. Zamenhof took General Sébert's hand, "may calm heads like yours always prevail."

"No more of this utopian skylarking, then?"

"Not for the immediate future," Dr. Zamenhof agreed.

"Yes," General Sébert sighed, settling back into his chair and eying a bevy of beautiful tubercular girls, "the immediate future, like all of the past, will have to do without universal brotherhood, I'm afraid."

DR. ZAMENHOF, HOWEVER, was afraid of no such thing. Though Hilel-ismo and its beardless twin, Homaranismo, may have been rejected, he knew who he was, and on the opening night of the congress, he took ad-vantage of the power conferred upon him not only by his superior posi-tion in our movement — he was, after all, the creator of Esperanto! — but by the moment itself to expound upon la interna ideo, the inner idea.

After thanking the gracious land of Switzerland and its king for a warm welcome, Dr. Zamenhof apologized to the crowd assembled at his feet for his inability to deliver a dry and meaningless speech. "Not only do I detest such speeches, but given everything that is now occurring in my native land, where millions of people are fighting for their most elemental rights, such a passionless speech would be a sin!"

General Sébert, on the dais, stiffened; Professor Cart sighed.

Undeterred, Dr. Zamenhof reminded us that, of course, according to the Boulogne Declaration, politics did not belong at these gatherings. "However" — he pounded his lectern — "the hatred between peoples that is the fundamental cause of all political strife is something that cannot *not* touch us as Esperantists either!"

He spoke in a calmer voice: "You know, we're not as naïve as people think. We don't believe that a universal language will turn men into an-gels. We know very well that evil men will remain evil. But as the world grows darker and men grow crueler, we must clarify for ourselves the inner idea of Esperantism."

The Boulogne Declaration, unanimously accepted at the First

Universal Congress, defined an Esperantist as any person who uses Esperanto.

"An Esperantist is therefore not only a person who dreams of unifying mankind through Esperanto but even one who uses Esperanto for practical reasons, or for economic benefit, or only for amusement, or even, God forbid, for ignoble and misanthropic purposes."

At these words, Dr. Zamenhof threw a searing look at the marquis. He was sitting close to the front and not far from me. In response, the marquis stood and tossed the crook of his elegant cane over his arm and applauded wildly.

"No one is compelled to believe in the inner idea," Dr. Zamenhof counseled us reassuringly. "But the Boulogne Declaration, which made such a belief a private matter, did not make it an *impermissible* one! And neither does anyone have the right to demand that each Esperantist see in Esperanto only a practical concern! Should we rip from our hearts the part of Esperanto that is the most important and the most holy?

"Oh, no, no, never!"

His "Ho, ne, ne, neniam!" rang throughout the brightly lit auditorium like a fire alarm.

"With this Esperanto," he spit out the words, "serving only the goals of practicality and commerce, we have nothing in common!" He roared: "Better we should tear to pieces and burn everything we've written on behalf of Esperanto, better we should rip the green star from our breasts!"

I imagined that by now the marquis would at least be blushing. But no, his teeth sparkled in a wide, open, and admiring smile, and one could even detect a tear glittering behind his pince-nez.

"The time will someday come," Dr. Zamenhof continued, holding the crowd enthralled, despite his shrill tenor, "when Esperanto, having become the possession of all mankind, will lose its inner idea; when it will be merely a language, and one will no longer fight battles for it. But now, we know what inspires our battles. Not practical use, no, but only the holy idea of brotherhood and justice between peoples!"

Then, like one of the ancient prophets he so reminded me of, Dr. Zamenhof threw down the gauntlet, demanding that those of us listening to him declare ourselves either for or against the inner idea.

"Why did they even join with us, these people who want Esperanto only as a language? Didn't they fear that the world would blame them for conspiring in the greatest of crimes, namely the desire to work little by little for the unification of mankind?"

The glowering expression disappeared from his face and he grinned at us, as though we were children who, after a stern talking-to, had been forgiven by our father. "You remember how happy we were in Boulogne, at the 'unforgettable congress,' and you all know very well what it was that inspired us: the inner idea. Let the world mock us or call us utopianists. Let us be fiery about the name utopianist! Let each of our new congresses strengthen in us the love of the inner idea, and little by little, our annual congresses will finally become a constant festival of human love and brotherhood."

Dr. Zamenhof stopped abruptly. We waited for him to continue, but instead he bowed, and for a moment after, there was nothing but silence. Then a great cry filled the hall; it sounded like the shelves in a crystal shop collapsing. The French intellectuals, lined up on the dais, smiled sheepishly, clapping their hands in postures that were equal parts reluctance, irony, and distress.

A voluble and unpredictable fellow, the Marquis de Beaufront suddenly leapt upon the stage, the split tails of his tuxedo jacket flapping behind him like the feathers of some ungainly bird. "Majstro!" he called out, and then to the auditorium: "Sinjorinoj kaj sinjoroj!" He waved his hands about, attempting to silence the crowd.

A prisoner to his own sense of politeness, Dr. Zamenhof stood frozen on the spot, uncertain what was coming next and clearly not knowing what to do. The audience retook its seats and settled down, expecting the marquis no doubt to make an announcement of some sort. Perhaps he would bestow an honor upon the Majstro or address a cautionary word or two about fire exits or lost personal items. Instead, shouting to the upper balconies, he announced that he had been, that very afternoon, to visit Ernest Naville, the ninety-year-old philosopher who was serving as the honorary president of our congress. Too frail to attend, Naville had nevertheless publicly endorsed the teaching of Esperanto in all Swiss schools.

"He repeated to me his interest in our great enterprise," the marquis burbled, "as well as his admiration for the work of our Majstro and his sympathy with us all. Finally, asking me to pass along his greetings to the congress, he said, as I was about to leave him, 'Let us kiss each other as brothers!' and he kissed me twice. Twice, yes!" The marquis cast an affectionate and sentimental look at Dr. Zamenhof. "As I cannot keep that twofold kiss to myself, I beg our dear Majstro to allow me to pass it on to him, and through him, to Esperantists everywhere!"

Like a pugilist, the marquis pulled Dr. Zamenhof to him with his long arms. Holding him captive against his chest, he placed a lingering kiss upon his cheek. Dr. Zamenhof seemed to go limp, his arms slack at his side. Finally the marquis released him, and he remained where he was, paralyzed, while the marquis sank into Dr. Zamenhof's chair on the dais, his hand over his heart, apparently overcome with the emotion of it all.

Fraŭlino Loë and I looked at each other through the unshatterable silence that filled the auditorium. Biting her lip and rounding her shoulders, she stifled a derisive laugh. I was about to essay a derogatory comment of my own, hoping to force the laughter from her throat—the pearling gaiety of her amusement always lightened my heart—when an uproar shook the room, causing me to jump: "Vivu Zamenhof! Vivu de Beaufront!" people on all sides of us were shouting.

Though I was pleased to take the marquis' exuberant gesture as a sign that he'd repented from his derisive attacks upon Hilelismo, not everyone was equally convinced. Carlo Bourlet, leaning into me, whispered a single bitter word: "Judas!"

(A curious note: When asked later about the event, Ernest Naville expressed confusion. "A kiss?" he wondered in astonishment. "I never kissed anyone, certainly not that man and certainly not twice. But why do you ask?")

HANS BERNFELD HAPPENED to be in Lausanne on business during the congress. Over the years, his daughter had tried in vain to interest him in Esperanto, but possessing a dozen languages already, he felt no need for eine Traum-Sprache, a dream language, as he called it. "As in a dream, everything makes sense, until you awaken and discover that all you've been speaking is gibberish." And so, though he was no more than fifty kilometers away, he'd declined to join us.

He avoided me on principle, anyway.

Moments before Fraŭlino Bernfeld and I would legally divorce a few years later, sitting across from each other in Rabbi Chajes's office at the Stadttempl on Seitenstettengasse, preparatory to my signing, upon her insistence, a rabbinic degree of divorce, she revealed to me the truth about our wedding in Geneva. The events leading up to it had not proceeded as I'd imagined. As I recalled the moment, the two of us were once again elated by Dr. Zamenhof's speech, and in the heightened flush, our hearts open and unfearful about the future of mankind and of ourselves, I'd taken her by the hand and suggested, or rather demanded, that we wait no longer but immediately find "somewhere in the free republic of Switzerland!" a rabbi who might marry us that very night. Though Loë made some demurrals — there was the question of her father and her family and the large circle of her acquaintances — she acceded to my wishes.

"Good!" I shouted my joy to the ceilings of Victoria Hall. "Let us find this rabbi then and summon him immediately!"

Fraŭlino Loë, however, convinced me that tomorrow would be early enough, as it would give her sufficient time to telegraph her father in order to urge him to attend.

In reality, everything had been prepared in advance. Unbeknownst to me, Loë had already contacted a Rabbi Himmelglocke, who had already procured two witnesses and hired a local handyman to erect a wedding canopy in the sanctuary of the little pink synagogue two blocks from Victoria Hall. The alacrity with which Herr Bernfeld answered his daughter's telegram raised no alarums of suspicion in my mind either, though his reply to her summons was waiting for her at breakfast the following day.

He'd written to express his displeasure at his daughter's rashness, while promising to arrive as quickly as possible. His telegram concluded: "DO NOT GO THROUGH WITH ANYTHING UNTIL WE HAVE SPOKEN!"

In this whirlwind of preparations — the good rabbi balked at my request that he conduct the ceremony in Esperanto, and Dr. Zamenhof, no keeper of Sabbaths, was not to be permitted, as we'd wished, to sign the wedding contract—it never occurred to me how astonishing it was that, with a single day's notice, the fraŭlino had found in the foreign shops of Geneva a perfectly tailored wedding dress (in which, parenthetically, she looked magnificent). Her hair, freed from its usual binding, was a mass of unruly curls. In addition, she wore long sheer gloves of patterned lace and, beneath her wide skirts, though neither I nor anyone else could see them, matching stockings that immodestly concealed the soft intoxicating flesh of her legs.

We'd scheduled the ceremony for four o'clock, hoping to give her father time to arrive. When half an hour had passed and Herr Bernfeld was still not present, Rabbi Himmelglocke insisted we begin. He had other duties to attend to, as did the witnesses, and our guests, congress participants all, needed to prepare for the evening's festivities. As we were instructed to wear them beneath our top hats, yarmulkes were found for me, for Dr. Zamenhof, and for the three other Jewish Esperantists whom we'd asked to hold up the chupah with him. These included Drs. Javal and Ilia Ostrovski, physician to the recently deceased writer Anton Chekhov and the designer of the Esperanto flag. A prayer shawl was procured for me as well. Those who'd come to celebrate were divided, first by the rabbi and then by themselves, into three groups: men on one side of the sanctuary, women on the other, French intellectuals in the back, where they stood, keeping a cool distance from the exotic proceedings.

The hall was lit by candlelight. Dr. Zamenhof's eyes were shining. A violinist played. My thoughts, as ever, were elsewhere: How many times have I stood beneath a wedding canopy? I wondered. And will this really be the last? (I couldn't possibly have known then that this, the first marriage of my own contrivance—if one didn't count Fraŭlino Loë's clandestine hand in the affair—would be only the third among, at the most recent counting, seven.) Or will Ita hound me beyond her grave to my own? There seemed little likelihood of that, and I congratulated myself on taking a stand against her. I had made my choice: rather than waiting forever for Ita in a Szibotya of my own making, I'd entered the braver newer world of our virgin century with Fraŭlino Loë, meanwhile trading our old sad dzjargon for the glories of la lingvo universala, and my father's linguistic idiocies for Dr. Zamenhof's visionary schemes.

When Fraŭlino Loë appeared in the sanctuary, holding a bouquet of daisies dyed Esperanto green, I knew I'd made the correct choice. She was radiant, a study in white. She was, in fact, so beautiful I could barely look at her and instead lowered my gaze to her small feet, shod in white leather and peeking out from beneath the great, frothy bell of her wedding gown. With each of her tiny steps down the center aisle, the ensemble made a charming rustling sound. As she encircled me the seven requisite times, I caught a whiff of her perfume—cinnamon, honey, clove—and I nearly swooned. I mumbled a prayer of thanks and swore to whatever deity there was to raise our children in an Esperantan home, so that, as a family, we might lead the way to international brotherhood and peace.

Fraŭlino Loë revolved around me with such an hypnotic gait that I did, in fact, become hypnotized. Or at least partially so. I could feel myself standing outside the moment, gazing down upon it, as it were, from inside the synagogue's domed ceiling. Removed from the proceedings in this way, I watched everything with a clarity that was astonishing to me. While Rabbi Himmelglocke was reading the wedding contract in Aramaic, in response to the sound of a door opening, Fraŭlino Loë turned her head. Daylight from the front door spilled in through the second door, momentarily flooding the room. Loë nodded nearly imperceptibly, pleased it seemed, and I looked in that direction as two figures entered the sanctuary: Loë's father, the great Hans Bernfeld, in his long black coat and his luxuriant black beard and, behind him, his amanuensis Herr Goldberg. The little scrollwork of Herr Bernfeld's flaring nostrils was as articulated as the curls in a violin head as he literally turned up his nose at the proceedings before him.

Loë's face darkened in response.

In the strange disembodied state I was inhabiting, I knew exactly what he was seeing: me, a silly man, completely beneath his daughter in status, in fortune, in intellect. He looked at our beloved Majstro and saw him for the humbug that he was: a Don Quixote in a ridiculous top hat, a child pretending to be a man, daydreaming of his useless utopias, making speeches all over the world in an incomprehensible idioglossia. In an age more humane than ours, he would have been put down like a dog. Herr Bernfeld next glanced at Klara, crying into her kerchief. What was she but a simpering little cow, an addlepated Jewess, following her deranged husband, Sancho Panza–like, from kingdom to kingdom as he made a bigger and bigger ass of himself, squandering in the meantime her valuable dowry, which could have been invested towards excellent profit, and destroying their children's names as well as their fortunes?

What were we all, really, but a silly bunch of Jewish dreamers, clowns, and buffoons?

Herr Bernfeld extended his hand, his palm raised towards Herr Goldberg, and lightly gestured with his fingers. Herr Goldberg removed a dossier from his briefcase, which he placed inside Herr Bernfeld's open hand. Imprisoning Loë in his gaze, Herr Bernfeld indicated the dossier while giving her the blackest of looks.

She dropped her eyes to the floor and refused to look at him. He had no choice: surveying the sanctuary like a great predatory bird scratching out a place to sit, with Herr Goldberg, as always, a step and a half behind him, Herr Bernfeld searched for a seat. He moved first towards the women's section before ruling it out. He lifted his eyes towards the balconies, uncertain why the women were not seated there where they belonged. Backing away from the men, repelled, I assumed, by their too-Jewish faces and their bold, misshapen noses, he had no choice but to stand in the back with the French, which he did, shaking hands and exchanging greetings, before adopting for himself their posture of uncomfortable disdain.

By this time, Rabbi Himmelglocke was chanting the Seven Blessings. Loë's veil had been raised, and she was offered the wine to sip. She drank tentatively, choking a little, but then she took one sip after another and seemed so little inclined to release the silver goblet that Rabbi Himmelglocke had to pry it from her hands. He peered into the bell-shaped vessel and saw that there was no longer sufficient wine for me. Scowling, he refilled the goblet and forced it brusquely into my hand.

My drinking was disturbed by his hand clapping. "מזל טוב!," he exclaimed, and my feeling of disembodiment ended. I was again myself, and I recalled, from my previous times beneath the chupah, that I was now expected to break the glass that the good rabbi had wrapped in a silk handkerchief and was placing upon the floor at my feet. I raised my foot, but before I could lower it, Loë picked up her skirts and dashed towards the doors, tripping over the cloth and crushing the little goblet herself.

"Fraŭlino!" I cried as she hurried from the sanctuary.

"Go after her!" Dr. Zamenhof advised me.

"Go! Go!" Dr. Javal seconded blindly.

I did as they commanded. "Fraŭlino!" I shouted again, running to the exit.

"Congratulations, old man."

As I passed their frosty group, I heard the Frenchmen pressing their salutations upon Herr Bernfeld, whom they seemed to have gotten to know, in a single half hour, better than I had during the many years I'd been courting his daughter.

I found la novan sinjorinon Sammelsohn downstairs in the room set aside for the bride and groom to spend a private moment alone together, her enormous wedding dress crumpled in a heap about her. She sat with her head upon the arm of the divan, weeping inconsolably, or at least as far as my abilities to console her were concerned.

Indeed, my presence only seemed to add to her distress. "Go away! Please go away!" she cried.

I was at my wit's end, when a rapping sounded at the door.

"Loë," I said. "There's someone at the door, my darling." I addressed her trembling back. "Should I answer it?" I said. "I will, if my doing so won't distress you any further. However, if you'd rather I didn't, I won't, of course."

Before I could do anything, the door was pushed open from outside.

"Dr. Sammelsohn," Herr Bernfeld greeted me with a coldness all the more icy given the circumstances: I was his son-in-law now, the husband of his only daughter, and the father, I supposed, of his potential heirs. He was carrying the dossier I'd seen Herr Goldberg hand him.

"Herr Bernfeld," I said, returning the greeting in kind.

"If you'll excuse us and wait outside for a moment, Doktor."

"Outside?"

"Are you deaf, man?"

"Wait outside my own yichud?"

I turned from his unsmiling face to Loë's trembling back. Her shoulders juddered in anguish, her wailing swelled at the sound of her father's voice. Should I stand my ground as Loë's husband or surrender my place as her lord and master to its former occupant? Everything—my relations with my father-in-law, my marriage to his daughter, our future happiness—depended upon how I behaved in this moment, I knew.

Either I make my stand now or spend the rest of my life groveling in Herr Bernfeld's majestic shadow.

"I'll be outside if you need me," I said. Herr Bernfeld and I traded places. I was now outside the room, craning my neck to get a last glimpse of my new wife, when he slammed the door in my face. I lay my ear against the paneling but could hear nothing. The musicians Loë had hired were in the upstairs reception hall playing for our guests, guests who were, no doubt, at that moment, waiting to celebrate our arrival into that hall as man and wife. The music interfered with my eavesdropping. From the few sounds coming through the door, however, I could guess that harsh words were being exchanged. I heard intonations of recriminations, invocations of a dead wife, counterinvocations of a dead mother. Did I only imagine it or was a face slapped? And if so, was it his or, more improbably, hers?

After that, if that indeed is what I'd heard, everything went quiet and, a moment later, the door opened from within. Herr Bernfeld moved through its frame, closing it behind himself. Ashen-faced, he brushed past me without a word and quickly ascended the stairs to the small foyer above.

"Herr Bernfeld?" I said, going after him. Turning, he gazed down his long, slender nose at me, as though he were the millionaire he was and I a beggar who had dared to call him by his name. "The reception is that way," I said, indicating that once he left the synagogue and entered the garden, he should follow the building round to the back, on the right. "There's an entrance after a few stairs down."

"I'm well aware of that," he said, returning his hat to his head. With a click of his fingers, he summoned Herr Goldberg, who appeared, out of nowhere, carrying his master's cloak. "Herr Goldberg," Herr Bernfeld said, nodding. The two men exited without a glance backwards through the big double doors of the synagogue—the afternoon sun poured into the dark shul with such intensity I had to shield my eyes—and then like phantoms at daybreak, they were gone.

My instinct, now that I'd seen the trick performed, was to disappear myself, but I lacked the nerve. It was impossible to enter the reception hall without Loë on my arm; neither did I feel secure in approaching her inside the bridal chamber. There was nothing to do but wait for her to emerge, sitting outside her door in the chair the shomer had hastily abandoned when Herr Bernfeld barged past him.

I SAT DOWN and stood up and sat down again.

How much time passed in this way, I cannot say — my emotions were too roiled for me to keep track of the time — but the band seemed to have started its repertory over. The music filtered down through the ceiling above me. Certainly they were performing "Kiss Me Again" and "Because You're You" for a second time.

My mind went to the dossier I'd seen Herr Goldberg handing to Herr Bernfeld in the synagogue. I shuddered to think what was in it. Knowing Herr Bernfeld, I've no doubt he'd hired a detective to look into my past. And what would he find there? Everything I'd been hiding from his daughter, all depicted in the worst possible light: that I'd been married twice, that I'd ruined my first wife and turned her against her family before coldly divorcing her, that the abandonment of my second wife drove her to suicide, that upon my arrival in Vienna, according to a certain Dr. Freud, I'd attempted to rape the woman I was courting, claiming in my defense that she was possessed by a demon. How appalling it all seemed minus one's subjective justifications.

At one point, Dr. Zamenhof wandered down the stairs, in conversation with a Professor Couturat. Dr. Zamenhof looked at me queerly, alarmed to find me on the wrong side of the bridal chamber door, while Professor Couturat, knowing nothing of Jewish custom and having evinced no interest in my person, ignored me, or rather continued to ignore me, or rather failed to see me at all, pursuing his conversation with Dr. Zamenhof instead, the persistent tone of which precluded Dr. Zamenhof from even addressing me.

Transporting little dishes of hors d'oeuvres and flutes of Champagne, they took shelter inside the synagogue's tiny library, where they were soon joined by a third man, a Professor Leau. Despite his physical superiority — Professor Leau possessed the dashing good looks of a matinee idol—he seemed to defer to the stubbier Professor Couturat in all matters, at times even standing behind him like an Oriental wife.

From my chair outside the bridal chamber, I could see them through the doorway of the library as now one, and now the next, paced before it, each speaking passionately, it seemed, although I couldn't hear a word they were saying; though I watched them from this small distance, my mind was on other things, naturally. I had only two thoughts, really. The first, concerning Loë, beat like a drum inside my brain: When will she call for me? When will she summon me? And what have I done *now* to alienate her affections? The second (namely: I wish *I* had a kite) announced itself whenever I thought of the children I happened to have glanced, during Herr Bernfeld's departure, through the open doorway of the synagogue, playing in the square with their tails and their twine. If I possessed a thought concerning Dr. Zamenhof, it was probably something along these lines: How good it is to see the Majstro basking in the admiration he so richly deserves from even the haughtiest of our French intellectuals.

"HUSBAND," LOË SAID.

The door of the bridal chamber opened, and naturally, I lost track of Dr. Zamenhof and the two professors still conversing in the library. I started to rise from my chair, but before I could, Loë crossed the threshold and fell at my knees. She laid her head across my lap.

"Why can he not understand how much I love you!"

"Oh, darling," I said, caressing her hair.

"Why would he come all this way? Just to ruin this day for me, for us!"

"Oh, no, no, it's not ruined, Loë, no."

"He thinks just because I threw that bracelet away when I was nine, he knows everything there is to know about me!"

"Bracelet?"

"When I was nine." She nodded tearfully.

"He told me it was a necklace."

"You see!" She laughed for a moment and wiped away a tear. "That's how much he knows!" Then she began to cry all over again. "And now everything is ruined!"

"It isn't, believe me!" I said, lifting her head and kissing her brow. "The reception is still going on. You can hear it upstairs."

"Oh, Kaĉjo, you're so sweet and kind! Thank God I married you."

"What did he say to you?"

She blew her nose. "It doesn't matter what he said, although it was terrible, terrible. I called him a liar, and I told him I never wanted to see him again."

"What was in that dossier?"

She shook her head. "Let's not talk about that. Never. Let's never talk about that. Rather kiss me instead."

Her kisses were wet and salty from her tears and from some sort of moisture that was coming from her nose. I gave her my handkerchief, and she prettied herself. It took a while, but eventually I convinced her to come upstairs with me to join the others. However, by the time we made our way as a couple to the reception hall, the band were packing up their instruments and most of the guests had gone.

Loë and I returned to Vienna as man and wife and established our residence in her apartments. Relations with her father appeared to have been irreparably damaged, and though we lived in the same building with him and saw him often — for meals and family gatherings and such — the chill between father and daughter never thawed. Loë exhibited towards him what I can only describe as a cordial hostility. They were correct with each other, polite and precise, but there was an unmistakable hatred in her attitude that was quite obviously breaking the old gentleman's heart. I tried to befriend him, but he would have none of it. Though I attempted, in his presence, to bring the conversation round to subjects that might interest him, he continued to treat me with disdain, a circumstance that only incensed Loë further, so that I stopped speaking to him altogether out of fear of worsening the situation.

Despite everything, I was taken on by the firm of Bernfeld & Sons, Inc., so that I might at least appear to earn a salary commensurate with the needs of the class to which I now belonged. Neither the Bernfeld daughters nor the Bernfeld sons-in-law were granted positions of authority inside the family empire — a network of markets and economies overseen by the six Bernfeld brothers and their sons exclusively — and my workdays were an empty canvas. With little to do, I established a free clinic in our offices and saw to the ocular needs of our Viennese employees. My hours were my own, and I'm certain no one would have noticed had I run off to join Herr Franz's Marvelous & Astonishing Puppet Theater, an idea I spent far too many afternoons in contemplation of.

As the time for the Delegation Committee neared, everything changed, however, and my office was suddenly inundated with mail. Multi-colored brochures, pamphlets, grammars, dictionaries began arriving upon my desk at a furious rate, forwarded through Paris from all across the world.

Like the other members of the Delegation Committee, I received pro-
spectuses for nearly two hundred artificial languages and also Professors
Couturat and Leau's compendious *Histoire de la langue universelle*.

THE DELEGATION COMMITTEE was the brainchild of these two Frenchmen whom I'd seen Dr. Zamenhof speaking with at my wedding. May I
say: as far as French intellectuals went, they were la vraie chose. Inspired,
as had been so many of their countrymen, by the Paris Exhibition of
1900, dazzled by the array of international congresses that had been held
in its wake, Louis Couturat and Léopold Leau were convinced that the
time for a universal language had at last arrived. Putting aside their own
work — Professor Couturat was a philosopher of renown, Professor Leau
a prominent mathematician — they formed la Délégation pour l'adoption
d'une langue internationale, and they hoped, through their delegation,
to influence the prestigious International Association of Academies into
deciding, once and for all, which artificial language deserved to be adopted universally. Should the association, a federation of the most important scientific organizations, find itself unwilling to cooperate — and
this proved to be the case: the association declared itself incompetent
in the matter — the delegation, according to its own bylaws, was free to
appoint its own committee to examine the question and, afterwards, to
found a society to promote the chosen scheme.

Having secured the participation of a host of intellectual illuminati
(they bandied about such names as Bergson and James with ease) — it
was their plan to bestow upon Esperanto two gifts of incalculable worth:
the renunciation of its many rivals and the ringing endorsement of a
body of illustrious men.

Dr. Zamenhof expected little from their delegation. Further, he believed the enterprise was fraught with danger. Their committee possessed no political power, no power at all, really, besides the illustrious
reputations of its participants. "And anyone who hasn't been convinced
by the facts or by the strength of our movement will not be convinced
by even a thousand Ostwalds!" he told them at my wedding. "Worse: informed by your committee that there are many artificial languages, more

or less of equal worth, people will say to themselves that although one prestigious committee has chosen one language today, that's no guarantee that tomorrow another, more prestigious committee will not choose another!"

"Pish!" Professor Couturat answered him. "We'd have to have selected our committeemen very poorly for that to happen!"

"Indeed," Professor Leau said, "we'd have to be perfect comedians to perpetuate such a buffoonery!"

HOW I CAME to sit on the Delegation Committee is a story in itself.

Though it was more than a year away, and though la Tria Universala Kongreso lay before it, talk of the Delegation Committee threatened to overwhelm the Geneva congress, and the excitement was palpable. Everywhere one looked, one saw les professeurs Couturat et Leau—planning, scheming, conferring, dashing off to send a telegram to this or that distant luminary. Though both Henri Bergson and William James had declined to sit upon the committee, the professors' enthusiasm for the work remained undiminished.

And one afternoon, when Dr. Zamenhof, Loë, Klara and I had taken a respite from the busying work of the congress, Professor Couturat emerged so unexpectedly from a grove of trees in the Parc de l'Ariana, I was reminded of the character of Rumpelŝtilskino in *Fabeloj de la Fratoj Grimm,* which I was then reading.

"One last thing!" he cried.

"Forgive us for detaining you," Professor Leau said, following him out. "The ladies especially."

"However, the matter is urgent," Professor Couturat said, dropping his pince-nez into his pocket and bowing hastily.

"Professor Couturat and I have been conferring," Professor Leau explained to all of us, while Professor Couturat bore in on Dr. Zamenhof, "and we're of the opinion that Rector Boirac's presence on the committee is an absolute necessity. A must! He's your best advocate."

"Unanimous votes from the committee will certainly gather around his name."

"Oh, it would be laughable," Professor Couturat said, and Professor Leau obliged him by laughing, "and useless, of course—"

"Useless," Professor Leau echoed.

"—if the whole of the committee were formed of Esperantists. Nonetheless, we believe it's essential that Esperanto have at least one strong supporter there."

"En fin: Rector Boirac."

"If he doesn't agree . . ." Professor Couturat pulled an exaggerated frown.

"We don't see what Esperantist we could put in his place."

"Perhaps the marquis?" Dr. Zamenhof suggested, no doubt thinking of our staunchest anti-reformer.

"The marquis?" Professor Couturat repeated with a blank face.

"The marquis?" Professor Leau repeated as well.

"De Beaufront," Dr. Zamenhof elaborated helpfully.

A series of complicated expressions crossed Professor Couturat's face.

"That would be impossible, I'm afraid," Professor Leau said, translating Professor Couturat's grimaces.

"You can't expect us to throw an unknown individual—"

"One without professional or academic standing—"

"—in among the august specialists whose participation in the Delegation Committee we foresee."

Dr. Zamenhof conceded the point. "I'll speak to Rector Boirac."

"Do."

"And urge him to agree. The rector is the necessary link between Esperanto and the delegation, the living symbol of our alliance."

"With him . . ." Professor Leau said.

"Everything will succeed; without him . . ." Professor Couturat made a small clicking sound with his mouth.

"Nothing is certain."

Dr. Zamenhof frowned. "Yes, but I'm only wondering . . ."

"Wondering?" Professor Couturat smiled impatiently.

". . . is it fair?" Dr. Zamenhof said.

"Fair?" Professor Couturat repeated.

"To the creators and proponents of the other artificial languages to so stack the deck in favor of our cause?"

"The other languages?" Professor Couturat scoffed. "As you yourself have said, none of these are more than theoretical schemes."

"Not living languages at all!" Professor Leau said.

"What hope do they have of succeeding?"

"None," Dr. Zamenhof said, "with the cards so stacked against them."

"None, in fact," Professor Couturat stated emphatically, "even if they weren't."

STILL, IT WASN'T easy convincing Rector Boirac to join the Delegation Committee. To begin with, as a government official, he lacked the freedom to leave his academic post in Dijon and come to Paris for indefinite periods of time. Unable to partake in the committee's decisions fully, he would nevertheless seem to have sanctioned them with his own name. And secondly, he didn't trust Professor Couturat.

"Let me ask you only this, kara sinjoro," Rector Boirac said to Dr. Zamenhof, as the two sat in the hotel bar over a late afternoon glass of kvass, smoking their interminable cigarettes. "Why would he want me, of all people, the president of the Esperantiso Language Committee, to sit on his committee when he's promised a lack of partisanship to the competing schemes?"

"Why indeed?" Dr. Zamenhof sighed. "I brought the matter up with him myself."

"Yes? And?"

"He assured me it has nothing to do with partisanship. It's a foregone conclusion that Esperanto will prevail."

"But . . ."

"I know, I know."

"He's a strange little man."

Dr. Zamenhof shrugged. How could he not? How many times had he himself been called a strange little man? He made a clicking noise with his tongue. "He appears sincere, if a bit unworldly. Certainly he won't be able to deliver everything he hopes, and yet, if we can't stop him—and I suggest we can't—we might as well profit from all he wants to give us."

Rector Boirac threw back his head and forced the last drops of his drink down his throat before signaling to the bartender for two more. "And on the days when I can't be present at the meetings?" he asked.

Dr. Zamenhof blew out a cloud of cigarette smoke before nodding towards me. "We'll send Dr. Sammelsohn here as your second."

Loë and I were sitting at the next table over, listening in to their conversation, a fact that must have been obvious to Dr. Zamenhof, otherwise he would never have addressed me so directly. Embarrassed to have been caught out eavesdropping, I pretended not to have heard him at first.

"Dr. Sammelsohn," he said, ignoring my silly pretense, "Rector Boirac and I are discussing the possibility of sending you to Paris to sit upon the Delegation Committee as his second."

"Ah, yes," I said, deciding not to ask them to fill me in on all the details I'd already heard. "Anything I can do for the movement. And as you know, I have the time."

"Good." Dr. Zamenhof lowered his voice. "I thought it might not hurt for you and the sinjorino to get away from Vienna for a while."

"Ho, Kaĉjo," Loë whispered, gripping my hand, clearly pleased that her husband should be so honored with such an important position. But how important was it, really? I was to be a mere second to Rector Boirac. As far as honors went, surely this was a minor one.

"ON THE CONTRARY," Dr. Zamenhof told me the next day at an icecream stand in the Jardin Botanique, "do not for a moment imagine that a second is less essential than the man he supports. No, he is, in every way, the more essential man."

"The more essential?"

Dr. Zamenhof nodded. "Should the principal fall, the second remains. However, if the second falls, there is no one." He lowered his voice and stood more closely to me. "Also, I must tell you this in strictest confidence: I'm not certain how much we can trust Rector Boirac."

"I'm astonished to hear this," I said.

Dr. Zamenhof's eyes narrowed. "What do we know of his true feelings?"

"Surely you don't suspect him of reformist tendencies?"

"Of course not." Dr. Zamenhof glanced about, as though searching the garden for spies. "However, the other day, he said something quite odd to me concerning the letter *H*."

"The letter *H*?"

Dr. Zamenhof pointed with his chin. "We were sitting on a park bench not far from here. And naturally, I was reiterating to him how dangerous even the most innocent attempts at improvement could be for us at this delicate time, and do you know what he told me?"

"No."

"Do you know what he said to me?"

"I have no idea."

"He said: 'So you've given no more thought to reforming the super-signs, then?' 'Oh, what an absurdity!' I cried. 'Our enemies claim that because of these supersigns, Esperanto can't be printed universally. And yet, with the *H*,' I said, 'thanks to the letter *H*,' I told him, 'we can be printed in printing houses anywhere in the world!' 'Yes,' the rector said, 'thanks to the letter *H*—which is a kind of reform, isn't it?'"

Dr. Zamenhof gave me a significant look.

"I'm sure he meant nothing by it."

"Are you?"

"Yes," I said.

"You're quite sure?"

"Yes!" I protested.

Dr. Zamenhof scrutinized me with an intensity I found unnerving.

"Well. Keep your ears and eyes open in Paris," he said. "That's all I ask."

On one score at least, Dr. Zamenhof had been right. I was only too happy to leave the ill-fitting life that had been forced upon me in Vienna. As soon as we arrived in Paris, both Loë and I seemed to relax. Out from beneath the shadow of her father, we walked the bridges and the narrow streets of the Île St. Louis in the autumn light, feeling more ourselves again. We breakfasted each morning at a café overlooking the Seine, reading the morning newspapers or discussing the artificial language schemes we'd immersed ourselves in the night before. I'd had no lovers during my student days, and so it was with an unidentifiable sense of nostalgia that I woke up every morning with this dear woman in my bed, in whose sweet company I dallied before dashing off, with my notebooks and pamphlets underneath my arm, like a university student, to the Collège de France.

CHAPTER 14

Monsieur Couturat was a professor at the collège, and the Delegation Committee convened in a large meeting hall there. I had no idea what I expected to find that first morning, but upon entering its chambers, I was struck by an immediate sense of disappointment. Professor Couturat had always spoken of his committee as though it represented the will of mankind: the members of la Délégation pour l'adoption d'une langue internationale included several thousand scientific academies and university faculties and many hundreds of other such organizations — everything from commercial schools to bicycle clubs from across the globe — each with a large membership. From these great numbers, 331 delegates had been chosen, out of which 253 had elected twelve men to sit on the committee, of whom four had shown up in Paris that day. Though other committee members would drift in and out of these sessions, it was these four men, with Professors Couturat and Leau acting as nonvoting secretaries, who had somehow been empowered to choose a universal language on behalf of the entire world.

Not that these four weren't imposing: they were, and Rector Boirac among them. I greeted him with a firm handshake. "Any subsequent word from that impish sprite?" I couldn't help asking. I'd never gotten a chance to speak with him about that night at la Unua Universala Kongreso, and I inquired about it now, hoping to make it all seem as little important to me as possible.

The rector frowned professionally. "Oh, yes, with the fraŭlino, you mean, at the —"

"At the first congress, yes," I said, nodding.

"Naturally, upon my return to Dijon, I began researching the event."

"Yes? And? Any discoveries?"

"Well, no. Unfortunately, just as I was on the point of arriving at some definitive conclusions, my lab burned to the ground. All my notes were irretrievably lost."

"Oh dear!"

"These spirits can be quite destructive, Dr. Sammelsohn. However, as far as that night in Boulogne is concerned, I wouldn't make too much of it. I can only assume that the highly suggestible mind of the young woman in question—"

"A Fraŭlino Zinger, if I'm recalling correctly."

"—found itself dominated by the mind of a member of our audience whose neurosis was so overwhelmingly potent, so overwhelmingly powerful, that it spilled the banks of his own mind, so to speak, and flooded everyone else's in the room."

I bared my teeth in as good-natured a smile as I could. "Fascinating," I said.

"Isn't it?"

I bid him good morning, and as I did, I banished from my mind, as I had a thousand times since my encounters with Fraŭlino Zinger, the picture of Ita reborn as a pretty little Parisienne, roller-skating down la rue de Quelque Chose, her cheeks rosy with the cold, her pigtails flying. The last thing I wanted intruding upon this august scene was a communiqué from Ita, scrawled via some unnatural means onto our collective perception like an angry graffito.

I MOVED ON and was next introduced to Jan Baudouin de Courtenay, a rangy-looking man with a concise grey beard. A professor of linguistics at the University of St. Petersburg, he had dragged the art of philology, it was said, kicking and screaming into our new century, forcing it to behave like a science. Among his many discoveries were the phoneme, the morpheme, the grapheme, the syntagm, and a host of other queer-sounding -*agm*s and -*eme*s. A French Catholic by birth, he considered himself an atheistic Pole, and though he could speak two dozen languages, he greeted me that morning in Yiddish: אַהאַ! דאָקטער סאַמעלזאָן, גוט מאָרגן! He lowered his voice. "I don't know about you," he said, "but the pretentiousness of this occasion is already beginning to nauseate me."

The angularly bookish man next to him, peering coolly through his rimless spectacles, was Otto Jespersen. A linguist at the University of Copenhagen, he'd revised the teaching of English worldwide, and the battles he'd fought on behalf of modern learning, he told me, had been severe. "And as a consequence, I have no patience for the cant that passes for high-mindedness nor for junk-thoughts passed down from generation to generation and held dear for no good reason!"

The robust German bear of a man standing in the center of the room, his rosy-golden beard reaching the topmost button of his vest, his laughter thundering throughout the chamber, was Wilhelm Ostwald. Destined to win the Nobel in two years, he'd made his name as a chemist and, in addition to publishing twenty-two books and 120 scientific papers, he found time to carry on a lively correspondence concerning pigments with painters and to lecture housewives on the chemistry of cooking, all the while agitating on behalf of causes as varied as world peace and the standardization of book sizes ("the hypotenuse oblong" being the preferred dimension). Teaching at Harvard the year before, he'd undertaken a lecture tour of America to promote Esperanto and had done much to advance our cause in the New World.

"No, no, no, it's much simpler than that," he was saying to Professors Jespersen and Leau. "The energetic imperative simply mandates that all things must act so that crude energy, as one might call it, is transformed into its highest form with the least loss to itself."

"Now, you're going to have to give us an example," Professor Jespersen said jovially.

"Happiness?" Professor Leau suggested, speaking over him, and the two professors nodded at each other, as though they'd contrived an unbeatable chess move against a formidable opponent.

"The energetic formula for happiness?" Professor Ostwald bellowed. "Nothing simpler: it's $H = E^2 - U^2$."

"$H = E^2 - U^2$?" Professor Leau, the mathematician, repeated.

"$H = E^2 - U^2$?" Professor Jespersen puzzled over the strange formula.

"Happiness equals Energy squared minus Unpleasantness squared," Professor Couturat supplied the solution as he joined their little group.

"Indeed," Professor Ostwald boomed. "One need only take the two extremes: heroic men achieve H by increasing their total expenditure of E, while men of timid temperaments prefer to maintain their contentment by decreasing amounts of U."

AS SECRETARIES, MESSIEURS Couturat and Leau had prepared the moment well. Croissants and jam were laid out at every seat. Waiters poured piping hot coffee into porcelain cups. The handsome Leau, dashing from chair to chair, served as amanuensis not only to Professor Couturat but to himself, slipping the two volumes of their *Histoire de la langue universelle* at the place of each committeeman.

Upon seeing me, Professor Couturat let his gaze go slack, as though he hadn't seen me at all, and then apparently remembering who I was, he moved through the small crowd and greeted me with a moist kiss on each cheek.

Lightly clapping his hands, Professor Leau cried, "Gentlemen, gentlemen, it's ten of the clock, and time we were called to order. Professor Couturat," he called to his friend, "will the esteemed professor address our illustrious committee and remind us of the sacred task that we are here to perform in these chambers for the good of all mankind?" Gesturing towards Professor Couturat with an open palm, Professor Leau stimulated the chamber to applause with his own brisk clapping.

Nodding his head humbly, applauding silently in return, Professor Couturat stepped to the table in order to address his committee. This was, there was no doubt about it, his shining hour, the culmination of his seven long years of selfless labor. One could almost see his eyes growing misty behind his pince-nez as he took in the five or six eminent gentlemen who, at his request, were seated now before him. The sun breached the clouds and shone through the tall windows behind him, draping a mantle of light upon his narrow shoulders.

With a raised knuckle, he lightly brushed aside the wings of his mustache.

"Gentlemen," he said, clearing his throat, "may I begin by reminding each man here of how we all felt in 1900 when the Paris Exposition demonstrated that the world had been made anew? No longer would borders and nationalities divide us! No longer would scientists of one nation be unable to speak with scientists from another!" He shook his head, as though in wonderment. "May I say that there was only one other time when I felt like this; and that was upon that rare and grace-filled morning when I stood poised to enter the royal archives of the Hanover Library, armed with nothing but a bibliographic catalog prepared by Herr Bodemann, the chief librarian of that royal institution."

I shifted in my seat. Though I'd meet Professor Couturat only once before, at the Second Universal Congress, I'd already heard him tell this story twice.

"That catalog," his voice trembled with emotion, "with its classification of the archive's great stores—principally the unedited and unpublished manuscripts of Gottfried Leibniz—guided my researches. Better yet, let us say it rendered them possible. Days passed, weeks, months, gentlemen, during which I neither saw daylight nor heard a word spoken in my native tongue. And yet, on that final morning, when I left the depths of that archive to return to Paris, to my apartments on la rue Nicole, I was no longer the same man who had departed them half a year before. Neither the world nor I would ever be the same. No," he said, "I knew then, as the world would soon know, that Leibniz's metaphysic proceeds from his logic and not"—he looked every man at the table in the eye—"his logic from his metaphysic!"

He was silent for a moment, allowing the weight of his great discovery to impress itself upon us. I nearly laughed. Surely, I thought, he's joking. The statement seemed absurd. But when I glanced about and saw that no one else was laughing, I quickly stifled my own laughter.

"Be that as it may," he said, "the world needs a universal language. Just as Leibniz once dreamt. To that end, Professor Leau and I, as you know, founded our delegation." He removed his glasses and twirled them on their ribbon. "Many people, including Mesdames Couturat et Leau—isn't that right, Professor Leau?"—amid warm laughter, Professor Leau nodded his head ruefully—"warned us that our hopes were foolish, that our work would produce nothing but gossamer dreams. And yet, in the few intervening years," Professor Couturat nodded towards Rector Boirac, "I'm happy to say that Dr. Zamenhof's Esperanto has proven to the world that a universal language is no dream at all. Why, I myself attended the congress in Boulogne two years ago, where for more than eight days—for more than eight days, gentlemen!—nearly a thousand people from twenty different lands communicated with each other via the only language they held in common: Esperanto. In a word, this was the most sensational refutation of every pseudoscientific objection by all those know-nothings who would presume to judge an international language without knowing it and who, without penalty, are free nevertheless to assert the opposite of the truth. Although"—he raised an eyebrow—"when one sees how, thanks to the great success of Esperanto, the whole question of a universal language has fallen into the hands of utopianists, fanatics, and enthusiasts, one can hardly blame the cynics." He clicked his tongue against the roof of his mouth. "No, of course, despite its proven brilliance, Esperanto is not the only international language. And over the next two weeks, we shall be looking into more than two hundred such schemes. The question remains: which language is best? which the most perfect? which the most useful to the greatest number of persons?"

Professor Couturat next went over the rules that were to govern us: each language scheme was to be presented before the committee by a representative chosen by the language's creator. In no instance should the author himself present his own case. After each presentation, members of the committee were free to question the presenters. Appointments for presentations were to last, it was hoped, no more than twenty to thirty minutes. At the end of our sessions, the committee would vote upon which language to adopt.

"I think that's everything," Professor Couturat said. "And if not, well, as I'm fond of reminding Madame Couturat: wise are those who hold their tongues."

OUR WORK BEGAN immediately.

Placing his fountain pen in the seam of his cahier, Professor Leau left the room and brought back the first of the presenters. They were seated in the hallway—I'd see them whenever I left the chambers in search of a bathroom or a telephone—each staring mutely at his competitors, some holding elaborate charts or other presentational devices, and their mind-goggling presentations continued on for days. Interspersed with our own private discussions, ably led by Professor Ostwald, we heard reports on Apolema, Balta, Blaia Zimondal, Dil, Dilpok, Lingua Filosofica Universale pei Dotti, Monoglottica, Orba, Spelin, Spokil, and Völkerverkehrsspache, among numerous others.

The tedium was relieved only twice. Once, comically so, when a Mr. Streiff, presenting his own Bopal before the committee claimed that its superiority lay in the ease with which it could be committed to memory, and then couldn't, under the scrutiny of an increasingly short-tempered Jespersen, remember a single word of it; next, and unnervingly so (at least for me), when a man named Boleslas Gajewski entered our chambers as an advocate for Solresol, a language invented eighty years earlier by the musician Jean-François Sudre.

"Thank you for welcoming us here today, gentlemen," Monsieur Gajewski said, laying his violin case upon our conference table. He was accompanied by a small boy, his son, I presumed, although the two looked nothing alike. The child stared at the members of the committee without saying a word, indeed, practically without blinking, while Monsieur Gajewski tuned his violin.

The boy, I remember thinking, looked a little ill and underfed.

At Monsieur Gajewski's request, Professor Ostwald and Professor Baudouin jotted down a few sentences on scraps of paper. These were kept from the boy, whom Monsieur Gajewski had stationed at the far end of the room. Screwing a monocle into his eye, Monsieur Gajewski read each sentence silently before scratching out a phrase on his violin. The child, listening intently, turned to the blackboard and, with a piece a chalk, transcribed each of Professors Ostwald's and Baudouin's sentences faultlessly upon it.

"Marvelous," Professor Ostwald roared.

"Yes, although I've seen such things performed in a circus," Professor Jespersen said. More loudly, he called to Monsieur Gajewski: "Would you mind turning your back to the boy, Monsieur Gajewski? Oh, and young man," he addressed the child, "if you would, please face away from your father."

"He's not my father, sir," the child answered politely.

"Then from Monsieur Gajewski." Professor Jespersen smiled with all the warmth of a man who hadn't had a bowel movement in days. The boy complied, though it mattered little. Even with their backs turned to each other — as a precaution, I supposed, against some secret signaling — the child was able to translate our colleagues' sentences without error.

"Now," Monsieur Gajewski said to me and Rector Boirac, "would you gentlemen kindly do the same?" He stepped away from our table as we hatched out half a dozen lines between us. I could barely think of what to write. *The heart is crooked; who can know it?* was one of my contributions, as well as *The future is a thing of the past.* I've forgotten what Rector Boirac jotted down, but nothing dissimilar. "Please hand the slips of paper to the boy, without my seeing," Monsieur Gajewski said.

With the sort of studiousness available only to a nine-year-old, the child looked earnestly, indeed almost sadly, at the slips of paper we'd handed him, as Monsieur Gajewski tied three colorful kerchiefs over his own eyes.

"Gaston," he said, "I'm ready now."

The boy secreted the pieces of paper into his pocket and stationed himself next to his master. The two seemed to lock hands, although upon closer inspection, it was evident that the child was fingering various parts of Monsieur Gajewski's hand — the fingertips, the knuckles, the vales between his digits — as though it were the neck of a guitar. Monsieur Gajewski's Adam's apple juddered over his cravat. He cleared his throat.

"The past is also a thing of the future, Yankl," he recited, and my heart nearly leapt into my throat. I looked at Rector Boirac, but he had noticed nothing.

Gaston again fretted at the Monsieur Gajewski's large hand.

"Didn't I promise you we'd meet in Paris, my dear?" Monsieur Gajewski recited.

And finally: "I only want to return the love you have given me."

I said nothing out loud, of course, but inwardly, I was trembling.

"Let me see those papers, Gaston," Professor Jespersen said, smirking behind his beard. He scanned the lines before returning the pages to the boy. "Well, not quite a hundred percent, is it?"

Monsieur Gajewski pulled off his blindfold and snatched the slips out of the little boy's hands.

"Gaston!" he cried.

The little boy shook his head. A terrible look passed between them: a silent threat from Monsieur Gajewski, a mute denial from the boy, the unspoken promise of retribution when the two had left our chamber. All signs of life drained from Gaston's face; indeed, he seemed to have disappeared into himself.

Monsieur Gajewski tried to push on, explaining to us that Monsieur Sudre had based his invention upon the tonic scale — "Solresol may be spoken, sung, played upon an instrument, whistled, or as Gaston and I have demonstrated to you today, although imperfectly, communicated via touch" — but it was too late. By the time Monsieur Gajewski had taken seven sheets of colored paper from his violin case, Professor Couturat was already standing.

"Thank you very much, Monsieur . . . Gajewski," he said, referring to his notes. "However, I think the committee can understand the rest of it on principle."

"On principle, yes. Very good, sir," Monsieur Gajewski said.

"We're running over time," Professor Leau added more kindly.

"Over time, yes, I understand," Monsieur Gajewski growled, unable to mask the violence of his anger. "Monsieur Sudre lived and died and gave his life to Solresol, with no one to advocate on his behalf until now, but you're running out of time, I see."

"Léopold," Professor Couturat said firmly.

"Thank you, Monsieur Gajewski," Professor Leau said, rising.

"No, no, thank *you,* thank *you,* Messieurs," Monsieur Gajewski said, recovering slightly. "I'll only leave you with this grammar that I published at great expense to myself several years ago."

"We've all seen copies of it already, thank you," Professor Couturat said.

In reaction to the two Frenchmen, now both standing, Monsieur Gajewski hurried to gather his things, packing up his fiddle and muttering ill-tempered commands to Gaston, who I caught, at one point, gazing, I thought, a little too earnestly at me.

(If he was, as in that moment I feared, the latest incarnation of Ita, there was little I could do, I told myself, to prevent his early death that evening at the hands of his enraged master, and I renounced for the thousandth time any thoughts I might have had of a Parisian dalliance with Ita. Clearly we wouldn't be consummating our love any time soon!)

CHAPTER 15

The days passed and the sessions wore on.

Idiom Neutral—the most recent reformation of Volapük—was presented to the committee by Eugène Monseur, a professor of Sanskrit from the University of Bruxelles. Professor Monseur's demonstration—interrupted with twitters whenever one of us, forgetting his academic title, addressed him simply as Monsieur Monseur—was less a positive defense of Idiom Neutral than a zealot's denunciation of Esperanto.

"All these -*ajn*s and -*ojn*s!" he complained. "One sounds like a Chinaman with a toothache! A Chinaman suffering from a rotten tooth that should be pulled out by its roots, by its Slavonic roots, gentlemen, if you understand my meaning."

A bit of historical elucidation here: Idiom Neutral was created by Volapükists who, having conceived a desire to preserve Volapük, replaced Father Scheyler's strange inventions with variants more resembling those of western European speech until the language bore no relationship to Volapük at all.

"You see where these reforms will lead you?" Rector Boirac whispered to me, as Monsieur Monseur took his leave, although not quietly enough that the rest of the committeemen didn't hear him. "Ah, speaking of which, here's the marquis now. Sinjoro Markizo!" he cried, standing up.

The Marquis de Beaufront strutted into the chamber, twirling his cane. "Ho! Karaj amikoj!" he cried, heading for our chairs. Pulling me to his chest, he pressed his lips against each of my cheeks, leaving a moist impression. Clasping my hand between both of his, he intoned: "Forteco, kuraĝo, eleganteco, ĉu ne?" He made a great show of speaking Esperanto with the rector and afterwards with Professor Couturat, who nodded blankly, so that I doubted, despite his claiming to be an Esperantist, that he understood unu vorton de kio diris la markizo.

"Gentlemen, gentlemen, to order!" Professor Ostwald pounded his gavel.

"Oui," Professor Leau concurred, briskly clapping his hands.

Professors Jespersen and Baudouin left off their conversation and returned to their seats, as did the rest of us. A waiter from the collège refilled our cups. A few committeemen lit cigarettes or pipes, and everyone settled in.

"We all know the marquis, I believe?" Professor Couturat said. "Welcome, Monsieur Marquis. Gentlemen, the Marquis de Beaufront has graciously elected to take time away from his young charges to speak with us today about Esperanto, isn't that right, Monsieur Marquis? And how *are* the children?"

Le Marquis Pierre Josselin Gerard Eugène Albert Louis de Beaufront looked at Professor Couturat with a wounded sense of incomprehension: why, before such an illustrious committee, would the professor refer to the fact that having lost his fortune, the poor fellow must now tutor the children of his wealthier friends? Reading through his pince-nez, held at chest level in his hand, he busied himself with papers he'd taken from a leather portfolio. "They're well, Professor," he answered tartly, letting the spectacles fall against his vest.

"Gentlemen," he said in that velvety and solemn voice of his, "illustrious friends, dear colleagues. I speak to you today on behalf of Dr. Zamenhof, who, in abiding, as others have not, by the restrictions imposed upon him by your august committee, has remained far from these proceedings and has elected me, in his stead, to present and defend—yes, and to defend, if it comes to that"—in jest, he affected the stance of a pugilist, to no small laughter—"the one artificial language in the world that needs no introduction and no defense at all."

He shook his head at us, as though he were a schoolman confronting a gang of rowdies. "I daresay, were it not for the great renown and practical success achieved internationally by Esperanto, none of us would be here today. This committee and the delegation it represents would not exist. Certainly none of you men would be taking time away from his essential endeavors to concern himself with as quixotic a chimera as a world language."

The marquis turned his back on our table, strolled over to the tall windows, and gazed out through them. "The fall of Volapük, wounded first by its own deficiencies, and then killed like Othello"—he spun around dramatically—"by its former friends, did much harm to our cause, and as a consequence, Esperanto had to pitch its tent on a windswept ledge where the world said nothing could survive, and yet, in that high and rocky place, gentlemen, we have not only survived, we have flourished!"

I can only reproduce this scene now with chagrin. This should have been the marquis' finest hour, the culmination of his twenty long years of self-sacrificing devotion to our cause. For twenty years, when it came to the question of Esperanto, the marquis had been the staunchest of conservatives, and in that hour, he championed his position (a position, I might add, even more extreme than Dr. Zamenhof's) with a fiery elegance. Had it all ended here, without its subsequent and multiple dénouements, there might now be de Beaufront Streets running alongside the many Zamenhof Streets throughout the world or at least (as would perhaps be more appropriate) crossing them at every turn.

Instead one need only consult an atlas to realize that there are none.

With more pathos than I'd ever heard it before, the marquis next recounted the story of his abandoning Adjuvanto. "Gentlemen, I, the son of nobility and a student of Müller's, was neither too proud nor too foolish to submit to another man's greater genius, though he was a nobody, not a grand intellectual like ourselves, but an impoverished oculist with no formal training in the lingual arts, and as it turns out, a Jew." His nostrils flared, and his tone grew even more oleaginous. "On the contrary, it was with love in my heart for all mankind that I burned my own project in a self-inflicted auto-da-fé: dictionaries, grammars, flash cards, the works! The chambermaid, hearing a fire crackling on the hottest day in July, ran into my rooms, thinking to save me from some dire mishap. Understanding everything in a glance, she threw herself upon the fire, plunging her hands into the flames to save whatever remnant she could, singeing herself pitiably. 'Non, non, old mother,' I cried. 'Non, non! Let it go, let it burn.' 'But, Master, your work!' she wept, as I salved her burnt fingers with my tender kisses."

Moved to silence by his own words, the marquis stared at an empty space in the room, as though seeing the scene before him once again. We were all silent for a moment, until, coughing, Professor Jespersen cleared his throat and said, "I'd like to address the question of the supersigns, if I may?"

The marquis, regaining his composure with apparent difficulty, replied, "By all means, by all means, certainly."

Professor Jespersen stood and removed his glasses. "It appears to me," he said, twirling them by their stems, "that, here, Idiom Neutral has the advantage over Esperanto, possessing as it does a natural alphabet unblemished by circumflexed consonants that Esperanto alone, of the hundreds of languages we've studied so far, dares to offer to the world."

These two combatants, sizing each other up, proceeded to joust over the supersigns, the accusative endings, the plural -*js*, and a host of other philological concerns, the marquis parrying each of Professor Jespersen's potentially lethal thrusts with consummate skill, I thought. Their debate was enthralling, and the marquis' performance—deft, witty, inspiring— left the men of the committee stimulated and amused.

SO MUCH SO, in fact, I imagined the marquis' presentation might prove decisive for the committee. However, the discussion that followed it turned quite fractious.

"I say we've heard enough!" Rector Boirac surprised everyone by pushing away from the table, his forehead flushing scarlet. "How much longer can this go on? Yes, it's been a fascinating intellectual voyage. Marvelous that so many cranks and eccentrics can scare up cab fare to appear in the Fifth Arrondissement, each with his own more or less inadequate scheme. Gentlemen, gentlemen!" Rector Boirac was forced to raise his voice as the others grew restive. "I move that this committee immediately vote to accept Esperanto en bloc and let this exercise in intellectual pharisaism end so that we can all go home to our wives and our dinner, happy to have contributed to the welfare of mankind."

"The table recognizes Professor Jespersen," Professor Ostwald barked above the commotion Rector Boirac's outburst had pulled in its train, pounding his gavel like a smithy hammering an anvil. Professor Jespersen unfolded his long body and stood with his hands pinioning his coattails against his hips. He scowled in Rector Boirac's direction, before turning, in this guise, to take in every face around the table.

"Perhaps it would have been more prudent of me, like many of our good friends, to have remained a distant observer of this committee and its goals." He laughed grimly and shook his head. "Certainly doing so would have spared me many a vexation." Inside the opening of his beard, his mouth became a bloodless line. "There have been too many days of work and too many nights without sleep since this whole rigmarole began!"

"Hear, hear!" everyone chorused.

"However," he raised his hands to silence the grumbling he himself had elicited, "because of a certain impetuosity in my nature, once I have determined which course is right, it is impossible for me to remain passive. Now," he said sharply, "Rector Boirac is correct. Perhaps our good secretaries have been too meticulous, too thorough in their researches. It's a failing we all, as scholars, should aspire to, and let me be the first to say it: Bravo, Messieurs Couturat et Leau! Bravo!"

"Bravo, congratulations, good work, gentlemen!" was heard around the table.

"However," Professor Jespersen silenced us again, "in contradiction to what Rector Boirac maintains, a number—a very small number, granted—but a number of worthy candidates for an international language have shown themselves in the course of our discussions and— forgive me, Rector Boirac—if I insist upon insisting"—he had begun to lose his temper—"that in a matter of such consequence for the whole of mankind, it *will not do* to leave a final choice to mere chance—"

"Mere chance?" Rector Boirac barked out.

"Gentlemen, gentlemen!" Professor Ostwald pounded his gavel.

"—nor," Professor Jespersen shouted down both men, "to the most vociferous of propaganda campaigns!"

"Do you realize what an idiot you're sounding?" Rector Boirac nearly screamed.

"I won't be threatened or intimidated," Professor Jespersen called back.

"What do you propose? What is Professor Jespersen proposing?" Rector Boirac attempted to draw the table into the argument. "That we tear down our twenty years of building? Burn the books we've published for more than twenty years? Destroy the printing houses, disband our organizations?"

"Certainly no one is suggesting that," Professor Couturat replied fretfully.

"Sir," Professor Jespersen spoke more mildly, "I am not, as you well know, a practical man. I am, rather, a scientist, and I can only examine the matter before me with scientific detachment and clarity. Were I asked to judge the question of which language has most successfully built up its structures and marshaled its resources, then, of course, I would honestly concede, and gladly so, to Esperanto." Rector Boirac and Professor Jespersen looked sadly into each other's faces. "But that is not the question we have been called here to decide. Rather, we're here to decide which language is *best*, not which has been the most successfully propagandized."

"Volapük lived and died, Otto," said a Dr. Förster who, along with a Dr. Bouchard and a Professor Eötvös, was attending the proceedings that day. "Let it rest in peace."

"Let us be honest." Professor Jespersen dropped his shoulders. "Let us speak plainly with one another, shall we? We all know that there are simply too many unreasoned and eccentric idiosyncrasies in Esperanto"— Rector Boirac nearly coughed up his coffee—"deriving no doubt," Professor Jespersen continued over the commotion, "and I say this with only admiration for Dr. Zamenhof's bold assay—deriving no doubt from the fact that the man is not a linguist."

"Not a linguist?" Professor Baudouin said. "Otto!"

"He's an oculist, for God's sake!" Professor Jespersen laughed, straightening his tie. "Why, I'd no sooner presume to suggest he allow me to write my own prescription for eyeglasses!" Laughter rose up from the table on all sides, bathing Professor Jespersen in its warmth.

"So what do you suggest, then?" Rector Boirac thundered.

Professor Jespersen exhaled furiously. The polemics were clearly wearing on his nerves. "What do I suggest?" He returned to his seat. "A simple and elegant principle, and one with which our friend Ostwald here would no doubt agree, as it uses the least amount of energy to attain the greatest amount of good for the largest number of people."

"Oh?" Professor Ostwald said, intrigued.

"I suggest, simply, that in assessing the internationality of a word, we count up the number of people who know that word already in some form in their native language and cleanse the vocabulary of whatever language we decide must be our committee's choice from the obscure and little known choices resorted to by Dr. Zamenhof, who quite obviously worked without regard to scientific principle!"

"Then," Professor Baudouin raised his voice, glowering at the men before him, "we have no other work before us today than to vote Chinese in as the international language and be done with it!"

"Chinese?" Professor Eötvös said.

"What does Chinese have to do with an international language?" Dr. Bouchard said.

Professor Baudouin had not finished. "You gentlemen from the western half of Europe have fallen once again, as you so often do, into the trap of thinking your small principalities represent some superior norm. The elements you can't abide in Dr. Zamenhof's Esperanto are precisely what make it so appealing to the majority of Europeans. Simply because a man is a Pole or a Russian does not mean he can't have an original or a superior thought!"

"You're saying then, I take it," Professor Jespersen challenged him, "that Esperanto simply can't be improved?"

"Don't be an ass, Otto. Of course, it can be improved, just as French or German can be improved. However, just as I wouldn't presume to dictate those improvements to the French or the German, neither would I do so with the Esperantists, who represent a substantial community of speakers. Rather, we must leave these sorts of changes up to the actual—"

At the word *ass*, however, the uproar Professor Baudouin caused drowned out the rest of what he was saying.

"We have a committee that oversees such things," Rector Boirac shouted, though no one seemed to be listening to him. "There are procedures! There are rules!"

"I thought you were here as a private citizen, Rector Boirac," Professor Jespersen said abrasively.

"A private citizen who just happens to be the president of the Esperanto Language Committee," Dr. Bouchard said chidingly.

"Look," Professor Jespersen ripped his glasses from his face and threw them down upon his notepad, "a language *must* change or die. You *cannot* impose your will upon a living language."

"That's true for a natural language, Otto," Professor Baudouin said, "but not for an artificial one!"

"Oh, rubbish!" Professor Jespersen complained.

"Do you really think, Otto," Professor Ostwald asked, "that Idiom Neutral with its fifteen verb forms can be made to work worldwide?"

"No, of course not, not as it stands now, but we would change all that with improvements."

"But that is *not* the mandate of this committee!" Rector Boirac roared.

Exhausted by the bickering, I left the chamber and hurried to the nearest door, my shoes clacking against the marble floors of the hallway. Outside, the sky was grey and the air was sharp with the threat of winter. Taking refuge beneath a barren tree, I lit a small cigar and took a calming puff.

"Hey, since when are you smoking again?" Loë said.

"Ah, what are you doing here?" I exhaled, greeting her. With my gloved hand, I stirred the cloud of smoke until it thinned.

"You know I don't approve."

"No, and neither do I."

"Still, give us a puff all the same."

Glancing over her shoulders to make certain no one was watching her, Loë accepted my cigar. With her head lowered, she took in a mouthful of smoke. "I've come to take you to lunch, Kaĉjo. How has the day been so far?"

"Oh God! Terrible, just awful, in fact! No, I have such a headache! Just look at me!" I lifted my hands to show her how much they were trembling. I paced back and forth, the gravel of the cinder path crunching beneath my shoes. "None of the procedures are being followed! Inventors are presenting their own languages! A Professor Peano, after presenting his own language, was invited to sit on the committee! And no one can agree on anything! I mean, what good is an international language if there's more than one? Do you see what I mean?"

In this vexed state of mind, I couldn't help eying Loë with a smallness of spirit. "I'll light you your own, if you wish," I addressed her sharply. She'd ceased passing back the cigar and was keeping it to herself, puffing in and out quickly, the smoke leaving her mouth in small staccato bursts.

"Oh God, no," she said. "You know how I hate these things."

Before I could stop her, she'd tossed the one-franc cigar onto the gravel and, raising her skirts, stamped it out with the toe of her shoe. "You shouldn't be smoking in any case. You're not as young as you once were, you know."

"It's absurd," I said, lighting the other one I'd purchased. "The inventors can't even speak to one another. Their years of selfless labor have left them with nothing but an idiolect, understood by one solitary person or, as in the case of Mr. Streiff's Bopal, not even that!"

"If the deficiencies of these other schemes are that obvious to you, Kaĉjo, surely the other men on the committee will see them."

"You're right, you're right," I said.

"They're not fools. And after Esperanto is presented to the world as a fait accompli, no one will ever bother again about Dilpak or Blague Blague or whatever it's called."

"Langue Bleu," I said.

"Where on earth do they come up with these names?"

WE ATE OUR lunch at a café overlooking le pont St. Louis. Though I'd worried that it had been a mistake to ask Loë to join me on this trip, my fears were unfounded. Away from Vienna, beyond Herr Bernfeld's unhelpful reach, we were discovering ourselves again. As I watched her slathering apricot jam upon her croissant, taking as much care with it as a bricklayer might with his trowel, I couldn't help exulting in her beauty: her hands were so small; her fingers so elegantly articulated; her lips plump and pouty, as though they'd been stung by a bee. Delicate lines appeared on either side of her mouth whenever she chewed.

What were the chances, I asked myself, given the sad history of my sentimental education, that I, Ya'akov Yosef Sammelsohn, might find myself in a pleasant café on a quiet street on an island in the Fourth Arrondissement overlooking the grey waters of the Seine with a beautiful woman who, acting upon her own desires, had become my wife?

If I hadn't already decided to renounce Ita forever, I would have done so then and there.

"What if I skip the afternoon session?" I said to Loë, walking along the river back towards the collège. "We could go back to our hotel room and take a little nap."

I put my arms around her waist and leaned in to kiss her. She struggled to unclasp herself from the bracelet of my arms. "Not here! Kaĉjo!"

"Isn't it time we had a little infanon of our own?"

"Perhaps, but this isn't the place to talk about it."

"Let's go back to the hotel then, and make a little idon, shall we?"

"I admit it's enticing," she said, finally moving nearer to me.

"And we'll raise the little prince speaking only Esperanto, keeping him away from the harsh world of multiple international languages, as though he were the Buddha himself."

"All right, all right," she said, and she kissed me, rising on the tips of her toes. "But not now."

"No?"

"You've got work to do."

Another kiss. We were in Paris, after all.

"Tonight," she said. "I promise."

"Tonight then."

She took my arm and, like Ariadne, escorted me through the labyrinth of my own dour thoughts, back to the Collège de France. In that moment, I felt possessed of a perfect happiness. In Loë's presence, everything made sense. The men of the committee will come to their senses, Professor Couturat will live up to the promises he had made (*in writing*, I might add) to Dr. Zamenhof. Esperanto will be endorsed by the committee as the international language. Little by little, the entire world will begin speaking it, an occurrence that will usher in a golden age. The dark world of separation and exile—known only too well to me from my childhood in Szibotya—will disappear, and with a dawning sense of excitement, and perhaps even with a sense of adventure, men will begin recognizing one another as brothers. Science and technology, no longer the private domain of separate nations, will progress rapidly as a world-wide endeavor, unhampered for the first time since the fall of Latin by a confusion of tongues. Man's health and his living conditions, as a consequence, will improve; as privation and suffering disappear, the need for war will cease. No longer forced to live in fear, every man will tend to his garden until the entire world is one rich and thriving garden.

Loë and I arrived back at the chamber as the presentation of Novlatin was ending and the committeemen were preparing to depart for lunch. Professors Couturat and Leau were leaving with Rector Boirac. A good sign, I thought, although when the rector caught my eye, he lifted his eyes to the ceiling and pantomimed an exaggerated sigh, his arms raised slightly, his palms exposed. I understood his gesture as a signal of chagrin—a lunch in the company of Messieurs Couturat et Leau could be a trial—though, in retrospect, I realized, he looked like a martyr being carried down from his cross.

That evening, when Professor Ostwald insisted on buying drinks for everyone in a tavern across from the Sorbonne, I found it difficult to get away. Five drinks into it, he further insisted upon giving over his views on immortality and individuality and was stopped only when Professor Baudouin borrowed a guitar from one of the students and Professor Jespersen a fiddle, and the three men sang songs from their own university days. They were tipsy and sentimental, and the crowd of students who encircled them, aware of who these illustrious gentlemen were, loved it.

"Thank you," Professor Ostwald intoned, unsteady on his feet. "And I hope we've passed the audition."

"Where's Couturat?" he said, joining me, a moment later, at the bar.

"Dinner appointment." I sipped my drink.

"And Leau?"

"No idea."

"Baudouin"—he pointed with his forehead towards the door, where the linguist could be seen leaving with two girls, one on each arm—"is off to one of his mysterious political confabulations. Best not to inquire too deeply there. That leaves only you and Jespersen and me, I suppose."

"For?"

"Why, for dinner, of course! At my expense, naturally. No, I'm insisting."

THOUGH THE NIGHT air seemed to sober my companions, it did nothing to diminish their high spirits. "That's the effect of Paris," Professor Jespersen said, taking in a deep breath.

"No, not of Paris," Professor Ostwald corrected him, "but of the Latin Quarter. Don't you feel it? I always feel like this when I'm here . . ."

"Ah, yes," Professor Jespersen concurred, looking about him, his eyes gleaming.

"It has its own genius loci."

As we strolled past l'Église St. Séverin and la Bibliothèque de l'heure joyeuse, and a thousand and one other bookshops, I knew what my companions meant: the winding narrow streets of the quarter were vibrant with activity. All about us, students were lugging their books, and downing their coffees and their beers, immersed in philosophical inquiries. Everything lay before them; all roads remained equally open. Here, in this kingdom of the mind, I told myself, one could become anything one wished. Strolling through its streets in the company of these two dignitaries, I couldn't help feeling I'd finally arrived where I always belonged.

"Yes, that's exactly it!" Professor Ostwald said, wrapping his ursine arm about my shoulder and rubbing my hair with his hand. "That's exactly how I feel. As though I'm finally home indeed."

Professor Jespersen said, "It's been a marvelous week, hasn't it been?"

"Em," Professor Ostwald concurred, stroking his rosy-golden beard.

"Even though," Professor Jespersen added ruefully.

"Ha!" Professor Ostwald laughed.

"I know, I know!" I complained.

"I could have done without those endlessly tedious demonstrations."

"What *were* they thinking!" Professor Ostwald shook his head.

"Couturat and Leau," I said, shaking mine.

"Their book come to life, I suppose, day after day, before the eyes of a captive audience."

"Well, thank *God* that's over and done with, and we can finally get down to what matters!"

"And how do you see us proceeding?" I asked Professor Ostwald.

"Excellent question," he said, pulling me a bit closer to himself. "An excellent question. You're an astonishingly excellent chap. Isn't he, Professor Jespersen? An astonishingly excellent chap?"

"Sammelsohn? Oh, yes. First rate. No doubt about it. Happy to have him on board."

"Well," Professor Ostwald rubbed his hands together as he steered us into the restaurant he'd chosen, "my first action will be to found a scientific journal in the new language, a popular magazine, nothing too erudite, you understand. But we'll need an editor. I couldn't take on the responsibility myself."

"What about Sammelsohn here?" Professor Jespersen said, as the waiter showed us to our table.

"But would he do it?" Professor Ostwald asked Professor Jespersen. "That's the question."

"Well, I'm flattered to be considered for the position," I said. "But of course I would. No, I *will*! Certainly, I'll do it. The decision requires no further thought, gentlemen. Consider me in."

"Ah, excellent!" Professor Ostwald said.

"Good," Professor Jespersen said, "and I'll make contributions on linguistics."

THE WAITER PLACED a napkin in my lap. I took a sip of water. Professor Ostwald had insisted I telephone Loë and invite her to join us. While we waited for her to arrive by taxi, Professor Ostwald ordered a few dishes in advance. Soon, a rare Chablis from the Château Duhart-Milon was perspiring in a brass tub at our table; plump oysters, garlanded by lemons and garlic, lay on a bed of iridescent ice; next to them were ramekins of caviar and a tray of escargot, with little tools for extracting the snails from their shells.

"Here. Let me assist you with that," Professor Ostwald said, taking the utensils from my hands and removing a number of escargot on my behalf. "It's clear you've never eaten these before."

"No, I haven't." I laughed, abashed.

With his large hands, Professor Ostwald squeezed a bit of lemon juice onto the snails and dipped them into the garlicky butter before laying them out on a tiny plate for me.

"Good, aren't they?"

"Very good," I said, pretending to enjoy them.

When Loë arrived, there were kisses all around. Professor Ostwald stood and kissed Loë's hand; Professor Jespersen stood and kissed her hand as well; I stood and she bussed me on the cheek—we were in Paris, after all—after which, Professor Ostwald, overcome with affection, kissed both her cheeks as well.

"Damned attractive woman you've got there, Sammelsohn," he said to me.

"Welcome, Madame Sammelsohn, welcome," Professor Jespersen said gallantly, his eyes sparkling behind his severe glasses. "Professor Ostwald, your husband, and I, like Caesar with Gaul, have divided the world into three."

"Oh?" Loë asked playfully, infected by the high spirits of the table. "And what have we inherited?"

"Professor Ostwald is planning on founding a magazine," I explained, "and I'm to be its editor."

"And I will contribute and solicit contributions on linguistics from others," Professor Jespersen said.

"Our offices will be right here in Paris," I told her.

"Where else?" Professor Ostwald bellowed.

"You're eating *that*?" Loë said quietly, noting my oysters.

"When in Rome." I shrugged, as Professor Jespersen poured a glass of the Chablis for her.

"Shall we start with the consommé?" Professor Ostwald peered into the menu.

"Order for everyone, Wilhelm," Professor Jespersen said. "You're familiar with the menu."

"Yes, do," Loë said.

She and Professor Jespersen smiled at each other.

Professor Ostwald removed his reading glasses and stuck their stems into his mouth. "All right," he said, chuckling. "We're going to have a marvelous night, even if it bankrupts me." He signaled to the waiter. "We'll begin with the consommé," he told the man, "followed by the salad of duck gizzards—everyone's up for that?—the veal tongue, a gâteau of chicken livers, sweetbreads, the rissole of lamb's feet with artichoke hearts and basil . . . oh, and let's see, hmm, what else does anyone want?"

The ordering went on and on, until finally the waiter departed and returned a moment later with an even rarer Merlot. We all raised our glasses in celebration.

"To the Delegation and to its Committee!"

"To its honest members!" Loë said.

"Hear, hear," Professor Jespersen said.

We drank and settled back in our chairs, smiling at one another.

"So I take it," Loë said, between sips, "that the work of the committee is over?"

"All but." Professor Jespersen nodded. "All but."

"And Esperanto has been accepted?"

"Oh—well—now," Professor Ostwald said, and the conversation faltered.

"Oh," Loë said. "I just naturally assumed that if my husband were involved . . ."

"Esperanto. Of course, Esperanto," Professor Ostwald said in his blustery way. "It's a foregone conclusion."

"Although"—Professor Jespersen carefully swallowed an oyster—"there may be a few minor reforms."

Loë arched an eyebrow. I imagined I was the only one to note the indignation howling in that small gesture.

"Loë," I warned her quietly.

"I understand your concern," Professor Jespersen said, "but the issue for me—and perhaps for Professor Ostwald as well"—he nodded towards Professor Ostwald, who nodded back, albeit reluctantly, having no idea what Professor Jespersen was on the verge of saying—"is not emotional, but rather scholarly and practical. The question is, which is the most perfect language?"

"But surely there's no created language more perfect than Esperanto."

Professor Jespersen blew on his soup. Taking a spoonful, he nodded. "Still."

"All those -*ojn*s and -*ajn*s," Professor Ostwald said, knurling up his nose.

"Oh, that's the least of it," Professor Jespersen said.

"Although the decision hasn't yet been made," I reminded everyone.

"The Delegation Committee," Loë remarked, "is authorized—has in fact authorized itself!"—I smiled on her behalf towards the others—"to decide only which among the *existing* languages is best. It has no authority to reform any of those languages. That's what Esperanto's own language committee is for."

"As Professor Baudouin so ably pointed out during this afternoon's session," I reminded everyone.

"But that's just it," Professor Ostwald said, fretting into his beard.

"Madame, don't be absurd!" Professor Jespersen said, more boldly.

"Absurd?" Loë said. Her throat had turned a vibrant scarlet.

"The Esperanto Language Committee is a chaos in which nothing can get done. Perhaps even intentionally so."

"No one's making that claim," Professor Ostwald said quickly.

"On the contrary, Wilhelm, someone *is* making that claim. *I* am making that claim!" Professor Jespersen's reddish face was flushing even more redly than usual. "Ostrich policies!" he cried. "You can't tell me that Dr. Zamenhof doesn't hide behind the Language Committee, doesn't issue his dictatorial edicts through its mouth, doesn't rely on its incompetence to table all talk of desperately needed reform!"

Hearing himself, Professor Jespersen attempted to refashion his tone. "Don't misunderstand me, madame. Everyone agrees on Esperanto in principle. Still, there is nothing that can't be made better."

"In principle," I said, when Loë said nothing.

Professor Jespersen threw up his hands. "I ask you only this: how could a language invented by a fifteen-year-old boy *not* require improvements? No matter how brilliant that boy was, Esperanto is still the work of a single man, with all his individual blindnesses, whereas the committee possesses many capable men, each able to correct the other's mistakes, don't you see?"

"Chiefly editors and doctors," Loë said.

"There *is* a linguist or two," he replied coldly.

"Two, I believe," she said.

"Two," he conceded.

"In any case," Professor Ostwald took over, "when did a committee ever produce anything of value? No, I'm afraid, Otto, you're entirely incorrect there. Rather it's to the lone wolf of genius that humanity owes everything of worth!"

"Well, and what do you have to say to all of this?" Loë fixed me with a determined look.

I'd been poking through my salad of duck gizzards, pushing to the side of my plate anything that looked as though it had once digested food itself. I raised my head to look at Loë—she was speaking a little too loudly for my comfort—and laid down my fork. "Lower your voice, darling, please," I murmured, an admonition that succeeded only in making her raise it.

"You're here as Rector Boirac's second!" she said.

"Here, in Paris, at the committee meetings, yes, I am Rector Boirac's second," I said through my teeth while contriving to maintain a pleasant face. Though they were pretending not to, both Professors Ostwald and Jespersen were listening to our conversation. "But not at this dinner table."

"Oh!" She looked at me as though seeing me for the first time. "I can't believe you're being such an idiot!"

"Loë!" I said.

"Excuse me," she said, standing.

"Loë!" I said again, rising from my chair.

"Madame," Jespersen and Ostwald said politely. They stood as Loë made her way to the powder room. When we sat, Professor Ostwald cast an indulgent look at me. "Women," he clucked.

Professor Jespersen shook his head. "They understand so very little."

Professor Ostwald poured everyone more wine.

"What do you think of Couturat's theory of derivations?" Professor Jespersen asked him after a moment.

"I'm not convinced of its value." Holding the stem between his fingers, Professor Ostwald watched the liquid rise inside his glass. "In any case, we'll speak of it later."

"And why is that?" Professor Jespersen asked.

"Because here he is now," Professor Ostwald said, pointing with his chin, as Professors Couturat and Leau marched in with the marquis between them.

"The poor man looks as though he's being led to his execution," Professor Ostwald said wryly.

I'd noted the same thing. The marquis shuffled in so lifelessly between his apparent captors, he did in fact appear as though he expected to find not an elegant dinner, but a firing squad waiting for him behind the door of the private dining chamber into which the three men disappeared.

"Or if not his execution, then something worse," Professor Jespersen said.

"Worse?" Professor Ostwald snorted. "And what could be worse than that?"

"Another lecture on the subjunctive in Mundolingo, I suppose."

"Ach, Gott!" Professor Ostwald roared. "No, you're correct there! I'd much rather be shot!"

"WHAT IN GOD'S name were you thinking?" Loë asked me on our walk back to the hotel.

"I wasn't thinking anything. I merely accepted Professor Ostwald's dinner invitation."

"But can't you see what they're up to?"

"They're not up to anything, Loë!"

"How can you be so blind?"

"Must you suspect everyone?"

"Those damned egoists!"

"They're not egoists!"

"They're nothing but egoists!"

"Yes, but must they be *damned* egoists?"

"Nothing exists for them but their own points of view!"

"They have strong opinions. They're accomplished men, and so naturally they have strong opinions."

"Emphasis on 'men.'"

"Ah." I could only sigh.

"Well, why *are* there no women on Professor Couturat's committee?"

"I have no idea. Perhaps none accepted his invitation."

"It's 1907, for God's sake!"

"Worse. It's October, so it's almost 1908."

"Am I the only one living in the modern world?"

"*I'm* living in the modern world."

"Oh, please!" She gave me a cutting look. "You really have no sense of who you are, do you, Kaĉjo?" Her laughter was scalding. "Sometimes you're just such a Galitsyaner, aren't you?"

"Loë. Enough."

"These men tell you they're impressive, and so you believe them. Well, why shouldn't you? You've done it your entire life. The rebbe tells you he can fly to Heaven and, so of course, you believe him! Why would he say it, if it wasn't true?"

"We're not having this conversation!"

"No, we *are* having this conversation!"

"I am not having this conversation!"

"No, you *are* having this conversation! Do you know how frustrating it is for me, as a woman, to have to leave everything in your questionable hands?"

As we crossed le pont de la Tournelle to the narrow streets of the Île St. Louis, I surrendered all hopes of the amorous night I'd been promised. Instead, we sat up in our nightclothes until nearly three, with Loë quizzing me on every detail of every day of the committee's meetings, details we'd already thoroughly discussed, and razzing me on my naïveté, which she was certain would sabotage our case before the committee.

"Let me tell you something, Dr. Sammelsohn," she said when it was nearly dawn. "If anything unfortunate should happen during these last committee days, I'm not sure I'll be able to forgive you. Do you understand me?"

I sighed and closed my eyes. "Yes, I understand you. But, Loë, don't worry!"

"I don't know why Dr. Zamenhof would send such a Galitsyaner to defend his work. Just look at you! Bedazzled by a couple of university professors!"

Sleep was out of the question, and in the morning, despite copious amounts of coffee, I was good for little.

WHICH WAS UNFORTUNATE because, immediately following the morning's session, Rector Boirac was recalled to Dijon by his academic duties there.

"There's been another fire," he said as I bundled him into a cab outside the collège gates. "It shouldn't be too great a problem. The meetings are scheduled to continue until the end of the week, and I'll be back the day after tomorrow."

I handed him his hat. "You're certain?" Our breaths made small clouds in the cold morning air.

"Absolutely." He regarded me with a small smile. "I wouldn't leave otherwise."

I nodded, conceding to his superior wisdom.

"Continue with your reports to General Sébert. And if you get in over your head, call him."

"I won't."

"Call him?"

"Get in over my head."

"But if you do, do."

"I will," I said, "but I won't."

He bit into his cigar, lit it, and tossed the match into the street.

"Nu, ĝis la revido." He seated himself inside the motorcar.

"Ĝis la," I said.

The engine barked and thundered, and I shivered as his taxi trundled off.

CHAPTER 17

The dénouement played out as anyone might have guessed.

After lunch, when those of us remaining returned to the committee chamber, we discovered that in the interim someone had placed a proposal on the table. There were copies pressed from a mimeographed stencil at every committeeman's chair. Professor Baudouin pointed the pamphlet out with his cane as soon as we'd entered the room. "What's this?" he asked suspiciously.

"Professor Leau?" Professor Couturat said.

Professor Leau shrugged and shook his handsome head.

"Most irregular," Professor Ostwald grumbled.

"Hm," Professor Jespersen said in a hollowish way.

"It appears"—Professor Couturat affixed his pince-nez in order to leaf through the pamphlet—"to be an additional scheme, with a grammar and a partial dictionary." He read through it irritably, giving each page a cursory perusal before flipping to the next.

"A proposed system of reforms," Professor Leau added helpfully, standing in much the same posture as his friend.

"And who is the author?" Professor Ostwald demanded.

Professor Couturat turned back to the first page of the document, as we all did, and the sound of rustling pages filled the hall. "The work is pseudonymous," Professor Couturat said, looking up from the sheets. "The author gives his name only as Ido."

"Did you say *Ita*?"

"Ido," Professor Leau corrected me.

"He's not Japanese, is he?" Dr. Eötvös said.

"No, no, *Ido* means 'child' in Esperanto," I explained.

"Ah, yes, so it does, so it does," Professor Ostwald said, blushing, flustered. "Out of context, which is to say, rather, speaking in French"—he gestured with one finger, making little circles near his ear — "I didn't hear it."

"Upon cursory examination," Professor Leau said, "it appears to address much of what has been complained about in Esperanto."

"Exactly the sort of thing we've been asking for," Professor Ostwald said.

"Well, not exactly," Professor Leau purred.

"Neither of you two" — Professor Ostwald pointed with his great ursine head towards Professors Couturat and Leau — "are this Monsieur Ido, by any chance?"

"No," Professors Couturat and Leau both said, each looking at the other.

At which point, the committee, as though one man, bowed its head and read the pamphlet through in silence.

"Where is Boirac?" Professor Baudouin whispered.

"Couldn't be here today," I said.

"Well, I suggest you say something and quickly."

"Me?"

"Who else?" Professor Baudouin scowled. "You're Boirac's second."

"Of course," I said, but before I could stand and speak, before I could even examine my fly to see that it was properly buttoned, a familiar, oleaginous voice boomed out in the chamber: "May I speak?" We all looked up and saw the Marquis de Beaufront, standing in the doorway, dashing in a mauve frock coat.

"In Rector Boirac's absence," Professor Leau explained, "I took it upon myself to phone the marquis." He dropped his voice and said to me: "I hope I haven't offended."

"Not at all," I assured him, "not at all." I was in fact relieved to see the marquis. Whatever problems I had with the fellow — he was, on his best days, an egomaniacal and duplicitous boor — he was the strongest defender against the array of reformists who continued to bedevil Esperanto like a cloud of annoying bees.

"Step forward, Marquis, and address the committee," Professor Leau said.

The marquis took his time approaching the table, rapping his cane against the floor, scowling like an irritated choirmaster at a group of out-of-tune tenors. Unidentifiable ribbons—war medals? aristocratic insignia of some kind?—decorated the lapel of his morning coat; a boutonnière bloomed through the buttonhole on the other side. Rooting his cane to the floor, he stared down at the black-and-white tiles and pushed a long and weary sigh through his nose. He removed his pince-nez and steamed the lenses with his breath, one at a time, before wiping each with a monogrammed kerchief. (I was perturbed, sitting near him, to observe that the initials of the monogram were not his own, but those of his employer, the Graf de Maigret, and that the insignia on his chest were simple Catholic medallions.) Returning his spectacles to their place, the marquis shot poisonous looks at the committee through them. With a flourish, he removed a copy of Ido's proposals from the inside pockets of his morning coat (at the time, it didn't occur to me to wonder how he'd come into possession of it) and slapped it against his open palm. "Well, gentlemen, I've had the opportunity to look over this . . . this little . . . *pamphlet,*" he said, spitting out the word.

NOW WAS WHEN I should have been at my most alert, when I should have been most on guard. Rector Boirac had departed the scene; the Trojan Horse of the Ido pamphlet had been rolled into the committee chambers; the conspirators had all put on their most pleasing masks; however, at that moment, I was at my most distracted. As the marquis was speaking, I happened to glance over his shoulder, my attention drawn to a diminutive figure standing on the other side of the tall chamber windows, peering in with his hands cupped on either side of his face, shielding his eyes from the sun.

Following Monsieur Gajewski's departure from our committee chambers, I tried to convince myself that it was utter foolishness to imagine, because of one or two irregularities during their presentation, that Gaston was Ita reborn. More, it was madness to think so! Upon what evidence could one draw such a conclusion? One need only look at the facts: demonical possessions were, as Dr. Freud steadfastly maintained, the misdiagnosed hysterias of yesteryear; Rector Boirac's metagnomical presentation of cryptesthesia during the First Universal Congress was, by his own admission, an example of group trance; Fraŭlino Zinger, I think we can all agree, was a strange woman; and university laboratories, like any buildings, occasionally burn to the ground. There was nothing mysterious in any of this nor in the boy's return. He had obviously been sent to the collège by an anxious Gajewski to spy upon the committee in order to ascertain how Solresol's case was proceeding before it.

Nevertheless, I felt a strong hand had to be taken against him, that he needed to know that I, at least, would have nothing more to do with him, no matter who or what he might be.

I slipped out of the committee chambers and into the collège court-yard. I had no thought of leaving the chambers for any length of time. Debate over the worthlessness of the Ido pamphlet, I felt certain, would fill the rest of the afternoon. It was exactly the sort of intellectual bone upon which Professor Couturat liked to gnaw. Also, I told myself, the marquis was here to defend against its proposals, and if I knew these two men, they'd be at it all day.

"Ho! Little man!" I shouted at the boy. He was leaning against the window, his breath fogging the glass. At the sound of my voice, he jumped back and regarded me with a mixture of dread and alarm. At this distance, I couldn't be sure he was the same child who'd assisted Monsieur Gajewski. Perhaps this boy was merely a beggar hoping to receive a coin from the illustrious men inside. Nevertheless, I called out to him: "There's no need for you to fear me."

He said nothing, but standing on the balls of his feet, he flexed his small fists and glanced about nervously, preparing, I assumed, the most propitious avenue of escape.

"Gaston?" I said. "That's your name, isn't it? Gaston?"

He nodded slightly, his chest heaving beneath the fabric of his shirt.

"Come here for a moment, boy. I merely wish to speak with you."

I took a step nearer, hoping neither to frighten nor to propel him into flight.

"You're here on Monsieur Gajewski's behalf. Isn't that correct?"

He glanced at the street, his eyes cutting between me and the various gateways in the wall of the courtyard.

"By which I mean you haven't come here to tell *me* anything, have you?" I touched my chest with both hands as I said the word *me*. I glanced over my shoulder: there seemed to be no one but ourselves in the court-yard. "That is to say: you're not here to see *me* by any chance, are you?"

I took an additional step towards him. The child was trembling. As I drew nearer, I searched for evidence of the beating I assumed he had received following Solresol's disastrous presentation.

"Odd how you changed those sentences the other day. Why would you have done such a thing?" I took another step. "What happened there? You may confide in me . . . if there's anything you wish to say . . . specifi-cally to me?"

The wind ruffled the cowlicks in his hair, and I began to feel inordi-nately foolish. Once again, I'd let my guilty imagination run wild. Ita was dead, the poor girl I knew in Szibotya was dead. The Ita I knew afterwards did not exist, nor had she ever. And the Ita I'd been hoping to meet in Paris for an amorous idyll was only a figment of my imagina-tion. I nodded curtly at the boy, dismissing him, and was on the point of returning to the committee chambers—I'd already removed a cigar from my pocket and was lighting it—when the little fellow gave out a war whoop and bounded off. However, he ran not towards the street, as I'd expected him to, but towards me, his fists raised high, like a Red Indian, his knucklebones blanching. I couldn't help laughing at the ri-diculousness of the sight, the boy charging at me with all the feroc-ity of his tiny person, preparing, it seemed, a lethal strike. However, when he kicked me in the shins and pummeled me in my solar plexus, I was so caught off-guard, I lost my wind and actually toppled to the ground.

"Gaston!" I cried hoarsely, as he dashed towards la rue des Écoles. "Come back, you wretched child!" He refused to obey me. "Arrêt!" I shouted from the ground. I should have let the encounter end there, but instead I dashed after him, and by the time I reached the collège gates, all I could see was the flash of his little suit as he tore around the corner of the Sorbonne.

"Arrêtez ce garçon!"

Though various onlookers glanced up at the sound of my command,

none did as I bid him, and I had to run after the little felon myself. Naturally, he had the advantage over me. He knew the territory better than I,
who knew it not at all, and thanks to his small stature, he was able to rip
through the crowds and the environments I had to blunder around. At
times, I had the impression I wasn't chasing him at all, but that he was
leading me. Certainly, he kept peering over his shoulder to ascertain if
I was still behind him; and though he could have easily been checking
whether he had lost me or not, at times he seemed to be taking especial
care not to lose me. Very soon we reached a cul-de-sac, our progress
halted by a wall, which the boy tried unsuccessfully to scale. Stopped
short, he turned to face me, bouncing on his feet. He dashed to the left,
but the way was blocked; to the right, but that way was blocked as well.
With a little fancy dodgery, he could have barged past me, but I bore
down upon him and soon had him snared. It was Monsieur Gajewski's
boy, after all, as I was able to confirm at closer range. He had the same
underfed look, the same bruised puddles beneath his eyes, and he was
wearing the same tiny suit with the same little black foulard.

"So, it *is* you then!" I cried.

"No, monsieur."

"Why did you come back to the collège?"

"You've mistaken me for someone else, monsieur."

"You were standing there, looking through the windows!"

"But it wasn't I!"

"Stop lying to me!"

He drew in his cheeks and looked as though he were sucking on a
bitter candy.

"Don't you dare laugh at me!" I said.

"I wasn't, monsieur."

"Don't you *dare* laugh at me."

I had grabbed him by the shirt front and the collar, and I lifted him
from the ground. He weighed next to nothing. I held him in midair,
bracing his back against the wall. "How many times will you just show
up like this and ruin my life like this, eh?"

"Please, monsieur, you're hurting me!"

"How dare you! How dare you just show up whenever you feel like it!

Oh, yes, that was very funny, wasn't it, what you did with those sentences the other day?"

"Monsieur! I did as well as I could!"

I pounded his little body against the wall.

"And how dare you call my wife a whore!"

"I didn't, monsieur!"

"When you're not even fit to lick her boot! Listen to me!" I said, pushing my face into his. "It's over between us! Do you understand me?" I could feel his feet kicking at my stomach, his knees pedaling against my chest. It did him no good. I was enraged and consequently I had the strength of, if not one hundred men, then a hundred small boys, against whom he was powerless. "Do you hear me? That oath meant nothing! There were no witnesses! I owe you nothing and . . . good Lord! You're a little boy! I mean, my God, what on earth were you thinking?"

"Monsieur, please . . ." he cried.

"What?" I shouted at him.

"Don't kill me!" he said.

His body was convulsing, tears were running down his cheeks, he seemed to have wet his pants. His legs, bicycling uselessly in midair, were dripping with urine. The absurdity of the situation pierced me like a poisoned arrow. I trembled at the murderous crime I'd been on the point of committing. What was I doing? What was I thinking? I cursed my father and the Szibotyer Rebbe! Was I never to be liberated from the ridiculous superstitions they had stuffed into my brain? I relaxed my grip on the boy and lowered him to the street. He remained nearly motionless, crouching next to the wall, stunned perhaps, unsure what I intended for him. I didn't know myself. I ran my hand through my hair. Good Lord!

"I'm . . . I'm sorry," I said, reaching out to touch the lad's hair, hoping to reassure him, but as I did, he sprang away. Who could blame him? I myself would have run from the madman I'd become, if only I knew how. Before he could get too far, however, Monsieur Gajewski, traveling the street with his dog, rounded the corner and caught him by the sleeve.

"Hoy, Gaston!" he cried, and the boy shrieked in alarm. "What are you doing here with Dr. Sammelsohn?" Monsieur Gajewski demanded, looking between us and trying to decipher what was surely, under the best of circumstances, an incomprehensible tableau.

"Monsieur Gajewski." I nodded towards him.

"Answer me!" Monsieur Gajewski thundered at the child, and the dog, an Alsatian, began snarling.

"Nothing, master," Gaston cried, shrinking against the wall.

"Was he bothering you, Dr. Sammelsohn?"

"On the contrary. Not in the least, Monsieur Gajewski."

"Were you bothering him, Gaston?"

"No, I wasn't!"

"He wasn't," I reiterated.

"What did you take from him?" Monsieur Gajewski demanded. The boy shook his head. "What did you take from him, Gaston?"

"I took nothing!"

"He took nothing, sir!"

"Don't you lie to me, Gaston."

Monsieur Gajewski smiled into the sunlight, as though the boy's denials were, in equal parts, amusing and embarrassing to him. Then he cracked the boy across the face with the back of his hand. The dog yowled.

"Gajewski!" I screamed. I was horrified. The man possessed all the signs of drunkenness: his step was uncertain, he was sweating profusely, he reeked of alcohol and, to a lesser degree, of vomit, his hair was dirty, and he was on the street midday without a hat.

"Now tell me what you took from him, Gaston?" he demanded, ignoring me. "Tell me the truth, boy."

"I took nothing!"

"Liar!" Monsieur Gajewski slapped him once more.

"Gajewski, please," I cried. "You mustn't harm him. He's entirely innocent in this matter."

Monsieur Gajewski pushed the boy against the wall and went through his pockets, turning them out one after the other, and discovering within them a treasure trove of childish things: a pen knife, a few sous, a mandolin pick.

"Is this yours, Dr. Sammelsohn?" With one arm flat against the little man's chest, Monsieur Gajewski kept him pinioned against the wall; with his other hand, he offered me what I recognized immediately as my own wallet. Reflexively, I patted my own pockets and found it missing. Gaston must have taken it when he'd knocked me to the ground and pummeled me in the stomach.

"Is it yours, sir?" Monsieur Gajewski repeated. "Identify it, if you will."

I had no choice but to confirm that the billfold was indeed mine. Monsieur Gajewski drew in a deep breath. He shifted his feet and pressed the enormous weight of his body more fully against the arm that kept Gaston pinned in place. The boy soiled his pants.

"Monsieur Gajewski," I cried, nearly hysterical myself, "calm yourself, man, and consider that no harm has actually been done."

"Gaston." Monsieur Gajewski shook his head sadly. "How could you steal a wallet from a member of the Delegation Committee?"

"I . . . I didn't," the boy said, unable to meet the gaze of his tormentor.

"Gajewski, please." I reached out for his shoulder, but he repelled my hand. "Stop this now. I'm insisting! As a doctor! But also as a member of the Delegation Committee." I had no idea which title would impress him more.

"I take you in, I give you a home, and this is how you repay me?"

"No harm was done, Gajewski. The wallet has been returned. Perhaps he'd found it in the street and was simply bringing it to me."

"Do you know how long I've been working on behalf of Solresol, Gaston? You do know, my darling, I know, because I told you all about it. We've spoken of it, haven't we? Many, many nights, haven't we?"

"I didn't *do* anything," the child protested.

"Gajewski, leave him! It won't make any difference to the outcome of the committee's decision, I can assure you of that!"

"And yet you decide to wreck everything with your thievery!"

Monsieur Gajewski raised his fist like a cudgel over Gaston's head. I saw that the skin on his knuckles was broken from where he'd already beaten him. Gaston swallowed and raised his eyes, cringing at the sight of Monsieur Gajewski's fist hovering over his head. Then he turned his gaze on me. Locking his eyes on mine, he smiled a queer smile, almost a smirk, it seemed. His eyes flashed, and he raised one little eyebrow and one corner of his cheek in what—if only for a brief moment—appeared to be a perfect gloat of triumph.

"Gaston?" I said. And then: "Gajewski, no!"

"You miserable orphan! You . . . you ruined my life!" Monsieur Gajewski cried, raining his fist down upon the boy.

The Alsatian went wild with snarling. Gaston's neck snapped under the first blow. His legs went slack. His eyes were instantly glassy. Heedlessly, Monsieur Gajewski kept battering away at him, holding his little body in place, gripping his collar and his little foulard in one hand, punishing him with the other.

"גוואַלד! פּאָליציייש! העלפֿט! גוואַלד!‏," I cried—*Help! Police! Help! Murder!*—before I realized I was speaking in Yiddish. I found the first policeman I could and directed him back to the alleyway, and then I ran—there was no help for the boy, I knew that—stopping only once to double over and vomit in the street.

BY THE TIME I returned to the committee chambers, most of the committeemen had left. In fact, only Professor Leau remained, seated at the table, jotting something down in his cahier.

"Where is everyone?" I asked.

Professor Leau gave me an odd look. I'm certain I looked a shambles.

"Gone," he said simply.

"Gone?"

"Everyone left after the voting, of course?"

"The *voting*?"

Professor Leau squinted up at me over the ovals of his reading glasses. "Weren't you here?"

"Certainly I wasn't, no."

"Ah, yes, that's right," he said. "I thought I saw you leaving. Well, not long after that, Professor Couturat declared that the committee's theoretical discussions had reached their natural conclusion, and that it was time to put the matter to a vote." He searched through the pages of his cahier. "As you can see, it's noted here that the president of the Esperanto Language Committee abstained."

"Abstained?"

He shrugged good-naturedly in that handsome way of his. "You were Rector Boirac's second, weren't you?"

"And . . . and what language was ultimately voted on?" I said.

"Oh." He smiled. "I'm pleased to report that Idiom Neutral finally met its defeat."

"Ah. Very good."

"Yes, even Professor Jespersen abandoned his support of it. Many of its forms, he conceded at last, are ungraceful."

"And so then, that means . . . ?"

"Esperanto won the day."

"Thank God!"

"After which, Professor Couturat called for another vote."

"Another vote?"

"This one proposing that certain reforms be adopted into it—"

"Certain reforms!"

"—along the lines of those proposed by Monsieur Ido in his pamphlet, which the marquis, acting as Dr. Zamenhof's representative, accepted and approved."

"The marquis . . . *endorsed* the reforms? But he wasn't even entitled to vote!"

"Naturally not. Nevertheless, his opinion on the matter carried great weight with the members of the committee, and in light of this, the measure passed by a majority," Professor Leau said, reading from his notes, "with the president of the Esperanto Language Committee once again noted as abstaining."

"But I didn't even vote!"

"Which"—Professor Leau pointed to his cahier—"is why I noted your abstention."

"But these abstentions do not accurately reflect the will of either Rector Boirac or myself!"

"Oh." His handsome face crumbled into a sympathetic scowl. "Well, that *is* unfortunate."

"You must allow me to change my vote."

"I'm sorry, Dr. Sammelsohn. After the voting, the committee was dis-
solved, again by unanimous consent, minus your abstention, and I can't
very well put into the minutes observations of events that didn't occur."

My legs buckled, and I fell into a chair.

I looked out the room's tall windows at the murky October sky.
Throughout the committee meetings, as I'd been instructed to do by
Rector Boirac, I had given a daily report, via telephone, to general Sébert,
but each day, by a means unknown to me, the general seemed to have
already obtained a detailed précis of the day's events, which, at some
point in the afternoon, he must have shared with Loë — since our arrival
in Paris, the two had become fast friends — as there was nothing I could
tell either of them — to Sébert via telephone; or to Loë, upon meeting her
later for dinner — that they didn't already seem to know.

(The general, after a long career of military strategizing, had obviously thought to make one of the collège's secretaries, or perhaps one of
our waiters, his spy.)

I sat trembling in the now-empty chamber. I knew the news of my
perfidy, through the agency of General Sébert's spy, had probably already
reached my wife, and suddenly, I was no longer a grown man sitting in
a splendid chamber in the Collège de France, but a boy in his father's
gazebo, General Sébert's unknown spy substituting for my sister, whose
back I watched, in memory, receding into the distance as she raced
through our father's orchards, shrilling his and my mother's names into
the air, ferrying back to them the report of my treachery, whose consequence, I knew, would be my eviction from their lives.

How could it be any different with Loë? Forgiveness wasn't exactly
her métier.

With a leaden foot, I made my way back to our hotel, doubting she
would even be there when I arrived, and knowing that, if she were, she
would most likely have already booked herself a separate room.

BOOK THREE

ON THE DEVIL'S ISLAND;

or, My Life and Death in the Warsaw Ghetto

I felt terrible, of course. Overestimating the quality of my character, as he was wont to do with all men, Dr. Zamenhof had invested me with his trust, and I had failed him. I'd fallen asleep at my post. At the precise moment my presence was most needed in the committee chambers, I was loose upon the streets, chasing down a young pickpocket, and not because he'd picked my pocket (which he had done) but because I was under the impression he was the metempsychosical reappearance of my second wife.

Did I truly believe that a spiteful Ita had lured me out of the committee chambers in order to destroy the happiness I had found without her? Had I but thought the matter through, had I banked the fires of my heart, had I cooled my head with the balm of sweet reason, not only might Gaston yet be alive—the image of myself, cowering, as his tormentor pummeled him to death fills me with shame to this very hour—but the world might also now possess, as its common heritage, an international auxiliary language. One mustn't underestimate its loss. Without it, we live that much farther outside the precincts of Eden.

However, whether I believed in this scenario of a vengeful, heartbroken dybbuk hardly mattered, as I was shortly to discover. Ita or no, we were surrounded by schemers and cheats.

MUST I REHEARSE all the heartbreaking details?

Let me say only this: there is no spectacle less edifying than a turf war fought between intellectuals and idealists. Though no blood was spilled, many fortunes were lost and men's good names blackened and their years of visionary labor squandered. The Delegation Committee, as it turned out, was a fraud, a swindle, a Potemkin village designed to wrest the international language movement out of Dr. Zamenhof's utopian hands. Professor Couturat and the Marquis de Beaufront had been in cahoots the entire time (and with Rector Boirac away in Dijon and myself otherwise engaged, there was no one to stand in their way).

As the treachery of these men became clear, Dr. Zamenhof refused to have anything further to do them, but that only made it easier for Professor Couturat to push forward with his schemes, and he began to act as though the committee hadn't chosen Esperanto at all, but rather a new language of its own devising called Ido after its pseudonymous author.

Oh, yes, Esperanto might have been good enough for an Ostjude like me or Dr. Zamenhof, who, no matter how sophisticated we became, were still holding our breath, certain the Messiah was only one or two tram stops away, but the rest of the world needed something else: an international language enlightened by French culture, designed for the Western tongue, crafted to convey its most subtle and sublime philosophies. Ido, invented by hard-hearted scientists according to rock-hard scientific principle, would serve the needs of this real world without the burden of ungainly idealisms and other such fairy-lighted nonsense.

The war between Esperanto and Ido had begun. Abandoning his philosophical work, Professor Couturat pitched himself into battle. Between his scathing attacks on his opponents and his condemnation of the fissiparous tendencies of his own Ido Academy, he became that most uncompromising of men: the infallible pope of a small schismatic church, issuing his denunciations, broadcasting his excommunications, publishing his accusations in a universal language understood by only a tiny minority of men. Dr. Zamenhof, hoping to remain above the fray, was unable to defend himself against Professor Couturat's bloodying attacks.

And by the time it was all over, both men were dead, and the international language movement lay in ruins. Esperanto's great gains were sundered, and the worldwide momentum towards a universal language had splintered, exactly as Dr. Zamenhof had warned at my wedding, in a thousand schismatic directions.

AND WHO WAS this mysterious Ido, this phantom linguist who'd graced the table with his reforms mere hours before the committee, unable to pledge itself wholeheartedly to Esperanto, might have floundered without them? Naturally, we were all shocked when the marquis unmasked himself as the culprit in the pages of *L'Espérantiste*. A closet reformer, what sort of defense could a man like that have presented before the Delegation Committee on Esperanto's behalf?

Still, upon further reflection, it made a kind of sense. Everything about the man was false. He had secrets hidden within his secrets. To begin with, he wasn't even a marquis. Rather, the title had come to him late in his life and had been conferred upon him by no monarch grander than himself. Nor had he lost a family fortune. There's little difference in appearance between a lost fortune and none at all, and the marquis exploited this fact. Even further: his name wasn't Beaufront. Beaufront, as it turned out, was simply un beau front, a handsome façade. He'd been christened Louis Eugène Albert Chevreux, the bastard son of Louise Chevreux, his father unknown. Certainly he'd never mastered yogic breathing techniques under the tutelage of Swami Sri Giri, nor had he assisted Max Müller at Oxford on his translations of the Rig-Veda. Even the gazette in which he claimed to have read about Dr. Zamenhof's books carried no such item; and his beloved Adjuvanto, it goes without saying, existed only as a smaller fiction within the grander fiction he'd created of himself.

"Of course, the marquis was Ido!" I said, slapping my hand against the pages of *L'Espérantiste*. And now, he'd even confessed to it!

There was only one problem: as with everything else about the marquis, this confession was a lie.

SECRETS LIKE THESE cannot be kept forever, and when rumors of his authorship of the Ido pamphlet threatened to destroy the integrity of the Delegation Committee's decision, Professor Couturat did what any man in his situation would do: he placed a letter, written ostensibly to de Beaufront, identifying the marquis as the author of the pamphlet, into an envelope addressed to Otto Jespersen in care of the University of Copenhagen and sent it off.

(Whether he placed a corresponding letter to Professor Jespersen in an envelope addressed to the marquis, I do not know, but I wouldn't be surprised: in his deceptions, Professor Couturat possessed the thoroughness of a stage magician.)

The ploy worked. Puzzled to receive a letter from Professor Couturat that addressed him not as "Cher monsieur," his customary salutation, but as "Mon cher ami," Professor Jespersen was horrified by what he read next. If the marquis *were* Ido, and if Professor Couturat knew of this, what did it suggest about the integrity of the Delegation Committee's decision to endorse Ido's reforms?

(The answer: something less damning than what the truth itself would suggest—that Professor Couturat was Ido; that he had conspired with or perhaps even blackmailed the marquis into capitulating to Ido's reforms; that all those long and tedious days in Paris had been exactly what Dr. Zamenhof claimed they were: a comedy prepared in advance in which Professor Jespersen and the other experts, there for the sake of their prestige, were manipulated like puppets, an assertion Professor Jespersen had consistently denied.)

(When news of all this reached me, I dashed from my apartments in the Karlsplatz, where I'd returned following my expulsion from the Bernfeld household, and I ran to the Prater, hoping to find Herr Franz in residence at his Marvelous & Astonishing Puppet Theater. I intended to propose to him that we collaborate on a puppet show chronicling my life in the international language movement—I would author the script; he would design the figures—if for no other reason than that I relished a scene in which the marionette version of Otto Jespersen, suited in his academic gowns, his arms tangled up in his strings, his wooden forehead blushing beneath a patina of red paint, declares to an audience of mocking children that he is not now nor has ever been a puppet in the hands of a wily Couturat! The theater, however, had disappeared without a trace; in its place stood a key-making concession run by an unfriendly looking fellow with a large mustache.)

The letter caused Professor Jespersen enormous torment, and after many a sleepless night, he wrote to Professor Couturat, demanding the truth: Was the marquis Ido? When Professor Couturat confirmed this unhappy fact, Professor Jespersen insisted, in strongly worded letters to both men, that the fact be made immediately known. And when at last the marquis published his confession, Professor Jespersen was appeased and the matter closed, and Professor Couturat was free to devote his considerable intellectual and financial resources to the battle against Esperanto.

THE MARQUIS BURNED his correspondence with Professor Couturat, and so we'll never know what brought the two together as conspirators. Some have suggested that, unlike Dr. Zamenhof, the marquis couldn't resist a bribe; others that Professor Couturat knew a certain problematical something about de Beaufront's private life. Whatever the truth, it seems to me that Professor Couturat and the marquis were after the same thing: an Esperanto sans the inner idea. Distressed over Dr. Zamenhof's insistence upon making la lingvon universalan one more branch of le mystification Juiv, the marquis seized upon the opportunity to switch to a less ethereal horse in midstream, trading in the Hindenburg of Esperanto for the swift lifeboat of Ido an hour before he felt certain the former would crash and burn. And what did he have to lose, after all, except a handful of superfluous supersigns and the accusative -n?

LOË WAS WAITING for me at our hotel when I arrived from that final committee meeting, her bags stacked next to her chair in the atrium. She had a copy of Ido's pamphlet rolled up in one hand and was slapping it against the palm of the other.

"What in God's name are you doing with that piece of filth?" I said, coming in from la rue St. Louis.

"The general sent it to me," she said.

"Ah, General Sébert? Did he? Well, throw it out. I'll have nothing to do with it. This Monsieur Ido, whoever he is, is no friend of ours, and he's certainly no son of Dr. Esperanto's."

"You sound indignant."

"I am. The Delegation Committee was a complete farce!"

"Really?"

"Indeed."

"Well, if that's so . . ."

"Yes?"

". . . then where were you, I'm wondering, when it was time for you as Boirac's second to denounce these men for the blackguards you knew them to be?" She ripped her reading glasses from her face and glared at me through no lenses but her own astigmatic exasperation. "Not out chasing little boys in the streets, I hope."

"Sébert!" I cried. No doubt the general's spy had apprised her of everything.

"Don't!" Loë repulsed my hands when I reached for her shoulders. I peeked at the hotel's concierge stationed at his desk. He dropped his gaze and pretended not to be following our conversation. Why must we always argue in front of bellhops and doormen?

"Unpack your bags and stay," I said. "Let's talk this over."

"But these aren't my bags, Kaĉjo."

"They're not?"

"No, they're yours."

"Mine?"

"I had them packed for you. I'm sending you home. I'll be staying on in Paris. Perhaps the general and I can straighten out this mess. Albert," she called over my shoulder to the concierge, "ring for a taxi for Dr. Sammelsohn. It should be here in a minute," she told me.

"Loë," I said again.

"How could you just let them steal everything from us?" Once again she slapped the pamphlet against her hand. "This has Couturat's fingerprints all over it. Any child could see that. It's all so very Leibnizian!"

I ARRIVED IN Vienna and took a cab to our apartment. Herr Bernfeld met me at the door.

"I've taken the liberty of having your things boxed up and sent to your rooms in the Karlsplatz," he said, screwing in his monocle. "There's no telling when my daughter will return and no reason for you to stay on here, really, haunting the place like a ghost. Your continued employment at the firm is, naturally, out of the question."

"Naturally."

"However, I've spoken with Dr. Koller about the possibility of your returning to the clinic."

"And?"

"I am happy to report I've managed a fifteen percent rise in your salary."

He was sorry to have heard about the debacle in Paris, he told me. However, had he been consulted, he would have warned us against exactly this sort of treachery.

"Esperanto may be capable of reform, but not so men's hearts."

He held my hand in parting, and despite everything, I was grateful for the warmth of his touch.

And seven years later, when the Serbian madman Gavrilo Princip assassinated the archduke Franz Ferdinand, and Europe set to cannibalizing itself, none of it, I regret to say, took me by surprise—neither the ferocity of the hatreds evinced on all sides nor the lethal shortsightedness of men who had earlier possessed loftier temperaments. Hadn't I lived through the entire thing in miniature, my naïveté burnt to cinders by the Idists? After witnessing excellent men devouring one another in the service of a benevolent idea, the Great War seemed little more than a fully staged version of an opera I'd already seen as a chamber piece.

All about me, men of good sense, men who should have known better—and by that, I mean writers, doctors, artists—felt their blood quickening at the thought of a good, purgative war. And while these men, in their last moments of freedom, set about proposing marriage to girls or purchasing new piping for their military costumes, I simply took mine out of its trunk—it stank of moth balls, perspiration, and the odium of military life—and spent nothing on its rehabilitation. As for girls, I had none to propose to.

Still, the emperor needed all his sons, not merely the enthusiasts, and having been long in the reserves—the Thirty-fifth Yeomanry was my home—I was mustered into the medical corps as an officer and sent to the Eastern Front with a truckload of optical equipment. In no more than two hours, my assistants and I—these were a Dr. Gleissner and a Dr. Winternitz—had been captured by a Russian lieutenant and locked inside a tavern and promptly forgotten. "The war is over for us, lads," I told them, happy to have spent nothing smartening up my uniform. We spent the night and the next day and the night after that requisitioning the tavern's whiskey and sleeping across its long tables, while the battle of

Przemyśl raged on in the distance. We could hear the howitzers booming and the planes groaning overhead.

At daybreak of the second day, I ordered Dr. Gleissner to open up the
tavern door, which he did, although not without difficulty, bruising his
shoulder in the process. The morning light poured in, momentarily blinding us. Birdsong filled the air. Venturing out, we discovered the corporal
who had been our guard, sitting not far from the door with a bullet wound
in his head. "Take his gun," I gave the order to Dr. Winternitz, "and his
eyeglasses, I suppose." We stashed these inside our truck and roared away,
traveling no more than three kilometers before running out of petrol. We
took turns pushing the truck after that. We might have abandoned it, I
suppose. However, it contained valuable medical supplies belonging to the
emperor. We pushed deeper into the countryside and, as we traveled, I began to recognize the hills and the dales and the little rivers. We weren't far
from Szibotya, I knew. We sheltered, in fact, for three days in my father's
old gazebo. It was in ruins by then. My parents were long dead, Father having perished in the Szibotya pogroms of 1905, Mother succumbing a few
days later, some say of a broken heart, others by less gentle means.

I couldn't bring myself to approach the house. Instead, I lay on my
stomach in the grass, watching from a distance, as either Dr. Gleissner
or Dr. Winternitz knocked upon the door to beg some food. The woman
of the house brought out whatever she could. Periodically, as though she
knew I was there, she'd raise a hand and cup it to her brow, shielding her
eyes from the sun and peering into the orchard, searching for me, or so
it seemed, among the cherry trees.

After three days, I could take no more of this, and I gave the order
to push on. Though we'd discussed it not at all beforehand, and though
we'd pushed the damned thing all the way from Galicia, we abandoned
the optical truck at the city gates of Vienna. Let the emperor come and
claim his property if he wants it! Affecting limps and contriving slings,
so we might at least appear to have been wounded, Dr. Gleissner and Dr.
Winternitz and I bid one another farewell before stealing back into our
former lives.

I unlocked the door of my rooms in the Karlsplatz and slept for what seemed like a thousand and one nights in the soft sheets of my bed. Hobbling in on crutches the next morning, my arm in a sling, I reported not to the army board, where I was obligated by law and by my own failing sense of patriotism to report, but to the Allgemeines Krankenhaus, where I quietly took up my old position. After a decent interval, I unlaced the sling and replaced my crutches with a sturdy cane. I was nearly forty. Who was going to think anything of it?

EVEN AFTER THE armistice, terrible privations ensued. The war had cost its sponsors billions, and we were all paying for it now. The only man I knew who avoided absolute ruin was my former father-in-law, Herr Bernfeld (now Baron Bernfeld, if that title meant anything still). Bernfeld & Sons, Inc., had actually profited from the war. At their father's urging, a Bernfeld resided in nearly every European capital, and the brothers had sold arms to every side, trafficking in a dozen different currencies, so that by war's end, the corporation had lost not one sou nor one heller nor one pfennig nor one penny nor one ruble to the new inflation.

Of the hundred million men mobilized on all sides, sixty million had been wounded and thirteen million killed, and though I'm loath to admit it, this left a considerable number of war widows in my immediate vicinity. While in other cities, jubilant soldiers marched in their victory parades, it was the women belonging to men they had slaughtered who paraded through my apartment and into my bed, a long line of comely widows, each a numbingly infinite variation on but a single theme. And though we were all very kind to each other, and grateful, I suspect, for these hours of reprieve, the sense that we were standing in for others—they for Loë, and I for scores of men—performing on their behalf an act they would not (in Loë's case) or could not (in the case of the dead) perform, made of our couplings a grinding and repetitive business.

And one grey morning, bleary from a short night in the arms of a not terribly beautiful stranger, breathing in the soft fumes of her halitus, I extricated myself from bed and stood at my window, my thoughts turning east. Dr. Zamenhof had not survived the war, it's true, but his children had, and among them, as I recalled, were two lovely daughters.

God only knew how they were faring, orphaned and alone. As I stirred a curative dose of sugar into my coffee, for the first time in what seemed like ages, I sensed a glimmer of hope rising with the sun.

Perhaps a visit from Uncle Kaĉjo was in order.

OR ONKLO KAĈJO, rather.

As the porter led me into the vestibule, I calculated how many years had passed since Fraŭlino Loë and I had visited, and the answer I arrived at was: nearly twenty-five! Certainly I was no longer the young swain I'd been. On the contrary, in the intervening years, I'd become that most ridiculous of persons: a bachelor in his late middle years. Upon our greeting one another, however, I could detect no astonishment in either Adamo's or Zofia's eyes at the grey-bearded gentleman standing before them.

No, as I'd been an adult when they were children, I appeared to them as I always had, as an old man; and this was my first indication, received as soon as I'd crossed their threshold, that Zofia would never consent to be my lover, to say nothing of my wife. Additionally — and it pains me to confess this — she was no longer la bela junulino I remembered from the early congress days. Gone was the little girl who'd so dopily anticipated my proposal to her onklino Loë. In her place stood a stout matron with an incipient mustache. (She'd had a rough few years, I'd learn over dinner that evening, serving as a medic in either the Russian or the Polish army, I can't remember which, while her brother served, as a medic as well, in the opposing corps.)

Nevertheless, she greeted me warmly. "This way, Onklo Kaĉjo, and we'll show you to your room."

Dr. Adamo, tall and courtly, took my arm, and guided me towards the stairs. "You remember Lidja, of course," he said.

"Of course," I said, although when I'd seen her last, she'd been a toddler in her mother's arms, and this was an image that I found *I* couldn't excise from *my* mind. Though a willowy woman in her twenties, she seemed as much a baby to me as she always had, and I realized with a pang that my dream of finding a bride among la Zamenhofidinoj was simply one more impossible scheme.

(Why must everything concerning the Zamenhofs fall into that category?)

It was all I could do not to turn around, descend the stairs, hail a taxi, depart for the train stations, and return to Vienna at once. In fact, the only thing that stopped me from doing so, besides my own social cowardice—which has stopped me from doing half the things I've wanted to my entire life—was the sight of Wanda Zamenhof, Dr. Adamo's young wife, who, at that moment, joined us, stepping into the foyer from the kitchen, drying her hands on a kitchen towel.

The introductions were quickly made, and I took her in with the rapacity of an old starving wolf, devouring her optically from the cap of her ruby-blonde head to the meat of her calf, and was startled, as I did, to find a child hiding behind her shapely legs.

"Well, well, well, who's this then?" I said, crouching down to greet him. His fingers digging into his mother's thigh, he hid his eyes against her skirt. The adults all laughed. The boy was dressed in a little sailor's suit, which seemed an odd touch to me, given the family's pacifism. He'd obviously wanted to greet the visitor but had found himself, at the decisive moment, too shy to do so.

"Now, Lutek," one of his aunts said, her admonition making him peek out at me.

I offered him my hand. "Doktoro Jakovo Jozefo Sammelsohn."

"Ludovic Zamenhof," he said in his tiny voice.

(His parents had named him after his grandfather, of course.)

"Care for a lollipop?" I reached into my coat pocket for the sweet.

He shook his head fiercely and withdrew even further behind his mother's skirts. Still crouching, I gazed up the tower of her legs. Staring down at the two of us, she took the candy from my hand, and by way of apologizing for her son's rudeness, said, "Perhaps he'll feel differently after dinner, Dr. Sammelsohn."

AS THEY WERE too polite to do so, it was I who brought Loë up, later in the evening, when we were all seated around the dining room table.

"Yes, we occasionally hear from la sinjorino," Dr. Adamo replied. "In fact, she recently sent funds for Father's tomb."

"Ah, did she?" I said.

"I believe she's on the point of remarrying," Zofia said.

I nodded grimly. "So I understand."

"And you've never thought of remarrying, Onklo?" Lidja asked.

As though caught off-guard, I glanced up from my aperitif, leaving my lips on the rim of the glass. Returning the drink to the table, I said, "Well, that's precisely why I'm here, Lilke."

"Oh?"

"Yes, to see which of the two of you will have me."

The laughter occasioned by this remark was so open and affectionate, so joyous and mirthful and sweet, I couldn't fail to understand how ridiculous, how utterly impossible, the notion of my marrying one of them seemed.

At the sound of his parents' and aunts' laughter, little Ludovic let out a squeal.

"Don't worry, Dr. Sammelsohn," Wanda said, pressing her hand onto the top of mine.

"Kaĉjo," I corrected her.

"I'll be happy to adopt you." She said this in what I hoped was at least a mildly flirtatious way, and once again, the table erupted in laughter.

"Would you like that?" Zofia asked Ludovic. "Would you like an elder brother?"

"No!" the boy screamed at his aunt. To his mother, he said, "No, Panjo! Only me!" He began to cry in earnest, his face as red as a beet, his lungs thundering like a bull-roarer.

"Aw, now, now, Lutek, no, no," his aunt Lidja cautioned him, tutting her tongue.

"It was just a joke," his father explained, helpless to placate the boy. "No one's adopting Onklo Kaĉjo." He pulled an apologetic face at me. "Isn't that right, Onklo?"

DESPITE THE WEEKLY meetings of the Warsaw Esperanto Society, held in their parlor; despite Poland's new postwar independence; despite the Jewishness of the Zamenhofs themselves, the Zamenhof household was a Russian household, and it wasn't long before I'd become one of those characters one finds in a Russian play. You know what I mean: a friend, though not a dear friend, living for ancient and unexplained reasons on the family estate.

None of the women paid any attention to me. Lidja, under the spell of Bahá'íism, spent her days learning the sacred Bahá'í texts and petitioning the Holy Guardian Shoghi Effendi for permission to travel to the holy city of Haifa; Doktorino Zofia was busy with her house calls and her hospital rounds; Wanda was a happily married woman devoted, through her own work as an oculist, to that of her husband. Even the maid demonstrated no true interest in my person. Though at the age of thirteen, I was a boy a jilted girl might throw herself into the river over, the only member of the Zamenhof household who seemed to identify me as a sexual threat was its three-year-old son.

Nevertheless, I delighted in the warm atmosphere of their home, and my visits, which lasted longer than I intended, began occurring more frequently than necessary. Sometimes I spent half the year in the little room Zofia had set aside for me, reading my books and pining away for Wanda. I was here, I told myself, to help Dr. Adamo run his father's old consultancy, and not to steal his wife, and yet, each time I visited, Wanda seemed only more beautiful to me. I denied my feelings as much as I could, and certainly I acted upon none of them. I held her yarn when she knitted, I lit her cigarettes, I brought her cups of tea, aware that to press my suit further was to risk my place inside their little family. Still, especially in the early years, when she still possessed the weighted breasts of a new mother, it was all I could do, as we listened in the parlor to Dr. Adamo playing cello in an amateur quartet, not to stare at her bosom and imagine myself falling asleep there, my head in the soft cleft between them.

I WAS IN Warsaw when Dr. Zamenhof's monument was unveiled. His grave had been marked until then by the humblest of markers, and among Klara's final wishes had been the hope that samideanoj the world over might raise the funds for an appropriately magnificent tomb. The work had been fraught with difficulties. The sculptor, a local madman named Lubelski, had insisted upon Aberdeen marble — "Ah, the grey of

Aberdeen, Dr. Sammelsohn," he told me after I'd volunteered to take over the project on behalf of the Zamenhofs, "is a grey of which Warsaw, which knows much of grey, knows nothing!"—and as a consequence, the work had taken ages. When the stone finally crossed the North and the Baltic seas, and I traveled to Danzig to meet Pan Lubelski and to claim it, I was mortified, as was he, to see that certain typographical errors had crept into the inscription. As though Idist pranksters had sabotaged it, the inscription contained circumflex accents where none was needed.

Clutching at his heart, Pan Lubelski nearly rent his garment at the sight of these diacritical marrings. "Miecystam Lubelski shall never permit his name to remain on such a monstrosity!" he told me, referring to himself, as was his habit, in the third person. Instead, he browbeat me into purchasing a new ticket for him to Aberdeen, and he boarded the ship and disappeared with the stone. I was afraid I'd see neither of them again, but shortly before the ninth anniversary of Dr. Zamenhof's death, the one turned up with the other in tow. Klara, however, had not lived to see the day. She lay buried beside her husband, a circumstance that made the occasion even more bittersweet.

According to the newspapers, nearly five hundred people attended the ceremony. I don't know how they calculate such things, but I can attest to the fact that the crowd was enormous. A crisp stand of Esperanto flags snapped in the breezes above the monument, which Pan Lubelski had draped with a heavy black cloth. The greenery surrounding the Zamenhofs' graves had been landscaped into the shape of a five-pointed star. An honor guard of students, bearing more flags, stood at attention, and next to them were representatives from the Jewish community and the Esperanto Society and various other organizations. Reporters and photographers jostled with government officials for a place near the front. I stood as close to Wanda as decency permitted. My lovesickness was then at its most feverish. Her somber clothing and her pale complexion gave her a soulful look, and I found myself imagining her, standing years and years hence in a similar attitude at my grave, mourning the love neither of us had had the courage to declare.

At eleven o'clock precisely, Professor Odo Bujwid, an ancient friend of Dr. Zamenhof's, cut the ribbon, and with a magician-like flourish, Pan

Lubelski ripped the black cloth away. The monument was unveiled: a tower of granite blocks upon which sat a beribboned globe. A small, sad cheer went up. The choir, cued by its director, sang "L'Espero." Various speeches were made. Dr. Adamo, representing the family, placed a white wreath at the foot of the tomb, and other wreaths soon followed.

At one point, my attention was arrested by a sight I hadn't thought to anticipate. A couple I couldn't quite identify stood on the far side of the Zamenhofs' grave. The woman, her hands in a fur muff, seemed distraught; the gentleman, in a bowler hat, less so. Indeed, he looked rather bored. Once he even dropped his head back and yawned before opening his watch and glancing at the sky, checking his timepiece against the position of the sun. It was only when the woman caught my glance and looked at me directly that I realized—with an alarmed constriction of the heart—that it was Loë and the most recent of her many husbands.

SHE'D HAD SEVERAL between our marriage and the present moment, and I was pleased to see that she came to the reception, following the ceremony, without him. She stood across the Zamenhofs' parlor with a drink in her hand, leaning her head against the wall, dressed from head to toe in black, the corona of her golden hair shot through with handsome ribbons of grey. I couldn't help staring at her, though she refused to return my glance or acknowledge me in any way.

As those of us gathered around the piano finished singing "L'Espero" and the poet Leo Belmont began sharing his memories of the Majstro, Loë allowed me to look at her for the first time without turning away. She nodded her head almost imperceptibly towards a door before departing the room. An electric jangle shivered my spine. I tamped my cigar out and searched for a place to leave my glass. Though I nearly knocked over an end table, righting the vase before it fell, no one seemed to notice as I crossed the parlor—Wanda was busy greeting late-arriving well-wishers—and slipped out of the room.

There was no one in the hallway by the time I'd entered it, and I walked its lengths wondering if I hadn't imagined the entire thing. The day, the monument, Pan Lubelski's arrogance, the crowd of samideanoj, the Majstro's absence and Klara's had had an oppressive effect on me. In my current mental state, it would have been easy to imagine all sorts of things. I wouldn't have been surprised to have seen a Minotaur in the middle of the parlor, sharing its memories of the day the Majstro had liberated it from its labyrinth.

But no, finally, a door cracked open, and through it, I heard a suddenly too-familiar voice whispering: "Ho, Kaĉjo! In here, darling. I'm in here."

THE ROOM WAS the laundry room. Clean-smelling sheets had been hung up to dry, and the afternoon sun, blazing through the windows, projected violent rose and blue rectangles on their snowy-white surfaces. Folded and stacked in wicker baskets were our sleeping garments. Loë stood before the heater, fretting her fingers together and apart. The years had been extraordinarily kind to her, I must say. She seemed a richer version of herself, older, yes, but even more striking, the small amount of extra weight making her hips and bust beneath her clothing appear as though they'd ripened. She met my eye, and I was overcome by a sense of lust-inflected remorse, if such a sentiment exists.

"Oh, now I've forgotten what it was I wanted to tell you." She lifted her hands in a gesture that wasn't quite a shrug, and for a small time, neither of us said anything at all.

Finally, I said, "Well . . ."

And she said, "Yes?"

But then I shook my head as though I too had forgotten what I'd wanted to say.

"The monument was quite . . ."

"Oh, that Lubelski . . ." I laughed ruefully.

"No, no, you did a wonderful . . ."

"What a madman to work with, really."

She lowered her head and laughed through her nose.

"And was that your . . . ?"

"Husband?" She supplied the word I couldn't bring myself to pronounce.

"Ah. So he *is* your. . . ?"

"Husband. Oh, yes. Oskar," she said, and she laughed, as though at

something ludicrous. She bit her underlip. Her tooth left a small inden-
tation in its skin. "But I suppose there are other, more pleasant topics to
discuss."

"I suppose," I said.

"And have you . . . ?" she said, peeking up at me from beneath her
brow. I shook my head to indicate that I didn't understand her. "Married?" she said.

"Oh," I said. "No. Well."

"Remarried, I should have said." She shrugged prettily. "Married
again, I meant."

"No. There's been . . . no one, really." I shrugged as well.

"No one? Really?"

"They're all . . . married, I suppose. Including—"

"Don't say it, Kaĉjo."

"—you." I refused to be censored.

"Ho!" she said.

"Well. Just look at you."

"Enough!"

"You're just so beautiful."

Too late to stop me from pronouncing the word, she covered my mouth
with her hand. And then, of course, I kissed her, or rather she kissed
me, or rather I'm not certain who kissed whom. Perhaps we'd kissed
each other. Certainly, I'd started by kissing her hand, which she'd placed
against my mouth, but instantly, her arms were around my neck, mine
were around her back, and we were grappling, as though we couldn't
quite bring ourselves near enough to each other. Her face flushed against
mine, and I could feel its heat. The tears on my cheek—hers? mine? I
couldn't be certain—were hot.

"Oh, no, no, no," she said. Breaking away from me, she dried her
cheeks with the heel of her hand, and the little muscle between her eyebrows tightened. Straightening her clothes, she looked as if she were
about to call a policeman. She took a step away from me. "You're not
preying on these people, are you, Kaĉjo?"

"On the Zamenhofs, you mean?"

"Because they're still very much in grief, you know."

"How dare you suggest such a thing!"

"Are you out of money?"

"Am I what? Loë!"

"Because Father gave you a very generous settlement, I understand."

"Yes, he did. You needn't remind me of that. I'm well aware of it, thank you!"

"Then what are you doing here?"

"Can't a friend simply visit his friends?"

"Of course, he may. However, you've all but moved in!"

"Moved in? No, Loë! I'm simply here to help with the monument. Why? Has someone complained?"

"No, but they should have, the way you look at her!"

"I have no idea what you're talking about."

"Are you in love with her?"

"Don't be ridiculous!"

"Are you?"

"She's a happily married woman, Loë!"

"Just tell me the truth!"

"And a mother besides!"

"Stop lying to me! Just tell me: are you in love with her, Kaĉjo?"

"I'm not, but if I were, why would you even care?"

"Ha! So you are, then!"

"Am I? I suppose I am. Or maybe not! I don't know. Should I be?" I pushed my hand through my hair. "I don't think I am. Although I might be."

Loë drew in a breath. Then, as though they were hammers beating anvils, she hurled her fists against the lapels of my jacket. "God damn you! God damn you! God damn you!"

I captured her wrists and, though we tussled, she was unable to free herself. Our wrestling was sufficiently violent, however, that her hair clasp opened and a wing of her hair came undone. Manacling her wrists, I forced her against the wall and pressed my body against hers. I kissed her and, as she kissed me back, I felt all the sorrows of our long separation dropping away. All I wanted was to erase the years and to awaken beside her in the bed we'd shared on Papagenogasse. However, when I released her hands and folded her into my arms and kissed her again, I felt the dull thwack of her elbows against my chest.

"How dare you!" She slapped me half a dozen times in the face. "I'm a married woman! Wanda is a married woman! What *is* wrong with you?" She repinioned her hair and straightened her waistcoat. "Must you make everyone's life a misery?"

Despite Loë's admonition, I lingered in Warsaw, and so I wasn't in Vienna when the chancellor of Germany arrived, having sent his armies in before him. Nor did I witness the citizens of my country gathering en masse in the Heldenplatz to welcome him in as their liberator. And from what were they being liberated, one might ask? Why, from me, I suppose. I took it personally, in any case. It was hard not to when, as a consequence, my citizenship was revoked and my passport nullified. Listening to Herr Hitler's speeches over the wireless or struggling through as much of *Mein Kampf* as I could, I'd noticed a curious thing: the chancellor spoke of us in the singular. It was always der Jude! der Jude! der Jude! who troubled him. And so, although grammatically at least, only one of us seemed to be bothering him, I wasn't convinced I wasn't that one. And if I were dieser Jude! who so perturbed the chancellor of Germany, why didn't I run farther from him, one might also ask? After all, I was an old hand at being driven from my home. However, I no longer possessed a usable passport, and I very much doubted I'd have been given a certificate to emigrate; the Zionists distributed these mainly to their friends. Also, having driven me from Vienna, I told myself the Germans would never follow me to Warsaw, but of course, there, I was wrong.

I WAS LYING in bed in my room in the Zamenhofs' house when I heard the first explosions. By the time the call rang out for all able-bodied men to report to the Vistula, the city was under attack. The German planes kept coming, one squadron after another, wave after wave, firing on anything they chose. The Zamenhofs' house went up in flames after an incendiary bomb was dropped upon it. During the weeks of siege that followed the fall of the city, the Zamenhofs themselves were arrested, targeted specifically, I believe, as the Majstro's children. (As incredible as it may seem, upon their earlier entry into Vienna, the Germans took time out of a busy schedule of looting and murder to stop by Vienna's Esperanto Museum in order to destroy the few childhood notebooks of Dr. Zamenhof's that had survived his father's auto-da-fé.) I ran to the Jewish Council, hoping to secure their release, but no help was forthcoming from there. "People are being arrested, Dr. Sammelsohn?" they screamed at me. "Of course, they're being arrested! What did you expect? There's a war on!" And so I made my way, recklessly perhaps, or recklessly indeed, to the occupier's headquarters at Pawiak Prison.

It was there that I first encountered Rav Kalonymos Kalmish Szapira, the holy Piaseczna Rebbe, and though I didn't know it then, he would shortly become the third of the father figures who haunt these pages, Drs. Freud and Zamenhof having preceded him. At that moment, he was descending the front steps of the prison with a young man in his arms, and he grabbed me by the elbow as I passed them, as though hooking me with a cane.

"I wouldn't go in there, Dr. Sammelsohn, if I were you."

A tallish man, he glowered at me from behind the elegant sable of his beard, his hat knocked onto the back of his head, his spectacles low on his nose. I had no idea who he was and assumed he was simply an ordinary rabbi. Judging, however, by the jubilant expressions passing between him and the young man, I could only surmise he had just done exactly what he was warning me against.

I stopped and smiled sheepishly. Embarrassed by my own theatrical heroics, I said, "Apparently you've managed it, however."

"Yes," he said, "but I'm not unarmed."

Now it was his turn to give me an embarrassed smile. Indeed, he blushed, and although I'm certain he meant nothing of the kind, I found myself looking for a gun or a telltale bulge beneath his long frock coat.

"It's not cowardice, you know," Reb Kalonymos said kindly.

"No, isn't it?"

"Not at all."

"But who will save the Zamenhofs, then?"

He shrugged unhappily. "There's only so much each of us can do."

As this was not merely a consoling gesture, but a statement of fact, I turned from the prison's façade. It wasn't difficult, in truth, to lose enthusiasm for the task. "Very well then," I said. As there was nothing more to do, I bid him good day, meanwhile congratulating the young man on his release. However, as I turned to descend the stairs, the rebbe lightly touched my arm. "A moment, Dr. Sammelsohn."

"Yes, what is it?"

"If I'm not mistaken," he said, "you're a descendant of the holy Seer of Lublin?"

"On my mother's side, yes, that's correct."

"As am I."

"Ah," I said.

"Which makes us cousins, I suppose."

It was an odd thing to be discussing, I felt, given our circumstances. However, it proved to be considerably less odd than what the rebbe said next. "Perhaps this isn't the time or the place," he said, leaning into me and dropping his voice, "but I was wondering if you'd be kind enough to pay me a visit."

"A visit?"

"Sooner might be better than later, I think."

"At your home?"

"If it's still standing."

"Certainly," I said.

"Excellent, as there's a literary matter I wish to discuss with you."

A LITERARY MATTER?

I couldn't believe I'd heard him correctly. These were the days of house arrests and firing squads. Our lives were a chaos. People were being murdered in the streets. Against all codes of war, even after they'd conquered our city, the Germans kept firing on its civilian population. Rebbe Szapira knew this as well as anyone. After our meeting on the steps of Pawiak Prison, I'd made some inquiries and discovered that his son had been wounded only the day before when a German soldier let loose a riptide of shrapnel, and a small piece of it had burst through the rebbe's window. The poor man had bled so profusely, though it meant braving a storm of bullets and incendiary bombs, he was taken to the hospital. Or rather he was taken from hospital to hospital, as each was full, and none had any supplies. (Among the German's übermenschliche achievements, it seemed that they had sped up time; the distance between the present and the future had collapsed; and we were dying too quickly to be accommodated.) Help was found at last at the hospital on Blonda Street, but the rebbe's daughter-in-law and his sister-in-law were killed when an incendiary bomb exploded at the hospital entrance. The rebbe himself had only moments before gone off in search of a Dr. Binswanger, or he would have been killed as well. Upon his return, confronted by the terrible scene, he'd ordered one of his students to see that the women were taken to the cemetery, and another to gather up their jewelry, lest someone desecrate their bodies by robbing them. When this second student was captured by a German patrol and charged with looting from the dead, the rebbe put aside all other concerns and dashed to the prison to explain everything and to plead for the boy's life.

His son died from his wounds on the second day of Sukkos, and the rebbe, in strict conformity with the Law, put off his mourning until the holy day was done. Then tearing his garment and sitting, he cried, "The war is already lost for me. May God have mercy on the people of Israel."

Could a man really write a book under these circumstances?

NONE OF OUR Yiddish writers ever thought to translate Proust, nor had his monumental novel been written when I was a child reading stolen books in my father's gazebo, and yet, each time I encountered an Hasidic rebbe, I felt I'd gorged myself on madeleines. I could never enter Rav Szapira's study without feeling the hand of Reb Yudel on my neck, and the creeping resentment I continually felt in the rebbe's presence, I knew, had little to do with the man himself.

"Ah, good afternoon, good afternoon, Dr. Sammelsohn!" he said the first time I visited him, rising to greet me. "You've come at last! Just as I knew you would! Tea?" He rubbed his hands together as though he were a nervous waiter.

"Thank you, no," I said. I had no wish to take anything from the rebbe's precious stores.

"Oh, please don't deprive me of the joy of caring for a guest. If you must deprive me of something, let it be tea but not that."

I couldn't help laughing. "If the rebbe insists," I said.

"If the rebbe insists! He insists! The rebbe insists!" He opened a door behind his desk and called out to someone in another part of the house, "Darling?" To me, he said, "My daughter will be only too happy to see to our needs. She's all I have now, really." He reseated himself and folded his hands together before him. "Now, so tell me — how is our illustrious doctor?"

"The times are difficult for everyone, I suppose."

"Of course, of course, though not the worst we've seen."

"No?" I shot him an incredulous look.

"Perhaps not ourselves personally, but our people."

"Oh. That," I said. "Yes."

It was a grim subject, and so I let it drop.

"You're still at . . . ?"

"The Zamenhofs'," I said, finishing his sentence. "Though I'm back on Dzika Street, the new house on Królewska having been blown to bits."

"You knew the father, I believe?"

"Dr. Zamenhof was a friend of mine, yes."

"I don't wish to be harsh . . ." He hesitated. "But a man will always pay for his blindnesses." He shook his head. "Hilelismo, Homaranismo. Nariŝkajtismo is more like it: nonsensismo. Though I had nothing personally against the man."

"Indeed, no one did," I said with a tight smile. I wasn't going to argue with the rebbe. I knew from long experience that one can't win with these fanatical pietists.

"Dreaming of his useless utopias." He made a little clicking sound with his tongue. "He wanted to do away with national borders and now: look! the borders have fallen. He wished to do away with religion, and now: look! our religion is illegal. As a physician, I'd diagnose it as a classic case of premature messianism. At times, a man will rush so passionately that all he accomplishes is smashing his head against the doorjamb."

As a physician. This is as good a place as any, I suppose, to mention that, in addition to his other many accomplishments—according to his Hasidim, the rebbe was the wonder of his generation, a brilliant theologian, and a ladder of piety whose topmost rung reached to the Heavens—he was not only a violinist of professional caliber but a self-taught doctor whose prescriptions were, nevertheless, recognized by all the pharmacists in the city.

"In any case," I said, hoping to change the subject, "the rebbe wished to speak to me about a literary matter?"

"Ah! Yes!" His face brightened. "Though may I show you something first?"

"Certainly," I said, and I followed him to a cabinet, where he unlocked first one drawer and, not finding what he was searching for, the next.

"Yes, here it is." He handed me a stack of papers. "Well?" he asked expectantly, looking over the rims of his spectacles at me.

I examined the sheets, but could see nothing out of the ordinary. "It appears to be a religious treatise of some kind."

"A treatise, yes, but as you can see, there's one remarkable feature. If you'll look carefully, you'll notice that the handwriting changes exactly here, right in the middle of this sentence."

I peered more closely at the work. "Yes, I see it now."

"The rebbetzin and I were very close." Reb Kalonymos pushed his spectacles onto his forehead. "And once, I was in the middle of recording a talk I'd given, when, for reasons I can no longer remember, I was called away. A medical emergency or a spiritual one of some kind. In any case, when I returned, though the hour was quite late and I was quite exhausted, I wished to finish the work, lest I forget some of the ideas that had come out of my mouth when I'd delivered the talk, you see? However, sitting down at my desk, I discovered there was no need, no need at all. In my absence, the rebbetzin had picked up my pen and finished it herself, beginning exactly where I'd left off. I read it through and saw that nothing needed changing. On the contrary, everything was as I had intended it, or even better."

His eyes glistened with the memory. He smiled apologetically and, with a trembling hand, reached for the pages, which were clearly dear to him.

"I haven't touched my violin since the day of her death. And you?" he said, tucking the manuscript back into its drawer as carefully as if he were tucking a child into bed. "You've never been married, isn't that right?"

"No, I have actually. More than once, in fact."

He appeared momentarily puzzled. "Oh, yes. The little retarded girl. I'd forgotten."

"Forgotten?"

"And the Bernfeld daughter, and the first one as well — what was her name? Hindele? — when you were a child."

"I don't recall ever mentioning any of this to the rebbe."

"To the rebbe!" he said. "Let us do away with this tedious third-person address, shall we? We must learn to speak in complete honesty for what I have in mind." Gesturing with his hand, he invited me to return to our chairs at his desk. "Shall we get down to cases, then?"

"Fine," I said. "But if we're to speak with each other in complete honesty, please tell me how it is you knew about my wives."

"Oh!" The rebbe took off his glasses and gave me a flirtatious look. "I made some inquiries, that's all. After we'd encountered each other on the prison steps. Oh, surely, Dr. Sammelsohn, you don't believe that a rebbe can read a man's life story in the lines of his face, do you?"

"Can he?"

"Can you?" he said, laughing.

"No," I said.

"Then how could I? I'm not the Szibotyer Rebbe, after all. No, in these modern times, Dr. Sammelsohn, so much has been lost. I can't, for example, remember any past lives, nor the sonnets I wrote when I was an Italian rabbi."

He smiled mischievously at me. If I didn't misunderstand him, he was referring to the fantastical story the Szibotyer Rebbe had told my friend Shai and me the night he'd exorcised the dybbuk from Khave Katznelson.

"But there's no one you could have asked about that!" I protested.

"No, as a matter of fact, there isn't. In any case, moving on." He cleared his throat, coughing into his hands. "As I've indicated to you, I'm writing a book."

My head was spinning.

"A book?" I have to admit that this was as flummoxing as anything he'd yet said.

"You're amazed?" he said.

"Amazed? No," I lied.

"Astonished?"

"Well . . ." I demurred.

"Astounded . . ."

I squinted at him.

". . . to the point of muteness perhaps?"

I got up and walked to the window.

"Out with it, just out with it, Dr. Sammelsohn! Just tell me what it is you're thinking."

I turned to him and, as gently as I could, I said, "Is this really the time for books?"

He looked me in the eye, smiling beneath his mustache. "Oh, Dr. Sammelsohn, it's clear you haven't thought the matter through."

"No, I haven't," I said. "I haven't thought about it at all beyond my initial confoundment."

"Yes, that's clear."

"Then perhaps the rebbe will enlighten me."

"Your reaction is a purely emotional one."

(I suppose he was right. Like a good diagnostician, he'd put his finger on my most sensitive wound. From the books Reb Sender stuck beneath my nose before I could even read, to the novels Avrum the Book Peddler had forced upon me, to Dr. Freud and Dr. Breuer's *Studies on Hysteria* and Dr. Fliess's *On the Causal Connection between the Nose and the Sexual Organ,* to Dr. Esperanto's *Unua Libro* and Professors Couturat et Leau's *Histoire de la langue universelle,* I'd been driven nearly mad by books. For personal reasons, I'd exclude the copy of Dr. Albrecht's *Mysteries of Females or, The Secrets of Nature* Loë brought with her to Boulogne-sur-Mer, but otherwise I couldn't remember when a book had ever done me any good.)

The rebbe said, "One need only ask himself this, Dr. Sammelsohn: if books are so dangerous they must be burned, then isn't the most efficient act of sabotage the writing of a book?"

"Sabotage?"

Nodding, the rebbe stroked his beard.

"You can't be serious."

"Dr. Sammelsohn, this isn't simply a book. You must understand that. Things are dire. Fewer and fewer of my people come to me on Shabbos. I can't blame them. It's not a pleasant thing to be out in the streets these days. A hundred souls might turn up, but these are my Hasidim. If I were to ask one or two for an opinion, what is he going to tell me? How can he criticize me? He can't, he won't. But a cousin, a descendant, like myself, of the seer, and a freethinker besides? Now there's a man whose opinion might be worth a złoty or two!"

"If we *are* truly cousins."

"But of course, we're truly cousins! On our mothers' sides. We've been over this! You know it as well as I, although perhaps what you don't know is how deep the connection runs."

"If I'm understanding you correctly, you wish me to—"

"Sit in on my talks during the Third Meal, to which I'm inviting you as an honored guest, to listen critically to everything I say, remembering everything you hear. At the end of the Sabbath, because of the curfew, you'll remain here, and you can sleep in my son's room. You'll write down everything you remember—along with any thoughts you've had about what I've said—I'll write down all I remember, and on Sunday morning, we'll compare notes, draw up a fair copy of the talk, after which you'll be completely free of me until the following Sabbath or holy day, whichever comes first. And in this way, believe me, Dr. Sammelsohn, we'll bring our enemies to their knees. So what do you say?"

What could I say to him?

"Are you in?"

The enterprise sounded preposterous to me.

"You'd be doing me an extraordinary service," he said.

When I continued to hesitate, he added, "Please don't think I'm asking you to do this work for nothing. In exchange for the services you will render to me, I will do for you what a good rebbe always does."

"And what is that, if you don't mind my asking?"

He leaned forward and dropped his voice to a whisper. "Do I really need to answer that, Dr. Sammelsohn? I think it's clear to both of us."

"I have no idea what you're talking about!"

"Ah!" he said, as the door opened and a young woman entered the room, carrying our tea in on a silver tray. "This is my daughter, Rekhl Yehudis. My dear, Dr. Sammelsohn is a cousin of ours."

The rebbe's daughter and I nodded to each other, she demurely keeping her gaze lowered.

"Thank you, my darling," he said, ushering her out again. I'd already taken a bite of the mandelbrot she had brought us and had begun sipping my tea when the rebbe lifted his own cup and began intoning an elaborate blessing over it.

"Amen," I said when he had finally finished with it.

"Well, Dr. Sammelsohn?" he said, putting down his cup. "What have you decided?"

I spun my teacup on its saucer. Every fiber of my being shrieked in protest against accepting his offer. The times were perilous, and if writing a book of Hasidic theology wasn't already an illegal act, punishable most likely by death, it soon would be. Risking one's life for such a quixotic misadventure seemed foolish in the extreme, and yet—I don't know why; perhaps it was the look his daughter had given me—I felt incapable of refusing him.

"Good! Excellent!" he cried, clapping his hands. "You've no idea how happy you've made me!" He opened his desk drawer and withdrew from it ten or so sheets of paper. "These are the pieces I've already done. Take them with you, read them over, and tell me what you think. I'm relying on your complete and honest opinion. It's one thing to write a book for one's Hasidim, quite another for the entire world. And—it goes without saying—be careful with those, as they're my only copy."

"Perhaps I should just read them here then," I suggested, already beginning to regret my decision.

"True, nothing is safe on the streets. Sit outside my study in the hallway, where you can read them in peace, and leave them with my daughter when you're done."

I did as he'd commanded me, taking a seat on the hard wooden bench outside his study. There were only two sermons, both from the High Holy Days, and they were exactly the sort of tripe I'd had stuffed down my throat as a child. As I shuffled through the pages, I half-expected Reb Sender to cuff me on the ears. All the usual Hasidic malarkey was here: stories of captive princes estranged from their fathers; God forgiving our sins as a monarch might our taxes; the typical Hasidic standing on its head of who exactly is in need of repentance—God or ourselves?—all leading to one ineluctable conclusion: we must repent and, if we repent, God and man, the stars of creation's longest-running Punch and Judy show (this is my own commentary, of course, and not the rebbe's), will once again, or at least for another year, be reconciled.

I dropped the pages into my lap. My head began to pound with a terrible headache. What had I gotten myself into?

With their great love of regimentation, the Germans began making new laws as though they were counterfeiting money, and one never knew, from day to day, what might be newly illegal, nor what penalties these new crimes might carry. At last it was decided that Germans, Poles, and Jews could no longer live higgledy-piggledy across the city wherever they wished. No, separate peoples required separate quarters. Wasn't this an elementary principle of life? Certainly it was! And if people weren't inclined to obey this principle, then, of course, it had to be mandated by law. Jews must live with Jews in a Jewish quarter; Poles with Poles in a Polish quarter; and Germans with Germans alone.

We made the trade as best as we could. Those of us living outside the Jewish Quarter abandoned our homes and piled the little we were allowed onto carts, which we hauled into apartments that had been similarly abandoned by others living in the wrong section of town. I took as many refugees as I could into the Zamenhofs' old house on Dzika Street. (Among the Germans' numerous small cruelties was the restoration to Zamenhof Street of its former savage name.) Though I'd originally inhabited Dr. Adamo's childhood bedroom, most nights now I slept on the sofa in Dr. Zamenhof's consultancy.

Things couldn't get much worse. At least that's what we told ourselves. Surely, this is the end of it, we said. And when the Germans sealed the quarter, we actually breathed a sigh of relief. Walls have two sides, and though we were being walled in, it wasn't difficult for us to imagine that they had walled themselves out. Typhus was the official reason, although as a doctor, I knew this was absurd. I'd never heard of a single case. Still, who cared what lies they told about us as long as they left us alone? The ghetto was our natural home. Hadn't we always lived in ghettos? And weren't we happiest there where we could more fully be ourselves? We'd set up our own housing committee, our own community kitchens, our own free loan societies and live as a free society of slaves. Why, we even had a Jewish postman, the first in Poland! Just like in Palestine!

Or so the common thinking ran. I was less sanguine myself. Roaming the ghetto's streets, I felt as if we'd all become trapped in Dr. Rosenberg's dream. How many years had it been since Dr. Freud had impressed me into his Tarock game and Dr. Rosenberg, dozing in the small hours, had dreamt he was Captain Dreyfus on Devil's Island, exiled to that fearsome place for an act of treason he hadn't committed? Both Dr. Freud and Dr. Rie had made light of their friend's fears. Innocent or guilty, Dreyfus is but a single man, not a representative of our race, and his tragedy has nothing to do with us, they said. Everyone knows you simply can't trust the French!

As I stood on Bonifraterska Street, watching the Jewish laborers place the last bricks into the wall, sealing us in, I only wished they'd been correct. But here I was, here we all were, a million or so Captain Dreyfuses, trapped inside our own Devil's Island, our very existence deemed an act of treason.

IT WAS ANOTHER castaway, however, who came to mind when I was in the presence of the holy Piaseczna rebbe. *Rubinchek Cruzoe* was one of the romances I read in Yiddish as a child. The diary, purportedly, of a shipwrecked Hasid, the book recounts its protagonist's efforts at retaining his piety while cut off from all humanity, cast away upon an island. And if the rebbe were Alter-Lieb Rubinchek—such was always my next thought—who was I but his man Shabbos, the savage he hoped to turn into an observant Jew?

I admit that the reluctance I felt in regard to the rebbe didn't spring from any qualms I had about squandering what were surely my last days on a book I was convinced would never see the light of the printed page. Nor did the idea of dying trouble me. Nor the idea of dying as a Jew among Jews. As I'd lived exclusively among Jews, I was content to die, if I must, among them. Rather, it was the prospect of dying among the *pious,* irritated by their every saintly gesture, aggravated by their every reverent word, that I found intolerable, their inability, for instance, to answer even a simple question such as *How are you?* with anything more pertinent than a *Thank God!*

The child-like reverence in which his Hasidim held the rebbe was particularly galling to me. His disciples believed him capable of the most astonishing of things. Many of these so-called miracles seemed like simple rabbinical card tricks to me: he'd saved a wealthy disciple's London business by urging the man to make a large donation to his school; he'd been consulted by the dean of the Telz Yeshiva when the latter came to Warsaw for a delicate medical procedure. (Only in our little cloistered world would a Lithuanian Talmudist's seeking out the medical advice of a Poylisher rebbe be a miracle tantamount to the fishes and the loaves!) The most preposterous of these stories involved a student of the rebbe's who'd been called up for the draft. Unlike most of his fellows, among whom, let's be honest, there might be enough muscles for the needs of one Cossack woman—or so the story goes—this young fellow was exceptionally strong. He had no chance of receiving an exemption, which meant serving in the tsar's army for no fewer than twenty-five years.

On the day of his physical examination, the rebbe called the young man into his study. The two sat by the stove, speaking of this and that—a bisele toyre, a bisele khasides, a bisele tsayko-analisiz—when apropos of nothing, the rebbe dipped his finger into the ashes of the stove and used it to trace a few words onto the young man's forehead. Just as quickly, he erased whatever it was he had written there with a kerchief.

"Listen to me," he told the young man. "On your way into town this afternoon, do not look into the face of another human being, and in the army offices, meet the eye of no one. Do you understand me?"

Of course, the boy didn't understand, but he did as he was told, carrying out the rebbe's instructions with perfect fidelity. Whatever the rebbe had written on his forehead made him appear monstrous and deformed, and as result, people in the streets fled from him in terror. At the army offices, nurses screamed and doctors fainted dead away. His fellow inductees, horrified, scrambled for cover, jumping out of windows. Finally, some higher-up was found who, clutching a kerchief to his nose, wrote out an exemption certificate before pointing the boy towards the door.

When the young man returned to the yeshiva, he asked the rebbe what it was that he had written that made people react to him in such a way?

"Oh, nothing extraordinary," the rebbe said. "Just a word or two in the language the angels use."

Nothing bound me to the rebbe, of course. I could have fabricated any number of excuses or told him outright that I no longer wished to assist him. I could have simply stopped coming to his house on Saturday afternoons. Our lives were sufficiently precarious that any number of unforeseen obstacles might have precluded my arriving there. I'm not sure why, but every Saturday, as the sky began to drain of color above our prison of jagged rooftops, I traced my way along the few blocks between Dzika and Dzielna streets, the cityscape worsening each week, becoming more and more corpse-strewn, timing my entrance at the rebbe's house so that I arrived well after the afternoon prayers, which I had no interest in praying, when the rebbe was already seated and lingering over the Sabbath's final meal, his Hasidim ringed about him, one tuneless tune bleeding into another.

Their numbers were dwindling. Each week, fewer braved the patrols and broke the laws forbidding their attendance there. Others had been starved to death or murdered. No one ever asked me what I was doing there. My presence was tolerated, I imagined, if not completely understood. I was merely the rebbe's cousin. Or his personal physician. Or perhaps they'd been told I was assisting him with a book. Whatever the case, I'd take my seat as unobtrusively as possible and listen to their singing. I won't say I relaxed or enjoyed myself precisely—we were all living in a state of vigilant fear—but at times their deep, sonorous voices unjangled my nerves. (At other times, their singing only increased my nervousness: God alone knew if our voices could be heard outside and who the devil was listening.) And then finally, in response perhaps to some inner prompting or a silent signal from the Heavens, the rebbe would slide back his chair, its legs scraping against the wooden floor, and standing, he'd tuck his hands into the sleeves of his kapote and begin to speak.

It's impossible for me to replicate his talks. Although he prepared them—mentally, at least; he wrote nothing down beforehand—while working as a slave in Schultz's Shoe Factory, they were fiercely learned and complex. As I listened to him each week, however, I noticed a curious thing. The rebbe seemed to be addressing two audiences, alternating between the two. The first were his Hasidim, the ever-more-bedraggled captives who came to him hoping for some illumination on the wretched state of their lives. These the rebbe urged to use our desperate times as a spur towards self-reflection and repentance, in response to which, he felt certain, the Holy Blessed One would be compelled, indeed, forced by His Own Goodness, so to speak, into treating us with kindness and mercy.

Redemption was only a matter of our asking for it, of our crying out with as much purity of heart as we could muster given the grinding circumstances of our lives.

And of course, it was the Holy One Himself whom the rebbe's second audience comprised. Quite audaciously, the rebbe seemed to have challenged the Holy Blessed One, Master of our Universe, to a kind of theological disputation, the high stakes of which were our immediate ransom. Drawing upon a formidable arsenal of theological weaponry, skillfully citing theolegal and scriptural precedent, he used all his cunning to arouse the slumbering conscience of our Creator. Reading the Torah backwards and forwards, turning it inside and out, spinning the sacred law on its head until, like a prism, it threw off a thousand and one new and unheard-of interpretations, he reminded the Holy One not only of His promises but of His many promises to keep those promises. Using the Holy One's own words against Him, like a prosecutor, the rebbe returned again and again to this one incontrovertible fact: the Holy One had obligated Himself, by His own holy law, into rising up in our defense.

I have to say, at those times, when the rebbe directed the full force of his person towards the Heavens, hurling himself against its barricades, demanding of its many offices a response to his damning list of charges, the silence of the Divine reply was as deafening as thunder.

HE SIGHED AND dropped his glasses onto the desk before him.

"To tell you the truth, Dr. Sammelsohn, I didn't think it would take this long."

"Didn't think what would take this long?"

"Before the Holy One answered our pleas."

We were in his study, transcribing the talk he'd given the day before. Not that he seemed to need my help. On the contrary, Reb Kalonymos recalled his every word with an astonishing precision. His sterling memory made mine seem like a dull and lusterless trap. Our work was finished for the day, and he'd taken our few new pages and stacked them beneath the older ones. The ink and paper were costing him dearly, I knew, and the manuscript was thickening at an alarming rate.

"You think I'm mad, don't you?" he said, "that what I'm doing, or rather what I'm attempting to do, is mad." He waited for me to answer him, but I found nothing to say.

The rebbe crossed his arms. "Still, we're taught as schoolboys that the Holy One not only studies the Torah but is obligated, so to speak, to adhere to its laws."

"Yes, so we're taught," I said, and I thought: And only a schoolboy would continue to believe it.

"Taught? What am I saying?" The rebbe waved the remark away. "It's not a matter of our being taught, but of one's deeply knowing. *Of course* the Holy One lives according to the Law. How could it be otherwise, and yet . . ."

"And yet?" I wondered aloud.

"No," he censored himself. "We must simply push on, that's all. There's something more mysterious at hand, although at the moment, I cannot tell you what."

He fingered the manuscript lying like a brick on the desk between us, gazing upon it with a mixture of pride (it was, after all, growing proof of his accomplishments as an author) and despair (the larger it became, the more it spoke of its failure to move its Audience).

And what a curious book it was. Given the circumstances of its creation, I often wondered if it would even survive us? And if it did, who would ever read it?

I PROMISE YOU: I had nothing but the purest of intentions regarding Rekhl Yehudis; and when I entered the rebbe's kitchen, in search of a cup of tea, romance was the furthest thing from my mind. Still, there she was with her back towards me and her delicate shoulders trembling, staring out through the rain-soaked windows. I saw instantly that she was crying. Only the most blackhearted of Bluebeards would have trifled with such a child, given her situation: in the wake of her mother's death, she was an orphan; in the wake of her brother's, a mourner; via our dubious state, a captive. Also, unlike in my own family, where the son had been a thorn in the bouquet of all those pretty sisters, Rekhl Yehudis had played second fiddle to her brother. At least in her father's affections. Perhaps she'd been her mother's favorite. I couldn't know. But now, with her mother dead and her brother as well, there seemed only so much love even a magician like Reb Kalonymos could conjure up on her behalf. This thought created within me even more compassion for her: having been a hated child, I could only sympathize with one who had been the lesser loved.

Certainly, I could have reversed my course and backed silently out of the room, but her beauty arrested me. Not her physical beauty, which, as she was starving like the rest of us, was diminished, but an inner radiance that, despite our terrible circumstances, she yet possessed, and that reminded me not a little of my sisters. Perhaps hunger had robbed me of the ability to act quickly. Whatever the reasons, I found myself paralyzed, standing in place in the doorway, staring at the picture she made — a sorrowful girl with the rain-soaked light coloring her face — not a thought moving in my brain, until at last she had no choice but to turn and greet me.

"So sorry," I stammered, pulled out from my famished daze. "But I'm afraid I . . . didn't see you there."

She nodded sympathetically, as though what I had said made sense. Her face was red and blotchy from crying, and she pushed her tears away with the heel of her hand.

"Are you all right, fraylin?" I took a step towards her. "You haven't been crying, have you?"

"No," she said, although this assertion, so transparently false, only made her cry more. We were forbidden from touching each other by the rules governing this rabbinic household, and it was all I could do not to reach out to her and enfold her in my arms, so that she might give unchecked expression to her grief. I offered her my handkerchief instead. As she reached for it gratefully, however, our hands brushed, and I felt that oddly shocking, illicit electricity of sexual contact, made even more delicious by the stricter rules of the household forbidding it. It was all I could do not to kiss her hand or press my cheek against it, wetting it with my own tears. Ignoring our touch, she dried her eyes with the rag I'd presented to her and said, "It's all so very sad, isn't it, Dr. Sammelsohn?"

I nodded, standing as near to her as propriety allowed. She folded her arms and, with her chin trembling, gazed at the ceiling rafters. "Oh, how I wish you could have been here when my mother was alive." She looked at the floor and shook her head. "All the cooking and the baking and the feasting! You wouldn't believe it now, Doctor, but this kitchen was always filled with clouds of steam and, oh, all sorts of delicious vapors. A never-ending banquet! How I used to love to walk by and stick my head in and hear the oil sizzling and the dumplings boiling. The smells would wake me in the morning sometimes, and it was all I could do to finish dressing before dashing down to help. One of the cooks was sweet on me, and she'd give me a little taste of whatever it was she was preparing, before assigning me a chore." She laughed a small laugh. "Visitors and relatives and servants everywhere, the clatter of silverware, of drawers opening, of rolling pins pounding, I can't tell you! The men praying and singing with my father, the women cooking and talking and laughing. It was a proper court then, with music and dancing and . . ." Her breast lifted and fell heavily. "You could feel the presence of God here. But now?" She gave out a shrug. "Now I don't know."

She dropped her head and smiled at something. "Shall I tell you a secret?" she said.

"If you wish, fraylin."

"When I was a little girl, I believed that nothing made God happier than His frequent visits to our house." She closed her eyes. Two tears slid down her cheeks. "Oh, who knows anything anymore?"

"Things will return to how they once were," I said. What else could I say?

"You're a sweet liar."

"Still, we must hold on." I attempted to remove all playfulness from my voice. She was still holding my handkerchief, and she looked at it as though noticing it for the first time.

"And now"—she pulled the handkerchief through one hand—"it's all I can do to scrounge up a cup of tea for our good doctor, who brings so much joy to our good father's life."

"On the contrary, fraylin, it's he who has done much for me," I said, although, in fact, I could think of nothing at all the rebbe had done on my behalf.

"He cherishes his Sunday mornings with you, you know. You've been so like a son to him."

"I doubt that."

"But it's true."

"A son nearly fourteen years his senior!" I exclaimed with a sense of theatrical heartiness.

"No!" she cried. "You don't look it at all." And she hit me playfully on the arm with my handkerchief.

"Now, fraylin, it's you who are so very sweetly lying."

"No, but really, you're . . . I don't know . . . quite boyish. And besides, what does it matter how old a man is when he's as . . ."

But here, she stopped herself. I'm not certain which one of us dropped his gaze first, I only know that soon we were both looking at the floor.

"Here. Let me have your cup, and I'll brew up what little tea we have and bring it in to both you and my father."

I surrendered the teacup and, as I did so, she pressed my hand gently but firmly inside her own. The embrace was tender and warm and—unless I'm a terrible judge of such things—not a little erotic.

We existed in a kind of traumatized dream-state. The thin membrane between sanity and madness seemed to have ruptured, and if you described your day to someone outside the ghetto, he'd no doubt assume you were recounting a dream: *The sidewalks were littered with corpses, it was wintertime, I was starving, and the government had forced everyone to turn in their fur coats.* We knew from the broadcasts we tuned in to over our contraband radios—by "we," I mean the ever-changing group of refugees who slept on top of one another inside the Zamenhofs' apartment—that there was no stopping the Germans as they marched across Europe, flattening everything in their path. Liberation was another dream, and every hour took its toll. Almost every day now, I saw at least two or three people dropping dead in the street, often helped along into the next world by the Jewish police, who had traded their wooden-tipped shoes for rubber-toed boots, the better to splinter our bones, without risking theirs, whenever they kicked us. I have to say: they were the worst among us. Each had been charged with a daily quota of deportees, and if they failed to round up the requisite number, members of their own families made up the shortfall. Perhaps this goes a long way in explaining their brutality. In matters of life and death, a certain shortsightedness is to be expected, I suppose, and every hour, though it be one's last, counts. Still, we were all marked for death, the Jewish policemen included, and everyone knew it.

The deportation center, the Umschlagplatz, was directly behind the Zamenhofs' old house, and in the twilight sometimes, when I imagined no one could see me, I'd make my way to the roof and look down into its hellish precincts. It was there that the truckloads of captives were taken for deportation, men, women, children, escorted in under armed Ukrainian guard.

Even from the heights of the rooftop, I couldn't block out their screams. The entrance was like the maw of some mythological beast whose hunger could not be satisfied. You could buy your way out with only a hundred złotys, but only the rich could afford that, and with prices going up every day, it was only a matter of time before they took their place in line as well.

There were doctors working in the Umschlagplatz. I could see their white smocks moving among the prisoners in the twilight from my roof. They were part of the ruse, it seemed, employed by the enemy as a way of keeping order. (Certainly, you'd tell yourself, if the authorities have gone to the trouble of hiring a doctor to put a plaster on my foot, which the Ukrainian or the Lithuanian or the Latvian guard has broken, these same authorities can't be sending me to my death now. It didn't add up.)

I tried not to think about it, and I attempted, as well as I could, to avoid being swept up in one of the Jewish policemen's raids, an easy enough task on the days I wore my smuggler's uniform—thanks to my fluency in German, I'd been impressed into service by the underground— however, on days when I appeared in the streets only as myself, my fate was as insecure as anyone's. And naturally, when the German captain let himself into Dr. Zamenhof's consultancy and asked for me by name, I assumed I'd been betrayed, my smuggling exposed by someone who knew me.

As with so much else in my life, however, I was wrong.

"HERR DOKTOR SAMMELSOHN?"

"Ja, bitte?" I said, not daring to look him in the face.

"Herr Doktor Jakob Josef Sammelsohn?"

"Ja, ja," I said.

"*You're* Herr Doktor Jakob Josef Sammelsohn?"

"I am," I said, although at that moment my greatest wish was not to be.

"Well," he muttered, as though disappointed to have found me, "come along." When I didn't obey him immediately, he raised his voice and said, "Get your coat and come along, Doctor. That's all now. Please."

"But my patients," I said, grasping at straws. When I turned towards my lone patient, who a moment before had been sitting in the waiting room, I found that he had fled. Perhaps he'd never been there to begin with. Food, as I've said, was scarce, and though I continued to smuggle it in, I shared it with as many people as I could, principally the children living in the Zamenhofs' house. I could barely remember the last time I'd eaten a full meal, and thanks to the starvation with which I lived, it was impossible at times to tell what was truly happening. My mind seemed to drift constantly. Still, this captain seemed real enough, and I did as he commanded me, putting on my coat and making my way towards the door. Glancing over my shoulder, I glimpsed the patient who had disappeared standing now in the darkness of the back room. He nodded at me, his face a picture of forlorn encouragement. I was clearly doomed, and we both knew it. I wasn't even a Pole, but a former Austrian living illegally in Warsaw and a Jew.

(Although the Germans had nullified my passport, I wasn't exactly a man without a country. I *had* a country. It merely happened to be an imaginary one. For two thousand years, my people had lived in the Land of Zion as though it were real; and although this is perhaps not the place to say it, now that it's real, I regret that we too often treat it as though it were imaginary.)

"Don't forget your hat, Herr Doktor," the captain said, taking my elbow and steering me out the door. On the street, he added: "You should lock up, don't you think? To discourage vandals," he explained.

Ah, that's how it is with Germans, I thought. They think nothing of killing a man, but every door must be locked and every window bolted. I banished this thought from my mind, however. There was no profit in feeling superior to a man who, literally or figuratively, has a gun pointed at one's back.

"Down this street," the captain said, a step behind me. Though I couldn't bring myself to look him in the face, I was exquisitely aware of his presence — the thudding of his boots, the rasping of his breath — and I trembled each time he touched my elbow to steer me this way or that. Against his solid hand, I was embarrassed to feel my own insubstantial trembling.

"Only a little farther, Herr Doktor."

"And where, may I ask, is the good captain taking me?"

"Never mind. Never you mind that." He spat.

I considered pestering him with questions in order to make his job as unpleasant as possible, but found I lacked the spirit for the game. Besides, it was impossible to awaken a conscience in an enemy without one. I looked at the sky above the rows of tired old houses, at the midwinter sun struggling up behind them. I tried to remain philosophical: all the attention I'd lavished upon my life, all the care I'd taken with its every detail, and this is where it had gotten me.

Hadn't I had enough of these old hurts, these old wounds, and all the comical feints they'd inspired? Perhaps Ita had been right all along, perhaps it was better to jump into the next life, as into a pool of water, and emerge from the other side, newly reborn. (If, on the other hand, as we'd seen with Ita, one merely enters one's new life with a new iteration of one's old problems, surrounded by reincarnated versions of the people one once knew, there seemed little point in dying.)

"Up these stairs, Herr Doktor. Careful now. There's a tricky step." I considered running for it, but being shot in the street at that moment seemed less preferable than being shot in an interrogation room twenty minutes later. "In here, in here," he said, pushing me through the door of an apartment. "Sit!" he barked, and I sat. He walked past me and, as he did, he lifted my hat from my head and dropped it onto my lap. Grinning obscenely, he rapped with his knuckles against an interior door.

"Fine, fine," a voice answered him from within.

For the first time, I felt free to study my captor. A typical specimen, I thought, barrel-chested with powerful shoulders. On closer inspection, he appeared slightly stooped, as though the effort of standing erect was costing him dearly. His face was wide and jowly. There was something almost feral about him. He seemed a wild, ferocious dog.

Having received his answer at the door, he took a seat behind me—I could hear the legs of his chair creaking beneath his weight—and I imagined that would be the last I'd see of him.

Soon, I thought, he'll put a bullet through my head.

THE DOOR OPENED, and a second man entered the room. "Ah!" he said, seeing the two of us together. "Excellent work, brother."

I must say: this fellow couldn't have been more different from the first. Trim and dignified, he wore a precise little beard on the point of his chin. It was silver, as was his elegant pompadour. His black vest was still unbuttoned and he was busily rolling down his shirtsleeves. He looked as if he'd just finished his morning shave. "So you've managed to find our good doctor, have you? Marvelous! No, no, Dr. Sammelsohn, don't get up, don't get up!" he said, extending his hand and moving towards my chair. "You haven't changed a bit. Has he, brother? Not a bit. Ah, but it's extraordinary to see you again!"

It's extraordinary to see me again? Did I know these men? I looked about the apartment, at the table and the sofa, at the antique lamp glowing on the desk. None of it seemed familiar. I peered into the face of the man standing before me. He smiled expectantly, his eyes gleaming behind a thick pair of black-rimmed glasses. His lower teeth were crooked, and this gave his chin an asymmetrical, though not an unattractive cast.

"Ha! He's amazed!" the captain chortled behind me.

"Astonished is more like it," the other fellow said, peering diagnostically into my eyes.

"It never fails!"

"It never does, does it?"

"I . . . I'm sorry," I stammered, "but I don't recall our ever having met."

"He doesn't recall our ever having met!" The captain hawked up a vulgar laugh. The other fellow shook his head and tutted his tongue.

"They tend to forget," he said.

"Human beings, he means," the captain whispered in my ear.

"They forget that they've forgotten.

"And then that is forgotten as well."

I'm hallucinating from hunger, was my next thought.

"Possibly," the man in the vest agreed, although I was certain I hadn't spoken these words aloud. Or perhaps they've already murdered me, I thought.

"No, I can assure you that hasn't happened yet."

"Yet?" I said.

And with that, he began to laugh, and his companion, the hulking dog-man standing behind me, began to laugh as well, and that glorious sound, a sound I remembered having heard only once before—at the side of Fräulein Eckstein's hospital bed—filled the dingy little apartment until I couldn't keep from giggling myself. "I'm not hallucinating, then?" I said.

"Oh, well, no, we never said you weren't! There are many avenues into the true world, Dr. Sammelsohn, and hallucination has a long and noble tradition."

"More reliable than dreams," שמנגלפ growled.

"On the contrary, don't believe him, Dr. Sammelsohn. His is the minority opinion."

"But it isn't. Just the opposite: it's he who hasn't kept up with the literature."

אשריל braised שמנגלפ with a searing scowl. "Must you contradict everything I say?"

"I don't contradict everything you say. However, in this case, Dr. Sammelsohn, he's incorrect, and the scholarly conclusions are mixed."

The two angels glared at each other with such ferocity that I feared they'd come to blows, but then they began to laugh again, and I couldn't help laughing as well, and once again, that delicious golden sound filled the room. My shoulders relaxed, my belly unknotted, and tears began streaming down my face.

שמנגלפ HELD OUT a starched kerchief. "Aw, here you go, Dr. Sammelsohn."

"Thank you." I said, and drying my tears, I apologized for my weeping.

"Oh, no, no, tush, tush! Don't be silly," אשריל said.

"We sympathize completely," שמנגלפ said. "The passage of time"—he made a small rolling gesture with his hand—"the sense of loss."

"Not to mention," אשריל nodded towards the window, "these deplorable conditions."

My brain was on fire. I seemed to have only the slightest idea of what was taking place before me. My medical training, as well as the time I'd spent with Dr. Freud, made me believe, as I told myself it was reasonable to believe, that I'd undergone a psychic fracturing of some kind. Confronted with the brutality I was doubtlessly at that moment experiencing at the hands of my torturers or fearing I would in the next moment experience, my mind had retreated into a world of fantasy where sense could seem to be made of it all. Still, amazed to hear myself, I next said, "אשריל! שמנגלפ!—but why on earth are you here?"

"Forgive me, Dr. Sammelsohn," שמנגלפ said, "if I suggest that you're not thinking clearly."

"No, I assumed not," I said, pointing to my head, happy to have my self-diagnosis of madness confirmed. That it had been confirmed by a figure who was himself an element of my delusion did not strike me as ironical as it perhaps should have.

"No. Why else would we be here, he means," שמנגלפ said.

Looking back and forth between the two, I shrugged. "I have no idea truly."

"It's אָאָעָאָ אָ אָעָ עָעוִויא," אשריל said.

"Ita?" I said.

"She's been reborn," שמנגלפ said.

Reborn? Ita? These words chilled me to the bone. Still, I supposed it made a kind of sense. Hadn't the three of them always been mixed up together?

"Or rather reborn *again,* we should say."

"Ah, yes, that's right," אשריל said. "You met her once before in Paris, I believe."

"Gaston," שמנגלפ whispered, and as he pronounced the name, I once again saw the poor unfortunate being pummeled to death by Monsieur Gajewski.

I blushed at the memory. "I *thought* that was Ita. However, I wasn't certain, you see."

"No, of course not," שמנגלפ said.

"The entire system works on just that very principle of doubt," אשריל explained.

"It's not that. Rather, it's the fact that . . ." I took a moment and looked at my hands resting on my knees. "No, it's just that Gaston seemed, I have to say, a little too much like the Ita I once knew, that we all knew, in fact: violent, vindictive, spiteful, addicted, as I believe you once told me, to short lives and unhappy deaths."

שמנגלפ shrugged. "I suppose that's true."

"Whereas" — I couldn't help shaking my finger at them — "I seem to recall striking a bargain with the two of you."

"A bargain?" אשריל said, squinting myopically behind his thick glasses.

"A bargain?" שמנגלפ swallowed his laughter. "Do you recall making any bargains, brother?"

"A bargain?" אשריל repeated.

I hesitated, uncertain how one approaches an angelic being with a grievance, but my anger had emboldened me, and so I persisted. "A bargain indeed! As I recall, you two made me a promise. You promised me that if I coerced Ita into abandoning Fräulein Eckstein's body and submitting to your authority, you'd see to it that she was remanded to the Highest of Heavens, her soul restored to its original purity."

"Oh, yes, *that* bargain." אשריל tutted his tongue. "Now, of course, I remember."

"Well, you kept your part of it, at least," שמנגלפ said.

"As did we, as we did," אשריל reassured me.

"No, it's true, Dr. Sammelsohn. My fellows and I never laid so much as a glove on her, though many of the lads were eager to do so, although not necessarily a glove, if you understand my meaning."

"As a matter of celestial record, אָאָעְאָ אָ אָעְ עְעוֹוִיא was not required to undergo the usual purifying torments, which never had much effect on her anyway."

"He says that as though our methods don't work nearly one hundred percent of the time. They do, Dr. Sammelsohn. Justice is justice, though

no one said it would be pretty."

"And yet," I felt compelled to belabor the point, "there was Ita, alive again and loose on the streets of Paris, creating mischief, as though she hadn't progressed one jot in spiritual refinement."

The two figures — I cannot call them men, though in every wise they resembled men — exchanged complicated looks. שמנגלפ fiddled with his truncheon. אשריל coughed into his fist.

"We were hoping this wouldn't come up."

"Wouldn't come up!"

"Please, Dr. Sammelsohn, don't make more of this than it is."

אשריל cleared his throat. "At the end of the process, אַאְעְעָאֶא אֶעֶ עָעוּוִיא was asked to perform a small favor, that's all."

"A favor?"

"A small, simple favor."

"Which was?"

"Ah, Dr. Sammelsohn!" שמנגלפ sighed. "Must we go into all that?"

אשריל explained: "To use her God-given talents for mischief and destruction one final time, after which the sins accumulated during all her previous lives would be forgiven and, in her next life, she would be free to start anew."

"Her expertise was required," שמנגלפ said.

"Her expertise?"

"For mischief and destruction, as we've said."

"And what exactly was it that Heaven needed her to destroy?" I said, stunned by this piece of news.

The two brothers looked at each other.

"Tell me," I insisted.

"Tell him," שמנגלפ said, dropping his head.

"Me? Why should it be me? It was your idea."

"You're the so-called good angel!"

"Oh, please! Do you know how much harder it is to do the good, Dr. Sammelsohn?"

"Ach, not this again!" שמנגלפ said, crossing his broad arms against his chest. "Here we go again!"

"Evil is simple, easy," אשריל said.

"Spoken like a true amateur!"

"A man can destroy in a morning what has taken centuries to build: cities, civilizations, cultures."

"These arguments are so tedious!"

"Certainly, there's more good than evil in the world—otherwise nothing could endure—but it's only a little more, a fraction at best, if even that."

"And Esperanto?" I said, suddenly fearing I understood him too well. "How did Esperanto fit into this balance?"

"Oh, well, that's just it, you see," אשריל said unhappily.

שמנגלפ wagged his thick finger at me. "That Dr. Zamenhof of yours got just a little too close for comfort, I must say. One really can't force the hand of the Messiah, Dr. Sammelsohn. Everyone knows this."

"What . . . what are you saying?" I sputtered. "That Ita, working on behalf of Heaven, intentionally destroyed the Esperanto movement in order to . . . to . . . to what? . . . to delay the coming of the Messiah?"

"Oh, no, not at all! Not at all!" אשריל said, but then he immediately corrected himself: "Well, actually, I suppose that's exactly it."

"We couldn't rely on Professor Couturat to do the job alone, although, as it turned out, he succeeded beyond our wildest dreams."

"But-but-but," I stammered, "why on earth would Heaven wish to delay the coming of the Messiah?"

"Oh, Dr. Sammelsohn, don't ask us that please," אשריל said.

"We don't make the rules."

"No, we simply carry them out."

"In other words," שמנגלפ said in German, giving his brother an amused look and straining to finish his sentence before laughter choked it off, "we were only following orders!"

(For reasons I wouldn't understand for many years, שמנגלפ and אשריל burst out laughing, after which אשריל, drying his eyes on his sleeve, said, "אַאָעָאָאָעָעֶעוּוִיא was right. All the emotions in a human body! Whoever thought it!")

"But it wasn't only אַאָעָאָאָעָעֶעוּוִיא on that Parisian street," אשריל told me.

"Or didn't you recognize Zusha the Amalekite?"

"In the guise of Master Gajewski!"

"And your own father!"

"In the guise of the dog."

"A new entry for Dr. Freud's chart!"

"Which, thank Heaven, he burned."

I stared at the two of them, the German officer and the Jewish professor. No, it's definitive, I thought. I'm definitely hallucinating.

"We never denied it, we never denied that," אשריל said.

"That snarling wolfhound was my father?"

They both affirmed this terrible fact with a shrug.

"But I didn't even pet him!" I exclaimed, feeling suddenly very glum.

"No, well, why would you have? He'd only have bitten your hand."

"Listen to me, Doctor," אשריל said. "אָאָעֶעְאָ אָ עָ עְעוּוִיאָ was no neophyte. She'd been through the whirling vortex of lives nearly a hundred times before. She understood exactly what she was agreeing to."

"Oh, yes! This was hardly אָאָעֶעְאָ אָ עָ עְעוּוִיאָ's first time at the ball."

"And though she agreed to our request, it wasn't without asking for a favor of her own in return."

"One can *do* that?" I exclaimed.

אשריל shrugged unhappily. "Regrettably, things have loosened up over the course of the last five hundred years or so."

"Not one of my favorite topics," שמנגלפ growled.

"Nor mine."

"And this favor?" I said. "What exactly was it?"

"Oh, no, you don't want to know that, Dr. Sammelsohn, believe me."

"But I do!"

"I don't think you do, Dr. Sammelsohn," שמנגלפ said, and he began to beat his truncheon against the meat of his palm and became so menacing, I had no choice but to drop the matter.

"In any case," אשריל said, trying to put a good face on things, "we're not at liberty to reveal it to you."

"And yet," שמנגלפ lifted his two arms in the air, "is our being here not miracle enough for you, Dr. Sammelsohn? I mean, here we all are again!"

"Yes! All of us together again!"

"Take me to her," I said.

"Naturally," שמנגלפ said.

"Actually," אשריל purred, "we assumed that would have been your first request."

"I'M TELLING YOU, Dr. Sammelsohn," אשריל peered at me through his thick glasses, "you won't even recognize her."

"But of course, he wouldn't recognize her anyway, would he?" שמנגלפ said.

"No, that's true. Physically, she's nothing like herself, but internally, she's also changed."

We were sitting on a park bench in a square near the corner of Leszno and Karmelicka, שמנגלפ keeping track of the time on his watch. "Any minute now, any minute now," he said.

"I know you don't believe us, Dr. Sammelsohn, but your love has transformed her."

"My love!" I could only scoff. "Gentlemen, surely you're mocking me. When I review my life, my principal regret is that Zusha the Amalekite didn't succeed in strangling Ita with his shoestring!"

שמנגלפ shrugged. "Fine. Regret it. It wouldn't have done you any good. She'd only have been reborn again."

"Correct."

"And again."

"We don't call them gilgulim for nothing." He made a circular motion with his hand.

I gathered my collars against the cold and pulled my hat brim down. Was there any point in allowing myself to be hoodwinked by these two — what were they even? — phantoms? angels? psychoid disturbances? Did I even wish to see Ita again? It was a question I hadn't even bothered asking myself in the wild tumult of events. Why would I want to see her? She'd been a disaster from first to last. As herself, she'd wrecked my childhood; as a dybbuk, she'd destroyed my romance with Fräulein Eckstein; as a miserable street urchin, she'd sabotaged my marriage to Loë while bringing down the Esperanto movement and (if the angels were to be believed) delaying the arrival of the Messiah! What possible good could come from meeting her in a fourth incarnation even if, as אשריל and שמנגלפ assured me now, she'd repented of her evil ways?

"No, I've had enough of this!" I cried. "I refuse to be made a fool of by my own hallucinations!" I began to stand, but שמנגלפ thudded the back of his fist against my chest and forced me back onto the park bench.

"Look!" he said. "There she is now!" He pointed to a woman who was leaving an apartment house across the way. She stood at the top of the building's exterior stairs, buttoning her coat before descending to the sidewalk. She looked in both directions at the curb before committing to the street, as the usual ghetto traffic, more rickshaws than cars by that time, sped by.

"Ah." אשריל nodded gently. "I'd forgotten how lovely she's become."

שמנגלף gave him a stern look. "What's happening to you here, brother?"

"Why, whatever do you mean?"

"Don't let this little masquerade of ours go to your head."

I paid their argument little mind. My attention was riveted on the young woman. She wore a white medical smock beneath her winter coat and was carrying a black medical bag.

"The limp"—whispering, שמנגלף directed my attention to her irregular gait—"has carried over, you see."

"As we told you," אשריל whispered in my other ear, "she's a doctor."

"And what does she do—murder her patients?"

"No, Heaven forbid!" שמנגלף exclaimed. "She's completely reformed herself, Dr. Sammelsohn! How many times must we tell you that?"

I nearly got up to greet the woman, but she walked right past us, paying no attention to me or to my companions.

"Oh, this is all nonsense!" I cried. Nevertheless, with the angels trailing behind me, I followed her for a block, keeping a respectable distance between us. אשריל was correct: despite the brutality of the times and the wasting effect it was having upon all of us, despite the limp, which made of her walking an asymmetrical affair, she moved with a pleasing femininity. As I reduced the distance between us, I could see that beneath her hat, her hair was sensibly pinned and, despite her youth, streaked with grey.

First she and then I rounded a corner and simultaneously we caught sight of a soldier. The young doktershe turned around so quickly, she was walking straight towards me or (why not give in to the madness?) straight towards the three of us. In fact, she nearly walked into me, and as she did, she eyed me, I thought, with an odd flash of recognition. Having confirmed on closer inspection that she did not know me after all, she shook her head, seeming quite literally to be shaking off the impression.

"Doktershe," I said, greeting her with a tip of my hat.

"Ah! Ah, ha! Dr. Sammelsohn, did you see? Did you see that?" אשריל said, as the young woman moved past us and disappeared into the crowd.

"See what?"

"The way she looked at you! How she seemed to recognize you!"

"Oh, nonsense!"

"What's nonsensical about it?" he said.

"What *isn't* nonsensical about it? Must I elaborate? To begin with, and I hate to keep harping on this, but there's no way for me to know whether you two are even real!"

"As we," אשריל attempted to keep an even tone, masking his exasperation with me, his dullest student, "have, in all fairness, admitted to you."

"Why he must keep throwing it in our faces, brother! That's what I'd like to know. And why must he lump us in together? After all, perhaps you're a hallucination but I'm not."

אשריל seemed appalled by the idea. "Right, right! I suppose if only one of us were real, it would have to be you."

שמנגלפ pointed his chin at me. "What even makes him think *he's* real? Perhaps we're hallucinating you, Dr. Sammelsohn, or did you never think of that?"

"Even if you weren't hallucinations," I persisted, nearly shouting at them, "you could simply pick out any woman from a crowd and tell me she was Ita."

"And what possible motive would we have for doing that?" אשריל said.

"No, the way she studied you, Dr. Sammelsohn! You saw it. I know you saw it. That flare of recognition!"

"He's right," אשריל said. "Why *would* she recognize him? It makes no sense at all."

"Oh, you two are completely incorrigible!" I threw up my hands. "I don't know what I saw. I only know what you're trying to convince me I saw. And in any case"—I looked at my watch—"I'm late for an appointment."

"With the rebbe?"

"Yes, with the rebbe! And whatever you do, please *do not* follow me there."

B ut of course they did. They followed me everywhere. Despite my doubts concerning their materiality, I ran into them at every turn, especially שמנגלפ, who, with his band of punitive angels, descended upon the ghetto periodically, dressed in their black leathers, with their truncheons and their pistols and their whips. Their violence revolted me. However, far worse was the fact that whenever שמנגלפ finished whatever grim task he was overseeing—pistol-whipping an old man; shooting a child he'd caught smuggling—he'd call out to me from across the square with a wave of his broad arm. "Hoi, Dr. Sammelsohn! A good afternoon to you, sir!"

It was all I could do to pull my collars up and pretend I didn't know him.

"Despite everything, I love this job," he said one day after a particularly unpleasant episode, joining us at the Café Leszno. "There's nothing quite like a little murder and mayhem to stir a soul to repentance."

Picking up my knife, he used it to clean away the blood from under his fingernails.

"Brother," אשריל said, "can't we talk about something other than your work for a change?"

"Like what? Yours? Don't make me yawn! But no, I suppose you're right." He lowered his jowly cheek into his palm and looked at me. "I keep forgetting I'm not among specialists here, as I am with my gang."

"Must be nice having an army," אשריל said wistfully.

"To tell you the truth," שמנגלפ said, "I don't think you could handle the responsibility."

As opposed to שמנגלפ, אשריל specialized in the miraculous rescue. More than once, I'd seen him pulling some poor soul out of harm's way, pushing him from a building moments before the Jewish police arrived, or routing him away from a trap. Once I even saw him unloading a line of soldiers' guns right behind their backs. He made certain ammunition found its way to the underground, and he performed all these tasks with such a light and gentle hand that many of the recipients of his charities had no idea he'd come to their aid.

As for Ita—or for the woman the angels insisted was Ita—I'd encounter her periodically, limping through the streets in her white medical smock, and the odd happiness I'd felt at seeing her again, at discovering that she was still alive, never failed to fill me with a blushing sense of confusion.

The angels brought her up continually. Indeed, no conversation could proceed between us, it seemed, without her being mentioned at least once. More often, she formed the whole of our conversation. I refused to demonstrate any interest in her person before the two of them, but this didn't stop them. They'd pretend to forget that I could hear them and discuss some secret something or other in front of me until my curiosity was piqued. Perhaps it was all part of the byzantine protocol of the Heavenly Court for which they worked. Perhaps a mortal must ask for information before the Angelics may give it to him. I had no idea. And at times, I was too heartsick to even wonder about it.

"He's not even listening to us," one of them might say.

"Dr. Sammelsohn, are you even listening to us?" שמנגלפֿ waved his hand before my eyes.

"She's moved into a new apartment—that's what we're trying to tell you."

"It's *outside* the ghetto."

"Yes, that's the amazing thing!"

"It's directly across from where you stay when you're smuggling."

"Could you please keep your voices down!"

"In fact, looking through your window, you can see directly into hers."

THE LESS SAID about my smuggling, the better. There was nothing heroic about it. Thanks to my fluency in German, I'd been impressed into the underground and given a key to an empty apartment. Inside the apartment was a wardrobe, and inside of the wardrobe was the uniform of a German captain. (The underground employed a small cabinet of tailors, and one of these, a diminutive fellow with a hump on his back, had paid me a clandestine visit two or three weeks previous.) Whenever I put it on, I couldn't look at myself in the mirror. The transformation was too dispiriting. At my age and with the lowish rank my handlers had assigned to me, no one would mistake me for anything but a lifelong military man who hadn't had the verve to succeed. Invisible to the German soldiers I encountered, I was nevertheless terrifying to the Poles and the Jews who crossed my path. Though a gun came with the uniform, I didn't have the nerve to inquire if it was loaded. I hoped not. Having it made me nervous.

Though Chłodna Street was in the Aryan Quarter, it linked the large ghetto with the smaller one, and we were all forced, at various times, to cross it. Doing so filled me with terror. How ludicrous to suppose I wouldn't be unmasked here and shot! Despite my gleaming leather boots and my oiled revolver, despite my clean-shaven cheeks stinging against the morning air, despite the sneer I wore, for good measure, between those cheeks, what was I but an overdressed Jew? (And why shouldn't I believe what they had always told us about ourselves, that our smell was different from theirs, that the shape of our eyes gave us away, that our nose, our gait, the very curve of our spine marked us from a hundred meters away?) There was always a throng gathered at the Chłodna crossing, men and women stamping and fretting on both sides of the street, preoccupied with the business of saving their lives. At the guard's shrill whistle, it was all I could do not to throw up my hands and surrender. Though my presence had provoked the whistling, it wasn't to stop me, I realized, but to permit me, a German captain, to cross.

We saluted each other, this guard and I, traffic grinding to a halt on either side of me. I stepped into the street, the swarm of nervous Jews keeping a respectful distance behind me.

Only in the Polish Quarter did the dread drop from my shoulders. Here, children chased one another in parks, and lovers were quarreling. I found a bench, hidden in a grove of trees, where I vomited and wept. Eventually, I made my way to the address I'd been asked to memorize. And there, I'd sit in the back room until I heard another key turning in the front door and a bag falling on the parlor table, followed by a brisk rapping, in code. After that, the door was shut and the lock locked. Twenty minutes later, I'd enter the parlor and conceal whatever contraband had been left there—food, guns, messages, bullets, whatever—in the thousand pockets sewn secretly into my uniform by my humpbacked tailor.

In truth, I would never have searched for Ita myself, nor even made inquiries into her whereabouts. Nothing would have been more frightening to a Jewish woman living a double life in the Polish Quarter than having a German officer asking after her. But as it turned out, I didn't need to. The angels were correct: the woman whom they endeavored to convince me was Ita (the name would have meant nothing to her, I suppose) did in fact keep an apartment directly across from the one the underground had assigned me; and it was also true, as the angels had additionally claimed, that because my rooms were a story higher than hers, I could see into her windows from my own, and never more clearly than at dusk.

How to justify this Peeping Tomfoolery? If I believed that אשריל and שמנגלפ were little more than feverish projections appearing in the Magic Lantern of my brain, manifesting from a combination of hunger, anxiety, and despair, it made no sense to credit their preposterous claims. Whoever she was, I was convinced this young doctor was not Ita, and yet, for reasons I can't explain, it was impossible to repress the thrill I experienced each time I caught sight of her through the twin veils of our windows, undoing her coat or removing her hat, tossing it onto a table and letting her hair drop about her shoulders.

She was a not unattractive woman, and each time she turned her back on me in order to light her stove, for instance, I couldn't help admiring her backside and her shapely flanks.

Unable to stop myself, I reached for the binoculars with which, along with the gun and the whistle, and half a dozen other wartime accoutrements, my uniform came equipped, and unclasped them from their holster.

One evening, I watched as she dragged a big brass tub into the middle of her kitchen and began filling it with water heated on the stove. I resolved to put an end to this ocular trespass and had even begun drawing the curtains when she lifted both her arms to unbutton the top of her dress. Instead, I adjusted the focus on my binoculars as she lowered her arms and reached behind herself for the lower buttons. Letting the garment fall to the floor, she stepped out of it before picking it up with her bare foot and placing it on a chair. Reaching back again with both arms, she unhooked her brassiere, and her two small breasts fell from their binding. With a little skip, she stepped out of her underpants, and though I cautioned myself to turn away, to look away, instead, I admired the dark triangle of her sex as she lifted first one leg and then the next over the rim of the tub.

A low moan escaped from my mouth, and I chided myself. Hadn't I been warned against making noise of any kind. The walls were thin, and this apartment was assumed by the residents of the building to be empty. But even worse: wasn't this exactly the way I'd encountered Ita that first time in Vienna, attending Dr. Herzl's play at the Carl, dressed in the costume of another man, gazing at her through a lorgnette?

Had nothing in my life changed or progressed since that night? I threw down the field glasses, and as I did, I found myself thinking of my father, his saturnine face appearing in my mind's eye. When I was young enough that it mattered, he'd broken something deep within me. Thanks to that brokenness, I'd lurched through my life with a crooked gait, listing to the side, never quite arriving where I intended, and the more I attempted to straighten myself, the crookeder I became. I was an old man now, and my tormentor was long dead, but, as with any ancient hurt, the wound ached from time to time.

Why had he forced Ita, this eternal bride, onto me? Were we truly fated to each other? Would we just keep chasing each other through the millennia, as we had since the giving of the Torah, if Dr. Freud's chart was to be believed? I'd broken all my promises to her, and in return she'd destroyed everything I loved, all for the sake of some selfish reward. Though neither שמנגלפ nor אשריל would reveal to me the terms of the bargain she'd made with them, it wasn't egoism that made me suspect it had to do with me. When had Ita ever thought of anything *but* her all-consuming passion for my person? One had only to watch שמנגלפ and

אשריל, like shadchens hoping to marry off two mamzers, to understand what she was up to: at last, after chasing each other through various worlds and incarnations, we'd reunite and consummate our love. That our earthly reunion should occur under the inhuman conditions of the ghetto, I chalked up to Heaven's great irony. When, after all, had God ever kept His word beyond the strict measure of the Law? If a reunion with me was indeed the favor she'd requested of the Celestial Courts, Heaven, I felt certain, would see to it that our life together was as short and painful as possible.

Raising her arm, the woman across the way, whoever she was, brought a palmful of bathwater to her shoulder and her neck. She lathered her underarm and her chest with soap, and she threw the water against her bosom in order to rinse it off. Finally, I could take no more of it. I left the apartment, though no contraband had been delivered. Slamming the door and thundering down the stairs, I ran out to the street and returned to the Zamenhofs' old house in the ghetto, where I spent a sleepless night, my body alive with electric trembling.

MEANWHILE, AS THE saying goes, the rebbe neither slumbered nor slept. In addition to his weekly words of encouragement, those fractious disputations with the Holy One held before a dwindling jury of his Hasidim, he was praying to the Same while meditating on the higher realms and performing whatever other feats a rebbe of his caliber performs. It was around this time, if I'm remembering correctly, that he conceived of the idea of immersing in a mikve as a further act of sabotage.

"Ah, Cousin," he said, removing his glasses and laying them on top of the growing pile of manuscript pages during one of our Sunday morning sessions, "Rosh Hashanah has now passed, and soon it will be Yom Kippur."

He tossed a melancholy glance through the grey panes of his study window.

"I suppose that's true," I said. I recognized a certain tone in his voice that I didn't like, as it always seemed to mean he was planning some new scheme.

"And during these great days of awe . . . I don't know," he said. "It's hard not to feel the compulsion . . ."

"The compulsion, Cousin?"

He hesitated. ". . . to immerse in a mikve."

"Ah, yes, of course," I said, "but."

"Yes: but," he agreed.

"That would be impossible," I added, as though I were speaking to a child, to a precocious child, a brilliant child, a child with amazing gifts and talents and abilities, but a child nonetheless. "You know as well as I the mikves have all been closed. You've seen the signs yourself," I reminded him.

Like pious Hasidim, l'havdil, the Germans seemed to know where every ritual bath in the city was, and with their usual conscientiousness, they'd hung a sign on each, which read OPENING THE MIKVE OR EMPLOYING IT WILL BE PUNISHED AS SABOTAGE, SUBJECT TO BETWEEN TEN YEARS IN PRISON AND DEATH.

"Strange, isn't it? Ten years in prison, death." The rebbe gave a little shrug with his hands.

"Yes, for a bath, yes, I suppose, it is extreme."

He was silent for a moment; then cocking his head to the side, as if he'd only just heard me, he said, "For a bath, did you say?"

"Regretfully," I said. "The mikve is, of course, not a bath." Or at least not in the rebbe's view. However, I had no interest in arguing with him over this or anything else, for that matter. Working on his book was a sufficiently draining experience. The last thing I wanted was an encyclopedic lecture on the efficacy of ritual immersion and the proper care and feeding of the Jewish soul. And the last thing I wanted after that was to go traipsing after him on a mad trip to a mikve. If he were truly my cousin, he was the only family I had, and all I wanted, really, was to sit in his home, as a visiting relative might, and wait for the war to end.

I pointed towards our manuscript. "Perhaps we should return to our work."

"I don't mean to be harsh, Cousin —"

"Nor I, nor I."

"—but I'm afraid that here the enemy, may their name be blotted out, knows considerably more than you do."

I put down my pen. "I'm certainly willing to concede that possibility."

"Only ask yourself: isn't their phraseology a tad queer?"

"Their phraseology?"

"On the warning signs, I mean. Isn't it queer that immersing in a mikve should be considered an act of sabotage?"

"They're merely playing with us, tormenting us. That's all it is."

"Yes, of course," the rebbe said, "although I think not. For what is a mikve, my dear cousin, but the very waters of mercy! By immersing in a mikve, a man is purified, all his sins forgiven. Now don't you see? Once our sins are forgiven, there will be no need for the Holy One to punish us further. Nor any justification for His continuing to do so."

"Though God might forgive us," I said, hoping to extinguish the fire I sensed stirring up in him, "I'm not so sure about the Germans."

"Oh, please! Don't be ridiculous! Do you really imagine our enemies could have achieved all they have—and may it soon crumble to dust!—without the aid of Heaven?"

"Well," I said, "it's illegal and that's that."

"That's true," the rebbe agreed, "it's illegal."

"And that's that," I said.

"Ten years in prison is no laughing matter."

"Nor is death."

He puffed a little on his pipe before tamping it out.

"And yet you risk it every day. With your smuggling and your . . ." He searched for an additional word, but could find none, and so he simply repeated "smuggling."

"And who told you about that?"

"Who told me about that? Are you still so naïve? Everyone talks to me. And as a consequence, I know everything."

"Whatever I'm doing—" And here, I stopped myself, not wanting to incriminate him. "That is to say: whatever I *may or may not be* doing, this is an entirely different matter."

"Is it?"

I lowered my voice and leaned in nearer to him. "If I'm smuggling items into the ghetto, and I assure you, my dear cousin, that I'm not, it's because the children here are in need of medicine. And if occasionally I carry in arms for the underground, which I don't, it's only because I've been asked to, although of course, I haven't been. And if I'm out there anyway, what would be the point of leaving these hypothetical weapons ownerless, when others have theoretically risked their lives to get them to me? However, there is no need for you to so pointlessly endanger yourself."

"No, you're right," he said. "I suppose you're right. It's needlessly risky, and no, you're right, you're right, our daily work calls to us." He patted the manuscript affectionately. I picked up my pen and straightened my notes and prepared to read through them with him, but then he cried, "Oh, how you shame me! You risk your life to help your people merely because someone has asked you to! Well, have I not been asked? No, even further: commanded!"

"Commanded? By whom?"

"By the very voice of Heaven!" he said, his face suddenly filling with an electric glow.

"Oh dear God!"

"No, it's clear," he cried. "Someone must sabotage our enemies by going to the mikve!"

"Don't be absurd!"

Finally, at last, he calmed himself and seemed to relent. "No, no, I suppose you're right. To risk one's life over such a trifle is . . ."

"Precisely."

"Over such a small thing . . ."

"Exactly."

"Over a bath, really, when you get down to it."

"Although as you pointed out," I conceded, hoping to further placate him, "it's not merely a bath, but still."

"No, that's right, you're correct. It's not a trifle."

"No."

"Performing the will of Heaven!"

Ah, here we go! I thought.

"It's decided, then." The rebbe pushed his glasses onto his forehead.

"As the Day of Atonement is upon us, we must go to the mikve. Don't try to talk me out of it, Cousin. If we risk our lives to obey God's commandments, surely He'll spare those lives, and in this way, we'll bring our enemies to their knees!"

The rebbe replaced his glasses onto the bridge of his nose and, as though nothing of significance had transpired between us, we returned to our work. Whenever I stole a glance at him, however, I could see the effect his decision was having upon him. He seemed happier than he had been for days, happier perhaps than I'd ever seen him. He even hummed a little to himself, grinning from time to time inside his extravagant beard. He was like a man with a secret mistress, knowing that the time until he saw her wouldn't be long.

CHAPTER 7

I told myself it wasn't up to me to talk him out of his decision. To begin with, he would never have listened to me. Who was I, after all? Only his cousin, the unbeliever. Also, the idea seemed so preposterous, I was certain one of the rebbe's closer associates, the once well-to-do Hasidim who formed a kind of advisory board around him, would dissuade him from it. I was appalled, however, to see that even these men were helpless in this regard. Each time one of them tried to convince the rebbe to cancel the trip, the rebbe used the conversation as a way to better organize his plans.

"The rebbe can't be serious," I heard one of them saying. "Why, we'd have to proceed by cover of darkness."

"Ah, by cover of darkness, you're suggesting? Setting out at dawn, you mean?"

"No, the rebbe would have to *arrive* at dawn, or even earlier!"

"Of course. Excellent thinking."

"And the idea of taking a car is sheer madness!"

"What would you suggest, then?"

"A wagon would be less conspicuous, though slower."

"Good. Round up a wagon."

"And you'll never be able to convince the owner of the mikve to open it."

"Have you tried?"

"What would be the purpose?"

"Talk to Reb Itzik, and let me know if he agrees."

Everything had to be prepared in strictest secrecy, although this posed no problem for the rebbe. He kept a million secrets, not only those of his Hasidim, who told him everything and upon whose foreheads, I was becoming convinced, he could read the rest, but the secrets of the cosmos as well. Everything Heaven allowed a man to know, the rebbe knew, and he kept his mouth shut about most of it.

A secret rendezvous with a mikve was child's play for a man like that.

HOWEVER, EVERYTHING WENT wrong from the start.

A small group of us gathered in the rebbe's kitchen. We'd slept at his house, as there was no other way to be there before five, the hour when Jews were first permitted on the streets. Though I considered it folly to risk my life for a freezing bath in the bitterest days of October, I'd grown rather protective of the rebbe and had no intention of letting him out of my sight. Besides, he'd insisted I come.

No one said anything as we moved about the kitchen. Though my heart was in my throat, the rebbe seemed calm enough. Indeed, his face appeared radiant. At last, he'd gotten his wish: he was a saboteur, and there was nothing the enemy could do about that. The Germans, in any case, hardly seemed to figure into his calculations. They were, at most, a minor detail in the larger conversation he was holding with the Holy One. True, they were fierce — I'd seen one place a pistol to the head of a child and pull the trigger and go about his day as though he'd done nothing more than kick a dog — but when it came to goodness and mercy, the rebbe was equally as fierce.

Our wagon driver failed to arrive at the appointed time, and it was decided we should set out on foot, hoping he'd find us along the way. There must have been ten of us, descending the stairs as quietly as we could, moving along with a sort of rustling hum. The janitor was asleep, and we were forced to rouse him, as he possessed the only key to the front gate.

"And what possible reason could Jews have for needing to be out at this godforsaken hour?" he complained, squinty with sleep.

What would we tell him? Even if he weren't groggy, I'm certain it would have been impossible to explain that we were off to the baths in order to bring the German army to defeat. He wasn't a bad fellow, simply a man with whom there was little point in discussing the niceties of Hasidic theology.

Instead we offered him a tip, and he unlocked the gate.

The distance between the rebbe's house and the mikve was not inconsiderable, and we walked silently in pairs. Periodically, we'd hear footsteps from someone other than ourselves, and these moments were terrifying. The night trolley clattered down its tracks, and we ran to board it, but it was an Aryans-only trolley, and the driver turned us away. A car approached, its headlights blinding us. However, it passed without stopping, and we all breathed a sigh of relief. At this hour, the gates of the houses were all locked, and there would have been nowhere to hide.

A SHADOWY FIGURE met us in the courtyard next door to the mikve. Without a word, he waved his hand and bid us to follow him. We entered a cellar that was so dark we'd been instructed beforehand where to walk, for how many steps, where to turn left, where right. At last, we reached a hole in the wall, and I climbed through it after the man in front of me, tearing the skin on my shins against its roughened edges. On the other side of the hole, though the darkness was equally thick, I could sense we were standing on a platform made of boards. "Jump!" someone whispered, and I jumped, landing with such force that my teeth knocked together with a resounding clop.

Someone lit a match, and I saw that we were now standing in a tiled changing room outside the mikve. Slowly the morning light began to shine through the windows near the ceiling. Others had already immersed themselves by the time we'd arrived, their emaciated bodies in various states of nakedness. For all our secrecy, word must have gotten out and they'd somehow beaten us here.

"Cousin, pay attention to where your thoughts go beneath the water," the rebbe told me before he immersed himself. I peered at him through the dark curtain of water. Without my glasses, he was an indistinct watery blur, floating weightlessly, his beard rising before his face.

I drew in a lungful of air and plunged down, hewing through the cold water. As I did, I found myself thinking about my own shipwrecked life. Why had I even come to Warsaw in the first place? Did anyone even know I was still here? The Zamenhofs had all disappeared. It'd been years since I'd had word from any of my own siblings, years since I'd received the news that Sore Dvore and her husband, Zelig Mintz, had perished from malaria in the Promised Land. I had only the vaguest notion where any of the others had been when the war began. My parents were dead, of course, and Aunt Fania had died, leaving Uncle Moritz to face the German invasion alone.

I had no idea where Loë was. Even Ita seemed to have forgotten all about me.

How's that for eternal love?

Floating to the bottom of the tiled pool, I doubted that even God could find me here. Despite His fabled omniscience, I knew He'd look for me in the only place I ever looked for myself, which was inside my father's gazebo, reading my forbidden books while the pink cherry blossoms shimmered in the cool Galician breeze.

I IMAGINE MY powers of spiritual discernment were not as sophisticated nor as subtle as the rebbe's, and yet, as far as I could see, his piety had moved Heaven not at all. In the days after we'd emerged from the mikve, the world, or at least our small portion of it, only seemed greyer. People were hungry, if not hungrier, and the streets were filled with even more corpses than before.

Even the rebbe seemed to have lost heart. "But none of this makes any sense," he insisted to me. "It's one thing for the Holy One to rebuke us with suffering, quite another for these rebukes to destroy everything in the world that's holy."

It was a Sunday morning, and though it wasn't the thick of winter, the day was frozen solid. A heavy snow had fallen during the night, the temperatures had plummeted. We'd finished our work earlier than usual, and the rebbe saw me to the door. As we stepped out onto the landing, our breaths steaming forth in great cottony puffs, we were confronted by a terrible sight. All along the street, at various points, either huddled together or alone, were children, some barefoot, most bare-kneed, many of them lacking a winter coat, this one cradling a book in his hands; that one, a doll.

When I looked closer, I realized that none of them was moving. My first thought was that they must be playing at some game, at statues, perhaps, but then of course I realized they'd frozen in the night.

A cry erupted from the rebbe's throat.

Plastered to the sides of buildings were posters designed by the Judenrat, celebrating the Month of the Child. Each bore the legend A CHILD IS THE HOLIEST THING.

"Dr. Sammelsohn, help me!" the rebbe said, and before I knew it, he'd ripped one of the posters down and was using it to cover the child nearest him. For some reason, I couldn't move. I felt as though I were frozen to the ground as well. Instead, I watched as Reb Kalonymos ran from one wall to the next, pulling down poster after poster, covering each child with the tatters.

"Forgive me, children," he told them. "It's all that I have."

"Master of the Universe!" he screamed. "This far? this far?"

Then: "Dr. Sammelsohn! Help me!"

Then: "Children, forgive me!"

Then: "Master of the Universe, this far?"

"שמנגלפ! אשריל!‏" I remember roaring when I was next conscious of myself. I knew what I looked like, but a madman shouting indecipherable names as he sank to his knees in the middle of a city square wouldn't, in those days, have attracted any special attention, and no one seemed to bother about me. "שמנגלפ! אשריל!‏," I continued to call, until my voice grew hoarse and the two stood before me, אשריל in his woolen overcoat, שמנגלפ in his leather one.

"What kind of angels are you, anyway?" I demanded of them.

"Doctor, please! You pierce us to the quick!" אשריל said.

"What does he mean, what kind of angels are we? We're angel angels," שמנגלפ said, pounding his fist with his truncheon. "And whatever we are, I can assure you we don't have time for these sorts of theological speculations with a man who owes his continuing existence to—"

"Brother!" אשריל silenced him.

"When the Romans were martyring Rabbi Akiva," I jeered, "what did your forefathers do?"

שמנגלפ spat. "You see, that shows you how little he understands!"

"He doesn't literally mean our forefathers," אשריל told him, attempting, it seemed, to keep the conversation on a politer keel.

"'This far, Master? This far?' That's what your ancestors said, that's what the angels of that era had the nerve to say, and to the Holy One Himself!"

"Yes, and you heard what the Holy One said back to them. If they didn't stop complaining, he'd return the universe to chaos and desolation! Is that what you want, Dr. Sammelsohn? Chaos and desolation?"

Given the chaos and desolation in which we lived our daily hours, the question couldn't have seemed more irrelevant. All three of us realized this, I think. אשריל sighed. Flicking his glasses onto his forehead, he rubbed his eyes. שמנגלפ let his truncheon drop and stared at his gleaming boots. I looked down at the mud and at the snow dampening my trousers. My bare hands were raw and freezing. At that moment, rain began to fall in dense, windy sheets. "Oh, wonderful! That's just wonderful!" I said, crossing one leg beneath the other and sitting in the mud.

"Horrible," שמנגלפ muttered under his breath. "Just . . ."

"Dr. Sammelsohn." אשריל kneeled near me. "You have to understand."

"No, he doesn't! This is none of his business!"

"Things are not as they should be, nor as they used to be."

"Why don't you just draw him a map?" שמנגלפ said. "Why don't you just take him up into the Heavens and show him exactly what you mean!"

"And would that be so wrong?" אשריל challenged him.

"Would that be wrong?" שמנגלפ laughed darkly. "Brother, think!"

"Why not?"

"Why not? Must I tell you why not? Because I won't permit it, that's why not?"

"Oh, *you* won't permit it?"

"Yes, *I* won't permit it!"

"And what if *I*—" אשריל started to say, but before he could finish his sentence, שמנגלפ had grabbed him by his tie, his shirt front, and the lapels of his coat. Pushing his fist into אשריל's chest, he knocked him against the trunk of a tree. אשריל's glasses flew from his forehead, his hat tumbled to the ground. שמנגלפ, his chest heaving, raised his truncheon over him.

"Oh, don't be so fucking tedious!" אשריל said, forcing שמנגלפ's hand from his lapels.

שמנגלפ gave out a strangled cry. Wielding his truncheon, he repeatedly struck it against the iron railing of a park bench until it shattered and all he was holding was its nib. "You think I'm happy with the situation?" he roared. "I am not! I am not happy with the situation. But I do my best. I do what's asked of me, which doesn't mean I agree with every policy from on high. But still, what are our choices, brother?"

"Well," I said, getting up and moving away. There'd be no help from this quarter, I could see. I left them arguing behind me. But, brother, what if this, and No, brother, we can't that, back and forth, back and forth, until אשריל cried, "Dr. Sammelsohn!" and ran after me. Wanting nothing more to do with them, however, I kept walking, blowing into my hands, trying to warm them.

"Will you come with us, then?" he said, catching up with me.

"Come with you?" His words seemed to have no meaning. "Where?"

"It's never been done before, you know that, don't you?" שמנגלפ said, catching up with us as well.

"I know. I know that," אשריל said.

"Maybe once or twice before but that's it."

WE ALL STOOD in the middle of Tłomackie Place Square facing in the same direction.

"Perhaps you should stand between us, Dr. Sammelsohn."

I had no idea what they were up to, but it seemed useless to resist. It's difficult to describe what next occurred. The two of them began reciting or rather chanting in a kind of susurrous rasp — the words are impossible for me to reproduce — and the sky, slowly at first, but then more quickly, began to roil. The dark rain-filled clouds began to form into whirling coils, as the wind picked up. My hat blew off, and אשריל grabbed my arm when, by instinct, I began to dash after it. "Forget it!" שמנגלפ barked into the gales, grappling me to his side. "Let it go, Dr. Sammelsohn. Let it go!"

With his chin pointed high, אשריל searched the skies. "Can you see it, brother?"

"Not yet."

"There? Is it there?"

שמנגלף peered through the lashing storm. "I don't think so."

"What is it you're looking for?"

"There! Isn't that it?" אשריל said.

"I believe so," שמנגלף said. "Finally." He pointed with his truncheon. "Do you see it, Dr. Sammelsohn, that little black rectangle among those purplish clouds way up there?"

I squinted, looking through the storm, expecting to see—what? I don't know. The longer I stood in Tłomackie Place Square, the more ridiculous the enterprise seemed. However, despite my cynicism, I couldn't deny that in the quadrant of the sky where שמנגלף was pointing, there seemed to be a black doorway.

"Do you mean that little black doorway?" I said.

"Precisely," שמנגלף said.

"Now, watch this," אשריל said.

As I did, the firmament, as though it were a blanket, seemed to rumple. Behind the fabric, so to speak, it seemed as though a staircase was being lowered, the cloth conforming to the shape of the stairs. Step after step, it descended towards us, each step appearing larger as it grew nearer, until it stopped with a clunk at our feet.

"Careful, Doctor," אשריל said, as, in step with both of them, I placed my foot cautiously upon the lowest stair. Each angel held me by an arm. "The rain will have made it slippery."

"One mustn't fall."

"Especially from the upper reaches."

"And Heaven forbid someone should push you off!" שמנגלף said. Holding me by the shoulder with one arm, he made me shake with the other.

"Brother, stop it!" אשריל said. "You're scaring him."

שמנגלף gave out a barking laugh.

AS FOR ME, I never felt more certain that these angels were, as Dr. Freud had once endeavored to convince me, figments of my imagination, hallucinations brought on by fatigue, stress, and a consequential derangement of my senses. Thanks to starvation, the freezing temperatures, and the grinding conditions of our life, I assumed I was simply dying in the middle of Tłomackie Place Square. Or perhaps I was already dead, having been unable to endure one more moment of my captivity.

As we climbed the numinous stairway, I felt certain that if I turned my head and looked behind me, I would see my body, a lifeless, forlorn figure, lying in the snow. Surely, the experience of ascending a staircase into the firmament was the last gasp of the neurons in my brain, a vision the dying mind throws up, like a dream, to seal one more firmly inside this new and eternal sleep. Each time I thought to peer below me in order to verify this impression, however, אשריל or שמנגלפ prevented me from looking back, either with remonstrations or by slyly distracting my attention.

"I wouldn't do that, Dr. Sammelsohn, oh no!" one of them might say, or: "Hey, hey, watch your step there! It's slippery."

I had no idea how long our mad ascent was taking. Indeed, I'd lost all sense of time. The air had begun to thin, and soon we were above the rain line, and the sky-embossed steps beneath our feet became not only less slippery but brighter and warmer in color. With the rains receding, it seemed safe enough to stop and tie my shoes. As I did, אשריל said, "You see, Dr. Sammelsohn, if this *were* an hallucination, I very much doubt your mind would have included as mundane a detail as the need to tie a shoe."

Only when we'd attained the threshold of the black door did my guides permit me to look down. I could see Warsaw far below us, its cars moving along its streets like toys, the cemetery with its tiny white monuments to the east, the train tracks to the north, the trolleys rumbling down Chłodna. I searched for a glimpse of my corpse, lying in Tłomackie Place Square, where I was sure I'd find it, but at this height, it was impossible to see such a small detail.

"This way, Dr. Sammelsohn, this way." שמנגלפ pulled me in by the arms. I ducked my head beneath the lintel of the black doorway, and we entered what appeared to be the upside-down bowl of the Heavens.

"Look up, Dr. Sammelsohn," אשריל commanded me.

I did. The planets seemed to be wheeling directly above our heads. The stars were so near I could feel their heat upon my face. I was reminded of the Planetarium in the Deutsches Museum, which I had visited in Munich once with Loë. There, the planets traveled on rails, powered by electric motors, and the stars were projected onto the wall by electric bulbs, while here, the friction of their breezing against the stratosphere created the most beautiful music I'd ever heard. It sounded like harps, flutes, and the voices of women and children.

"But this is the real thing, Dr. Sammelsohn," שמנגלף said, "and not some German planetarium. Do you have any idea how long it took to build all this?"

"No, how long?"

"One day." He roared with laughter.

"Oh, yes, well," I said, somewhat chagrined. "Perhaps I did have some idea."

"This way." אשריל took my arm. "There's still so much to see."

Together, the brothers went searching for a doorway hidden in the back wall of the cosmos. Searching blindly with their hands—the atmosphere here was particularly dark and cold—they at last found the knob. "Ah, yes. Here it is!" They pulled the door open, and the light from the stairwell flooded the room. I followed them, slightly unnerved by the whiff of urine that greeted us in the stairwell. After we'd opened a door marked with a large numeral 2, the scent was replaced by the smell of baking bread. A pang pierced my heart. Here, exactly as I had been taught as a child, was the Heavenly Bakery, where angelic bakers were busy preparing the manna that will be enjoyed by the righteous at the end of time. Their magnificent ovens were working at full blast. Apprentices in smocks and caps were running with floury wheelbarrows. Master bakers were shouting their orders, opening their oven doors, inspecting their loaves, while their assistants slathered the long work tables with oil and pounded down mountains of dough with giant rolling pins. The scent of coffee filled the air. The music I'd heard below, produced by the circuits of the planets, now blared out of the radios each baker listened to at his station.

"Is there someplace we could sit and order a little something?" I said, suddenly feeling quite famished.

אשריל shook his head.

"Look at them working," שמנגלפ said, thrusting his hands into his pockets. "They have no idea what's in store, do they?"

Exchanging silent greeting with the master baker, the angels led me to a storeroom in the back. Behind a pallet stacked high with flour bags was a rickety ladder leading to an opening in the ceiling, a sort of attic door. We climbed through this opening and arrived in what appeared to be an antiquarian book shop. Outside the shop's windows, a golden light turned the façades of the marble buildings pink. אשריל greeted an old man in a velvet yarmulke and a black vest who was sitting behind a counter, stroking his beard and reading. שמנגלפ whispered something in his ear, and the old fellow got up from his stool, searching through the riot of keys that dangled from his belt. Shuffling to the door, he unlocked it, and we slipped through it to the street.

Outside, doves were cooing, and the smell of citrus seemed to be everywhere. "The Old City's not so crowded today," שמנגלפ said, drawing in a breath.

"Must be a bus strike," אשריל said, frowning.

"But where are we?" I demanded to know.

"Why, this is the Celestial Jerusalem," אשריל explained.

"The *Celestial* Jerusalem?"

"Yes, it hovers above its more terrestrial twin."

My companions seemed to know the place quite well, and we strode through its streets, past cisterns and reflecting pools, past windmills and cafés, until we came to the Celestial Temple. Its looming façades reflected the complex palette of the dying sun. Leading me through the crowds in the courtyard, we snuck in through a door below a bridge and caught a glimpse of the archangel Michael in his holy garments, or so my guides informed me, offering up the souls of the righteous on the Temple altar. They stood, like pilgrims waiting to enter a shrine, the line winding through the courtyard and out into the streets, filling every passageway and alley.

"Has death undone so many?" I said.

"Best not to think about it," שמנגלפ said. "It'll only make you gloomy."

We entered the next level—the fifth, by my reckoning—via a rusty elevator whose mechanical innards wheezed as it shuddered between floors. We were let out in an opulent concert hall, its walls a shimmering blond spruce. There were rows and rows of empty choir stalls. Indeed, they seemed to stretch for miles. My guides allowed me to ascend the conductor's podium, and from this pinnacle, I couldn't see the end of them. An exquisite Bösendorfer stood, black and gleaming, in the center of the hall, surrounded by a goodly number of harps.

"And where are the angels?" I said.

"The angels?" אשריל said.

"The hosts of angels whose job it is, if I'm remembering my lessons correctly, to sing the praises of the Holy One from this very room."

"No, no, Dr. Sammelsohn," אשריל said. "That's only during the night." He pushed his eyeglasses onto his forehead and peered into the sheet music that had been left on the conductor's stand. After humming a few bars, he added, "During the day, it's up to the Jewish people to sing those praises."

I raised my hand to silence him, so that I might listen for these songs, but I heard nothing.

"Precisely," שמנגלפ said grimly.

I blushed. I was as guilty as anyone in this regard.

"But even at night," אשריל said, kicking the toe of his shoe against the wooden floor, "the singing is morose."

"Dirge-like," שמנגלפ agreed.

"They just mumble, and at times, you can barely make out the tune."

"Perhaps it's fear."

"Fear?" I said.

"Fear closes down the heart, I'm afraid."

"Even the hearts of angels break, Dr. Sammelsohn," שמנגלפ said. "Or didn't you know that?"

"Fear, despair, whatever," אשריל said.

At these sad words, the three of us fell into a silence made all the more profound by the impeccable acoustics of the room. One could have heard a pin drop, or a heart breaking, for that matter. I didn't know what to say. אשריל let out a long sigh; and שמנגלפ seemed to growl a little to himself. I thought I heard someone, from a distance, calling my name. I was certain I'd imagined it, until I noticed that אשריל and שמנגלפ had turned their heads in the direction of the sound, and then I heard it again.

Someone was calling me.

"OH, THANK GOD, Dr. Sammelsohn, I've found you!"

It was the rebbe, of course. Who else could it have been? Who else would have been in the choir room at this time, singing God's praises?

"I've brought you your hat." He ran towards me, the wings of his black coat flapping behind him, his footsteps thocking against the wooden floor, cradling my shabby grey fedora in his hands.

"You were in the square at Tłomackie Place," he said, a little breathless now, "and as I was approaching you in order to greet you, I saw it fly from your head. I ran to retrieve it, naturally, and having done so, I called out to you, but in the excitement of the moment, what with all that thundering and the storming, I suppose you didn't hear me. I thought I'd follow you." He looked at the two angels. "One must return lost objects to their proper owners, after all."

He was quoting the Talmudic law to them, it seemed to me, in the hopes that it might provide him with a legal excuse for being here, if אשריל or שמנגלפ were inclined to throw him out as a poacher from this Heavenly precinct.

Instead, אשריל bowed. "Your Holiness," he said.

"Rav Szapira," שמנגלפ said, doing the same.

The rebbe nodded and encouraged them to stand, clearly embarrassed by their adulation. Not knowing what else to do, he glanced about the room. "Ah, is that a Bösendorfer?" He pointed towards his ear. "I thought I recognized the tone."

Allow me to stop for a moment to dwell on this curious tableau: here we were, two Jews, one religious, one not, in our wintry overcoats and our hats, with our hateful armbands pinned to our sleeves, standing in the Choir Room of the Fifth Level of Heaven in the company of our angelic escort, one dressed, more or less, in the costume of a professor from the Old World, the other, in his black leathers, as a thug from the New, and yet the harmony between us was serene.

"Shall we proceed, then?" the rebbe said to אשריל and שמנגלפ. "And with your permission, may I join in with you?" The angels nodded in agreement.

"Thanks to my brushing up on what are known in our tradition as the Hekhaloth texts," the rebbe whispered to me, as he took my arm, "I was able to make my way past all the previous guards."

"Guards?" I said.

"Naturally."

"I didn't see any guards."

"I'm not certain I'd have been as successful the rest of the way."

אשרי and שמנגלף hurried us along a knotted rope bridge. Upon entering the Sixth Heaven, however, we discovered it was in a complete disarray. I cupped my handkerchief to my nose. "What *is* that smell?"

"Rats," שמנגלף said.

"It appears they've broken into the storehouses."

"And what exactly is stored here?"

"Tsk, tsk, tsk," שמנגלף said, inspecting the damage.

"Trials and vexations," אשריל told me.

"Trials and vexations?" I said.

"Well, yes."

I looked about. The place was indeed a wreck. Doors were bursting open, some were hanging off their hinges. Snow and hail had spilled out across the floor, and it was difficult not to slip on the mess. Noxious dew was dripping from more than one vat, and a military magazine stocked with storms had been ransacked, it appeared, as had several cellars holding what שמנגלף told us were very precious reserves of smoke and ash. Also a laboratory in which a rare bacterium was kept had been pilfered.

"And all so close to the Holy Blessed One," the rebbe said with a tone of wonder in his voice. Like me, he'd covered his face with a handkerchief.

אשריל and שמנגלף were hanging back, I'd noticed, near the exit doors.

"Perhaps we shouldn't have brought them here," אשריל said glumly.

"No, no, I want to see it all. I must see it all." The rebbe circled around, taking in the room. "Now, if I'm not mistaken, that door is all that separates us from the Seventh Heaven and the Throne of the Merciful One Himself." He pointed down a long passageway toward a door that appeared to be on fire.

"Not exactly, Your Holiness," אשריל said. "Behind that door is another door, and behind it is another door as well. There are twelve, in fact, each hotter and more blazing than the last."

"The Throne itself is guarded by the archangel Metatron." שמנגלפ lowered his voice and whispered this odd-sounding name, and the rebbe nodded, as though he were familiar with the figure. "But you'll have to take our word for it, as unfortunately . . ." שמנגלפ said, looking helplessly at his brother.

"Ah, yes, unfortunately . . . well . . . how to put this?"

"They're renovating at the moment."

"And consequently, it's closed to the public."

"We're sorry to have brought you all this way, gentlemen." שמנגלפ clapped his hands together as though he were a tour guide at the end of a tour. "However Heavens One through Six are not nothing."

"You may return to your homes content to have seen the greater part of it, certainly."

The two angels shrugged at each other, as though they knew their bluff was as ludicrous as it seemed.

"In any case," אשריל warned, "there's no way through the corridor of fire."

Looking again at the twelve burning doors, I was inclined to take him at his word. There seemed little point in our proceeding. Even if we made it through the doors alive—and I assumed we would not—the Holy One (of this, I was certain) would never deign to answer our petition for clemency and mercy. This was the same deity, after all, who'd enlisted Ita as a special emissary to return to Earth for the purpose of destroying the Esperanto movement! Six celestial and one terrestrial level below us, children were freezing to death on the streets of Europe! If God could turn a blind eye to that, what good would the petition of two miserable Jews do, even though one of them was an Hasidic master?

Surely, the rebbe was on the point of conceding as much, and it was only a matter of moments before we turned back and descended to Earth. However, he pushed his hat onto the back of his head and scratched his beard, and said, "Dr. Sammelsohn."

"Yes, my cousin?"

"Shelter with me beneath my talis and do not release it until we are through the corridor of fire. Do you understand me?"

"I understand you, yes. However . . ."

"Good."

שמנגלף and אשריל clucked their tongues and grumbled, as I sputtered out a litany of protests. Meanwhile, the rebbe simply and quietly withdrew his prayer shawl from some inner pocket of his outer coat. Does he keep the damned thing on him all the time, I wondered? Reciting the appropriate blessing, he whipped it into the air, wrapping it about his shoulders and his head. Holding it above him as though it were a tent, he beckoned me to join him beneath it.

What could I do? His insistence upon forging on had clearly consternated our angelic hosts; only the reverence in which they held him seemed to be keeping them from restraining us bodily. I hated to act against their wishes—surely, they'd already compromised themselves in bringing us this far—and I was equally loath to get myself into trouble. And yet I had to wonder: What's the worst that could happen to me? Either I was already dead or the journey back to Earth would kill me, and if it didn't, the Germans certainly would. All things considered, wasn't burning up in the divine conflagration between the Sixth and the Seventh Heavens the preferable course?

The rebbe pulled back the sides of his jacket, and I saw that he had two rams' horns, on either side of his waist, tucked into his belt. They looked like pistols and he, having tied his handkerchief over the lower half of his face, like a Mexican bandito. Why not go out in a blaze of glory? I thought.

"This isn't your fight, Dr. Sammelsohn. You know that," אשריל said to me, as I joined the rebbe beneath his talis.

"But perhaps it is," I said, tying my own handkerchief about my face. "Perhaps it's everyone's fight."

"Ready, Dr. Sammelsohn?" the rebbe said.

"Ready, Your Holiness."

"Now, when I give the signal, we shall charge forward. And whatever you do, do not let go of the corners of my prayer shawl."

We huddled together, and the thought occurred to me that he would probably never find the courage to give the signal, but once again I was wrong. Before I'd even prepared myself inwardly, the rebbe blew a blast on the ram's horn and shrilled out the word "Now!"

I closed my eyes as we charged towards the first door. I could feel the heat of the flames scorching my skin. I crammed my fedora tighter upon my head, and the hair on the back of my hand was singed. Cringing, I moved closer to the rebbe, pressing in as near to him as I could. Nevertheless, I smelled smoke, and I worried that perhaps his talis was burning. Few must have passed this way before us, and certainly no mortals, because *corridor of fire,* as a description, turned out to be a gross understatement. *Long corridor of fire* or perhaps even *endless corridor of fire* might have been more apt. The smoke was so thick at times, and the heat so scalding, I assumed we'd suffocate before reaching its end.

"Careful, Cousin, careful," the rebbe whispered. "Every step is perilous." The ram's horn he'd tucked into his gartl scraped against my hip. His mouth was so near my ear I could feel his breath through the hairs of his mustache. To quell my fear, I told myself again and again that what I was experiencing, what I imagined I was experiencing—the staircase, the angels, the various levels of Heaven, even the rebbe's presence beside me—was a vision created from a lack of oxygen reaching my brain. Though I felt myself high above Warsaw in the corridor between the Sixth and the Seventh Heavens, reason told me I was lying in the mud and the snow, far below, dying, perhaps with a helpful bullet delivered to my brain by some passing soldier. However, before I knew it, we'd pushed through the corridor of burning doors and had entered a large and beautiful library.

IT WAS EMPTY, except for one man, or one being rather. Even in comparison to the archangel Michael, this was an impressive fellow: tall—seven feet? eight?—extraordinarily lithe with a long flowing white beard. His arms were so muscular, they bulged inside the fabric of his sleeves. He was stationed behind a tall escritoire, the sort of writing desk at which one doesn't sit, but rather stands. He put down his quill and looked over his glasses at us, trembling before him. He consulted his wristwatch and adjusted it and made a note in his ledger book. "Precisely on time," he said. With a great rustling of his wings—at one point, I tried to count the pairs, stopping at thirty-two—he moved towards us. In the meantime, the rebbe had released me from the shelter of his talis—I felt naked in the presence of this hierarch without it—and was adjusting it, as a shul-goer will, about his shoulders. I didn't know what to expect. Surely we were poachers here, and I feared a fire might at any moment be exhaled from this being's nostrils in which at least one of us—the one without the protective prayer shawl, I assumed—would be incinerated.

Instead, the archangel Metatron greeted us pleasantly enough. "Gentlemen, welcome, welcome! Your merits, Rav Szapira, and in your case, Dr. Sammelsohn, other arrangements, I see, have brought you safely through the portal of fire. That's all to the good. I'd offer you a drink or even a meal, but"—he removed his eyeglasses and looked about the room—"I'm afraid we're a bit understaffed at the moment. Permit me, however, to introduce myself. I am Metatron, King of Angels, Prince of the Divine Face, Chancellor of Heaven, Angel of the Covenant, Watchman of the Night, and Teacher of Prematurely Deceased Children." He bowed his head. "At your service."

I didn't know what to say. Stunned into muteness, I took a moment to gaze about the room. I'm certain that, as time has gone by, I've forgotten much of what I saw there; however, I can attest to this: although the room resembled an ancient library with tall shelves and high ladders, and thick, plush chairs, upon closer examination, it all seemed to have been fashioned out of letters, words, sentences, a dense handwritten script that vibrated or even more precisely hummed continuously.

The rebbe finally spoke, and I was grateful that he did. I knew I didn't possess words sufficiently supple or eloquent to address a hierarch of such exalted stature, and certainly not within the Heavenly precincts. It's one thing to speak to אשריל and his brother, שמנגלף, on our groaning little planet; quite another to converse face to face with God's Personal Valet. Also, the rebbe possessed a solid religious education, something I sorely lacked, and had spent nearly all of his life in a mystical trance, meditating on the Powers That Eternally Be. I'm exaggerating, of course, but he was in his element here, whereas I felt far outside my own.

"Divine Sir," the rebbe bowed his head, "allow a humble Jew to greet you. We stand before you, as I think perhaps you know, because my cousin here, Ya'akov Yosef ben Alter Nosn, challenged your brothers and sons אשריל and שמנגלפ on their relative cowardice vis-à-vis the Holy One, Blessed be He."

Each time the rebbe mentioned the Lord's name, from nowhere seemingly — or rather from everyplace at once — a chorus of angelic voices sang out: יהא שמה רבא מברך לעלם ולעלמי עלמיא May His great name be blessed forever and ever!

The archangel Metatron tilted his head and scrutinized me. "Your cousin?"

"Yes, Your Majesty."

"Dr. Sammelsohn is your *cousin*?"

The rebbe nodded. "And a descendant of the holy Seer of Lublin, as am I."

The archangel Metatron grumbled, and I regretted that the rebbe had mentioned my name, that he'd brought me into the story at all, making me, in this way, its protagonist. I was more comfortable as a minor side character, the role I'd played my entire life with Dr. Freud and Dr. Zamenhof, and with my father and my mother and my sisters and even my wives. Forced to speak now by the expectation that I would, I blustered, "Well, I might have said something or other. As I'm sure His Majesty knows, our life on earth is at a particularly low point, and perhaps I was overly critical in comparing the angels' seeming complacence with the moral stance their forefathers — "

" — took in the case of Rabbi Akiva, yes, I know all about that," the archangel Metatron said. "Although forefathers isn't the correct word."

"As they informed me."

"And *I* found Dr. Sammelsohn's hat," the rebbe said, "and followed him in order to return it."

The archangel Metatron moved his gaze from the rebbe's face to my fedora, which I still wore, apparently uncertain what made this hat so irreplaceable a trip through the Divine Palaces was necessary for its return. "But surely you're here for other reasons as well," he said.

And the rebbe nodded. "Indeed, I was wondering . . . that is to say, I'd assumed, from all my years of toiling in the vineyards of the Holy One's holy Torah"—here, the voices rang out: "May His great name be blessed forever and ever!"—"that we might find Him"—the voices sang: "Blessed be He!"—"on His holy throne, so to speak"—the voices: "Blessed be the glory of God from His place!"—"where we might successfully petition Him for His mercy or at least come to understand the divine withholding of it." The rebbe looked about the room with a calculated nonchalance. "And where, by the way, *is* the Lord's holy throne?" he said.

In answer to this impertinent question, the archangel Metatron, King of Angels, et cetera, et cetera, drew himself up to his full height. His many sets of wings bristled—they sounded like an army on the march—and I assumed at that moment that we'd be chased out, flung from those lofty heights like mice swept out of a cupboard. But, no, he simply said, "Would that all humanity had made the ascent you two have done today." He seemed in the grip of some terrible emotion. "May we sit?" He pointed with his forehead to three armchairs in a nearby chamber. "Over here. Away from all this paperwork."

We did as he asked, and I was amazed to feel the chair, although constructed out of humming script, sink comfortably beneath my weight.

"The text you see forming the chair," the archangel answered my unuttered question, "is the mathematical formula for 'chair.' The chairs you know on Earth are the product of this equation. The same holds true with everything you see here: the books, the ladders, et alia."

The rebbe scanned the tall shelves of books behind Metatron's head.

"Yes, it's there," the archangel told him.

"What's where?" I said, looking between the two of them.

The rebbe laughed modestly.

"The book your rebbe is writing," the archangel explained. "You'll find it on the shelf and also listed in our card catalog."

"And the publication date?" the rebbe asked innocently enough, I thought.

A sort of fire flickered in the archangel's eyes. "Let's not get greedy, shall we?"

"Fair enough, fair enough," the rebbe demurred.

THE ARCHANGEL LEANED back in his chair and crossed his legs. He gripped the top of his thigh with both hands and interlaced his fingers around it. There were so many of them, it took a moment for his wings to settle in around his shoulders. At last, he said, "Ah, well, you've asked the right question there, haven't you? Indeed, where *is* the Holy One's throne? You've made it to the Seventh Heaven, you've braved the store-houses of ills in the Sixth. You've passed through the Door of Fire, and here you are, in the fabled Seventh, hoping to challenge and confront your Creator, to awaken His Exalted Conscience and to stir Him into action, to remind Him that He is not only the Maker of Peace but also, as it says in our holy books, a Man of War, so that you might say to him: 'Look down, look down, see how Your people are suffering. Arouse Your-self and come to our aid.' Or words to that effect, yes?"

The archangel Metatron glanced between us. Light from a skylight fell diagonally across his bearded face. "Perhaps I can ring for a little coffee or tea. Would either of you care for a little something?"

We nodded and shrugged in the polite way of guests who fear their presence might be inconveniencing their host. Nevertheless, the arch-angel Metatron lifted a bell from the coffee table and shook it. Its little ringing seemed to echo down many adjoining hallways and corridors. The archangel Metatron listened for a moment, hearing apparently noth-ing in response. "Oh, dear." He sighed. "I'm afraid we'll have to make do with nothing for the nonce."

He picked at a thread on his gown and brushed away a bit of lint from the fabric. "I can tell you in confidence that I have long been in the Divine Service — it's been aeons and aeons since I walked the earth as a humble shoemaker — and though times have been dark, I've never seen them quite as dark as these." He shook his head at some private thought. "Oh, gentlemen, how I wish you could have seen this place in the old days!" He closed his eyes and hugged himself. "All the cooking and the preparing and the feasting! You wouldn't believe it now, but the Heavenly Kitchens were once filled with clouds — What am I saying: clouds? — with whole *stratospheres* of delicious vapors. All for the never-ending banquets for the righteous! Oh, how I used to love walking these corridors, sticking my head into the kitchens. The smells would draw me from my writing table, and it was all I could do to finish my bookkeeping before dashing in to help. Of course, they never let me, but one of the sous-chefs was sweet on me, and she would always give me a little taste of whatever she was preparing before chasing me out again. The Seraphim, the Cherubim, the holy Chayyos running in and out, the clatter of silverware, of drawers opening, of rolling pins pounding, the Heavenly Choirs, the Earthly choirs as well, all singing the Holy One's praises." He smiled sadly. "It was a proper Heaven then, gentlemen, with music and dancing . . ." His enormous chest lifted and fell. "You could feel the presence of the Holy One in these halls then. But now?" He shrugged. Glancing over the top of his spectacles, he peered into the sky-embossed ceilings above us and, as though he'd caught a glimpse of cobwebs in a corner, he scowled. "Now you can't even get a fucking cup of tea."

The rebbe brought his fist to his lips and coughed. He cleared his throat politely. "And where, so to speak, *is* the Holy One?" He seemed to be pressing the issue as gently as he could, and the archangel Metatron gave him a piercing look, as though taking in the measure of the man in order to determine exactly how much of the truth he might reveal to him.

"Weeping," he said simply.

"Weeping?" the rebbe asked.

"The Holy Blessed One is weeping. Oh, yes, he has a place for it. But you would know that, wouldn't you?" the archangel said to the rebbe. "It's called the Mistarim."

"Concealment," the rebbe translated softly for me.

"It's an actual place?" I said.

The archangel Metatron nodded. I leaned back in my chair and gazed at the clouds in the ceiling above me, and for a moment, I couldn't help imagining the Holy One sneaking out of a window, as I had done after my marriage to Ita, and I couldn't help feeling sympathy for the Lord.

"As God is infinite," the archangel explained, "so is His pain infinite. There are some things, Dr. Sammelsohn, so great, so immeasurably large, that they cannot be seen at all. The Holy One's pain is an example of just such a thing."

"If the world could hear the Holy One's weeping," the rebbe added, "it could never bear it."

"Of course not," the archangel confirmed. "Everything would return to chaos and desolation. Instead, the Holy One chose to disappear, so to speak, to slip through the cracks of the Mistarim, and His absence, as you well know, has been as traumatic on Earth as it has been in Heaven. Now, the Holy One's pain has grown so large and so great that even I cannot hear His weeping."

I DON'T KNOW how long we sat together in silence, but it felt like a very long time. The sorrow between us was palpable. I glanced at the rebbe. He seemed pale, unnerved, drained of vitality. "Well, you've cleared up everything," he finally said, "thank you. And now perhaps I can finish my book." After a long moment, he stood, and the archangel Metatron stood as well. He bowed at the rebbe's feet, the span of his enormous wings stretching out before him, and the next thing I knew, I was lying facedown in the mud in the Tłomackie Place Square in a not dissimilar position.

"Dr. Sammelsohn! Cousin!" I heard the rebbe's voice from very far away. "Wake up, wake up! Oh, dear, we've got to get you out of here!"

I raised my head. The rebbe was standing over me, his beard flecked with mud, his hat askew. Mud darkened the knees of his trousers as well. He was holding on to my hat, which he placed on my head before lifting me from the ground. He threw my arm over his shoulders and carried me to his home.

THERE, ONE OF the rebbe's Hasidim met us at the door.

"Bad news," he said.

"Bad news?" The rebbe held on to me more tightly.

The Hasid ducked his head. "It's the rebbe's daughter, I'm afraid."

"Rekhl Yehudis?"

"She's gone."

"Gone?"

"Kidnappers. Or so we suspect." The man smiled unhappily. "In any case, she hasn't been home since Wednesday."

"Wednesday? How long have we been away?" the rebbe said to no one in particular.

• • •

I MUST HAVE blacked out again because soon I was in the middle of the street, the traffic roaring on either side of me. A cloud of thoughts buzzed around my head like angry flies. Rekhl Yehudis had been kidnapped! The Zamenhofs were gone! My world was disappearing! Everyone I knew had gone missing! Like God, they'd disappeared into the Mistarim! The conviction suddenly overwhelmed me: I no longer wished to live. I'd been walking along Nowolipie Street, but I made an abrupt turn and veered down Karmelicka, towards the Umschlagplatz. I'd turn myself in, I'd surrender, I'd accept my loaf of bread and my jar of beet marmalade, and I'd let myself be transported east, where, as so many of us had been murdered, I'd be murdered as well.

It wasn't a far walk. The entrance to the Umschlagplatz was at the point in the road where what had once been Zamenhof Street met Dzika Street. People were being herded in through the station's many doors. Trucks roared up in fleets, and the Jewish policemen turned their captives over to the Ukrainian and the Lithuanian guards. I won't say they herded us in like sheep. Rather, let me say that we were herded in like men and women who had no weapons of their own. The rain had turned to snow again, and the sky was frozen an iron grey. I was jostled in through the entrance along with everyone else. Inside, hundreds of people were milling about. I shivered and hugged myself. I had no idea when the last train had departed, nor how long anyone had been waiting, but it seemed a long time. People were clearly running out of food.

"The next train?" I asked a man sitting on his suitcase, but he only stared into space. As I looked about for someone else to approach, I began to regret my decision to turn myself in. In one area, a man and a woman and two small children were lying in a puddle of blood. The children's skulls had been smashed in and their shoes stolen. Had they tried to escape? I wondered. Or were they shot merely as a warning to the crowd, which, I realized, had begun to outnumber its guards.

I rubbed my arms, hoping to get warm. I had no idea where I'd left my gloves. My clothes were covered in mud, and I'd apparently forgotten my coat at the rebbe's. At uneven intervals, trucks drove up to the gates, and new crowds were deposited. There was no concealing anyone's despair now. As the hours lengthened, women began wailing, children began shrieking, and the guards began shooting anyone who wasn't moving quickly enough. Because they'd turned off the water that supplied the trains, we were all mad with thirst. Outside in the streets, I could hear gunshots and shrieking. Inside, people were begging for water and moaning. The elderly sat on boxes or lay next to one another on the ground. Children were losing their strength, their heads nodding on their necks, their eyes glassy, their lips dry and cracking.

As the crowd swelled, people were getting lost in the crush, calling out for one another. I couldn't stop sighing. A young man was selling yesterday's newspapers at exorbitant rates. A cordon of soldiers marched through, taking the strongest-looking among us, firing their guns overhead or sometimes even into the throng. Eventually, a train huffed into the station, and we all surged towards it. There was more shooting and screaming and wailing. The guards pushed at us with their rifle butts. The doors of the cattle cars opened and the tangy scent of chlorine made it difficult to breathe. No one, I realized, had given me the three loaves of bread and the kilogram of beet marmalade that had been promised to anyone who turned himself in. One more lie, I supposed. Was I ready to die? I didn't know. I only knew that I was hungry and tired and thirsty and too weary to resist. I attempted to make my way to one of the cars but couldn't make it through the crowds. In fact, I was knocked back and pushed to the ground. "Please! Someone!" I cried, shielding my head with my hands. A shoe clipped my cheek, I was kicked in the ribs, someone stepped upon my hand. Through the legs of the people walking over me, I saw a figure dashing towards me, a doctor in a white medical smock. Bending over me, she took hold of my arms. "Hurry! This way," she said.

I STRUGGLED TO my feet, grasping her smock. "This way," she said, and her voice forbade contradiction; nevertheless, I said, "But, Doktershe, I was hoping to board that train."

"Follow me." I hadn't the will to resist, and so I followed her away from the tracks and the crowds. It was only after I'd begun to calm down that I realized—mostly because of her limp—that this was Ita, or not Ita, but the young doctor אשריל and שמנגלפ had so unrelentingly tried to convince me was Ita.

"Wait here," she said, and she left me in a part of the Umschlagplatz inhabited only by the dead. They were transported to the Jewish cemetery on Okopowa Street in carts used for that purpose exclusively. Perhaps, I thought, I'd been crushed by the mob and was now dead myself. But if I were dead, I reasoned, the dead themselves probably wouldn't appear dead to me. Or would they? I didn't really know.

An hour passed, and the train I'd tried to board roared out of the station. I peered into the crowd left behind, wondering what to do next, when I saw her again, this Dr. Ita—to this day, I don't know her true name—moving briskly towards me with (I had to squint to make sure I was seeing this correctly) אשריל and שמנגלפּ in her train. I laughed a bitter little laugh. Ah, so here it is then, at last, the long-promised, long-deferred reunion between אַאָעְאָ אָ אָעָעוּוֹיא and me. One more of Heaven's cruel jokes. We were once again alive at the same moment and in the same place, and this slaughterhouse is the venue Heaven has chosen for our reunion? One kiss—is that what was to be granted us?—before the angel of death bludgeons us both with his truncheon?

However, the doktershe didn't offer to kiss me. Instead, she gave me an order: "Climb onto the cart and pretend you're dead, and do it quickly, before somebody sees."

"Do as she says, Dr. Sammelsohn," שמנגלפּ told me, gazing at the soldiers behind us, one hand on his revolver, the other upon his truncheon, poised and ready, if need be, it seemed, for battle.

"It's all been ordained," אשריל assured me. "There's no getting out of this, my friend."

"Hurry, hurry!" שמנגלפּ barked.

I didn't hesitate. Choking back my sense of revulsion, I clambered onto the cart. The figures there were cold and hardened. They didn't move against my weight as one might have expected. Horrified, trembling, I found a small depression among them and lay down within it and pretended to be dead.

"Keep perfectly still," the doktershe whispered into my ear. She even stroked my hair a little bit. "Keep your eyes closed, and don't move a muscle until you've made it to the cemetery."

"If she knew who you really were," אשריל whispered to me as well, "she'd tell you how much she loved you. But, of course, Dr. Sammelsohn, she doesn't remember any of that."

"As far as she knows," שמנגלפֿ said, "she's merely acting on a strange impulse, an impulse she'll never be able to explain to herself. Which is not an uncommon experience, I'm told, among you human beings."

Ita took a limping step backwards, and the driver mounted the wagon. Picking up the reins, he alerted the horses of his intention, and the wagon began to move, its wheels slipping in the muddy ground. I kept my eyes open a slit, so I could see her. In her white medical smock, its edges smeared with dirt and blood, she kept watch over the cart as it juddered off, with אשריל and שמנגלפֿ standing on either side. The distance between us grew. שמנגלפֿ lifted his truncheon in a salute of farewell. After the cart rounded a corner, I could see nothing more of them.

I shivered, aware of the inert bodies beneath mine, swaying with the movement of the cart. My head was on the breast of some poor woman's coat. I tried not to look at my companions' faces or at their grey hands. We passed beneath the arch of one of the Umschlagplatz's doorways and were soon out on the street, the horses' hooves clopping against the cobblestones, the sky wheeling above my head. Snow fell on my face, and I let it. The wind blew a freezing blast and, for a moment, I feared I might sneeze. I didn't. The cemetery was outside the ghetto wall, and it was there that the driver abandoned us, with no guard of any kind. The fear of typhus was too great, I supposed; and certainly, I imagined him telling himself, these dead were dead enough, and could do no one any further harm.

When I was certain I was alone, I scrambled off my bier. My legs collapsed, and I retched violently, the force buckling me in two. I fell onto my hands and knees, and vomited again. Wiping the damp grass and the snow from my hands, I stood. I was struck primarily by the ridiculousness of my situation. Though free, I had no place to go and also no means of getting there. My choices seemed to be starving here in the cemetery or taking my chances in the world, where no doubt I would be quickly recaptured and returned to the Umschlagplatz. Twice I headed towards the cemetery gates, and twice I doubled back.

   • • •

IT WAS AN hour or so before nightfall when I heard my name being called softly. The rebbe had entered the cemetery from Karolkowa Street, the two angels behind him.

"Greetings, Dr. Sammelsohn," אשריל said. "I see you made it out safe and sound."

"Thank Heaven," שמנגלף said.

"Cousin!" the rebbe said again, kissing me and holding me to his breast. "Thank God, you're alive. I've managed to bring you a few essential things."

Food and money, I hoped, and a coat and warm gloves, but he seemed to be carrying nothing at all.

"A blessing," he said.

"Food and money," אשריל laughed, shaking his head. "They never learn, do they?"

"Bow your head, my son," the rebbe said, and he intoned the patriarchal blessing.

"You're coming with me, of course," I said, when he was done.

"Oh, no. Not at all. No, I'll remain here where perhaps I may yet do some good. Who knows?"

"But they'll kill you."

I looked at the two angels for help, but they avoided my glance.

"Perhaps," the rebbe said. "However, one may unite with the Holy One in grief as well as in joy. And also, don't forget, I've got a book to finish. After which, my dearest cousin, I plan to bury it in one of Ringelblum's milk cans. Perhaps after the war, if I don't survive—"

"He won't," אשריל whispered.

"—you'll be kind enough to dig it up and see that it's published."

"I'll see to it, Dr. Sammelsohn," אשריל said. "You needn't concern yourself."

"You know," the rebbe said, "it was only in your merit that we were able to storm the Gates of Heaven yesterday. You thought you were clinging onto me, but in fact, I was clinging onto you."

"In my merit?"

"Yes, as we told you," שמנגלף confirmed, "אַאָעעָאָ אָ אָעַ עָעוּוֹויא made a deal with the Heavenly Court."

אשריל nodded. "She would do what Heaven wished—"

"Esperanto, the Messiah, et cetera."

"—if we'd see to it that you were protected throughout these dark days."

"They've kept their parts of the bargain," the rebbe said. "Now you must keep yours."

It was all a bit confusing, I have to say.

"Ita bargained with the Heavenly Court on my behalf, ransoming me like a captive?"

"She loved you, you see," אשריל said.

What was there to say to that? Nothing, and so we all stood for a moment in silence, until שמנגלפ coughed conspicuously, as though to remind us that time was short and there was something that still needed doing.

"Oh! Oh, yes," the rebbe said. "Yes, there *is* something more." He bent to the ground and dug through the snow. He lifted his mud-encrusted index finger towards my forehead. "Allow me just to write a little something across your brow, if I may."

Before I could protest, his finger was moving across my forehead, and when he was done, he quickly brushed off whatever he had written there.

"And what was that?" I said.

"Oh, never you mind about that," he answered sternly.

But שמנגלפ said, "It's the name of your beloved, of course."

"אַאָעְאָאָ אָעָ עְ עָ עוֹוִיא," אשריל said, reading.

"The bride your father chose for you. After all, you're leaving here under her protection."

"Speak to no one," the rebbe said, holding me firmly by the shoulders. "Look no one in the eye until you're safely away. Do you understand me?"

"Not really."

"Well, just do what you're told, then, for once in your life."

We kissed each other, and he handed me a satchel filled with food and water. Taking off his coat and his gloves, he gave them to me as well.

"Go. Before it gets too dark," he said.

I lifted the satchel and kissed him again. I bowed my head towards the two angels, who bowed theirs in return, and I left the three of them without looking back.

Well, actually, I looked back once, but they had disappeared.

I swung the satchel across my shoulder and snuck out of the cemetery. By nightfall, the city was far behind me. I began to breathe a bit more freely in the countryside. The forests were so quiet. I slept inside a warm barn, covered in hay, and in the morning, I began walking again. I had no precise idea where I was going, but the important thing, I told myself, was to keep heading south, towards Istanbul, where I thought I might find a ship to Haifa. As I walked, I thought about Ita, and I played the events of the last few days over again in my mind. Did I truly believe that Ita had been so touched by my simple expression of love for her that she'd move Heaven and Earth on my behalf? I have to say: the farther I got from the ghetto, the harder it was to believe. I'd had my fill of myths and dreams. I was walking into a realer world, I told myself, a truer world. I was walking into history. I was heading towards Palestine, towards the Promised Land, and it was only there, I knew, that a man could live as a Jew, and a Jew could live in peace.

ACKNOWLEDGMENTS

My work and research on this novel was supported in part by the National Endowment for the Arts and the University Research Committee of Emory University. Heartfelt thanks to Herbert Mayer and his staff at the Sammlung für Plansprachen und Esperantomuseum der Österreichische Nationalbibliothek, Detlev Blanke, Tadzio Carvelaro, James Chandler, Boris Kolker, Steven Nadler, Stefen Schaden, and Jefim Zajdman, all of whom graciously answered my many questions and requests; to Eugenia Amis, Nechoma Hiller Birnbaum, Julia House, Olivia Hay Jones, Marc Miller, Reed Travis, and Miriam Udel for help with translations (all the errors of which are mine); to Jeffrey Allen, Max Apple, Ben Austen, Bruce Cockburn, J. M. Coetzee, Rick Ehrstin, Shalom Goldman, Jim Grimsley, Dara Horn, Rodger Kamenetz, Michael Kramer, James Magnuson, Moshe Manheim, Laura Otis, Alex Shakar, Arianna Skibell, Barbara Freer Skibell, Paula Vitaris, Bret Wood, and numerous other friends and colleagues for their sensitive readings and discussions of the novel as it progressed; to Jude Grant for her heroic copyediting (six languages in three alphabets); and to Elisabeth Scharlatt and Wendy Weil.

I AM INDEBTED as well to the many writers, scholars, and historians whose work informs the historical background of *A Curable Romantic*. A bibliography of these works may be found at www.josephskibell.com.